# TO SAY
# NOTHING OF THE DOG

Also by
CONNIE WILLIS

LINCOLN'S DREAMS
DOOMSDAY BOOK
IMPOSSIBLE THINGS
UNCHARTED TERRITORY
BELLWETHER REMAKE

# TO SAY NOTHING OF THE DOG

## or

## How We Found The Bishop's Bird Stump At Last

CONNIE WILLIS

BANTAM BOOKS
NEW YORK LONDON TORONTO SYDNEY AUCKLAND

To Say Nothing of the Dog
A Bantam Spectra Book/January 1998

BOOK DESIGN BY JAMES SINCLAIR

ISBN 0-553-09995-7 (hc)

Bantam Books are published by Bantam Books, a division of Bantam Doubleday Dell
Publishing Group, Inc. Its trademark, consisting of the words "Bantam Books" and the
portrayal of a rooster, is Registered in U.S. Patent and Trademark Office and in other
countries. Marca Registrada. Bantam Books, 1540 Broadway, New York, New York
10036.

Printed in the United States of America

*"... a harmless, necessary cat"*
William Shakespeare


*"God is in the details."*
Gustave Flaubert

To Robert A. Heinlein

Who, in Have Space Suit, Will Travel,
first introduced me to Jerome K. Jerome's
Three Men in a Boat,
To Say Nothing of the Dog

*In loving memory*
*of Lorena and Bertie*

# CHAPTER ONE

A Search Party—Wartime Headgear—The Problem of Nepotism—
Royal Headgear—The Bishop's Bird Stump Is Missing—
Jumble Sales—A Clue to Its Whereabouts—Astronomical
Observations—Dogs—A Cat—Man's Best Friend—
An Abrupt Departure

There were five of us—Carruthers and the new recruit and myself, and Mr. Spivens and the verger. It was late afternoon on November the fifteenth, and we were in what was left of Coventry Cathedral, looking for the bishop's bird stump.

Or at any rate I was. The new recruit was gawking at the blown-out stained-glass windows, Mr. Spivens was over by the vestry steps digging up something, and Carruthers was trying to convince the verger we were from the Auxiliary Fire Service.

"This is our squadron leader, Lieutenant Ned Henry," he said, pointing at me, "and I'm Commander Carruthers, the post fire officer."

"Which post?" the verger said, his eyes narrowed.

"Thirty-six," Carruthers said at random.

"What about him?" the verger said, pointing at the new recruit, who was now trying to figure out how his pocket torch worked and who didn't look bright enough to be a member of the Home Guard, let alone AFS.

"He's my brother-in-law," Carruthers improvised. "Egbert."

"My wife tried to get me to hire her brother to work on the fire watch," the verger said, shaking his head sympathetically. "Can't walk across the kitchen without tripping over the cat. 'How's he supposed to put out incendiaries?' I asks her. 'He needs a job,' she says. 'Let Hitler put him to work,' I says."

I left them to it and started down what had been the nave. There was no time to lose. We'd gotten here late, and even though it was only a bit past four, the smoke and masonry dust in the air already made it almost too dark to see.

The recruit had given up on his pocket torch and was watching Mr. Spivens digging determinedly into the rubble next to the steps. I sighted along him to determine where the north aisle had been and started working my way toward the back of the nave.

The bishop's bird stump had stood on a wrought-iron stand in front of the parclose screen of the Smiths' Chapel. I picked my way over the rubble, trying to work out where I was. Only the outer walls of the cathedral and the tower, with its beautiful spire, were still standing. Everything else—the roof, the vaulted ceiling, the clerestory arches, the pillars—had come crashing down into one giant unrecognizable heap of blackened rubble.

All right, I thought, standing on top of a roof beam, that was the apse, and along there was the Drapers' Chapel, although there was no way to tell except by the blown-out windows. The stone arches had come down, and there was only the bayed wall left.

And here was the St. Laurence Chapel, I thought, scrabbling over the rubble on my hands and knees. The clutter of stone and charred beams was five feet high in this part of the cathedral, and slippery. It had drizzled off and on all day, turning the ash to blackish mud and making the lead slates from the roof as slick as ice.

The Girdlers' Chapel. And this must be the Smiths' Chapel. There was no sign of the parclose screen. I tried to judge how far from the windows it would have stood, and started digging.

The bishop's bird stump wasn't underneath the mass of twisted girders and broken stone, and neither was the parclose screen. A broken-off length of kneeling rail was, and part of a pew, which meant I was too far out into the nave.

I stood up, trying to orient myself. It's amazing how much destruction can distort the sense of space. I knelt down and looked up the church toward the choir, trying to spot the base of any of the north aisle pillars to see how far out into the nave I was, but they were hopelessly buried.

I needed to find where the arch had been and work from there. I looked back up at the Girdlers' Chapel's east wall, aligned myself with it and the windows, and started digging again, looking for the supporting pillar of the arch.

It had been broken off six inches from the floor. I uncovered the space around it, then, sighting along it, tried to estimate where the screen would have been, and started digging again.

Nothing. I heaved up a jagged piece of the wooden ceiling, and under it was a giant slab of marble, cracked across. The altar. Now I was too far in. I sighted along the new recruit again, who was still watching Mr. Spivens dig, paced off ten feet, and started digging again.

"But we *are* from the AFS," I heard Carruthers say to the verger.

"Are you certain you're with the AFS?" the verger said. "Those coveralls don't look like any AFS uniform I've ever seen."

He wasn't having any of it, and no wonder. Our uniforms had been intended for the middle of an air raid, when anyone in a tin helmet can pass for official. And for the middle of the night. Daylight was another matter. Carruthers's helmet had a Royal Engineers insignia, mine was stencilled "ARP," and the new recruit's was from another war altogether.

"Our regular uniforms were hit by a high explosive," Carruthers said.

The verger didn't look convinced. "If you're from the fire service, why weren't you here last night when you might have done some good?"

An excellent question, and one that Lady Schrapnell would be sure to ask me when I got back. "What do you mean you went through on the fifteenth, Ned?" I could hear her asking. "That's a whole day late."

Which was why I was scrabbling through smoking roof beams, burning my finger on a still-melted puddle of lead that had dripped down from the roof last night, and choking on masonry dust instead of reporting in.

I pried up part of an iron reinforcing girder, nursing my burnt finger, and started through the heap of roof slates and charred beams. I cut the finger I'd burnt on a broken-off piece of metal and stood up, sucking on it.

Carruthers and the verger were still at it. "I never heard of any Post Thirty-six," the verger said suspiciously. "The AFS posts in Coventry only go up to Seventeen."

"We're from London," Carruthers said. "A special detachment sent up to help out."

"How'd your lot get through?" the verger said, picking up his shovel aggressively. "The roads are all blocked."

It was time to lend assistance. I went over to where they were standing. "We came round Radford way," I said, fairly sure the verger wouldn't have been out that direction. "A milk lorry gave us a lift."

"I thought there were barricades up," the verger said, still clutching his shovel.

"We had special passes," Carruthers said.

Mistake. The verger was likely to ask to see them. I said hastily, "The Queen sent us."

That did it. The verger's tin helmet came off, and he came to attention, his shovel like a staff. "Her Majesty?"

I placed my ARP helmet over my heart. "She said she couldn't look Coventry in the face till she'd done something to help. 'Their beautiful, beautiful cathedral,' she said to us. 'You must go up to Coventry straight-away and offer them whatever help you can.'"

"She would," the verger said, shaking his bald head reverently. "She would. 'Their beautiful, beautiful cathedral.' It sounds just like her."

I nodded solemnly at the verger, winked at Carruthers, and went back to my digging. The rest of the collapsed arch was underneath the roof slates, along with a tangle of electrical cords and a broken memorial tablet that read, "May you know rest et—," a wish which apparently had not been granted.

I cleared a space three feet wide around the pillar. Nothing. I crawled over the rubble, looking for the rest of the pillar, found a fragment of it, and began digging again.

Carruthers came over. "The verger wanted to know what the Queen looked like," he said. "I told him she was wearing a hat. She did, didn't she? I can never remember which one wore the hats."

"They all did. Except Victoria. She wore a lace cap affair," I said. "And Camilla. She wasn't queen long enough. Tell him Her Majesty saved Queen Victoria's Bible when Buckingham Palace was bombed. Carried it out in her arms like a baby."

"She did?" Carruthers said.

"No," I said, "but it'll keep him from asking why you're wearing a bomb squad helmet. And it might get him talking about what was saved last night."

Carruthers pulled a piece of paper from the pocket of his coveralls. "The altar candlesticks and cross from the high altar and the Smiths' Chapel were saved by Provost Howard and the fire watch and taken to the police station. Also a silver paten and chalice, a wooden crucifix, a silver wafer box, the Epistles, the Gospels, and the regimental colors of the Royal Warwickshire Regiment, Seventh Battalion," he read.

It matched the list in Provost Howard's account of the raid. "And not the bishop's bird stump," I said, surveying the rubble. "Which means it's here somewhere."

"No luck finding it?" Carruthers asked.

"No," I said. "I don't suppose there's any chance anyone arrived earlier and has already found it?"

"Nobody of ours," Carruthers said. "Davis and Peters couldn't even get to the right year. It took me four tries to get this close. The first time I came through I landed on the nineteenth. The second time I ended up in the middle of December. The third time I ended up spot-on target, right month, right day, ten minutes before the raid started. And in the middle of a field of marshmallows halfway to Birmingham."

"Marshmallows?" I said, thinking that I couldn't have heard right. Marshmallows didn't grow in fields, did they?

"*Marrows*," Carruthers said, sounding irritated. "In a field of vegetable marrows. And it wasn't anything to joke about. The farmer's wife thought I was a German paratrooper and locked me in the barn. I had the devil of a time getting out."

"What about the new recruit?" I said.

"He came through right before I did. I found him wandering about in the Warwick Road, no idea of where to go. If I hadn't found him he'd have fallen in a bomb crater."

Which might not have been a bad thing, considering. The new recruit had given up watching Mr. Spivens and was back trying to figure out how to switch on his pocket torch.

"It took us two hours to get here," Carruthers said. "How about you, Ned? How many tries before you got this close?"

"Just the one. I only just got pulled off jumble sales to try when you weren't having any luck."

"Jumble sales?"

"Lady Schrapnell got the idea the bishop's bird stump might have been sold at one of the cathedral's jumble sales," I said. "You know, to raise money for the war effort. Or given to a scrap iron drive, so she sent me to every church and community function from September on. I say, you don't know what a penwiper's used for, do you?"

"I don't even know what a penwiper is."

"Neither do I," I said. "I've bought seven. Two dahlias, a rose, a kitten, a hedgehog, and two Union Jacks. One's got to buy something, and since I couldn't bring anything I bought back through the net with me, it had to be something I could slip onto the fancy goods table without being caught, and penwipers are small. Except for the rose. It was nearly as big as a soccer ball, made out of layers and layers of bright fuchsia wool sewn together, and pinked round the edges. And what I can't see is what on earth the use of something like that would be, except of course for people to buy at jumble sales. They all had them, the Evacuated Children Charity Fair, the ARP Gas Mask Fund Baked Goods Sale, the St. Anne's Day Sale of Work—"

Carruthers was looking at me oddly. "Ned," he said, "how many drops have you made in the past week?"

"Ten," I said, trying to remember. "No, twelve. There was the Trinity Church Harvest Fête, the Women's Institute Victory Drive Sale of Work, the Spitfire Benefit Tea. Oh, and the bishops' wives. Thirteen. No, twelve. Mrs. Bittner wasn't a drop."

"Mrs. Bittner?" Carruthers said. "The wife of the last bishop of Coventry?"

I nodded. "She's still alive. And still living in Coventry. Lady Schrapnell sent me out to interview her."

"What could she possibly know about the old cathedral? She wouldn't even have been born when it burned."

"Lady Schrapnell had the idea that if the bishop's bird stump survived the fire, it might have been put in storage somewhere in the new cathedral, so she sent me to interview the bishops' wives because, and I quote, 'Men don't know where anything's kept.' "

Carruthers shook his head sadly. "And did the wives know?"

"They'd never even *heard* of it except for Mrs. Bittner, and she said it wasn't there when they packed up everything before they sold the new cathedral."

"But that's good, isn't it?" he said. "If it isn't here either, that means it wasn't in the cathedral when the raid happened, and you can tell Lady Schrapnell she won't need to have a reconstruction of it in the cathedral for the consecration."

"You tell her," I said.

"Perhaps it was removed for safekeeping," he said, looking at the windows. "Like the east windows."

"The bishop's bird stump?" I said incredulously. "Are you joking?"

"You're right," he said. "It isn't the sort of thing you'd want to keep from being blown up. Victorian art!" He shuddered.

"Besides," I said, "I've already been to Lucy Hampton rectory—that's where they took the windows—to check. It wasn't there."

"Oh," Carruthers said. "Could it have been moved to somewhere else in the church?"

That was an idea. Perhaps one of the Altar Guild ladies, unable to stand the sight of it, had stuck it in a corner behind a pillar or something.

"Why is Lady Schrapnell so obsessed with this stump thing anyway?" Carruthers said.

"Why is she so obsessed with every detail of this project?" I said. "Before she assigned me to the bishop's bird stump, it was monuments. She wanted a copy of every inscription on every monument in the cathedral, including the one on Captain Gervase Scrope's tomb, which went on forever."

Carruthers nodded sympathetically. "Organ pipes," he said. "She's had me all over the Middle Ages measuring organ pipes."

"The real question, of course, is, why is she so obsessed with rebuilding Coventry Cathedral?" I said.

"Her great-great-something grandmother went to Coventry and—"

"I know, I know, the experience changed her great-great-something grandmother's life, and when Lady Schrapnell found her diary, it changed *her* life, and she decided to rebuild the cathedral exactly as it was just before it burned down in honor of, et cetera, et cetera. I've heard that speech a number of times. Also the one about how God—"

"—is in the details," Carruthers quoted. "I despise that speech."

"The one I hate the most is the 'leave no stone unturned' speech. Give me a hand." I pointed to the end of a large stone.

He stooped down and got hold of the other side of it.

"One, two, three," I said, "lift," and we heaved it across the aisle, where it rolled into what was left of a pillar and knocked it down.

The bishop's bird stump wasn't under the stone, but the wrought-iron stand it had stood on was, and one of the crosspieces of the parclose screen, and, under a chunk of red sandstone, a half-charred stem of a flower. There was no telling what sort of flower, there weren't even any leaves left, and it might have been a stick or an iron rod except for the inch or so of green at one end.

"It stood in front of a screen?" Carruthers said, crunching through the glass.

"This screen. On this stand," I said, pointing at the wrought-iron stand. "As of November the ninth, the Prayers for the RAF Service and Baked Goods Sale. Two crocheted antimacassars, a pansy penwiper, and half a dozen rock cakes. Extremely aptly named."

Carruthers was looking round at the glass. "Could the blast have knocked it to some other part of the nave?" he asked.

"It wasn't high explosives that destroyed the cathedral, it was incendiaries."

"Oh," he said. He looked over at the verger, who was coming toward us. "Queen Victoria's Bible, did you say?"

"Yes. Complete with the births, deaths, and nervous breakdowns of all those Georges," I said. "Find out if anything was taken away for safekeeping to anywhere besides Lucy Hampton before the fire."

He nodded and went back over to the verger, and I stood there looking at the wrought-iron stand and wondering what to do next.

The majority of the bombs that had fallen on the cathedral had been incendiaries, but Carruthers was right. Concussion can do peculiar things, and there had been a number of explosions in the vicinity, from HEs to gas mains going. The bishop's bird stump might have been blown into the central aisle of the nave, or the choir.

I cleared away more masonry, trying to see what direction the glass from the Drapers' Chapel had taken. Most of it seemed to have sprayed south and west. I should be looking in the other direction, toward the back of the nave.

I went back to the screen and started digging south and west from it. No stone unturned.

The bells began to strike the hour, and we all stopped what we were doing, even Mr. Spivens, and looked up at the tower. With the roof gone, we could see the spire, rising above the smoke and dust unharmed. The bells sounded beautiful, undimmed by the destruction that lay around us.

"Look, there's a star," Carruthers said.

"Where?" I said.

"There," he pointed.

All I could see was smoke. I said so.

"*There*," he said. "Above the spire. Above the smoky pall of war, above the wrack of destruction. Untouched by man's inhumanity to man, a high herald of hope and beauty, of better times to come. A sparkling symbol of a resurrection it yet kens not."

"It yet kens not?" I looked at him, worried. "A high herald of hope and beauty?"

One of the first symptoms of time-lag is a tendency to maudlin sentimentality, like an Irishman in his cups or a Victorian poet cold-sober. Carruthers had been on at least four drops in the past day, two of them within hours of each other, and who knew how many others researching the organ pipes. He'd said himself he hadn't had any sleep.

I frowned, trying to remember the checklist of time-lag symptoms. Maudlin sentimentality, difficulty in distinguishing sounds, fatigue—but he'd heard the bells, and everyone associated with Lady Schrapnell's reconstruction project was suffering from sleep deprivation. The only sleep I'd gotten in the past week was during the St. Crispin's Day War Effort Bazaar. I'd dozed off during the "Welcome" and slept through half the "Introductions of the Organizing Committee."

What were the other symptoms? Tendency to become distracted by irrelevancies. Slowness in answering. Blurred vision.

"The star," I said. "What does it look like?"

"What do you mean what does it look like?" Carruthers said, not at all slow to answer. "It looks like a *star*."

The bells stopped chiming, their echoes lingering in the smoky air.

"What do you *think* a star looks like?" Carruthers said, and stomped off toward the verger.

Irritability was a definite symptom. And the net guidelines specifically stated that time-lag sufferers were to be immediately "removed from the environment" and from duty, but if I did that, I would have to explain to Lady Schrapnell what we were doing in Oxford instead of Coventry.

Which was why I was here poking about in the rubble in the first place, because I didn't want to try and explain why I hadn't landed at eight o'clock on the fourteenth in front of the cathedral like I'd been supposed to, and it was no good trying to explain that it was because of the slippage because Lady Schrapnell didn't believe in slippage. Or time-lag.

No, so long as Carruthers wasn't completely incoherent, it was better to stay here, find the bishop's bird stump, and then go back and be able to tell Lady Schrapnell, yes, it had been in the cathedral during the raid, and then get some sleep. Sleep, that knits the ragged sleeve of non-AFS uniforms, that soothes the sooty brow and shuts out sorrow, blessing the weary soul with blissful, healing rest—

Carruthers came over, looking neither fatigued nor distracted. Good.

"Ned!" he said. "Didn't you hear me calling?"

"Sorry," I said. "I was thinking about something."

"You must have been. I've been calling for five minutes," he said. "Did she have Dookie with her?"

I must have misheard that, too, or else Carruthers was more time-lagged than I'd thought. "Dookie?" I said cautiously.

"Yes, Dookie!" he said. "Did she have Dookie with her?"

Oh, no, I was going to have to get him back to Oxford without making the verger suspicious, get him to Infirmary, and then try to get back here to finish searching the cathedral and probably end up in a marrows field halfway to Liverpool.

"Ned, can't you hear me?" Carruthers was saying worriedly. "I said, 'Did she have Dookie with her?' "

"With whom?" I said, wondering how I was going to convince him he needed to be taken out. Time-lag victims never think they're time-lagged. "Lady Schrapnell?"

"No," he said, very irritably. "Her Majesty. The Queen. When she commissioned us to come up here. 'Their beautiful, beautiful cathedral,' and all that." He pointed to the verger, who was heading toward us. "He asked me if she had Dookie with her when we saw her, and I didn't have any idea who that was."

I didn't either. Dookie. It seemed unlikely that that would have been her nickname for the King. For her ne'er-do-well brother-in-law, perhaps? No, Edward had already abdicated by 1940, and the Queen wasn't calling him anything.

The Queen's dog, I thought, but that didn't help particularly. In her later years as the Queen Mum, she'd had Welsh corgis, but what had she had during World War II? A Yorkshire terrier? A toy spaniel? And what gender, if any? And what if Dookie was her maid instead? Or a nickname for one of the princesses?

The verger came up. "You were asking about Dookie," I said. "Afraid Dookie wasn't with Her Majesty. Up at Windsor for the duration. Terrified of the bombs, you see."

"It takes some of them that way," the verger said, looking over toward where Mr. Spivens and the new recruit were. "Weak nerves."

The new recruit had finally figured out how the pocket torch worked. He'd switched it on and was playing the beam on the blackened walls of the chancel and on Mr. Spivens, who was apparently digging a tunnel into the rubble next to the steps.

"Blackout?" I mentioned to Carruthers.

"Oh, Lord," Carruthers said. "Put that out!" he shouted, and clambered over toward him.

"Week before last I go up on the roofs, and what do I find?" the verger said, looking over at the chancel, where Carruthers had grabbed the torch away from the new recruit and was switching it off. "My brother-in-law, careless as you please, striking a match. 'What do you think you're doing?' I say. 'Lighting my cigarette,' he says. 'Why don't you light some flares while you're at it,' I say, 'and set them out so the Luftwaffe will be certain to know where to find us?' 'It was only one match,' he says. 'What harm could it do?' "

He looked around bleakly at what the Luftwaffe had so obviously found, and I wondered if he considered his brother-in-law accountable, but he said instead, "Poor Provost Howard." He shook his head. "It was a blow to him, losing the cathedral. Wouldn't go home. Stayed here all night."

"All night?" I said.

He nodded. "Watching for looters, I suppose." He looked sadly at the rubble. "Not that there was much left to pinch. Still, if anything did survive, you don't want people making off with it."

"No," I agreed.

He shook his head sadly. "You should have seen him, walking up and down across the rubble, back and forth. 'Go home and have a lie down,' I told him. 'Let me and Mr. Spivens take a turn.' "

"So someone's been here the whole time since the fire," I persisted.

"Pretty near," he said, "except when I went home to tea. And this morning it started to rain and I sent my brother-in-law home for my mackintosh and an umbrella, but he never came back, so I had to go home and get them myself. Getting dark," he added, looking nervously at the sky to the east. "The jerries will be back soon."

Actually they wouldn't. The Luftwaffe had decided to go after London tonight instead. But it was getting dark. The far end of the church, where Carruthers was yelling at the new recruit over blackout regulations, was in gloom, and the blown-out east window gaped on a darkening blue-black haze of smoke crisscrossed by searchlights.

"We'd best do what we can before night falls," I said, and went back over to where I'd been digging and surveyed the rubble, trying to guess how far the bishop's bird stump had been knocked by the blast. If it hadn't been carted off by looters. The verger had been gone for at least an hour having his tea, during which time anyone could have walked in through the nonexistent south door and carried off anything they liked. Including the bishop's bird stump.

I must be getting light-headed from lack of sleep. No one, even badly shell-shocked, would steal it. Or buy it at a jumble sale. This was the bishop's bird stump. Even the munitions scrap iron drive would turn it down. Unless of course someone recognized its potential as a psychological weapon against the Nazis.

So it had to be here somewhere, along with the rest of the parclose screen and the section of memorial tablet that read, "—ernal," and I'd better get busy if I was going to find them before dark. I picked up a kneeling cushion, still smouldering and smelling strongly of feathers, laid it in the aisle, and started digging toward the back of the nave.

I found a kneeling rail, a single bronze candlestick, and a charred hymnal, open to "From All That Dwell Below the Skies." There was a sheet of paper stuck inside the back cover.

I pulled it out. It was an order of service for Sunday the tenth of November. I opened the folded sheet, blackened fragments flaking away as I did.

I squinted, trying to read it in the gloom, wishing I had the new recruit's pocket torch. ". . . and red carnations on the High Altar," it read, "were given in remembrance of Lieutenant David Halberstam, RAF. The pulpit arrangement of pink begonias and the bouquet of yellow chrysanthemums in the bishop's bird stump were donated and arranged by the Flower Committee of the Ladies' Altar Guild, Chairwoman Lo—"

The rest of the chairwoman was burnt away, but at least we had proof that the bishop's bird stump had been in the cathedral five days ago. So where was it now?

I kept digging. It got darker, and the moon that had been such an aid to the Luftwaffe the night before came up and promptly disappeared into the murk of smoke and dust.

This part of the church seemed to have fallen in all in one piece, and I almost immediately ran out of things I could lift by myself. I looked over at Carruthers, but he was deep in royal conversation with the verger and, presumably, getting some information out of him. I didn't want to bother him.

"Give me a hand!" I called to the new recruit instead. He was squatting next to Mr. Spivens, watching him burrow into the tunnel. "Over here!" I shouted, gesturing to him.

Neither of them paid any attention. Mr. Spivens had nearly disappeared into the tunnel, and the new recruit was fiddling with his pocket torch again.

"Hullo!" I shouted, "Over here!" and several things happened at once. Mr. Spivens reappeared, the new recruit reared back and fell over, the pocket torch came on, its beam sweeping the sky like one of the searchlights, and a long dark animal shot out of the tunnel and across the top of the rubble. A cat. Mr. Spivens took off after it, barking wildly.

I went over to where the new recruit was sitting gazing interestedly after them, switched off the torch, helped him up, and said, "Come help me with these timbers."

"Did you see that cat?" he said, looking over to where it had disappeared under the chancel steps. "It was a cat, wasn't it? They're smaller than I thought they'd be. I thought they'd be more the size of a wolf. And they're so *fast!* Were all of them black like that?"

"All of them that had been crawling about in a burnt-out cathedral, I should think," I said.

"A real cat!" he said, dusting off his non-AFS coveralls and following me. "It's just so amazing, seeing a creature that's been extinct for nearly forty years. I've never seen one before."

"Take hold of that end," I said, pointing at a length of stone gutter.

"It's *all* so amazing," he said. "Actually *being* here, where it all started."

"Or ended," I said dryly. "Not that one, the one on top."

He lifted, his knees straight, staggering a little. "It's just so exciting! Lady Schrapnell said working on Coventry Cathedral would be a rewarding experience, and it is! Seeing *this* and knowing that it isn't really destroyed, that it's rising out of the ashes at this very minute, resurrected and restored to all its former glory."

He sounded time-lagged, but probably wasn't. All of Lady Schrapnell's new recruits sound time-lagged.

"How many drops have you done?" I asked.

"This is my first," he said, his face eager, "and I still can't quite believe it. I mean, here we are in *1940*, searching for the bishop's bird stump, unearthing a treasure of the past, the beauty of a bygone era."

I looked at him. "You've never actually seen the bishop's bird stump, have you?"

"No," he said, "but it must be truly amazing. It changed Lady Schrapnell's great-great-grandmother's life, you know."

"I know," I said. "It's changed all of our lives."'

"Here!" Carruthers called from the Drapers' Chapel. He was on his knees. "I've found something."

He was in the wrong direction for blast, and at first all I could see was a tangle of timbers, but Carruthers was pointing at something in the midst of the tangle.

"I see it!" the verger said. "It looks like metal."

"Use your torch," Carruthers said to the new recruit.

The recruit, who'd forgotten how to switch it on, messed with it for a bit and then switched it on in Carruthers' face.

"Not on me," Carruthers said. "Under there!" He snatched it away from him and shone it on the pile of timbers, and I caught a glint of metal. My heart leaped.

"Get those timbers off there," I said, and we all went at the pile.

"Here it comes," the verger said, and Carruthers and the new recruit hauled it up out of the rubble.

The metal was black with soot, and it was badly crushed and twisted, but I knew what it was, and so did the verger. "It's one of the sand buckets," he said, and burst into tears.

It was physically impossible for the verger to be suffering from time-lag, unless it was somehow contagious. He was giving a good imitation of it, though.

"I saw that bucket only last night," he blubbered into a very sooty handkerchief, "and now look at it."

"We'll clean it up," Carruthers said, patting him awkwardly. "It'll be as good as new," which I doubted.

"The handle's blown clean off," the verger said. He blew his nose loudly. "I filled that bucket with sand myself. Hung it up by the south door myself."

The south door was at the other end of the church, with the full length of the nave and rows and rows of solid oak pews between it and the Drapers' Chapel.

"We'll find the handle," Carruthers said, which I also doubted, and they knelt as if in prayer and started digging through the timbers.

I left them and the new recruit, who was peering under the steps, presumably looking for cats, and went back over to where the roof had fallen in in one piece.

And stood there in what had been the center aisle, trying to reason out where to look. The blast had knocked the sand bucket nearly half the length of the church in the opposite direction of the blast from the Smiths' Chapel window. Which meant the bishop's bird stump could be anywhere.

And it was dark. The searchlights had come on, sweeping the sky in long arcs, and off to the north an orange-brown glow from a fire Posts One through Seventeen hadn't yet got under control lit the sky, but neither of them gave any light, and the moon was nowhere to be seen.

We wouldn't be able to work much longer, and Lady Schrapnell would meet us in the net, demanding to know where we'd been and why we hadn't found the bishop's bird stump. She'd send me back to try again, or, worse, she'd put me back on jumble sale duty, with all those dreadful penwipers and embroidered tea cloths and hard-as-rock cakes.

Perhaps I could simply stay here, enlist in the Infantry and get sent to somewhere safe and quiet, like the beaches of Normandy. No, D-Day wasn't until 1944. To North Africa. El Alamein.

I shoved aside a burnt end of a pew and lifted the stone beneath it. Under it was pavement, the sandstone floor of the Dyers' Chapel. I sat down on a piece of coping.

Mr. Spivens trotted over and began scrabbling at the pavement. "It's no use, boy," I said. "It's not here." I thought despairingly of the sweet-pea penwipers I would have to purchase.

Mr. Spivens sat down at my feet, looking up at me sympathetically.

"You'd help if you could, wouldn't you, boy?" I said. "It's no wonder they call you man's best friend. Faithful and loyal and true, you share in our sorrows and rejoice with us in our triumphs, the truest friend we ever have known, a better friend than we deserve. You have thrown in your lot with us, through thick and thin, on battlefield and hearthrug, refusing to leave your master even when death and destruction lie all around. Ah, noble dog, you are the furry mirror in which we see our better selves reflected, man as he could be, unstained by war or ambition, unspoilt by—"

And found myself yanked back to Oxford and hauled off to Infirmary before I'd even finished patting him on the head.

# C H A P T E R   T W O

The Spanish Inquisition—Oxford, City of Dreaming Spires—
Escape—Entanglement—Extrication—Explication—The Playing
Fields of Merton—Eavesdropping—Difference Between Literature
and Real Life—Some Sort of Nymph—An Important Clue—Lady
Windermere's Fan—A Good Idea

Your partner says you're suffering from advanced time-lag, Mr. Henry," the nurse said, fastening a tach bracelet round my wrist.

"Listen," I said, "I'm aware that I may have got a bit carried away on the dog thing, but I must get back to Coventry immediately."

It was bad enough that I'd landed fifteen hours later than I was supposed to have. Now I'd also left the cathedral only partly searched, which was as bad as not searching at all, and even if I was able to get back there at something close to the time I'd left at, there would still be all those missing moments, during which the verger, led by the cat, might have found the bishop's bird stump and given it for safekeeping to his brother-in-law, whence it would pass out of history altogether.

"It's essential I return to the ruins," I said. "The bishop's bird stump—"

"Preoccupation with irrelevancies," the nurse said into her handheld. "Appearance dirty and disheveled."

"I was working in a burnt-out cathedral," I said. "And I must get back there. The—"

She popped a temp into my mouth and stuck a monitor on my wrist.

"How many drops have you made in the last two weeks?" she said.

I watched her punch the reads into her handheld, trying to remember what the legal limit on drops was. Eight? Five?

"Four," I said. "The person you should be examining is Carruthers. He's even dirtier than I am, and you should have heard him, going on about the stars and the 'future ye ken not.' "

"What symptoms are you experiencing? Disorientation?"

"No."

"Drowsiness?"

That was more difficult. Everyone under Lady Schrapnell's lash was automatically sleep deprived, but I doubted that the nurse would take that into consideration, and at any rate it didn't manifest itself so much as drowsiness as a sort of "walking dead" numbness, like people bombarded night after night in the Blitz had suffered from.

"No," I said finally.

"Slowness in Answering," she said into the handheld. "When's the last time you slept?"

"1940," I said promptly, which is the problem with Quickness in Answering.

She typed some more. "Have you been experiencing any difficulty in distinguishing sounds?"

"No," I said, smiling at her. Infirmary nurses usually resemble something out of the Spanish Inquisition, but this one had an almost kindly face, the sort an assistant torturer, the one who straps you to the rack or holds the door to the Iron Maiden open for you, might have.

"Blurring of vision?" she asked.

"No," I said, trying not to squint.

"How many fingers am I holding up?"

Slowness in Answering or not, this question required some thought. Two was the most likely number, being easily confused with both three and one, but she might have chosen five to confuse me, and if that was the case, should I answer four, since the thumb isn't technically a finger? Or might she be holding her hand behind her back?

"Five," I said finally.

"How is that possible when according to you, you only made four drops?"

No matter how far my guess had been from the actual number of extended fingers, this was surely an inappropriate response. I considered asking her to repeat the question, but decided she would type in Difficulty in Distinguishing Sounds. I decided on a frontal attack.

"I don't think you understand the seriousness of the situation," I said. "The cathedral's consecration is seventeen days from now, and Lady Schrapnell—"

The nurse handed me a stiff card and went back to making incriminating remarks into the handheld. I looked at the card, hoping it wasn't something I was supposed to read as a further test of Blurring. Especially as it appeared to be blank.

"It's essential that the bishop's bird stump—" I said.

The nurse flipped the card over. "Tell me what you see."

It appeared to be a postal card of Oxford. Seen from Headington Hill, her dear old dreaming spires and mossy stones, her hushed, elm-shaded quads where the last echoes of the Middle Ages can still be heard, murmuring of ancient learning and scholarly tradition, of—

"That's about enough of that," she said, and wrenched the card out of my hand. "You have an advanced case of time-lag, Mr. Henry. I'm prescribing two weeks' bed rest. And no time travel."

"Two weeks?" I said. "But the consecration's in seventeen days—"

"Let other people worry about the consecration. You need to focus on getting rest."

"You don't understand—"

She folded her arms. "I certainly don't. I suppose your devotion to duty is admirable, but why you should want to risk your health to rebuild an archaic symbol of an outmoded religion is beyond me."

I *don't* want to, I thought. Lady Schrapnell wants to, and what Lady Schrapnell wants, Lady Schrapnell gets. She had already overcome the Church of England, Oxford University, a construction crew of four thousand who informed her daily it was impossible to build a cathedral in six months, and the objections of everyone from Parliament to the Coventry City Council, to rebuild her "archaic symbol." I didn't stand a chance.

"Do you know what fifty billion pounds could do for medicine?" the nurse said, typing things into the handheld. "We could find a cure for Ebola II, we could vaccinate children all over the world against HIV, we could purchase some decent equipment. With what Lady Schrapnell is spending on the stained-glass windows alone, Radcliffe Infirmary could build an entire new facility with the latest in equipment." The handheld spit out a strip of paper.

"It isn't devotion to duty, it's—"

"It's criminal carelessness, Mr. Henry." She tore off the strip and handed it to me. "I want you to follow these instructions to the letter."

I looked bleakly at the list. The first line read, "Fourteen days' uninterrupted bed rest."

There was nowhere in Oxford I could get uninterrupted bed rest, or in England, for that matter. When Lady Schrapnell found out I was back, she'd track me down and interrupt me with a vengeance. I could see her storming in, flinging the covers off, and leading me by the ear over to the net.

"I want you to eat a high-protein diet and drink at least eight glasses of fluid daily," the nurse said. "No caffeine, no alcohol, no stimulants."

A thought struck me. "Could I be admitted to Infirmary?" I said hopefully. If anyone could keep Lady Schrapnell out, it would be those Grand Inquisitors, the ward nurses. "Put in isolation or something?"

"Isolation?" she said. "Certainly not. Time-lag isn't a disease, Mr. Henry. It's a biochemical imbalance brought about by disruption of the internal clock and the inner ear. You don't need medical treatment. All you need is rest and the present."

"But I won't be able to sleep—"

Her handheld began to bleep. I jumped.

"Exaggerated Nervousness," she said, typing it into the handheld, and to me, "I want to run a few tests. Take off your clothes and put this on," she said, taking a paper gown out of a drawer and dumping it on my legs. "I'll be back directly. The fastening tapes go in the back. And wash up. You're covered in soot."

She went out and shut the door. I got off the examining table, leaving a long black smear where I'd been sitting, and went over to the door.

"Worst case of time-lag I've ever seen," she was saying to someone. I hoped it wasn't Lady Schrapnell. "He could write rhymed verse for the dailies."

It wasn't Lady Schrapnell. I knew because I couldn't hear whoever it was answer.

The nurse said, "He's showing undue anxiety, which isn't a usual symptom. I want to run a scan to see if I can find out the source of the anxiety."

I could tell her right now the source of my anxiety, which was *not* undue, if she'd only listen, which wasn't likely. And fierce though she was, she was no match for Lady Schrapnell.

I couldn't stay here. When you have a scan, they strap you into a long enclosed tube for an hour and a half and communicate with you by microphone. I could hear Lady Schrapnell's voice booming at me through the earphones, "*There* you are. Come out of that contraption immediately!"

I couldn't stay here, and I couldn't go back to my rooms. They were the first place she'd look. Perhaps I could find somewhere in the infirmary and sleep long enough to be able to think clearly what to do.

Mr. Dunworthy, I thought. If anyone could find me somewhere quiet and unlikely to hide, it would be Mr. Dunworthy. I put the paper gown, somewhat soot-smudged, back in the drawer, tugged on my boots, and climbed out the window.

Balliol was just down the Woodstock Road from Infirmary, but I didn't dare risk it. I went round to the ambulance entrance, up to Adelaide and through a yard to Walton Street. If Somerville was open, I could cut through its quad to Little Clarendon and down Worcester to the Broad, and come in through Balliol's back gate.

Somerville was open, but the journey took a good deal longer than I thought it would, and when I did reach the gate, something had happened to it. It had been twisted in on itself, and the ironwork scrolls had been bent into prongs and hooks and points, which kept catching on my coveralls.

At first I thought it was bomb damage, but that couldn't be right. The Luftwaffe was supposed to hit London tonight. And the gate, including prongs and points, had been painted a bright green.

I tried sidling through crabwise, but the epaulet on my non-AFS uniform caught on one of the hooks, and when I tried to back out, I got even more entangled. I flailed about wildly, trying to free myself.

"Let me help you there, sir," a polite voice said, and I turned around, as much as I was able, and saw Mr. Dunworthy's secretary.

"Finch," I said. "Thank God you're here. I was just coming to see Mr. Dunworthy."

He unhooked the epaulet and took hold of my sleeve. "This way, sir," he said, "no, not that way, through here, that's it. No, no, *this* way," and led me, finally, to freedom.

But on the same side I'd been when I started. "This is no good, Finch," I said. "We've still got to get through that gate into Balliol."

"That's Merton, sir," he said. "You're on their playing fields."

I turned and looked where he was pointing. Finch was right. There was the soccer field, and beyond it the cricket ground, and beyond that, in Christ Church Meadow, the scaffolding-and-blue-plastic-covered spire of Coventry Cathedral.

"How did Balliol's gate get here?" I said.

"This is Merton's pedestrian gate."

I squinted at the gate. Right again. It was a turnstile gate, designed to keep bicycles out.

"The nurse said you were time-lagged, but I had no idea . . . No, this way." He took hold of my arm and propelled me along the path.

"The nurse?" I said.

"Mr. Dunworthy sent me over to Infirmary to fetch you, but you'd already left," he said, guiding me between buildings and out onto the High. "He wants to see you, though what use you'll be to him in your condition I can't quite see."

"He wants to see *me?*" I said, confused. I had thought I was the one who wanted to see him. I thought of something else. "How did he know I was in Infirmary?"

"Lady Schrapnell phoned him," he said, and I dived for cover.

"It's all right," Finch said, following me into the shop doorway I'd ducked into. "Mr. Dunworthy told her you'd been taken to the Royal Free Hospital in London. It'll take her at least half an hour to get there." He pulled me forcibly out of the doorway and across the High. "Personally, I think he should have told her you'd been taken to Manhattan General. How *do* you put up with her?"

You keep a sharp eye out, I thought, following Finch into the walkway next to St. Mary the Virgin's and keeping close to the wall.

"She has no sense of the proper way of doing things," he said. "Won't go through the proper channels, won't fill up requisition forms. She simply *raids* the place—paper clips, pens, handhelds."

And historians, I thought.

"I never have any idea of what supplies to order, if I had time to order anything. I spend all my time trying to keep her out of Mr. Dunworthy's office. She's in there constantly, harping on something. Copings and brasses and lectionaries. Last week it was the Wade Tomb's chipped corner. How did it get chipped and when did it get chipped, before the raid or during it, and what sort of edges does it have, rough or smooth? Must be completely authentic, she says. 'God is—' "

" 'In the details,' " I said.

"She even tried to recruit me," Finch said. "Wanted me to go back to the Blitz and look for the bishop's bathtub."

"Bird stump," I corrected.

"That's what I said," he said, looking hard at me. "You're having difficulty distinguishing sounds, aren't you? The nurse said you were. And you're obviously disoriented." He shook his head. "You're not going to be any use at all."

"What does Mr. Dunworthy want to see me about?"

"There's been an incident."

"Incident" was the euphemism the AFS employed to mean a high-explosive bomb, houses reduced to rubble, bodies buried, fires everywhere. But surely Finch didn't mean that sort of incident. Or perhaps I was still having Difficulty Distinguishing Sounds.

"An incident?" I said.

"Calamity, actually. One of his historians. Nineteenth Century. Pinched a rat."

Oh, definitely Difficulty, although there had been rats in the Victorian era. But no one would have pinched one. It would pinch you back, or worse. "What did you say?" I asked cautiously.

"I said, 'Here we are,' " Finch said, and we were. There was Balliol's gate, though not the side one, the front gate and the porter's lodge and the front quad.

I started through the quad and up the stairs to Mr. Dunworthy's room, but I was apparently still disoriented because Finch took my arm again and led me across the garden quad to Beard.

"Mr. Dunworthy's had to turn the Senior Common Room into an office. She has no respect at all for the sported oak or the notion of knocking, so Mr. Dunworthy's had to devise an outer and inner office, though I personally think a moat would have been more effective."

He opened the door to what had been the buttery. It now looked like a physician's waiting room, with a row of cushioned chairs against the wall and a pile of fax-mags on a small side table. Finch's desk stood next to the inner door and practically in front of it, no doubt so Finch could fling himself between it and Lady Schrapnell.

"I'll see if he's in," Finch said and started round the desk.

"Absolutely not!" Mr. Dunworthy's voice thundered from within. "It's completely out of the question!"

Oh, Lord, she was here. I shrank back against the wall, looking wildly for somewhere to hide.

Finch grabbed my sleeve, and hissed, "It's not her," but I had already deduced that.

"I don't see why not," a female voice had answered, and it wasn't Lady Schrapnell, because it was sweet rather than stentorian, and I couldn't make out what she said after "why not."

"Who is it?" I whispered, relaxing in Finch's grip.

"The calamity," he whispered back.

"What on earth made you think you could bring something like that through the net?" Mr. Dunworthy bellowed. "You've studied temporal theory!"

Finch winced. "Shall I tell Mr. Dunworthy you're here?" he asked hesitantly.

"No, that's all right," I said, sinking down on one of the chintz-covered chairs. "I'll wait."

"Why on earth did you take it into the net with you in the first place?" Mr. Dunworthy shouted.

Finch picked up one of the ancient fax-mags and brought it over to me.

"I don't need anything to read," I said. "I'll just sit here and eavesdrop along with you."

"I thought you might sit on the mag," he said. "It's extremely difficult to get soot out of chintz."

I stood up and let him put the opened mag on the seat and then sat down again.

"If you were going to do something so completely irresponsible," Mr. Dunworthy said, "why couldn't you have waited till after the consecration?"

I leaned back against the wall and closed my eyes. It was rather pleasant listening to someone else being read out for a change, and by someone besides Lady Schrapnell, even though it was unclear what exactly the calamity was guilty of. Particularly when Mr. Dunworthy yelled, "That is no excuse. Why didn't you simply pull the cab out of the water and leave it on the bank? Why did you have to carry it into the net with you?"

Cab-toting seemed even less likely than rat-pinching, and neither one seemed in need of rescue from a watery grave. Rats especially. They were always swimming away from sinking ships, weren't they? And had they had taxis in the Nineteenth Century? Horse-drawn hansom cabs, but they were too heavy to carry even if they would fit into the net.

In books and vids, those being eavesdropped upon always thoughtfully explain what they are talking about for the edification of the eavesdropper. The eavesdroppee says, "Of course, as you all know, the cab to which I refer is Sherlock Holmes's hansom cab which had been accidentally driven off a bridge during a heavy fog while following the Hound of the Baskervilles, and which I found it necessary to steal for the following reasons," at which point said theft is fully explained to the person crouched behind the door. Sometimes a floor plan or map is thoughtfully provided next to the frontispiece.

No such consideration is given the croucher in real life. Instead of outlining the situation, the calamity said, "Because bane came back to make sure," which only confused the issue further.

"Heartless monster," she said, and it was unclear whether she was refer-ring to the bane that had come back or to Mr. Dunworthy. "And it would only have gone back to the house, and he'd have tried it again. I didn't want him to see me because he'd know I wasn't a contemp and there wasn't anyplace to hide but the net. He'd have seen me in the gazebo. I didn't think—"

"Exactly, Miss Kindle," Mr. Dunworthy said. "You didn't think."

"What are you going to do?" the calamity said. "Are you going to send it back? You're going to drown it, aren't you?"

"I do not intend to do anything until I have considered all the possi-bilities," Mr. Dunworthy said.

"Utterly heartless," she said.

"I am extremely fond of cabbies," he said, "but there is a good deal at stake here. I must consider *all* the consequences and possibilities before acting. I realize that's an alien notion to you."

Cabbies? I wondered why he was so fond of them. I have always found them entirely too talkative, especially the ones during the Blitz, who apparently paid no attention to the admonition that "Loose lips sink ships." They were always telling me how someone had been buried alive in the rubble or got blown up— "Head was all the way across the street in a shop window. Milliner's. Riding in a taxi just like you are now."

"Are you sending *me* back?" she said. "I told them I was going out sketching. If I don't come back, they'll think *I've* drowned."

"I don't know. Until I decide, I want you in your rooms."

"Can I take it with me?"

"No."

There was a sinister-sounding silence, and then the door opened, and there stood the most beautiful creature I'd ever seen.

Finch had said Nineteenth Century, and I'd expected hoop skirts, but she had on a long, greenish gown that clung to her slim body as if it were wet. Her auburn hair trailed about her shoulders and down her back like water weeds, and the whole effect was that of a Waterhouse nymph, rising like a wraith out of the dark water.

I stood up, gawping as foolishly as the new recruit, and took off my ARP helmet, wishing I had cleaned up when the nurse told me to.

She took hold of her long, trailing sleeve and wrung it out on the carpet. Finch grabbed a fax-mag and spread it under her.

"Oh, good, Ned, you're here," Mr. Dunworthy said from the door. "Just the person I wanted to see."

The nymph looked at me, and her eyes were a dark clear greenish-brown, the color of a forest pool. She narrowed them. "You're not sending *that*, are you?" she said to Mr. Dunworthy.

"I'm not sending anyone. Or anything, until I've thought about it. Now go change out of those wet clothes before you catch cold."

She gathered up her dripping skirts with one hand, and started out. At the door she turned back, her rosy lips open to impart some final benediction, some last word to me perhaps of love and devotion. "Don't feed her. She's had an entire place," she said, and drifted out the door.

I started after her, bewitched, but Mr. Dunworthy had his hand on my arm. "So Finch found you all right," he said, steering me around behind Finch's desk and into the inner office, "I was afraid you'd be off in 1940 at one of those church bazaars Lady Schrapnell keeps sending you to."

Outside the window I could see her crossing the quad, dripping gracefully on the pavement, a lovely . . . what were they called? Dryads? No, those were the ones that lived in trees. Sirens?

Mr. Dunworthy came over to the window. "This is all Lady Schrapnell's fault. Kindle's one of my best historians. Six months with Lady Schrapnell, and look at her!" He waved his hand at me. "Look at you, for that matter. The woman's like a high-explosive bomb!"

The siren passed out of my vision and into the mist she had emerged from, only that wasn't right. Sirens lived on rocks and shipwrecked sailors. And it sounded like dryads. Delphides? No, those were the ones who went about predicting doom and disaster.

". . . had no business sending her in the first place," Mr. Dunworthy was saying. "I tried to tell her, but would she listen? Of course not. 'No stone unturned,' she says. Sends her off to the Victorian era. Sends you off to jumble sales to buy pincushions and tea towels!"

"And calves' foot jelly," I said.

"Calves' foot jelly?" he said, looking at me curiously.

"For the sick," I said. "Only I don't think the sick eat it. *I* wouldn't eat it. I think they give it to the next jumble sale. It makes the rounds from year to year. Like fruitcake."

"Yes, well," he said, frowning. "So now a stone *has* been turned, and she's created a serious problem, which is what I wanted to see you about. Sit down, sit down," he said, motioning me toward a leather armchair.

Finch got there first with a fax-mag, murmuring, "So difficult to get soot out of leather."

"And take off your hat. Good Lord," Mr. Dunworthy said, adjusting his spectacles, "you look dreadful. Where have you been?"

"The soccer field," I said.

"I gather it was a somewhat rough game."

"I found him in the pedestrian gate by Merton's playing fields," Finch explained.

"I thought he was in Infirmary."

"He climbed out the window."

"Ah," Mr. Dunworthy said. "But how did he get in this condition?"

"I was looking for the bishop's bird stump," I said.

"On Merton's playing fields?"

"In the cathedral ruins just before he was brought to Infirmary," Finch said helpfully.

"Did you find it?" Mr. Dunworthy said.

"No," I said, "and that's the reason I came to see you. I wasn't able to finish searching the ruins, and Lady Schrapnell—"

"—is the least of our worries. Which is something I never thought I'd find myself saying," he said ruefully. "I gather Mr. Finch has explained the situation?"

"Yes. No," I said. "Perhaps you'd better review it for me."

"A crisis has developed regarding the net. I've notified Time Travel and—Finch, did Chiswick say when he'd be here?"

"I'll check on it, sir," he said, and went out.

"A very serious situation," Mr. Dunworthy said. "One of our historians—"

Finch came back in. "He's on his way over," he said.

"Good," Dunworthy said. "Before he gets here, the situation is this: One of our historians stole a fan and brought it back through the net with her."

A fan. Well, that made a good deal more sense than a rat. Or a cab. And it explained the pinching part. "Like Lady Windermere's mother," I said.

"Lady Windermere's mother?" Mr. Dunworthy said, looking sharply at Finch.

"Advanced time-lag, sir," Finch said. "Disorientation, difficulty in distinguishing sounds, tendency to sentimentalize, impaired ability to *reason logically*," he said, emphasizing the last two words.

"Advanced?" Dunworthy said. "How many drops have you made?"

"Fourteen this week. Ten jumble sales and six bishops' wives. No, thirteen. I keep forgetting Mrs. Bittner. She was in Coventry. Not the Coventry I was in just now. Coventry today."

"Bittner," Mr. Dunworthy said curiously. "This wasn't Elizabeth Bittner, was it?"

"Yes, sir," I said. "The widow of the last bishop of Coventry Cathedral."

"Good Lord, I haven't seen her in years," he said. "I knew her back in the early days when we were first experimenting with the net. Wonderful girl. The first time I saw her I thought she was the most beautiful creature I'd ever seen. Too bad she had to fall in love with Bitty Bittner. She was absolutely devoted to him. How did she look?"

Hardly like a girl, I thought. She'd been a frail, white-haired old lady who had seemed ill-at-ease through the whole interview. She had probably thought Lady Schrapnell was going to recruit her and send her off to the Middle Ages. "She looked very well," I said. "She said she had some difficulty with arthritis."

"Arthritis," he said, shaking his head. "Hard to imagine Lizzie Bittner with arthritis. What did you go and see her for? She wasn't even born when the old Coventry Cathedral burned down."

"Lady Schrapnell thought the bishop's bird stump might have been stored in the crypt of the new cathedral and that since Mrs. Bittner was there when the cathedral was sold, she might have supervised the cleaning out of the crypt and have seen it."

"And had she?"

"No, sir. She said it had been destroyed in the fire."

"I remember when they had to sell Coventry Cathedral," he said. "People had lost interest in religion, attendance was down at the services . . . Lizzie

Bittner," he said fondly. "Arthritis. I suppose her hair's not red anymore either?"

"Preoccupation with irrelevancies," Finch said loudly. "Miss Jenkins said Mr. Henry had a severe case of time-lag."

"Miss Jenkins?" Mr. Dunworthy said.

"The nurse who examined Mr. Henry at Infirmary."

"Lovely creature," I said. "A ministering angel, whose gentle hands have soothed many a fevered brow."

Finch and Mr. Dunworthy exchanged looks.

"She said it was the worst case of time-lag she'd ever seen," Finch said.

"Which is why I came to see you," I said. "She's prescribed two weeks of uninterrupted bed rest, and Lady Schrapnell—"

"Will never allow that," Mr. Dunworthy said. "The cathedral's consecration is only seventeen days away."

"I tried to tell the nurse that, sir, but she wouldn't listen. She told me to go to my rooms and go to bed."

"No, no, first place Lady Schrapnell would look. Finch, where is she?"

"In London. She just phoned from the Royal Free."

I started up out of the chair.

"I told her there'd been a mistake in communications," Finch said, "that Mr. Henry'd been taken to the Royal Masonic."

"Good. Ring up the Royal Masonic and tell them to keep her there."

"I've already done so," Finch said.

"Excellent," Mr. Dunworthy said. "Sit down, Ned. Where was I?"

"Lady Windermere's fan," Finch said.

"Only it wasn't a fan the historian brought through the net," Mr. Dunworthy said. "It was—"

"Did you say brought through the net?" I said. "You can't bring anything through the net from the past. It's impossible, isn't it?"

"Apparently not," Mr. Dunworthy said.

There was a scuffling sound in the outer office. "I thought you said she was at the Royal Free," Mr. Dunworthy said to Finch, and a short, harried-looking man burst in. He was wearing a lab coat and carrying a bleeping handheld, and I recognized him as the head of Time Travel.

"Oh, good, you're here, Mr. Chiswick," Mr. Dunworthy said. "I want to talk to you about an incident concerning—"

"And I want to talk to you about Lady Schrapnell," Chiswick said. "The woman's completely out of control. She pages me night and day, wanting to know why we can't send people more than once to the same time and place, why we can't process more drops per hour *even though* she has systematically stripped me of my research staff *and* my net staff and sent them running all over the past looking at almsboxes and analyzing flying buttresses." He waved the bleeping handheld. "That's her now. She's paged me six times in the last hour, demanding to know where one of her missing historians is! Time Travel agreed to this project because of the opportunity the money afforded us to advance our research into temporal theory, but that research has come to a complete stop. She's appropriated half my labs for her artisans, and tied up every computer in the science area."

He stopped to punch keys on the still bleeping handheld, and Mr. Dunworthy took the opportunity to say, "The theory of time travel is what I wanted to discuss with you. One of my historians—"

Chiswick wasn't listening. The handheld had stopped bleeping, and now it was spitting out inch upon inch of paper. "Look at this!" he said, tearing off a foot and brandishing it before Mr. Dunworthy. "She wants me to have one of my staff telephone every hospital in the greater London area and find this missing historian of hers. Henry, his name is, Ned Henry. One of my staff. I don't *have* any staff! She's taken every single one of them except Lewis, and she tried to take him! Luckily, he—"

Mr. Dunworthy broke in. "What would happen if an historian brought something from the past forward through the net?"

"Did *she* ask you that?" he said. "Of course she did. She's gotten it into her head to have this bishop's bird stump she's so obsessed with if she has to go back in time and steal it. I've told her and told her, bringing anything from the past to the present would violate the laws of the space-time continuum, and do you know what she said? 'Laws are made to be broken.'"

He swept on, unchecked, and Mr. Dunworthy leaned back in his desk chair, took off his spectacles, and examined them thoughtfully.

"I tried to explain to her," Chiswick said, "that the laws of physics aren't mere rules or regulations, that they're *laws*, and that the breaking of them would result in disastrous consequences."

"What sort of disastrous consequences?" Mr. Dunworthy said.

"That is impossible to predict. The space-time continuum is a chaotic system, in which every event is connected to every other in elaborate, nonlinear ways that make prediction impossible. Bringing an object forward through time would create a parachronistic incongruity. At best, the incongruity might result in increased slippage. At worst, it might make time travel impossible. Or alter the course of history. Or destroy the universe. Which is why such an incongruity is not possible, as I *tried* to tell Lady Schrapnell!"

"Increased slippage," Mr. Dunworthy said. "An incongruity would cause an increase in slippage?"

"Theoretically," Mr. Chiswick said. "Incongruities were one of the areas Lady Schrapnell's money was to enable us to research, research which now has gone completely by the wayside in favor of this idiotic cathedral! The woman's impossible! Last week she ordered me to decrease the amount of slippage per drop. Ordered me! She doesn't understand slippage either."

Mr. Dunworthy leaned forward and put his spectacles on. "Has there been an increase in slippage?"

"No. Lady Schrapnell simply has no concept of the workings of time travel. She—"

"The field of marrows," I said.

"What?" Mr. Chiswick turned and glared at me.

"The farmer's wife thought he was a German paratrooper."

"Paratrooper?" Chiswick said, and his eyes narrowed. "You're not the missing historian, are you? What's your name?"

"John Bartholomew," Mr. Dunworthy said.

"Whom, I see from his condition, Lady Schrapnell has recruited. She must be stopped, Dunworthy." The handheld began bleeping and spitting again. He read aloud. " 'No info yet on Henry's whereabouts. Why not? Send location immediately. Need two more people to go to Great Exhibition, 1850, check on possible origins of bishop's bird stump.' " He crumpled the readout and threw it on Mr. Dunworthy's desk. "You've got to do something about her now! Before she destroys the university!" he said, and swept out.

"Or the known universe," Mr. Dunworthy murmured.

"Should I go after him?" Finch asked.

"No," Mr. Dunworthy said. "Try to get in touch with Andrews, and call up the Bodleian's files on parachronistic incongruities."

Finch went out. Mr. Dunworthy took off his spectacles and peered through them, frowning.

"I know this is a bad time," I said, "but I wondered if you had any idea where I might be able to go to convalesce. Away from Oxford."

"Meddling," Mr. Dunworthy said. "Meddling got us into this, and more meddling will only make it worse." He put his spectacles back on and stood up. "Clearly the best thing to do is wait and see what happens, if anything," he said, pacing. "The chances that its disappearance would affect history are statistically insignificant, particularly from that era. Whole batches of them were routinely thrown in rivers to keep the numbers down."

The number of fans? I thought.

"And the fact that it came through the net is in itself a proof that it didn't create an incongruity, or the net wouldn't have opened." He wiped his spectacles on the tail of his jacket and held them up to the light. "It's been over a hundred and fifty years. If it were going to destroy the universe, it would very likely have done so by now."

He exhaled onto the lenses and wiped them again. "And I refuse to believe that there are two courses of history in which Lady Schrapnell and her project to rebuild Coventry Cathedral could exist."

Lady Schrapnell. She'd be back from the Royal Masonic any time now. I leaned forward in the chair. "Mr. Dunworthy," I said, "I was hoping you could think of somewhere where I could recover from the time-lag."

"On the other hand, there's a good chance that the reason there wasn't an incongruity is that it was returned before there could be any consequences, disastrous or otherwise."

"The nurse said two weeks' bed rest, but if I could just get three or four days—"

"But even if that is the case," he stood up and began pacing, "there's still no reason not to wait. That's the beauty of time travel. One can wait three or four days, or two weeks, or a year, and still return it immediately."

"If Lady Schrapnell finds me—"

He stopped pacing and stared at me. "I hadn't thought about that. Oh, Lord, if Lady Schrapnell were to find out about it—"

"If you could just suggest somewhere quiet and out of the way—"

"Finch!" Mr. Dunworthy shouted, and Finch came in from the outer office, carrying a readout.

"Here's the bibliography on parachronistic incongruities," he said. "There wasn't much. Mr. Andrews is in 1560. Lady Schrapnell sent him there to examine the clerestory arches. Should I try to get Mr. Chiswick back here?"

"First things first," Mr. Dunworthy said. "We need to find Ned here a place where he can rest and recuperate from his time-lag without interruption."

"Lady Schrapnell—" I said.

"Exactly," Mr. Dunworthy said. "It can't be anywhere in this century. Or the Twentieth Century. And it needs to be somewhere peaceful and out of the way, a country house, perhaps, on a river. The Thames."

"You're not thinking of—" Finch said.

"He needs to leave immediately," Mr. Dunworthy said. "Before Lady Schrapnell finds out about it."

"Oh!" Finch gasped. "Yes, I see. But Mr. Henry's in no condition to—" Finch said, but Mr. Dunworthy cut him off.

"Ned," he said to me, "how would you like to go to the Victorian era?"

The Victorian era. Long dreamy afternoons boating on the Thames and playing croquet on emerald lawns with girls in white frocks and fluttering hair ribbons. And later, tea under the willow tree, served in delicate Sèvres cups by bowing butlers, anxious to minister to one's every whim, and those same girls, reading aloud from a slim volume of poetry, their voices floating like flower petals on the scented air. "All in the golden afternoon, where Childhood's dreams are twined, In Memory's mystic band—"

Finch shook his head. "I don't think this is a good idea, Mr. Dunworthy."

"Nonsense," Mr. Dunworthy said. "Listen to him. He'll fit right in."

*"...when you have eliminated the impossible, whatever remains, however improbable, must be the truth."*

*Sherlock Holmes*

# CHAPTER THREE

A Straightforward Job—Angels, Archangels, Cherubim, Powers,
Thrones, Dominions, and the Other One—Drowsiness—I Am
Prepped in Victorian History and Customs—Luggage—The
Inspiring Story of Ensign Klepperman—More Luggage—Difficulty
in Distinguishing Sounds—Fish Forks—Sirens, Sylphs, Nymphs,
Dryads, and the Other One—An Arrival—Dogs Not Man's Best
Friend—Another Arrival—An Abrupt Departure

Do you think that's a good idea?" Finch said. "He's already suffering from advanced time-lag. Won't that large a jump—?"

"Not necessarily," Mr. Dunworthy said. "And after he's completed his assignment, he can stay as long as he needs to to recover. You heard him, it's a perfect holiday spot."

"But in his condition, do you think he'll be able to—" Finch said anxiously.

"It's a perfectly straightforward job," Mr. Dunworthy said. "A child could do it. The important thing is that it be done before Lady Schrapnell gets back, and Ned's the only historian in Oxford who's not off somewhere chasing after misericords. Take him over to the net and then ring up Time Travel and tell Chiswick to meet me there."

The telephone bipped, and Finch answered it, then listened for a considerable length of time. "No, he *was* at the Royal Free," he said finally, "but they decided to run a TWR, so they had to transport him to St. Thomas's. Yes, in Lambeth Palace Road." He listened again, holding the receiver some distance from his ear. "No, this time I'm certain." He rang off. "That was Lady Schrapnell," he said unnecessarily. "I'm afraid she may be returning soon."

"What's a TWR?" Mr. Dunworthy said.

"I invented it. I think Mr. Henry had best get over to the net to be prepped."

Finch walked me over to the lab, which I was grateful for, especially as it seemed to me we were going completely the wrong direction, though when we got there, the door looked the same, and there was the same group of SPCC picketers outside.

They were carrying electric placards that read, "What's wrong with the one we already have?," "Keep Coventry in Coventry," and "It's Ours!" One of them handed me a flyer that began, "The restoration of Coventry Cathedral will cost fifty billion pounds. For the same amount of money, the present Coventry Cathedral could not only be bought back and restored, but a new, larger shopping center could be built to replace it."

Finch pulled the tract out of my hand, gave it back to the picketer, and opened the door.

The net looked the same inside, too, though I didn't recognize the pudgy young woman at the console. She was wearing a white lab coat, and her halo of cropped blonde hair made her look like a cherub rather than a net technician.

Finch shut the door behind us, and she whirled. "What do *you* want?" she demanded.

Perhaps more an archangel than a cherub.

"We need to arrange for a jump," Finch said. "To Victorian England."

"Out of the question," she snapped.

Definitely an archangel. The sort that tossed Adam and Eve out of the Garden.

Finch said, "Mr. Dunworthy authorized it, Miss . . ."

"Warder," she snapped.

"Miss Warder. This is a priority jump," he said.

"They're *all* priority jumps. Lady Schrapnell doesn't authorize any other sort." She picked up a clipboard and brandished it at us like a flaming sword. "Nineteen jumps, fourteen of them requiring 1940 ARP and WVS uniforms, which the wardrobe department is *completely* out of, and all the fixes. I'm three hours behind schedule on rendezvous, and who knows how many more *priority* jumps Lady Schrapnell will come up with before the day's over." She slammed the clipboard down. "I don't have time for this.

Victorian England! Tell Mr. Dunworthy it's completely out of the question."
She turned back to the console and began hitting keys.

Finch, undaunted, tried another tack. "Where's Mr. Chaudhuri?"

"Exactly," she said, whirling round again. "Where *is* Badri, and why isn't
he here running the net? Well, I'll tell you." She picked up the clipboard
threateningly again. "Lady *Schrap*nell—"

"She didn't send him to 1940, did she?" I asked. Badri was of Pakistani
descent. He'd be arrested as a Japanese spy.

"No," she said. "She made him drive her to London to look for some
historian who's gone missing. Which leaves me to run Wardrobe *and* the
net *and* deal with people who waste my time asking stupid questions." She
crashed the clipboard down. "Now, if you don't have any more of them, I
have a *priority* fix to calculate." She whirled back to the console and began
pounding fiercely at the keys.

Or perhaps an arch-archangel, one of those beings with enormous wings
and hundreds of eyes, "and they were terrible to see." What were they called?
Sarabands?

"I think I'd better go fetch Mr. Dunworthy," Finch whispered to me.
"You'd best stay here."

I was more than glad to comply. I was beginning to feel the drowsiness
that the nurse at Infirmary had questioned me about, and all I wanted to
do was sit down and rest. I found a chair on the far side of the net, took a
stack of gas masks and stirrup pumps off another one so I could put my feet
up on it, and stretched out to wait for Finch and try to remember the name
of arch-archangels, the ones "full of eyes round about." It began with an "S."
Samurai? No, that was Lady Schrapnell. Sylphs? No, those were heavenly
sprites, who flitted through the air. The water sprites began with something
else. An "N." Nemesis? No, *that* was Lady Schrapnell.

What were they called? Hylas had come upon them while he was fetching
water from a pond, and they had pulled him into the water with them,
twining their white arms about him, tangling him in their trailing auburn
hair, drowning him in the dark, deep waters. . . .

I must have dozed off because when I opened my eyes, Mr. Dunworthy
was there, and the tech was threatening him with her clipboard.

"It's out of the question," she was saying. "I've got four fixes to do, eight
rendezvous, *and* I've got to replace a costume one of *your* historians got
wet and ruined." She flipped violently through the sheets on the clipboard.
"The soonest I can fit you in is Friday the seventh at half-past three."

"The seventh?" Finch gurgled. "That's next week!"

"It must be today," Mr. Dunworthy said.

"Today?" she said, raising the clipboard like a weapon. "*Today?*"

Seraphim. "Full of eyes all around and within, and fire, and out of the fire went forth lightning."

"It won't require calculating new time coordinates," Mr. Dunworthy said. "We're using the ones Kindle came through from. And we can use the drop you've got set up at Muchings End." He looked round at the lab. "Where's the tech in charge of Wardrobe?"

"In 1932," she said. "Sketching choir robes. On a *priority* jump for Lady Schrapnell to see whether their surplices were linen or cotton. Which means *I'm* in charge of Wardrobe. And the net. And everything else around here." She flipped the pages back down to their original position and set it down on the net console. "The whole thing's out of the question. Even if I could fit you in, he can't go like that, and, besides, he'd need to be prepped on Victorian history and customs."

"Ned's not going to tea with the Queen," Mr. Dunworthy said. "His assignment will only bring him into limited contact with the contemps, if any. He won't need a course in Victoriana for that."

The seraphim reached for her clipboard.

Finch ducked.

"He's Twentieth Century," she said. "That means he's out of his area. I can't authorize his going without his being prepped."

"Fine," Mr. Dunworthy said. He turned to me. "Darwin, Disraeli, the Indian question, *Alice in Wonderland*, Little Nell, Turner, Tennyson, *Three Men in a Boat*, crinolines, croquet—"

"Penwipers," I said.

"Penwipers, crocheted antimacassars, hair wreaths, Prince Albert, Flush, frock coats, sexual repression, Ruskin, Fagin, Elizabeth Barrett Browning, Dante Gabriel Rossetti, George Bernard Shaw, Gladstone, Galsworthy, Gothic Revival, Gilbert and Sullivan, lawn tennis, and parasols. There," he said to the seraphim. "He's been prepped."

"Nineteenth Century's required course is three semesters of political history, two—"

"Finch," Mr. Dunworthy said. "Go over to Jesus and fetch a headrig and tapes. Ned can do high-speed subliminals while you," he turned back to the seraphim, "get him dressed and set up the jump. He'll need summer clothes, white flannels, linen shirt, boating blazer. For luggage, he'll need . . ."

"Luggage!" the seraphim said, sprouting eyes. "I don't have time to collect luggage! I have nineteen jumps—"

"Fine," Mr. Dunworthy said. "We'll take care of the luggage. Finch, go over to Jesus and fetch some Victorian luggage. And did you contact Chiswick?"

"No, sir. He wasn't there, sir. I left a message."

He left, colliding with a tall, thin young black man on his way out. The black man had a sheaf of papers, and he looked no older than eighteen, and I assumed he was one of the pickets from outside and held out my hand for a leaflet, but he went up to Mr. Dunworthy and said nervously, "Mr. Dunworthy? I'm T.J. Lewis. From Time Travel. You were looking for Mr. Chiswick?"

"Yes," Mr. Dunworthy said. "Where is he?"

"In Cambridge, sir," he said.

"In Cambridge? What the devil's he doing over there?"

"Ap-applying for a job, sir," he stammered. "H-he quit, sir."

"When?"

"Just now. He said he couldn't stand working for Lady Schrapnell another minute, sir."

"Well," Mr. Dunworthy said. He took his spectacles off and peered at them. "Well. All right, then. Mr. Lewis, is it?"

"T.J., sir."

"T.J., would you go tell the assistant head—what's his name? Ranniford—that I need to speak with him. It's urgent."

T.J. looked unhappy.

"Don't tell me he's quit as well?"

"No, sir. He's in 1655, looking at roof slates."

"Of course," Mr. Dunworthy said disgustedly. "Well, then, whoever else is in charge over there."

T.J. looked even unhappier. "Uh, that would be me, sir."

"You?" Mr. Dunworthy said in surprise. "But you're only an undergraduate. You can't tell me you're the only person over there."

"Yes, sir," T.J. said. "Lady Schrapnell came and took everyone else. She would have taken me, but the first two-thirds of Twentieth Century and all of Nineteenth are a ten for blacks and therefore off-limits."

"I'm surprised that stopped her," Mr. Dunworthy said.

"It didn't," he said. "She wanted to dress me up as a Moor and send me to 1395 to check on the construction of the steeple. It was her idea that they'd assume I was a prisoner brought back from the Crusades."

"The Crusades ended in 1272," Mr. Dunworthy said.

"I know, sir. I pointed that out, also the fact that the entire past is a ten for blacks." He grinned. "It's the first time my having black skin has been an actual advantage."

"Yes, well, we'll see about that," Mr. Dunworthy said. "Have you ever heard of Ensign John Klepperman?"

"No, sir."

"World War II. Battle of Midway. The entire bridge of his ship was killed and he had to take over as captain. That's what wars and disasters do, put people in charge of things they'd never ordinarily be in charge of. Like

Time Travel. In other words, this is your big chance, Lewis. I take it you're majoring in temporal physics?"

"No, sir. Comp science, sir."

Mr. Dunworthy sighed. "Ah, well, Ensign Klepperman had never fired a torpedo either. He sank two destroyers and a cruiser. Your first assignment is to tell me what would happen if a parachronistic incongruity had occurred, what indications we would have of it. And don't tell me it couldn't happen."

"Para-chron-istic incon-gruity," T.J. said, writing it on the top of the papers he was holding. "When do you need this, sir?"

"Yesterday," Mr. Dunworthy said, handing him the bibliography from the Bodleian.

T.J. looked bewildered. "You want me to go back in time and—"

"I am *not* setting up another drop," Warder cut in.

Mr. Dunworthy shook his head tiredly. "I *meant* I need the information as soon as possible," he said to T.J.

"Oh," T.J. said. "Yes, sir. Right away, sir," and started for the door. Halfway there, he stopped and asked, "What happened to Ensign Klepperman?"

"Killed in the line of duty," Mr. Dunworthy said.

T.J. nodded. "That's what I thought."

He went out and Finch came in, carrying a headrig.

"Ring up Ernst Hasselmeyer in Berlin and ask him if he knows anything about parachronistic incongruities, and if he doesn't, ask him who does," Mr. Dunworthy said. "And then I want you to go over to the cathedral."

"The cathedral?" Finch said, alarmed. "What if Lady Schrapnell's there?"

"Hide in the Drapers' Chapel," Mr. Dunworthy said. "See if there's anyone over there who works in Time Travel, anyone at all. There has to be someone around with more experience than an undergraduate."

Finch said, "Right away, sir," and crossed over to me. He put the headrig in my ear. "The subliminal tapes, sir," he said.

I started to roll up my sleeve for the hypnotic.

"I don't think it's a good idea for you to use drugs in your condition," he said. "You'll have to listen to them at normal speed."

"Finch," Mr. Dunworthy said, coming over. "Where's Kindle?"

"You sent her to her rooms, sir," Finch said.

He touched the headrig. "Queen Victoria ruled England from 1837 to 1901," the tape said in my ear.

"Go and ask her how much slippage there was on the drop," Mr. Dunworthy said to Finch. "The one where—"

"—she brought unprecedented peace and prosperity to England."

"Yes," Mr. Dunworthy said. "And find out how much slippage there's been on the others—"

"—remembered as a decorous, slow-paced society—"

"—and telephone St. Thomas's. Tell them under no circumstances to let Lady Schrapnell leave."

"Yes, sir," Finch said and went out.

"So Lizzie Bittner is still living in Coventry?" Mr. Dunworthy asked.

"Yes," I said. "She moved back from Salisbury after her husband died," and then, because something more seemed to be expected, I said, "She told me all about the new cathedral and how Bishop Bittner had tried to save it. He reintroduced the Coventry morality plays in an attempt to shore up attendance and put up displays of the Blitz in the ruins. She took me on a tour of what had been the ruins and the new cathedral. It's a shopping center now, you know."

"Yes," he said. "I always thought it made a better shopping center than a cathedral. Mid-Twentieth-Century architecture was nearly as bad as Victorian. It was a nice gesture, though. And Bitty liked it. It was originally sold to the Church of the Hereafter or something, wasn't it? I suppose you've checked with them to make certain they don't have it?"

I nodded, and then he must have left, though I don't remember that part. A sound like the All-Clear after an air raid had started blasting in one ear, and the tapes were talking about the subservient role of women in the other.

"Women held little or no power in Victorian society," the headrig said. Except Queen Victoria, I thought, and saw that Warder was coming toward me with a wet cloth. She scrubbed roughly at my face and hands and then smeared a white lotion above my upper lip.

"The role of the Victorian woman was that of nurse and helpmeet," the headrig said, "of 'the angel in the house.' "

"*Don't* touch your lip," Warder said, pulling the measuring tape from around her neck. "Your hair will have to do. There's not enough time for fenoxidils." She encircled my head with the tape. "Part it in the middle. I said, *don't* touch your lip."

"Women were thought to be too high-strung for formal education," the subliminal said. "Their lessons were confined to drawing, music, and deportment."

"This whole thing's ridiculous." She wrapped the tape around my neck. "I should never have come to Oxford. Cambridge has a perfectly good degree in theatrical design. I could be costuming *The Taming of the Shrew* right now instead of doing three jobs at once."

I stuck a finger between the tape and my Adam's apple to prevent strangulation.

"Victorian women were sweet, softspoken, and submissive."

"You know whose fault this is, don't you?" she said, snapping the tape as she pulled it free. "Lady Schrapnell's. Why on earth does she want to rebuild Coventry Cathedral anyway? She's not even English. She's an American! Just because she married a peer doesn't mean she has the right to come over here to our country and start rebuilding our churches. They weren't even married that long."

She yanked my arm up and jammed the tape in my armpit. "And if she was going to rebuild something, why not something worthwhile, like Covent Garden Theatre? Or support the Royal Shakespeare or something? They were only able to mount two productions last season, and one of those was an old-fashioned nude production of *Richard II* from the 1990s. Of course, I suppose it would be asking too much of someone from Hollywood to appreciate art! Vids! Interactives!"

She took rapid, careless measurements of my chest, sleeve, and inseam, and disappeared, and I went back to my chairs, leaned my head against the wall, and thought about how peaceful it would be to be drowned.

This next part is a bit muddled. The headrig discussed Victorian table-settings, the All-Clear mutated into an air-raid siren, and the seraphim brought me a stack of folded trousers to try on, but I don't remember any of it very clearly.

Finch lugged in a pile of Victorian luggage at one point—a portmanteau, a large carpetbag, a small satchel, a Gladstone bag, and two pasteboard boxes tied with string. I thought perhaps I was to choose from among them, like the trousers, but it developed that I was to take them all. Finch said, "I'll fetch the rest," and went out. The seraphim settled on a pair of white flannels and went off to look for suspenders.

"The oyster fork is placed on the soup spoon, tines angled toward the plate," the headrig said. "The oyster spear is placed to its left. The shell is held steady in the left hand, and the oyster lifted whole from the shell, detaching it, if necessary, with the spear."

I drowsed off several times and the seraphim shook me awake to try various articles of clothing on me and wipe off the white lotion.

I touched the new mustache gingerly. "How does it look?" I said.

"Lopsided," the seraphim said, "but it can't be helped. Did you pack a razor for him?"

"Yes," Finch said, coming in with a large wicker hamper, "a pair of hair-brushes from the Ashmolean and a brush and soap mug. Here's the money," he said, handing me a wallet nearly the size of the portmanteau. "It's mostly coins, I'm afraid. Bank notes from that era have deteriorated badly. There's a bedroll, and I've packed the hamper full of provisions, and there are tinned goods in the boxes." He scurried out again.

"The fish fork is placed to the left of the meat and salad forks," the headrig droned. "It is recognizable by its pointed, slanted tines."

The seraphim handed me a shirt to try on. She was carrying a damp white dress over her arm. It had trailing sleeves. I thought about the water nymph, wringing it out on the carpet, the very picture of beauty. I wondered if water nymphs used fish forks and if they liked men with mustaches. Had Hylas had a mustache in the painting by Waterhouse? It was called *Hylas and the*...what? What were they called? It began with an "N."

More muddled parts. I remember Finch coming in with *more* luggage, a covered wicker basket, and the seraphim tucking something in my waistcoat pocket, and Finch shaking me on the shoulder, asking me where Mr. Dunworthy was.

"He's not here," I said, but I was mistaken. He was standing next to the wicker basket, asking Finch what he'd found out.

"How much slippage was there on the drop?" Mr. Dunworthy said.

"Nine minutes," Finch said.

"Nine minutes?" he said, frowning. "What about her other drops?"

"Minimal. Two minutes to a half hour. The drop is in an isolated part of the grounds, so there isn't much chance of being seen."

"Except the one time it counted," Mr. Dunworthy said, still frowning. "What about coming back?"

"Coming back?" Finch said. "There's no slippage on return drops."

"I am aware of that," Mr. Dunworthy said, "but this is an unusual situation."

"Yes, sir," Finch said, and went over, conferred with Warder for a few minutes, and came back. "No slippage on the return drop."

Mr. Dunworthy looked relieved.

"What about Hasselmeyer?" Mr. Dunworthy said.

"I have a message through to him."

The door opened and T.J. Lewis hurried in with a thin stack of papers. "I've read the available research," he said. "There's not much. Setting up the necessary equipment to test for incongruities is extremely expensive. Time Travel was planning to build it with the money from the cathedral project. Most temporal physicists don't believe incongruities are possible. Except for Fujisaki."

"Fujisaki thinks they're possible? What's his theory?"

"He has two theories. One is that they're not incongruities, that there are objects and events in the continuum that are nonsignificant."

"How is that possible? In a chaotic system, every event is linked to every other."

"Yes, but the system's nonlinear," T.J. said, looking at the papers, "with feedback and feedforward loops, redundancies and interference, so the effect of some objects and events is multiplied enormously, and in others it's cancelled out."

"And a parachronistic incongruity is an object whose removal has no effect?"

T.J. grinned. "Right. Like the air historians bring back in their lungs or," he looked at me, "the soot. Its removal doesn't cause any repercussions in the system."

"In which case the object shouldn't be returned to its temporal location?" Mr. Dunworthy asked.

"In which case it probably can't be returned," T.J. said. "The continuum wouldn't allow it. Unless it was nonsignificant in its returned state, too. Unfortunately, this sort of incongruity's pretty much limited to air and soot. Anything larger has a significant effect."

Even penwipers, I thought, leaning my head against the wall. I had bought an orange one shaped like a pumpkin at the Autumn Choir Festival and Salvage Drive and then forgotten it, and when I tried to come back, the net wouldn't open. I wondered drowsily how it had come to open for the fan.

"What about living things?" Mr. Dunworthy asked.

"Harmless bacteria, possibly, but nothing else. The effect of life-forms on the continuum is exponentially greater than for inanimate objects, and exponentially greater again for intelligent life-forms because of the complexity of interactions they're capable of. And of course nothing that could have an effect on the present or future. No viruses or microbes."

Mr. Dunworthy cut him off. "What's Fujisaki's other theory?"

"His second theory is that there are incongruities, but that the continuum has built-in defenses that counteract them."

"Slippage," Mr. Dunworthy said.

T.J. nodded. "The mechanism of slippage prevents nearly all potential incongruities by removing the time traveller from the area of potential danger. Fujisaki's theory is that the amount of slippage is limited, and that an incongruity occurs when the slippage can't increase radically enough to prevent the parachronism."

"What happens then?"

"Theoretically it could alter the course of history, or, if it were severe enough, destroy the universe, but there are safeguards in the modern net to prevent that. As soon as the danger of incongruities was realized, the net was modified to automatically shut down whenever the slippage reaches dangerous levels. And Fujisaki says that if an incongruity did occur, which it can't, there are other lines of defense that would correct the incongruity and would manifest themselves as," he read from the paper, "radically increased slippage in an area surrounding the incongruity, an increase in coincidental events—"

Mr. Dunworthy turned to me. "Did you experience any coincidences in Coventry?"

"No," I said.

"What about your jumble sales?"

"No," I said, thinking how nice it would have been if I had experienced one, if, strolling between the coconut shy and the plum-cake raffle, I had run bang into the bishop's bird stump.

Mr. Dunworthy turned back to T.J. "What else?"

"Increased slippage in the peripheral temporal areas."

"How large an area?"

He bit his lip. "Fujisaki says most incongruities are corrected within fifty years, but this is all theoretical."

"What else?"

"If it were really serious, a breakdown in the net," T.J. said.

"What sort of breakdown?"

He frowned. "Failure of the net to open. Malfunction in destination. But Fujisaki says those are all statistically unlikely," T.J. said, "and that the continuum is essentially stable or it would have been destroyed by now."

"What if there was no radical increase in slippage, but it was definitely an incongruity?" Mr. Dunworthy said. "Would that mean it had been corrected before it could have any effect on the continuum?"

"Yes," T.J. said. "Otherwise there'd have to be slippage."

"Good. Excellent job, Ensign Klepperman," Mr. Dunworthy said. He went over to the seraphim, who was violently banging keys at the console. "Warden, I want a list of all the drops we've done to the 1880s and '90s with the recorded amount of slippage and the normal parameters."

"It's *Warder*," the seraphim said. "And I can't do it now. I've got a rendezvous."

"The rendezvous can wait." He went back over to T.J. "Lewis, I want you to look for unusual slippers."

Or at least that's what I thought he said. The All-Clear had started up again, and now it was accompanied by a steady, thumping throb, like ack-ack guns.

"And chicken drops."

"Yes, sir," T.J. said and left.

"Finch, where's the hat?" Mr. Dunworthy said.

"Right here," Finch said, and that couldn't be right either. I had white flannels and a waistcoat, but no hat. And Victorians always wore hats, didn't they? Top hats and those hard round affairs, what were they called? It began with an "N."

The seraphim was leaning over me, which meant I must have sat down again. She stood me up to try on blazers.

"Put your arm in this one," she said, thrusting a maroon-striped one at me. "No, your *right* arm."

"The sleeves are too short," I said, looking at my bare wrists.

"What's your name?"

"My name?" I said, wondering what that had to do with the sleeves being too short.

"Your *name!*" she said, yanking off the maroon-striped blazer and shoving a red one at me.

"Ned Henry," I said. The sleeves of this one came down over my hands.

"Good," she said, stripping it off and handing me a dark-blue-and-white one. "At least I won't have to come up with a contemp name for you." She tugged on the sleeves. "That'll have to do. And don't go diving into the Thames. I haven't time to do any more costumes." She clapped a straw boater on my head.

"The hat *was* here. You were right, Mr. Dunworthy," I said, but he wasn't there. Finch wasn't either, and the seraphim was back at the console, banging away at the keys.

"I can't believe Badri isn't back yet," she said. "Leaving me with this lot. Set the coordinates. Come up with a costume. And meanwhile, I've got an historian waiting three-quarters of an hour to come through. Well, your *priority* jump can jolly well wait for unmarried girls were constantly accompanied by chaperones, usually an older maiden aunt or cousin, and were never allowed to be alone with a man until after their engagement, Ned, pay attention."

"I am," I said. "Unmarried girls were always accompanied by chaperones."

"I told you I didn't think this was a good idea," Finch, who was there, too, said.

"There's nobody else to send," Mr. Dunworthy said. "Ned, listen carefully. Here's what I want you to do. You'll come through on June the seventh, 1888, at ten A.M. The river is to the left of the dessert fork, which is used for gateaux and puddings. For such desserts as Muchings End, the dessert knife is used with the . . ."

Knife. Nice. Naiads. That was what they were called. *Hylas and the Naiads.* He went to fill his water jug, and they pulled him into the water with them, down and down, their hair and their wet sleeves twining about him.

"As soon as it's returned, you can do whatever you like. The rest of the two weeks is yours. You can spend it boating on the river or to the right of the dessert plate, with the blade pointing inward." He clapped me on the shoulder. "Have you got that?"

"What?" I said, but Mr. Dunworthy wasn't listening. He was looking at the net. There was a loud hum that threatened to drown out the ack-ack guns, and the veils on the net began to lower.

"What's that?" Mr. Dunworthy said to the seraphim.

"The rendezvous," she said, pounding keys. "I couldn't very well leave him there forever. I'll do your drop as soon as I bring him through."

"Good," Mr. Dunworthy said. He clapped me on the shoulder. "I'm counting on you, Ned," he said through the hum.

The veils touched the floor, draping gently. The hum rose in pitch till it sounded like the All-Clear, the air shimmered with condensation, and Carruthers appeared inside the net. He began fighting with the veils to get out.

"*Stand still* and wait till the veils have raised," the seraphim ordered, pounding keys. The veils rose a foot and a half and stopped.

"Wait?" Carruthers said, ducking under them. "*Wait?* I've been *waiting* for two bloody hours!" He flailed at the fabric of the veils. "Where the bloody hell *were* you?"

He worked himself free and limped toward the console. He was covered in mud. He had lost one of his boots, and the front of his non-AFS uniform had a long, flapping tear in the back of one leg. "Why the hell didn't you come get me as soon as you got the fix and saw where I'd landed?"

"I was *interrupted*," she said, glaring at Mr. Dunworthy. She crossed her arms militantly. "Where's your boot?"

"In the mouth of a bloody great mastiff! I was lucky to get away with my foot!"

"That was an authentic AFS Wellington," she said. "And what have you done to your uniform?"

"What have I done to my *uniform?*" he said. "I've just spent two hours running for my life. I landed in that same damnable marrows field. Only I must have come through later than last time because the farmer's wife was ready for me. With dogs. She'd recruited a whole bloody pack of them to aid in the war effort. She must have borrowed them from all over Warwickshire."

He caught sight of me. "What the hell are you doing here?" he demanded, limping over. "You're supposed to be in Infirmary."

"I'm going to 1888," I said.

"I told that nurse she wasn't to tell Lady Schrapnell you were back," he said disgustedly. "Why's she sending you to the Nineteenth Century? Is this about the great-grandmother?"

"Great-great-great-great," I said. "No. The doctor prescribed two weeks' uninterrupted bed rest, and Mr. Dunworthy's sending me there for it."

"He can't," Carruthers said. "You can't. You've got to go back to Coventry and look for the bishop's bird stump."

"I *was* looking for it," I said, "and you pulled me out. Remember?"

"I had to. You were a raving lunatic. Going on about dogs, man's noblest ally in war and peace, his truest friend through thick and thin. Pah! Look at that!" He held up the long strip of torn coverall. "Man's truest friend did that!" He showed me his stockinged foot. "Man's noblest ally nearly took my foot off! How soon can you be ready to go?"

"The nurse said no drops for two weeks. Why did you send me to Infirmary if you wanted me to go back?"

"I thought they'd give you an injection or a pill or something," he said, "not forbid you to do drops. Now how are we supposed to find the bishop's bird stump?"

"You didn't find it after I left?"

"I can't even find the cathedral. I've been trying all afternoon, and the marrows field was the closest I got. The bloody slippage—"

"Slippage?" Mr. Dunworthy said alertly. He came over to where we were standing. "Has there been more slippage than usual?"

"I told you," I said, "the marrows field."

"What marrows field?"

"The one halfway to Birmingham. With the dogs."

"I'm having trouble getting back to Coventry Cathedral on the fifteenth, sir," Carruthers explained. "I've tried four times today, and the closest I can get is the eighth of December. Ned's got the closest of anyone so far, which is why I need him to go back and finish searching the rubble for the bishop's bird stump."

Mr. Dunworthy looked puzzled. "Wouldn't it be simpler to look for the bishop's bird stump *before* the raid, on the fourteenth?"

"That's what we've been *trying* to do for the past two weeks," Carruthers said. "Lady Schrapnell wanted to know if it was in the cathedral at the time of the raid, so we arranged a jump to the cathedral at a quarter till eight, just before the start of the raid. But we can't get near the place. Either the date's off, or if we do come through at the target time, we're sixty miles away in the middle of a marrows field." He indicated his muddy uniform.

"We?" Mr. Dunworthy said, frowning. "How many historians have tried?"

"Six. No, seven," Carruthers said. "Everyone who wasn't off doing something else."

"Carruthers said they'd tried everybody," I put in, "and that was why they'd pulled me off jumble sales."

"What about the jumble sales?"

"They're a sale where they sell things they want to get rid of, things they bought at the last jumble sale, most of it, and things they've made to sell. Tea caddies and embroidered needle cases and penwipers and—"

"I *know* what a jumble sale is," Mr. Dunworthy said. "Was there any slippage on those jumps?"

I shook my head. "Just the usual. Mostly spatial, so no one would see me come through. Behind the rectory or back of the tea tent."

He turned abruptly to Carruthers. "How much were the Coventry drops off by, the ones in which you came through *in* Coventry?"

"It varies," he said. "Paulson came through on the twenty-eighth of November." He stopped and calculated. "The average is about twenty-four hours, I'd say. The closest we've been able to get to the target is the afternoon of the fifteenth, and now I can't even get there. Which is why Ned needs to go. The new recruit's still there, and I doubt if he even knows how to get back on his own. And who knows what trouble he's likely to get into."

"Trouble," Mr. Dunworthy murmured. He turned to the tech. "Has there been increased slippage on all the drops, or just the ones to Coventry?"

"*I* don't know," she said. "I'm a wardrobe tech. I'm *only* filling in for Badri. *He's* the net tech."

"Badri, yes," he said, brightening. "Good. Badri. Where is he?"

"With Lady Schrapnell, sir," Finch said. "And I'm afraid they may be on their way back by now," but Mr. Dunworthy didn't seem to hear him.

"While you've been filling in," he said to Warder, "have you run any jumps that weren't to the cathedral on November 14th, 1940?"

"One," she said. "To London."

"How much slippage was there?" he persisted.

She looked like she was going to say, "I don't have time for this," and then apparently thought better of it and began pounding keys. "Locational, no slippage. Temporal, eight minutes."

"So it is Coventry," he said to himself. "Eight minutes which way? Early or late?"

"Early."

He turned back to Carruthers. "Did you try sending someone to Coventry earlier and having them stay till the raid?"

"Yes, sir," Carruthers said. "They still ended up after the target time."

Mr. Dunworthy took off his spectacles, examined them, and put them back on. "Does the amount of slippage seem to be random or is it getting progressively worse?"

"Worse," he said.

"Finch, go ask Kindle if she noticed any coincidences or discrepancies while she was at Muchings End. Ned, you stay here. I've got to talk to Lewis." Mr. Dunworthy went out.

"What was that all about?" Carruthers said, looking after him.

"Lady Windermere's fan," I said, and sat down.

"Stand up," the seraphim said. "The drop's ready. Get in place."

"Shouldn't we wait for Mr. Dunworthy?" I asked.

"I have nineteen drops scheduled, not to mention another *priority* jump for Mr. Dunworthy, and—"

"All right, all right," I said. I gathered up the satchel, portmanteau, Gladstone, and wicker basket, and went over to the net. The veils were still only a foot and a half from the floor. I set down one armful on the floor, lifted the veil, ducked under, and began pulling the bags in after me.

"The Victorian era was a time of rapid technological and scientific change," the headrig said. "The invention of the telegraph, gas lighting, and Darwin's theory of evolution were significantly altering the fabric of society."

"Pick up your luggage and stand on the X," she said.

"Travel in particular was changing rapidly. The invention of the steam locomotive, and, in 1863, the first underground railway, made it possible for Victorians to go faster and farther than ever before."

"Ready?" she said, her hand poised over the keyboard.

"I think so," I said, checking to make sure everything was inside the veils. One corner of the covered wicker basket was sticking out. "Wait," I said, and scraped it inside with my foot.

"I said, ready now?" she said.

"Easy and affordable travel had the effect of broadening the Victorians' horizons and breaking down the rigid barriers of class which—"

The seraphim flung the veils up, yanked the headrig out of my ear, and went back to the console.

"Ready *now*?" she said.

"Yes."

The seraphim began tapping keys.

"Wait!" I said. "I don't know where it is I'm going."

"June seventh, 1888," she said, and resumed tapping.

"I mean, after that," I said, trying to find an opening in the veils. "I didn't hear all of Mr. Dunworthy's instructions. Because of the time-lag." I pointed at my ear. "Difficulty in Distinguishing Sounds."

"Difficulty in evidencing intelligence," she said. "I don't have *time* for this," and flounced out of the room, slamming the door behind her.

"Where's Mr. Dunworthy?" I heard her say in the corridor, probably to Finch.

Mr. Dunworthy had said something about Muchings End, and about a boat, or was that the headrig? "It's a perfectly straightforward job," he'd said.

"Where is he?" I heard the seraphim say again, and her voice sounded uncomfortably like Lady Schrapnell's.

"Where is who?" Finch said.

"You know perfectly well who," she said in stentorian tones. "And don't tell me he's in hospital. I've had enough of your wild goose chases. He's here, isn't he?"

Oh, Lord.

"Come away from that door and let me pass," Lady Schrapnell roared. "He *is* here."

I dropped the luggage with a thud and looked wildly about for somewhere to hide.

"No, he's not," Finch said bravely. "He's over at Radcliffe Infirmary."

There was nowhere to hide, at least in this century. I ducked under the veils and sprinted for the console, praying the seraphim had truly made all the necessary preparations.

"I said, let me pass," Lady Schrapnell said. "Badri, make him come away from the door. Mr. Henry's here, and I intend to see that he goes to look for my bishop's bird stump instead of malingering in the present, pretending to have time-lag."

"But he does have time-lag," Finch said. "A very serious case. His vision's blurred, he has Difficulty Distinguishing Sounds, and his reasoning faculties are severely impaired."

The console screen said, "Ready. Hit 'send.'" I measured the distance to the net.

"He's in no condition to make any drops," Finch said.

"Nonsense," Lady Schrapnell said. "Now come away from that door this instant."

I took a deep breath, punched "send," and dived head-first for the net.

"Please believe me," Finch said desperately. "He's not here. He's over at Christ Church."

"Get out of my way!" she said, and there was the sound of a scuffle.

I skidded face-first onto the X. The veils lowered on my foot. I yanked it inside.

"Mr. Henry, I know you're in here!" Lady Schrapnell said, and the door burst open.

"I told you," Finch said. "He's not here."

And I wasn't.

*"Journeys end in lovers meeting."*
*William Shakespeare*

C H A P T E R   F O U R

An Abrupt Arrival—Difference Between Literature and Real
Life—Similarity of Train Whistles to Air Raid Sirens—Benefits of
Adrenaline—I Contemplate My Mission—*Howard's End*—A Timely
Newspaper—Two Ladies—A Late Arrival—Contact!—"Oxford,
City of Dreaming Spires"—A Fashion Plate—Fate—The Mystery
of Rabbits Hypnotized by Snakes Solved—An Introduction

I came through face-down on railroad tracks, stretched across them like
Pearl White in a Twentieth-Century serial, except that she didn't have
so much luggage. The portmanteau, et al, were scattered around me,
along with my boater, which had fallen off when I dived for the net.

Lady Schrapnell's voice was still booming in my ears, and I got to my feet
and looked about cautiously, but there was no sign of her. Or of a boat or a
river. The railway tracks were on a grassy embankment, with trees growing
below and beside them.

The first rule of time travel is "Ascertain exact time-space location,"
but there didn't seem to be any way of doing that. It was clearly summer—the sky overhead was blue and there were flowers growing between the ties—but no signs of civilization other than the train tracks. So
sometime after 1804.

In vids, there is always a newspaper lying on the ground with a helpful
headline like "Pearl Harbor Bombed!" or "Mafeking Relieved!" and a clock
above it in a shop window thoughtfully showing the time.

I looked at my watch. It wasn't there, and I squinted at my wrist, trying to remember whether Warder had taken it off me when she was trying shirts on. I remembered she'd tucked something in my waistcoat pocket. I pulled it out, on a gold chain. A pocket watch. Of course. Wristwatches were an anachronism in Nineteenth Century.

I had trouble getting the pocket watch open and then difficulty reading the extinct Roman numerals, but eventually I made it out. A quarter past X. Allowing for the time I'd spent getting the watch open and lying on the tracks, bang on target. Unless I was in the wrong year. Or the wrong place.

As I didn't know where I was supposed to have come through, I didn't know if I was in the right place or not, but if there's a small amount of temporal slippage, there usually isn't much locational slippage either.

I stood up on a rail to look down the tracks. To the north, the tracks headed into deeper woods. In the opposite direction, the woods seemed thinner, and there was a dark plume of smoke. A factory? Or a boathouse?

I should gather up my bags and go see, but I continued to stand on the rail, taking in the warm summer air and the sweet scent of clover and new-mown hay.

I was a hundred and sixty years away from pollution and traffic and the bishop's bird stump. No, that wasn't true. The bishop's bird stump had been given to Coventry Cathedral in 1852.

Depressing thought. But there wasn't any Coventry Cathedral. St. Michael's Church hadn't been made a bishopric till 1908. And there wasn't a Lady Schrapnell. I was more than a century away from her snapped orders and from vicious dogs and from bombed-out cathedrals, in a more civilized time, where the pace was slow and decorous, and the women were softspoken and demure.

I gazed about me at the trees, the flowers. Buttercups grew between the tracks, and a tiny white flower like a star. The nurse at Infirmary had said I needed rest, and who couldn't rest here? I felt totally recovered just standing here on the tracks. No blurring of vision. No air-raid sirens.

I had spoken too soon. The air-raid siren started up again and then as abruptly stopped. I shook my head, trying to clear it, and then took several long, deep breaths.

I wasn't cured yet, but I soon would be, breathing in this clear, pure air. I gazed up at the cloudless sky, at the plume of black smoke. It seemed higher in the sky and nearer—a farmer burning weeds?

I longed to see him, leaning on his rake, untouched by modern worries, modern haste, longed to see his rose-covered cottage with its white picket fence, its cozy kitchen, its soft feather bed, its—

The air-raid siren sounded again in short sharp blasts. Like a factory whistle. Or a train.

Adrenaline is an extremely effective drug. It galvanizes the body into action and has been known to produce impossible feats of strength. And speed.

I snatched up the satchel, the hamper, the portmanteau, the carpetbag, the boxes, and my hat, which had somehow fallen off again, chucked them all down the near side of the embankment, and chucked myself after them before the plume of black smoke had cleared the trees.

The covered basket that Finch had been so concerned about was still on the tracks, sitting squarely on the far rail. The adrenaline leaped across, scooped it up, and rolled down the embankment as the train thundered past in a deafening roar.

Definitely not totally recovered. I lay at the bottom of the embankment for a considerable time contemplating that fact and trying to start breathing.

After a while I sat up. The embankment had been fairly high, and the basket and I had rolled a considerable way before coming to a stop in a mass of nettles. As a result, the view was very different than that from the tracks, and I could glimpse, beyond a thicket of alders, a corner of some white wooden structure and a glimpse of fretwork. It could definitely be a boathouse.

I disentangled the basket and myself, climbed up the embankment, and looked carefully up and down the tracks. There was no smoke in either direction, and no sound at all. Satisfied, I sprinted across the tracks, gathered up my etc., looked in both directions, bolted back across, and set off through the woods toward the boathouse.

Adrenaline also tends to clear the brain, and several things became remarkably clear as I trudged toward the boathouse, the foremost of which was that I had no idea what to do when I got there.

I distinctly remembered Mr. Dunworthy saying, "Here are your instructions," and after that a jumble of Stilton spoons and collars and the All-Clear, and then he'd said the rest of the two weeks was mine to do with as I liked. Which obviously meant that a portion of it wasn't. And when I'd got in the net, Finch had said, "We're counting on you."

To do what? There was something about a boat and a river. And a Something End. Audley End. No, that didn't sound right. It began with an "N." Or was that the water nymph? Hopefully, it would come back to me when I got to the boathouse.

It wasn't a boathouse. It was a railway station. There was a carved wooden sign on the wall above a green bench. Oxford, it said.

And what was I supposed to do now? Oxford had boathouses and a river. But if I'd come through at the railway station, perhaps I was supposed to take a train to this Something End and then a boat from there. I seemed to remember Mr. Dunworthy saying something about a railway. Or had that been the headrig?

My coming through at the railway station might have been due to slippage, and I was really supposed to have come through down at Folly Bridge. I distinctly remembered something having been said about a boat and the river.

On the other hand, I had a great deal of luggage for a boat.

I looked across the tracks to the platform. On the far side of the green bench was a glass-covered notice board. The train schedule. I could look at it, and if Something End was listed, I'd know I was supposed to take the train, especially if one was due shortly.

The platform was empty, at least for the moment. The distance up to it looked high, but not impossible, and the sky was unsullied blue in both directions. I looked up and down the tracks and then at the door to the waiting room. Nothing. I checked the tracks three or four more times, just to be safe, and then sprinted across them, heaved my luggage over the edge, and clambered up after it.

The platform was still uninhabited. I piled my luggage on the end of the bench and strolled over to the notice board. I read the headings: Reading, Coventry, Northampton, Bath. It was very likely one of the smaller stations: Aylesbury, Didcot, Swindon, Abingdon. I read the entire list. There wasn't a single End among them.

And I couldn't go into the station and ask when the next train to Something End was. What was it? *Something* End. Howard's End? No, that was a novel by E.M. Forster. It hadn't even been written yet. Something End. There was a pub in the Turl called The Bitter End, but that didn't sound right either. It began with an "N." No, that was the naiad. An "M."

I went back over to the bench and sat down, trying to think. Mr. Dunworthy had said, "Here are your instructions," and then something about oyster spears and tea with the Queen. No, that *had* to have been the headrig. And then, "We're sending you through to the seventh of June, 1888."

Perhaps I'd better find out if I was really on the seventh of June, 1888, before I worried about anything else. If I was in the wrong time, I had no business going anywhere, by train or by boat. I needed to stay here till Warder got the fix, realized I was in the wrong time, and set up a rendezvous to take me back. At least it wasn't a field of marrows.

And it had occurred to me, now that I was recovering a bit, that Warder would have set my watch for the time in the past. In which case, it proved absolutely nothing at all.

I stood up and went over to the station window to see if there was a clock inside. There was. It said twenty to eleven. I pulled out my pocket watch and checked it against the clock. Twenty to XI.

In books and vids there's always a newsboy hawking papers with the date neatly visible for the time traveller to see, or a calendar with the dates marked off with an X. There was no sign of a calendar, a newsboy, or a friendly porter who'd volunteer, "Lovely weather for June seventh, isn't it, sir? Not like last year. We hadn't any summer at all in '87."

I went back to the bench and sat down, trying to concentrate. Marlborough End, Middlesex End, Montague End, Marple's End.

A train whistle (which I instantly recognized as such) sounded, and a train tore through the station without stopping, with a roar and a sudden wind that blew my boater with it. I went running after it, caught it, and was putting it back on when a paper, apparently caught in the same draft, blew against the back of my legs.

I unwrapped myself from it and looked at it. It was a sheet from a newspaper. The *Times.* 7 June 1888.

So I was at the right time, and all I had to work out was what I was supposed to do now.

I sat down and put my head in my hands, trying to concentrate. Carruthers had come through without his boots and Warder had slammed her clipboard down and Mr. Dunworthy had said something about a river and a contact. A contact.

"Contact Tennyson," he'd said, only that wasn't the name. But it had begun with a "T." Or an "A." And Finch had said something about a contact, too. A contact.

That explained why I didn't know what to do. All I'd been told was that I was to meet a contact, and he or she would tell me. I felt a surge of relief. The contact would explain everything.

So now the only question was, who was it and where was he or she? "Contact someone," Mr. Dunworthy had said. What was the name? Chiswick. No, that was the head of Time Travel. Correction, the ex-head of Time Travel. "Contact—" Klepperman. Ensign Klepperman. No, that was the sailor who'd been killed in the line of duty. Because he hadn't known what he was doing.

"Contact—" Who? As if in answer, another train whistle blew several deafening blasts, and a train pulled into the station. Spitting sparks and great whooshes of steam, the train came to a stop. A porter jumped down from the third car, deposited a plush-covered stool in front of the door, and got back on the train.

Several minutes went by, and the porter reappeared, carrying a hatbox and a large black umbrella. He extended his hand to a frail old lady, and then a younger one, as they stepped down.

The elderly lady was wearing crinolines and a bonnet and lace mitts, and for a moment I was afraid I was in the wrong year after all, but the younger one had a long, flared skirt and a hat that tilted forward over her brow. She had a sweet face, and when she spoke to the porter, telling him what bags they had, her voice was both softspoken and demure.

"I told you he wouldn't be here to meet us," the old lady said in a voice with Lady Schrapnellian overtones.

"I'm certain he will be here shortly, Auntie," the young woman said. "Perhaps he was delayed on college business."

"Poppycock," the old lady said, a word I had not ever expected to hear anyone say. "He's off fishing somewhere. Disgraceful occupation for a grown man! Did you write to tell him when we were coming?"

"Yes, Auntie."

"And told him the time, I hope?"

"Yes, Auntie. I'm certain he'll be here shortly."

"And in the meantime we're left to stand here in this dreadful heat."

The weather had seemed pleasantly warm, but then I wasn't wearing black wool buttoned to the neck. Or lace mitts.

"Absolutely sweltering," she said, fishing in a small beaded purse for a handkerchief. "I feel quite weak. *Care*ful with that!" she boomed at the porter, who was struggling with a huge trunk. Finch had been right. They did travel with steamer trunks.

"Quite faint," Auntie said, fanning herself weakly with the handkerchief.

"Why don't you sit down over here, Auntie," the young woman said, leading her over to the other bench. "I'm certain Uncle will be here momentarily."

The old lady sat down in a whoomph of petticoats. "Not like that!" she snapped at the porter. "This is all Herbert's fault. Getting married! And just when I was coming to Oxford. Don't scratch the leather!"

It was obvious neither of these ladies was my contact, but at least I no longer seemed to be having Difficulty Distinguishing Sounds. And I could understand what they were saying, which isn't always the case in the past. My first jumble sale I hadn't understood one word in ten: skittles and shies and sales of work.

Also, I seemed to have overcome my Tendency to Sentimentality. The younger lady had a pretty heart-shaped face, and even prettier ankle-shaped ankles, which I'd caught a white-stockinged glimpse of when she alighted from the train, but I hadn't felt any inclination to dissolve into rapturous comparisons with sylphs or cherubim. Better still, I had been able to come up with both words without any trouble. I felt completely cured.

"He's forgotten us completely," Auntie said. "We'll have to hire a fly."

Well, perhaps not completely cured.

"There's no need for us to hire a carriage," the young woman said. "Uncle won't have forgotten."

"Then why isn't he here, Maud?" she said, arranging her skirts so they took up the entire bench. "And why isn't Herbert here? Marriage! Servants have no business marrying. And how did Herbert meet anyone suitable to marry? I absolutely forbade her to have followers, so I suppose that means it's someone unsuitable. Some person from a music hall." She lowered her voice. "Or worse."

"It's my understanding that they met at church," Maud said patiently.

"At church! Disgraceful! What is the world coming to? In my day, church was a duty, not a social occasion. Mark my words, a hundred years from now, one will not be able to distinguish between a cathedral and a music hall."

Or a shopping center, I thought.

"It's all these sermons on Christian love," Auntie said. "Whatever happened to sermons on duty and knowing one's place? And punctuality. Your uncle could benefit from a sermon on—where are you going?"

Maud was heading for the station door. "To look at the clock," she said. "I thought perhaps the reason Uncle isn't here yet is that the train might have been early getting in."

I helpfully pulled out my pocket watch and opened it, hoping I could remember how to read it.

"And leave me here alone," Auntie said, "with who knows *what* sort of persons?" She crooked a lace-mitted finger at Maud. "There are *men*," she said in a stage whisper, "who hang about public places waiting for their chance to engage unaccompanied women in conversation."

I snapped the pocket watch shut, put it back in my waistcoat pocket, and tried my best to look harmless.

"Their object," she whispered loudly, "is to steal unprotected women's luggage. Or worse."

"I doubt if anyone could *lift* our luggage, Auntie, let alone steal it," Maud whispered back, and my opinion of her shot up.

"Nevertheless, you are in my care, since my brother has not seen fit to meet us, and it is my duty to protect you from *harmful influences*," Auntie said, looking darkly at me. "We are not staying here one moment longer. Put those in the cloakroom," she said to the porter, who had succeeded finally in wrestling the trunks and three large bandboxes onto a luggage barrow. "And bring us the claim check for them."

"The train is about to leave, madam," he protested.

"I am not taking the train," she said. "And engage us a fly. With a respectable driver."

The porter looked desperately at the train, which was emitting great gouts of steam. "Madam, it is my duty to be on the train when it departs. I shall lose my job if I'm not on board."

I thought of offering to get them a carriage, but I didn't want Auntie to take me for Jack the Ripper. Or was that an anachronism? Had he started his career by 1888?

"Pish-tosh! You shall lose your job if I report your insolence to your employers," Auntie was saying. "What sort of railway is this?"

"The Great Western, madam."

"Well, it can scarcely call itself great when its employees leave the passengers' luggage on the platform to be stolen by *common criminals*," another dark look at me. "It can scarcely call itself great when its employees refuse to aid a helpless old lady."

The porter, who looked as though he disagreed with the word "helpless," glanced at the train, whose wheels were starting to turn, and then at the station door, as if gauging the distance, and then tipped his hat and pushed the barrow into the station.

"Come, Maud," Auntie said, rising out of her nest of crinolines.

"But what if Uncle comes?" Maud said. "He'll just miss us."

"It will teach him a useful lesson on punctuality," Auntie said. She swept out.

Maud followed in her impressive wake, giving me a smile of apology as she went.

The train started up, its great wheels turning slowly, then faster as it gathered steam, and started out of the station. I looked anxiously at the station door, but there was no sign of the poor porter. The passenger cars moved slowly past, and then the green-painted luggage van. He wasn't going to make it. The guard's van pulled past, its lantern swinging, and the porter burst through the door, ran down the platform after it, and made a flying leap. I stood up.

He caught the railing with one hand, swung himself up onto the bottom step, and clung there, panting. As the train cleared the station he shook his fist at the station door.

And no doubt in future years he became a socialist, I thought, and worked to get the Labour Party voted in.

And what about Auntie? No doubt she had outlived all her relatives and left her servants nothing in her will. I hoped she'd lasted well into the Twenties and had to put up with cigarettes and the Charleston. As for Maud, I hoped she'd been able to meet someone suitable to marry, though I was afraid she hadn't, with Auntie's eagle eye constantly on her.

I sat on for several minutes, contemplating their futures and my own, which was decidedly less clear. The next train from anywhere wasn't until 12:36, from Birmingham. Was I supposed to meet my contact here? Or was I supposed to go into Oxford and meet him there? I seemed to remember Mr. Dunworthy saying something about a cabby. Was I supposed to take a hansom cab into town? "Contact," Mr. Dunworthy had said.

The station door burst open, and a young man shot through it at the same speed as the porter had previously. He was dressed like I was, in white flannels and slightly crooked mustache, and was carrying his boater in his hand. He ran onto the platform and strode rapidly to the far end of it, obviously looking for someone.

My contact, I thought hopefully. And he was late, which was why he hadn't been here to meet me. As if in confirmation, he stopped, pulled out his pocket watch, and flipped it open with impressive dexterity. "I'm late," he said, and snapped it shut.

And if he was my contact, would he announce himself as such, or was I supposed to whisper, "Psst, Dunworthy sent me"? Or was there some sort of password I was supposed to know the answer to—"The marmoset sails at midnight," to which I was supposed to respond, "The sparrow is in the spruce tree"?

I was debating "The moon sets on Tuesday" versus the more straight-forward "I beg your pardon. Are you from the future?" when he turned back my way, gave me the barest of glances, strode past me to the other end of the platform, and peered down the tracks. "I say," he said, coming back, "has the 10:55 from London arrived yet?"

"Yes," I said. "It pulled out five minutes ago." Pulled out? Was that an anachronism? Should I have said "departed" instead?

Apparently not, because he muttered, "I knew it," and clapped his boater on his head and disappeared into the station.

A moment later he was back again. "I say," he said, "you haven't seen any agèd relicts, have you?"

"Age-ed relicts?" I said, feeling as if I were back among the jumble sales.

"A deuce of dowagers, 'fall'n into the sere, the yellow leaf,' " he said. "Crookbacked and crabbèd with age. 'You are old, Father William,' and all that. They would have come in on the train from London. In bombazine and jet, I should imagine." He saw my incomprehension. "Two ladies of advanced age. I was supposed to meet them. I don't suppose they'd have come and gone, would they?" he said, looking vaguely round.

He must be referring to the two ladies who'd just left, though he couldn't possibly be Auntie's brother and Maud could hardly be described as of advanced age.

"They were both elderly?" I said.

"Antiquated. I had to meet them once before, during Michaelmas term. Did you see them? One was very likely in a crotchet and a fichu. The other's a spinster of the sparse, sharp-nosed sort, all blue stockings and social causes. Amelia Bloomer and Betsey Trotwood."

It wasn't them, then. The names were wrong, and the stockings I'd seen descending from the train had been white, not blue.

"No," I said. "I didn't see them. There was a young girl and a—"

He shook his head. "Not my party. Mine were absolutely antediluvian, or they would be if anyone still believed in the Flood. What would Darwin call it, do you suppose? Pre-Pelasgian? Or Ante-Trilobitian? He must have got the trains mixed again."

He strode over to the board, examined the schedule, and straightened in disgust. "Drat!" he said, another word I'd thought existed only in books. "The next train from London's not until 3:18, and by then it will be too late."

He slapped his boater against his leg. "Well, that's that, then," he said. "Unless I can get something out of Mags at the Mitre. She's always good for a crown or two. Too bad Cyril isn't here. She likes Cyril." He clapped his boater back on his head and went into the station.

And so much for his being my contact, I thought. Drat!

And the next train from anywhere wasn't until 12:36. Perhaps I was supposed to have met the contact where I'd come through, and I should take my luggage and go back to that spot on the tracks. If I could find it. I should have marked the spot with a scarf.

Or was I supposed to meet him down by the river? Or go somewhere by boat to meet him? I squeezed my eyes shut. Mr. Dunworthy had said something about Jesus College. No, he had been talking to Finch about getting the provisions. He had said, "Here are your instructions," and then something about the river and something about croquet and Disraeli and . . . I squeezed my eyes shut, trying to force the memory.

"I say," a voice said. "I'm sorry to disturb you."

I opened my eyes. It was the young man who'd missed meeting the age-ed relicts.

"I say," he said again, "you weren't going on the river, were you? Well, of course you are, I mean, boater, blazer, flannels, you're hardly dressed for an execution, are you, and there's nothing else on in Oxford this time of year. Occam's Razor, as Professor Peddick would say. What I meant was, had you made plans to go with friends, a house party or something, or were you going on your own?"

"I—" I said, wondering if he could be my contact after all, and this was some sort of intricate code.

"I say," he said, "I'm going about this all wrong. We haven't even been properly introduced." He shifted his boater to his left hand and extended his right. "Terence St. Trewes."

I shook it. "Ned Henry," I said.

"What college are you?"

I was trying to remember if Mr. Dunworthy had mentioned someone named Terence St. Trewes, and the question, phrased so casually, caught me off-guard.

"Balliol," I said, and then hoped against hope he went to Brasenose or Keble.

"I *knew* it," he said happily. "One can always spot a Balliol man. It's Jowett's influence. Who's your tutor?"

Who had been at Balliol in 1888? Jowett, but he wouldn't have had any pupils. Ruskin? No, he was Christ Church. Ellis? "I was ill this year," I said, deciding on caution. "I'm coming up again in the autumn."

"And in the meantime, your physician's recommended a trip on the river to recover. Fresh air, exercise, and quiet and all that bosh. And rest that knits the ravelled sleeve of care."

"Yes, exactly," I said, wondering how he knew that. Perhaps he was my contact after all. "My physician sent me down this morning," I said, in case he was and was waiting for some sign from me. "From Coventry."

"Coventry?" he said. "That's where St. Thomas à Becket's buried, isn't it? 'Who will rid me of this turbulent priest?' "

"No," I said. "That's Canterbury."

"Then which one's Coventry?" He brightened. "Lady Godiva," he said. "And Peeping Tom."

Well, so he wasn't my contact. Still, it was nice being in a time when those were the associations for Coventry and not ravaged cathedrals and Lady Schrapnell.

"Here's the thing," Terence said, sitting down next to me on the bench. "Cyril and I were planning to go on the river this morning, had the boat hired and noinbob put down to hold it and our things all packed, when Professor asks me if I can meet his agèd relatives because he's got to go write about the battle of Salamis. Well, one doesn't say no to one's tutor, even if one is in a devil of a hurry, especially when he was such a brick about the whole Martyr's Memorial thing, not telling my father and all, so I left Cyril down at Folly Bridge to watch our things and make certain Jabez didn't rent the boat out from under us which he's done on more than one occasion, including that time Rushforth's sister was up for Eights, even with a deposit, and legged it up St. Aldate's. I could see I was going to be late, so when I got to Pembroke, I hailed a hansom. I only had enough for the balance of the boat, but I was counting on the agèd relics anteing up. Only he'd got the trains mixed and I can't draw against my next quarter allowance because I put it all on Beefsteak in the Derby, and Jabez for some reason *refuses* to extend credit to undergraduates. So here I am, stuck like Mariana in the South, and there's Cyril, 'like patience on a monument, smiling at grief.' " He looked at me expectantly.

And, oddly enough, though this was far worse than the jumble sales and I'd only understood about one word in three and none of the literary allusions, I'd got the gist of what he was saying: he didn't have enough money for the boat.

And of what it meant: he definitely wasn't my contact. He was only a penniless undergraduate. Or one of Auntie's "ruffians" who hung about railway stations engaging people in conversation and trying to borrow money. Or worse.

"Hasn't Cyril any money?" I asked.

"Lord, no," he said, stretching out his legs. "He never has a shilling. So I was wondering, since you were planning to go on the river and so were we, if we mightn't combine resources, like Speke and Burton, only of course the sources of the Thames have already been discovered, and we wouldn't be going upriver, at any rate. And there won't be any savage natives or tsetse flies or things. Cyril and I wondered if you'd like to go on the river with us."

"Three men in a boat," I murmured, wishing he were my contact. *Three Men in a Boat* has always been one of my favorite books, especially the chapter where Harris gets lost in Hampton Court Maze.

"Cyril and I are going downriver," Terence was saying. "We were thinking of taking a leisurely trip down to Muchings End, but we could stop anywhere you'd like. There are some nice ruins at Abingdon. Cyril loves ruins. Or there's Bisham Abbey, where Anne of Cleves waited out the divorce. Or if you had in mind simply drifting along, enjoying the 'current that with gentle murmur glides,' we could simply drift."

I wasn't listening. Muchings End, he'd said, and I knew as soon as I heard it, it was the name I'd been trying to remember. "Contact someone," he'd said, and this was clearly the someone. His references to the river and my physician's orders, his crooked mustache and identical blazer, couldn't all be coincidences.

I wondered why he didn't simply tell me who he was, though. There was no one else on the platform. I looked in the station window, trying to see if the station agent was eavesdropping, but I couldn't see anything. Or perhaps he was just being cautious in case *I* wasn't the right person.

I said, "I'm—" and the station door opened, and a portly middle-aged man wearing a bowler and a handlebar mustache came out. He tipped the bowler, grunted something undistinguishable, and went over to the notice board.

"I should like very much to go with you to *Muchings End*," emphasizing the last two words. "A trip on the river will be a restful change from *Coventry*."

I fished in my trouser pocket, trying to remember what Finch had done with the purse full of money. "How much do you need for the hire of the boat?"

"Sicksunthree," he said. "That's for a week's hire. I've already put noin bob down."

The purse was in my blazer pocket. "I'm not certain if I brought enough with me," I said, tipping the bank note and coins out in my hand.

"There's enough there to *buy* the boat," Terence said. "Or the Koh-i-noor. This your kit?" he said, indicating my stacked luggage.

"Yes," I said, and reached for the portmanteau, but he'd already grabbed it and one of the twine-tied boxes up in one hand, and the satchel and hamper in the other. I grabbed the other box and the carpetbag and the covered basket up and followed him.

"I told the hansom driver to wait," he said, starting down the steps, but there was nothing outside the station except a mangy spotted hound, lazily scratching its ear with its hind leg. It paid no attention as Terence passed, and I felt another surge of jubilation that I was years and years from vicious dogs and downed Luftwaffe pilots, in a quieter, slower-paced, more decorous time.

"Uncivilized blighter," Terence said. "I told him to wait. We'll have to get a cab on Cornmarket."

The hound shifted position and began licking its private parts. All right. Not entirely decorous.

And not all that slow. "Come along then," Terence said. "There's no time to lose," and took off up Hythe Bridge Street at a near-gallop.

I followed at as fast a clip as I could manage, considering the luggage and Hythe Bridge Street, which was unpaved and badly rutted. It took all my attention to keep my footing and juggle the luggage.

"Come along then," Terence said, pausing at the top of the hill. "It's nearly noon."

"Coming," I said, adjusting the covered basket, which was slipping, and struggled up the hill to the top.

When I got there, I stopped, gaping as badly as the new recruit had at the cat. I was in the Cornmarket, at the crossroads of St. Aldate's and the High, under the mediaeval tower.

I had stood here hundreds of times, waiting for a break in the traffic. But that was in Twenty-First Century Oxford, with its tourist shopping centers and tube stations.

This, this was the real Oxford, "with the sun on her towers," the Oxford of Newman and Lewis Carroll and Tom Brown. There was the High, curving down to Queen's and Magdalen, and the Old Bodleian, with its high windows and chained books, and next to it the Radcliffe Camera and the Sheldonian Theatre. And there, down on the corner of the Broad, was Balliol in all its glory. The Balliol of Matthew Arnold and Gerard Manley Hopkins and Asquith. Inside those gates was the great Jowett, with his bushy white hair and his masterful voice, telling a student, "Never explain. Never apologize."

The clock in Cornmarket's tower struck half past eleven, and all the bells in Oxford chimed in. St. Mary the Virgin, and Christ Church's Great Tom, and the silvery peal of Magdalen, far down the High.

Oxford, and I was here in it. In "the city of lost causes" where lingered "the last echoes of the Middle Ages."

" 'That sweet city with her dreaming spires,' " I said, and was nearly hit by a horseless carriage.

"Jump!" Terence said, lunging for my arm, and pulled me out of the way. "Those things are an absolute menace," he said, looking longingly after it. "We're never going to find a hansom in this mess. We're better off walking," and plunged in amongst a host of harried-looking women with aprons and market baskets, murmuring, "Sorry," to them and tipping his hat with the hamper.

I followed him down Cornmarket, through the bustling crowd and past shops and greengrocers'. I glanced in the window of a hatter's at the people reflected there, and stopped cold. A woman with a basket full of cabbages crashed into me and then went round me, muttering, but I scarcely noticed.

There hadn't been any mirrors in the lab, and I had only been half aware of the garments Warder was putting on me. I had had no idea. I looked the very image of a Victorian gentleman off for an outing on the river. My stiff collar, my natty blazer and white flannels. Above all, my boater. There are some things one is born to wear, and I had obviously been fated to wear this hat. It was of light straw with a band of blue ribbon, and it gave me a jaunty, dashing look, which, combined with the mustache, was fairly devastating. No wonder Auntie had been so anxious to hustle Maud off.

On closer inspection, my mustache was a bit lopsided, and my eyes had that glazed, time-lagged look, but those could be remedied shortly, and the overall effect was still extremely pleasing, if I did say so my—

"What are you doing, standing there like a sheep?" Terence said, grabbing my arm. "Come along!" He led me across Carfax and down St. Aldate's.

Terence kept up a cheerful stream of chatter as he went. "Look out for the tram rails. I tripped over one last week. Worse for the carriages, though, just the right size to catch their wheels, and over they go. Well, over I went, and lucky for me that the only thing coming was a farm wagon and a mule old as Methuselah, or I'd have gone to meet my Maker. Do you believe in luck?"

He crossed the street and took off down St. Aldate's. And there was *The Bulldog* with its painted pub signboard of angry proctors chasing an undergraduate, and the golden walls of Christ Church, and Tom Tower. And the walled deanery garden, from which came the sound of children laughing. Alice Liddell and her sisters? My heart caught, trying to remember when Charles Dodgson had written *Alice in Wonderland*. No, it had been written earlier, in the 1860s. But there, across the street, was the shop where Alice had bought sweets from a sheep.

"The day before yesterday I'd have told you I didn't believe in luck," Terence said, trotting past the path to Christ Church Meadow. "But after yesterday afternoon, I'm a true believer. So many things have happened. Professor Peddick getting the trains mixed, and then you being there. I mean, you might have been going somewhere else altogether, or you mightn't have had the money for the boat, or you mightn't have been there at all, and then where would Cyril and I have been? 'Fate holds the strings, and Men like children move but as they're led: Success is from above.'"

A hansom cab pulled up beside us. "Tack ye summers, gemmun?" the driver said in a completely unintelligible accent.

Terence shook his head. "By the time we got all our luggage in, it's faster to walk. And we're nearly there."

We were. There was Folly Bridge, and a tavern, and the river, with a ragtag of boats tied up to its edge.

" 'Fate, show thy force. What is decreed must be, and be this so,' " Terence said, crossing the bridge. "We go to meet our destiny." He started down the steps toward the dock. "Jabez," he called out to the man standing on the riverbank. "You haven't rented our boat, have you?"

Jabez looked like something out of *Oliver Twist*. He had a scruffy beard and a decidedly unfriendly manner. He was standing with his thumbs in a pair of impossibly dirty braces, and his hands were, if possible, even dirtier.

At his feet lay an enormous brown-and-white bulldog, its ugly flattened snout resting on its paws. Even at this distance, I could see its powerful shoulders and belligerent underslung jaw. Bill Sikes in *Oliver Twist* had had a bulldog, hadn't he?

I didn't see any sign of anyone who might be Terence's friend Cyril, and I wondered if Jabez and his dog had murdered him and thrown him in the river.

Terence, obliviously chattering, hurried down the bank toward the boat. And the monster. I followed cautiously, keeping well to the rear and hoping it might ignore us like the hound at the station, but as soon as it saw us, it sat up alertly.

"Here we are," Terence called out gaily, and the bulldog took off at a run for us.

I let go of the satchel and box with a thud, clapped the covered basket to my chest like a shield, and looked wildly about for a stick.

The bulldog's wide mouth opened as he ran, revealing foot-long canines and row upon row of sharklike teeth. Bulldogs had been used for fighting in the Nineteenth Century, hadn't they? Fighting bulls, that was how they'd gotten their name, wasn't it? Leaping for the bull's jugular and hanging on? That was how they'd gotten that mashed-in nose, too, and those heavy jowls, wasn't it? The flat muzzle had been bred into them so they could breathe without letting go.

"Cyril!" Terence cried, but no one appeared to save us, and the bulldog shot past him and straight for me.

I dropped the covered basket, and it rolled off toward the riverbank. Terence dived for it. The bulldog paused and then took off for me again.

I had never understood what would hypnotize a rabbit into standing there and staring at an approaching snake, but now I realized it must be the snake's unusual method of movement.

The bulldog was running straight toward me, but it was more a roll than a run, and there was a lateral component to it, so that although he was clearly going directly for my throat, he nevertheless was canting to the left, so much that I thought he might miss me altogether, and by the time I realized he wouldn't, it was too late to run.

The bulldog flung himself at me and I went down, trying to protect my jugular with both hands and wishing I had been more sympathetic to Carruthers.

The bulldog had his front paws on my shoulders and his wide mouth inches from mine.

"Cyril!" Terence said, but I didn't dare turn my head to see where he was. I hoped, wherever he was, that he had a weapon.

"Good boy," I said to the bulldog, not very convincingly.

"This basket of yours nearly went in the drink," Terence said, moving into my field of vision. "Best catch I've made since the match against Harrow in '84." He set the basket down on the ground beside me.

"Could you . . ." I said, cautiously taking one hand away from my neck to point at the bulldog.

"Oh, of course, how thoughtless of me," Terence said. "You two haven't been properly introduced." He squatted down beside us. "This is Mr. Henry," he said to the bulldog, "the newest member of our merry band and our financial savior."

The bulldog opened his huge mouth in a wide, drooling grin.

"Ned," Terence said, "allow me to introduce Cyril."

# CHAPTER FIVE

Bulldogs' Tenacity and Fierceness—Cyril's Family Tree—More Luggage—Terence Packs—Jabez Packs—Riding a Horse—Christ Church Meadow—The Difference Between Poetry and Real Life—Love at First Sight—The Taj Mahal—Fate—A Splash—Darwin—A Rescue from a Watery Grave—An Extinct Species—Natural Forces—The Battle of Blenheim—A Vision

How do you do, Cyril?" I said, not attempting to get up. I had read somewhere that any sudden movement could cause them to attack. Or was that bears? I wished Finch had brought me a tape on bulldogs instead of butlers. Bulldogs nowadays are solid marshmallow. Oriel's mascot has a pleasant disposition and spends all of his time lying in front of the porter's lodge, hoping someone will come along and pet him.

But this was a Nineteenth-Century bulldog, and the bulldog had originally been bred for bull-baiting, a charming sport in which bulldogs, specifically bred for tenacity and a ferocious disposition, latched onto vital arteries, and the bull, understandably annoyed, attempted to gore the dogs and/or toss them on his horns. When had bull-baiting been outlawed? Surely before 1888. But it would take some time, wouldn't it, to breed all that tenacity and fierceness out of them?

"Delighted to make your acquaintance, Cyril," I said hopefully.

Cyril made a sound that might have been a growl. Or a belch.

"Cyril comes from an excellent family," Terence was saying, still squatting beside my prostrate form. "His father was Deadly Dan out of Medusa. His great-great-grandfather was Executioner. One of the great bull-baiters of all time. Never lost a fight."

"Really?" I said weakly.

"Cyril's great-great-great grandfather fought Old Silverback." He shook his head in admiration. "Eight-hundred-pound grizzly bear. Latched onto his muzzle and didn't let go for five hours."

"But all that tenacity and fierceness has been bred out of them?" I said hopefully.

"Not at all," Terence said.

Cyril growled again.

"I shouldn't think they ever had it," Terence continued, "except as an occupational necessity. Being clawed by a bear would make anyone ferocious, I should think. Wouldn't it, Cyril?"

Cyril made the low rumble again, and this time it sounded definitely like a belch.

"A heart of gold Executioner had, so they say. Mr. Henry's going on the river with us, Cyril," he said, as if the bulldog didn't still have me down and thoroughly drooled on, "as soon as we load the boat and settle up with Jabez." He pulled out his pocket watch and snapped it open. "Come along, Ned. It's nearly a quarter to twelve. You can play with Cyril later." He picked up both bandboxes and started for the dock.

Cyril, apparently desiring to help, got off me and ambled over to sniff at the covered basket. I picked myself up, rescued the basket, and followed Terence down to the river.

Jabez was standing on the dock next to a large pile of luggage, his arms folded militantly. "They think I'm going to let them pack the boat before they pay," he said to no one in particular, "but Jabez has seen *that* trick before." He thrust an impressively dirty hand under my nose. "Farnsecks."

I had no more idea of what "farnsecks" was than "noinbob." "Here," I said, handing Terence my purse, "you settle up with him, and I'll fetch the rest of the luggage."

I gathered up the portmanteau and the satchel, which had been knocked halfway up steps when Cyril hit me, and took them down to the dock, Cyril waddling amiably along beside me.

Terence was standing in the boat, which was a peeling dark green and had *Victory* stencilled on its prow. It was battered-looking but large, which was a good thing, since the pile of luggage on the dock turned out to be Terence's.

"A beauty, isn't she?" Terence said, taking the portmanteau from me and stowing it under the middle seat. "We'll have her loaded and be on the river in no time."

It took somewhat longer than that. We stowed Terence's luggage, which consisted of a large Gladstone bag, two bandboxes, a valise, three hampers, a wooden crate, a tin box, a roll of rugs, and two fishing poles, in the prow, and mine in the stern, which completely filled the boat, so that we had to pull it all out and start again.

"We need to go at this scientifically," Terence said. "Large items first, then fill in with the smaller."

We did, starting with the Gladstone and ending with the rugs which we unrolled and crammed into corners. This time there was a space approximately a foot wide in the middle. Cyril immediately came over and lay down in it.

I felt I should volunteer to leave some of my bags behind, but as I had no idea what was in them, I decided I'd better not.

"I knew I should have brought Dawson," Terence said. "Dawson's a wonder at packing."

I assumed that Dawson was his valet. Then again, it might be his pet raccoon.

"When I came up to Oxford, he managed to fit all Cyril's and my earthly possessions in a single trunk with room left over. Of course, if he were here, there'd be *his* luggage to consider. And him." He looked speculatively at the luggage. "Perhaps if we started with the smallest first—"

Eventually I suggested we tip Jabez an additional noinbob (whatever that was) and have him try. He did, jamming and mashing things in by brute force, and keeping up a running monologue. "Keep Jabez waiting half the day for his money," he muttered, cramming the satchel under a seat, "and then expect him to pack the boat, as if he was a common servant. And then stand there watching Jabez like a pair of fools."

We were. At any rate I was. Watching him with a sort of sick fascination. He had apparently not had the fierceness and tenacity bred out of him. I hoped there was nothing fragile in any of the boxes. Cyril, evicted from the boat, had gone back to sniffing at the covered basket, which must contain food. Terence pulled out his pocket watch and asked Jabez if he couldn't go faster, which seemed to me extremely unwise.

"Faster, he says," Jabez said, smashing in the side of Terence's bandbox. "If they hadn't brought along everything they own, it wouldn't take this long. You'd think they were going to find the sources of the Nile. Serve 'em right if she sinks."

Jabez finally succeeded, after much dark muttering and some denting of the valise, to get everything stowed. It wasn't scientific, and the pile in the prow looked like it might topple over at any moment, but there was space for the three of us.

"Right on schedule," Terence said, snapping his watch shut and stepping into the boat. "Avast, mateys, we're off. Step lively now."

Cyril ambled into the boat, lay down on the boards, and went to sleep.

"Ahoy, Ned," Terence said. "Time to shove off."

I started for the boat, and Jabez stepped in front of me, his hand outstretched for a tip. I gave him a shilling, which was apparently too much. He broke into a snaggled smile and stepped back immediately, and I climbed into the boat.

"Welcome aboard," Terence said. "This first bit's rather tricky to navigate. You row to start, and I'll be cox."

I nodded and sat down at the oars, looking dubiously at them. I'd rowed some at school, but only with automatically coordinated supraskims. These oars were wooden and weighed a ton. And they didn't appear to have any linkage. When I tried to move them together, one hit the water with a flat splash, and the other didn't even make contact with it.

"Sorry," I said, trying again. "I haven't done much rowing since my illness."

"It will come back to you," Terence said cheerily. "It's like riding a horse."

The second time I got both oars in the water, and could hardly get them out again. I gave a mighty pull, as if I were lifting roof beams in Coventry Cathedral, and sent a fountain of water over everything in the boat.

"Pair of fools!" Jabez said to no one in particular. "Never been in a boat before. They'll be drowned before they get to Iffley, and what'll become of Jabez's boat then?"

"I say, I'd better row to start," Terence said, scrambling over to change places with me, "and you be cox." He took the oars and lowered them expertly into the water together and out again with scarcely a splash. "Just till we're through this tricky bit."

This tricky bit was the bridge, and then a veritable forest of skiffs, punts, rowboats, and two large yellow-and-red-painted barges. Terence rowed energetically past them, shouting orders to me to pull the tiller lines straight, which I was trying to do, but the boat seemed to have something of the same tendency as Cyril and kept canting to the left.

In spite of my best efforts, we were drifting steadily sideways toward some willows and a wall.

"Hold her to starboard," Terence shouted, "to starboard!"

I had no idea what starboard was, but I pulled experimentally on the tiller lines until the boat more or less straightened, and by that time we were past the boats and opposite a wide grassy field.

It took me a moment to realize the field was Christ Church Meadow, though not the one I knew. No dozers, no scaffolding, no billowing sheets of plastic. No cathedral rising up out of heaps of red sandstone and mortar and roof slates. No workmen shouting orders to the robot masons. No Lady Schrapnell shouting orders at the workmen. No pickets protesting the ruination of the environment, education, the skyline of Oxford, and things in general.

A trio of cows were placidly chewing their cuds where the west tower and its spire now stood, swathed in blue plastic and waiting for Lady Schrapnell and the Coventry City Council to complete the bell negotiations.

A dirt path led past them, and, halfway up it, two dons strolled toward Christ Church's honey-colored walls, their heads bent together, discussing philosophy or the poems of Xenophon.

I wondered again how Lady Schrapnell had managed to talk them into letting her build there. Back in the Nineteenth Century, the city had tried for thirty years to build a mere road across Christ Church Meadow before it finally lost to the university, and later, when the tube came to Oxford, the outcry at the mention of a tube station there had been even greater.

But temporal physics had reached a point in its research where it couldn't go anywhere without building a nuclear-powered fine-structure oscillator. And there was no money to be gotten from the multinationals, who'd lost interest in time travel forty years ago, when they found out they couldn't rape and pillage the past. No money for buildings, either, or for fellowships or salaries. No money, period. And Lady Schrapnell was an extremely determined woman and extremely rich. And she had threatened to give the money to Cambridge.

"No, no," Terence said, "you're steering us into the bank!"

I hastily pulled on the lines and we headed back out into the current.

Ahead lay the college boathouses and the green-arched mouth of the Cherwell, and beyond that the gray tower of Magdalen and the long sweep of the Thames. The sky overhead was a gauzy blue, and, ahead, piled white clouds caught the sun. Near the far bank there were water lilies, and between them the water was a deep, clear brown, like the Waterhouse nymph's eyes.

" 'Dark brown is the river,' " I quoted, " 'golden is the sand,' " and then hoped that had been written before 1888.

" 'It flows along forever, with trees on either hand,' " Terence said, so apparently it had.

"Although actually it doesn't," Terence said. "After this next bit it's mostly all fields till Iffley. It doesn't flow along forever, either, of course, only as far as London. That's the thing about poetry, it's scarcely ever accurate. Take the Lady of Shalott. 'She loosed the chain and down she lay; The broad stream bore her far away.' She lies down in the boat and goes floating down to Camelot, which couldn't possibly happen. I mean, one can't steer lying down, can one? She'd have ended up stuck in the reeds a quarter of a mile out. I mean, Cyril and I always have trouble keeping the boat headed in a straight line, and we're not lying down in the bottom of the boat where one can't see anything, are we?"

He was right. As a matter of fact, we were drifting directly toward the bank again, which here was overhung by spreading chestnuts with spreading dark-green leaves.

"Turn it to starboard," Terence said impatiently.

I tugged on the lines, and the boat headed straight for a duck who'd built a floating nest out of sticks and chestnut leaves.

The duck squawked and flapped its wings.

"To starboard!" Terence said. "To the right!" He back-paddled furiously, and we missed the duck and headed back out toward the middle.

"I've never understood how a river works," Terence said. "If one's pipe or one's hat falls in, even if it's only a foot from shore, it goes bang into the current, straight out to sea, and round the Cape to India, which is probably what happened to poor Princess Arjumand. But in a boat, when one *wants* to be in the current, it's all eddies and whirlpools and side currents, and one's lucky if he doesn't end up in the middle of the towpath. And even if the Lady of Shalott didn't end up in the reeds, there's the problem of the locks. To starboard, man! Starboard, not port!" He snapped his pocket watch open, looked at it, and began rowing even more energetically, shouting at me periodically to hold her to starboard.

But in spite of the boat's unfortunate leftist leanings and the fact that I seemed to have signed on with Captain Bligh, I felt I could finally begin to relax.

I had met my contact, who was clearly very good—he had the role of Oxford undergraduate down perfectly—and we were on our way to Muchings End. Christ Church Meadow was an open field and Lady Schrapnell was a hundred and sixty years away.

I still couldn't remember what it was I was supposed to do at Muchings End, but bits of it were coming back. I distinctly remembered Mr. Dunworthy saying, "as soon as it's returned," and telling Finch, "it's a perfectly straightforward job," and something about a nonsignificant object. I still couldn't remember what the nonsignificant object I was supposed to return was, but it was obviously somewhere in that pile of luggage in the prow, and if all else failed I could leave it all at Muchings End. And presumably Terence knew. I'd ask him as soon as we were safely away from Oxford. We were obviously going to an appointment in Iffley, and possibly that was where I'd find out exactly what the plan was.

In the meantime, my job was to rest and recover from the ravages of time-lag and Lady Schrapnell and all those jumble sales, lean back and follow doctor's orders and Cyril's example. The bulldog had rolled over on his side and was snoring happily.

If the Victorian era was the perfect infirmary, the river was the perfect ward. The healing warmth of the sun on my neck, the soothing dip of the oars in the water, the restful scenery, green upon green upon green, the comforting drone of bees and Cyril's snoring and Terence's voice.

"Take Lancelot," he was saying, apparently back on the subject of the Lady of Shalott. "Here he is in his armor and his helmet, riding along on his horse with his shield and lance, and he's singing 'Tirra-lirra.' 'Tirra-lirra'! What sort of a song is that for a knight to be singing? 'Tirra-lirra.' Still, though," he said, pausing in his pull on the oars, "he did get the part about falling in love right, even though he made it a bit overdramatic, all that bit about 'The web flew out and floated wide. The mirror crack'd from side to side.' Do you believe in love at first sight, Ned?"

The image of the naiad, wringing out her sopping sleeve on Mr. Dunworthy's carpet, rose unbidden before me, but that was clearly a side-effect of time-lag, the result of hormones out of balance, and so, very probably, was this. "No," I said.

"Neither did I until yesterday," Terence said, "or in Fate either. Professor Overforce says there's no such thing, that it's all accident and random chance, but if that's so, why was she out on the river just at that spot? And why had Cyril and I decided to go boating instead of reading Appius Claudius? We were translating 'Negotium populo romano melius quam otium committi,' you see. 'The Romans understand work better than leisure,' and I thought, that's exactly why the Roman Empire fell, they understood work better than leisure, and I certainly don't want that to happen to the dear old British Empire, so off Cyril and I went and hired a boat and started up toward Godstow, and as we were passing through this wooded bit, I heard a voice so sweet it could have been a fairy's calling 'Princess Arjumand! Princess Arjumand!' and I looked over at the bank, and there she was, the most beautiful creature I'd ever seen."

"Princess Arjumand?" I said.

"No, no, a girl, dressed all in pink, with golden curls and a sweet, fair, beautiful face. Red cheeks and a mouth like a rosebud, and her nose! I mean, 'She hath a lovely face' simply doesn't cover it, although what can one expect from someone who would go about on his horse singing, 'Tirra-lirra'? I sat there, hanging onto the oars, afraid to move or speak for fear she was an angel or a spirit or something who would vanish at the sound of my voice, and just then she looked up and saw me and said, 'O, sir, you haven't seen a cat, have you?'

"And it was just like 'The Lady of Shalott,' only without the curse, and the mirrors breaking and flying about. That's the thing with poetry, it tends to exaggerate. I hadn't any inclination to lie down in the bottom of the boat and die of a broken heart at all. I rowed smartly in, hopped ashore, and asked her what sort of cat and where had she last seen it. She said, black with a white face and the dearest little white feet, and that it had gone missing two days before and she was afraid something had happened to it, and I said, never fear, that cats have nine lives. And just then a chaperone person who turned out to be her cousin came along and told her she shouldn't talk to strangers, and she said, 'O, but this young man has kindly offered to help me,' and her cousin said, 'That's very good of you, Mr.—?' and I said St. Trewes, and she said, 'How do you do? I am Miss Brown and this is Miss Mering,' and then she turned to her and said, 'Tossie, I'm afraid we must be going. We shall be late for tea.' Tossie! Have you ever heard such a beautiful name? 'O name forever sweet! forever dear! The sound of it is precious to mine ear!' Tossie!" he said rapturously.

Tossie? "Then who's Princess Arjumand?" I said.

"Her cat. It's named after the Indian maharani they named the Taj Mahal after, though one would think it would be called the Taj Arjumand in that case. Her father was out in India, the Mutiny and Rajahs and never the twain shall meet and all that."

I was still lost. "Princess Arjumand's father?"

"No. Miss Mering's father, Colonel Mering. He was a colonel in the Raj, but now he collects fish."

I didn't even ask what "collecting fish" was.

"At any rate, the cousin said they had to be going, and Toss—Miss Mering said, 'O, I do hope we meet again, Mr. St. Trewes. We are going tomorrow afternoon to see the Norman church at Iffley at two o'clock,' and her cousin said, 'Tossie!' and Miss Mering said she was only telling me in case I found Princess Arjumand, and I said I would search most diligently, and I did, I went up and down the river with Cyril, calling 'Puss, puss!' all last night and this morning."

"With Cyril?" I said, wondering if a bulldog was the best searcher under the circumstances.

"He's nearly as good as a bloodhound," he said. "That's what we were doing when we ran into Professor Peddick and he sent us along to meet his antique relatives."

"But you didn't find the cat?"

"No, and not likely to, either, this far from Muchings End. I'd assumed Miss Mering lived near Oxford, but it turns out she's only visiting."

"Muchings End?" I said.

"It's downriver. Near Henley. Her mother'd brought her up to Oxford to consult a medium—"

"A medium?" I said weakly.

"Yes, you know, one of those persons who tips tables and dresses up in cheesecloth with flour on her face to tell you your uncle's very happy in the afterlife and his will's in the top lefthand drawer of the sideboard. I've never believed in them myself, but then again, I've never believed in Fate either. And that's what it must have been. My meeting Miss Mering, and your being on the railway platform and her telling me she and her cousin were to go to Iffley this afternoon.

"Only I hadn't enough money for the boat, which is why it must be Fate. I mean, what if you hadn't wanted to go on the river and hadn't had the cost of Jabez? We shouldn't be going to meet her at Iffley right now, and I might never have seen her again. At any rate, these mediums are apparently very good at finding missing cats as well as wills, so they came up to Oxford for a séance. But the spirits didn't know where Princess Arjumand was either, and Miss Mering thought it might have followed her up from Muchings End, which didn't seem very likely. I mean, a dog might follow one, but cats—"

Only one thing in all this tangled account was clear—he was not my contact. He knew nothing about what it was I was supposed to do at Muchings End. If it *was* Muchings End and I hadn't gotten that wrong, too. I had gone off with a contemp and a complete stranger—to say nothing of the dog—and left my contact waiting on the station platform or the tracks or in a boathouse somewhere. And I had to get back there.

I looked back at Oxford. Its distant spires shone in the sun, already two miles behind. And I couldn't jump overboard and walk back because that would mean leaving my luggage behind. I'd already abandoned my contact. I couldn't abandon my luggage as well.

"Terence," I said. "I'm afraid I—"

"Nonsense!" someone ahead of us shouted, and there was a splash that nearly swamped the boat. The covered basket, which was sitting on the top of the Gladstone bag, almost went overboard. I grabbed for it.

"What is it?" I said, trying to see round the curve.

Terence looked disgusted. "Oh, it's very likely Darwin."

I kept imagining I was cured, when clearly I was obviously still suffering from a considerable residue of time-lag and was still having Difficulty Distinguishing Sounds. "I beg your pardon?" I said cautiously.

"Darwin," Terence said. "Professor Overforce taught him to climb trees and now he's taken to jumping down on innocent passersby. Turn the boat, Ned." He gestured the direction I was to turn us in. "Bring us away from the bank."

I did so, trying to see round the bend and under the willows.

"Landed bang in the middle of a punt with two Corpus Christi men and their girls last week," Terence said, rowing us toward the middle of the river. "Cyril completely disapproves."

Cyril did, in fact, look disapproving. He had sat up, more or less, and was looking toward the willows.

There was another, louder splash, and Cyril's ears went back alertly. I followed his gaze.

Either I had been mistaken about my Difficulty, or my Blurring of Vision had taken on new dimensions. An elderly man was floundering in the water beneath the willows, splashing wildly and uselessly.

Good Lord, I thought, it *is* Darwin.

He had Darwin's white beard and muttonchop whiskers and his balding head, and what looked like a black frock coat was floating around him. His hat, upside down, was floating several yards from him, and he made a grab for it and went under. He came up choking and flailing, and the hat drifted farther out.

"Good heavens, it's my tutor, Professor Peddick," Terence said. "Quick, turn the boat, no, not that way! Hurry!"

We rowed frantically over, me with my hands in the water, paddling, to make us go faster. Cyril stood up with his front paws on the tin trunk like Nelson on the bridge at Trafalgar.

"Stop! Don't run Professor Peddick over," Terence said, pushing the oars away from him and leaning over the side.

The old man was oblivious to us. His coat had billowed up like a lifejacket around him, but it obviously wasn't keeping him afloat. He went under for more than the third time, one hand still reaching ineffectually for his hat. I leaned over the edge of the boat and grabbed for him.

"I've got his collar," I shouted, and suddenly remembered that the one Warder had put on me was detachable, and fumbled for the collar of his frock coat instead. "I've got him," I said, and yanked upward.

His head rose out of the water like a whale's, and, also like a whale, spewed a great gasping spout of water all over us.

" 'Then once by man and angels to be seen, In roaring he shall rise.' Don't let go," Terence said, clamping Professor Peddick's hand onto the side of the boat and fishing for the other one. I'd lost my grip on his neck when he spouted, but his hand had come up, too, when he breached, and I grabbed for that and pulled, and his head came up again, shaking water like a dog.

I have no idea how we got him into the boat. The gunwale dipped sharply underwater, and Terence shouted, "Cyril, no! Ned, back up! We're going under! No, don't let go!" but our masses of luggage apparently acted as ballast and kept us from upsetting, even though Cyril came over at the last minute to look at the proceedings and add to the weight on this side of the boat.

Finally, I got a grip on one of his arms, and Terence maneuvered around till he was on the professor's other side, bracing his foot against the portmanteau so the boat didn't capsize and got a grip on the other, and we were able to haul him, drenched and pathetic, over the side and into the boat.

"Professor Peddick, are you all right, sir?" Terence said.

"Perfectly all right, thanks to you," he said, wringing out his sleeve. What I had taken to be a frock coat was actually a black gabardine academic robe. "Fortuitous thing you came along when you did. My hat!"

"I've got it," Terence said, leaning out over the water. What I had taken to be a hat was a mortarboard, complete with the tassel.

"I know I packed blankets. I remember Dawson setting them out," Terence said, rummaging in his luggage. "What on earth were you doing in the water?"

"Drowning," Professor Peddick said.

"You very nearly were," Terence said, digging in the tin box. "But how did you come to be in the water? Did you fall in?"

"Fall in? *Fall* in?" the professor said, outraged. "I was *pushed.*"

"Pushed?" Terence said, taken aback. "By whom?"

"By that murderous villain Overforce."

"*Professor* Overforce?" Terence said. "Why would Professor Overforce push you in the water?"

"Larger matters," Professor Peddick said. "Facts are inconsequential in the study of history. Courage is unimportant, and duty and faith. Historians must concern themselves with larger matters. Pah! A lot of scientific rigamarole. All history can be reduced to the effects of natural forces acting upon populations. Reduced! The Battle of Monmouth! The Spanish Inquisition! The Wars of the Roses! Reduced to natural forces! And populations! Queen Elizabeth! Copernicus! Hannibal!"

"Perhaps you'd better begin at the beginning," Terence said.

"*Ab initio.* An excellent plan," Professor Peddick said. "I had come to the river to reflect upon a problem I was having with my monograph on Herodotus's account of the battle of Salamis by that method which Mr. Walton recommends as the perfect aid to thinking, 'a rest to his mind, a cheerer of his spirits, a diverter of sadness, a calmer of unquiet thoughts.' But, alas, it was not to be. For I had come to '*piscatur in aqua turbida.*'"

Oh, good, I thought, another one who makes no sense and spouts quotations. And in Latin.

"One of my pupils, Tuttle Minor, had told me he'd seen a white gudgeon just here along the bank while practicing for the Eights. Nice boy, wretched recitations and worse penmanship, but very sound on fish."

"I *knew* I'd packed them," Terence said, coming up with a green wool blanket. "Here," he said, handing it to the professor. "Take that off and put this round you."

Professor Peddick unbuttoned his robe. "His brother, Tuttle Major, was the same way. Dreadful penmanship." He pulled his arm out of one sleeve and stopped, a peculiar expression on his face, and stuck his arm into the other sleeve.

"Always blotted his essays." His hand groped wildly in the sleeve. "Translated '*Non omnia possumus omnus*' as 'No possums allowed on the omnibus.'" He made one last wild gyration and pulled his arm out of the sleeve, "Thought he'd never be able to sit exams," and opened his closed hand to reveal a tiny white fish.

"Ah, *Ugobio fluviatilis albinus*," he said, peering at its flopping. "Where's my hat?"

Terence produced the professor's mortarboard, and Professor Peddick dipped it in the river and then dropped the fish into the water-filled hat. "Excellent specimen," he said, leaning over it. "Assistant to the Head of the Exchequer now. Advisor to the Queen."

I sat there watching him examine the fish and marvelling at what we'd caught. A genuine eccentric Oxford don. They're an extinct species, too, unless you count Mr. Dunworthy, who is really too sensible to be eccentric, and I had always felt a bit cheated that I hadn't been there in the glory days of Jowett and R.W. Roper. Spooner was the most famous, of course, because of his gift for mangling the Queen's English. He'd told a delinquent student, "You have tasted a worm," and announced the morning hymn one Sunday as "Kinquering Congs Their Titles Take."

My favorite don was Claude Jenkins, whose house was so messy it was sometimes impossible to open the front door, and who had arrived late for a meeting and apologized by saying, "My housekeeper has just died, but I've propped her up on a kitchen chair, and she'll be all right till I return."

But they had all been personalities: Professor of Logic Cook Wilson, who after two hours of steady orating, said, "After these preliminary remarks . . ." Mathematics professor Charles Dodgson who, when Queen Victoria wrote him praising *Alice in Wonderland* and requesting a copy of his next book, sent her his mathematical treatise *Condensations of Determinants,* and the professor of classics who thought a barometer would look better if placed horizontally rather than vertically.

And of course Buckland, with his household menagerie and his trained eagle who had strutted, wings half spread, down the aisle of Christ Church Cathedral during morning prayers. (Church must have been exciting in those days. Perhaps Bishop Bittner should have tried introducing animals to Coventry Cathedral when attendance lagged. Or Spoonerisms.)

But I had never expected to actually meet one in the flesh, and here he was, an excellent specimen, interestedly peering at a fish swimming in his mortarboard, and orating on the subject of history.

"Overforce propounds the theory that the study of history as a chronicle of kings and battles and events is obsolete," Professor Peddick said. " 'Darwin has revolutionized biology,' he says—"

Darwin. The same Darwin whom Professor Overforce had taught to climb trees?

" '—and so must history be revolutionized,' Overforce claims. 'It must no longer be a chronicle of dates and incidents and facts. They are no more important than a finch or a fossil is to the theory of evolution.' "

Actually, I thought, they were utterly important.

" 'Only the laws underlying the theory of history are important, and they are natural laws.' 'But what of the events that have shaped history for good or ill?' I asked him. 'Events are irrelevant,' Overforce said. Julius Caesar's assassination! Leonidas's stand at Thermopylae! Irrelevant!"

"So you were fishing on the riverbank," Terence said, spreading the professor's robe out to dry over the luggage. "And Professor Overforce came along and pitched you in?"

"Yes," Professor Peddick said, pulling off his boots. "I was standing under a willow, hooking a worm to my line—gudgeons prefer blood-worms but *Pseudococcidae* will do—when that imbecile Darwin flung himself out of the branches and plummeted toward me like one of Satan's angels 'hurled headlong flaming from th' ethereal sky, With hideous ruin and combustion down,' and landed with a great splash that made me drop my line." He looked darkly at Cyril. "Dogs!"

A dog, I thought gratefully. Darwin is Professor Overforce's dog. Which still didn't explain what it was doing jumping out of trees.

"He'll end by killing someone." Professor Peddick took off his socks, wrung them out, and put them back on again. "Leaped out of a tree on the Broad last Tuesday and knocked Trinity's bursar flat. The man's completely unbalanced. He fancies himself another Buckland," Professor Peddick said, "but Buckland, for all his faults, never trained his bear to jump out of trees. Tiglath Pileser was always extremely well-behaved, and so were the jackals, though one wouldn't want to dine at his house. Liable to be served crocodile. I remember one dinner party at which the meat course was vole. But he had two excellent Crucian carp."

"Darwin made you drop your line . . ." Terence prompted, trying to get the professor back on track.

"Yes, and when I turned round, there was Overforce, laughing like one of Buckland's hyenas. 'Out fishing?' he said. 'Tch, tch. You will never attain the Haviland Chair idling your time away like that.' 'I am pondering the effects of Themistocles's deception of the Persians at Salamis,' I said, and he replied, 'An even more idle pursuit than fishing. History is no longer a chronicle of mere events. It is a science.'

" 'Mere events!' I said. 'Do you consider the Greeks' defeat of the Persian fleet a mere event? It shaped the course of history for hundreds of years!' Overforce waved his hand as if to dismiss them. 'Events are irrelevant to the theory of history.' 'Do you consider the Battle of Agincourt irrelevant?' I said. 'Or the Crimean War? Or the execution of Mary Queen of Scots?' 'Details!' he said. 'Did details matter to Darwin or Newton?' "

As a matter of fact, they had. As Lady Schrapnell is so fond of saying, "God is in the details."

" 'Darwin! Newton!' I said," Professor Peddick went on. " 'You disprove your own argument by your examples. It is the individual that matters in history, not the population. And it is forces other than natural ones that shape history. What of courage and honor and faith? What of villainy and cowardice and ambition?' "

"And love," Terence said.

"Exactly," Professor Peddick said. " 'What of Antony and Cleopatra's love? Was that irrelevant to history?' I asked him that while he was in the water. 'What of Richard the Third's villainy?' I said. 'What of Joan of Arc's fervor? It is character, not populations, that affect history!' "

"In the water?" I said blankly.

Terence echoed, "You pushed Professor Overforce in the water?"

"A push is an event, an incident, a fact," Professor Peddick said, "and therefore irrelevant to Overforce's theory. I said that to him when he shouted at me to pull him out. 'Natural forces acting upon populations,' I said."

"Good Lord," Terence said. "Turn the boat around, Ned. We've got to go back. I do hope he isn't drowned by now."

"Drowned? Impossible! A drowning is unimportant in his theory of history, though it be the drowning of the Duke of Clarence in a vat of malmsey! 'What of murders?' I said to him while he was splashing about, waving his arms and calling for help. 'And what of help? They are irrelevant, for both require intention and morality, of both of which you have denied the existence. Where in your theory are purpose and plan and design?' 'I *knew* it!' Overforce said, thrashing wildly. 'Your theory of history is nothing but an argument for a Grand Design!' 'And is there not evidence for a Grand Design?' I said, offering my hand to him to pull him out. 'Is there only chance in your theory of history? Is there no free will? Are there no acts of kindness?' I said, and pulled Overforce up onto the bank. 'Surely you must admit now that the individual and the event are not irrelevant to history,' I said, quite reasonably. And the villain pushed me in!"

"But he is all right?" Terence said anxiously.

"All right?" Professor Peddick said. "He is wrongheaded, ignorant, prideful, opinionated, puerile, and violent! All right?"

"I mean, he's not in danger of drowning."

"Of course not," Professor Peddick said. "He has no doubt gone off to expound his misguided theories to the Haviland Committee! And left me to drown! If you two had not come along when you did, I should have shared the Duke of Clarence's fate. And Overforce, that villain, would have had the Haviland Chair!"

"Well, at least no one's *killed* anyone," Terence said. He looked anxiously at his pocket watch. "Ned, take the lines. We must hurry if we are to take the professor home and be back to Iffley before the afternoon's gone."

Good, I thought. When we get back to Folly Bridge I can make some excuse for not going on to Iffley with Terence—seasickness or a relapse or something—and go back to the railway station. And hope my contact was still there.

"Iffley!" Professor Peddick said. "Just the place! Splendid dace fishing there. Tuttle Minor said he saw a split-tailed rainbow half a mile above Iffley Lock."

"But shouldn't you go back?" Terence said unhappily. "You should get out of those wet clothes."

"Nonsense. Nearly dry. And this is too good an opportunity to miss. You've fishing lines, I presume, and bait?"

"But what about Professor Overforce?" I said. "Won't he be worried about you?"

"Ha! He's gone off to write about populations and teach his dog to ride a bicycle! Populations! History is made by individuals, not populations! Lord Nelson, Catherine de Medici, Galileo!"

Terence looked longingly at his pocket watch. "If you're certain you won't catch cold," he said. "The thing is, I've an appointment at Iffley at two o'clock."

"Then 'Press on! while yet ye may!' " Professor Peddick said. " '*Vestigia nulla retrorsum,*' " and Terence took up the oars with determination.

The willows dwindled to bushes and then to grass, and ahead around a long curve of the river I could see a gray church tower. Iffley.

I pulled out my pocket watch and counted out the Roman time. Five minutes till II. Terence would be on time for his appointment at least. And hopefully mine would wait for me.

"Stop!" the professor said and stood up in the boat.

"Don't—" Terence said and dropped the oars with a clatter. I grabbed for him and caught the rug as it fell around his feet. The boat swayed dangerously, and water slopped over the gunwales. Cyril blinked, bleary-eyed, and wobbled to his feet, and that was all we needed.

"Sit," I commanded, and Professor Peddick looked around bewilderedly and sat down.

"St. Trewes, we must take the boat to shore immediately," he said, pointing at the bank. "Look."

We all, even Cyril, looked at a grassy meadow covered in Queen Anne's lace and buttercups.

"It is the very image of the field of Blenheim," Professor Peddick said. "Look, yonder the village of Sonderheim and beyond it Nebel Brook. It proves my point exactly. Blind forces! It was the Duke of Marlborough who won the day! Have you an exercise book? And a fishing line?"

"Wouldn't it be better to do this later? This afternoon, after we've been to Iffley."

"The attack against Tallard happened in early afternoon in just this light," Professor Peddick said, pulling on his boots. "What sort of bait did you bring?"

"But we haven't time," Terence said. "I've this appointment—"

" *'Omnia aliena sunt, tempus tantum nostrum est,'* " Professor Peddick quoted. " 'Nothing is ours except time.' "

I leaned forward and whispered to Terence, "You could leave us here and come back for us after your appointment."

He nodded, looking happier, and began bringing the boat in toward the bank. "But I need you to go with me," he said, "to work the tiller. Professor Peddick, I'm going to put you ashore to study the battle, and we'll go on to Iffley and then come back and collect you." He began to look for a place to land.

It took an eternity to find a spot where the bank sloped enough for the professor to be able to climb it, and even longer to locate the fishing equipment. Terence rummaged through the Gladstone bag between frantic looks at his pocket watch, and I dug into the tin box, looking for the fishing line and a box of flies.

"Here it is!" Terence said. He thrust the flies into the professor's pocket, reached for an oar, and pushed us up flat against the bank.

"Land ho," Terence said, popping up and standing with one foot on the muddy bank. "Here you go, Professor."

Professor Peddick looked vaguely around, picked up his mortarboard, and started to put it on.

"Wait!" I said, rescuing it. "Have you got a bowl or something, Terence? For the white gudgeon."

We rummaged again, Terence through one of the bandboxes, I in my satchel. Two starched collars, a pair of black patent shoes three sizes too small for me, a toothbrush.

The covered basket Cyril had been sniffing at. It had the food in it, and presumably, a pot to cook it in. I dug through the jumble in the stern and then under the seat. There it was, perched on the prow. I reached for it.

"A kettle!" Terence said, holding one up by the handle. He handed it to me.

I emptied the fish and the water into it and handed the mortarboard to Professor Peddick. "Don't put it on just yet," I said. "Wait till the water's evaporated."

"An apt pupil," the professor said, beaming. " '*Beneficiorum gratia sempiterna est.*' "

"All ashore that's going ashore," Terence said, and had him out of the boat and up the bank before I could set the kettle down.

"We'll be an hour," he said, clambering back into the boat and grabbing the oars. "Perhaps two."

"I shall be here," Professor Peddick said, standing on the very edge of the bank. " '*Fidelis ad urnum.*' "

"He won't fall in again?" I said.

"No," Terence said, not very convincingly, and went at the oars as if it were Eights Week.

We pulled rapidly away from Professor Peddick, who had stooped to peer at something on the ground through his pince-nez. The box of flies fell out of his pocket and skittered halfway down the bank. He bent farther and reached for it.

"Perhaps we should . . ." I said, and Terence gave a mighty pull around a bend, and there was the church and an arched stone bridge.

"She said she'd be waiting on the bridge," Terence panted. "Can you see her?"

I shaded my eyes and looked at the bridge. There was someone standing near the north end of it. We pulled rapidly closer to the bridge. A young woman holding a white parasol. In a white dress.

"Is she there?" Terence said, yanking on the oars.

She was wearing a white hat with blue flowers on it, and under it her auburn hair shone in the sunlight.

"Am I too late?" Terence said.

"No," I said. But I am, I thought.

She was the most beautiful creature I'd ever seen.

*Non semper ea sunt quae videntur.*
*(Things are not always what they seem.)*
Phaedrus

# C H A P T E R  S I X

An English Rose—Ruffles—Cyril Guards the Boat—A Message
from the Other Side—Seeing the Sights—A Butler—Signs
and Portents—In a Country Churchyard—A Revelation—An
Alias—Explanations—A Water-Logged Diary—Jack the Ripper—A
Problem—Moses in the Bulrushes—More Aliases—An Even
More Unexpected Development

I know, I had said the naiad was the most beautiful creature I'd ever seen, but she had been wet and dirty, and, even though she looked like she'd risen out of a Pre-Raphaelite pond, unmistakably Twenty-First Century.

Just as the creature on the bridge was unmistakably Nineteenth. No historian, no matter how casually she caught up her trailing white skirts with a kid-gloved hand, no matter how erect she held her head on her aristocratic neck, could hope to capture the quality of stillness, of clear-eyed innocence of the girl on the bridge. She was like a delicate blossom, capable of growing only in a single time, adapted only to the select hothouse environment of the late Victorian era: the untouched flower, the blooming English rose, the angel in the house. She would be extinct in only a handful of years, replaced by the bicycling bloomer girl, the cigarette-smoking flapper and the suffragette.

A terrible melancholy swept over me. I could never have her. Standing there with her white parasol and her clear greenish-brown-eyed gaze, the image of youth and beauty, she was long since married to Terence, long since dead and buried in a churchyard like the one at the top of the hill.

"To port," Terence said. "No, to port!" He rowed rapidly toward the side of the bridge, where there were several stakes, presumably for tying the boat up.

I grabbed the rope, jumped out into squishy mud, and looped the rope.

Terence and Cyril were already out of the boat and climbing the steep bank up to the bridge.

I tied a very lumpish-looking knot, wishing Finch had included a subliminal tape on half-hitches and sheepshanks, and that there were some way to lock the boat.

This is the Victorian era, I reminded myself, when people could trust each other and the earnest young man gets the girl and is probably already kissing her on the bridge.

He wasn't. He was standing on the muddy bank, looking vaguely round. "I don't see her," he said, looking directly at the vision, "but her cousin's here, and there's the landau," he pointed at an open carriage standing on the hill next to the church, "so she must still be here. What time is it?" He pulled out his pocket watch to look at it. "You don't suppose they've sent her cousin to tell me she's not to see me. If she—" he said, and broke into a wide smile.

A girl in ruffles appeared on the bank above us. Her white dress had ruffles on the skirt and ruffles on the yoke and ruffles on the sleeves. Her parasol had ruffles round the edges, too, and her short white gloves, and all of the ruffles were in motion, like flags being carried into battle. There weren't any ruffles on her hat, but, to compensate, it had a large batch of fluttering pink ribbons, and her blonde hair under the hat curled and bounced with every stray breeze.

"Look, Cousin, it's Mr. St. Trewes," she said, and started down the slope, which set everything into a flurry of motion. "I told you he would come!"

"Tossie," the vision in white said reprovingly, but Tossie was already running toward the towpath, catching her flounced skirts up just enough to reveal the toes of very small feet in white boots, and taking dainty little steps.

She reached the edge of the riverbank and stopped—comparatively, that is—fluttered her eyelashes at us, and addressed Cyril. "Did the dearie doggums come to see his Tossie? Did he know his Tossie missed her sweetums Cyril?"

Cyril looked appalled.

"He's been goodums, hasn't he?" Tossie cooed. "But his master's been a naughty bad boy. He didn't come and didn't come."

"We were delayed," Terence interjected. "Professor Peddick—"

"Tossie was afwaid her tardy boy'd forgotten all about her, wasn't her, Cywil?"

Cyril gave Terence a look of resignation and ambled forward to have his head petted.

"O! O!" Tossie said, and somehow managed to make it sound exactly like I'd seen it written in Victorian novels. "O!"

Cyril stopped, confused, and looked at Terence, and then started forward again.

"Bad, bad dog!" Tossie said, and pursed her lips into a series of tiny screams. "The horrid creature will muss my dress. It's silk muslin." She fluttered her skirts away from him. "Papa had it made for me in Paris."

Terence lunged forward and grabbed Cyril, who had already backed away, by his collar. "You frightened Miss Mering," he said sternly, and shook his finger at him. "I apologize for Cyril's behavior," he said, "and for my tardiness. There was a near-drowning, and we had to save my tutor."

The cousin came up. "Hello, Cyril," she said kindly and bent to scratch him behind the ears. "Hello, Mr. St. Trewes. How nice to meet you again." Her voice was quiet and cultured, without a hint of baby-talk. "Does your being here mean you've found Princess Arjumand?"

"Yes, do tell us," Tossie said belatedly. "Have you found my poor lost Juju?"

"Alas, no," Terence said, "but we intend to continue the search. This is Mr. Henry. Mr. Henry, Miss Mering and Miss Brown."

"How do you do, Miss Mering, Miss Brown," I said, tipping my straw boater as the subliminals had instructed.

"Mr. Henry and I have hired a boat," he gestured toward the foot of the bridge, where the nose of the boat was just visible, "and we intend to explore every inch of the Thames."

"That's very good of you," Miss Brown said, "but I have no doubt that when we return home this evening, we shall find she has returned safe and sound."

"Home?" Terence said, dismayed.

"Yes!" Tossie said. "We're to return to Muchings End tonight. Mama has had a message that we are needed there."

"I hope nothing unfortunate has happened to call you home," Terence said.

"Oh, no," Tossie said, "it wasn't a message like that. It was from the Other Side. It said, 'Return to Muching's End to await your happy Fate,' so Mama is determined to go at once. We're taking the train this evening."

"Yes," Miss Brown said. "We should be returning to Madame Iritosky's." She extended a kid-gloved hand. "Thank you for your kindness in looking for Princess Arjumand. So nice to have met you, Mr. Henry."

"Oh, but we mustn't go back now, Cousin Verity," Tossie said. "Our train isn't till half-past six. And Mr. St. Trewes and Mr. Henry haven't seen the church."

"It is a long way to Madame Iritosky's home," Cousin Verity protested, "and your mother particularly said we were to be back for tea."

"We've plenty of time," Tossie said. "We'll tell Baine to drive very fast. Wouldn't you like to see the church, Mr. St. Trewes?"

"I'd love to," Terence said fervently. Cyril trotted happily up between them.

Tossie hesitated prettily. "Shouldn't Cyril stay by the boat?"

"Oh, yes, of course," Terence said. "Cyril, you must stay."

"He could wait outside the lychgate," I offered, but it was no use. Terence was too far gone.

"Stay, Cyril," he commanded.

Cyril gave him the look Julius Caesar must have given Brutus, and lay down on the shadeless bank, his head on his paws.

"Don't let any bad, bad mans steal the boat," Tossie said. "You must be a brave, brave doggums." She unfurled her parasol and started up the path. "It's the cunningest little church. So quaint and old-fashioned. People come from miles about to see it. I do love sights, don't you? Mama has promised to take us to Hampton Court next week." She led the way up the hill, chattering to Terence, and the vision and I followed.

Tossie was correct about the church, and people did "come from miles about to see it," if the signs posted were any indication. They began at the foot of the hill with a hand-lettered placard that said, "Keep to path." This was followed by, "No tours during church services," "Keep off grass," and "Picking flowers forbidden."

"Mama says we're to have a séance in the Gallery at Hampton Court. The spirit of Catherine Howard walks there, you know. She was one of Henry the Eighth's wives. He had eight wives. Baine says he only had six, but if that were true, why would his name be Henry the Eighth?"

I glanced at Miss Brown, who was smiling gently. At close quarters she was even more beautiful. Her hat had a veil, caught up behind into a fall of sheer white over her auburn hair, and through it her fair skin and pink cheeks looked almost ethereal.

"Henry the Eighth's wives were all beheaded," Tossie was saying. "I should hate to be beheaded." She gave her blonde curls a toss. "They clipped off your hair and dressed you in a horrid plain shift without any decoration at all."

Or ruffles, I thought.

"I do hope it won't just be Catherine Howard's head," she said. "It is sometimes, you know, not the entire spirit. When Nora Lyon came to

Muchings End, she materialized a spirit hand. It played the accordion." She looked coyly at Terence. "Do you know what the spirits told me last night? That I would meet a stranger."

"What else did they tell you?" Terence asked. "That he was tall, dark, and handsome, I suppose."

"No," she said, perfectly serious. "They rapped out 'Beware,' and then the letter 'C.' Mama thought it was a message about Princess Arjumand, but I think it meant the sea, only we aren't anywhere near it, so it must mean the stranger will arrive by the river."

"Which I have," Terence said, far gone.

We were nearing the crest of the hill. An open carriage stood at the top with a driver in, of all things, full morning dress: swallowtail coat and striped trousers. He was reading a book, and the horse was grazing listlessly at the grass. I was surprised there wasn't a "No parking" sign.

As we came up, the driver closed the book and sat up stiffly at attention. "I was afraid we couldn't come after all," Tossie said, walking past the carriage without so much as a glance at the driver. "Madame Iritosky's boy was to have driven us, but he was in a trance, and Mama wouldn't let us take the landau alone. And so then I thought, Baine can drive us. That's our new butler. Mama stole him from Mrs. Chattisbourne, who was dreadfully angry. Good butlers are so difficult to find."

That explained the striped trousers and the stiffness—Finch's tape had been very clear. Butlers did not drive carriages. I looked at him. He was younger than I'd expected, and taller, with a rather haggard expression, as if he hadn't been getting enough sleep. I could relate to that. I felt as though I'd been up for centuries.

Finch's tapes had said that butlers were supposed to be poker-faced, but this one wasn't. He looked distinctly worried about something. I wondered what. This outing, or the prospect of working for someone who thought Henry the Eighth had eight wives? I tried to sneak a look at his book as we passed. It was Carlyle's *The French Revolution.*

"I don't like our butler," Tossie said as if he wasn't there. "He's always cross."

Apparently Cousin Verity didn't like him either. She kept her gaze straight ahead as we passed. I nodded to the butler and tipped my hat. He picked up his book and resumed reading.

"Our last butler was much nicer. Lady Hall stole him from us when she came to visit. Imagine, while she was staying under our roof! Papa says servants shouldn't be allowed to read books. It ruins their moral fibers. And gives them ideas."

Terence opened the gate to the church. It had a sign on it which read, "Close gate when you leave."

He and Tossie walked up to the door. It was plastered with signs—"No visitors after four o'clock." "No visitors during services." "No photographs or daguerreotypes allowed." "For assistance contact Mr. Egglesworth, Churchwarden, Harwood House, do not disturb except in case of EMERGENCY." I was surprised Luther's Ninety-Nine Objections weren't on there, too.

"Isn't the church cunning?" Tossie said. "Look at those sweet zigzags carved over the door."

I recognized them even without tapes as dogtoothed ornamentation dating from the twelfth century, the result of having spent the last several months on Lady Schrapnell's cathedral. "Norman architecture," I said.

"I do so love dear old-fashioned churches, don't you?" Tossie said, ignoring me. "So much simpler than our modern ones."

Terence opened the simple old-fashioned note-covered door, Tossie furled her parasol, and went in. Terence followed her, and I expected Cousin Verity to follow suit. Finch's tapes had said Victorian young ladies were never allowed to go anywhere unchaperoned, and I had assumed that Cousin Verity, vision though she was, was that chaperone. She had certainly looked disapproving enough down on the riverbank, and the church would be dimly lit and full of opportunities for hanky-panky.

And it was clear from the sign on the door that the churchwarden wasn't inside. But Miss Brown didn't so much as glance toward the half-opened door or the shadowy darkness within. She opened the iron gate, which was decorated with a sign that read "No spitting," and walked into the churchyard.

She paced silently among the graves, past several signs directing us not to pick the flowers or lean against the tombstones, past a badly tilting obelisk, against which somebody obviously had.

I tried to think of what one said to a Victorian young lady when alone with her. Finch's tapes hadn't given any guidelines as to proper topics of conversation for a young man and a young lady who'd just met.

Not politics, since I had no idea what they were in 1888, and young ladies weren't supposed to bother their pretty heads about affairs of state. And not religion, since Darwin was still controversial. I tried to remember what people had said in the Victorian plays I'd seen, which consisted of *The Admirable Crichton* and *The Importance of Being Earnest*. Class issues and witty epigrams. A butler with ideas was clearly not a popular idea in these parts, and I couldn't think of any witty epigrams. Besides, humor is always fraught with peril.

She had reached the last of the tombstones and was looking at me expectantly.

The weather. But how was I supposed to address her? Miss Brown? Miss Verity? Milady?

"Well," she said impatiently. "Did you get it back all right?"

It was not exactly the opening line I had expected. "I beg your pardon?" I said.

"Baine didn't see you, did he?" she said. "Where did you leave it?"

"I'm afraid you've confused me with someone else . . ."

"It's all right," she said, looking toward the church. "They can't hear us. Tell me exactly what happened when you brought it back through the net."

I must be having some sort of relapse of the time-lag. None of this was making any sense.

"You didn't drown it, did you?" she said angrily. "He promised he wasn't going to drown it."

"Drown what?" I said.

"The cat."

This was worse than talking to the nurse in Infirmary. "The cat? You mean Tossie—Miss Mering's cat that's lost? Princess Arjumand?"

"Of course I mean Princess Arjumand." She frowned. "Didn't Mr. Dunworthy give her to you?"

"Mr. Dunworthy?" I gaped at her.

"Yes. Didn't he give the cat to you to bring back through the net?"

The light began to dawn. "You're the naiad in Mr. Dunworthy's office," I said wonderingly. "But you can't be. Her name was Kindle."

"That's my name. Miss Brown is my contemp name. The Merings don't have any relatives named Kindle, and I'm supposed to be a second cousin of Tossie's."

The light was still breaking. "You're the calamity," I said, "who brought something forward through the net."

"The cat," she said impatiently.

A cat. Of course. That made much more sense than a cab or a rat. And it explained the peculiar look Mr. Dunworthy'd given me when I mentioned Lady Windermere's fan. "It was a cat you brought through the net," I said. "But that's impossible. You can't bring things forward through the net."

Now she was the one gaping. "You didn't know about the cat? But I thought they were going to send the cat through with you," and I wondered uneasily if they had intended to. Finch had told me to wait when I was standing there in the net. Had he gone to fetch the cat, and I'd made the jump before he could give it to me?

"Did they tell you they were sending it back with me?" I asked.

She shook her head. "Mr. Dunworthy refused to tell me anything. He told me I'd caused enough trouble already, and he didn't want me meddling any further. I just assumed it was you because I saw you in Mr. Dunworthy's office."

"I was there to speak to Mr. Dunworthy about my time-lag," I said. "Infirmary prescribed two weeks' bed rest, so Mr. Dunworthy sent me here to get it."

"To the Victorian era?" she said, looking amused.

I nodded. "I couldn't get it in Oxford because of Lady Schrapnell—"

She looked even more amused. "He sent you here to get away from Lady Schrapnell?"

"Yes," I said, alarmed. "She isn't here, is she?"

"Not exactly," she said. "If you don't have the cat, do you know who they sent it through with?"

"No," I said, trying to remember that conversation in the lab. "Contact someone," Mr. Dunworthy had said. Andrews. I remembered now. Mr. Dunworthy had said, "Contact Andrews."

"They said something about contacting Andrews," I said.

"Did you hear them say anything else? When they were sending him through to? Whether the jump worked?"

"No," I said, "but I was dozing a good deal of the time. Because of the time-lag."

"When exactly did you hear them mention Andrews?"

"This morning, while I was waiting for my jump," I said.

"When did you come through?"

"This morning. At ten o'clock."

"Then that explains it," she said, looking relieved. "I was worried when I got back and Princess Arjumand wasn't there. I was afraid something had gone wrong, and sending her back through the net hadn't worked, or that Baine had found her and thrown her in again. And when Mrs. Mering insisted on coming to Oxford to consult Madame Iritosky on her disappearance, and your young man showed up, I got truly worried. But everything's all right. They obviously sent her through after we left for Oxford, and the visit was a good thing. It put us all out of the way so no one would see her being put back, and Baine's here, so he can't drown her before we get back. And the jump must have been successful, or you wouldn't be here. Mr. Dunworthy said he was suspending all drops to the Nineteenth Century till the cat was returned. So everything's all right. Mr. Dunworthy's experiment worked, Princess Arjumand will be there waiting to greet us when we get back, and there's nothing to worry about."

"Wait," I said, thoroughly confused. "I think you need to begin at the beginning. Sit down."

I indicated a wooden bench with a sign on it: "Do not deface." Next to it was a carved heart with an arrow through it and under it, "Violet and Harold, '59." She sat down, arranging her white skirts gracefully about her.

"All right," I said. "You brought a cat forward through the net."

"Yes. I was at the gazebo, that's where the drop is, just behind it in a little copse, it's on a ten-minute on and off rendezvous. I'd just come through from reporting to Mr. Dunworthy, and I saw Baine, that's the butler, carrying Princess Arjumand—"

"Wait. What were you doing in the Victorian era?"

"Lady Schrapnell sent me here to read Tossie's diary. She thought there might be some clue in it as to the whereabouts of the bishop's bird stump."

Of course. I might have known all this had something to do with the bishop's bird stump. "But what does Tossie have to do with the bishop's bird stump?" I had a sudden horrible thought. "Please tell me she isn't the great-great-grandmother."

"Great-great-great-great. This is the summer she went to Coventry, saw the bishop's bird stump—"

"—and had her life changed forever," I said.

"An event she referred to repeatedly and in great detail in the voluminous diaries she kept for most of her life, which Lady Schrapnell read and became obsessed with rebuilding Coventry Cathedral, and had *her* life changed forever."

"And ours," I said. "But if she read the diaries, why did she have to send you back to 1888 to read them?"

"The volume in which Tossie originally recorded the life-changing experience—the one Tossie wrote in the summer of 1888—is badly water-damaged. Lady Schrapnell's got a forensics expert working on it, but she's only made limited progress, so Lady Schrapnell sent me to read it on the spot."

"But if she referred to it in great detail in the other diaries—?" I said.

"She didn't say exactly *how* it changed her life or on what date she went there, and Lady Schrapnell thinks there may be other details in the volume that are important. Unfortunately, or perhaps I should say fortunately, since Tossie writes the way she talks, she keeps her diary under better lock and key than the Crown Jewels, and so far I haven't been able to get at it."

"I'm still confused," I said. "The bishop's bird stump didn't disappear till 1940. What use is a diary written in 1888?"

"Lady Schrapnell thinks there might be a clue as to who gave it to the church. The donations records for Coventry Cathedral were burnt up during the air raid. She thinks whoever donated it, or their descendants, might have taken it away for safekeeping at the beginning of the war."

"Whoever donated it was probably trying to get rid of it."

"I know. But you know Lady Schrapnell. 'No stone unturned.' So I've been following Tossie around for two weeks, hoping she'll leave her diary lying out. Or go to Coventry. She's got to go soon. When I mentioned Coventry, she said she'd never been there, and we know she went sometime in June. But so far nothing."

"So you kidnapped her cat and demanded her diary as ransom?"

"*No,*" she said. "I was coming back from reporting to Mr. Dunworthy, and I saw Baine, that's the butler—"

"Who reads books," I said.

"Who's a homicidal maniac," she said. "He was carrying Princess Arjumand, and when he got to the riverbank, a perfectly lovely June. The roses have been so pretty."

"What?" I said, disoriented again.

"And the laburnum! Mrs. Mering has an arbor of laburnum that is ever so picturesque!"

"Begging your pardon, Miss Brown," Baine said, appearing out of nowhere. He gave a stiff little bow.

"What is it, Baine?" Verity said.

"It's Miss Mering's pet cat, ma'am," he said uncomfortably. "I was wondering if Mr. St. Trewes's being here meant that he had located it."

"No, Baine," she said, and the temperature seemed to drop several degrees. "Princess Arjumand is still missing."

"I was concerned," he said and bowed again. "Do you wish the carriage to be brought around now?"

"No," she said frostily. "Thank you, Baine."

"Mrs. Mering requested that you return in time for tea."

"I am aware of that, Baine. Thank you."

He still hesitated. "It is half an hour's drive to Madame Iritosky's home."

"Yes, Baine. That will be all," she said and watched him till he was nearly to the carriage before she burst out, "Cold-blooded murderer! 'I was wondering if Mr. St. Trewes might have found the cat.' He knows perfectly well he hasn't. And all that about being concerned! Monster!"

"Are you certain he was trying to drown her?" I said.

"Of course I'm certain. He flung her as far out as he could throw her."

"Perhaps it's a contemp custom. I remember reading they drowned cats in the Victorian era. To keep the population down, of all things."

"That's newborn kittens, not full-grown cats. And not pets. Princess Arjumand's the thing Tossie loves most, next to herself. The kittens they drown are farm cats, not pets. The farmer just up the road from Muchings End killed a batch last week, put them in a sack weighted with stones and threw it in his pond, which is barbaric but not malicious. *This* was malicious. After Baine threw her in, he dusted off his hands and walked back toward the house *smiling*. He clearly intended to drown her."

"I thought cats could swim."

"Not in the middle of the Thames. If I hadn't done something, it would have been swept away in the current."

"The Lady of Shalott," I murmured.

"What?"

"Nothing. Why would he want to murder his mistress's cat?"

"I don't know. Perhaps he has something against cats. Or perhaps it isn't just cats, and we'll all be murdered in our beds some night. Perhaps he's Jack the Ripper. He was operating in 1888, wasn't he? And they never did find out his true identity. All I know is, I couldn't just stand there and let Princess Arjumand drown. It's an extinct species."

"So you dived in and saved it?"

"I *waded* in," she said defensively, "and caught hold of her and brought her back on shore, but as soon as I did, I realized no Victorian lady would have waded in like that. I hadn't even taken off my shoes. I didn't think. I just acted. I ducked in the net, and it opened," she said. "I was only trying to get out of sight. I didn't mean to cause a problem."

A problem. She had done something temporal theory said was impossible. And possibly caused an incongruity in the continuum. No wonder Mr. Dunworthy had asked Chiswick all those questions and been grilling poor T.J. Lewis. A problem.

A fan was one thing, a live cat was another. And even a fan won't go through. Darby and Gentilla had proved that, back when time travel had first been invented. They'd built the net as a pirate ship for plundering the treasures of the past, and they'd tried it on everything from the *Mona Lisa* to King Tut's tomb and then, when that didn't work, on more mundane items, like money. But nothing except microscopic particles would come through. When they tried to take any object, even a halfpence or a fish fork, out of its own time, the net wouldn't open. It didn't let germs through either, or radiation, or stray bullets, which Darby and Gentilla and the rest of the world should have been grateful for, but weren't particularly.

The multinationals who'd been backing Darby and Gentilla lost interest, and time travel had been handed over to historians and scientists, who'd come up with the theories of slippage and the Law of Conservation of History to explain it, and it had been accepted as a law that if one tried to bring something forward through the net, it wouldn't open. Till now.

"When you tried to bring the cat through, the net opened, just like that?" I said. "You didn't notice anything out of the ordinary about the drop, no delays or jolts?"

She shook her head. "It was just like any other jump."

"And the cat was all right?"

"She slept through the whole thing. Fell asleep in my arms in the drop and didn't even wake up when we got to Mr. Dunworthy's office. Apparently that's how time-lag affects cats. It puts them right out."

"You went to see Mr. Dunworthy?"

"Of course," she said defensively. "I took the cat to him as soon as I realized what I'd done."

"And he decided to try to send it back?"

"I pumped Finch, and he told me they were going to check all the drops to the Victorian era, and if there weren't any indications of excessive slippage, that meant the cat had been returned before its disappearance could cause any damage, and they were going to send it back."

But there *was* excessive slippage, I thought, remembering Mr. Dunworthy asking Carruthers about Coventry. "What about the trouble we were having in Coventry?"

"Finch said they thought it was unrelated, that it was due to Coventry's being an historical crisis point. Because of its connection to Ultra. It was the only area of excessive slippage. There wasn't any on any of the Victorian drops." She looked up at me. "How much slippage was there on your drop?"

"None," I said. "I was spang on target."

"Good," she said, and looked relieved. "There was only five minutes on mine when I came back. Finch said the first place an incongruity would manifest itself was in the increased slip—"

"Oh, I *do* love country churchyards," Tossie's voice said, and I leaped away from Verity like a Victorian lover. Verity remained serene, opening her parasol and standing up with a calm grace.

"They're so delightfully rustic," Tossie said and hove into view, flags flying. "Not at all like our dreadful modern cemeteries." She stopped to admire a tombstone that had nearly fallen over. "Baine says churchyards are unsanitary, that they contaminate the water table, but I think it's wonderfully unspoilt. Just like a poem. Don't you, Mr. St. Trewes?"

" 'Beneath those rugged elms that yew trees shade,' " Terence obligingly quoted, " 'where heaves the turf in many a mouldering heap—' "

The bit about "the mouldering heap" seemed to confirm Baine's theory, but neither Terence nor Tossie noticed, Terence particularly, who was declaiming, " 'Each in his narrow cell forever laid, The rude forefathers of the hamlet sleep.' "

"I *do* love Tennyson, don't you, Cousin?" Tossie said.

"Thomas Gray," Verity said. " 'Elegy Written in a Country Churchyard.' "

"Oh, Mr. Henry, you must come and see the inside of the church," Tossie said, ignoring her. "There's the dearest decorated vase. Isn't it, Mr. St. Trewes?"

He nodded vaguely, gazing at Tossie, and I saw Verity frown. "We must see it, by all means," she said, and caught up her skirts with a gloved hand. "Mr. Henry?"

"By all means," I said, offering her my arm, and we all went into the church, past a large sign that read, "Trespassers will be prosecuted."

The church was chilly and smelled faintly of old wood and mildewing hymnals. It was decorated with stout Norman pillars, a vaulted Early English sanctuary, a Victorian rose window, and a large placard that proclaimed "Keep out of chancel" on the altar railing.

Tossie blithely ignored it and the Norman slate baptismal font and swept up to a niche in the wall opposite the pulpit. "Isn't it the cunningest thing you've ever seen?"

There was no question she was related to Lady Schrapnell, and no question where Lady Schrapnell had got her taste from, though Tossie at least had the excuse of being a Victorian, and part of an era that had built not only St. Pancras Railway Station, but the Albert Memorial.

The vase that sat in the niche looked like both, though on a less grandiose scale. It only had one level and no Corinthian pillars. It did, however, have twining ivy and a bas-relief of either Noah's ark or the battle of Jericho.

"What is it supposed to be depicting?" I asked.

"The Slaughter of the Innocents," Verity murmured.

"It's Pharaoh's Daughters Bathing in the Nile," Tossie said. "Look, there's Moses' basket peeping out from among the rushes. I do wish we had this in our church," Tossie said. "The church at Muchings End hasn't anything in it but a lot of old things. It's just like that poem by Tennyson," Tossie said, clasping her hands together. "Poem to a Greek Vase."

And the last thing we needed was Terence quoting Keats's "Ode on a Grecian Urn." I looked desperately at Verity, trying to think of something to get us out of here and somewhere we could talk. The dogtoothed ornamentation? Cyril? Verity was looking round calmly at the stone vaulting, as if we had all the time in the world.

" 'Beauty is truth, truth beauty,' " Terence said. " 'That is all ye know—' "

"Do you suppose it's haunted?" Verity said.

Terence stopped quoting. "Haunted?"

"Haunted?" Tossie said happily and gave a miniature version of a scream, a sort of screamlet. "Of course it is. Madame Iritosky says that there are certain places that act as portals between one world and the next," she said.

I glanced at Verity, but she looked serene, untroubled by Tossie's having just described the net.

"Madame Iritosky says that spirits often hover near the portal by which their souls passed to the Other Side," Tossie explained to Terence. "That's why séances fail so often, because they're not close enough to a portal. That's why Madame Iritosky always holds her séances at home, instead of travelling to people's homes. And a churchyard would be a *logical* portal." She looked up at the ribbed vaulting and gave another screamlet. "They could be here with us now!"

"I should imagine the churchwarden would know of any spirits," Verity said helpfully.

Yes, and would have put up a sign saying, "No manifestations," I thought. "Absolutely no ectoplasm."

"Oh, yes!" Tossie said and gave another of her little screamlets. "Mr. St. Trewes, we must ask the churchwarden!" They went out the door, consulted the sign, and started off for Harwood House and the churchwarden, who would no doubt be delighted to see them.

"All Mr. Dunworthy would tell me was that he was sending me back to two hours after I'd rescued the cat," Verity said, picking up where she'd left off, "and to report back if there was any unusual slippage or coincidental happenings, and I assumed that meant Princess Arjumand was already back at Muchings End. But when I came through, she wasn't there. Tossie had discovered she was missing and had the whole household out searching for her, and I began to worry that something had gone wrong. And before I could report back to Mr. Dunworthy and find out what had happened, Mrs. Mering had hauled us all off to Oxford, and Tossie had met Count de Vecchio."

"Count de Vecchio?"

"A young man at one of the séances. Rich, handsome, charming. Perfect, in fact, except that his name begins with a 'V' and not a 'C.' He's interested in theosophy," she said. "He was also interested in Tossie. He insisted on sitting next to her at the table so he could hold her hand, and he told her not to be afraid if she felt a touch on her feet, that it was only the spirits. That's why I suggested the walk by the Thames, to get her away from him, and then Terence came rowing by, and his name doesn't begin with a 'C' either. And he seemed so smitten with her. Not that that's unusual. Every young man who meets Tossie is smitten with her." She looked up at me from under her veil. "Speaking of which, why aren't you?"

"She thinks Henry the Eighth had eight wives," I said.

"I know, but I'd have thought with your time-lag you'd have been in poor Titania's condition, wandering about ready to fall in love with the first girl you saw."

"Which was you," I said.

If she had been the untouched English rose she looked like, she'd have blushed a becoming pink under that veil, but she was Twenty-First Century.

"You'll get over it," she said, sounding just like the Infirmary nurse, "as soon as you've had a good night's sleep. I wish I could say the same for Tossie's suitors. Especially Terence. Tossie seems so taken with him. She insisted on coming to Iffley this afternoon even though Mme. Iritosky had arranged a special séance for finding Princess Arjumand. And on the way over in the carriage, she asked me what I thought of plum cake for a bride's cake. That's when I got truly worried that my taking the cat had caused an incongruity and Count de Vecchio and Terence would never have met Tossie if she hadn't come to Oxford, and neither of their names begins with a 'C.'"

I was getting lost again. "Why do their names need to begin with a 'C'?"

"Because that summer—*this* summer—she married someone whose name begins with a 'C.'"

"How do you know? I thought the diary was unreadable."

"It is." She walked over to a pew and sat down next to a sign that read, "Sitting in pews allowed only during services."

"Then couldn't the 'C' refer to that trip to Coventry that changed her life forever?" I said. "Coventry begins with a 'C.'"

She shook her head. "Her diary entry for May 6, 1938 says, 'This summer we shall have been married fifty years, and I am happier than I ever thought possible being Mr. C-something's wife,' but the middle of his name is blotted out, and the letter 'w' of 'wife.'"

"Blotted?"

"An ink stain. Pens did that in those days, you know."

"And you're certain it's a 'C' and not a 'G'?"

"Yes."

That seemed to rule out not only Count de Vecchio and Terence but also Professor Peddick and Jabez. And thankfully, me.

"Who is this Mr. Chips or Chesterton or Coleridge she's supposed to marry?" I said.

"I don't know. It's no one she's ever mentioned and no one who's ever been to Muchings End. I asked Colleen, the parlor maid. She'd never heard of him."

There was the sound of distant voices from outside. Verity stood up. "Walk with me," she said. "Pretend we're examining the architecture." She strolled over to the baptismal font and looked interestedly at it.

"So you don't know who this Mr. C is, but you know it's someone Tossie hasn't met yet and you know she married him this summer," I said, examining a sign that said, "Do not remove church furnishings." "I thought Victorians went in for long engagements."

"They do," she said, looking grim, "and after the engagement, the banns have to be read out in church for three successive Sundays, not to mention meeting the parents and sewing a trousseau, and it's already nearly the middle of June."

"When were they married?"

"We don't know that either. The church at Muchings End was burned during the Pandemic, and her later diaries don't mention the date."

I thought of something. "But surely they mention his name, don't they? The May sixth entry can't have been the only time she mentioned her husband in fifty years."

She looked unhappy. "She always refers to him as 'my darling husband' or 'my beloved helpmeet.' 'Darling' and 'beloved' underlined."

I nodded. "And exclamation points." I'd had to read some of the diaries for references to the bishop's bird stump.

We strolled over to the side aisle. "The diaries stopped for several years after this summer's," Verity said, "and then started up again in 1904. By that time they were living in America, and he was working in silent films under the stage name of Bertram W. Fauntleroy, which he changed to Reginald Fitzhugh-Smythe in 1927, when the talkies came in."

She stopped in front of a stained-glass window half-covered with a sign that read, "Do not attempt to open." "He had a long and distinguished career playing British aristocrats," she said.

"Which means it was likely he was an aristocrat himself. That's good, isn't it? It means at least he wasn't a tramp who wandered by." I thought of something. "What about his obituary?"

"It lists his stage name," she said, "and so does hers." She smiled wryly at me. "She lived to the age of ninety-seven. Five children, twenty-three grandchildren, and a major Hollywood studio."

"And nary a clue," I said. "What about Coventry? Could she have met this Mr. C there, while she was looking at the bishop's bird stump, and that's the event that changed her life forever?"

"It's possible," she said. "But that's another problem. They haven't said anything about a trip to Coventry. Mrs. Mering's talked about going to Hampton Court to see Catherine Howard's ghost, but they've never so much as mentioned Coventry, and they didn't go before I got here. I know because I asked—"

"—the upstairs maid," I finished.

"Yes. And we know Tossie went there sometime in June. That's why I've been so worried about their coming to Oxford to see Madame Iritosky.

I was afraid Princess Arjumand's disappearance had made them come to Oxford when they should have been going to Coventry, or that Mr. C might have come to Muchings End while Tossie was here and missed meeting her. But if Mr. Dunworthy and T.J. have returned Princess Arjumand, that means the cat's simply wandered off. And who knows? Mr. C may be the one who finds her and brings her back. Perhaps that's why they got engaged so suddenly, because she was grateful to him for returning Arjumand."

"And it isn't as if you've been away from Muchings End long," I said. "Only a day. If Mr. C did come calling, the maid would no doubt ask him to wait in the parlor till you returned."

"What do you mean?" she said. She stood up abruptly, her skirts rustling.

"I just assumed," I said, surprised. "Weren't the Victorians the ones with parlors? Didn't their maids ask callers to wait?"

"When did you come through?" she demanded.

"This morning," I said. "I told you. Bang on target. Ten o'clock, June the seventh, 1888."

"This is the tenth of June," she said.

The tenth. "But the newspaper—"

"—must have been an old one. I came through on the night of the seventh. We came to Oxford on the eighth, and we've been here three days."

I said blankly, "Then there must have been—"

"—increased slippage," she said, "which is an indication that there's been an incongruity."

"Not necessarily," I said. "I left rather in a hurry." I explained about Lady Schrapnell. "Warder might not have finished setting the coordinates. Or she might have made a mistake. She'd done seventeen drops already."

"Perhaps," she said doubtfully. "Where did you come through? Folly Bridge? Is that where you met up with Terence?"

"No, the railway station. He was there to meet his tutor's relatives, but they didn't arrive." I explained about his asking me if I were going on the river and about his financial problems. "So I paid the balance on the boat."

"And if you hadn't been there, he wouldn't be here," she said, looking even more worried. "Could he have gotten the boat if you hadn't lent the money to him?"

"Not a chance," I said, thinking about Jabez, and then, at her worried expression, "He said something about trying to borrow money from someone named Mags at the Mitre," I said. "But he was determined to see Tossie again. I think he would have run the entire way to Iffley if he hadn't had the money."

"You're probably right," she said. "There's a great deal of redundancy in the system. If he hadn't met her here, he might very well have met her at Muchings End. He said yesterday he had been thinking of going downriver. And three days' slippage isn't all that much." She frowned. "Still, though, it seems a lot for a pleasure trip. And it's more than on the other Victorian drops. I'd better report it to Mr. Dunworthy when I get back to—"

"—certain the spirits will bring us word of Princess Arjumand," Tossie's voice said, and she fluttered in with Terence, who had his hat in his hands. "Madame Iritosky is famous for locating lost objects. She told the Duchess of Derby where her lost brooch was and the Duchess gave her a reward of a thousand pounds. Papa said, of course she knew where it was, she'd put it there herself, but Ma*ma*," she said, putting the accent on the last syllable, "knows it was the workings of the spirit world."

Verity stood up and draped her skirts. "What did the churchwarden say?" she said, and I was amazed at her composure. She looked the serene English maiden again. "Is Iffley Church haunted?"

"No," Terence said.

"Yes," Tossie said, looking up at the vaulting. "And I don't care what he says, cross old bear. They are here now, spirits from another time and place. I can feel their presence."

"What the churchwarden said was that it wasn't haunted, but he wished it were," Terence said, "because 'hants' didn't get mud all over the floor or take down his notices. Or bother the churchwarden when he was having his tea."

"Tea!" Tossie said. "What a lovely idea! Cousin, go and tell Baine to serve tea."

"There isn't time," Verity said, pulling on her gloves. "We are expected back at Madame Iritosky's."

"Oh, but Mr. St. Trewes and Mr. Henry have not seen the mill yet," Tossie said.

"They shall have to see it after we are gone," Verity said, and swept out of the church. "We do not want to miss our train to Muchings End." She stopped at the lychgate. "Mr. St. Trewes, would you be so good as to tell our butler to bring the carriage round?"

"My pleasure," Terence said, tipping his hat, and started toward the tree where Baine sat reading.

I'd hoped Tossie would go with him so I could talk to Verity, but she stayed by the lychgate, pouting and snapping her parasol open and shut. And what sort of excuse could give us a few moments alone? I could hardly suggest she follow Terence with Verity already concerned about her attraction to him, and she was the type to give orders, not take—

"My parasol," Verity said. "I must have left it in the church."

"I'll help you find it," I said, and opened the door with alacrity, scattering notices everywhere.

"I'll return to Oxford and report to Mr. Dunworthy as soon as I get the chance," she whispered as soon as the door was shut. "Where will you be?"

"I'm not certain," I said. "On the river somewhere. Terence talked about rowing down to Henley."

"I'll try to get word to you," she said, walking toward the front of the nave. "It may be several days."

"What do you want me to do?"

"Keep Terence away from Muchings End," she said. "It's probably just an infatuation on Tossie's part, but I don't want to take any chances."

I nodded.

"And don't worry. It's only three days' slippage, and Mr. Dunworthy wouldn't have sent you through if Princess Arjumand hadn't already been safely returned. I'm certain everything's fine." She patted my arm. "You get some sleep. You're supposed to be recovering from time-lag."

"I will," I said.

She retrieved the white parasol from underneath the kneeling rail and started toward the door, and then stopped and smiled. "And if you meet anyone named Chaucer or Churchill, send them along to Muchings—"

"Your carriage, miss," Baine said, looming in the door.

"Thank you, Baine," she said coldly and swept past him.

Terence was handing Tossie into the carriage. "I do hope we shall meet again, Mr. St. Trewes," Tossie said, no longer pouting. "We take the train home this evening to Muchings End. Do you know it? It's on the river, just below Streatley."

Terence took off his boater and held it over his heart. " 'Till then, good-bye, fair one, adieu!' "

The carriage lurched forward. "Baine!" Tossie protested.

"I beg your pardon, miss," Baine said and clucked the reins.

"Goodbye," Tossie called back to us, waving a handkerchief and everything else on her person. "Goodbye, Mr. St. Trewes!" The landau rolled away.

Terence watched it till it was out of sight.

"We'd better go," I said. "Professor Peddick will be waiting."

He sighed, looking longingly after the dust cloud it had left. "Isn't she wonderful?"

"Yes," I said.

"We must start immediately for Muchings End," he said, and started down the hill.

"We can't," I said, trotting after him. "We have to take Professor Peddick back to Oxford, and what about his agèd relicts? If they're on the afternoon train, they'll need to be met."

"I'll arrange with Trotters to meet them. He owes me a favor for that translation of Lucretius I did," he said without stopping. "It will only take an hour to row Peddick back. We can put him off at Magdalen by four. That will still give us four hours of daylight. We should be able to make it past Culham Lock. That will put us at Muchings End by noon tomorrow."

And so much for my blithely promising Verity to keep Terence away from Tossie, I thought, following him down to the boat.

It wasn't there.

*"This is the cat*
*That killed the rat*
*That ate the malt*
*That lay in the house that Jack built."*

*Mother Goose*

# CHAPTER SEVEN

Importance of Locks in Victorian Era—"Loose lips sink ships"—Tristan and Isolde—Pursuit—The French Revolution—An Argument Against Tipping—A Traumatized Cat—Soot—The Bataan Death March—Sleep—The Boat Is Found at Last—An Unexpected Development—Importance of Meetings to History—Lennon and McCartney—I Search for a Tin-Opener—What I Found

Cyril was there, in the same position in which we had left him, his head disconsolately pressed against his paws, his brown eyes reproachful.

"Cyril!" Terence said. "Where's the boat?"

Cyril sat up and looked round in surprise.

"You were supposed to guard the boat," Terence said sternly. "Who took it, Cyril?"

"Could it have drifted off, do you think?" I said, thinking about the half-hitch.

"Don't be ridiculous," Terence said. "It's obviously been stolen."

"Perhaps Professor Peddick came and got it," I said, but Terence was already halfway across the bridge.

When we caught up to him, he was looking downstream at the river. There was no one on it except for a mallard duck.

"Whoever stole it must have taken it back up the river," Terence said, and ran the rest of the way across the river and back up to the lock.

The lock-keeper was standing on top of the lock, poking at the sluice with his boathook.

"Did our boat go back through the lock?" Terence shouted to him.

The lock-keeper put his hand to his ear and shouted back, "What?"

"Our boat!" Terence shouted, cupping his hands around his mouth. "Did it go back through the lock?"

"What?" he bellowed back.

"Did our boat" Terence said, pantomiming the shape of a boat, "go back—" he made a sweeping motion upriver, "through the lock?" He pointed exaggeratedly at the lock.

"Boats go through the lock?" the lock-keeper shouted. "Of course boats go through the lock. What else do you think it's for?"

I glanced around, looking for someone, anyone else who might have seen the boat, but Iffley was completely deserted. Not even the churchwarden was in evidence, putting up "No shouting" signs. I remembered Tossie had said he was having his tea.

"No! *Our* boat!" Terence shouted. He pointed first at himself and then at me. "Did it go back through the lock?"

The lock-keeper looked indignant. "No, you can't go through the lock without a boat! What sort of foolery are you up to?"

"*No,*" Terence shouted. "Someone's stolen the boat we hired!"

"Wire?" The lock-keeper shook his head. "The nearest telegraph's in Abingdon."

"No. Not *wire. Hired!*"

"Liar?" he said and raised his pole threateningly. " 'Oo you callin' a liar?"

"No one," Terence said, backing up. "*Hired!* The boat we hired!"

The lock-keeper shook his head again. "What you want's Folly Bridge. Man name of Jabez."

Cyril and I wandered back down to the bridge, and I stood there, leaning over it and thinking about what Verity had told me. She'd saved a cat from drowning and then stepped into the net with it, and the net had opened.

So it must not have caused an incongruity, because if it would have, the net wouldn't have opened. That's what had happened the first ten times Leibowitz had tried to go back to assassinate Hitler. The eleventh he'd ended up in Bozeman, Montana in 1946. And nobody's ever been able to get close to Ford's Theater or Pearl Harbor or the Ides of March. Or Coventry.

I thought T.J. and Mr. Dunworthy were probably right about the increased slippage around Coventry, and I wondered why it hadn't occurred to us before. Coventry was obviously a crisis point.

Not because the raid had done significant damage. The Luftwaffe had only damaged, not destroyed, the aircraft and munitions factories, and they were up and running again within three months. They'd destroyed the cathedral, of course, which had enlisted outrage and sympathy from the States, but even that hadn't been critical. The Blitz had already stirred up plenty of American support, and Pearl Harbor was only three weeks away.

What was critical was Ultra, and the Enigma machine which we'd smuggled out of Poland and were using to decipher the Nazis' codes, and which, if the Nazis had found out we had it, could have changed the course of the entire war.

And Ultra had warned us of the raid on Coventry. Only obliquely, until late in the afternoon of the fourteenth, which had made it impossible to do more than notify Command and take impromptu defensive measures, and those (because history's a chaotic system) had cancelled each other out. Command had decided the main attack would be on London, no matter what Intelligence said, and sent their planes up accordingly, and the attempts to jam the pathfinder beams had failed because of an error in calculations.

But secrets are always pivotal events. A stray word could have endangered the safety of the Intelligence setup. And if something, anything, had happened to make the Nazis suspicious — if the cathedral had been miraculously saved or the entire RAF had shown up over Coventry, even if someone had talked — "Loose lips sink ships" — they would have changed their code-machines. And we would have lost the battles of El Alamein and the North Atlantic. And World War II.

Which explained why Carruthers and the new recruit and I had ended up in the rubble and the marrows field. Because around a crisis point, even the tiniest action can assume importance all out of proportion to its size. Consequences multiply and cascade, and anything — a missed telephone call, a match struck during a blackout, a dropped piece of paper, a single moment — can have empire-tottering effects.

The Archduke Ferdinand's chauffeur makes a wrong turn onto Franz-Josef Street and starts a world war. Abraham Lincoln's bodyguard steps outside for a smoke and destroys a peace. Hitler leaves orders not to be disturbed because he has a migraine and finds out about the D-Day invasion eighteen hours too late. A lieutenant fails to mark a telegram "urgent" and Admiral Kimmel isn't warned of the impending Japanese attack. "For want of a nail, the shoe was lost. For want of a shoe, the horse was lost. For want of a horse, the rider was lost."

And around those attractors, there was radically increased slippage and net closures.

Which must mean Muchings End wasn't a crisis point, and the cat hadn't changed history, particularly since it would only have required a few minutes' slippage to prevent the whole thing. Verity wouldn't even have had to have ended up in Bozeman, Montana. If she'd come through five minutes later, the cat would already have gone under. Five minutes earlier, and she'd have been inside the house and missed the whole thing.

And it wasn't as if this were Queen Victoria's cat (in spite of her name) or Gladstone's or Oscar Wilde's. It was hardly in a position to affect world events, and 1888 wasn't a critical year. The Indian Mutiny had ended in 1859 and the Boer War wouldn't start for another eleven years. "And it's only a cat," I said out loud.

Cyril looked up, alarmed.

"Not here," I said. "It's probably safely back at Muchings End by now," but Cyril got up and began looking warily about.

"No! Thieves, not sheaves!" Terence was yelling, his voice drifting toward us over the water. "Thieves!"

"Sieves?" the lock-keeper bellowed back. "This is a lock, not an ironmonger's."

Eventually, he waved his arm dismissively at Terence and went inside the lockhouse.

Terence hurried over. "Whoever took it went that way," he said. "The lock-keeper pointed downstream."

I was not at all sure of that. It seemed to me just as likely that the gesture had meant, "Go on, I've had it with talking to you," or even, "Get the bloody hell out of here!" And the opposite direction was better in regard to keeping Terence away from Tossie.

"Are you certain?" I said. "I thought he pointed upstream."

"No," Terence said, already across the bridge. "Definitely downstream," and galloped off down the towpath.

"We'd better hurry," I said to Cyril, "or we'll never catch up to him," and we set off after him, past the straggle of Iffley's cottages and a line of tall poplars and up a low hill, from which we could see a long stretch of river. It glittered emptily. "Are you sure they went this way?"

He nodded without slackening his pace. "And we'll find them and get the boat back. Tossie and I are meant to be together, and no obstacle can keep us apart. It's fated, like Tristan and Isolde, Romeo and Juliet, Héloïse and Abelard."

I didn't point out that all of the aforementioned had ended up dead or severely handicapped, because it was all I could do to keep up. Cyril wobbled after us, panting.

"When we catch up to them, we'll go back and fetch Professor Peddick and take him back to Oxford and then row down below Abingdon and camp for the night," Terence said. "It's only three locks away. If we work at it, we should be able to make Muchings End by teatime tomorrow."

Not if I could help it. "Won't that be a rather tiring journey?" I said. "My physician said I wasn't to overtire myself."

"You can nap while I row. Tea's the best time. They have to ask you to stay, it's not like dinner or something, it doesn't require a formal invitation or dressing or anything. We should be able to make Reading by noon."

"But I'd hoped to see some of the sights along the river," I said, racking my brain to think what they were. Hampton Court? No, that was below Henley. So was Windsor Castle. What had the three men in a boat stopped to look at? Tombs. Harris was always wanting to stop and look at somebody or other's tomb.

"I'd hoped to see some tombs," I said.

"Tombs?" he said. "There aren't any interesting ones along the river, except for Richard Tichell's at Hampton Church. He threw himself out of one of the windows of Hampton Court Palace. And at any rate, Hampton Church is past Muchings End. If Colonel Mering likes us, we might be asked to dinner. Do you know anything about Japan?"

"Japan?" I said.

"That's where the fish are from," he said obscurely. "The best thing, of course, would be if we were asked to stay a week, but he doesn't like houseguests, says it disturbs them. The fish, I mean. And he went to Cambridge. Perhaps we could pretend to be spiritualists. Mrs. Mering's mad for spirits. Did you pack evening clothes?"

The time-lag must be catching up with me. "Do spiritualists wear evening clothes?" I asked.

"No, long, flowing robe sort of things, with sleeves you can hide tambourines and cheesecloth and things in. No, for dinner, in case we're asked."

I had no idea whether there were evening clothes in my luggage or not. When we caught up to the boat, *if* we caught up to the boat, I needed to go through my bags and see exactly what Warder and Finch had sent with me.

"It's too bad we haven't found Princess Arjumand," Terence said. "That would get us an invitation to stay. The lost lamb and the fatted calf and all that. Did you see Tossie when she ran down the bank and asked me if I'd found her? She was the loveliest creature I'd ever seen. Her curls bright as gold and her eyes, 'blue as the fairy-flax, her cheeks like the dawn of day!' No, brighter! Like carnations! Or roses!"

We went on, Terence comparing Tossie's various features to lilies, berries, pearls, and spun gold, Cyril thinking longingly of shade, and me thinking about Louis the Sixteenth.

It was true that Princess Arjumand wasn't Queen Victoria's cat and Muchings End wasn't Midway Island, but look at Drouét. He hadn't been anybody either, an illiterate French peasant who normally would never have made it into the history books.

Except that Louis the Sixteenth, escaping from France with Marie Antoinette, leaned out the window of his carriage to ask Drouét directions, and then, in one of those minor actions that change the course of history, tipped him a banknote. With his picture on it.

And Drouét tore ahead through the forest to raise a force to stop the carriage, and failing that, dragged a cart out of a barn and across the road to block their way.

And what if an historian had stolen the cart, or waylaid Drouét, or warned Louis's driver to take another road? Or what if, back at Versailles, an historian had stolen the banknote and replaced it with coins? Louis and Marie would have made it to their loyalist army, put down the Revolution, and changed the entire course of European history.

For want of a cart. Or a cat.

"We should be coming to Sandford Lock soon," Terence said cheerfully. "We can ask the lock-keeper if he's seen the boat."

In a few minutes, we came to the lock, and I thought we were going to have to endure another interminable and incomprehensible conversation, but this time Terence's earnest shouts failed even to bring the lock-keeper out, and after several minutes he said, undaunted, "There'll be someone at Nuneham Courtenay," and set off again.

I didn't even ask how far Nuneham Courtenay was, for fear of the answer, and beyond the next bend in the river there was a line of willows next to the towpath, obscuring the view. But when we came round the bend, Terence was standing in front of a thatched cottage, looking thoughtfully at a little girl in the front garden. She was sitting on a swing in a blue-and-white-striped pinafore whose petticoats billowed up around her, holding a white cat and talking to it.

"Dear sweet pussy," she said, "you love to go up in a swing, don't you? Up in the air so blue?"

The cat didn't answer. It was sound asleep.

Cats weren't extinct yet in the Forties, so I'd seen them before, but, except for that sooty streak in the cathedral, I had yet to see one that was awake. Verity had said time-lag had made the cat she brought through the net sleepy, but I wasn't convinced this wasn't their normal state. The black-and-orange calico at the Nativity of the Virgin Mary Fête had slept the entire duration of the fête on top of a crocheted afghan on the Fancy Works Table.

"I say, what do you think?" Terence said, indicating the little girl.

I nodded. "She might have seen the boat. And she can't be any worse than the lock-keeper."

"No, no. Not the child. The cat."

"I thought you said Miss Mering's cat was black," I said.

"It is. With white feet and a white face," he said. "But with a bit of boot-blacking in the right spots—"

"No," I said. "You said she was very attached to her pet."

"She is, and she'll be extremely grateful to the person who finds it. You don't think some soot, carefully applied . . ."

"No," I said, and walked over to the swing. "Have you seen a boat?"

"Yes, sir," she said politely.

"Excellent," Terence said. "Who was in it?"

"In what?" she said.

"In the boat," Terence said.

"Which boat?" she said, petting the cat. "There are lots and lots of boats. This is the Thames, you see."

"This was a large green boat with a great deal of luggage piled in it," Terence said. "Did you see it?"

"Does he bite?" the little girl asked Terence.

"Who? Mr. Henry?" Terence said.

"Cyril," I said. "No, he doesn't bite. Did you see a boat like that? With a lot of luggage?"

"Yes," she said, and got off the swing, shifting the cat to her shoulder. It didn't wake up. "It went that way," she said and pointed down the river.

"We know that," Terence said. "Did you see who was in the boat?"

"Yes," she said, patting the cat as if she were burping a baby. "Poor, dear pussy, did the big dog frighten you?"

The cat slumbered on.

"Who was in the boat?" I said.

She transferred the cat back to her arms and cradled it. "A reverent."

"A reverend? You mean, a clergyman? A verger?" I said, wondering if the churchwarden had posted a sign saying, "No docking," and carted the boat off as punishment.

"Yes," she said. "Wearing a robe."

"Professor Peddick," I said.

"Did he have white hair?" Terence said. "And muttonchop whiskers?"

She nodded, picking the cat up under the front legs and holding it out in front of her like a doll. "What a wicked dog, to frighten you so!"

The cat still didn't wake up.

"Come on, then," Terence said, already far ahead. "We should have thought of that," he said when the wicked dog and I caught up to him, "that it was Professor Peddick who took the boat. He can't have gone far."

He gestured at the river, winding slowly off to the southwest between the flat fields. "It looks exactly like the plain of Marathon."

It might have been a spitting image, for all I knew, but either the resemblance hadn't struck Professor Peddick or he could row faster than I thought. Neither he nor the boat were anywhere to be seen.

Terence didn't seem bothered. "We're bound to spot him soon."

"What if we don't catch up to him?" I said.

"We shall," he said. "There's a lock five miles from here. He'll have to wait to go through it."

"Five miles?" I said weakly.

"And we must catch up to him. That's how Fate works. Like Antony and Cleopatra."

Yet another love story that hadn't turned out well.

"Would Antony have let a little thing like a lost boat stand in his way? Though I suppose in his case it would have been a barge."

We struggled on. The Victorian sun beat down, Terence hurried on at an energetic pace, comparing Tossie to angels, fairies, sprites, and Cleopatra (a truly bad end); Cyril began to take on the demeanor of a Bataan Death March participant; and I thought longingly of sleep and tried to calculate how long I had been up.

I had been here since ten, and my pocket watch said nearly IV, so that was six hours, and I had spent three hours in the lab being prepped, an hour in Mr. Dunworthy's office, a half hour on the playing fields of Oxford, ditto in Infirmary, which added up to eleven, and that didn't count the two hours I'd spent looking for the bishop's bird stump and the hour I'd spent looking for the cathedral, and the five hours I'd spent at the Harvest Charity Bazaar and Scrap Metal Drive. Nineteen.

When had I gone through to the bazaar, in the morning or the afternoon? Afternoon, because I was just heading back to my rooms for dinner when Lady Schrapnell caught me and put me on jumble sale duty.

No, that was the day before. Or the day before that. How long had I been doing jumble sales? Years. I had been up for years.

"We're going to have to give this up," I said, thinking wearily of how far it was back to Oxford. Perhaps we could sleep in the church in Iffley. No, it was only open until four. And no doubt there was a "No sleeping in pews" sign tacked to the hymnal rack.

"Look!" Terence cried. He pointed to a willow-covered island in the middle of the river. "There he is!"

It was definitely Professor Peddick. He was bending over at the very edge of the river, his robe fluttering, peering through his pince-nez at the water.

"Professor Peddick!" Terence shouted to him, and he nearly toppled in.

The professor grabbed hold of an uncertain-looking willow branch and steadied himself. He adjusted his pince-nez and peered at us.

"It's us," Terence shouted, cupping his hands round his mouth. "St. Trewes and Henry. We've been looking for you."

"Ah, St. Trewes," Peddick shouted. "Come over. I've found some excellent shallows, perfect for chub."

"You must come over here and fetch us," Terence said.

"Hitches?" Professor Peddick said, and I thought, here we go again.

"*Fetch* us," Terence said. "You've got the boat."

"Ah," Professor Peddick said. "Stay there." He disappeared into a thicket of willows.

"Let's hope he remembered to tie up the boat," I said.

"Let's hope he remembers where he left it," Terence said, sitting down on the bank.

I sat down next to him, and Cyril lay down and immediately rolled over on his side and began to snore. I wished I could do the same.

Now we'd have to row the professor all the way back to Oxford, which would take at least three hours, *if* we could talk him out of stopping at every fish and meadow.

But perhaps this was all to the good. Verity had said to keep Terence away from Muchings End, and this was certainly doing that. It would be dark by the time we reached Oxford. We'd have to spend the night, and in the morning perhaps I could talk Terence into going upriver to Parson's Pleasure. Or going down to London or to a horse race. When was Derby Day?

Or, who knows, with a good night's sleep he might come to his senses and see Tossie for the twittering ignoramus she was. Infatuation was a lot like time-lag, an imbalance of chemicals, cured by a good night's sleep.

There was no sign of the professor. "He's found a new variety of chub and forgotten all about us," Terence said, but presently the boat appeared, nosing around the end of the island, Professor Peddick's sleeves billowing like black sails as he rowed.

The boat pulled up downstream from us, and we scrambled down the towpath to it, Cyril wobbling after us.

I turned to urge him. "Come along, Cyril," I said, and crashed into Terence, who had stopped short and was staring down at the boat.

"You cannot imagine the wonderful discoveries I've made," Professor Peddick said. "This island is the very image of the location of the battle of Dunreath Mow." He held up the pan. "I want to show you the double-gilled blue chub I've found."

Terence was still staring strickenly at the boat.

I couldn't see any scrapes or dents except for the ones that had been there when Jabez rented it to us, and there didn't seem to be any holes. The boards of the stern and the bow looked perfectly dry.

The boards of the stern. And the bow. "Terence . . ." I said.

"Professor Peddick," Terence said in a strangled voice. "What's happened to our things?"

"Things?" Professor Peddick said vaguely.

"The luggage. Ned's portmanteau and the baskets and—"

"Ah," the professor said. "Under the *Salix babylonica* on the far side of the island. Climb in. I shall ferry you across like Charon bearing souls over the River Styx."

I climbed in and helped Terence get Cyril in, propping his front legs on the gunwale while Terence hoisted his rear legs over and then clambered in himself.

"Wonderful gravel bottoms," Professor Peddick said, and began rowing across. "Perfect spot for dace. Lots of midges and flies. I caught a trout with a red ridge-gill slit. Have you a net, St. Trewes?"

"A net?"

"For trawling. I do not want to endanger the mouth by using a hook."

"There really isn't time for fishing," Terence said. "We must repack the boat as quickly as we can and then start back."

"Nonsense. I've found a perfect place to camp."

"Camp?" Terence said.

"No use in going home and then having to come back again. Chub bite best near sundown."

"But what about your sister and her companion?" He pulled out his pocket watch. "It's nearly five o'clock. If we leave now, you can be there to see them at dinner."

"No need," he said. "A pupil of mine has already met them."

"*I'm* that pupil, Professor," Terence said.

"Nonsense. This pupil was boating along the Thames while I was working on my—" He peered at Terence through his pince-nez. "By George, you are."

"I met the 10:55," Terence said, "but your sister and her companion weren't on it, so they must have come in on the 3:18."

"Didn't come," he said, peering into the water. "Good grass for perch."

"I know your sister didn't come," Terence persisted, "but if she arrived on the 3:18—"

"Not my sister," he said, pushing up the sleeve of his robe and sticking his hand in the water. "Her companion. Ran off and got married."

"Married?" I said. The woman on the platform had talked about someone getting married.

"In spite of my sister's best efforts. Met him at church. Classic example of individual action. History is character. She brought my niece instead."

"Your niece?" I said.

"Lovely girl." He brought up a slimy piece of trailing brown grass. "Wonderful at labelling specimens. Too bad you weren't there to meet them when they arrived so you could have met her."

"I was, but they weren't there," Terence said.

"You're certain?" Professor Peddick said, handing the grass to me. "Maudie's letter was quite clear about the time." He patted his coat pockets.

"Maudie?" I said, hoping I'd misheard.

"Named after her poor dear mother, Maud," he said, looking through his pockets. "Would have made a good naturalist if she were a boy. Must have lost the letter when Overforce tried to murder me. Certain it was the 10:55. Might have been tomorrow's train, though. What day is it? Ah, here we are, arrived at last in paradise, 'the Elysian plain at the ends of the earth, where fair-haired Rhadamanthys is.' "

The boat hit the shore with a jolt hard enough to wake Cyril, but it was nothing to the jolt I'd just had. Maud. I had made Terence miss meeting the "agèd relics." If it hadn't been for me, Professor Peddick's sister and niece would still have been sitting on the platform waiting for Terence when he skidded in. And if I hadn't told him no one of that description had come in on the train, he'd have caught up with them on their way to Balliol. But he had said "agèd relics." He had said they were "positively antediluvian."

"Can you get the rope, Ned?" Terence said, pulling the nose of the boat into the shore.

Meetings are notoriously pivotal in the complex chaotic course of history. Lord Nelson and Emma Hamilton. Henry VIII and Anne Boleyn. Crick and Watson. John Lennon and Paul McCartney. And Terence was supposed to have met Maud on that railway platform in Oxford.

"*Ned?*" Terence said. "Can you get the rope?"

I took a giant step onto the muddy bank with the rope and tied the boat up, thinking this was the last thing I should be doing.

"Hadn't we better leave for Oxford now to meet your niece? And sister," I added. They wouldn't be at the station, but at least they'd have met. "We can leave this luggage here and come back for it. Two ladies, travelling alone. They'll need someone to see to their luggage."

"Nonsense," Professor Peddick said. "Maudie's perfectly capable of ordering their luggage sent and hiring a fly to take them to the hotel. She's extremely sensible. Not silly like other girls. You'd like her, St. Trewes. Have you any mealworms?" he asked, and set off toward the willows.

"Can't you convince him?" I said to Terence.

He shook his head. "Not where fish are concerned. Or history. The best thing to do is to set up camp before it gets dark." He went over to where our various suitcases and boxes were piled under a large willow tree and began rummaging through them.

"But his niece—"

"You heard him. Sensible. Intelligent. His niece is probably one of those dreadful modern girls who have opinions and think women should go to Oxford." He pulled out a skillet and several tins. "A most unpleasant sort of girl. Not like Miss Mering. So pretty and innocent."

And silly, I thought. And he shouldn't have met her. He should have met Maud. "You'd like her," Professor Peddick had said, and I had no doubt Terence would have, with her dark eyes and sweet face. But I had looked suspicious, and Verity had acted without thinking, and now Terence and Tossie, who would otherwise never have met, were planning rendezvouses, and who knew what complications that would cause?

"We shall meet her in the morning, at any rate," Terence said, slicing meat pie. "When we take Professor Peddick back tomorrow."

He would meet her in the morning. Chaotic systems have redundancies and interference and feedforward loops built in, so the effect of some events is not multiplied enormously, but cancelled out. "Missing you one place, we meet another." Terence had missed meeting Maud today, but he would meet her tomorrow. And, in fact, if we took him back tonight we might be too late and Professor Peddick's sister would not be receiving visitors, and he'd miss meeting her again. But tomorrow morning, she'd be wearing a pretty dress and Terence would forget all about Muchings End and ask Maud to go punting up to the Port Meadow for a picnic.

If he was meant to meet her. And Professor Peddick's sister might well have thought the porter looked suspicious or felt a draft and gone off in a hired fly before Terence got there even if I hadn't been there. And Terence, in a hurry to hire the boat, would still have gone off to Folly Bridge without ever meeting her. T.J. had said the system had self-correction capabilities.

And Verity was right. Princess Arjumand had been returned, the incongruity, if there even was one, had been repaired, and I should be resting and recovering, which meant food and sleep, in that order.

Terence was spreading out a blanket and putting tin plates and cups on it.

"What can I do to help?" I said, my mouth starting to water. When was the last time I'd eaten? A cup of tea and a rock cake at the Women's Institute Victory Drive Sale of Work was all I could remember, and that was at least two days and fifty-two years ago.

He dug in the hamper and brought up a cabbage and a large lemon. "You can spread out the rugs. Two of us can sleep in the boat, the other on shore. And if you can find the silverware and the ginger beer, you can set them out."

I went over and got the rugs and began spreading them out. The island was apparently owned by the churchwarden in Iffley. Signs were posted on virtually every tree and on a number of stakes pounded into the bank. "No Thoroughfare," "Keep Off," "Private Land," "Trespassers Will Be Shot," "Private Waters," "No Boats," "No Fishing," "No Dumping," "No Camping," "No Picnicking," "No Landing."

I rummaged through Terence's boxes and found an assortment of peculiar-looking utensils. I chose the ones which most closely resembled forks, spoons, and knives, and set them out.

"I'm afraid we're rather roughing it," Terence said. "I'd intended to stop for provisions along the way, so we've had to make do. Tell Professor Peddick dinner is served, such as it is."

Cyril and I went and found Professor Peddick, who was leaning precariously over the water, and brought him back.

Terence's idea of roughing it consisted of pork pie, veal pie, cold roast beef, a ham, pickles, pickled eggs, pickled beets, cheese, bread and butter, ginger beer, and a bottle of port. It was possibly the best meal I had ever had in my life.

Terence fed the last bits of roast beef to Cyril and picked up a tin. "Drat!" he said, "I've gone off and left the tin-opener behind, and here I've brought a tin of—"

"Pineapple," I said, grinning.

"No," he said, looking at the label, "peaches." He bent over the hamper. "But there might be a tin of pineapple in here somewhere. Though I should imagine they'll both taste about the same without a tin-opener."

We could try opening it with the boathook, I thought, smiling to myself. That was what they'd done in *Three Men in a Boat*. And nearly killed George. It was his straw hat that had saved him.

"Perhaps we could open it with a pocket-knife," Terence said.

"No," I said. They had tried a pocket-knife before they tried the boathook. And a pair of scissors and the hitcher and a large rock. "We shall have to do without," I said sagely.

"I say, Ned," he said, "you haven't a tin-opener in among your luggage, have you?"

Knowing Finch, I probably did. I unbent my legs, which had gotten stiff, went down to the willows, and started through the luggage.

The satchel had three collarless shirts, a set of formal evening clothes that were far too small for me, and a too-large bowler hat in it. It was a good thing I was only going on the river.

I tried the hamper. This was more promising. It held several large spoons and an assortment of utensils, including one with a blade like a scimitar and another with two long handles and a revolving barrel pierced with holes. It was possible one of these was a tin-opener. Or some sort of weapon.

Cyril came over to help.

"You don't know what a tin-opener looks like, do you?" I said, holding up a flat grid affair at the end of a long handle.

Cyril looked in the satchel and then went over and sniffed at the covered basket.

"Is it in there?" I said, and unfastened the loop-and-peg arrangement that held the lid on, and opened the basket.

Princess Arjumand looked up at me with her gray eyes and yawned.

*"Cats, it has been well said, will be cats, and there seems nothing to be done about it."*

*P. G. Wodehouse*

# CHAPTER EIGHT

Pandora's Box—Underwear as a Topic of Conversation in the Victorian Era—My Mistake—Commands Suitable for Use With a Cat—King John's Mistake—Importance of a Good Night's Sleep—Opening a Tin—Cat-Calls—A Swan—Mrs. O'Leary's Cow—Hansel and Gretel—The Perfect End to a Perfect Day

What are you doing here?" I said.

But it was obvious what she was doing here. Mr. Dunworthy had sent her through with me, and I was supposed to return her to Muchings End before her disappearance caused any consequences.

But I had been three days late and forty miles off. And too time-lagged to realize what I was supposed to do. And in the meantime, Mrs. Mering had gone to Oxford and consulted a medium, and Tossie had met Terence and Count de Vecchio, and Terence had missed meeting Maud.

And the incongruity hadn't been repaired. It was right here, looking up at me.

"You're not supposed to be here," I said numbly.

The cat gazed up at me with its gray eyes. They had strange vertical pupils, like slits, and flecks of green in them. I had had no idea they had eyes that color. I had thought all cats had bright yellow eyes that glowed in the dark.

I had also thought dogs chased cats, but Cyril was simply sitting there, looking at me with an expression of utter betrayal.

"I didn't know she was here," I said defensively.

But how could I not have? What had I thought Finch would bring me in a basket—a covered basket!—at the last minute? A round of cheese? Why else would he have said he didn't think sending me was a good idea because I was time-lagged?

Well, he was certainly right. I hadn't even tumbled to it when Terence told me Tossie'd lost her cat. Or when Verity'd asked me where it was. Stupid, stupid, stupid.

I could have given it to Verity to take back to Muchings End. Or to Tossie. I could have made some excuse to go back to the boat and then pretended I'd found it walking along the riverbank. If I'd known I'd had it. If I'd so much as thought to look in the luggage. Stupid, stupid, stupid.

The cat was moving. She yawned and stretched delicately, extending one white paw. I leaned over the basket, trying to see her other feet. I couldn't see anything but black fur.

A wild thought occurred to me. What if this wasn't Princess Arjumand after all? Tossie had said it was black with a white face, but no doubt there had been hundreds or even thousands of white-faced black cats in 1888. They had had to drown kittens to keep the population down.

"Princess Arjumand?" I said tentatively.

There was no flicker of response in her gray eyes.

"Princess Arjumand," I said more firmly, and she closed her eyes.

It wasn't Princess Arjumand. It was the lock-keeper's cat, or the churchwarden's, and it had crawled in the basket while we were in Iffley Church.

The cat yawned again, revealing a pink tongue and a lot of sharp little teeth, and stood up.

Cyril moved back like an ARP warden faced with an incendiary.

The cat stepped out of the basket and sauntered away on four white feet, her white-tipped tail in the air. She had white on her hindquarters as well, with rather the effect of pantaloons. Tossie hadn't mentioned pantaloons, I thought hopefully, and then remembered this was the Victorian era. Well-bred people didn't discuss pantaloons, or any sort of underwear, did they? And how many white-pawed cats were there who were likely to have stowed away in my luggage and then fastened the lid?

She was nearly out of the clearing.

"Wait!" I said. "Princess Arjumand!" and then remembered the proper command. "Stay," I said firmly. "Stay."

She kept walking.

"Come back here," I said. "Stay. Stop. Whoa."

She turned and looked curiously at me with her large gray eyes.

"That's it," I said, and began to advance slowly. "Good cat."

She sat down on her haunches and began to lick her paw.

"*Very* good cat," I said, moving forward. "Stay . . . stay . . . that's it."

She rubbed her paw delicately over her ear.

I was less than a foot away from her.

"Stay . . . good . . . stay . . . ," I said and lunged for her.

She bounded lightly away and disappeared into the trees.

"I say, have you found it yet?" Terence called out from the direction of the riverbank.

I sat up, dusting off my elbows, and looked at Cyril. "Don't you say a word." I stood up.

Terence appeared, carrying the tin of peaches. "*There* you are," he said. "Any luck?"

"None at all," I said. I walked rapidly back to the luggage. "I mean, I haven't finished looking through everything."

I jammed the lid on the basket and opened the satchel, hoping fervently it didn't contain any surprises. It didn't. It contained a pair of lace-up boots that couldn't have been more than a size five, a large spotted handkerchief, three fish forks, a large filigreed silver ladle, and a pair of escargot tongs. "Would this work?" I said, holding them up.

Terence was rummaging through the hamper. "I doubt . . . here it is," he said, holding up the scimitar-looking object with the red handle. "Oh, you've brought Stilton. Excellent." He went off, clutching the tin-opener and the cheese, and I went back over to the edge of the clearing.

There was no sign of the cat. "Here, Princess Arjumand," I said, lifting up leaves to look under the bushes. "Here, girl."

Cyril nosed at a bush, and a bird flew up.

"Come, cat," I said. "Heel."

"Ned! Cyril!" Terence called, and I dropped the branch with a rustle. "The kettle's boiling!" He appeared, holding the opened tin of peaches. "What's keeping you?"

"I thought I'd just tidy up a bit," I said, sticking the escargot tongs in one of the boots, "get everything packed so we can make an early start."

"You can do it after your dessert," he said, taking me by the arm. "Come along now."

He led us back to the campfire, Cyril looking warily from side to side, where Professor Peddick was pouring out tea into tin cups.

"*Dum licet inter nos igitur laetemur amantes,*" he said, handing me a cup. "The perfect end to a perfect day."

Perfect. I'd failed to return the cat, kept Terence from meeting Maud, made it possible for him to get to Iffley to see Tossie, and who knew what else?

There was no use crying over spilt milk, even if that was an unfortunate metaphor, because it couldn't be put back in the bottle, no matter how hard one tried, and what exactly would be a good metaphor? Opening Pandora's box? Letting the cat out of the bag?

Whatever, there was no use crying over it, or thinking about what might have been. I had to get Princess Arjumand back to Muchings End as soon as possible, and before any more damage was done.

Verity had said to keep Terence away from Tossie, but she hadn't known about the cat. I had to get it back to the site of its disappearance immediately. And the quickest way to do that was to tell Terence I'd found it. He'd be overjoyed. He'd insist on starting to Muchings End immediately.

But I didn't want to create any more consequences, and Tossie might be so grateful to him for returning Princess Arjumand she'd fall in love with him instead of Mr. C. Or he might start wondering how the cat had got so far from home and insist on setting off after its kidnapper the way he had after the boat and end up going over a weir in the dark and drowning. Or drowning the cat. Or causing the Boer War.

I'd better keep the cat hidden until we got to Muchings End. If I could get it back in the basket. If I could find it.

"If we were to find Princess Arjumand," I said, I hoped casually, "how would one go about catching her?"

"I shouldn't think she'd need catching," Terence said. "I should think she'd leap gratefully into our arms as soon as she saw us. She's not used to fending for herself. From what Toss—Miss Mering told me, she's had rather a sheltered life."

"But suppose she didn't. Would she come if you called her by name?"

Terence and the professor both stared at me in disbelief. "It's a *cat*," Terence said.

"So how would one set about catching her if she were frightened and wouldn't come? Would one use a trap or—"

"I should think a bit of food would do it. She's bound to be hungry," Terence said, staring out at the river. "Do you suppose she's looking at the river as I am, ' 'mid the cool airs of Evening, as she trails her robes of gold through the dim halls of Night'?"

"Who?" I said, scanning the riverbank. "Princess Arjumand?"

"No," Terence said irritably. "Miss Mering. Do you suppose she's looking at this same sunset? And does she know, as I do, that we are fated to be together, like Lancelot and Guinevere?"

Another bad end, but nothing compared to the one we were all going to come to if I didn't find that cat and get it back to Muchings End.

I stood up and began picking up plates. "We'd best clear things away and then get to bed so we can make an early start tomorrow."

"Ned's right," Terence said to Professor Peddick, pulling himself reluctantly away from the river. "We'll need to start early for Oxford."

"Is Oxford necessary, do you think?" I said. "Professor Peddick could go with us down to Muchings End, and we could take him back later."

Terence was looking at me disbelievingly.

"It would save two hours at the least, and there must be any number of historical sights along the river Professor Peddick could study," I said, improvising. "Ruins and tombs and . . . Runnymede." I turned to Professor Peddick. "I suppose it was blind forces that led to the signing of the Magna Carta."

"Blind forces?" Professor Peddick said. "It was *character* that led to the Magna Carta. King John's ruthlessness, the Pope's slowness in acting, Archbishop Langton's insistence on *habeas corpus* and the rule of law. Forces! I'd like to see Overforce explain the Magna Carta in terms of blind forces!" He drained his teacup and set it down decisively. "We must go to Runnymede!"

"But what about your sister and your niece?" Terence said.

"My scout can provide anything they need, and Maudie's a resourceful girl. That was King John's mistake, you know, going to Oxford. He should have stayed in London. The entire course of history might have been different. We won't make that mistake," he said, and picked up his fishing pole. "We shall go to Runnymede. Only thing to do."

"But your sister and your niece won't know where you've gone," Terence said, frowning questioningly at me.

"He can send a telegram from Abingdon," I said.

"Yes, a telegram," Professor Peddick said and hobbled off toward the river.

Terence looked worriedly after him. "You don't think he'll slow us down?"

"Nonsense," I said. "Runnymede's down near Windsor. I can take him down in the boat while you're at Muchings End with Miss Mering. We could be there by midday. You'd have time to wash up so you can look your best. We could stop at the Barley Mow," I said, pulling the name of an inn out of *Three Men in a Boat*, "and you could have your trousers pressed and your shoes shined."

And I can sneak out while you're shaving and return the cat to Muchings End, I thought. If I can find the cat.

Terence still looked unconvinced. "It *would* save time, I suppose," he said.

"Then it's settled," I said, scooping up the cloth and stuffing it into the hamper. "You wash the dishes and I'll make up the beds."

He nodded. "There's only room for two of us in the boat. I'll sleep by the fire."

"No," I said. "I will," and went to get the rugs.

I spread all but two in the bottom of the boat and took the others into the clearing.

"Shouldn't you put them near the fire?" Terence said, piling dishes up.

"No, my physician said I shouldn't sleep near smoke," I said.

While Terence rinsed the dishes, standing ankle-deep in the river with his trousers rolled up, I stole a lantern and a rope, wishing Professor Peddick had brought along a fishing net.

I should have asked Terence what sort of food cats ate. Some of the Stilton was left. Did cats like cheese? No, that was mice. Mice liked cheese. And cats liked mice. I doubted if we had any mice.

Milk. They were supposed to like milk. The woman running the coconut shy at the Harvest Fête had been complaining about a cat getting into the milk left on her doorstep. "Clawed the cap straight off," she'd said. "Impudent creature."

We hadn't any milk, but there was a bit of cream left in the bottle. I pocketed it, a saucer, a tin of peas and one of potted meat, a heel of bread, and the tin-opener, and hid them in the clearing, and then went back to the campfire.

Terence was digging in the boxes. "Where has that lantern got to?" he said. "I know there were two in here." He looked up at the sky. "It looks like rain. Perhaps you'd better sleep in the boat. It'll be a bit crowded, but we can manage."

"No!" I said. "My physician said river vapors were bad for my lungs," a pathetic reason since I had just had my physician recommending a trip on the river for my health. "She said I should sleep inland."

"Who?" Terence said, and I remembered too late that women hadn't been physicians in Victorian England. Or solicitors or prime ministers.

"My physician. James Dunworthy. He said I should sleep inland and away from others."

Terence straightened up, holding the lantern by its handle. "I *know* Dawson packed two. I watched him. I've no idea where it got to."

He lit the lantern, removing the glass cover, striking a match, and adjusting the wick. I watched him carefully.

Professor Peddick came up, carrying the kettle with his two fish in it. "I must notify Professor Edelswein of my discovery. The *Ugubio fluviatilis albinus* was thought to be extinct in the Thames," he said, peering at it in the near-darkness. "A beautiful specimen." He set it down on the hamper and got out his pipe again.

"Shouldn't we be going to bed?" I said. "Early start and all that?"

"Quite right," he said, opening his tobacco pouch. "A good night's sleep can be critical. The Greeks at Salamis had had a good night's sleep the night before." He filled his pipe and tamped the tobacco down with his thumb. Terence took out *his* pipe. "The Persians, on the other hand, had spent the night at sea, positioning their ships to prevent the Greeks from escaping." He lit his pipe and sucked on it, trying to light it.

"Exactly, and the Persians were routed," I said. "We don't want that to happen to us. So." I stood up. "To bed."

"The Saxons, too, at the Battle of Hastings," Professor Peddick said, handing his tobacco pouch to Terence. They both sat down. "William the Conqueror's men were rested and ready for battle, while the Saxons had been on the march for eleven days. If Harold had waited and allowed his men to rest, he would have won the Battle of Hastings, and the whole course of history might have been changed."

And if I didn't get the cat back, ditto.

"Well, we don't want to lose any battles on the morrow," I said, trying again, "so we'd best get to bed."

"Individual action," Professor Peddick said, puffing on his pipe. "That's what lost the Battle of Hastings. The Saxons had the advantage, you know. They were drawn up on a ridge. Being on a defended height is the greatest military advantage an army can have. Look at Wellington's army at Waterloo. And the battle of Fredericksburg in the American Civil War. The Union army lost twelve thousand men at Fredericksburg, marching across an open plain to a defended height. And England was a richer country, fighting on their own home ground. If economic forces are what drives history, the Saxons should have won. But it wasn't forces that won the Battle of Hastings. It was character. William the Conqueror changed the course of the battle at at least two critical points. The first came when William was unhorsed during a charge."

Cyril lay down and began to snore.

"If William had not gotten immediately to his feet and pushed back his helmet so that his men could see that he was alive, the battle would have been lost. How does Overforce fit that into his theory of natural forces? He can't! Because history is character, as is proved by the second crisis point of the battle."

It was a full hour before they knocked the tobacco out of their pipes and started down to the boat. Halfway there, Terence turned and came back. "Perhaps you'd better take the lantern," he said, holding it out to me, "since you're sleeping on shore."

"I'll be perfectly all right," I said. "Good night."

"Good night," he said, starting down to the boat again. " 'Night is the time for rest.' " He waved to me. " 'How sweet when labors close, To gather round an aching breast the curtain of repose.' "

Yes, well, it would be, but I had a cat to find first. I went back to the clearing to wait for everyone to go to sleep, trying not to think about how every moment the cat was loose the number of consequences multiplied exponentially.

It might have been eaten by a wolf. Did Victorian England have wolves? Or found by an old woman in a cottage and taken in. Or picked up by a passing boat.

The locks are closed, I told myself, and it's only a cat. How much of an effect on history can an animal have?

A big one. Look at Alexander the Great's horse Bucephalus, and "the little gentleman in the black fur coat" who'd killed King William the Third when his horse stepped in the mole's front door. And Richard the Third standing on the field at Bosworth and shouting, "My kingdom for a horse!" Look at Mrs. O'Leary's cow. And Dick Whittington's cat.

I waited half an hour and then cautiously lit the lantern. I took the tins out from their hiding place and pulled the tin-opener out of my pocket. And tried to open them.

It was definitely a tin-opener. Terence had said it was. He'd opened the peaches with it. I poked at the lid with the point of the scimitar and then with the side of it. I poked at it with the other, rounded edge.

There was a space between the two. Perhaps one fit on the outside of the tin as a sort of lever for the other. Or perhaps it went in from the side. Or the bottom. Or perhaps I was holding it the wrong way round, and the scimitar thing was the handle.

That resulted in a hole in the palm of my hand, not exactly the idea. I rummaged through the satchel for a handkerchief to wrap round it.

All right, look at the thing logically. The point of the scimitar had to be the part that went through the tin. And it had to go through the lid. Perhaps there was a specific place in the lid where it fit. I examined the lid for weaknesses. It hadn't any.

"Why did the Victorians have to make everything so bloody complicated?" I said and saw a flicker of light at the near edge of the clearing.

"Princess Arjumand?" I said softly, holding up the lantern, and I had been right about one thing. Cats' eyes did glow in the dark. Two were shining yellowly at me from the bushes.

"Here, cat," I said, holding out the heel of bread and making "tsk"ing noises. "I've got some food for you. Come here."

The glowing eyes blinked and then disappeared. I stuck the bread in my pocket and started carefully for the edge of the clearing. "Here, cat. I'll take you home. You want to go home, don't you?"

Silence. Well, not exactly silence. Frogs croaked, leaves rustled, and the Thames made a peculiar gurgling sound as it flowed past. But no cat sounds. And what sounds did cats make? Since all the cats I'd ever seen had been asleep, I wasn't sure. Meowing sounds. Cats meowed.

"Meow," I said, lifting branches to look under the bushes. "Come here, cat. You wouldn't want to destroy the space-time continuum, would you? Meow. Meow."

There the eyes were again, past that thicket. I set off through it, dropping bread crumbs as I went. "Meow?" I said, swinging the lantern slowly from side to side. "Princess Arjumand?" and nearly tripped over Cyril.

He wagged his nether half happily.

"Go back and sleep with your master," I hissed. "You'll just get in the way."

He immediately lowered his flat nose to the ground and began snuffling in circles.

"No!" I whispered. "You're not a bloodhound. You haven't even got a nose. Go back to the boat." I pointed toward the river.

He stopped snuffling and looked up at me with bloodshot eyes that *could* have been a bloodhound's and an expression that clearly said, "Please."

"No," I said firmly. "Cats don't like dogs."

He began snuffling again, what passed for his nose earnestly to the ground.

"All right, all right, you can come with me," I said, since it was obvious he was going to anyway. "But stay with me."

I went back into the clearing, poured the cream into a bowl, and got the rope and some matches. Cyril watched interestedly.

I held the lantern aloft. " 'The game's afoot, Watson,' " I said, and we set off into the wilderness.

It was very dark, and along with the frogs, river, and leaves were assorted slitherings and rattlings and hoots. The wind picked up, and I sheltered the lantern with my hand, thinking what a wonderful invention the pocket torch was. It gave off a powerful light, and one could point the beam in any direction. The lantern's light I could only direct by holding it up or down. It did give off a warm, wavering circle of light, but its only function seemed to be to make the area outside said circle as black as pitch.

"Princess Arjumand?" I called at intervals, and "Here, cat," and "Yoo hoo." I dropped bread crumbs as I went, and periodically I set the dish of cream down in front of a likely looking bush and waited.

Nothing. No glowing eyes. No meows. The night got darker and damper, as if it might rain.

"Do you see any sign of her, Cyril?" I asked.

We trudged on. The place had looked quite civilized this afternoon, but now it seemed to be all thornbushes and tangled underbrush and sinister clawlike branches. The cat could be anywhere.

There. Down by the river. A flash of white.

"Come on, Cyril," I whispered and started toward the river.

There it was again, in the midst of some rushes, unmoving. Perhaps she was asleep.

"Princess Arjumand?" I said and reached through the reeds to pick her up. "There you are, you naughty thing."

The white suddenly rose up, revealing a long, curving neck.

"Squaw-w-w!" it said, and exploded into a huge white flapping. I dropped the dish with a splash.

"It's a swan," I said unnecessarily. A swan. One of the ancient beauties of the Thames, floating serenely along the banks with their snowy feathers and their long graceful necks. "I've always wanted to see one," I said to Cyril.

He wasn't there.

"Squaww-w-w-k!" the swan said and unfolded its wings to an impressive width, obviously irritated at being awakened.

"Sorry," I said, backing away. "I thought you were a cat."

"Hiss-s-s-s!" it said, and started for me at a run.

Nothing in all those "O swan" poems had ever mentioned that they hissed. Or resented being mistaken for felines. Or bit.

I finally managed to escape by crashing through a thicket of some thorny variety, climbing halfway up a tree, and kicking at its beak with my foot until it waddled back to the river, muttering threats and imprecations.

I waited fifteen minutes, in case it was a trick, and then climbed down and began examining my wounds. Most of them were to the rear and difficult to see. I twisted round trying to see if there was blood, and saw Cyril, coming out from behind a tree, looking shamefaced.

"A rout," I said. "Just like the Persians. Harris had trouble with swans. In *Three Men in a Boat*," I said, wishing I'd remembered that chapter before now. "They tried to drag him and Montmorency out of the boat."

I picked up the lantern, which, amazingly, had fallen in an upright position when I dropped it. "If King Harold had had swans on his side, England would still be Saxon."

We set off again, staying away from the river and keeping a wary eye out for patches of white.

Polly Vaughn's boyfriend had killed her because he mistook her for a swan in the old poem. She'd been wearing a white apron, and he thought she was a swan and shot her with an arrow. I could sympathize completely. In future, I'd shoot first and ask questions later, too.

The night got darker and damper, and the bushes thornier. There were no patches of white or shining eyes and scarcely any sounds. When I dropped the last of the bread and called, "Here, cat!" my voice echoed in the black, empty stillness.

I had to face it, the cat was long gone, to starve to death in the wilderness or be murdered by an irate swan or be found in the bulrushes by Pharaoh's daughter and change the course of history. Cyril and I weren't going to find her.

As if in confirmation, the lantern began to smoke. "It's no use, Cyril," I said. "She's gone. Let's go back to camp."

That was easier said than done. I had been paying more attention to finding the cat than to the way we had come, and all thickets look alike.

I held the lantern close to the ground, looking for the trail of bread crumbs I'd left, and then remembered Hansel and Gretel were another couple who had come to a bad end.

"Show me the way, Cyril," I said hopefully, and he looked around alertly and then sat down.

The thing to do, of course, was to follow the river, but there was the possibility of swans to be considered, and surely the wolves hadn't eaten all the bread crumbs. I set off in a likely looking direction.

Half an hour later it began to drizzle, and the leaf-strewn ground turned wet and slick. We slogged on like Saxons who'd been marching for eleven days. And were about to lose England.

I had lost the cat. I had wasted hours of precious time, unaware I had her, and then let her get away. I had gone off with a total stranger, made Terence miss a possibly important meeting and . . .

A thought occurred to me. I had gone off with Terence, and we had shown up at exactly the right moment to save Professor Peddick from a watery grave. Would that have happened if Terence had met Maud, or had he been meant *not* to meet her so that he would be in the right place at the right time to save his tutor? Or was Professor Peddick supposed to drown, and I had the rescuing of him to add to my list of transgressions?

But if it was a transgression, I couldn't make myself feel too guilty about it. I was glad he hadn't drowned, even though he had complicated my life significantly, and I began to understand how Verity felt about rescuing the cat.

The cat, which was lost somewhere out in the rain. Like Cyril and I were. I had no idea where we were, I knew I had *never* seen a row of trees like that, or a tangle of thickets like that. I stopped and then started back the way we had come.

And there was the boat. And the clearing. And my bedroll.

Cyril saw it first and made a dash for it, wriggling happily, and then stopped dead. I hoped the swan hadn't taken up residence in it.

It hadn't. There, curled up in the middle of the rugs, sound asleep, was Princess Arjumand.

# C H A P T E R   N I N E

My First Night in the Victorian Era—Crowding—Snoring—
Rain—Importance of Weather to the Course of History—
Pneumonia—The Cat Is Missing—An Early Start—Professor
Peddick's Double-Gilled Blue Chub Is Missing—Abingdon—Rowing
Advice—Professor Peddick Is Missing—Souvenirs—The Telegram's
Sent—A Tardy Departure

My first night in the Victorian era was not exactly what the nurse in Infirmary had had in mind. Or what I'd had in mind, for that matter. It was a good deal less comfortable than I'd imagined, and a great deal more crowded.

I had intended to put Princess Arjumand back in the basket, with a strong lock and some rocks on the lid for good measure. But when I'd picked her carefully up, watching out for claws and sudden moves, she'd snuggled cozily into my arms. I carried her over to the basket and knelt down to deposit her. She looked up appealingly at me and began to hum.

I had read of cats purring, but I had always imagined it as more of a low growl, or perhaps a sort of static. This had nothing unfriendly or electromagnetic about it, and I found myself apologizing. "I have to put you in the basket," I said, petting her awkwardly. "I can't run the risk of your running away again. The universe is at stake."

The hum increased, and she laid a paw beseechingly on my hand. I carried her back over to the bed. "She'll have to be in the basket all day tomorrow," I said to Cyril, who had settled down in the middle of the rugs. "And I don't think she'll run away now that she knows me."

Cyril looked unimpressed.

"She was frightened before," I said. "She's quite tame now."

Cyril snorted.

I sat down on the rugs and took off my wet shoes, still holding the cat against me, and then tried to get into bed. Easier said than done. Cyril had staked out his claim and refused to move. "Move over!" I said, freeing one hand from holding the cat to push. "Dogs are supposed to sleep at the foot of the bed."

Cyril had never heard of this rule. He jammed his body up against my back and began to snore. I tugged at the rugs, trying to get enough to cover me, and turned on my side, the cat cradled in my arms.

Princess Arjumand paid no attention to the regulations of animals on the bed either. She promptly wriggled free and walked round the bed, treading on Cyril, who responded with a faint "oof," and kneading her claws in my leg.

Cyril shoved and shoved again, until he had the entire bed and all the covers, and Princess Arjumand draped herself across my neck with her full weight on my Adam's apple. Cyril shoved some more.

An hour into this little drama it began to rain in earnest, and everyone moved in under the covers and began jockeying for position again. Eventually both of them wore themselves out and fell asleep, and I lay there and worried about what Verity was going to say when she found out I had the cat and about the rain.

What if it rained all day tomorrow and we couldn't go to Muchings End? The weather had affected how many turning points of history, starting with the heavenly wind, the *kamikaze* that had destroyed the Kublai Khan's fleet when it tried to invade Japan in the thirteenth century?

Gales had scattered the Spanish Armada, a blizzard had determined the outcome of the battle of Towton, fog had diverted the *Lusitania* into the path of a German U-boat, and a low-pressure front over the forest of Ardennes had nearly lost the Battle of the Bulge for the Allies in World War II.

Even good weather could affect history. The Luftwaffe's raid on Coventry had been successful because of cold, clear weather and a full "bomber's moon."

Weather and its sidekick, disease. What if Professor Peddick caught cold from sleeping in the rain and had to be taken back to Oxford tomorrow? The United States President William Henry Harrison had caught cold standing in the rain at his inauguration and died of pneumonia a month later. Peter the Great had caught cold while sighting a ship and died within a week. And not just colds. Henry the Fifth had died of dysentery, and as a result the English lost everything they'd gained at Agincourt. The undefeatable Alexander the Great was defeated by malaria, and the face of the whole continent of Asia changed. To say nothing of the Black Death.

Weather, disease, changes in climate, shifts in the earth's crust—Professor Overforce's blind forces—all were factors in history whether Professor Peddick would admit it or not.

The problem, of course, as in so many wars, was that Professor Overforce and Professor Peddick were both right. They were just a century too early for chaos theory, which would have incorporated both their ideas. History was indeed controlled by blind forces, as well as character and courage and treachery and love. And accident and random chance. And stray bullets and telegrams and tips. And cats.

But it was also stable. I remembered distinctly T.J. saying that, and Mr. Dunworthy saying that if the incongruity had done any damage it would have shown up by now. Which meant that the cat had been returned to its original space-time location before it had caused any long-lasting consequences.

Or, the other possibility was that the cat's disappearance hadn't affected anything, but I knew that wasn't true. It had made me make Terence miss meeting Maud. And I wasn't taking any chances. I intended to return the cat to Muchings End as quickly as possible, which meant getting us on the river in the morning as quickly as possible.

Which meant it couldn't rain. It had rained at Waterloo, turning the roads to an impossible muck and bogging down the artillery. It had rained at Crécy, soaking the archers' bowstrings. It had rained at Agincourt.

Somewhere in the midst of worrying about the rain at the Battle of Midway, I must have fallen asleep, because I woke with a jerk to the gray light of dawn. It had stopped raining and the cat was gone.

I leaped up in my stocking feet and flung the rugs aside, trying to see if she was hidden in them somewhere, disturbing Cyril, who whuffled and rolled over.

"Cyril!" I said. "The cat's gone! Did you see where she went?"

Cyril shot me a look that clearly said, I told you so, and subsided among the covers.

"Help me look for her!" I said, yanking the rug out from under him.

I fumbled with my shoes. "Princess Arjumand!" I whispered frantically, "Where are you? Princess Arjumand!" and she strolled into the clearing, treading daintily on the wet grass.

"Where have you been?" I said. "I should have shut you in the basket!"

She sauntered past me to the disordered bed, lay down next to Cyril, and went to sleep.

I wasn't going to take a second chance. I got the carpetbag and emptied out the shirts and the escargot tongs. Then I got the fileting knife out of the hamper and made several short slashes in its sides with the point, making sure they went all the way through the lining. I arranged the too-small tweed jacket in the bottom for a nest and stuck the saucer next to it.

Princess Arjumand didn't even wake up when I put her in the carpetbag and closed the clasp. Perhaps Verity was right, and she was suffering from time-lag. I jammed the clothes in the portmanteau, and rolled up all but one of the rugs, which Cyril was on.

"Rise and shine, Cyril," I said. "Time to get up. We need to make an early start."

Cyril opened an eye and stared at me disbelievingly.

"Breakfast," I said, and, carrying the carpetbag, went down to the remains of the campfire. I gathered wood, laid the fire, and lit it like an old hand, and then looked through Terence's luggage till I found a map of the river, and sat down by the fire to plot our trip.

The map was an accordion-style which folded out to portray the full winding length of the Thames, which I certainly hoped we didn't have to cover. I had learned to read maps when I was an undergraduate, but this one suffered from a wealth of details: it not only listed villages, locks, islands, and all the distances between, but weirs, shallows, canals, towpaths, historic sights, and recommended fishing spots. I decided I'd better keep it out of Professor Peddick's hands.

It also provided an assortment of editorial comments, such as "one of the most charming views along the river" and "a rather difficult current just here," with the result that it was difficult to find the river in amongst all the wordage. Terence had said Muchings End was just below Streatley, but I couldn't find either.

I finally found Runnymede, which was listed as "the historical site of the signing of the Magna Carta, *not*, as certain river people would have you believe, the stone on Magna Carta Island. Good bream deeps. Poor for gudgeon, dace, and jack."

I worked my way up from Runnymede to Streatley, marked its place with my finger, and looked for Iffley. There it was: "Quaint mill, which people come from miles about to see, 12th cent. church, middling chub." We were halfway between Iffley and Abingdon, and twenty-three miles from Streatley.

Allowing half an hour for breakfast, we'd be on the river by six. We could easily be there in nine hours, even allowing for Professor Peddick to stop along the way and send a telegram to his sister. With luck, we'd have the cat back to the place where it had disappeared by three, and the incongruity corrected by five.

"We can easily be there by teatime," I told Cyril, folding the map up. I put it back in Terence's bag and got eggs, a slab of streaky bacon, and the skillet out of the hamper.

The birds began to sing, and the sun came up, streaking the water and the sky with ribbons of rosy-pink. The river flowed serene and golden within its leafy banks, denying incongruities—the placid mirror of a safe, untroubled world, of a grand and infinite design.

Cyril was looking up at me with an expression that clearly said, "Exactly how time-lagged *are* you?"

"I didn't get any sleep last night," I said. "Thanks to you. Come along."

I put the kettle on, sliced bacon, broke eggs into the skillet, and went down to the boat to wake Terence and his tutor up, banging on a pot lid with the Stilton spoon. "Time to get up," I said. "Breakfast's on."

"Good Lord," Terence said groggily, fumbling for his pocket watch. "What time is it?"

"Half-past five," I said. "You wanted to make an early start to be at Muchings End by teatime. Miss Mering, remember?"

"Oh," he said, and shot up out of the blankets. "You're right. Wake up, Professor Peddick."

" 'Morn, wak'd by the circling hours, with rosy hand unbarr'd the gates of light,' " Professor Peddick said from the stern, blinking sleepily.

I left them and ran back up to check on the eggs and the cat. She was sleeping soundly. And soundlessly, which was even better. I set the carpetbag over with the luggage and began dishing up the eggs.

"At this rate, we'll be on the river by six," I told Cyril, feeding him a strip of streaky bacon. "We'll be through the lock by half-past, we'll stop in Abingdon so the professor can send his telegram, we'll be to Clifton Hampden by eight, Day's Lock by nine, and to Reading by ten."

By ten we were still in Abingdon.

It had taken us two hours to load the luggage, which seemed to have expanded, and then, at the last minute, Professor Peddick discovered his double-gilled blue chub was missing.

"Perhaps an animal got it," Terence said, and I had a good idea which animal.

"I must catch another specimen," Professor Peddick said, unloading the fishing pole and tackle.

"There isn't time," Terence said, "and you've still got your albino gudgeon."

Yes, I thought, and it had better be put under lock and key, or *an animal* might get it, and we'd never get to Muchings End.

"We need to start, sir, if we intend to make Runnymede by tomorrow," Terence said.

" '*Non semper temeritas es felix,*' " the professor said, selecting a fly from his box. " 'Rashness is not always fortunate.' Remember, if Harold had not rushed foolishly into the fray, he would have won the battle of Hastings." He meticulously tied the fly to his line. "Early morning is not the best time for chub," he said, making practice casts. "They do not usually rise before late afternoon."

Terence groaned and looked beseechingly at me.

"If we leave now, we can be to Pangbourne by late afternoon," I said. I unfolded the map. "It says the Thames at Pangbourne has long been a favorite spot of the angler. It is a perfect spot for barbel." I read aloud, "Superior perch, roach, and gudgeon. Plenty of dace and chub. The weir stream is famous for large trout."

"At Pangbourne, you say?" Professor Peddick said.

"Yes," I lied. "It says, 'There are more fish of every kind at this spot on the Thames than at any other.' "

That did it. He got in the boat.

"*Thank* you," Terence mouthed and pushed off before he could change his mind.

I looked at my pocket watch. Twenty past VIII. Later than I'd hoped, but we could still be to Muchings End by five if things went well.

They didn't. Abingdon Lock was closed, and it took us a quarter of an hour to wake up the lock-keeper, who took it out on us by letting the water out of the lock at a trickle. In the meantime, the rearward stack of luggage had overbalanced, and we had to stop twice and tie it into place.

The second time Professor Peddick announced, "Do you see those water lilies? And that swift-moving current near the bank? Perfect for barbel," and clambered out of the boat before we could stop him.

"There isn't time," Terence said helplessly.

"Pangbourne," I reminded him.

"Pshaw," he said, and I would have been impressed at yet another Victorian exclamation if I hadn't had the carpetbag and the fate of the universe to worry about. "There can't be a more perfect spot than this."

Terence took out his pocket watch and looked despairingly at it. What would get him moving? The Battle of Hastings? Salamis? Runnymede?

"This is how I've always pictured Runnymede," I said, waving my hand at the meadow beside us, "the mist rising from the fields as King John and his men rode in. Where do you think the actual signing took place? Runnymede or Magna Carta Island?"

"Runnymede," he said. "The King is proved to have spent the night in Staines and ridden to the field in the morning."

"Ah," I said. "I believe Professor Overforce makes an extremely convincing case for Magna Carta Island."

"For Magna Carta Island?" he said disbelievingly.

"Extremely convincing," Terence said. "It goes along with his theory of history being the result of natural forces."

"Balderdash!" Professor Peddick said and flung the fishing pole down. Terence snatched it up and stuck it in the boat.

"Convincing case?" Professor Peddick steamed. "There is undisputable evidence that the signing took place in Runnymede." He climbed in the boat. I grabbed up the rope and cast off. "What sort of convincing case? There were far too many barons and lords to fit on the island, and King John was far too suspicious to let himself be in a situation with no avenue of escape. Natural forces!"

And so on till we reached Abingdon.

It was a quarter past nine by the time we got through the lock and up to the village.

Professor Peddick went off to send his telegram, and Terence went into the village to buy bread and sliced meat so we wouldn't have to stop and cook lunch.

"And a bottle of milk," I called after him. As soon as they were out of sight, I opened the carpetbag and checked on Princess Arjumand.

Still sleeping. I left the carpetbag open, set it between my knees, and took up the oars. Terence had done all the rowing this far, but he couldn't keep it up all day, not if we were going to make good time. And rowing was rowing. It couldn't be all that different from supraskims. Except that the oars were a good deal heavier. And less balanced. When I pulled back on them, nothing happened.

I sat up straight on the seat, braced my feet, spit on my hands, and yanked back on the oars.

This time something happened. The right oar came out of the water, the oar handles banged together violently, smashing my knuckles, the left oar came unshipped, and the boat swung around and headed straight for the stone wall of the bridge.

I scrambled to get the oar back in its oarlock and both of them in the water before we hit the bridge, banging my knuckles together again in the process, and bringing us up against the bank.

Cyril stood up and waddled over to the bank side of the boat, as if preparing to abandon ship.

All right, third time's a charm. I managed to push the boat away from the bank with an oar, get it out in the current, and tried again, watching to make sure the handles didn't hit me on the knuckles. They didn't. The left one swung up and hit me on the nose.

But on the fourth try, I got it, though rather clumsily, and after a few minutes I had mastered the fundamentals. I took the boat out across the current and then under the bridge and back again, rowing smartly and with a good deal of dash.

"No, no!" Terence said behind me. "Not like that. Throw your weight onto the sculls at the beginning of the stroke."

I looked back at him, standing on the bank, and both oars came out of the water and smacked me on the hand.

"Don't look back! Watch where you're going!" Terence shouted, which struck me as a bit unfair. "One hand over the other. Keep the trim. No, no, no!" he shouted, gesticulating with the bread in one hand and the milk bottle in the other. "Get forward. Open your knees. Keep her head out. Remember your seat."

There is nothing more helpful than shouted instructions, particularly incomprehensible ones. I did my best to follow the ones I could understand, which consisted of, "Open your knees," and was rewarded by Terence shouting, "No, no, no! Bring your knees together! Feather! You'll catch a crab! Head up!"

But eventually I got the hang of it and, keeping the trim, head up, weight on the sculls, knees open *and* closed, and keeping my seat fully in mind, I rowed back across to him.

"Slow and steady," Terence said as I brought the boat neatly up to the dock. "That's it. Very good. All you need's practice."

"Which I should have plenty of opportunity to get," I said, taking the milk bottle from him and sticking it in my pocket. "Let's go. Where's Professor Peddick?"

Terence looked round as if expecting to see him. "He hasn't come back from the telegraph office?"

"No," I said, climbing out and tying up the boat. "We'd best go look for him."

"One of us had best stay here with the boat," Terence said, looking severely at Cyril. "In case he comes back."

"Excellent idea," I said. While he was gone, I could check on the cat again and perhaps let it out.

"You should be the one to go," Terence said. "You're better at history." He pulled out his pocket watch and looked at it.

I took advantage of his distraction to pick up the carpetbag and hide it behind my back.

"Ten o'clock," he said, snapping the watch shut savagely. "I should have insisted on taking him home the moment we pulled him in."

"There wasn't time," I said. "Besides, you said yourself there's no stopping him if he's determined."

He nodded gloomily. "He's an unstoppable force. Like William the Conqueror. History is the individual." He sighed. "By the time we get there, she'll already be engaged."

"Engaged? To whom?" I said, hoping she'd mentioned other suitors and that one of them was the required Mr. C.

"I don't *know* to whom," he said. "A girl like Tossie—Miss Mering probably gets a dozen proposals a day. Where *is* he? We'll never get to Muchings End at this rate."

"Of course we will," I said. "It's Fate, remember? Romeo and Juliet, Héloïse and Abelard?"

"Fate," Terence said. "But what a cruel Fate, that keeps me from her even for a day!" He turned to gaze dreamily downriver, and I escaped with the carpetbag.

Cyril trotted after me. "You stay here, Cyril," I said firmly, and the three of us set off into the village.

I had no idea where the telegraph office might be or what one looked like, but there were only two shops. A greengrocer's and a shop with fishing gear and flower vases in the window. I tried the fishing shop first. "Where can I send a telegram?" I asked a smiling old woman in a mobcap. She looked just like the sheep in *Through the Looking Glass.*

"Out for a trip on the river?" she said. "I've lovely plates with views of Iffley Mill painted on them. They're inscribed, 'Happy Memories of the Thames.' Are you heading upriver or down?"

Neither, I thought. "Down," I said. "Where is the telegraph office?"

"Down," she said delightedly. "Then you've already seen it. Lovely, isn't it?" She handed me a fringed yellow satin pillow with the mill and "Souvenir of Iffley" stencilled on it.

I handed it back. "Very nice. Where can I send a telegram?"

"From the postal office, but I always think it's so much nicer to send a letter, don't you?" She whipped out writing paper. Each sheet had "Greetings from Abingdon," inscribed on the top. "Ha'pence a sheet and a penny for the envelope."

"No, thank you. Where did you say the postal office was?"

"Just down the street. Opposite the abbey gate. Have you seen it? We've got a lovely replica of it. Or perhaps you'd like one of our china dogs. Handpainted. Or we've some lovely penwipers."

I ended up buying a china bulldog that bore no resemblance to Cyril—or to a poodle for that matter—to get away, and sought out the gate and the postal office.

Professor Peddick wasn't there, and the mobcapped old woman behind the counter didn't know if he had been. "My husband's gone home for his dinner. He'll be back in an hour. Out for a trip on the river, are you?"

she said, and tried to sell me a vase with a picture of Iffley Mill painted on it.

He hadn't been in the greengrocer's either. I bought a souvenir tooth glass inscribed "Holiday Greetings from the River Thames." "Have you any salmon?" I asked.

"We do," yet another mobcapped old woman said and set a tin on the counter.

"I meant fresh," I said.

"You can catch it yourself," she said. "Abingdon's got the best fishing on the entire river," and tried to sell me a pair of rubber fishing waders.

I came out of the shop and said to Cyril, who had been waiting patiently outside each door, "Where to now?"

Abingdon had been built around a mediaeval abbey. The ruins, including the granary and a croft, were still there, and they seemed like the likeliest places for Professor Peddick to be, but he wasn't there. Or in the cloisters.

Neither was anyone else. I knelt down next to the cloister wall, set the bottle of milk on a stone, and opened the carpetbag.

Cyril sat down, looking disapproving.

"Princess Arjumand?" I said, lifting her out. "Want some breakfast?"

I set her down, and she walked a few feet across the grass and then took off like a shot and disappeared round the corner of a wall.

I told you so, Cyril said.

"Well, don't just stand there. Go after her," I said.

Cyril continued sitting.

He had a point. Our chasing after her in the woods hadn't been a roaring success. "Well, what do you suggest then?"

He lay down, his muzzle against the milk bottle, and it wasn't a bad idea. I got the saucer out of the carpetbag and poured some milk into it. "Here, cat," I called, setting it out in front of the wall. "Breakfast!"

As I say, it wasn't a bad idea. It did not, however, work. Neither did searching the ruins. Or the town square. Or the streets of half-timbered houses.

"You knew what cats were like," I said to Cyril. "Why didn't you warn me?"

But it was my fault. I had let her out, and she was probably on her way to London this morning to meet Gladstone and cause the fall of Mafeking.

We had come to the outskirts of the village. The road petered out and ended in a hay field crisscrossed with narrow streams.

"Perhaps she's gone back to the boat," I said hopefully to Cyril, but he wasn't listening. He was looking at a dirt path leading off toward a bridge over a narrow stream.

And there by the bridge was Professor Peddick, knee-deep in the stream with his trousers rolled up, holding a large net. Behind him on the bank was a tin kettle with water in it and, no doubt, fish. And Princess Arjumand.

"Stay here," I said to Cyril. "I mean it," and crept up on the crouched cat, wishing I'd had the foresight to buy a net.

Princess Arjumand crept toward the kettle, her white paws silent in the grass, and the professor, as intent as the cat, stooped and lowered the net slowly toward the water. Princess Arjumand peered into the kettle and stuck her paw experimentally into the water.

I pounced, clapping the open carpetbag over her and scooping her up like the fish she was after. So did Professor Peddick, bringing the net down and up again with a wriggling fish in it.

"Professor Peddick!" I said. "We've been looking everywhere for you!"

"Stickleback," he said, extracting the fish from the net and tossing it in the kettle. "Excellent pitches for trout along here."

"Terence sent me to fetch you," I said, extending a hand to help him up the bank. "He's anxious to get on to Pangbourne."

" 'Qui non vult fieri desidiosus amet,' " he said. "Ovid. 'Let the man who does not wish to be idle, fall in love,' " but he climbed out and sat down on the bank and put his shoes and socks back on. "Pity he never met my niece, Maudie. He'd have liked her."

I picked up the tin kettle and the net. It had "Souvenir of the River Thames," printed on the handle. Cyril was still sitting where I'd told him to stay. "Good boy!" I said, and he galloped over and crashed into my knees. Water slopped out of the kettle.

Professor Peddick stood up. "Onward. The day's half over," he said, and set off briskly for the village.

"You did send your telegram?" I asked him as we passed the postal office.

He put his hand inside his coat and pulled out two yellow slips. "The abbey has some small historical interest," he said, sticking them back inside his coat. "It was pillaged by Cromwell's men during the Protectorate." He stopped at the gate. "There's a Fifteenth-Century gateway here you should see."

"I understand Professor Overforce considers the Protectorate a result of natural forces," I said, and steered him, ranting, down to the dock where an old woman in a mobcap was trying to sell Terence a mug with a picture of Boulter's Lock on the side.

"Such a nice reminder of your trip downriver," she said. "Each time you take your tea, you'll think of this day."

"That's what I'm afraid of," Terence said, and to me, "Where have you been?"

"Fishing," I said. I climbed in the boat, set the carpetbag down, and reached out my hand to help Professor Peddick, who was bent over his kettle of fish, peering at them through his pince-nez.

"He *did* send his telegram, didn't he?" Terence said to me.

I nodded. "I saw the yellow slips."

Cyril had lain down on the quay and was deep in slumber. "Come along, Cyril," I said. "Professor? *Tempus fugit!*"

"Do you *know* how late it is?" Terence said, waving his pocket watch in front of my nose. "Drat! It's nearly eleven."

I sat down at the oars and put the carpetbag between my knees. "Don't worry," I said. "It's all clear sailing from here."

*"There is nothing—absolutely nothing—half so much worth doing as simply messing about in boats. . . ."*

*The Wind in the Willows*
*Kenneth Grahame*

C H A P T E R   T E N

Clear Sailing—A Non-Picturesque Stretch of River—Mystery of
Victorians' Sentimentality Regarding Nature Solved—Importance
of Jumble Sales to the Course of History—We See Three Men in a Boat,
To Say Nothing of the Dog—Cyril vs. Montmorency—The Episode
of the Maze—A Traffic Jam—A Teakettle—Importance of Trifles to
the Course of History—Another Swan—Shipwreck!—Similarities
to the *Titanic*—A Survivor—A Swoon

Amazingly, we did have clear sailing, or, rather, rowing. The river was
smooth and empty, with a fresh breeze blowing across it. The sun
glittered brightly on the water. I remembered my seat, kept my knees
both open and closed, feathered, kept the trim, and pulled strongly, and
by noon we were through Clifton Lock and could see the chalk cliff of
Clifton Hampden with the church perched atop it.

The map called this stretch "the least picturesque on the Thames" and
suggested we travel by rail to Goring to avoid it. Looking at the lush green
meadows, crisscrossed with flowering hedges, the riverbanks lined with
tall poplars, it was hard to imagine what the picturesque stretches would
look like.

There were flowers everywhere—buttercups and Queen Anne's lace and
lavender lady's smock in the meadows, lilies and blue flags growing along
the banks, roses and ivy-leaved snapdragons in the lockhouse gardens.

There were even flowers in the river. The waterlilies had pink cup-shaped blossoms, and the rushes were topped with nosegays of purple and white. Iridescent blue-green dragonflies darted between them, and monstrous butterflies flitted past the boat and came to rest momentarily on the overbalanced luggage, threatening to topple it over.

Off in the distance, a spire could be glimpsed rising above a clump of elm trees. The only thing lacking was a rainbow. No wonder the Victorians had waxed sentimental about nature.

Terence took the oars, and we rowed round a curve in the river, past a thatched cottage decked with morning glories and toward an arched bridge built of golden-tinted stone.

"Dreadful what's been done to the river," Terence said, gesturing at the bridge. "Railway bridges and embankment cuts and gasworks. They've completely spoilt the scenery."

We passed under the bridge and round the curve. There were scarcely any boats on the river. We passed two men in a fishing punt, moored under a beech tree, and they waved at us and held up an enormous string of fish. I was grateful Professor Peddick was asleep. And Princess Arjumand.

I'd checked on her when Terence and I changed places, and she was still out cold. Curled up inside the carpetbag with her paws tucked under her furry chin, she didn't look capable of altering history, let alone destroying the continuum. But then neither had David's slingshot or Fleming's moldy petri dish or the barrel full of jumble sale odds and ends Abraham Lincoln had bought for a dollar.

But in a chaotic system, anything from a cat to a cart to a cold could be significant, and *every* point was a crisis point. The barrel had held a complete edition of Blackstone's *Commentaries,* which Lincoln could never have afforded to buy. They had made it possible for him to become a lawyer.

But a chaotic system has feedforward loops, too, and interference patterns and counterbalances, and the vast majority of actions cancel each other out. Most rainstorms don't defeat armadas, most tips don't cause revolutions, and most of the things one buys at a jumble sale don't do anything but gather dust.

So the chances of the cat changing the course of history, even if she'd been missing four days, were infinitesimal, especially if we continued to make such excellent time.

"I say," Terence said, unpacking the bread and cheese he'd bought for lunch in Abingdon, "if we're able to keep this up, we should be able to make Day's Lock by one," he said. "There's nobody on the river."

Except for a single boat coming up the river toward us with three men in it, all in blazers and mustaches, and with a small dog perched on the bow, looking alertly ahead. As they drew nearer, their voices came to us clearly across the river.

"How much farther before it's your turn, Jay?" the rower said to the one lying in the bow.

"You've only been rowing ten minutes, Harris," the one in the bow said.

"Well, then, how far to the next lock?"

The third man, who was stouter than the other two, said, "When do we stop for tea?" and picked up a banjo.

The dog caught sight of our boat and began barking. "Stop that, Montmorency," the bow-lier said. "Barking's rude."

"Terence!" I said, half-rising to my feet. "That boat!"

He glanced over his shoulder. "It won't hit us. Just hold the lines steady."

The banjo player strummed a few out-of-tune bars and began to sing.

"Oh, don't sing, George," rower and bow-lier said in unison.

"And don't you get any ideas about singing either, Harris," Jay added.

"Why not?" he said indignantly.

"Because you only think you can sing," George said.

"Yes," Jay said. "Remember 'The Ruler of the Queen's Navy'?"

"Diddle-diddle-diddle-diddle-diddle-diddle-dee," George sang.

"It *is* them!" I said. "Terence, do you know who that is? It's *Three Men in a Boat, To Say Nothing of the Dog*."

"Dog?" Terence said contemptuously. "You call that a dog?" He looked fondly at Cyril, who was snoring in the bottom of the boat. "Cyril could swallow him in one bite."

"You don't understand," I said. "It's the *Three Men in a Boat*. The tin of pineapple and George's banjo and the maze."

"The maze?" Terence said blankly.

"Yes, you know, Harris went in the Hampton Court Maze with this map and all these people followed him and the map didn't work and they got hopelessly lost and they had to call out for the keeper to come and get them out."

I leaned out for a better look. There they were, Jerome K. Jerome and the two friends he had immortalized (to say nothing of the dog) on that historic trip up the Thames. They had no idea they were going to be famous a hundred and fifty years from now, that their adventures with the cheese and the steam launch and the swans would be read by countless generations.

"Watch your nose!" Terence said, and I said, "Exactly. I love that bit, where Jerome is going through the lock at Hampton Court and someone calls out, 'Look at your nose!' and he thinks they mean his nose and they mean the nose of the boat has gotten caught in the lock!"

"Ned!" Terence said, and the three men in the boat waved and shouted, and Jerome K. Jerome stood up and began gesturing with his outstretched arm.

I waved back. "Have a wonderful trip!" I called. "Watch out for swans!" and pitched over backward.

My feet went up in the air, the oars hit the water with a splash, and the luggage in the bow toppled over. Still on my back, I made a grab for the carpetbag and tried to sit up.

So did Professor Peddick. "What happened?" he said, blinking sleepily.

"*Ned* didn't watch where he was going," Terence said, grabbing for the Gladstone bag, and I saw that we had hit the bank head-on. Just like Jerome K. Jerome had done in Chapter Six.

I looked over at the other boat. Montmorency was barking, and George and Harris appeared to be doubled over with laughter.

"Are you all right?" Jerome K. Jerome called to me.

I nodded back vigorously, and they waved and rowed on, still laughing, toward the Battle of the Swans and Oxford and history.

"I said, hold the lines steady," Terence said disgustedly.

"I know. Sorry," I said, stepping over Cyril, who had slept through the entire thing and who consequently missed his chance to meet a Truly Famous Dog. On the other hand, remembering Montmorency's proclivity for fights and his sarcastic manner, it was probably just as well.

"I saw someone I knew," I said, helping him pick up the luggage. "A writer," and then realized that if they were just now on their way upriver, *Three Men in a Boat* must not have been written yet. I hoped when it came out, Terence wouldn't read the copyright page.

"Where's my net?" Professor Peddick said. "These waters are perfect for *Tinca vulgaris.*"

It took us till noon to get the luggage stowed and tied down again and to disentangle Professor Peddick from his *Tinca vulgaris,* but after that we made excellent time. We were past Little Wittenbaum before two. If we didn't have any trouble at Day's Lock, we could still be to Streatley by dinnertime.

We came through Day's Lock in record time. And ran bang into a traffic jam.

The reason the river had been so empty before was because the entire armada had gathered here. Punts, canoes, outriggers, double-sculling skiffs, covered rowing boats, eights, barges, rafts, and houseboats jammed the river, all of them heading upstream and none of them in a hurry.

Girls with parasols chattered to girls with parasols in other boats and called to their companions to pull alongside. People on launches strung with banners reading, "Lower Middlesex Musical Society Annual Outing" and "Mothers' Beanfeast" leaned over the railings to shout to people in pleasure boats below.

Clearly none of them had to be anywhere at a certain time. Middle-aged men on houseboats sat on the decks reading the *Times* while their middle-aged wives, clothespins in their mouths, hung up the washing.

A girl in a sailor dress and a beribboned straw hat poled a flat skiff slowly among them and stood there laughing when the pole stuck in the mud. An artist in a yellow smock stood motionless on a raft in the middle of the melee, painting a landscape on an easel, though how he could see said landscape over the flower-decked hats and parasols and fluttering Union Jacks, I had no idea.

A rower from one of the colleges, in a striped cap and jersey, cracked oars with a pleasure party's paddles and stopped to apologize, and a sailboat nearly crashed into them from behind. I yanked on the lines and nearly crashed into all three.

"I'd best steer," Terence said, scrambling up to change places when our boat hit an empty slot between a four-oared outrigger and a dinghy.

"Excellent idea," I said, but rowing was worse. Facing backward, I couldn't see anything and had the feeling I was going to run into the Upper Slaughter Ironmongers' River Excursion at any moment.

"This is worse than the Henley Regatta," Terence said, pulling on the lines. He maneuvered the boat out of the main current and off to the side, but that was even worse. It brought us into the midst of the punts and houseboats that were being towed, their towlines stretched across our path like so many tripwires.

The people towing weren't in any hurry, either. Girls pulled a few feet and then paused to look laughingly back at the boat. Couples stopped to look longingly into each other's eyes, letting the towline go limp in the water, and then remembered what they were supposed to be doing and yanked it up sharply. Jerome K. Jerome had written about a couple who'd lost their boat and gone on, talking and towing the frayed rope, but it seemed to me a greater danger was decapitation, and I kept glancing anxiously behind me like Catherine Howard.

There was a sudden flurry of activity upriver. A whistle shrieked and someone cried, "Look out!"

"What is it?" I said.

"A bloody teakettle," Terence said, and a steam launch puffed through the crowd, scattering the boats and sending up a tremendous wash.

The boat rocked, and one of the oars unshipped. I made a grab for it and the carpetbag, and Terence raised his fist and cursed at the steam launch's vanishing wake.

"They remind one of Hannibal's elephants at the Battle of the Ticinus River," Professor Peddick, who had just awakened, said, and launched into a description of Hannibal's Italian campaign.

We were in the Alps and in traffic all the way to Wallingford. We sat in line for Benson's Lock for over an hour, with Terence taking out his pocket watch and announcing the time every three minutes.

"Three o'clock," he said. Or "A quarter past three." Or "Nearly half past. We'll never make it in time for tea."

I shared his sentiment. The last time I'd opened the carpetbag, Princess Arjumand had stirred ominously, and as we pulled into the lock I could hear faint meowings, which luckily were drowned out by the crowd noise and Professor Peddick's lecturing.

"Traffic was responsible for Napoleon's losing the battle of Waterloo," he said. "The artillery wagons became stuck in the mud, blocking the roads, and the infantry could not make its way past them. How often history turns on such trivial things, a blocked road, a delayed corps of infantry, orders gone astray."

At Wallingford the traffic abruptly disappeared, the punts stopping to camp and start supper, the Musical Society disembarking and heading for the railway station and home, and the river was suddenly empty.

But we were still six miles and another lock from Muchings End.

"It'll be nine o'clock before we get there," Terence said despairingly.

"We can camp near Moulsford," Professor Peddick said. "There are excellent perch above the weir there."

"I think we should stay at an inn," I said. "You'll want a chance to clean up. You'll want to look your best for Miss Mering. You can shave and have your flannels pressed and your shoes shined, and we can go to Muchings End first thing in the morning."

And I can sneak out with the carpetbag after everyone's gone to bed, and return the cat without being seen, so that by the time Terence gets there tomorrow morning the incongruity will already be correcting itself. And he'll find Tossie holding hands with Mr. Cabbagesoup or Coalscuttle or whatever his name is.

"There are two inns in Streatley," Terence said, consulting the map. "The Bull and The Swan. The Swan. Trotters says it brews an excellent ale."

"It hasn't any swans, has it?" I said, glancing warily at Cyril, who had awakened and was looking nervous.

"I shouldn't think so," Terence said. "The George and Dragon doesn't have a dragon."

We rowed on. The sky turned the same blue as my hatband and then a pale lavender, and several stars came out. The frogs and crickets started up, and more faint mewings from the carpetbag.

I pulled up sharply on the oars, making a good deal of splashing, and asked Professor Peddick exactly where his and Professor Overforce's theories differed, which got us to Cleve Lock, where I jumped out, fed the cat some milk, and then set the carpetbag in the bow on top of the luggage as far from Terence and Professor Peddick as possible.

"The action of the individual, that's the force driving history," Professor Peddick was saying. "Not Overforce's blind, impersonal forces. 'The history of the world is but the biography of great men,' Carlyle writes, and so it is. Copernicus's genius, Cincinnatus's ambition, St. Francis of Assisi's faith: It is character that shapes history."

It was fully dark, and the houses were lit by the time we reached Streatley.

"At last," I said as we sighted the quay, "a soft bed, a hot meal, a good night's sleep," but Terence was rowing straight past it.

"Where are you going?" I said.

"To Muchings End," he said, pulling hard on the oars.

"But you said yourself it's too late to call," I said, glancing yearningly back at the quay.

"I know," he said. "I only want a glimpse of where she lives. I won't be able to sleep, knowing she's so close, until I've seen her."

"But it's dangerous to be on the river at night," I said. "There are shoals and eddies and things."

"It's only a short way," Terence said, rowing determinedly. "She said it was just past the third island."

"But we won't be able to see it at night," I said. "We'll get lost and go over a weir and be drowned."

"There it is," Terence said, pointing at the shore. "She told me I'd know it by the gazebo."

The white gazebo gleamed faintly in the starlight, and beyond it, across a sloping lawn, was the house. It was enormous and extremely Victorian, with gables and towers and all sorts of neo-Gothic gingerbread. It looked like a slightly smaller version of Victoria Station.

Its windows were all dark. Good, I thought, they've gone to Hampton Court to raise Catherine Howard's ghost or off to Coventry. I'll be able to return the cat easily.

"There's no one there," I said. "We'd best start back to Streatley. The Swan will be all booked up."

"No, not yet," Terence said, gazing at the house. "Let me gaze a moment longer on the hallowed ground whereon she walks, the sacred bower wherein she rests."

"It does look as though the family has retired for the evening," Professor Peddick said.

"Perhaps they've only got the curtains drawn," Terence said. "Shh."

That seemed unlikely, given the pleasantness of the evening, but we obediently listened. There was no sound at all from the shore, only the gentle lap of water, the murmur of a breeze through the rushes, the soft chirrup of frogs croaking. A meowing sound from the bow of the boat.

"There," Terence said. "Did you hear that?"

"What?" said Professor Peddick.

"Voices," Terence said, leaning out over the gunwale.

"Crickets," I said, edging toward the bow.

The cat meowed again. "There!" Terence said. "Did you hear that? It's someone calling us."

Cyril sniffed.

"It's a bird," I said. I pointed at a tree by the gazebo. "In that willow. A nightingale."

"It didn't sound like a nightingale," Terence said. "Nightingales sing of summer 'in full-throated ease and pour their souls abroad in ecstasy.' This didn't sound like that. Listen."

There was a snuffling sound in the front of the boat. I whirled round. Cyril was standing on his hind legs, his front paws on the stack of luggage, sniffing at the carpetbag and nudging it with his flat muzzle toward the edge.

"Cyril! Don't!" I shouted, and four things happened at once. I dived forward to grab the carpetbag, Cyril started guiltily and backed against the wicker basket, Professor Peddick said, "Take care you do not step on the *Ugubio fluviatilis*," and leaned sideways to pick the kettle up, and Terence turned round, saw the carpetbag toppling, and dropped the oars.

I tried, in mid-lunge, to avoid the oar and the professor's hand, and fell flat, Terence intercepted the basket, the professor clutched his kettle of fish to his breast, and I caught the carpetbag by a corner just as it toppled over. The boat rocked dangerously. Water slopped over the bows. I got a better grip on the carpetbag, set it on the stern seat, and pulled myself to a sitting position.

There was a splash. I grabbed for the carpetbag again, but it was still there, and I peered at the bow, wondering if the oar had gone in.

"Cyril!" Terence shouted. "Man overboard!" He began stripping off his jacket. "Professor Peddick, take the oars. Ned, get the life preserver."

I leaned over the side of the boat, trying to see where he'd gone in.

"Hurry!" Terence said, pulling off his shoes. "Cyril can't swim."

"He can't swim?" I said, bewildered. "I thought all dogs could swim."

"Indeed. The term 'dog paddle' is derived from the instinctive knowledge of swimming *Canis familiaris* possesses," Professor Peddick said.

"He *knows* how to swim," Terence said, stripping off his socks, "but he can't. He's a *bull*dog."

He was apparently right. Cyril was dog-paddling manfully toward the boat, but his mouth and nose were both underwater, and he looked desperate. "I'm coming, Cyril," Terence said and dived in, sending up a wave that nearly sunk him altogether. Terence started to swim toward him. Cyril continued to paddle and sink. Only the top of his wrinkled brow was still above the water.

"Bring the boat to port, no, starboard. To the left," I shouted and began rummaging for the life preserver, which we had apparently packed on the bottom. "As bad as the *Titanic*," I said, and then remembered it hadn't sunk yet, but no one was listening.

Terence had Cyril by the collar and was holding his head up above the water. "Bring the boat closer," he shouted, spluttering, and Professor Peddick responded by nearly running him down. "Stop! No!" Terence shouted, waving his arm, and Cyril went under again.

"To port!" I shouted. "The other way!" and leaned over and grabbed Terence by the scruff of *his* neck. "Not me!" Terence gasped. "Cyril!"

Between us we hoisted a very waterlogged Cyril into the boat where he coughed up several gallons of the Thames. "Put a blanket round him," Terence said, clinging to the bows.

"I will," I said, extending my hand. "Now you."

"I'm all right," he said, shivering. "Get the blanket first. He catches chills easily."

I got the blanket, wrapping it round the massive shoulders that had proven Cyril's downfall, and then we set about the tricky business of getting Terence back in the boat.

"Keep low," Terence ordered, his teeth chattering, "we don't want anyone else to go in."

Terence was no better at following directions than Professor Peddick had been. He persisted in trying to get a leg up over the bow, a motion that caused the bow to slant at an angle almost as bad as that of the *Titanic*.

"You'll capsize us," I said, wedging the carpetbag under the seat. "Hold still and let us haul you in."

"I've done this dozens of times," Terence said, and swung his leg up.

The gunwale dipped all the way to water level. Cyril, bunched in his blanket, staggered, trying to keep his feet, and the pile of luggage in the bow tilted precariously.

"I've never tipped a boat over yet," Terence said confidently.

"Well, at least wait till I've shifted things," I said, pushing the portmanteau back into place. "Professor Peddick, move all the way to that side," and to Cyril, who had decided to come over, trailing his blanket, to see how we were doing, "Sit. Stay."

"It's all a matter of getting the proper purchase," Terence said, shifting his grip on the gunwale.

"Wait!" I said. "Careful—"

Terence got his leg into the boat, raised himself on his hands, and pulled his torso up onto the gunwales.

"God himself could not sink this ship," I murmured, holding the luggage in place.

"All in the balancing." He hoisted himself into the boat. "There, you see," he said triumphantly. "Nothing to it," and the boat went over.

I have no idea how we got to shore. I remember the portmanteau sliding down the deck at me, like the grand piano on the *Titanic,* and then a lot of swallowing of water and clutching at the life preserver, which turned out to be Cyril, sinking like a stone, followed by more swallowing, and the dead man's carry, and we were all sitting on the shore dripping and gasping for breath.

Cyril was the first to recover. He tottered to his feet and shook himself all over us, and Terence sat up and looked out at the empty water.

" 'And fast through the midnight dark and drear,' " he quoted, " 'Like a sheeted ghost, the vessel swept/Tow'rds the reef of Norman's Woe.' "

"*Naufragium sibi quisque facit,*" Professor Peddick said.

Terence gazed out at the dark water. "She's gone," he said, exactly like Lady Astor had, and I stood up, suddenly remembering, and waded into the water, but it was no use. There was no sign of the boat.

An oar lay half on shore, and, out in the middle of the river, the professor's kettle bobbed past, the only survivors of the shipwreck. There was no sign of the carpetbag anywhere.

" 'Down came the storm, and smote amain/The vessel in its strength,' " Terence quoted. " 'He cut a rope from a broken spar/And bound her to the mast.' "

Princess Arjumand hadn't had a chance, wedged under the seat like that. If I'd let her out when she meowed, if I'd told Terence I'd found her, if I'd come through where I was supposed to and hadn't been so time-lagged—

" 'At day-break, on the bleak sea-beach/A fisherman stood aghast,' " Terence recited. " 'To see the form of a maiden fair/Lashed close to a drifting mast,' " and I turned to tell him to shut up and saw, behind us, white in the starlight, the gazebo where I was to have returned the cat.

Well, I had returned her, all right, *and* finished the murder the butler had started. And this time Verity hadn't been there to rescue her.

" 'The salt sea was frozen on her breast,' " Terence intoned, " 'the salt tears in her eyes. . . .' "

I gazed at the gazebo. Princess Arjumand, unbeknownst in her wicker basket, had nearly been run over by a train, been rolled into the Thames and been knocked in by Cyril and Professor Peddick, and had been rescued each time, only to drown here. Perhaps T.J. was right, and she had been meant to drown, and no matter how much Verity or I or anyone meddled, it was fated to end this way. History correcting itself.

Or perhaps she had simply run out of lives. I could count five of the nine she had used up in the last four days.

I hoped that was it, and not my complete incompetence. But I didn't think so. And I didn't think Verity would think so either. She had risked life and limb and Mr. Dunworthy's wrath to rescue it. "I won't let you drown it," she'd said. I doubted very much she would accept the course of history as an excuse.

The last thing I wanted to do was face her, but there was nothing else for it. Cyril, in spite of shaking himself all over us, was drenched, and so was Professor Peddick, and Terence looked half-frozen.

" 'Such was the wreck of the Hesperus,' " he said, his teeth chattering so he could scarcely recite, " 'in the midnight and the snow.' "

We had to get dried off and out of these clothes, and there was no other house in sight besides Muchings End. We had to go wake up the household and ask for shelter, even though it meant facing Tossie and having her ask if we'd found her "precious darling Juju." Even though it meant telling Verity.

"Come along," I said, taking Terence's arm. "Let's go up to the house."

He didn't budge. " 'Christ, save us all from a death like this,' " he said, " 'on the reef of Norman's Woe.' Jabez is going to charge us fifty pounds."

"We'll worry about that later," I said. "Come along. We'll try the French doors first. There's a line of light under them."

"I can't meet the family of the girl I love like this," Terence said, shuddering. "I haven't any coat."

"Here," I said, taking off my blazer and wringing it out. "You can have mine. They won't care that we're not dressed for dinner. Our boat sank."

Professor Peddick came up, squelching as he walked. "I managed to save some of the luggage," he said, and handed me the carpetbag. "None of my specimens, though, I'm afraid. Ah, my albino *Ugubio fluviatilis.*"

"I can't go up to the house without any shoes," Terence said. "I can't be seen half-naked by the girl I love."

"Here," I said, struggling to untie my wet shoelaces with one hand. "Take mine. Professor Peddick, give him your socks," and while they wrestled with the problem of getting wet socks off and on, I sprinted over behind the gazebo and opened the carpetbag.

Princess Arjumand, only slightly damp, glared up at me from its depths for a long minute and then swarmed up my leg and into my arms.

Cats were supposed to hate getting wet, but she settled into my sopping wet sleeves contentedly and closed her eyes.

"I'm not the one who saved your life," I said. "It was Professor Peddick," but she didn't seem to care. She nestled deeper against my chest and, amazingly, began to purr.

"Oh, good, Princess Arjumand is here," Terence said, straightening the blazer. It had apparently shrunk somewhat, too. "I was right. She was here all along."

"I do not think it is proper for an Oxford don not to wear socks," Professor Peddick said.

"Balderdash," I said. "Professor Einstein never did."

"Einstein?" he said. "I don't believe I know of him."

"You will," I said, and set off up the sloping lawn.

Terence had apparently been right about their having drawn the drapes. As we made our way across the lawn, the drapes were pulled back, a faint, flickering light appeared, and we could hear voices.

"This is terribly exciting," a man's voice said. "What do we do first?"

"Join hands," a voice that sounded like Verity's said, "and concentrate."

"Oh, Mama, *do* ask about Juju," and that was definitely Tossie's. "Ask them where she is."

"Shh."

There was a silence, during which we crossed the remainder of the lawn.

"Is there a spirit here?" a stentorian voice called out, and I nearly dropped Princess Arjumand. It sounded exactly like Lady Schrapnell, but it couldn't be. It must be Tossie's mother, Mrs. Mering.

"Oh, Spirit from the Other Side," she said, and I had to fight the impulse to run, "speak to us here in the earthly plane."

We maneuvered our way through an herbaceous border and onto the flagged pathway in front of the French doors.

"Tell us of our fate," Mrs. Mering boomed, and Princess Arjumand climbed up my chest and dug her claws into my shoulder.

"Enter, O Spirit," she intoned, "and bring us news of our missing loved ones."

Terence knocked on the doors.

There was another silence, and then Mrs. Mering called, in a somewhat fainter voice, "Enter!"

"Wait," I said, but Terence had already pulled the doors open. The curtains billowed inward, and we stood blinking at the candlelit tableau before us.

Around a black-draped round table sat four people, their eyes closed, holding hands: Verity, wearing white, Tossie, wearing ruffles, a pale young man wearing a clerical collar and a rapt expression, and Mrs. Mering, who, thank goodness, did not look like Lady Schrapnell. She was much rounder, with an ample bosom and ampler chins.

"Enter, O Spirit from the Other Side," she said, and Terence parted the curtains and stepped inside.

"I beg your pardon," Terence said, and everyone opened their eyes and stared at us.

We must have made rather an interesting tableau ourselves, what with Terence's bleeding stripes and my stockinged feet and our general drowned rat appearance, to say nothing of the dog, who was still coughing up river. Or the cat.

"We have come—" Terence began, and Mrs. Mering stood up and put her hand to the ample bosom.

"They have come!" she cried, and fainted dead away.

# C H A P T E R   E L E V E N

Why the Victorians Were So Repressed—Dearum Dearum Juju
Weturned to Her Mistwess—Fish—A Misunderstanding—
Importance of Knocking—Introductions—Irish Names—
An Amazing Coincidence—More Fish—A Reluctant Departure—
Another Misunderstanding—I Go to Bed—A Visitor—A Crisis

t was actually more of a swoon than a faint. She slumped sedately to
the flowered carpet, managing to avoid hitting any of the furniture—no
small feat since the room contained a large round rosewood table, a small
triangular table with a tintype album on it, a mahogany table with a bouquet
of wax flowers under a glass dome on it, a horsehair sofa, a damask loveseat,
a Windsor chair, a Morris chair, a Chesterfield chair, several ottomans, a
writing desk, a bookcase, a knick-knack cabinet, a whatnot, a firescreen, a
harp, an aspidistra, and an elephant's foot.

She also fell very slowly, and during the time it took her to collapse onto
the carpet, I registered a number of impressions:

One, that Mrs. Mering wasn't the only one who looked like she'd seen a
ghost. The pale young man, who must be a curate, was as white as his clerical
collar, and Baine, over by the door, was clutching the doorjamb for support.
His expression wasn't one of guilty horror, though. If I hadn't known better
I'd have thought it was one of relief. Or joy. Which was distinctly odd.

Two, Verity's expression was definitely one of joy, and in my still time-
lagged state I actually thought for a moment that it might be directed at

me. Then it hit me that she must not have been able to report back yet. Tossie must have kept the household up again last night looking for Princess Arjumand, and so Verity didn't know I'd been in charge of returning the cat and muffed it, and I'd have to be the one to tell her.

Which was unfortunate because, Three, even with a night's sleep (more or less) and a moratorium on drops, she was still the most beautiful creature I'd ever seen.

And Four, that the reason Victorian society was so restricted and repressed was that it was impossible to move without knocking something over.

"Ma*ma!*" Tossie cried, and Baine, Terence, Professor Peddick, and I all started forward to break her fall and managed to crash into everything Mrs. Mering had avoided.

Terence caught Mrs. Mering, Baine turned up the gas so we could see what we'd run into, I righted the Dresden shepherdess and the stereopticon I'd knocked over, and the clergyman sat down and began mopping his forehead with a large white handkerchief. Terence and Baine helped Mrs. Mering onto a maroon velvet sofa, knocking over a bust of Pallas in the process, and Verity began fanning her.

"Baine!" she said, "tell Colleen to bring the smelling salts."

"Yes, miss," Baine said, still looking overcome by emotion, and hurried out.

"O, Ma*ma!*" Tossie said, starting toward her mother. "Are you all—" and caught sight of the cat, which had climbed up my chest in all the excitement.

"Princess Arjumand!" she screamed and swooped at me. "Darling, darling Princess Arjumand! You've come back to me!"

Darling Princess Arjumand had to be removed from my shirtfront a claw at a time. I handed her to Tossie, who clutched the cat to her ecstatically, emitting a series of delighted screams.

"O, Mr. St. Trewes," she cooed, turning to Terence, "you've brought my dearum dearum Juju back to me!" She nuzzled dearum Juju. "Was oo awl wost in the scawy dawk, sweetums? Was oo fwightened? But Mr. St. Trewes was wooking for oo, wasn't he? Can oo say sank oo to the nice mannums, darwing Juju?"

Cyril, standing next to me, snorted loudly, and even "darwing Juju" looked disgusted. Well, good, I thought, this should bring Terence to his senses, we can go back upriver to Oxford, Tossie can marry Mr. C, and the continuum will be restored.

I looked at Terence. He was beaming besottedly at Tossie. "No need to thank me, truly," he said. "You bade me find your precious pet. 'Tis what you will. Your wish is my command, fair lady."

On the couch, Mrs. Mering moaned. "Aunt Malvinia," Verity said, rubbing her hands between hers. "Aunt Malvinia?" She turned to Tossie. "Cousin, fetch Baine and tell him we need a fire. Your mother's hands are like ice."

Tossie went over to a long tasseled panel of embroidered damask on the wall and tugged on the tassel.

I didn't hear anything, but there must have been a bell somewhere, because Baine appeared promptly. During his absence, he had apparently gained command of himself. His face and voice were impassive as he said, "Yes, miss?"

"Light the fire," Tossie said without looking up from the cat.

She'd said it almost rudely, but Baine smiled and said indulgently, "Yes, miss," and knelt by the hearth and began piling wood on the grate.

A maid with hair even redder than Verity's hurried in, carrying a minuscule bottle. "Oh, miss, has the mistress fainted then?" she asked Verity in a brogue that instantly identified her as Irish.

"Yes," Verity said, taking the bottle from her. She pulled the stopper out and passed it under Mrs. Mering's nose. "Aunt Malvinia," she said encouragingly.

"Oh, miss, was it haunts that did it?" the maid said, looking apprehensively around the room.

"No," Verity said, "Aunt Malvinia?" and Mrs. Mering moaned, but didn't open her eyes.

"I knew there was haunts in the house," the maid said, crossing herself. "I saw one, Tuesday last it was, out by the gazebo—"

"Colleen, fetch a damp cloth for Mrs. Mering's forehead," Verity said, "and a foot warmer."

"Yes, miss," the maid said, bobbed a curtsey, and went out, still looking fearfully around.

"O pwecious Juju," Tossie was cooing to the cat, "is oo a hungwy baby?" She turned to Baine, who had the fire laid and was about to light it. "Baine, come here," she said imperiously.

Even though he was in the act of lighting a spill of paper, Baine got immediately to his feet and came over to her. "Yes, miss?"

"Bring Juju a dish of cream."

"Yes, miss," he said, smiling at the cat. He turned to go.

"And a plate of fish."

Baine turned back. "Fish?" he said, raising an eyebrow.

Tossie's little chin went up. "Yes, fish. Princess Arjumand has been through a dreadful ordeal."

"As you wish," he said, every word dripping with disapproval.

"I do wish," she said, coloring. "Bring it immediately."

"Yes, miss," he said, but instead of leaving, he knelt by the hearth and methodically finished lighting the fire. He fanned it with the bellows and then carefully replaced them on the fire-irons stand before he stood up.

"I doubt we have any fish," he said and exited.

Tossie looked furious. "Ma*ma!*" she said, appealing to her mother, but Mrs. Mering was still out cold. Verity was spreading an afghan over her knees and arranging pillows behind her head.

I was beginning to shiver in my wet clothes. I made my way over to the fire, which was burning merrily, past the writing desk, a sewing table, and a small marble-topped table with a number of metal-framed photographs on it. Cyril was already there, dripping onto the warm hearth.

The maid Colleen hurried back in with a bowl of water. Verity took it from her, set it on the table next to a tall bronze vase full of peacock feathers, and wrung out the cloth.

"Oh, have the haunts taken her soul?" Colleen said.

"No," Verity said, laying the cloth across Mrs. Mering's forehead. "Aunt Malvinia," she said, and Mrs. Mering sighed and fluttered her eyelids.

A round gentleman with a bushy white mustache came in, carrying his newspaper. He was wearing a red smoking jacket and a strange red cap with a tassel on it. "What's all this?" he demanded. "Got so a man can't read the *Times* in peace."

"O Pa*pa,*" Tossie said. "Ma*ma*'s fainted."

"Fainted?" he said, coming over to see her. "What for?"

"We were having a séance," Tossie said. "We were attempting to find Princess Arjumand, and Mama was calling the spirits, and as she said, 'O come, spirits,' the curtains blew open, and there was a blast of chill air, and there Princess Arjumand was!"

"Harrumph," he said. "Knew this spiritualism nonsense was a bad idea. Lot of silliness."

Colonel Mering seemed to speak in a sort of shorthand, leaving off the subjects of his sentences. I wondered if they got somehow lost in his bushy mustache. "Hysteria," he said. "Gets women all worked up."

At this point, the curate cut in with, "A number of highly respected scholars and scientists are convinced of the validity of otherworldly phenomena. Sir William Crookes, the noted physicist, has written a respected treatise on the subject, and Arthur Conan Doyle is conducting—"

"Twaddle!" Colonel Mering said, which pretty much completed the collection of explosive Victorian disclaimers. "Cheesecloth and gullible women. Should be a law in Parliament against it." He stopped short at the sight of Terence. "Who are you? Blasted medium?"

"This is Mr. St. Trewes, Papa," Tossie interceded hurriedly. "He and his friends have returned Princess Arjumand," she said, holding the cat up for his inspection. "She was lost, and Mr. St. Trewes found her."

Colonel Mering looked at the cat with undisguised hatred. "Pah! Thought it had drowned, and good riddance."

"O Papa, you know you don't mean that!" She nuzzled the cat. "He doesn't mean the dweadful fings he says, does he, sweetum Juju? No, he doesn't-wuzn't."

The Colonel glared at Professor Peddick and then at me. "Suppose you're table-rappers as well?"

"No," I said. "We were out on the river and our boat capsized and—"

"Ohhh," Mrs. Mering moaned from the couch and fluttered her eyes open. "Husband," she said weakly, "is that you?" She reached out her hand to him. "O, Mesiel, the spirits!"

"Humbug! Lot of foolishness. Ruins your nerves and your health. Wonder someone wasn't hurt," the Colonel said, taking her hand. Verity relinquished her place, and Colonel Mering sat down next to his wife. "Settles it. No more séances. Absolutely forbid them in my house."

"Baine!" he said to the butler, who had just come in carrying a dish of cream. "Throw out the books on spiritism." He turned back to Mrs. Mering. "Forbid you to have any more to do with this medium Madame Idioskovitz."

"Iritosky," Mrs. Mering corrected. "O, Mesiel, you must not," she said, clutching at his hand. "You do not understand! You have always been a skeptic. But now you must believe. They were *here*, Mesiel. In this very *room*. I had just contacted Chief Gitcheewatha, Madame Iritosky's spirit control, and asked him regarding Princess Arjumand's fate, and—" she gave a screamlet just like Tossie's before going on, "—and there they were, carrying the cat in their ghostly arms!"

"Terribly sorry about that. Didn't mean to frighten you like that," Terence, who seemed to have caught the habit of chopping off subjects from Colonel Mering, said.

"*Who* is that?" Mrs. Mering demanded of her husband.

"Terence St. Trewes, at your service," Terence said and doffed his boater, which unfortunately still had a good deal of water in the brim. It sent a shower over Mrs. Mering.

"O, O, O," she said, uttering a whole series of screamlets, and waving her hands helplessly against the deluge.

"Most awfully sorry," Terence said and started to offer her his handkerchief. It was even wetter, and he stopped just in time and pocketed it again.

Mrs. Mering gave Terence a frosty look and turned back to her husband. "Everyone saw them!" She turned to the curate. "Reverend, tell Mesiel you saw the spirits!"

"Well . . ." the curate said uncomfortably.

"They were draped all in seaweed, Mesiel, and shining with an ethereal light," she said, clutching her husband's sleeve. "They had brought a message that poor Princess Arjumand had met a watery grave." She pointed at the French doors. "They came through those very doors!"

"Know we should have knocked," Terence said. "Didn't mean to barge in like that, but our boat went over and—"

"Who *is* this impertinent young man?" she asked her husband.

"Terence St. Trewes," Terence explained.

"Your spirits," Colonel Mering said.

"Terence St. Trewes," Terence said. "And this is Mr. Ned Henry and—"

"Spirits!" Colonel Mering said contemptuously. "Hadn't had all the lights out and been playing at table-rapping, you'd have seen they were punters who'd had a ducking. Watery grave? Bah!"

"Princess Arjumand's quite all right, Mama," Tossie said, thrusting the cat forward for her mother to see. "She isn't drowned. Mr. St. Trewes found her and brought her home. Didn't he, pwecious Juju? He did, yes, he did. He was *so* bwave, wasn't he? He was, he was!"

"*You* found Princess Arjumand?" Mrs. Mering said.

"Well, actually Ned was the one who—"

She glared silencingly at me and then back at him, taking in our wet clothes and bedraggled state, and, presumably, our non-spiritual nature.

I thought for a moment she might faint again, and Verity moved forward and took the stopper out of the smelling salts.

Then Mrs. Mering sat up on the couch, fixed Terence with a frosty eye, and said, "How *dare* you impersonate a spirit, Mr. St. Trewes!"

"I . . . we . . . our boat went over, and . . ." he stammered.

"Terence St. Trewes!" she went on, "what sort of name is that? Is it *Irish?*"

The temperature had dropped several degrees in the room, and Terence shivered a bit as he answered, "No, ma'am. It's an old family name. Dates back to the Conquest and all that. Knight who fought in the Crusades with Richard the Lionhearted, I believe."

"It *sounds* Irish," Mrs. Mering said.

"Mr. St. Trewes is the young man I told you about," Tossie said, "whom I met on the river and asked to search for Princess Arjumand. And he's found her!" She showed the cat to her mother.

Mrs. Mering ignored her. "On the river?" she said, and her stare was pure liquid nitrogen. "Are you some sort of bargeman?"

"No, ma'am," Terence said. "I'm an undergraduate. Second year. At Balliol."

"Oxford!" Colonel Mering snorted. "Bah!"

It looked like we were going to be tossed out on our ears in another couple of minutes, which might not be a bad thing, considering the way Tossie was carrying on about Terence. I wondered if this was some part of the continuum's correcting itself now that "pwecious Juju" had been safely returned. I hoped so.

I also hoped I would get a chance to talk to Verity before we were shown the gate. Since that first delighted look, she hadn't even glanced at me, and I needed at least to know what she'd found out from T.J. and Mr. Dunworthy, if anything.

"Do they teach you to break into people's homes at Oxford?" Mrs. Mering said.

"N-no," Terence stammered. "You said, 'Enter.' "

"I was *speaking* to the spirits!" she said stiffly.

"Suppose you're studying some damned modern subject," Colonel Mering said.

"No, sir. Classics, sir. This is my tutor, Professor Peddick."

"We didn't mean to intrude like this," Professor Peddick said. "These young gentlemen were kindly taking me downriver to Runnymede when—"

But the temperature had risen sharply, and the Colonel was smiling, or I thought he was, under his white mustache. "Not Professor Arthur Peddick? Wrote, 'On the Physical Characteristics of the Japanese Shubunkin'?"

Professor Peddick nodded. "Have you read it?"

"*Read* it? Wrote you only last week about my globe-eyed nacreous ryunkin," the Colonel said. "Astonishing coincidence, your showing up like this."

"Ah, yes," Professor Peddick said, peering at him through his pince-nez. "I've been intending to answer your letter. Fascinating species, the ryunkin."

"Utterly amazing that your boat should capsize here, of all places," the Colonel said. "What's the likelihood of that happening? Astronomical."

I looked over at Verity. She was watching them and biting her lip.

"You must come and see my Black Moor," the Colonel said. "Excellent specimen. All the way from Kyoto. Baine, fetch a lantern!"

"Yes, sir," Baine said.

"And a three-pound banded gudgeon," the Colonel said, taking hold of Professor Peddick's arm and leading him through the maze of furniture to the French doors. "Caught it only last week."

"Mesiel!" Mrs. Mering snapped from the couch. "Where on earth do you think you're going?"

"Out to the fishpond, my dear, to show Professor Peddick my goldfish."

"At this time of night?" she said. "Nonsense! He'll catch his death in those wet clothes."

"Quite right," Colonel Mering said, seeming to notice for the first time that the sleeve he was holding onto was sopping wet. "Must get you into dry things. Baine," he said to the butler, who was just leaving, "bring Professor Peddick some dry clothes at once."

"Yes, sir," Baine said.

"Mr. Henry and Mr. St. Trewes will both need fresh clothes as well," Verity said.

"Yes, miss."

"And bring some brandy," Colonel Mering said.

"And a fish," Tossie said.

"I doubt if these gentlemen have time for a glass of brandy," Mrs. Mering said, turning the thermostat down again. "It's extremely late, and they will be wanting to return to their lodgings. I presume you are staying at one of the river inns, Mr. St. Trewes? The Swan?"

"Well, actually—" Terence began.

"Won't hear of it. Nasty, common places. Appalling drains. Must stay here," Colonel Mering said, putting up his hand to ward off objections. "Plenty of room for you and your friends. Must stay as long as you like. Excellent trolling deeps here. Baine, tell Jane to make up rooms for these gentlemen."

Baine, who was trying to pour the brandy, fetch a lantern, and outfit half the people in the room, promptly said, "Yes, sir," and started out of the room.

"And bring in their luggage," Colonel Mering said.

"I'm afraid we haven't any luggage," Terence said. "When our boat capsized, we were lucky to make it to shore with our lives."

"Lost a beautiful albino gudgeon," Professor Peddick said. "Extraordinary dorsal fins."

"Shall have to catch it again," Colonel Mering said. "Baine, go see if you can salvage the boat and their belongings. Where's that lantern?"

It was a wonder Baine wasn't reading Marx, as downtrodden as he was. No, Marx was still writing it. In the Reading Room of the British Museum.

"I'll fetch it, sir."

"You will not," Mrs. Mering said. "It's far too late for fishpond excursions. I'm certain these gentlemen," the temperature plummeted, "are tired after their *adventure.* Boating! In the middle of the night. It's a wonder you weren't all swept over a weir and drowned," she said, looking as though she wished that that had happened. "I'm sure these gentlemen are *exhausted.*"

"Quite right," the curate said, "so I will take my leave. Good night, Mrs. Mering."

Mrs. Mering extended her hand. "O, Reverend, I am *so* sorry there were no manifestations tonight."

"Next time I do not doubt we shall be more successful," he said to Mrs. Mering, but he was looking at Tossie. "I shall look forward to our next excursion into the metaphysical. And of course to seeing you both day after tomorrow. I am certain it will be a brilliant success with you and your lovely daughter assisting."

He leered at Tossie, and I wondered if this might be the mysterious Mr. C.

"We are delighted to assist in any way," Mrs. Mering said.

"We *are* rather short of tablecloths," the curate said.

"Baine, take a dozen tablecloths to the vicarage at once," she said.

It was no wonder Baine had taken to pet-drowning in his spare time. Clearly justifiable homicide.

"I am delighted to have met all of you," the curate said, still looking at Tossie. "And if you are all still here the day after tomorrow, I should like to extend an invitation to our—"

"I doubt the gentlemen will be staying that long," Mrs. Mering said.

"Ah," the curate said. "Well, then, good night."

Baine handed him his hat, and he took his departure.

"You should have said good night to the Reverend Mr. Arbitage," Mrs. Mering said to Tossie, and there went that theory.

"Professor Peddick, you must at least see my globe-eyed nacreous ryunkin tonight," Colonel Mering said. "Baine, where's the lantern? Excellent coloration—"

"Aiyyyy!" Mrs. Mering said.

"What?" Terence said, and everyone turned and looked at the French doors as if expecting another ghost, but there was nothing there.

"What is it?" Verity said, reaching for the smelling salts.

"That!" Mrs. Mering said, pointing dramatically at Cyril, who was warming himself at the fire. "Who let that *dreadful creature* in?"

Cyril stood up, looking offended.

"I . . . I did," Terence said, hurrying over to grab Cyril by the collar.

"This is Cyril," Verity said. "Mr. St. Trewes's dog."

It was unfortunate that it was at that moment that Cyril's doggy nature asserted itself, or perhaps he was simply unnerved, as we all were, by Mrs. Mering. He shook himself all over, his jowls flapping wildly.

"O, dreadful dog!" Mrs. Mering cried, flinging up her hands even though he was half a room away. "Baine, take him outside at once!"

Baine started forward, and the thought crossed my mind that he might be some sort of serial pet murderer. "I'll take him out," I said.

"No, I will," Terence said. "Come along, Cyril."

Cyril looked at him disbelievingly.

"Terribly sorry," Terence said, tugging on Cyril's collar. "He was in the boat with us when it went over, and—"

"Baine, show Mr. St. Trewes the stable. Out!" Mrs. Mering said to Cyril, and he took off for the French doors like a shot, Terence right behind him.

"De naughty bad doggums is aww gone and dearum Juju don't have to be afwaid no more," Tossie said.

"O, this is all too much!" Mrs. Mering said, putting her hand dramatically to her forehead.

"Here," Verity said, sticking the smelling salts under her nose. "I'll be glad to show Mr. Henry to his room."

"Verity!" Mrs. Mering said in a voice that left no question of her being related to Lady Schrapnell. "That is *quite* unnecessary. The maid can show Mr. Henry to his room."

"Yes, ma'am," Verity said meekly and started across the room, catching her skirts up expertly so they didn't brush against the claw-footed table legs or the scrollwork aspidistra stand. As she reached for the bellpull's tassel, she murmured, "I am so glad to see you. I've been worried sick."

"I—" I said.

"Take me up to my room, Tossie," Mrs. Mering said. "I am feeling quite overcome. Verity, tell Baine I want a cup of chamomile tea. Mesiel, don't bother Professor Peddick with your silly fish."

Colleen appeared in the midst of her giving orders and was told to take me up to my room.

"Yes, ma'am," she said, bobbed a curtsey and led me up the stairs, stopping at the bottom to light a lamp.

The decorating notion that "Less is more" had apparently not been invented yet. The walls next to the stairway and above it were solid with gilt-framed portraits of various Mering ancestors in gold lace, knee-breeches, and armor, and the corridor was lined with an umbrella stand, a bust of Darwin, a large fern, and a statue of Laocoön entangled with an enormous snake.

Colleen led me halfway down the corridor and stopped outside a painted door. She opened it, curtsied, and held it open for me. "Your bedroom, sir," she said. Her Irish brogue made the "sir" sound like "sorr."

This room was not quite so crowded as the parlor. It only had a bed, a washstand, a nightstand, a wooden chair, a chintz-covered chair, a bureau, a looking-glass, and an enormous wardrobe which covered one entire wall—a blessing since the wallpaper consisted of trellises up which crawled enormous blue morning glories.

The maid set the lamp on the nightstand and darted across the room to take the pitcher off the washstand. "I'll just be bringin' you your hot water, sorr," she said, and ducked out.

I looked round the room. The Victorian interior decorating motto was apparently "No stone uncovered." The bed was covered with a bedspread which was in turn covered with a white openwork crocheted thing, the dressing table and the bureau were topped with bouquets of dried flowers and white linen scarves edged with tatting, and the nightstand was draped with a paisley shawl over which lay a crocheted doily.

Even the toilet articles on the bureau had knitted covers. I took them out and examined them, hoping they weren't as obscure as the kitchen utensils had been. No, those were brushes and that was a shaving brush and a mug with soap in it.

Twentieth Century has us use long-term depils on our drops, since shaving conditions are usually primitive, and I'd used one when I started my jumble sales, but it wouldn't last the whole time I was here. Had the safety razor been invented in 1888?

I took the knitted case off an enameled box and opened it and got my answer. In it lay two ivory-handled straight-edge razors with lethal-looking blades.

There was a knock on the door. I opened it, and the maid came in, lugging the pitcher, which was nearly as large as she was. "Your hot water, sorr," she said, setting the pitcher down and bobbing another curtsey. "If you'll be needing anything else, just ring the bell there."

She waved vaguely at a long ribbon embroidered with violets hanging above the bed, and it was a good thing I'd seen Tossie use a bellpull, or I would have taken it for part of the decorations.

"Thank you, Colleen," I said.

She stopped in mid-bob, looking uncomfortable. "Begging your pardon, sorr," she said, twisting the skirt of her apron in her hands, "it's Jane."

"Oh," I said. "Sorry. I must have misunderstood. I thought your name was Colleen."

She twisted some more. "No, sorr, it's Jane, sorr."

"Well, then, thank you, Jane," I said.

She looked relieved. "Good night, sorr," she said, bobbed her way out, and shut the door.

I stood there, looking at the bed almost in awe, scarcely able to believe I was actually going to get what I had come to the Victorian era for—a good night's sleep. It seemed almost too good to be true. A soft bed, warm covers, blissful unconsciousness. No rocks, no missing cats to search for, no rain. No jumble sales, no bishop's bird stump, no Lady Schrapnell.

I sat down on the bed. It sank in beneath me, smelling faintly of lavender, and entropy took over. I was suddenly too tired even to get undressed. I wondered how outraged Colleen—no, Jane—would be to come in and find me fully dressed in the morning.

I was still worried about incongruities and what I was going to tell Verity, but they would have to wait. And in the morning I would be rested, rejuvenated, finally cured of time-lag and able to reason out how to deal with the problem. If there was still a problem. Perhaps Princess Arjumand, safely back in the ruffled bosom of her owner, would restore balance and the incongruity would begin to heal itself. And if it didn't, why, after a good night's sleep I'd be able to *think*, able to reason out a plan of action.

The thought of that gave me the strength to spare the maid's sensibilities. I took off my soggy coat, hung it over the bedpost, and sat down on the bed and began pulling off my boots.

I made it as far as one boot and half a saturated sock before there was a knock.

It's the maid, I thought hopefully, bringing me a hot water bottle or a penwiper or something, and if her sensibilities are offended by a stockinged foot, so be it. I'm not putting my boot back on.

It wasn't the maid. It was Baine. He was carrying the carpetbag. "I have been down to the river, sir," he said, "and I regret that I was only able to save one of your baskets, your portmanteau, and this carpetbag, which was, unfortunately, empty and damaged." He indicated one of the slits I'd cut for Princess Arjumand. "It must have been caught in a weir before it washed onto the shore. I'll repair it for you, sir."

I didn't want him examining it closely and finding telltale cat hairs. "No, that's all right," I said, reaching for it.

"I assure you, sir," he said, "it can be sewn so that it's as good as new."

"Thank you," I said. "I'll take care of it."

"As you wish, sir," he said.

He crossed to the window and pulled the curtains shut. "We are still looking for the boat," he said. "I have notified the lock-keeper at Pangbourne Lock."

"Thank you," I said, impressed at his efficiency, and wishing he would go away so I could go to bed.

"Your clothes from the portmanteau are being washed and ironed for you, sir. I also retrieved your boater."

"Thank you," I said.

"Very good, sir," he said and I thought he was about to leave, but instead he just stood there.

I wondered if there was something I was supposed to say to dismiss him and what it was. One didn't tip butlers, did one? I tried to remember what the subliminals had said. "That will be all, Baine," I said finally.

"Yes, sir." He bowed slightly and started out, but at the door he hesitated again, as if there were something else.

"Good night," I said, hoping that was it.

"Good night, sir," he said and went out.

I sat down on the bed. This time I didn't even get the boot off before there was a knock.

It was Terence. "Thank goodness you're still up, Ned," he said. "You've got to help me. We've got a crisis on our hands."

*". . . the curious incident of the dog in the nighttime."*
*"The dog did nothing in the nighttime."*
*"That was the curious incident," remarked Sherlock Holmes.*

*Sir Arthur Conan Doyle*

# C H A P T E R   T W E L V E

A Rescue — Why English Country Houses Have a Reputation for Being
Haunted — Elizabeth Barrett Browning's Elopement — Visitors — A
Confession — The Mystery of Princess Arjumand's Drowning
Solved — More Visitors — The Charge of the Light Brigade — Rules
of Mystery Novels — The Least Likely Suspect — An Unpleasant
Discovery

The crisis was Cyril. "A stable! He's never slept outside, you know," Terence said, apparently forgetting about the night before.

"Poor Cyril!" he said, looking desperate. "Cast into outer darkness! With horses!" He paced the length of the room. "It's barbaric, expecting him to sleep outside after he's been in the river. And in his condition!"

"His condition?" I said.

"Cyril has a weak chest," he said. "A tendency to catarrh." He stopped pacing to peer out between the curtains. "He's probably already caught a cough. We've got to get him inside." He let the curtains drop. "I want you to sneak him up to your room."

"Me?" I said. "Why can't you sneak him up to your room?"

"Mrs. Mering will be watching out for me. I heard her tell the butler he was to see to it that the *animal* slept outside. *Animal!*"

"Then how can I get him in?"

"The butler will be watching me, not you. You should have seen the look on his face when I told him he had to stay. Absolutely betrayed. 'Et tu, Brute.' "

"All right," I said. "But I still don't see how I'm supposed to get past Baine."

"I'll go and ring for a cup of cocoa. That'll keep him out of your way. You're an absolute brick to do this. 'Best friend, my wellspring in the wilderness!' "

He opened the door and looked both ways. "All clear for the moment. I'll give it five minutes so you can put your boots back on, and then ring for the refreshments. If he does catch you, you can simply tell him you've come out for a smoke."

"And if he catches me on the way back with Cyril in tow?"

"He won't. I'll ask for a glass of claret, as well. Chateau Margaux, '75. These country houses never have a decent wine cellar."

He looked both ways again and sidled out, shutting the door softly behind him, and I went over to the bed and looked at my socks.

It is not an easy thing to put on a wet sock, let alone a wet boot on over it, and there was a certain reluctance involved. It took me well over five minutes to put them on and start down. I hoped that the Merings' wine cellar was at the opposite end of the house.

I opened the door a crack and peered down the corridor. I couldn't see anyone, or anything, for that matter, and wished I had paid more attention to the placement of the furniture and statuary.

It was so dark I debated going back for the lamp with the dangling crystals on it, trying to weigh which was worse: being caught by Mrs. Mering when she saw the light or being caught by Mrs. Mering after I'd crashed into the statue of Laocoön.

I decided the latter. If the servants were up, and I didn't see how they could not be, with all those tablecloths to wash and starch, they'd see the light and come scurrying up to ask me if there was anything else, sir. And my eyes were gradually adjusting to the darkness, enough at any rate to make out the outline of the corridor. If I kept to the very center of it I should be all right.

I felt my way to the head of the stairs, tripping over a large fern that rocked wildly on its stand before I managed to steady it, and what turned out to be a pair of boots.

I puzzled over those and what they meant the rest of the way to the staircase, and nearly tripped over another pair, Tossie's dainty white lace-up boots this time, and remembered the subliminals saying something about people putting their boots outside their doors at night for the servants to polish. No doubt after they were done with doing up the tablecloths and brewing cocoa and swimming down the Thames looking for stray boats.

There was more light here. I started down the stairs. The fourth step creaked loudly and when I looked anxiously back up the stairs there was Lady Schrapnell, glaring at me from the head of the stairs.

My heart stopped cold.

When it finally started up again, I realized she was wearing a pleated ruff and one of those long, pointed waists, and that Lady Schrapnell was still safely on the Other Side and this must be one of the Merings' Elizabethan ancestors. And no wonder Victorian country houses had a reputation for being haunted.

The rest of the way was easy, though I had a bad moment at the front door when I thought it was locked and I might have to go through that maze of a parlor and out the French doors, but it was only bolted, and it made scarcely any noise when I shoved the bolt back. And the moon was shining outside.

I had no idea which of several outbuildings shining whitely in the moonlight was the stable. I tried a potting shed and what turned out to be a henhouse before the whinny of horses, no doubt awakened by the hens, put me in the right direction.

And Cyril looked so pathetically glad to see me that I was sorry for the curses I'd been rehearsing for Terence. "Come along, old fellow," I said. "You have to be very quiet. Like Flush, when Elizabeth Barrett Browning eloped."

Which had been in these times, come to think of it. I wondered how she had managed to sneak down the stairs and out of a pitch-black house without killing herself. And carrying a suitcase and a cocker spaniel, too. I was beginning to have a lot of respect for the Victorians.

Cyril's version of being quiet consisted of heavy breathing punctuated by snorts. Halfway up the steps, he stopped cold, staring up at the head of the stairs.

"It's all right," I said, urging him on. "It's only a painting. Nothing to be afraid of. Careful of the fern."

We made it down the corridor and into my room without incident. I shut the door and leaned gratefully against it. "Good boy. Flush would be proud of you," I said, and saw that he had a black boot in his mouth, which he had apparently picked up along the way. "*No!*" I said and lunged for it. "Give me that!"

Bulldogs had originally been bred to grab a bull's nose and hang on for dear life. That trait persisted. I yanked and pulled and tugged to no avail. I let go. "Drop that boot," I said, "or I am taking you straight back out to the stable."

He looked at me steadily, the boot hanging from his mouth, laces dangling.

"I mean it," I said. "I don't care if you catch catarrh. Or pneumonia."

Cyril considered a moment longer and then dropped the boot and lay down with his flat nose just touching it.

I dived for the boot, hoping it belonged to Professor Peddick, who would never notice the teeth marks, or Terence, whom it would serve right. It was a woman's boot. And not Verity's. She had been wearing white ones, like Tossie's.

"This is Mrs. Mering's boot!" I said, shaking it at him.

Cyril responded by sitting up alertly, ready to play.

"This is serious!" I said. "Look at it!"

Actually, except for a great deal of drool, it did not seem to have sustained much damage. I wiped it off against my trouser leg and opened the door. "Stay!" I ordered Cyril and went to put it back.

I had no idea which was Mrs. Mering's door, and no way of seeing which had a boot missing, coming straight from my lit room. And no time to let my eyes adjust to the pitch-darkness. And *no* desire to have Mrs. Mering catch me crawling about the corridor on all fours.

I went back in the room, got the lamp, and shone it round the corridor till I found a door with one boot. Second from the end. And between it and my door the statue of Laocoön, Darwin, and a papier-mâché table with a large fern on it.

I ducked back in, shut the door, replaced the lamp, picked up the boot, and opened the door again.

"—tell you I saw a light," a voice that could only be Mrs. Mering's said. "An eerie, floating, ethereal light. A spirit light, Mesiel! You must get up!"

I shut the door, blew out the lamp, and crept back over to the bed. Cyril was in it, nicely ensconced among the pillows. "This is all your fault," I whispered, and realized I was still holding Mrs. Mering's boot.

I stuffed it under the covers, decided that would be *truly* incriminating, started to hide it under the bed, thought better of *that*, and stuck it between the springs and the feather-stuffed mattress. And then sat there in the dark, trying to determine what was happening. I couldn't hear any voices over Cyril's snoring, and there was no sound of doors opening nor any light under my door.

I gave it another few minutes and then took off my boots, tiptoed over to the door, and opened it a crack. Darkness and silence. I tiptoed back to the bed, cracking my big toe on the looking glass and my shin on the nightstand, lit the lamp again, and got ready for bed.

The last few minutes seemed to have sapped what little strength I had, but

I undressed slowly and carefully, noting how my collar and braces fastened and looking at the tie in the mirror as I untied it so that I could put it on in more or less the same arrangement tomorrow. Not that it mattered. I would already have cut my throat shaving. Or been revealed as a thief and a foot-fetishist.

I took off my still-soaking socks, put on the nightshirt, and got in bed. The springs sagged, the feather-stuffed mattress gave no support, the sheets were cold, and Cyril had all the covers. It felt wonderful.

Sleep, Nature's soft Nurse, the honeyed dew of holy rest, the balm of woe, sweet, blessed unravelling sleep.

There was a knock on the door.

It's Mrs. Mering, I thought, looking for her shoe. Or spirits. Or the Colonel, whom she made get up.

But there was no light under the door, and the knock, repeated, was too soft. It's Terence, I thought, wanting Cyril now that I've done all the work.

But in case it wasn't, I lit the lamp, put on the dressing gown, and flung the coverlet over Cyril to cover him up and then went and opened the door.

It was Verity. In her nightgown.

"What are you doing here?" I whispered at her. "This is the Victorian era."

"I know," she whispered back, sidling past me into the room. "But I've got to talk to you before I go report to Mr. Dunworthy."

"But what if someone comes in?" I said, looking at her white nightgown. It was a very modest sort of nightgown, with long sleeves and a high, buttoned-up neck, but I didn't think that would impress Terence. Or the butler. Or Mrs. Mering.

"No one will come in," she said, and sat down on the bed. "Everyone's gone to bed. And the walls in these Victorian houses are too thick to hear through."

"Terence has already been here," I said. "And Baine."

"What did *he* want?"

"To tell me he hadn't been able to salvage the luggage. Terence wanted me to sneak Cyril up from the stables."

At the mention of his name, Cyril emerged from the covers, blinking sleepily.

"Hullo, Cyril," Verity said, petting him on the head. He lay his head on her lap.

"What if Terence comes back to check on him?" I said.

"I'll hide," she said calmly. "You have no idea how glad I was to see you, Ned." She smiled up at me. "When we got back from Madame Iritosky's,

Princess Arjumand still wasn't here, and when I went to report back last night, Mrs. Mering caught me on my way out to the gazebo. I managed to convince her I'd seen a spirit and was chasing it, and then she insisted on getting everyone up and searching the entire grounds, so I couldn't go through and I didn't have any idea what had happened."

It really was too bad. The naiad was sitting on my bed in her nightgown, her Pre-Raphaelite auburn hair streaming down her back. She was here, smiling up at me, and I was going to have to ruin it all. Still, the sooner I got it over with, the better.

"And then this morning," she was saying, "I had to accompany Tossie to a meeting at the church, and—"

"I brought the cat through," I said. "It was in my luggage. Mr. Dunworthy must have told me I had it, but I was too time-lagged to hear him. I had it all along."

"I know," she said.

"What?" I said, wondering if I was experiencing Difficulty in Distinguishing Sounds again.

"I know. I reported back this afternoon and Mr. Dunworthy told me."

"But—" I said, trying to take this in. If she'd been back to 2057, then that radiant smile—

"I should have guessed when I saw you at Iffley," she said. "Sending historians on holiday isn't Mr. Dunworthy's style, especially not with Lady Schrapnell breathing down his neck and the consecration in only two weeks."

"I didn't know I had it till after I saw you at Iffley," I said. "I was looking for a tin-opener. I know you said to keep Terence away from Muchings End, but I thought it was more important to get the cat returned. The plan was for us to stop at an inn in Streatley, and I'd sneak her back during the night, but Terence insisted on rowing down, and then the cat started meowing, and Cyril started sniffing at it, and he fell in, and then the boat capsized and . . . you know the rest," I finished lamely. "I hope I did the right thing."

She bit her lip, looking worried.

"What? You don't think I should have brought her back?"

"I don't know."

"I thought I should get her back here before there were any other consequences."

"I know," she said, looking genuinely distressed. "The thing is, you weren't supposed to have brought her through in the first place."

"What?" I said.

"When Mr. Dunworthy found out about the Coventry slippage, he called off the drop."

"But—" I said. "I wasn't supposed to bring Princess Arjumand through? But I thought you said the Coventry slippage was unrelated, that it was due to a crisis point."

"It was, but while they were checking it, T.J. compared the slippage patterns to Fujisaki's research, and they decided the lack of slippage surrounding the original drop meant it was a nonsignificant event."

"But that's impossible. Animate creatures can't be nonsignificant."

"Exactly," she said grimly. "They think Princess Arjumand was nonanimate. They think she was intended to drown."

This was making no sense. "But even if she drowned, her body would still interact with the continuum. It wouldn't just disappear."

"That's what Fujisaki's research was about. She'd be reduced to her component parts, and the complexity of their separate interactions would drop exponentially."

Meaning her poor body would drift down the Thames, decomposing into carbon and calcium and interacting with nothing but the river water and hungry fishes. Ashes to ashes. Dust to nonsignificance.

"Which would make it possible," Verity said, "for her to be removed from her space-time location without any historical effect. Which meant she shouldn't be sent back from the future at all."

"So you didn't cause an incongruity by taking her through the net," I said. "But I did, by bringing her back."

She nodded. "When you didn't come, I was afraid they might have sent Finch or someone after you to tell you to drown Princess Arjumand."

"No!" I said. "No one's drowning anyone."

She rewarded me with one of her devastating smiles.

"If she's a nonsignificant event, we'll take her back to the future," I said firmly. "We're not going to drown her. But that doesn't make any sense," I said, thinking of something. "Her drowning, if that's what would have happened, would have had consequences, the same consequences her disappearance had: everyone looking for her, your going to Oxford, Tossie's meeting Terence."

"That's what I tried to tell Mr. Dunworthy," she said. "But T.J. said Fujisaki said those would have been short-term consequences without historical repercussions."

"In other words, they would have gotten over the cat," I said, "if I hadn't walked in with her."

"And you wouldn't have walked in with her, if I hadn't interfered in the first place," she said ruefully.

"But you couldn't let it drown," I said.

"No," she said, "I couldn't. And what's done is done, and I've got to tell Mr. Dunworthy and find out what we do next."

"What about the diary?" I said. "If there were references to her after the seventh, that would prove she hadn't drowned. Couldn't the forensics expert look for her name?"

Verity looked unhappy. "She did. The configuration of letters, actually—two very long words beginning with capital letters—but the only references are in the days immediately following, and she hasn't been able to translate them yet. Mr. Dunworthy says they may only be references to her being missing, or to her having drowned."

She stood up. "I'd better go report in. After you realized you had Princess Arjumand, what happened? When did Terence and Professor Peddick find out you had her?"

"They didn't," I said. "I kept her hidden till we got here. In a carpetbag. Terence thinks she was on the shore when we—" "Landed" wasn't quite the right word. "—arrived."

"And nobody else saw her?"

"I don't know," I admitted. "She got away twice. Once in the woods and once at Abingdon."

"She escaped from the carpetbag?"

"No," I said. "I let her out."

"You let her *out?*"

"I thought she was tame," I said.

"Tame?" she said, amused. "A cat?" She looked at Cyril. "Didn't you fill him in?" she said to him. She looked at me. "But you didn't see her interacting with anyone else?"

"No," I said.

"Well, that's good. Tossie hasn't met any other strange young men whose names don't begin with "C" since we came home."

"I take it Mr. C hasn't turned up," I said.

"No," she said, frowning, "and I haven't been able to get a look at Tossie's diary either. Which is why I need to report in. Perhaps the forensics expert has been able to decipher the name. Or one of the references to Princess Arjumand. And I need to tell them she's back and—"

"There's something else you need to tell them," I said.

"About Professor Peddick and the coincidence of his knowing Colonel Mering? I already thought of that."

"No," I said. "Something else. I made Terence miss meeting Professor Peddick's niece." I explained what had happened at the railway station.

She nodded. "I'll tell Mr. Dunworthy," she said. "Meetings—"

There was a knock on the door.

Verity and I froze. "Who is it?" I said.

"It's Baine, sir."

I mouthed silently at Verity, "Can I tell him to go away?"

"No," she mouthed back, flipped the bedclothes over Cyril, and started to crawl under the bed.

I grabbed her arm and mouthed, "The wardrobe."

"Coming, Baine," I called. "Just a minute," and opened the doors to the wardrobe. She dived in. I shut the door, opened it and shoved the tail of her nightgown in, shut it again, checked to make certain no bits of Cyril were sticking out from under the coverlet, stationed myself in front of the bed, and said, "Come in, Baine."

He opened the door, carrying a folded stack of shirts. "Your boat has been found, sir," he said, heading straight for the wardrobe.

I stepped in front of him. "Are those my shirts?"

"No, sir," he said. "I borrowed these from the Chattisbournes, whose son is in South Africa, until you can have your own things sent up."

My own things. And where exactly was I supposed to tell him to send? But I had more immediate problems. "Put the shirts in the bureau," I said, keeping between him and the wardrobe.

"Yes, sir," he said, and laid them neatly in the top drawer. "There is also a suit of evening clothes and one of tweeds, which I am having cleaned and altered to fit. They will be ready in the morning, sir."

"Good," I said. "Thank you, Baine."

"Yes, sir," he said and went out without even being told.

"That was a close—" I began and he came back in carrying a tray with a china cup, a silver pot, and a small plate of biscuits.

"I thought you might care for some cocoa, sir."

"Thank you."

He set it on the nightstand. "Would you like me to pour it out for you, sir?"

"No, thank you."

"There are additional bedcovers in the wardrobe, sir," he said. "Would you like me to put one on the bed?"

"No!" I said, moving to block him. "Thank you. That will be all, Baine."

"Yes, sir," he said, but he still stood there, fidgeting. "Sir," he said nervously, "if I might have your permission to speak . . ."

Either he knows Verity's in the wardrobe, I thought, or he knows I'm an impostor. Or both.

"What is it?" I said.

"I . . . just wanted to say . . ." again that nervous hesitation, and I saw that he looked pale and haggard, ". . . to say how very grateful I am to you for returning Princess Arjumand to Miss Mering."

It wasn't what I expected to hear. "Grateful?" I repeated blankly.

"Yes, sir. Mr. St. Trewes told me you were the one who had found her, after your boat capsized and you had swum ashore. I hope you don't think

I'm speaking out of my place, sir, but Miss Mering is extremely fond of her pet, and I would never have forgiven myself if anything had happened to her." He hesitated, looking nervous again. "It was my fault, you see."

"Your fault?" I said blankly.

"Yes, sir. You see, Colonel Mering collects fish. From the Orient. He keeps them in a pond in the rockery."

"Oh," I said, wondering if my time-lag symptoms were recurring again. I couldn't seem to see the connection.

"Yes, sir. Princess Arjumand has an unfortunate penchant for catching Colonel Mering's goldfish and eating them, in spite of my best efforts to prevent her from doing so. Cats, as you know, are quite impervious to threats."

"Yes," I said. "And cajoling and pleading and—"

"The only disciplinary measure that I have found to have any effect on her is—"

It all came suddenly, blindingly clear. "Throwing her in the river," I said.

There was a sound, like a gasp, from the wardrobe, but Baine didn't seem to notice. "Yes, sir," he said. "It doesn't cure her, of course. It's necessary to reinforce the message approximately once a month. I only throw her out a short way. Cats swim quite well, you know, when they are forced to. Better than dogs. But this last time she must have got caught in the current and—" He buried his face in his hands. "I feared she had drowned," he said despairingly.

"Here," I said, taking his arm and helping him into the chintz-covered chair. "Sit down. She hasn't drowned. She's perfectly all right."

"She ate the Colonel's silver Emperor fantail. An extremely rare fish. The Colonel had it shipped all the way from Honshu, at great expense," he said, anguished. "It had arrived only the day before, and there she was, sitting next to the dorsal fin, calmly licking her paws, and when I cried out, "Oh, Princess Arjumand! What have you *done?*' she looked up at me with an expression of utter innocence. I'm afraid I quite lost my temper."

"I quite understand," I said.

"No." He shook his head. "I carried her out to the river and flung her out as far as I could and then walked away. And when I came back—" he buried his face in his hands again, "there was no sign of her anywhere. I searched everywhere. These last four days I have felt like Dostoyevsky's Raskolnikov, unable to confess my crime, racked with guilt for having murdered an innocent creature—"

"Well, not quite innocent," I said. "She did eat the silver Emperor fantail."

He didn't even hear me. "She must have been carried away by the current and come ashore farther downstream, wet, lost—"

"Full of fantail," I said to keep him from burying his face in his hands again. And double-gilled blue chub, I thought.

"I couldn't sleep. I realized that I—I knew that Miss Mering would never be able to forgive me if any harm had come to her precious pet, yet I feared that with her good heart she might, and I would not be able to bear her forgiveness or forgive myself. Yet I knew I had to tell her, and I had determined to do so tonight, after the séance, and then the French doors opened, and it was a miracle. There was Princess Arjumand, safely returned, thanks to you!" He clasped my hands. "You have my most profound gratitude, sir! Thank you!"

"Perfectly all right," I said, pulling my hands away before he smothered them with grateful kisses or something. "Glad to do it."

"Princess Arjumand might have starved or frozen to death or been killed by wild dogs or—"

"No use worrying about things that didn't happen," I said. "She's safely home."

"Yes, sir," he said, and looked like he might go for my hands again.

I stuck them behind my back.

"If there is anything, *anything* I can do to return the service you have done me and show my gratitude, I would do it in an instant."

"Yes, well . . ." I said. "Thank you."

"No, thank *you*, sir," he said and, grabbing my hand from behind my back, shook it heartily. "And thank you for hearing me out. I hope I haven't spoken out of turn, sir."

"Not at all," I said. "I appreciate your telling me."

He stood up and straightened his lapels. "Would you like me to press your coat and trousers for you, sir?" he said, regaining his composure.

"No, that's all right," I said, thinking that the way things had gone thus far I might need them. "You can press them later."

"Yes, sir," he said. "Will there be anything else, sir?"

Probably, I thought, the way this night is going.

"No," I said. "Thank you. Good night, Baine. Get some rest. And don't worry. Princess Arjumand's home safe and sound, and no harm done." I hope.

"Yes, sir," he said. "Good night, sir."

I opened the door to let him out and held it open a crack to watch him till he reached the door to the servants' quarters and went through it, and then went over to the wardrobe and knocked quietly.

There was no answer.

"Verity?" I said, and pulled the double doors open. Verity was sitting huddled in the wardrobe, her knees hunched against her chest. "Verity?"

She looked up at me. "He wasn't going to drown her," she said. "Mr.

Dunworthy said I should have thought before I acted. He would have come back and rescued her if I hadn't interfered."

"But that's good news," I said. "It means she wasn't a nonsignificant event, and my returning her didn't create an incongruity."

She nodded, but without conviction. "Perhaps. But if Baine had rescued her, she wouldn't have been missing for four days. They wouldn't have gone to Madame Iritosky's, and Tossie would never have met Terence." She scrambled out of the wardrobe. "I've got to tell Mr. Dunworthy this." She started for the door. "I'll be back as soon as I can and tell you what I find out."

She put her hand on the door. "I won't knock," she whispered. "If Mrs. Mering hears knocking, she's liable to think it's spirits rapping. I'll scratch on the door, like this." She demonstrated. "I'll be back soon," she said, and opened the door.

"Wait," I said, and retrieved Mrs. Mering's boot from under the mattress. "Here," I said, thrusting it at Verity. "Set this in front of Mrs. Mering's door."

She took the boot. "I won't even ask," she said, grinned, and slid out the door.

I didn't hear any statuary crashes, or cries of, "The spirits!" from Mrs. Mering's room, and after a minute I sat down in the chair to wait. And worry.

I wasn't supposed to have brought the cat through. I remembered now Mr. Dunworthy saying, "Stay right there!" but I had thought he meant not to leave the net.

And it wouldn't be the first time a miscommunication had affected history. Look at the countless times when a message which had been misunderstood or failed to get through or fallen into the wrong hands had changed the outcome of a battle: Lee's accidentally dropped plans for Antietam, and the Zimmerman telegram, and Napoleon's illegible orders to General Ney at Waterloo.

I wished I could think of an instance in which a failure to communicate had had anything but disastrous results. I wasn't sure there were any. Look at Hitler's migraine on D-Day. And the Charge of the Light Brigade.

Lord Raglan, standing on a hill, saw the Russians trying to retreat with captured Turkish artillery and ordered Lord Lucan to stop them. Lord Lucan, not on a hill and possibly suffering from Difficulty in Distinguishing Sounds, didn't catch the word "Turkish," couldn't see any artillery except the Russian cannons pointed straight at him, and ordered Lord Cardigan and his men to charge straight at them. With predictable results.

"Into the Valley of Death rode the six hundred," I murmured, and heard a faint scratching on the door.

I didn't see how it could possibly be Verity. She'd scarcely been gone long enough to make it out to the gazebo and back, let alone to the future.

"Who is it?" I whispered through the door.

"Verity," she whispered back.

"I told you I'd scratch on the door," she said when I let her in. She had a brown paper parcel under her arm.

"I know," I said, "but you were only gone five minutes."

"Good," she said. "That means there wasn't any slippage, which is a good sign." She sat down on the bed, looking pleased with herself. The news must be good.

"What did Mr. Dunworthy say?" I asked.

"He wasn't there," she said happily. "He'd gone up to Coventry to see Elizabeth Bittner."

"Mrs. Bittner? The wife of the last bishop of Coventry?"

She nodded. "Only he didn't go to see her in her capacity as bishop's wife. She apparently worked on the net back in the early days. Do you know her?" she asked curiously.

"Lady Schrapnell had me interview her about the bishop's bird stump."

"Did she know where it was?"

"No."

"Oh. Can I eat your biscuits?" she said, looking hungrily at the tray on the nightstand. "I'm starving." She picked one up and took a bite out of it.

"How long were you there?" I asked.

"Hours," she said. "Warder wouldn't tell me where T.J. was—he was hiding from Lady Schrapnell, and he'd told Warder not to tell *anyone* where he was. It took me forever to track him down."

"Did you ask him about my making Terence miss meeting Maud?"

"Yes," she said. "Can I have your cocoa?"

"Yes. What did he say?"

"He said he thinks it's unlikely that Terence was supposed to have met Maud, or if he was, that the meeting was nonsignificant, because if it had been, the net wouldn't have opened."

"But if my bringing the cat through caused an incongruity?" I said.

She shook her head. "T.J. doesn't think it did. He thinks I caused it."

"Because of what Baine told us."

She nodded. "That, and the excessive slippage."

"But I thought that was supposed to be due to Coventry's being a crisis point."

She shook her head. "Not the area of slippage in Coventry. The one in Oxford. In April of 2018."

"2018? What crisis point is that?"

"It's not, to anyone's knowledge," she said. "That's why Mr. Dunworthy went to see Mrs. Bittner, to see if she remembers anything unusual about the drops or the time travel research they did that year that might account for it, but neither of them could remember anything. So if I caused the incongruity, then your bringing the cat back wouldn't have. It would have been correcting it, and so it should have made things better, not worse. And having Terence miss meeting someone would hardly make things better, especially if meeting them might have kept him from getting to Iffley in time to see Tossie. Which means Terence must not have been supposed to meet Maud, and we don't have to worry about it being a symptom the incongruity's getting worse."

"A symptom? What do you mean?"

"According to Fujisaki, the first line of defense is excessive slippage. Then, if that fails to correct the incongruity, there's an increase in coincidental happenings, and if *that* fails, then discrepancies appear."

"Discrepancies? You mean the course of history begins to alter?"

"Not at first. But the incongruity makes it destabilize. The way T.J. explained it was, that instead of there being a single fixed course of events, there becomes a superposition of probabilities."

"Like in Schrodinger's box," I said, thinking of the famous thought experiment with the Geiger counter and the bottle of cyanide gas. And the cat.

"Exactly," Verity said happily. "The course of events that will happen if the incongruity's corrected, and if it's not, both exist side by side, sort of. When the self-correction's completed, they collapse into one course of events or the other. But until that happens, there may be discrepancies between the observed and recorded events. Only the only record we have is Tossie's diary, and we can't read that, so there's no way to tell whether Terence and Maud's not meeting is a discrepancy or not."

She bit into another biscuit. "That's why I was gone so long. After I talked to T.J., I went over to the Bodleian to start a search on Terence and then over to Oriel to ask the forensics expert to look for references to him in the diary and to see if she'd found out Mr. C's name."

"And had she?" I said, thinking perhaps this was why Verity seemed so happy.

"No. She'd recovered one entire passage, which unfortunately was a description of a dress Tossie was having made. Four paragraphs of pintucks, Brussels lace, French embroidery, openwork insets, and—"

"Ruffles," I said.

"Ruffles and more ruffles," she said disgustedly. "And not a word about the cat or the trip to Coventry or the bishop's bird stump. I don't suppose you have any chocolate stashed away? Or cheese? I'm so hungry. I intended to go back to Balliol and eat dinner after I talked to the forensics expert, but on the way there, I ran into Lady Schrapnell."

"Lady Schrapnell?" I said. I'd nearly forgotten her in all the other crises. "She doesn't know where I am, does she? You didn't tell her, did you?"

"Of course not," she said, taking a swig of the cocoa. "I didn't tell her about the cat either. She demanded to know what I was doing there, and I told her I needed a new costume for day after tomorrow. Warder was livid."

"I can imagine."

"And then she stood there while I was being fitted, telling me all about you and how you'd gone off somewhere and Mr. Dunworthy wouldn't tell her where you were, and how T.J. Lewis refused to go back to 1940 to check on the bishop's bird stump just because the Twentieth Century was a ten for blacks, which was ridiculous, how dangerous could an air raid be?" She drained the last of the cocoa and peered into the pot. "And how the workmen were being completely impossible about the choir and told her the choir stalls wouldn't be completed for another month and how that was completely out of the question, the consecration was in thirteen days."

She poured the last drops of cocoa into her cup. "She wouldn't leave, even when Warder took me into the prep room to try on the dress. I had to have her go out and stall Lady Schrapnell while I telephoned the Bodleian and got the results of the search on Terence."

"And? Was he supposed to meet Maud?"

"I don't know," she said cheerfully. "The search didn't turn up anything. No medals, knighthoods, elections to Parliament, arrests, convictions, news stories. No mention at all in the official records."

"No marriage license?"

She shook her head and reached for the last biscuit. "His parish church was destroyed in the Blitz, and I didn't have time to do a global, but I left a message for Mr. Dunworthy with Warder, telling him to do one as soon as he got back from Coventry, but if Terence isn't mentioned in the official records, it means he didn't affect history, which means the meeting doesn't matter. Which goes along with what T.J. said about the discrepancies, which is that only the immediate area surrounding the incongruity is destabilized. And the meeting was four days from the time I rescued the cat, and Oxford Railway Station's over thirty miles from Muchings End, which is hardly the immediate vicinity. So it isn't a discrepancy, and the incongruity isn't getting worse."

"Umm," I said, wishing I were as convinced as she was.

"But if Tossie marries Terence instead of Mr. C, that would definitely be a discrepancy, so we need to steal the diary and find out who he is and get them married as soon as possible, and in the meantime we need to keep

Terence away from Tossie. And find the bishop's bird stump," she added, licking biscuit crumbs off her fingers.

"What?" I said. "I thought you didn't tell Lady Schrapnell where I was."

"I didn't," she said. "I told her you'd found out where the bishop's bird stump was and were off fetching it!"

"You *what?*" I said, sitting down on Cyril.

"She was determined to find you," she said. "The craftsmen have refused to make a reproduction of the bishop's bird stump, and she's furious. It was only a matter of time till she checked Warder's drop records and came after you," she said reasonably, "and that's all we need."

She had a point. "But what's going to happen when she finds out I don't have the slightest idea where the bishop's bird stump is and never did? The consecration's in two weeks, and I'm not supposed to be doing any drops."

"I'll help you," she said, "and we won't need to go anywhere. Poirot says all you need to solve a mystery is 'the little gray cells.' "

"Poirot?" I said. "Who's Poirot? The curate?"

"No," she said. "*Hercule* Poirot. Agatha Christie. He says—"

"Agatha Christie?" I said, completely lost.

"The mystery writer. Twentieth Century. My assignment before Lady Schrapnell took over Oxford *and* my life, was the 1930s, and it's an absolutely grim time: the rise of Hitler, worldwide depression, no vids, no virtuals, no money to go to the cinema. Nothing at all to do except read mystery novels. Dorothy Sayers, E.C. Benson, Agatha Christie. And crossword puzzles," she said, as if that explained everything.

"Crossword puzzles?" I said.

"Are not particularly useful to our present situation. But mystery novels are. Of course they're usually about murder, not robbery, but they always take place in a country house like this, and the butler did it, at least for the first hundred mystery novels or so. Everyone's a suspect, and it's always the least likely person, and after the first hundred or so, the butler wasn't anymore—the least likely person, I mean—so they had to switch to unlikely criminals. You know, the harmless old lady or the vicar's devoted wife, that sort of thing, but it didn't take the reader long to catch on to that, and they had to resort to having the detective be the murderer, and the narrator, even though that had already been done in *The Moonstone*. The hero did it, only he didn't know it. He was sleepwalking, in his nightshirt, which was rather racy stuff for Victorian times, and the crime was always unbelievably complicated. In mystery novels. I mean, nobody ever just grabs the vase and runs, or shoots somebody in a fit of temper, and at the very end, when you think you've got it all figured out, there's one last plot twist, and the crime's always very carefully thought out, with disguises and alibis and railway timetables and they have to include a diagram of the house in the frontispiece, showing everyone's bedroom and the library, which is where the body always is, and all the connecting doors, and even then you don't have a prayer of figuring it out, which is why they have to bring in a world-famous detective—"

"Who solves it with little gray cells?" I said.

"Yes. Hercule Poirot, that's Agatha Christie's detective, and he says it isn't at all necessary to go running about measuring footprints and picking up cigarette ends to solve mysteries like Sherlock Holmes. That's Arthur Conan Doyle's detective—"

"I know who Sherlock Holmes is."

"Oh. Well, anyway, Poirot says all you need is to use 'the little gray cells' and think about the problem."

"And we'll be able to find the bishop's bird stump. Here. In 1888," I said, unconvinced.

"Well, *it* won't be here, but we'll be able to find out where it is from here," she said, beaming. She settled herself on the bed. "Now, when was the last time you saw it?"

I was never going to get any sleep. I was going to have *Alice in Wonderland* conversation after *Alice in Wonderland* conversation until I died of exhaustion. Here, in the restful, idyllic Victorian era.

"Couldn't we do this in the morning?" I said.

"Everyone will be around then," she said, "and the sooner we find it, the sooner we can stop worrying about Lady Schrapnell barging in and demanding to know where it is. I've never actually seen it, you know. I've only heard stories. Is it truly as hideous as everyone says? It doesn't depict the Finding of the Infant Moses by Pharaoh's Daughters, does it, like that awful thing we saw at Iffley?"

She stopped. "I'm babbling, aren't I? Just like Lord Peter. That's Dorothy Sayers's detective. Lord Peter Wimsey. He and Harriet Vane solve mysteries together. It's terribly romantic, and I'm doing it again, aren't I? Babbling, I mean. Drops have that effect on me."

She looked ruefully at me. "And you're suffering from time-lag and supposed to be resting. I am so sorry."

She scrambled off the bed and picked up her paper-wrapped parcel. "It's sort of a cross between caffeine and alcohol. The effect drops have on me. Do they affect you that way? Sort of giddy and talkative?" She gathered up her shoes and stockings. "We'll both feel better in the morning."

She opened the door and peered out into the blackness. "Get some sleep," she whispered. "You look dreadful. You need to get your rest so you can help me keep Tossie and Terence apart in the morning. I've got it all worked out. I'll make Terence help me set up the fortune-telling tent."

"Fortune-telling tent?" I said.

"Yes, and you can help Tossie with the jumble sale."

CHAPTER THIRTEEN

Another Visitor—Variations on a Theme—*The Birds*—Importance of Butlers—An Old-Fashioned English Breakfast—Wildlife—The Bishop's Bird Stump—The One Little Fact—The Mystery of the Maid's Name Solved—I Am Prepped—The Mystery of the Origin of the Jumble Sale Solved—My Time in the States—Victorian Handicrafts—My Boater—Mr. C—A Surprise

Verity was not my final visitor. A half hour after she left there was another sound of scratching on the door, so faint I would not have heard it if I had been asleep.

I wasn't asleep. Verity, with her news of increased slippage and discrepancies, had pretty much put paid to that. Not to mention Lady Schrapnell and the bishop's bird stump.

And Cyril had somehow managed, in spite of his short legs, to sprawl over the entire width of the bed and both pillows so that there was only a narrow edge left, which I had a tendency to roll off of. I wrapped my feet round the bedpost and anchored the coverlet with my hands and thought about Lord Lucan and Schrödinger's cat.

It had been put into a box in Schrödinger's thought experiment, along with a doomsday device: a bottle of cyanide gas, a hammer hooked to a Geiger counter, and a chunk of uranium. If the uranium emitted an electron, it would trigger the hammer which would break the bottle. That would release the gas that would kill the cat that lived in the box that Schrödinger built.

And since there was no way to predict whether the uranium had emitted an electron or not, the cat was neither dead nor alive, but both, existing as side-by-side probabilities which would collapse into a single reality when the box was opened. Or the incongruity was repaired.

But that meant there was a fifty percent probability that the incongruity wouldn't be repaired. And for each moment the cat stayed in the box, the probability that the uranium would emit said electron became greater, and so did the likelihood that when the box was opened, the cat would be dead.

And the first line of defense had already failed. The coincidences of Tossie's meeting Terence and my meeting Terence and our rescuing Professor Peddick and his meeting the Colonel proved that. And discrepancies were the next step.

But Terence hadn't affected history, at least not directly, or his name would have been in the official records, and Oxford Railway Station was thirty miles and four days from Muchings End. And T.J. had said the immediate vicinity.

But what seemed to have escaped Verity in her time-lagged state was that even if their meeting wasn't in the immediate vicinity, Mrs. Mering's decision to take Tossie to Madame Iritosky's was, and that was what had led to her meeting Terence and to Terence's running into Professor Peddick and being asked to meet the agèd relics. And running into me. And what did immediate vicinity mean anyway? T.J. hadn't said. It might be years and hundreds of miles.

I lay there in the dark, going round and round, like Harris in the Hampton Court Maze. Baine hadn't intended to drown Princess Arjumand, but if she hadn't drowned and become nonsignificant, why hadn't the net refused to open for Verity? And if she *had* drowned, why had it opened for me?

And why had I come through at Oxford? To keep Terence from meeting Maud? I didn't see how that could possibly contribute to a self-correction. Or had it been to keep the cat away from Muchings End? I remembered dropping her basket at Folly Bridge when Cyril charged at me, and it nearly rolling into the river before Terence caught it. And my grabbing the carpetbag as it toppled, and sending Cyril into the drink. Had the course of history been trying to correct itself by drowning the cat, and I'd kept interfering?

But she couldn't have been intended to drown. Baine hadn't been trying to drown her when he threw her in. If Verity hadn't interfered, he would have dived in, morning coat and all, and saved her. Perhaps he'd thrown her out too far, and she'd been carried away by the current and drowned, in spite of Baine's best efforts. But that still didn't explain—

There was a faint scratching at the door. It's Verity, I thought. She forgot to explain Hercule Poirot's detecting methods. I opened the door.

There was no one there. I opened the door wider and looked down the hall in both directions. Nothing but blackness. It must have been one of Mrs. Mering's spirits.

"Mere," a small voice said.

I looked down. Princess Arjumand's gray-green eyes shone up at me. "More," she said, and sauntered past me, tail in the air, jumped on the bed, and lay down in the middle of my pillow.

This left me no room at all. Plus, Cyril snored. This in itself could have been got used to, but as the night progressed, it got louder and louder, till I was afraid it was going to wake the dead. Or Mrs. Mering. Or both.

And he seemed to do variations on a theme—a low rumble, like distant thunder, a snore, an odd whuffling sound which ruffled his jowls, a snort, a snuffle, a wheeze.

None of this bothered the cat, who had settled herself on my Adam's apple again and was purring (without variations) in my ear. I kept dozing off from cat-induced lack of oxygen and then waking up, lighting matches, and trying to read my pocket watch by them at II, III, and a quarter to IV.

I dozed off again at half-past V only to be awakened by the birds chirping the arrival of the sun. I had always been led to believe this was an idyllic, melodious sound, but this sounded more like a full-scale Nazi air raid. I wondered if the Merings had an Anderson shelter.

I fumbled for a match, realized I could read my pocket watch without it, and got up. I pulled on my clothes, put on my shoes, and began trying to rouse Cyril.

"Come along, boy, time to go back to the stable," I said, interrupting him in mid-whuffle with a shake. "You don't want Mrs. Mering to catch you in here. Come along. Wake up."

Cyril opened one bleary eye, closed it again, and began to snore loudly.

"Don't try to pull that!" I said. "It won't work. I know you're awake." I poked him in his midsection. "Come along. You'll get us both thrown out." I tugged on his collar. He opened the eye again and staggered to his feet. He looked like I felt. His eyes were bloodshot, and he was swaying gently, like a drunk after a night on the tiles.

"Good boy," I said encouragingly. "That's it. Off the bed. Down we go." Princess Arjumand chose that moment to yawn, stretch luxuriously, and settle comfortably into a nest of bedclothes. The message couldn't have been clearer.

"You're not helping," I said to her. "I know it's not fair, Cyril, but life is not fair. I, for instance, am supposed to be on holiday. Resting. Sleeping."

Cyril took the word "sleeping" for a command and sank back onto the pillows.

"*No,*" I said. "Up. Now. I mean it, Cyril. Come. Heel. Wake up."

One has not lived until one has carried a sixty-pound dog down a sweeping flight of stairs at half-past V in the morning. Outside, the grounds had the rosy flush of dawn, the grass bright with diamond dew, the roses just op'ing their sweet faces, all of which indicated I was still suffering from severe to terminal time-lag, which meant when I saw Verity at breakfast I would still be completely under her spell, even though she had told Lady Schrapnell I knew where the bishop's bird stump was.

In the meantime, the bird Luftwaffe must have gone back to refuel, and the world lay silent in the early light, a silence as much a part of the past as Victorian country houses and boating on the Thames, the stillness of a world that had yet no ken of airplanes and traffic jams, of incendiaries and pinpoint bombs, the still and holy hush of an idyllic world gone by.

It was too bad I wasn't in a position to appreciate it. Cyril weighed a ton, and set up a pathetic and piercing whine as soon as I set him down. I almost tripped over the slumbering stableboy on the way out, and, back inside the house, I nearly collided with Baine in the upper hall.

He was setting polished boots in neat pairs outside the bedroom doors. In the second before he saw me, I wondered when *he* slept.

"Couldn't sleep," I said, dropping the subjects of my sentences like Colonel Mering in my nervousness. "Went downstairs looking for something to read."

"Yes, sir," he said. He was holding Tossie's white boots. They had ruffles on the toes. "I find Mr. Toynbee's *The Industrial Revolution* very relaxing. Would you like me to fetch it for you?"

"No, that's quite all right," I said. "Feel as though I shall be able to sleep now."

Which was a blatant lie. I had far too many things to worry about to be able to fall asleep—how I was going to get my collar on and my tie tied in the morning. What Time Travel was going to discover about the consequences of my not returning Princess Arjumand to Muchings End for four full days. What I was going to tell Lady Schrapnell.

And even if I were able to stop worrying, there was no point in trying to sleep. It was already getting light. In a few minutes, sun would be streaming through the windows, and the bird Luftwaffe were already returning for a second raid. And I didn't dare fall asleep for fear of suffocation at the hands of Princess Arjumand.

She had taken over both pillows in my absence. I tried to push her gently to one side without waking her, and she stretched curvingly and began flipping her tail on my face.

I lay there under the lash and thought about the bishop's bird stump.

I not only didn't know where it was, I didn't have any idea what could possibly have happened to it. It had stood in the church for eighty years, and there was no indication it hadn't been there during the raid. In fact, there were a lot of indications that it had been. The order of service I'd found in the rubble proved it had been there four days before the raid, and I had seen it there myself on the day before that, the ninth, after the Prayers for the RAF Service and Baked Goods Sale.

I supposed it might have been removed for safekeeping at the last minute, but that hardly seemed likely when neither the Purbeck marble baptismal font nor the organ Handel had played on had been sent to the country or put down in the crypt, even though in retrospect they obviously should have been. And the bishop's bird stump looked far more indestructible than the marble baptismal font.

It *was* indestructible. The roof collapsing on it wouldn't have even chipped its cherubs. It should have been standing there in the ashes, rising above the rubble, untouched, unscathed, un—

When I woke, it was full daylight and Baine was standing over me with a cup of tea.

"Good morning, sir," he said. "I took the liberty of returning Princess Arjumand to her mistress's room."

"Good idea," I said, realizing belatedly that I had a pillow and was able to breathe.

"Yes, sir. It would be most distressing to Miss Mering to wake and find her gone again, though I can quite understand Princess Arjumand's attachment to you."

I sat up. "What time is it?"

"Eight o'clock, sir." He handed me the cup of tea. "I am afraid I was unable to retrieve the majority of your and Mr. St. Trewes's and Professor Peddick's luggage," he said. "These were all I was able to find."

He held up the size small suit of evening clothes Finch had packed for me. "I am afraid there has been considerable shrinkage, due to their immersion in the water. I have therefore sent for replacements, and—"

"Replacements?" I said, nearly spilling my tea. "From where?"

"Swan and Edgar's, of course, sir," he said. "In the meantime, your boating costume."

He had done more than press it. My shirt was bleached and starched to within an inch of its life, and the flannels looked like new. I hoped I would be able to figure out how to get into them. I sipped thoughtfully at my tea, trying to remember how the tie had gone.

"Breakfast is at nine, sir," Baine said. He poured out hot water from the ewer into the bowl and opened the box of razors.

The tie probably didn't matter. I would cut my throat shaving before I ever got to it.

"Mrs. Mering wishes everyone to be down to breakfast by nine o'clock as there are a great many preparations to be made for the church fête," he said, laying out the razors, "particularly as regards the jumble sale."

The jumble sale. I had almost managed to forget about it, or perhaps I was only in denial. I seemed to be doomed to attend bazaars and church fêtes no matter what century I went to.

"When is it to be held?" I asked, hoping he would say next month.

"The day after tomorrow," Baine said, draping a towel over his arm.

Perhaps we'd be gone by then. Professor Peddick would be eager to go on to Runnymede to see the meadow where the Magna Carta was signed, to say nothing of its excellent perch deeps.

Terence wouldn't want to go, of course, but he might not have any say in the matter. Mrs. Mering had taken a pronounced dislike to him, and I had a feeling she would like him even less when she found out he had designs on her daughter. And hadn't any money.

She might even pack us off directly after breakfast, pleading the preparations for the jumble sale, the incongruity could begin correcting itself, and I could take a nice long nap on the river while Terence rowed. If I hadn't killed myself with the straight razors before that.

"Would you care to have me shave you now, sir?" Baine said.

"Yes," I said, and bounded out of bed.

I needn't have worried about the clothes either. Baine fastened my braces and my collar, constructed the tie, and would have tied my shoes if I'd let him, I didn't know whether from gratitude or if this was the usual custom of the times. I would have to ask Verity.

"Which room is breakfast in?" I asked Baine.

"The breakfast room, sir," he said. "First door on your left."

I went tripping downstairs, feeling positively cheerful. A good old-fashioned English breakfast, bacon and eggs and orange marmalade, all served up by a butler, was a delightful prospect, and it was a beautiful day. Sun streamed in over the polished banisters and onto the portraits. Even Lady Schrapnell's Elizabethan ancestor looked cheerful.

I opened the first door to the left. Baine must have told me wrong. This was the dining room, almost entirely filled with a massive mahogany table and an even more massive sideboard with an assortment of covered silver dishes on it.

The table had cups and saucers and silverware on it, but no plates, and there was no one in the room. I turned to start back out and look for the breakfast room and nearly collided with Verity.

"Good morning, Mr. Henry," she said, "I hope you slept well."

She was wearing a pale-green dress with tiny pleats in the bodice and had a green ribbon bound round her piled-up auburn hair, and I obviously needed a good deal more sleep before I was over my time-lag. I noticed shadows under her green-brown eyes, but otherwise she was still the most beautiful creature I'd ever seen.

She went over to the sideboard. "Breakfast is served from the sideboard, Mr. Henry," she said, taking a flower-rimmed plate from a large stack. "The others will be down shortly."

She leaned toward me to hand me the plate. "I am *so* sorry I told Lady Schrapnell you knew where the bishop's bird stump was," she said. "I must have been more time-lagged than I realized, but that's no excuse, and I want you to know I'll do everything I can to help you find it. When's the last time anybody saw it?"

"I saw it on Saturday the ninth of November, 1940, after the Prayers for the RAF Service and Baked Goods Sale."

"And no one saw it after that?"

"No one's been able to get through after that till after the raid. The increased slippage around a crisis point, remember?"

Jane came in with a pot of marmalade, set it on the table, bobbed a curtsey, and left. Verity stepped over to the first of the covered dishes, which had a statuette of a flopping fish for a handle.

"And it wasn't found in the rubble after the raid?" she said, lifting the lid by the fish.

"No," I said. "Good Lord, what's that?" I was staring at a bed of blindingly yellow rice with strips of flaked white in it.

"It's kedgeree," she said, putting a small spoonful on her plate. "Curried rice and smoked fish."

"For breakfast?"

"It's an Indian dish. The Colonel's fond of it." She put the lid back on. "And none of the contemps mention having seen it from the ninth to the night of the raid?"

"It was listed in the order of service for Sunday the tenth, under the flower arrangements, so presumably it was there during the service."

She moved down to the next covered dish. This lid had a large antlered deer. I wondered briefly if they represented some sort of code, but the next one down was a snarling wolf, so I doubted it.

"When you saw it on the ninth," Verity said, "did you notice anything unusual about it?"

"You've never seen the bishop's bird stump, have you?"

"I mean, had it been moved? Or damaged? Did you notice anyone hanging about it or see anything suspicious?"

"You're still time-lagged, aren't you?" I asked.

*"No,"* she said indignantly. "The bishop's bird stump is missing, and it can't just have disappeared into thin air. So someone must have taken it, and if someone took it, there must be a clue to who it was. Did you notice anyone standing near it?"

"No," I said.

"Hercule Poirot says there's always something that no one noticed or thought was important," she said, picking up the Stag at Bay.

Inside was a mass of pungent-smelling brown objects. "What's that?"

"Devilled kidneys," she said, "braised in chutney and mustard. In Hercule Poirot mysteries, there's always one little fact that doesn't fit, and that's the key to the mystery." She picked up a charging bull by the horns. "This is cold ptarmigan."

"Aren't there any eggs and bacon?"

She shook her head. "Strictly for the lower classes." She held out a shellacked fish on a fork. "Kipper?"

I settled for porridge.

Verity took her plate and went over and sat down on the far side of the huge table. "What about when you were there after the raid?" she said, motioning me to sit down across from her. "Was there any sign of the bishop's bird stump having been in the fire?"

I opened my mouth to say, "The cathedral was completely destroyed," and then stopped, frowning. "Actually, there was. A charred flower stem. And we found the wrought-iron stand it stood on."

"Was the stem from the same kind of flower that was listed in the order of service?" Verity asked, and I was about to say there was no way to tell when Jane came in again, bobbed, and said, "Tea, ma'am?"

"Yes, thank you, Colleen," Verity said.

As soon as she'd gone, I said, "Why did you call the maid Colleen?"

"It's her name," she said, "but Mrs. Mering didn't think it was fashionable for a servant. Too Irish. English servants are what's *en vogue*."

"So she made her change it?"

"It was a common practice. Mrs. Chattisbourne calls all of her maids Gladys so she doesn't have to remember which is which. Weren't you prepped on this?"

"I wasn't prepped at all," I said. "Two hours of subliminals, real-time, which I was too time-lagged to hear. On the subservient status of women, mostly. And fish forks."

She looked appalled. "You weren't prepped? Victorian society's highly mannered. Breaches of etiquette are taken very seriously." She looked curiously at me. "How have you managed thus far?"

"For the past two days I've been on the river with an Oxford don who quotes Herodotus, a lovesick young man who quotes Tennyson, a bulldog, and a cat," I said. "I played it by ear."

"Well, that won't work here. You'll have to be prepped somehow. All right, listen," she said, leaning across the table, "here's the short course. Formality is the main thing. People don't say what they think. Euphemisms and politeness are the order of the day. No physical contact between the sexes. A man may take a lady's arm, or help her over a stile, or up the steps into a train. Unmarried men and women are never allowed to be alone together," she said, in spite of the fact that we seemed to be. "There must be a chaperone present."

As if on cue, Jane reappeared with two cups of tea and set them down in front of us.

"Servants are called by their first names," Verity said as soon as she'd gone, "except for the butler. He's Mr. Baine or Baine. And all cooks are Mrs., no matter what their marital status, so don't ask Mrs. Posey about her husband. This household has a parlormaid, that's Colleen—I mean, Jane—a scullery maid, a cook, a footman, a groom, a butler, and a gardener. It *had* an upstairs maid, a lady's maid, and a bootboy, but the Duchess of Landry stole them."

"Stole them?" I said, reaching for the sugar.

"They didn't eat sugar on their porridge," she said. "And you should have rung for the servant to pass it to you. Stealing each other's servants is their chief entertainment. Mrs. Mering stole Baine from Mrs. Chattisbourne and is currently in the process of trying to steal her bootboy. They didn't put milk on it either. No swearing in the presence of ladies."

"How about 'balderdash'?" I said. "Or 'pshaw'?"

"'Pshaw,' Mr. Henry?" Mrs. Mering said, sweeping in. "What are you pooh-poohing? Not our church fête, I hope? It benefits the restoration fund, *such* a worthwhile project, Mr. Henry. Our poor parish church is in such *desperate* need of restoration. Why, the baptismal font dates back to 1262. And the windows! Hopelessly mediaeval! If our fête is a success we hope to purchase all new ones!"

She heaped her plate with kippers and venison and wolf, sat down, and swept her napkin off the table and onto her lap. "The restoration project is all our curate Mr. Arbitage's doing. Until he came the vicar wouldn't even *hear* of restoring the church. I'm afraid he is quite old-fashioned in his thinking. He refuses even to consider the possibility of communication with the spirits."

Good man, I thought.

"Mr. Arbitage, on the other hand, *embraces* the idea of spiritism, and of speaking with our dear departed ones on the Other Side. Do you believe contact is possible with the Other Side, Mr. Henry?"

"Mr. Henry was inquiring about the church fête," Verity said. "I was just going to tell him about your clever idea of a jumble sale."

"O," Mrs. Mering said, looking flattered. "Have you ever been to a fête, Mr. Henry?"

"One or two," I said.

"Well, then, you know that there are donated fancy goods and jellies and needlework tables. *My* idea was that we also donate objects that we no longer have any use for, all sorts of things, dishes and bric-a-brac and books, a *jumble* of things!"

I was gazing at her in horror. This was the person who had started it all, the person responsible for all those endless jumble sales I'd been stuck at.

"You would be amazed, Mr. Henry, at the treasures people have in their attics and storerooms, sitting there covered in dust. Why, in my *own* attic I found a tea urn and a lovely celery dish. Baine, were you able to get the dents out of the tea urn?"

"Yes, madam," Baine said, pouring her coffee.

"Would you care for coffee, Mr. Henry?" Mrs. Mering asked.

I was surprised at how pleasant Mrs. Mering was being to me. It must be the politeness Verity had referred to.

Tossie came in, carrying Princess Arjumand, who had a large pink bow tied round her neck. "Good morning, Mama," she said, scanning the table for Terence.

"Good morning, Tocelyn," Mrs. Mering said. "Did you sleep well?"

"O yes, Mama," Tossie said, "now that my dearum-dearums pet is safely home." She snuggled the cat. "You slept cuddled next to me all night long, didn't you, sweetum-lovums?"

"Tossie!" Mrs. Mering said sharply. Tossie looked chagrined.

Obviously some sort of breach of etiquette, though I had no idea what. I would have to ask Verity.

Colonel Mering and Professor Peddick arrived, talking animatedly about the battle of Trafalgar. "Outnumbered twenty-seven to thirty-three," the Colonel was saying.

"Exactly my point," Professor Peddick said. "If it hadn't been for Nelson, they'd have lost the battle! It's character that makes history, not blind forces! Individual initiative!"

"Good morning, Papa," Tossie said, coming over to kiss the Colonel on the cheek.

"Good morning, Daughter." He glared at Princess Arjumand. "Doesn't belong in here."

"But she's had a terrible ordeal," Tossie said, carrying the cat over to the sideboard. "Look, Princess Arjumand, kippers," she said, put one on a plate, set it and the cat down, and smiled defiantly at Baine.

"Good morning, Mesiel," Mrs. Mering said to her husband. "Did you sleep well last night?"

"Tolerably," he said, peering under the wolf. "And you, Malvinia? Sleep well, my dear?"

This was apparently the opening Mrs. Mering had been waiting for. "I did not," she said, and paused dramatically. "There are spirits in this house. I heard them."

I knew I shouldn't have trusted Verity with her "The walls in these country houses are thick. One can't hear a thing through them."

"O, Mama," Tossie said breathlessly, "what did the spirits sound like?"

Mrs. Mering got a faraway look. "It was a strange, unearthly sound such as no living being could make. A sort of sobbing exhalation like breathing, though of course the spirits do not breathe, and then a . . ." she paused, searching for words, ". . . a shriek followed by a long painful gasp, as of a soul in torment. It was a dreadful, dreadful sound."

Well, I would agree with that.

"I felt as though it were trying to communicate with me, but could not," she said. "O, if only Madame Iritosky were here. I know she would be able to make the spirit speak. I intend to write to her this morning and ask her to come, though I fear she will not. She says she can only work in her own home."

With her own trapdoors and hidden wires and secret connecting passages, I thought, and supposed I should be grateful. At least she wasn't likely to show up and expose my harboring of Cyril.

"If she could have but heard the spirit's fearful cry, I know she would come to us," Mrs. Mering said. "Baine, has Mr. St. Trewes come down yet?"

"I believe he is coming momentarily," Baine said. "He took his dog for a walk."

Late for breakfast, *and* walking his dog. Two strikes against him, though Mrs. Mering didn't look as irritable as I'd thought she might.

"Hullo," Terence said, coming in, and without Cyril. "Sorry I'm late."

"That's perfectly all right," Mrs. Mering said, beaming at him. "Do sit down, Mr. St. Trewes. Would you care for tea or coffee?"

"Coffee," Terence said, smiling at Tossie.

"Baine, bring coffee for Mr. St. Trewes."

"We're all so delighted you've come," Mrs. Mering said. "I do hope you and your friends will be able to stay for our church fête. It will be such fun. We shall have a coconut shy and a fortuneteller, and Tocelyn will be baking a cake to raffle. Such an excellent cook, Tocelyn, and so accomplished. She plays the piano, you know, and speaks German *and* French. Don't you, Tossie, dear?"

"*Oui*, Mama," Tossie said, smiling at Terence.

I looked questioningly at Verity. She shrugged back an "I don't know."

"Professor Peddick, I do hope your pupils can spare you for a few days," Mrs. Mering was saying. "And Mr. Henry, *do* say you'll help us with the Treasure Hunt."

"Mr. Henry has been telling me he lived in the States," Verity said, and I turned and looked at her in astonishment.

"Truly?" Terence said. "You never told me that."

"It . . . it was when I was ill," I said. "I . . . was sent to . . . the States for treatment."

"Did you see Red Indians?" Tossie asked.

"I was in Boston," I stammered, silently cursing Verity.

"Boston!" Mrs. Mering cried. "Do you know the Fox sisters?"

"The Fox sisters?" I said.

"The Misses Margaret and Kate Fox. The founders of our spiritist movement. It was they who first received communications from the spirits by rapping."

"I'm afraid I didn't have that pleasure," I said, but she had already turned her attention back to Terence.

"Tocelyn embroiders beautifully, Mr. St. Trewes," she said. "You must see the lovely pillowcases she has sewn for our fancy goods stall."

"I am certain the person who purchases them will have sweet dreams," Terence said, smiling goopily at Tossie, " 'a dream of perfect bliss, too beautiful to last. . . .' "

The Colonel and the professor, still at Trafalgar with Nelson, pushed back their chairs and stood up, muttering, one after the other, "If you'll excuse me."

"Mesiel, where are you going?" Mrs. Mering said.

"Out to the fishpond," the Colonel said. "Show Professor Peddick my nacreous ryunkin."

"Do wear your greatcoat then," Mrs. Mering said. "And your wool scarf." She turned to me. "My husband has a weak chest and a tendency to catarrh."

Like Cyril, I thought.

"Baine, fetch Colonel Mering's greatcoat," she said, but they were already gone.

She turned back immediately to Terence. "Where do your people come from, Mr. St. Trewes?"

"Kent," he said, "which I always thought the fairest spot on earth till now."

"Might I be excused, Aunt Malvinia?" Verity said, folding her napkin. "I must finish my glove boxes."

"Of course," Mrs. Mering said absently. "How long have your family lived in Kent, Mr. St. Trewes?"

As Verity passed me, she dropped a folded note in my lap.

"Since 1066," Terence said. "Of course, we've improved the house since then. Most of it's Georgian. Capability Brown. You must come and visit us."

I unfolded the note under the table and sneaked a look at it. It read, "Meet me in the library."

"We should love to come," Mrs. Mering said eagerly. "Shouldn't we, Tocelyn?"

"*Oui*, Mama."

I waited for an opening and dived in. "If I might be excused, Mrs. Mering," I began.

"Absolutely *not*, Mr. Henry," she said. "Why, you haven't eaten a thing! You must have some of Mrs. Posey's eel pie. It is unparalleled."

It was, and so was the kedgeree, which she made Baine dump on my plate with a large shovel-like utensil. A kedgeree spoon, no doubt.

After some eels and as little kedgeree as possible, I made my escape and went to look for Verity, though I had no idea where the library was. I needed one of those diagrams like in Verity's detective novels.

I tried several doors and finally found her in a room lined from floor to ceiling with books.

"Where have you been?" Verity said. She was seated at a table covered with a litter of shells and pots of glue.

"Eating vile, unspeakable things," I said. "And answering questions about America. Why on earth did you tell them I'd been to America? I don't know anything about the States."

"Neither do they," she said imperturbably. "I had to do something. You haven't been prepped, and you're bound to make mistakes. They think all Americans are barbarians, so if you use the wrong fork, they'll put it down to your having spent time in the States."

"Thank you, I suppose," I said.

"Sit down," she said. "We need to plan our strategy."

I looked at the door, which had an old-fashioned key in the lock. "Should I lock the door?"

"It's not necessary," she said, selecting a flat pinkish shell. "The only person who ever comes in here is Baine. Mrs. Mering disapproves of reading."

"Then where did all this come from?" I said, indicating the rows of brown- and scarlet-bound books.

"They bought it," she said, swabbing glue on the shell.

"Bought what?"

"The library. From Lord Dunsany. The person Baine worked for before he came to the Chattisbournes. The Chattisbournes are who Mrs. Mering stole Baine from, though I think Baine actually chose to come. For the books." She stuck the shell down on the box. "Sit down. If anyone comes in, you're helping me with these." She held up a completed box. It was covered with shells of assorted sizes in the shape of a heart.

"That's absolutely hideous," I said.

"The entire Victorian era had the most atrocious taste," she said. "Be glad it's not hair wreaths."

"Hair wreaths?"

"Flowers made out of dead people's hair. The mother-of-pearl shells go along the edges," she said, showing me, "and then a row of cowrie shells." She shoved a glue pot at me. "I found out from Baine why Mrs. Mering's suddenly so friendly toward Terence. She looked him up in DeBrett's. He's rich, and he's the nephew of a peer."

"Rich?" I said. "But he didn't even have enough money to pay for the boat."

"The aristocracy are always in debt," she said, looking at a clamshell. "He's got five thousand a year, an estate in Kent, and he's second in line to the peerage. So," she said, discarding the clamshell, "our priority is to keep Tossie and Terence away from each other, which will be difficult with Mama matchmaking. Tossie's collecting things for the jumble sale this morning, and I'm going to send you with her. That'll keep them apart for at least half a day."

"What about Terence?" I said.

"I'm going to send him to Streatley after the Chinese lanterns for the fête. I want you to try to find out from Tossie if she knows any young men whose names begin with 'C.' "

"You've checked in the neighborhood for 'C''s, I suppose," I said.

She nodded. "The only two I've been able to discover are Mr. Cudden and Mr. Cawp, the farmer who's always drowning kittens."

"Sounds like a match made in heaven. What about Mr. Cudden?"

"He's married," she said glumly. "You'd think there'd be lots of Mr. C's. I mean, look at Dickens—David Copperfield, Martin Chuzzlewit, Bob Cratchet."

"Not to mention the Admirable Crichton," I said, "and Lewis Carroll. No, that won't work. It wasn't his real name. Thomas Carlyle. And G.K.

Chesterton. Eligible suitors all," I said. "What are you going to do while I'm with Tossie?"

"I'm going to search Tossie's room and try to find her diary. She's hidden it, and I had to cut my search short. Jane came in. But this morning they'll all be working on the fête, so I won't be interrupted. Failing that, I'll go through to Oxford and see what the forensics expert's been able to find out."

"Ask Warder how much slippage there was on the drop when you rescued Princess Arjumand," I said.

"Going through to Oxford with her, do you mean?" she said. "There's never any slippage on return drops."

"No," I said, "the drop where you came through and saw the cat."

"All right. We'd better get back in there." She stuck the cork in the glue pot, stood up, and rang for Baine.

"Baine," she said when he appeared, "have the carriage brought round immediately, and then come to the breakfast room."

"As you wish, miss," he said.

"Thank you, Baine," she said, picked up the shell-covered box, and led the way back to the breakfast room.

Mrs. Mering was still interrogating Terence. "O, how exquisite!" she said when Verity showed her the box.

"We still have a good deal to do for the fête, Aunt Malvinia," she said. "I so want the jumble sale to be a success. Have you your list?"

"Ring for Jane to bring it," Mrs. Mering said.

"She has gone to the vicarage to fetch the bunting," Verity said, and as soon as Mrs. Mering had left the room to get the list, "Mr. St. Trewes, may I prevail on you for a favor? The Chinese lanterns we had intended to string between the stalls have not been delivered. Would you be so good as to go to Streatley for them?"

"Baine can go," Tossie said. "Terence is to go with me to the Chattisbournes' this morning."

"Your mother cannot spare Baine, with the tea tent to be set up," Verity said. "Mr. Henry shall go with you. Baine," she said to the butler who had just come in, "bring Mr. Henry a basket in which to carry the jumble sale donations. Is the carriage waiting?"

"Yes, miss," he said, and left.

"But—" Tossie said, her mouth forming a pout.

"Here is the address," Verity said, handing Terence a sheet of paper, "and orders for the lanterns. This is *so* good of you," and hustled him out the front door before Tossie could even protest.

Baine brought the basket, and Tossie went to get her hat and gloves. "I don't see why Mr. Henry couldn't have gone for the lanterns," I heard her say to Verity as they went upstairs.

"Absence makes the heart grow fonder," Verity said. "Wear your hat with the polka-dot veil to show to Rose Chattisbourne."

Verity came back downstairs. "I'm impressed," I said.

"I've been taking lessons from Lady Schrapnell," she said. "While you're at the Chattisbournes', see if you can find out when Elliott Chattisbourne—he's the one whose clothes you're wearing—is coming home. She could have been secretly corresponding with him since he's been out in South Africa. Here comes Tossie."

Tossie fluttered down the stairs in the polka-dotted veil, carrying a reticule and a parasol, and we set off.

Baine ran to catch up with us. "Your hat, sir," he said breathlessly, handing me my boater.

My straw boater, which I had last seen floating down the river, the ribbon already beginning to fade pale blue onto the soggy straw. Baine had somehow restored it to its original state, the ribbon bright blue, the straw scrubbed and crisp.

"Thank you, Baine," I said. "I thought it was lost forever."

I put it on, feeling jauntier immediately and fully capable not only of keeping Tossie away from Terence but of being so charming she'd forget all about him.

"Shall we?" I said to Tossie and offered her my arm.

She looked up at me through the polka dots. "My cousin Verity says your hat makes you look feeble-minded," she said speculatively, "but I don't think it's *that* bad. Some men simply don't know how to wear hats. 'Don't you fink Mr. St. Twewes looks dashing in his boater?' my dearums Juju said to me this morning. 'Don't you fink he's the han'somest, han'somest mannums?' "

I had thought baby talk was bad, but baby talk from a cat—

"I knew a chap at school who lived near here," I said, changing the subject to something more productive. "I can't remember his name just now. Began with a 'C.' "

"Elliott Chattisbourne?"

"No, that's not it," I said. "It did begin with a 'C,' though."

"You knew him at school?" she said, pursing her lips. "Were you at Eton?"

"Yes," I said. Why not? "Eton."

"There's Freddie Lawrence. But he went to Harrow. Were you at school with Terence?"

"This was a medium-tallish chap. Good at cricket."

"And his name began with a 'C'?" She shook her curls. "I can't think of anyone. Does Terence play cricket?"

"He rows," I said, "and swims. He's a very good swimmer."

"I think he's terribly brave for rescuing Princess Arjumand," she said.

" 'Don't oo fink he's the bwavest knight in awl the world?' Juju asked me. '*I* fink he is.' "

This kept up the entire way to the Chattisbournes', which was just as well since I didn't know any other facts about Terence.

"Here we are," Tossie said, starting up the drive to a large neo-Gothic house.

Well, you survived that, I thought, and the rest of the morning's bound to go easier.

Tossie stepped up to the front door. I waited for her to ring the bell and then remembered it was the Victorian era and rang it for her, and then stepped back as the butler opened the door.

It was Finch. "Good morning, miss, sir," he said. "May I say who is calling?"

# CHAPTER FOURTEEN

A Surprise Appearance—Jeeves—In a Flower Garden—
Giggling—Dress Descriptions—An Overweight Cat—Sex and
Violence—Finch Is Not at Liberty to Say—Tales of the Wild
West—Amazing Treasures People Have in Their Attics—Home
Again—I Am Prepped—A Civilized Game—Bad News—Croquet
in Wonderland—More Bad News

I am not certain what I said or how we got in the house. It was all I could manage not to blurt out, "Finch! What are you doing here?"

It was obvious what he was doing. He was buttling. It was also obvious he had patterned himself on that greatest of all butlers, P.G. Wodehouse's Jeeves. He had the supercilious air, the correct speech, especially the poker-faced expression down cold. You'd have thought he'd never seen me before in his life.

He ushered us inside with a perfectly measured bow, said, "I will announce you," and started for the stairs, but he was too late.

Mrs. Chattisbourne and her four daughters were already hurrying down the stairs, burbling, "Tossie, dear, this *is* a surprise!"

She stopped at the foot of the staircase, and her daughters stopped, too, in a sort of ascending arrangement. They all, including Mrs. Chattisbourne, had turned-up noses and brownish-blonde hair.

"And who is this young gentleman?" Mrs. Chattisbourne said.

The girls giggled.

"Mr. Henry, madam," Finch said.

"So this is the young gentleman who found your cat," Mrs. Chattisbourne said. "We heard all about it from the Reverend Mr. Arbitage."

"O, no!" Tossie said. "It was Mr. St. Trewes who returned my poor lost Princess Arjumand to me. Mr. Henry is only his friend."

"Ah," Mrs. Chattisbourne said. "I am *so* pleased to meet you, Mr. Henry. Allow me to introduce my flower garden."

I had gotten so used to having people say nonsensical things to me in the last few days that it didn't even faze me.

She led me over to the stairs. "These are my daughters, Mr. Henry," she said, pointing up the stairs at them one by one. "Rose, Iris, Pansy, and my youngest, Eglantine. My own sweet nosegay, and *some* lucky gentlemen's," she squeezed my arm, "bridal bouquet."

The girls giggled in turn as she said their names and again at the end when she mentioned the bridal bouquet.

"Shall I serve refreshments in the morning room?" Finch said. "No doubt Miss Mering and Mr. Henry are fatigued from their walk."

"How marvellous of you to think of it, Finch," Mrs. Chattisbourne said, steering me toward the door on the right. "Finch is the most wonderful butler," she said. "He thinks of simply everything."

The Chattisbourne morning room looked exactly like the Merings' parlor, only floral. The carpet was strewn with lilies, the lamps were decorated with forget-me-nots and daffodils, and on a marble-topped table in the middle of the room was a poppy-painted vase with pink peonies in it.

It was just as crowded as the Merings', too, and being asked to sit down meant working my way through a maze of hyacinths and marigolds to a chair needlepointed in extremely realistic roses.

I sat down gingerly on it, almost afraid of thorns, and Mrs. Chattisbourne's four daughters sat down on a flowered sofa opposite and giggled.

I found out over the course of the morning that, except for Eglantine, the youngest, who looked about ten, they giggled at all times and at virtually everything that was said.

"Finch is an absolute gem!" Mrs. Chattisbourne said, for instance, and they giggled. "So efficient! He does things before we even know we want them done. Not at all like our last butler—what *is* his name, Tossie?"

"Baine," Tossie said.

"Oh, yes, *Baine*," she said with a sniff. "An appropriate name for a butler, I suppose, though I have always felt it is not the name that makes the butler, but the training. *Baine's* training was adequate, but hardly perfect. He was always reading books, as I recall. Finch never reads," she said proudly.

"Wherever did you find him?" Tossie said.

"That's the most amazing part of the whole thing," Mrs. Chattisbourne said. (Giggles.) "I went over to the vicar's to take him our dresser scarves for the fête, and he was sitting in the vicar's parlor. It seems he'd been employed by a family who'd gone out to India, and he was unable to accompany them because of a sensitivity to curry."

A sensitivity to curry.

"The vicar said, 'Do you know of anyone in need of a butler?' *Can* you imagine? It was Fate." (Giggles.)

"It sounds highly irregular to me," Tossie said.

"Oh, of course Thomas insisted on interviewing him, and he had the most glowing references."

All of them from people who'd gone out to India, no doubt, I thought.

"Tossie, I should be cross at your dear mother for hiring away—" she frowned in thought, "—I've forgotten the name again. . . ."

"*Baine*," Tossie said.

"For hiring away Baine, but how can I be when I've found the perfect replacement?"

The perfect replacement came into the room bearing a flowered tray with a cut-glass decanter and glasses on it. "Currant cordial!" Mrs. Chattisbourne cried. "The very thing! Do you see what I mean?"

Finch began pouring the cordial and passing it around.

"Mr. Henry," Mrs. Chattisbourne said. "Are you at school with Mr. St. Trewes?"

"Yes," I said. "At Oxford. Balliol."

"Are you married?" Eglantine asked.

"Eglantine!" Iris said. "It's rude to ask people if they're married."

"You asked Tossie if he was married," Eglantine said. "I heard you whispering."

"Hush," Iris said, turning, appropriately enough, carnation pink. (Giggles.)

"What part of England do you come from, Mr. Henry?" Mrs. Chattisbourne said.

It was time to change the subject. "I wished to thank you for your son's loan of clothing," I said, sipping the currant cordial. It was better than eel pie. "Is he here?"

"Oh, no," Mrs. Chattisbourne said. "Didn't the Merings tell you? Elliott is in South Africa."

"He's a mining engineer," Tossie volunteered.

"We have just had a letter from him," Mrs. Chattisbourne said. "Where is it, Pansy?"

The girls all got up and began looking for it with a good deal of giggling.

"Here it is, madam," Finch said, and handed it to Mrs. Chattisbourne.

"Dear Mother and Father and Posies," she read. "Here at last is the good long letter I had promised you," and it became obvious she intended to read the entire thing.

"You must miss your son a great deal," I said, trying to forestall her. "Will he be home soon?"

"Not until his two years' tour of duty is up, eight months from now, I'm afraid. Of course, were one of his sisters to marry, he would naturally come home for the wedding." (Giggles.)

She launched into the letter. Two paragraphs convinced me that Elliott was as silly as his sisters and had never been in love with anyone but himself in his life.

Three paragraphs convinced me Tossie didn't care two pins for him either. She looked positively bored.

By paragraph four I was wondering why Elliott had escaped being named Rhododendron or Mugwort, and gazing at the Chattisbournes' cat.

It was lying on a violet petit point footstool, and it was so enormous only a few violets showed round the edges. It was yellow, with yellower stripes, and even yellower eyes, and it returned my gaze with a heavy-lidded languor which I was beginning to feel myself, what with the currant cordial and Elliott Chattisbourne's prose. I thought longingly of being back at Muchings End. Under a tree. Or in a hammock.

"What are you wearing to the fête, Rose?" Tossie asked when Mrs. Chattisbourne paused to turn over the letter to the third page.

Rose giggled and said, "My blue voile with the lace insets."

"I'm wearing my white dotted swiss," Pansy said, and the older girls leaned forward and began to chatter.

Eglantine went over to the footstool, picked up the cat, and dumped it on my lap. "This is our cat, Miss Marmalade."

"*Mrs.* Marmalade, Eglantine," Mrs. Chattisbourne said, and I wondered if cats were given honorifics, like cooks.

"And how are you, Mrs. Marmalade?" I said, chucking the cat under the chin. (Giggles.)

"What are *you* wearing to the fête, Tossie?" Iris asked.

"The new dress Papa had made for me in London," Tossie said.

"Oh, what's it like?" Pansy cried.

"I've written a description of it in my diary," Tossie said.

Which some poor forensics expert will spend weeks deciphering, I thought.

"Finch," Tossie said, "do hand me that basket," and when he did, she reached under the embroidered cloth and brought out a cordovan leatherbound book with a gold lock.

And there went Verity's hopes of stealing a look at it while we were gone. I wondered if I could possibly sneak it out of the basket on the way home.

Tossie carefully unclasped a delicate gold chain with a tiny key on it from her wrist and unlocked the diary, and then painstakingly refastened it.

Perhaps I could ask Finch to steal it for me. Or perhaps he'd already thought of it, since Mrs. Chattisbourne claimed he could read minds.

"White mignonette organdie," Tossie read, "with an underdress of lilac silk. The bodice is made with a lace front, edged with a ruffle embroidered in ingrained colored silks of the softest shades of heliotrope, lilac, and periwinkle, worked in a pattern of violets and forget-me-nots inset with—"

The dress description was even longer than Elliott Chattisbourne's letter. I gave myself over to some serious petting of Mrs. Marmalade.

She was not only enormous, but extremely fat. Her stomach was huge and felt oddly lumpy. I hoped she wasn't suffering from something. An early form of the distemper that had wiped all the cats out in 2004 had been around in Victorian times, hadn't it?

"—and a pleated lilac sash with a rosette at the side," Tossie read. "The skirt is prettily draped and embroidered with a border of the same flowers. The sleeves are gathered, with shoulder and elbow ruffles. Lilac ribbons band—"

I felt cautiously along her underside as I petted her. Several tumors. But if it was leptovirus, it must be the early stages. Mrs. Marmalade's fur was soft and sleek and she seemed perfectly happy. She was purring contentedly, her paws kneading happily into my trouser leg.

I was clearly still suffering from Slowness in Thinking. She doesn't seem ill at all, I thought, even though she looks as though she's about to explode—

"Good Lord," I said. "This cat is pre—" and was struck in the back of the neck with a sharp object.

I stopped in mid-word.

Finch, behind me, said, "I beg your pardon, madam, there's a gentleman here to see Mr. Henry."

"To see me? But I—" and got clipped again.

"If you will excuse me, ladies," I said, made some sort of bow, and followed Finch to the door.

"Mr. Henry has spent the last two years in America," I heard Tossie say as I left the room.

"Ah," Mrs. Chattisbourne said.

Finch led me down the corridor and into the library, and pulled the door shut behind us.

"I know, no swearing in the presence of ladies," I said, rubbing my neck. "You didn't have to hit me."

"I did not strike you for swearing, sir," he said, "though you are quite right. You should not have done it in polite company."

"What did you hit me with anyway?" I said, feeling gingerly along my neckbone. "A blackjack?"

"A salver, sir," he said, pulling a lethal-looking silver tray out of his pocket. "I had no alternative, sir. I had to stop you."

"Stop me from what?" I said. "And what are you doing here anyway?"

"I am here on an assignment for Mr. Dunworthy."

"What sort of an assignment? Were you sent to help Verity and me?"

"No, sir," he said.

"Well, then, why are you here?"

He looked uncomfortable. "I am not at liberty to say, sir, except that I am here on a . . ." he cast about for a word, ". . . related project. I am on a different time-track from you, and therefore have access to information you have not discovered yet. If I were to tell you, it might interfere with your mission, sir."

"And hitting me on the back of the neck isn't interfering?" I said. "I think you've cracked a vertebra."

"I had to stop you, sir, from commenting on the cat's condition," he said. "In Victorian society, discussion of sex in mixed company was utterly taboo. It was not your fault that you did not know. You weren't properly prepped. I told Mr. Dunworthy I thought sending you without training and in your condition was a bad idea, but he was adamant that you should be the one to return Princess Arjumand."

"He was?" I said. "Why?"

"I am not at liberty to say, sir."

"And I wasn't going to say anything about sex," I protested. "All I intended to say was that the cat was preg—"

"Or anything resulting from sex, sir, or relating to it in any way." He lowered his voice and leaned toward me. "Girls were kept completely ignorant of the facts of life until their wedding night, when I'm afraid it proved a considerable shock to some of them. Women's bosoms or figures were never mentioned, and their legs were referred to as limbs."

"So what should I have said? That the cat was expecting? In the club? In a family way?"

"You should not have said anything at all on the subject. The fact of pregnancy in people *and* animals was studiously ignored. You shouldn't have referred to it at all."

"And after they're born and there are half a dozen kittens running all over the place, am I supposed to ignore that as well? Or ask if they were found under a cabbage leaf?"

Finch looked uncomfortable. "That's another reason, sir," he said obscurely. "We don't want to draw any more attention to the situation than necessary. We don't want to cause another incongruity."

"Incongruity?" I said. "What are you talking about?"

"I'm not at liberty to say. When you return to the morning room, I would refrain from all mention of the cat."

He truly did sound like Jeeves. "You've obviously been prepped," I said admiringly. "When did you have time to learn so much about the Victorian era?"

"I'm not at liberty to say," he said, looking pleased. "But I can say I feel as though this is the job I was born to."

"Well, since you're so good at it, tell me what I *am* supposed to say when I go back in there. Who am I supposed to say was here to see me?" I said. "I don't know anyone here."

"It won't be a problem, sir," he said, opening the library door with a gloved hand.

"Won't be a problem? What do you mean? I'll have to say something."

"No, sir. They will not care why you were called away, so long as it has afforded them the opportunity to discuss you in your absence."

"Discuss me?" I said, alarmed. "You mean as to my authenticity?"

"No, sir," he said, looking every inch the butler. "As to your marriageability." He led me across the corridor, bowed slightly, and opened the door with a gloved hand.

He was right. There was a sudden caught-out silence in the room, and then a spasm of giggles.

Mrs. Chattisbourne said, "Tocelyn has just been telling us about your brush with death, Mr. Henry."

When I almost said "pregnant"? I wondered.

"When your boat capsized," Pansy said eagerly. "But I suppose it is nothing compared to your adventures in America."

"Have you ever been scalped?" Eglantine said.

"Eglantine!" Mrs. Chattisbourne said.

Finch appeared in the door. "I beg your pardon, madam," he said, "but will Miss Mering and Mr. Henry be staying to lunch?"

"Oh, do stay, Mr. Henry!" the girls chimed. "We want to hear all about America!"

I spent lunch regaling them with a story of stagecoaches and tomahawks I'd stolen from Nineteenth-Century lectures I wished now I'd paid more attention to, and watching Finch. He signalled the proper utensil to use by whispering, "The fork with the three tines," in my ear as he set the courses in front of me and by signalling discreetly from the sideboard as I held their attention with lines like, "That night sitting round the campfire, we could hear their tomtoms in the darkness, beating, beating, beating." (Giggles.)

After lunch, Iris, Rose, and Pansy begged us to stay for a game of charades, but Tossie said we must go, and carefully relocked her diary and put it, not in the basket, but in her reticule. "Oh, but can't you stay for just a short while?" Pansy Chattisbourne begged.

Tossie said we still had to pick up contributions from the vicar's, for which I was grateful. I had had hock and claret at lunch and that, combined with the currant cordial and the residual effects of time-lag, made me want nothing but a long afternoon nap.

"Shall we see you at the fête, Mr. Henry?" Iris said, giggling.

I'm afraid so, I thought, hoping the vicar's wasn't far.

It wasn't, but first we had to stop at the Widow Wallace's (for a sauceboat and a banjo missing two strings), the Middlemarches' (a teapot with the spout broken off, a vinegar cruet, and a game of *Authors* missing several cards), and Miss Stiggins's (a bird cage, a set of four statuettes representing the Fates, a copy of *Through the Looking Glass,* a fish slice, and a ceramic thimble inscribed "Souvenir of Margate").

Since the Chattisbournes had already given us a hat pin holder, a cushion with crewelwork violets and sweet peas, an egg boiler, and a cane with a carved dog's head, the basket was already nearly full, and I had no idea how I was going to carry it all home. Luckily, all the vicar had to donate was a large cracked gilt-framed mirror.

"I will send Baine for it," Tossie said and we started back.

The walk home was a repeat of the walk there, except that I was more laden and a good deal more tired. Tossie prattled on about Juju and "bwave, bwave Tewence," and I thought about how glad I was my name didn't begin with a "C," and focused on finding a hammock.

Baine met us at the end of the drive and relieved me of my basket, and Cyril came running out to greet me. His unfortunate tendency to tilt to port, however, brought him up to Tossie's feet, and she began to cry, "O naughty, naughty, *bad* creature!" and emit little screamlets.

"Come here, Cyril, boy!" I called, clapping my hands, and he ambled over happily, wagging his whole body. "Did you miss me, boy?"

"What, ho, the travellers return," Terence called, waving from the lawn. " 'Back to the white walls of their long-left home.' You're just in time. Baine is setting up the wickets for a croquet match."

"A croquet match!" Tossie cried. "What fun!" and ran up to change her clothes.

"A croquet match?" I said to Verity, who was watching Baine pound stakes into the grass.

"It was this or lawn tennis," Verity said, "which I was afraid you hadn't been prepped in."

"I haven't been prepped in croquet either," I said, looking at the banded wooden mallets.

"It's a very simple game," Verity said, handing me a yellow ball. "You hit the ball through the wickets with a mallet. How did this morning go?"

"I was once a scout with Buffalo Bill," I said, "and I'm engaged to Pansy Chattisbourne."

She didn't smile. "What did you find out about Mr. C?"

"Elliott Chattisbourne's not coming home for another eight months," I said. I explained how I'd asked her about the chap whose name I'd forgotten. "She couldn't think of anyone it might be. But that's not the most interesting thing I—"

Tossie came running over in a pink-and-white peppermint-striped sailor dress and a large pink bow, holding Princess Arjumand in her arms. "Juju does so love to watch the balls," she said, setting her on the ground.

"And bat them," Verity said. "Mr. Henry and I shall be partners," she said. "And you and Mr. St. Trewes."

"Mr. St. Trewes, we are to be partners," she cried, running over to where Terence was supervising Baine.

"I thought the object was to keep Tossie and Terence apart," I said.

"It is," Verity said, "but I have to talk to you."

"And I have to talk to you," I said. "You'll never guess who I saw over at the Chattisbournes'. Finch."

"Finch?" she said blankly. "Mr. Dunworthy's secretary?"

I nodded. "He's their butler."

"What's he doing here?"

"He wouldn't tell me. He said it was 'a related project,' and that he couldn't tell me without interfering with ours."

"Are you ready?" Tossie called from the stake.

"Nearly," Verity said. "All right. The rules of the game are perfectly simple. You score points by hitting your ball through a course of six wickets twice, the four outside hoops, the center hoops, then back again in the opposite direction. Each turn is one stroke. If your ball goes through the wicket you get a continuation stroke. If your ball hits another ball, you get a croquet stroke and a continuation stroke, but if your ball goes through two hoops in one stroke, you only get one stroke. After you hit a ball, you can't hit it again till you've gone through your next hoop, except for the first hoop. If you hit a ball you've hit, you lose your turn."

"Are you *ready?*" Tossie called.

"Nearly," Verity said to her. "Those are the boundaries," she said to me, pointing with her mallet, "North, South, East, and West. That's the yard line, and that's the baulk line. Is all that clear?"

"Perfectly," I said. "Which color am I?"

"Red," she said. "You start from the baulk line."

"*Ready?*" Tossie called.

"Yes," Verity nodded.

"I go first," Tossie said, stooping gracefully and putting her ball on the grass.

Well, and how difficult could it be? I thought, watching Tossie line up her shot. A dignified Victorian game, played by children and young women in long, trailing dresses on lush green lawns. A civilized game.

Tossie turned, smiled prettily at Terence, and tossed her curls. "I hope I make a good shot," she said, and gave the ball a mighty whack that sent it through the first two hoops and halfway across the lawn.

She smiled surprisedly, asked, "Do I get another shot?" and whacked it again.

This time it nearly hit Cyril, who had lain down for a nap in the shade.

"Interference," Tossie said. "It hit its nose."

"Cyril hasn't got a nose," Verity said, placing her ball a mallet's head behind the first hoop. "My turn."

She didn't hit her ball quite so violently as Tossie had, but it wasn't a tap either. It went through the first hoop, and her next shot brought her within two feet of Tossie's ball.

"Your turn, Mr. St. Trewes," Tossie said, moving so her long skirt covered her ball. After his shot, when she walked over to him, her ball was a good yard farther away from Verity.

I went over to Verity. "She cheats," I said.

She nodded. "I wasn't able to find Tossie's diary," she said.

"I know. She had it with her. She read the dress description to the Chattisbourne girls."

"Your turn, Mr. Henry," Tossie said, leaning on her croquet mallet.

Verity had not said anything about the proper grip, and I hadn't been paying attention. I put my ball down by the wicket and took hold of the mallet with a sort of cricket bat grip.

"Fault!" Tossie called. "Mr. Henry's ball isn't the proper length from the hoop. You lose a turn, Mr. Henry."

"He does not," Verity said. "Move your ball back the width of a mallet head."

I did and then hit the ball more or less the right direction, though not through the hoop.

"My turn," Tossie said and thwacked Verity's ball completely off the court and into the hedge. "Sorry," she said, simpered demurely, and did the same thing to Terence's.

"I thought you said this was a civilized game," I said to Verity, crawling under the hedge to retrieve her ball.

"I said simple," she said.

I picked up the ball.

"Pretend you're still looking for it," Verity said under her breath. "After I searched Tossie's room, I went through to Oxford."

"Did you find out how much slippage there was on your drop?" I said, prying branches apart.

"No," she said, looking solemn. "Warder was too busy."

I was about to say that Warder always thought she was too busy, when she said, "The new recruit—I don't know his name—the one who was working with you and Carruthers—is stuck in the past."

"In the marrows field?" I said, thinking of the dogs.

"No, in Coventry. He was supposed to come through after he'd finished the rubble, but he hasn't."

"He probably couldn't find the net," I said, thinking of him messing with his pocket torch.

"That's what Carruthers said, but Mr. Dunworthy and T.J. are worried it's connected to the incongruity. They've sent Carruthers back to look for him."

"It's your *turn,* Verity," Tossie said impatiently. She started over to us. "Haven't you found it yet?"

"Here it is," I called and emerged from under the hedge, holding it aloft.

"It went out here," Tossie said, pointing with her foot to a spot several miles from where she hit it out.

"It's like playing with the Red Queen," I said, and handed Verity the ball.

My only goal on my next three turns was to get my ball on the same side of the court as Verity's, a goal that was repeatedly thwarted by "Off With Her Head!" Mering.

"I've got it," I said, limping over to Verity after one of Tossie's shots had sent Terence's ball straight into my shin, at which point Cyril had got up and moved to the far side of the lawn. "Mr. C is the physician who's called in to doctor Tossie's croquet casualties. What else did you find out?"

Verity lined up her shot carefully. "I found out who Terence married."

"Please don't say it was Tossie," I said, standing on my good leg and rubbing my shin.

"No," she said. She hit the ball neatly through the hoop. "Not Tossie. Maud Peddick."

"But that's good, isn't it?" I said. "That means I didn't ruin things by making Terence miss meeting Maud."

She pulled a folded sheet of paper out of her sash and handed it surreptitiously to me.

"What's this?" I said, sticking it in my breast pocket. "An excerpt from Maud's diary?"

"No," she said. "She's apparently the only woman in the entire Victorian era who didn't keep a diary. It's a letter from Maud St. Trewes to her younger sister."

"Your ball, Mr. Henry!" Tossie called.

"Second paragraph," Verity said.

I gave the red ball an enthusiastic whack that sent it straight past Terence's ball and into the center of the lilacs.

"I say, too bad!" Terence said.

I nodded and went crashing into the lilacs after it.

"Farewell, dear friend," Terence called gaily, waving his mallet. " 'Farewell! For in that fatal word—howe'er we promise—hope—believe—there breathes despair.' "

I found the ball, picked it up, and moved into the thickest part of the lilacs. I unfolded the letter. It was written in a delicate, spidery hand. "Dearest Isabel," it read, "I am so happy to hear of your engagement. Robert is a fine young man, and I only hope you will be as happy as Terence and I are. You worry that you met on the steps of an ironmonger's, a singularly unromantic location. Do not fret. My darling Terence and I first met at a railway station. I was standing with my Aunt Amelia on the platform of Oxford Railway Station—"

I stood there looking down at the letter. The platform of Oxford Railway Station.

"—scarcely a romantic location, yet I knew instantly, there amidst the luggage vans and steamer trunks, that he was my true mate."

Only she hadn't. I had been there, and she and her aunt had hired a fly and gone on.

"Can't you find it?" Terence called.

I hastily folded the letter and stuck it back in my pocket. "Here it is," I said, and emerged from the bushes.

"It went out here," Tossie said, indicating a totally fictitious point with her foot.

"Thank you, Miss Mering," I said and, measuring one mallet head's length from the edge with my mallet, placed it on the grass, and prepared to hit it again.

"Your turn is ended," Tossie said, going over to her ball. "It's my turn," she said, giving it an enormous whack that sent my ball right back into the lilacs.

"Roquet," she said, smiling sweetly. "Two strokes."

"Isn't she a topping girl?" Terence said, helping me look for my ball.

No, I thought, and even if she were, you're not supposed to be in love with her. You're supposed to be in love with Maud. You were supposed to meet her at the railway station, and this is my fault, my fault, my fault.

"Mr. Henry, it's your turn," Tossie said impatiently.

"Oh," I said and hit blindly at the nearest ball.

"Your fault, Mr. Henry," Tossie said impatiently. "You're dead."

"What?"

"You're dead on that ball, Mr. Henry," she said. "You've hit it once already. You can't hit it again till you've gone through the hoop."

"Oh," I said, and aimed for the wicket instead.

"Not *that* hoop," Tossie said, shaking her blonde curls at me. "I call a fault for attempting to skip a hoop."

"Sorry," I said, trying to focus.

"Mr. Henry is used to playing according to the American rules," Verity said.

I went over and stood next to her, watching Tossie line up her shot, setting it up like a billiards shot, calculating how the balls would ricochet off each other.

"There's worse," Verity said. "One of their grandsons was an RAF pilot in the Battle of Britain. He flew the first bombing raid on Berlin."

"Terence!" Tossie said. "Your *animal* is in the way of my double roquet."

Terence obediently went to shift Cyril. Tossie sighted along her mallet, measuring the angles at which the balls would collide, calculating the possibilities.

I stood there, watching Tossie line up her shot. Verity didn't say anything. She didn't have to. I knew all about that first bombing raid. It was in September of 1940, in the middle of the Battle of Britain, and Hitler had vowed that bombs would never fall on the Fatherland, and when they did, he had ordered the full-scale bombing of London. And then, in November, of Coventry.

Tossie swung her mallet. Her ball hit mine, ricocheted off, hit Verity's, and went straight through the hoop.

That bombing raid had saved the RAF, which the Luftwaffe had badly outnumbered. If the Luftwaffe hadn't switched to civilian bombing when they did, they would have won the Battle of Britain. And Hitler would have invaded.

# CHAPTER FIFTEEN

Nocturnal Visitors—A Fire—More Similarities to the *Titanic*—A
Spirit—Sleepwalking—Pearl Harbor—Fish—A Conversation with
a Workman—Finch—Up to No Good—Verity and I Go Boating
on the River—Proposals in Latin, Advantages and Disadvantages
of—Napoleon's Health Problems—Sleep—Similarity Between
Literature and Real Life—An Announcement

My second night at Muchings End was just as restful as the first. Terence
came in to ask me what Tossie had said about him while we were at the
Chattisbournes' and didn't I think her eyes were like "stars of twilight
fair," Cyril had to be carried down the stairs, and Baine brought me cocoa
and asked me if it was true that everyone in America carried a firearm.

I told him no.

"I have also heard that Americans are less concerned with ideas of class,
and that societal barriers are less rigid there."

I wondered what class had to do with guns and if he was considering
taking up a life of crime.

"It is certainly a place where everyone is free to seek his fortune," I said.
"And does."

"Is it true the industrialist Andrew Carnegie was the son of a coal miner?" he asked, and when I said I thought so, poured my cocoa and thanked me again for finding Princess Arjumand. "It is a delight to see how happy Miss Mering is now that her pet is back."

I thought she was happy because she'd trounced everyone at croquet, but I didn't say so.

"If there is ever anything I can do, sir, to return the favor—"

You wouldn't be willing to fly a bombing mission to Berlin, would you? I thought.

At the end of the croquet game, while Tossie was busy committing mayhem on Terence's ball, Verity had whispered to me to be certain I destroyed Maud's letter, that we were in no position to risk another incongruity. So as soon as Baine had left, I locked the door, opened the window, and held it over the flame of the kerosene lamp.

The paper flared up, curling at the edges. A fragment of it flew rapidly up, still burning, and over to the bouquet of dried flowers on the bureau. I leaped after it, crashing into the chair and making a wild grab that only sent it closer to the dried flowers.

Wonderful. In trying not to cause an incongruity, I was going to set the house on fire.

I made another slashing grab, and the burning paper twirled lightly out of my reach and settled slowly toward the floor. I dived under it, hands cupped to catch it, but it had already burnt up completely before it reached them, turned to ash and nonsignificance.

There was a scratching at the door, and I opened it to find Princess Arjumand and Verity. The cat promptly jumped up on the pillows and draped herself decoratively over them, and Verity perched on the end of the bed.

"Look," I said. "I don't think you have any business going through again. You've already made two trips in twenty-four hours, and—"

"I've already been," she said, smiling happily. "And I've got good news."

"Is it actually good news," I said skeptically, "or are you just happy because of the time-lag?"

"It's good news," she said, and then frowned. "At least they say it is. I wanted to see what they'd found out about the grandson and the bombing raid. T.J. says the raid on Berlin isn't a crisis point. He says there's no increased slippage either at the airfield *or* in Berlin, and he ran sims on the bombing raid, and the absence of Terence's grandson had no long-term effect in any of them. Can I have your cocoa?"

"Yes," I said. "Why didn't it?"

She scrambled off the bed and went over to the nightstand. "Because there were eighty-one planes involved and twenty-nine of them dropped bombs on Berlin," she said, pouring cocoa. "One pilot wouldn't have made a difference to the outcome, particularly since it wasn't the amount of damage done that made Hitler retaliate, but the idea of bombs falling on the Fatherland. And there were three more raids after that." She brought the cup and saucer over to the bed and sat down.

I had forgotten that there had been four raids. Good. That meant redundancy.

"And that's not all," she said, sipping cocoa. "Mr. Dunworthy says there's every indication that Goering had already decided to bomb London, and the bombing raid was simply an excuse. So he said not to worry, he can't see any way it would have changed the course of the war, but—"

I had known there was a "but."

"—there *is* a crisis point associated with the bombing that we should know about. It's August the twenty-fourth, the night the two German planes accidentally bombed London."

I knew about that. It was one of Professor Peddick's instances of individual action. And of accident and chance. The two German planes had been part of a big bombing raid on an aircraft factory at Rochester and the oil storage tanks at Thames Haven. The lead planes had been equipped with pathfinders, but the others hadn't, and two of the planes had got separated from the others, run into flak, and decided to jettison their bombs and run for home. Unfortunately, they had been over London at the time, and their bombs had destroyed the church of St. Giles, Cripplegate, and killed civilians.

In retaliation, Churchill had ordered the raid on Berlin, and in retaliation for *that*, Hitler had ordered the bombing of London in retaliation for the raid on Berlin. This is the cat that killed the rat that—

"Mr. Dunworthy and T.J. can't find any connection between Terence's grandson and the two German planes," Verity said, sipping cocoa, "but they're checking on it. And there's the possibility, since he was an RAF pilot, that he did something—shot down a Luftwaffe plane or something—that was pivotal. They're checking on that, too."

"And in the meantime, what are we supposed to do?"

"Everything we can to contain the situation and, if possible, get Terence back to Oxford to meet Maud. So tomorrow I want you to talk to Professor Peddick and convince him he needs to return to Oxford to see his sister and his niece. I'll work on Terence and make another stab at the diary."

"Do you think that's a good idea?" I said. "I've been thinking, this is a chaotic system, which means cause and effect aren't linear. Perhaps we're just making things worse by trying to fix them. Look at the *Titanic*. If they hadn't done anything to try to avoid the iceberg, they'd have—"

"Hit it head-on," Verity said.

"Yes, and the ship would have been damaged, but it wouldn't have sunk. It was their trying to turn it that made the iceberg scrape along the watertight compartments so that she went down like a stone."

"So you think we should just let Tossie and Terence get engaged?" she said.

"I don't know," I said. "Perhaps if we stop trying to keep them apart, Terence will realize what Tossie's really like and get over his infatuation."

"Perhaps," Verity said, eating cake seriously. "On the other hand, if somebody'd put enough lifeboats on the *Titanic* to begin with, nobody would have drowned."

She finished her cocoa and took the cup and saucer back over to the nightstand.

"What about the slippage in 2018? Have they found out what's causing that?" I said.

She shook her head. "Mrs. Bittner couldn't remember anything. 2018 was the year Fujisaki did his first work on the possibility of incongruities occurring, and they made modifications to the net so it would shut down automatically if the slippage became too great, but that was in September. The area of increased slippage was in April."

She opened the door and peered out. "Perhaps tomorrow morning Mr. C will come to help set up for the fête, and we won't have to do anything," she whispered.

"Or we'll hit an iceberg," I whispered back.

I realized as soon as I'd shut the door behind her that I hadn't asked her about Finch.

I waited five minutes to make sure Verity had made it safely back to her room and then put on my bathrobe and tiptoed carefully down the corridor, carefully avoiding the obstacles in the dark: Laocoön, whose situation I could empathize with; fern; bust of Darwin; umbrella stand.

I tapped softly on Verity's door.

She opened it immediately, looking upset. "You're not supposed to rap," she whispered, looking anxiously down the corridor to Mrs. Mering's room.

"Sorry," I whispered, sidling in the door.

Verity shut the door carefully. It made a soft snick. "What do you want?" she whispered.

"I forgot to ask you if you found out what Finch was doing here," I whispered back.

"Mr. Dunworthy wouldn't tell me," she said, looking worried. "He told me the same thing Finch told you, that it was a 'related project.' I think he was sent to drown Princess Arjumand."

"What?" I said, forgetting I was supposed to whisper. "*Finch?* You're joking."

She shook her head. "The forensics expert translated part of one of the references to Princess Arjumand. It said '. . . poor drowned Princess Arjumand.' "

"But how do they know that wasn't written while they were still looking for her? And why would they send Finch? He wouldn't harm a fly."

"I don't know," she said. "Perhaps they don't trust us to do it, and Finch was the only person available to send."

I could believe that, given Lady Schrapnell's penchant for recruiting anyone who wasn't nailed down. "But Finch?" I said, unconvinced. "And if that's what he's supposed to be doing, why would they send him to Mrs. Chattisbourne's instead of here?"

"They probably think Mrs. Mering will steal him away."

"*You* have had too many drops. We will talk about this in the morning," I said, looked out into the pitch-black hall, and slid out the door.

Verity shut the door silently behind me and I started back. Umbrella stand—

"Mesiel!" Mrs. Mering's voice cried. The corridor sprang into light. "I knew it!" Mrs. Mering said, and advanced on me holding a kerosene lamp.

The top of the stairs was too far away to make a run for it, and anyway, Baine was coming up them, carrying a candle. There wasn't even time to move away from my incriminating location in front of Verity's door. This was hardly what Mr. Dunworthy meant by "containing the situation."

I wondered if I could get away with saying I had just been downstairs to get a book. Without a candle. And where was said book? For a fantastic moment, I wondered if I could claim I was sleepwalking, like the hero in *The Moonstone*.

"I was—" I said, and was cut off by Mrs. Mering.

"I *knew* it!" she said. "You heard it, too, Mr. Henry, didn't you?"

Tossie's door opened and she peeked out, her hair in rag curlers. "Ma*ma*, what is it?"

"A spirit!" Mrs. Mering said. "Mr. Henry heard it, too, didn't you?"

"Yes," I said. "I had just come out to investigate. I thought it was an intruder, but there was no one here."

"Did you hear it, Baine?" Mrs. Mering demanded. "A rapping sound, very faint, and then a sort of whispering sound?"

"No, madam," Baine said. "I was in the breakfast room, setting out the silver for breakfast."

"But *you* heard it, Mr. Henry," Mrs. Mering said. "I *know* you did. You were white as a sheet when I came out in the corridor. There was a rapping and then whispers and a sort of—"

"Ethereal moan," I said.

"Exactly!" Mrs. Mering said. "I think there must be more than one spirit and they are speaking to one another. Did you see anything, Mr. Henry?"

"A sort of glimmer in white," I said, in case she'd seen Verity shutting the door, "just for a moment, and then it vanished."

"O!" Mrs. Mering said excitedly. "Mesiel! Come here! Mr. Henry has seen a spirit!"

Colonel Mering did not respond, and in the little silence before she called to him again, the faint sound of Cyril's snoring wafted down the corridor. We weren't out of the woods yet.

"There!" I said, pointing to the wall above Lady Schrapnell's portrait. "Did you hear that?"

"Yes!" Mrs. Mering said, mashing her hand to her bosom. "What did it sound like?"

"The sound of bells," I said, improvising, "and then a sort of sob—"

"Exactly," Mrs. Mering said. "The attic. Baine, open the attic door. We must go up."

At this point Verity finally made an appearance, clutching her wrapper and blinking sleepily. "What is it, Aunt Malvinia?"

"The spirit I saw two nights ago out by the gazebo," Mrs. Mering said. "It is in the attic."

Just then Cyril gave an enormous snuffling snort from the unmistakable direction of my room.

Verity instantly looked up at the ceiling. "I hear them!" she said. "Ghostly footsteps overhead!"

We spent the next two hours in the attic, tripping over cobwebs and looking for vanishing glimmers of white. Mrs. Mering didn't find any, but she did find a ruby glass fruit compote, a lithograph of Landseer's *The Monarch of the Glen,* and a moth-eaten tigerskin rug for the jumble sale.

She insisted on poor Baine carrying them down on the spot. "Amazing, simply amazing, the treasures one finds in attics," she said rapturously. "Don't you agree, Mr. Henry?"

"Umm," I said, yawning.

"I am afraid the spirit has departed," Baine said, coming back up the attic stairs. "We may only frighten it by our further presence."

"You are quite right, Baine," she said, and we were able, finally, to go to bed.

I was afraid Cyril might be at it again when we came down the corridor, but there was no sound from my room. Cyril and Princess Arjumand were sitting bolt upright in the middle of the bed, engaged in a nose (such as it was for Cyril) to nose staring match.

"No staring," I said, taking off my robe and crawling into bed. "No snoring. No sprawling."

There was none of the above. Instead, they paced round the bed, sniffing each other's tails (such as it was for Cyril) and looking daggers at each other.

"Lie down," I hissed, and then lay there in the dark, worrying about what to do and thinking about the accidental bombing of London.

It made sense that that was a crisis point. There had only been two planes involved, and very little would have been required to shift the course of events: they might have spotted a landmark and realized where they were, or their bombs might have fallen on a marrows field or in the Channel, or they might have been hit by flak. Or something even smaller, some tiny event that no one was aware of. It was a chaotic system.

So there was no way to tell what we should do, or not do, and how it would affect Terence's marrying Maud.

Cyril and Princess Arjumand were still pacing over the bed. "Lie *down*," I said, and, amazingly, Cyril did, flopping at my feet. Princess Arjumand walked over to him, sat down next to his head, and smacked him smartly on the nose.

Cyril sat up, looking aggrieved, and Princess Arjumand stretched out in his place.

If only it were that simple. Action and reaction. Cause and effect. But in a chaotic system, the effect wasn't always what one intended.

Look at the letter I'd tried to burn tonight. And the battleship *Nevada*. It had been damaged in the first wave of attack at Pearl Harbor, but not sunk, and it had fired up its boilers and tried to get underway and out of the harbor to where it could maneuver. And as a result it had nearly sunk in the channel, where it would have blocked the entire harbor entrance for months.

On the other hand, a radar technician at Opana Station had telephoned his superior officer at 7:05 A.M., nearly fifty minutes before the attack on Pearl Harbor, and reported a large number of unidentified planes coming in from the north. His superior officer had told him to ignore it, it was nothing at all, and gone back to bed.

And then there was Wheeler Field, where, trying to protect the planes from sabotage, they had parked them all in the middle of the field. Where it had taken the Japanese Zeros exactly two and a half minutes to destroy them all.

Lady Schrapnell's motto might be "God is in the details," but mine was rapidly becoming, "Damned if you do, damned if you don't."

I was still thinking about Pearl Harbor when I went down to breakfast. Tossie was standing at the sideboard, holding Princess Arjumand and taking the lids off each of the silver serving dishes and then putting them back on with a dissatisfied expression.

It was the first time I had felt any kinship with her. Poor thing, consigned to a life of frivolousness and wretched things for breakfast. Not allowed to go to school or do anything worthwhile, and eel pie besides. I was thinking I'd been too hard on her when she slammed down the snarling wolf dish, picked up the silver bell sitting next to it, and rang it violently.

Baine appeared in a moment, his arms full of coconuts and a length of purple bunting draped over his shoulders. "Yes, miss?" he said.

"Why is there no fish for breakfast this morning?" Tossie said.

"Mrs. Posey is engaged in preparing the cakes and refreshments for the fête tomorrow," Baine said. "I told her four hot dishes were sufficient."

"Well, they are not," Tossie snapped.

Jane came in with an armful of antimacassars, bobbed a curtsey at Tossie, and said hurriedly, "Beggin' your pardon, miss. Mr. Baine, the men are here with the tea tent, and Miss Stiggins's footman is wantin' to know where the extra chairs are to go."

"Thank you, Jane," Baine said. "Tell them I will be there directly."

"Yes, sorr," Jane said, bobbed, and ran out.

"I should like grilled trout for breakfast. Since Mrs. Posey is busy, *you* can prepare it," Tossie said, and if I'd been Baine I'd have beaned her with one of the coconuts.

Baine merely looked hard at her, clearly trying to maintain a poker face, and said, "As you wish, miss." He looked at Princess Arjumand. "If you will allow me to speak, miss, encouraging your pet to eat fish is not good for her. It only—"

"I do *not* allow you to speak," Tossie said imperiously. "You're a servant. Bring me the grilled trout immediately."

"As you wish, miss," he said, and started out, juggling his coconuts to keep them from falling.

"I want it served on a silver dish," Tossie called after him. "And tie up that horrid dog of Terence's. It tried to chase my dearums Juju this morning."

All right, that settled it. Tossie couldn't be allowed to marry Terence, and the hell with what our meddling might do to the continuum. A universe in which Cyril (and Baine) had to put up with that wasn't worth having.

I ran upstairs to Professor Peddick's room. He wasn't there, but I found Terence in his room. He was shaving.

"I've been thinking," I said, watching him brush soap on his face in fascination. "This is the third day Professor Peddick's been away from Oxford, and we still haven't been down to Runnymede. Perhaps we should go there today and then back to Oxford tomorrow. I mean, we're only in the way here, what with the jumble sale and all."

"I promised Miss Mering I'd stay and help with the fête," he said, scraping the lethally sharp blade along his cheek. "She wants me to be in charge of the Pony Ride."

"We could take him to Oxford on the train this afternoon," I said, "and be back in time for the fête. The professor's sister and niece are no doubt missing him."

"He sent them a telegram," Terence said, shaving his chin.

"But they may only be visiting for a short time," I said. "It would be a shame for him to miss them."

He looked unconvinced.

" 'Time is fleeting,' " I said, deciding perhaps a quote was what was needed, " 'and opportunities once miss'd, do ne'er return.' "

"True," Terence said, complacently drawing the blade across his jugular. "But people like Professor Peddick's relations always stay forever." He wiped the remains of the soap off with the towel. "The bluestocking niece has probably come up to campaign for women's colleges, or suffrage, or something, and they'll be in Oxford all term. Modern girls! Thank goodness Miss Mering is an old-fashioned girl, shy and demure and 'sweet as the dewy, milk-white thorn, dear as the raptured thrill of joy.' "

It was hopeless, but I continued to try for several more minutes, and then went to work on Professor Peddick.

I didn't make it. Mrs. Mering waylaid me on my way to the fishpond and sent me to put up placards in the village, and it was nearly noon by the time I got back.

Verity was on a ladder on the lawn, putting up Chinese lanterns between the stalls the workmen were hammering together. "Any luck with the diary?"

"No," she said disgustedly. "I've searched every ruffle and cranny of her room, and nothing." She stepped down off the ladder. "Any luck with Terence?"

I shook my head. "Where is he?" I said, looking round at the stalls. "He's not with Tossie, is he?"

"No," she said. "Mrs. Mering sent Terence to Goring for prizes for the fishing stall, and Tossie's over at the Chattisbournes' borrowing a ribbon for her hat. She should be gone all afternoon."

"For a ribbon?"

She nodded. "I told her she needed a special shade of lilac halfway between mauve and periwinkle, with just a hint of lavender blue. And the Chattisbourne girls will want to hear all about you. Both Tossie and Terence should be safely occupied till tea."

"Good," I said. "I'm going to work on Professor Peddick this afternoon."

"That is absolutely out of the question!" Mrs. Mering said, and nearly gave me a heart attack, she sounded so much like Lady Schrapnell. "The fête is tomorrow! My crystal ball must be here by then!"

I picked up a Chinese lantern so it would look like I was working and peered round the woolen goods stall at the half-constructed fortuneteller's booth.

A workman in a frock coat and top hat and a butcher's apron was cringing back against his carriage. "Felpham and Muncaster's greatly regret any inconvenience this may have caused," he was saying humbly, "and will earnestly endeavor—"

"Inconvenience!" Mrs. Mering shouted. "We are attempting to raise money for our restoration fund!"

I went back over to Verity. "The crystal ball didn't arrive."

"You'd think it would have foreseen that that would happen," she said, grinning. "If you're going to catch Professor Peddick, you'd best hurry. He and the Colonel are going fishing."

"It *must* be here by this afternoon at four," Mrs. Mering boomed.

"But, Mrs. Mering—"

"Four on the dot!"

"Do you know where Professor Peddick is?" I asked Verity.

"In the library, I think," she said, taking another Chinese lantern and catching up her skirt to climb the ladder. "He was looking up something about the Battle of Bannockburn. Before you go," she came back down the ladder a step. "I've been thinking over what you said about Finch, and you're right. He's not the type to drown a cat." She put her hand to her forehead. "I don't always think too clearly when I'm time-lagged."

"I know the feeling," I said.

"I haven't been able to think what Finch *is* doing here, though," she said. "Have you?"

I shook my head.

"I'm going through to see if the forensics expert's had any luck," she said. "I'll see what I can find out about Finch. Mr. Dunworthy wouldn't tell me, but perhaps I can get it out of Warder."

I nodded and went off to find Professor Peddick, taking the long way round to make sure Mrs. Mering didn't see me and waylay me again.

The professor wasn't in the library or the parlor. I went out to check at the stable and then started back toward the house to ask Jane if she knew where he was.

I was halfway there when Finch came out of the servants' door with Jane. He said something to her, and she giggled and then stood there watching him as he left, smiling and waving her apron at him.

I went over to her. "Jane," I said. "What was Finch doing here?"

"He brought the rock cakes for the fête tomorrow," she said, looking longingly after him. "I am wishin' he was our butler instead of Mr. Baine. Mr. Baine's always goin' on at me about reading books and how I should be trying to improve myself, do I want to be a maid all my life, but Mr. Finch is ever so nice, he never criticizes, he just talks."

"What did he talk to you about?" I said, trying to make the question casual.

"Oh, this and that. The fête tomorrow and was I going to buy any chances on the cake and Princess Arjumand's being lost. He was particular interested in Princess Arjumand, asked me all about her."

"Princess Arjumand?" I said sharply. "What did he say?"

"Oh, only how lucky it was she wasn't drowned, and had she ever had kittens, Miss Stiggins was saying she was such a pretty cat, she'd like to have one of the kittens, was she always with Miss Mering or did she wander off on her own sometimes and like that."

"Did he ask to see her?"

"He did," Jane said, "but I couldn't find her. I told him she was very likely out at the fishpond, trying to eat the Colonel's goldfish." She suddenly seemed to realize who she was talking to. "I didn't do nothing improper, did I, sorr, talking to him? We were working the whole time."

"No, of course not," I said. "I only asked because I thought he might have brought the curio cabinet for the jumble sale."

"No, sorr," she said. "Just the rock cakes."

"Oh," I said and took off for the fishpond, walking till I was out of Jane's sight and then breaking into a gallop. Verity had been right. Finch was after Princess Arjumand.

I ran across the lawn, where Mrs. Mering was still yelling at the workman, and past the spot where Verity had been hanging Chinese lanterns. The ladder was still there, but she wasn't, and I wondered if she had gone through to Oxford already.

I sprinted past the lilacs to the gazebo and then onto the path along the riverbank. There was no sign of Princess Arjumand or of her having recently been pitched in the river, and I remembered all over again how just a few minutes could have made an enormous difference.

"Princess Arjumand!" I called, and ran down the path and across the flower garden to the rockery.

The fishpond lay in the middle of the rockery, lined with brick and covered with waterlilies. Next to the pond sat Cyril, and on the edge of the pond sat Princess Arjumand, delicately swiping her paw into the water.

"Stop that," I said, and Cyril jumped and looked guilty.

Princess Arjumand continued to dip her paw unconcernedly in the water, as if she were trolling.

"All right, you two," I said. "You're under arrest. Come along." I scooped up Princess Arjumand and started back for the house, Cyril trudging behind with his head down.

"You should be *ashamed*," I said to him. "Letting her tempt you into a life of crime like that. Do you know what would have happened to you if Baine had found you?" and saw the shimmer of the net up by the gazebo.

I looked round anxiously, hoping there was no one else close enough to see it. It began to glow, and Cyril reared away from it and began to back, growling.

Verity emerged next to the gazebo and looked around. "Ned!" she said, catching sight of me, "How *nice* of you to come meet me!"

"What did you find out?" I said.

"And you brought Cyril," she said, patting him on the head. "And dearum-dearums Juju," she cooed, taking Princess Arjumand from me and cradling her in her arms. She waggled her fingers at Princess Arjumand's paws, and Princess Arjumand batted playfully at them. "How does oo stan' your mistwess talking ootsy-cutesy baby talk to oo?" Verity said. "Oo ought to swat her when her does it."

"Verity," I said. "Are you all right?"

"I'm perfectly all right," she said, still playing with the cat's paws. "Where's Terence?" she said, starting toward the lawn. "I need to tell him he can't be in love with Tossie because the fate of the free world is at stake. Also," her voice dropped to a stage whisper, "she cheats at croquet."

"How many drops have you had?" I demanded.

She frowned. "Sixteen. No, eight. Twelve." She peered at me. "It isn't fair, you know."

"What isn't?" I said warily.

"Your boater. It makes you look just like Lord Peter Wimsey, especially when you tilt it forward like that." She started for the lawn.

I took Princess Arjumand away from Verity, dumped her on the ground, and grabbed Verity's arm.

"I need to find Tossie," she said. "I have a thing or two to tell *her*."

"Not a good idea," I said. "Let's sit down a minute. In the gazebo." I led her toward it.

She came docilely. "The first time I ever saw you, I thought, he looks just like Lord Peter Wimsey. You were wearing that boater and—no, that *wasn't* the first time," she said accusingly. "The *first* time was in Mr. Dunworthy's office, and you were all covered in soot. You were still adorable, though, even if your mouth was hanging open." She looked at me quizzically. "Did you have a mustache?"

"No," I said, leading her up the gazebo steps. "Now, I want you to tell me exactly what happened in Oxford. Why did you make twelve drops?"

"Seven," she said. "T.J. wanted to test the slippage on drops to May and August of 1888. He's looking for surrounding areas of radically increased slippage," she said, sounding more coherent, and I wondered if the time-lag was just a temporary effect.

"He said our incongruity doesn't fit the pattern," she said. "There's supposed to be an area of moderately increased slippage surrounding the focus. Do you know why Napoleon lost the Battle of Waterloo? It rained. Buckets."

Nope. Apparently not temporary.

"Why did T.J. send you on all those drops?" I asked. "Why didn't he send Carruthers?"

"They can't get him out."

"No, it's the recruit they can't get out," I said.

She shook her head forcefully. "Carruthers."

I didn't know if what she was saying was true, or if she was confused. Or if we were even talking about the same thing—between Difficulty in Distinguishing Sounds, Blurring of Vision, and the sound of the ack-ack that was doubtless thudding in her ears, she might be having a different conversation entirely.

"Verity, I need to take you—" Where? Sleep was what she needed, but there was no way I could get her through the mine field between here and the house. The Reverend Mr. Arbitage would be on the lawn supervising the servants, Mrs. Mering would be there supervising the Reverend Mr. Arbitage, and Tossie might be back early from the Chattisbournes' and looking for a couple of suckers for a game of croquet.

The stable? No, we'd still have to cross a corner of the lawn to get there. Perhaps the best idea was to stay here in the gazebo and try to get Verity to lie down on one of the benches.

"And what is wrong with a Grand Design, I should like to know?" Professor Peddick said from the direction of the fishpond. "Of course Overforce can't envision a Grand Design. His idea of a plan is to train his dog to jump out of trees onto innocent bystanders."

"Come on, Verity," I said, raising her to her feet. "We can't stay here."

"Where are we going?" she said. "We're not going to the jumble sale, are we? I *hate* jumble sales. I hate shells and tassels and embroidery and tatting and scrollwork and all those beads they put on everything. Why can't they just leave well enough alone?"

"We cannot see the design because we are a part of it," Professor Peddick's voice, much nearer, said. "Can the thread in the loom see the pattern in the fabric? Can the soldier see the strategy of the battle he is fighting?" and I hustled Verity out of the gazebo and over behind the lilacs.

"Come on," I said, taking her hand as if she were a child. "We're going to go now. This way."

I led her behind the lilacs and down the path to the river. Cyril and Princess Arjumand followed us, Princess Arjumand twining herself around our legs as we walked and impeding our progress.

"Cyril," I whispered, "go find Terence."

"Good idea," Verity said. "I have a few things to say to Terence. 'Terence,' I'm going to say to him, 'how can you be in love with someone who hates your dog?' "

We reached the towpath. "Shh," I said, listening for Professor Peddick.

"Through art, through history, we may glimpse the Grand Design," he said. His voice sounded farther away. "But only for a fleeting moment. 'For His works are unsearchable and His ways past finding out,' " he said, his voice growing fainter. They must be going up to the house.

"I'll bet Maud Peddick loves dogs," Verity said. "She's a lovely girl. She doesn't keep a diary, she's patriotic—"

There was no one down at the dock. I propelled Verity rapidly down the path to the river.

"She's got a poem named after her," Verity said. " 'Come into the garden, Maud, I am here at the gate alone.' By Tennyson. Terence loves quoting Tennyson. When Maud Peddick screams, I'll bet it's the real thing and not some little baby scream. Oh, are we going in a boat?"

"Yes," I said, helping her in. "Sit down."

She stood, swaying slightly, in the stern, gazing wistfully out at the river. "Lord Peter took Harriet out boating," she said. "They fed the ducks. Are we going to feed the ducks?"

"You bet," I said, untying the rope. "Sit down."

"Oh, look," she said, pointing at the shore. "They want to come. Isn't that sweet?"

I jerked my head up and looked at the shore. Cyril and Princess Arjumand were standing side by side on the little dock.

"Can't Cyril come?" she said.

The thought of trying to rescue two dead weights if they went overboard was not appealing. On the other hand, if we took them with us, the Black Moor would be safe. And if Finch *was* trying to drown Princess Arjumand, she was safer with me.

"They can come," I said and hoisted Cyril, two legs at a time, into the boat.

Princess Arjumand promptly turned on her heel, flouncing her pretty tail in the air, and started for the fishpond.

"Oh, no you don't," I said and snatched her up, handed her to Verity, who was still standing up, and untied the rope.

"Sit down," I said and cast off. Verity sat down with a thump, the cat still in her arms. I jumped in, took up the oars, and started rowing out toward the current.

By going downstream, I could get her away faster, but we'd have to go past the house and a good section of the lawn, and I didn't want anyone to see us. I swung the boat upstream and rowed out of sight of Muchings End as rapidly as I could. There were a lot of boats on the river. One of them waved gaily to us, and Verity waved back. I rowed faster, hoping it wasn't one of the Chattisbourne girls.

I had thought we would be safe on the river, but I had forgotten how many people went boating in the afternoon, and fishing. It was obvious we weren't safe, and I began looking for some safe side stream or backwater we could pull into.

"I thought you said we were going to feed the ducks," Verity said accusingly. "Lord Peter and Harriet fed the ducks."

"We will, I promise," I said. On the far bank lay some weeping willows whose branches dipped almost down to the water. I rowed across the river toward them.

"Do you believe in love at first sight?" Verity said. "I didn't. And then I saw you standing there, all covered with soot—*when* are we going to feed the ducks?"

I rowed in under the willows, pushing against the bank with my oar to bring us round and close to the bank. We were completely hidden from the river here. The willow branches arched over us and down into the water, enclosing us in a pale-green bower. The sun shimmered through the leaves like the net as it was about to open.

I laid down the oars and looped the rope gently over a low-hanging branch. We should be safe here.

"Verity," I said, knowing this was probably hopeless. "What did you find out in Oxford?"

She was playing with Princess Arjumand, shaking the ribbons of her hat at her.

"Did you talk to the forensics expert?" I persisted. "Has she found out who Mr. C is?"

"Yes," she said.

"Yes," I said. "You know who Mr. C is?"

She frowned. "No. I mean, yes, I talked to her." She took off her hat and began untying one of the ribbons. "She said it's got between seven and ten letters, and the last one's an 'N' or an 'M.'"

It wasn't Mr. Chips then. Or Lewis Carroll.

"I told her to stop looking for references to Princess Arjumand," Verity said, "and to concentrate on Mr. C and the date of the trip to Coventry." She finished untying the ribbon and dangled it at Princess Arjumand.

"Good," I said. "You said Carruthers was stuck in Coventry. Didn't you mean the new recruit?"

"No," she said, playing with the ribbon. The cat reared up on her hind legs and batted at it with her white paws. "They got him out. Besides, this is different." She danced the ribbon up and down. Cyril came over to investigate.

"How is it different?" I asked patiently.

Cyril sniffed the dangling ribbon. The cat smacked him smartly on the nose and went back to the batting. "The new recruit couldn't find the net," she said. "It was open. Now it's not."

"When they try to bring Carruthers through, the net won't open?" I said, trying to get this straight, and she nodded.

T.J. had said net failure was a worsening sign of an incongruity.

"And they've tried more than once?"

"They've tried everything," she said, pulling the ribbon up sharply. The cat leaped for it, and the boat rocked. "T.J.'s even trying the battle of Waterloo."

She had said something about Waterloo before, but I'd assumed it was just babblings. "What exactly is T.J. doing?" I asked.

"Changing things," she said, holding the ribbon very still. Princess Arjumand watched her, ready to pounce. "Opening the gate at Hougoumont, bringing up D'Erlon's troops. Did you know Napoleon had terrible handwriting? It's worse than Tossie's diary. No one can decipher it."

She jerked the ribbon suddenly. Princess Arjumand leaped for it. The boat rocked. "*I* think he lost the battle because of his hemorrhoids."

Whatever T.J. was doing with Waterloo, it would have to wait. It was getting late, and Verity didn't seem to be getting appreciably better. I obviously couldn't take her back like this, and the only thing I could think of that might help was sleep.

"He couldn't ride with hemorrhoids," she said. "That's why he stayed the night at Fleurus. And *that's* why he lost the battle."

"Yes, you're probably right," I said. "I think you should lie down and rest."

She continued to dangle the ribbon. "It's terrible, really, how important a little thing like that can be. Like my saving Princess Arjumand. Who would have thought it would lose a whole war?"

"Verity," I said firmly and took the ribbon away from her. "I want you to lie down and rest now."

"I can't," she said. "I have to go steal Tossie's diary and find out who Mr. C is and then I have to go tell Mr. Dunworthy. I have to repair the incongruity."

"There's plenty of time for that," I said. "First you need to sleep." I pulled a slightly mildewed cushion out from under the prow and placed it on the seat. "You lie down right here."

She lay down obediently and put her head on the pillow. "Lord Peter took a nap," she said. "Harriet watched him sleep, and that's when she knew she was in love with him."

She sat up again. "Of course *I* knew it from the second page of *Strong Poison,* but it took two more books for Harriet to figure it out. She kept telling herself it was all just detecting and deciphering codes and solving mysteries together, but *I* knew she was in love with him. He proposed in Latin. Under a bridge. After they solved the mystery. You can't propose till after you've solved the mystery. That's a law in detective novels."

She sighed. "It's too bad. *'Placetne, magistra?'* he said when he proposed, and then she said, *'Placet.'* That's a fancy Oxford don way of saying yes. I had to look it up. I hate it when people use Latin and don't tell you what they mean. Do you know what Professor Peddick said to me yesterday? *'Raram facit misturam cum sapientia forma.'* I have no idea what he meant. Something about the Grand Design, I think. Do you believe in a Grand Design, Ned?"

"We'll talk about it later," I said, patting the pillow. "Right now you lie down."

She lay down again. "It *was* romantic, though, proposing in Latin. I think it was the boater that did it. She sat there, watching him sleep, and he looked *so* handsome in his boater. And his mustache. It's a little lopsided, did you know that?"

"Yes." I took off my blazer and put it over her shoulders. "Close your eyes and rest."

"Will you watch me sleep?" she said.

"I will watch you sleep."

"Good," she said, and closed her eyes.

Several minutes went by.

"Could you take your hat off?" Verity said drowsily.

I grinned. "Certainly."

I laid my boater beside me on the seat. She curled up on her side, her hands folded under her cheek, and closed her eyes. "It didn't help," she murmured.

Cyril settled into the bottom of the boat, and Princess Arjumand perched on my shoulders like a parrot and began to purr.

I looked at Verity. She had shadows under her eyes, and I realized that she hadn't had any more sleep the last two days than I had, racing out to the drop at all hours, planning strategies, spending who knew how many hours in Oxford, researching Terence's descendants, and talking to the forensics expert. Poor thing.

Cyril and Princess Arjumand were both asleep. I leaned forward, my elbow on my knee, and rested my cheek on my hand.

I watched Verity sleep.

It was almost as restful as sleeping myself. The boat rocked gently, and the sun through the leaves flickered softly in patterns of light and shade. She slept peacefully, quietly, her face still and untroubled in repose.

And I was going to have to face it. No matter how much sleep I got or she didn't, she was always going to look like a naiad to me. Even lying there with her greenish-brown eyes closed and her mouth half-open, drooling gently onto a mildewed boat cushion, she was still the most beautiful creature I'd ever seen.

" 'She hath a lovely face,' " I murmured, and, unlike Terence, thought that that covered it very well.

At some point I fell asleep myself, and at some later point my head must have fallen sideways. My elbow slipped off my knee, and I sat up with a jerk.

On my shoulders, Princess Arjumand meowed, irritated at being disturbed, and jumped down onto the seat beside me.

Verity and Cyril were both still asleep. Princess Arjumand yawned widely and stretched, and then went over to the side of the boat and looked in the water. She stood up, her paws on the gunwale, and dipped a dainty white paw in the water.

The shadowy light of the sun through the willows was more angled than it had been, and there was a golden tinge to it. I pulled out my pocket watch and snapped it open. Half-past III. We had best be getting back before anyone missed us. If we hadn't been missed already.

I hated to wake Verity up. She looked so peaceful, sleeping there, a faint smile on her lips as if she was dreaming of something pleasant. "Verity," I said softly and leaned forward to touch her on the shoulder.

There was a splash. I lunged for the side of the boat. "Princess Arjumand!" I said, and Cyril sat up, looking surprised.

There was no sign of the cat. I leaned over the gunwale, pushing up my sleeve. "Princess Arjumand!" I reached far under the water and felt around, trying to find her. "You are not drowning! Do you hear me? Not after we've risked the entire universe to save you!" I said, and she bobbed up and began swimming toward the boat, her fur wet and plastered to her head.

I grabbed her by the scruff of the neck and hauled her in. She looked like a drowned rat. Cyril ambled over, looking interested, and, I thought, pleased.

I pulled out my handkerchief and swabbed at her, but it obviously wasn't going to do the job. I looked in the prow for a blanket or a rug, but there wasn't anything. It was going to have to be my blazer.

I removed it gently from Verity's shoulders, wrapped Princess Arjumand in it, and began to rub her dry. "Fish are going to be the death of you, you know that, don't you?" I said, toweling her back and tail. "Cats only have nine lives, you know, and you've already used up six that I know of." I rubbed her tail. "You need to switch to a safer habit, like smoking."

Princess Arjumand began to struggle. "You're not dry yet," I said, and went on rubbing her.

She continued to struggle, and after a minute I unwrapped her from the blazer and let her go. She walked with rather bedraggled dignity past Cyril to the middle of the seat, sat down, and began to lick herself.

I draped my blazer over the prow to dry, and looked at my pocket watch again. A quarter to IV. I'd have to wake Verity up, even though she was obviously dead to the world if none of this had wakened her. I snapped my pocket watch shut.

Verity opened her eyes. "Ned," she said sleepily. "Did I fall asleep?"

"Yes. Do you feel better?"

"Better?" she said vaguely. "I . . . what happened?" She sat up. "I remember coming through and . . ." Her eyes widened. "I was time-lagged, wasn't I? I did all those drops to May and August." She put her hand to her forehead. "How awful was I?"

I grinned. "Worst case I've ever seen. Don't you remember?"

"Not really," she said. "It's all sort of a blur, and in the background there was this sound like a siren. . . ."

"The All-Clear," I said.

"Yes, and a sort of wheezing, snorting—"

"Cyril," I said.

She nodded. "Where are we?" she said, looking round at the willows and the water.

"About half a mile upstream from Muchings End," I said. "You were in no shape to see anyone till you'd had some sleep. Do you feel better now?"

"Um hmmm," she said, stretching. "Why is Princess Arjumand all wet?"

"She fell in while fishing," I said.

"Oh," she said, yawning.

"You're certain you feel better?" I said.

"Yes. Much."

"Good," I said, unlooping the rope. "Then we'd better be getting back. It's nearly time for tea." I took the oars and maneuvered us out from under the willows and onto the river.

"Thank you," she said. "I must have been in pretty bad shape. I didn't say anything humiliating, did I?"

"Only that Napoleon lost the battle of Waterloo because of his hemorrhoids," I said, rowing downstream, "a theory, by the way, that I wouldn't advise sharing with Professor Peddick and the Colonel."

She laughed. "No wonder you had to shanghai me. Did I tell you what T.J.'s doing with the battle of Waterloo?"

"Not exactly," I said.

"He's running incongruity simulations of the battle," she said. "Waterloo's a battle that's been analyzed in microscopic detail. An elaborate comp simulation of the battle was done in the Twenties." She leaned forward. "T.J.'s using that model and introducing incongruities that might change events. You know, like what if Napoleon had sent Ney a readable message instead of an indecipherable one? What if d'Erlon had been wounded?"

"What if Napoleon hadn't had hemorrhoids?"

She shook her head. "Only things an historian could have done," she said, "like switching messages or firing a musket ball. And then he's comparing the slippage configurations to our incongruity."

"And?"

"He just started," she said defensively, "and it's all just theoretical," which meant she didn't want to tell me.

"Did you find out from Warder how much slippage there was on your drop?" I asked.

"Yes," she said. "Nine minutes."

Nine minutes.

"What about the drops you did to May and August?"

"It varied. The average was sixteen minutes. That tallied with previous drops to the Victorian era."

We were nearly to Muchings End. I pulled out my pocket watch and looked at it. "We should be home in time for tea," I said, "and so there may not be any questions. If there are, we rowed up to Streatley to post signs for the jumble sale." I pulled on my damp blazer, and Verity straightened her hair and put on her hat.

Sixteen minutes, and Verity's drop had been nine. Even if her drop had had an average amount of slippage, she would have been too late, or too early, to rescue the cat and cause the incongruity. And at nine minutes, the slippage obviously hadn't been stretched to its limits. So why hadn't the net increased the slippage to the average? Or slammed shut before the incongruity could happen? And why had it slammed shut now, on Carruthers?

The dock was only a few hundred yards ahead. "With luck, no one will even know we've been on the river," I said, and pulled in toward the dock.

"Our luck seems to be out," Verity said.

I turned round in my seat. Tossie and Terence were running down to the riverbank, waving to us.

"Oh, Cousin, you'll never guess what's happened!" Tossie cried. "Mr. St. Trewes and I are engaged!"

# CHAPTER SIXTEEN

Chance of Rain—Another Swan—What People Buy at Jumble
Sales—Numbers Three, Seven, Thirteen, Fourteen, and Twenty-
eight—I Have My Future Predicted—Things Are Not What
They Seem—I Depart for the Other Side—The Battle of
Waterloo—Importance of Good Penmanship—A Fateful
Day—Number Fifteen—A Plan—An Unexpected Arrival

I t's not your fault," Verity said. We were arranging items in the jumble
sale stall the next morning, our first chance to talk since the "thrilling
news," as Mrs. Mering put it.

"It was my fault," Verity said, setting out a china wooden shoe with a
blue-and-white windmill on it. "I should never have let T.J. send me on so
many drops."

"You were only trying to find out something that might help us," I said,
unwrapping an egg-boiler. "I was the one who left Terence and Tossie alone."
I set it on the counter. "And gave him the idea. You heard him last night. He
wouldn't have proposed if I hadn't spouted that nonsense about 'fleeting
time' and 'miss'd opportunities.' "

"You were only doing what I told you to," she said, opening a Japanese fan.
" 'Turn the *Titanic,* Ned,' I said. 'Don't worry. We won't hit the iceberg.' "

"Not set up yet?" Mrs. Mering said, and we both jumped. "It's nearly time
for the fête to open."

"We'll be ready," Verity said, setting out a soup tureen in the shape of a head of lettuce. Mrs. Mering looked worriedly at the overcast sky. "O, Mr. Henry, you don't think it will rain, do you?"

Of course not, I thought. Fate is against me.

"No," I said, unwrapping an etching of Paolo and Francesca, another couple who had come to a bad end.

"O, good," she said, dusting off a bust of Prince Albert. "O, there is Mr. St. Trewes. I must go speak to him about the Pony Ride."

I watched her interestedly as she swooped down on Terence. She was wearing a blue garden party dress, with all the requisite Victorian puffs and frills and rosettes and insets of lace, but over it she had flowing robes striped in red, yellow, and purple, and round her forehead was a wide velvet band with a large ostrich feather stuck in it.

"She's the fortuneteller," Verity explained, setting out a pair of sewing scissors in the shape of a heron. "When she reads my fortune, I intend to ask her where the bishop's bird stump is."

"It may well be here," I said, trying to find a place to set the Widow Wallace's banjo. "It would fit right in."

She looked at the array of things on the counter. "It certainly is a jumble," she said, adding a mustache cup to the mess.

I looked critically at it. "It still lacks something," I said. I went and snatched a penwiper from Tossie's stall and stuck it between a paperweight and a set of tin soldiers. "There. It's perfect."

"Except for the fact that Tossie and Terence are engaged," she said. "I should never have assumed she'd stay at the Chattisbournes' all afternoon."

"The question is," I said, "not whose fault it is they got engaged, but what we're going to do now."

"What *are* we going to do now?" Verity said, rearranging a pair of Harlequin and Columbine figurines.

"Perhaps Terence will get a good night's sleep, come to his senses, and decide it was all a horrible mistake," I said.

She shook her head. "That won't help us. Engagements in Victorian times were considered nearly as serious as marriage. A gentleman couldn't just break an engagement without a dreadful scandal. Unless Tossie breaks it herself, there's no way Terence can get out of the engagement."

"Which means her meeting Mr. C," I said. "Which means our finding out who he is, and the sooner the better."

"Which means one of us reporting back to Mr. Dunworthy and finding out if the forensics expert has managed to decipher his name yet," she said.

"And that will be me," I said firmly.

"What if Lady Schrapnell catches you?"

"I will take that risk," I said. "*You* are not going anywhere."

"I think that's probably a very good idea," she said, putting her hand to her forehead. "I've been remembering some of the things I said in the boat yesterday." She ducked her head. "I want you to know that I only said those things about Lord Peter Wimsey and your hat because of the time-lag and the hormonal imbalance, and not because—"

"Understood," I said. "And I do not, when in my right mind, see you as a beautiful naiad, drawing me down and down into the deep to drown in your watery embrace. Besides," I said, grinning, "Pansy Chattisbourne and I are already promised to one another."

"Perhaps you'd like to buy her an engagement gift then," she said and held up a ceramic affair decorated with gilt lace, pink ceramic gillyflowers, and an assortment of small holes.

"What is it?" I said.

"I have no idea," she said. "You realize you'll have to buy *something*, don't you? Mrs. Mering will never forgive you if you don't."

She held up a wicker basket in the shape of a swan. "How about this?"

"No, thank you," I said. "Cyril and I are not fond of swans."

Verity set out a small lidded tin box that sugared violets had come in. "No one will buy this."

"That's where you're wrong," I said, unwrapping a waterstained copy of *An Old-Fashioned Girl* and setting it between two marble bookends carved in the likenesses of Dido and Aeneas, another couple who had gone up in smoke. Didn't history have any famous couples who had got married, settled down, and lived happily ever after?

"People will buy anything at jumble sales," I said. "At the Evacuated Children Charity Fair a woman bought a tree branch that had fallen on the table."

"Don't look now," Verity said, and her voice dropped to a whisper, "but here comes your betrothed."

I turned to see Pansy Chattisbourne bearing down on me. "Oh, Mr. Henry," she said, giggling, "do come help me set up the fancy goods stall," and dragged me away to arrange antimacassars and tatted handkerchief cases.

"I made these," Pansy said, showing me a pair of slippers crocheted in a design of pansies. "Heartsease. It means, 'I am thinking of you.'"

"Ah," I said, and purchased a bookmark embroidered, "Lay not up for yourselves treasures upon earth, where moths corrupt and thieves break in and steal. Matthew 6:19."

"No, no, no, Mr. Henry," Mrs. Mering said, swooping down on me and my cross-stitched tea cloths like some colorful bird of prey, "you're not supposed to be here. I need you over *here*."

She led me down the lawn past the knitted and crocheted goods stall and the fishing pond stall and the coconut shy and the tea tent to a spot at the end of the lawn where a plot of sand had been laid out inside a wooden frame. Baine was dividing the sand into foot-wide squares with the blade of a small shovel.

"This is our Treasure Hunt, Mr. Henry," she said, handing me a stack of folded pasteboard squares. "These are for numbering the squares. Have you any shillings, Mr. Henry?"

I fished out my purse and tipped it into my cupped hand.

She scooped up all the coins. "Three shillings for the minor prizes," she said, plucking out three silver coins and handing them back to me, "and the rest of this will do excellently for change at the woolen goods booth."

She handed me back a single gold coin. "And you'll need this," she said, "for purchasing treasures at the jumble sale."

Definitely related to Lady Schrapnell.

"I will let you choose which squares to bury the shillings and the Grand Prize in. Take care no one sees you," she said. "Avoid the corner squares and all the lucky numbers—Three and Seven and Thirteen—people always choose those first, and if someone finds the treasure early, we shan't make any money for the restoration. Also, avoid the numbers under twelve. Children always choose their age. And Fourteen. Today's the fourteenth of June, and people always choose the date. Make certain they only dig in one square. Baine, where is the Grand Prize?"

"Right here, madam," Baine said, handing her a brown-paper-wrapped parcel.

"The price for digging is tuppence a square or three for fivepence," she said, unveiling the parcel, "and here is our Grand Prize."

She handed me a plate with a painting of Iffley Mill and the words "Happy Memories of the Thames" on it. It looked just like the one the mobcap in Abingdon had tried to sell me.

"Baine, where is the shovel?" Mrs. Mering said.

"Here, madam," he said, and handed me a shovel and a rake. "For smoothing the sand down after you've hidden the treasure," he explained.

"Baine, what time is it?" Mrs. Mering asked.

"Five minutes to ten, madam," he said, and I thought she was going to swoon.

"O, we're not nearly ready!" she cried. "Baine, go and explain the fishing pond stall to Professor Peddick and bring out my crystal ball. Mr. Henry, there's no time to waste. You must bury the treasure immediately."

I started for the sand.

"And not Twenty-eight. That was last year's winning square. Or Sixteen. That's the Queen's Birthday."

She swept off, and I set about hiding the treasure. Baine had laid out thirty squares. Eliminating Sixteen, Twenty-eight, Three, Seven, Thirteen, Fourteen, and One through Twelve, to say nothing of the corners, didn't leave very many choices.

I took a sharp look round, in case there were any "Souvenir of the Thames" thieves lurking in the hedge, and stuck the three shillings in Twenty-nine, Twenty-three, and Twenty-six. No, that was a corner. Twenty-one. And then stood there, trying to decide what the least-likely looking square was and wondering if I had time to go through and report to Mr. Dunworthy before the fête started.

While I was debating, the bell from Muchings End Church began to toll, Mrs. Mering gave a screamlet, and the fête was declared officially open. I hastily buried the Grand Prize in Eighteen and began raking it over.

"Seven," a child's voice said behind me. I turned round. It was Eglantine Chattisbourne in a pink dress and a large bow. She was carrying the lettuce soup tureen.

"I'm not open yet," I said, raking several other squares and then stooping to place the cardboard numbers in them.

"I want to dig in Number Seven," Eglantine said, shoving fivepence at me. "I get three tries. I want seven for my first one. It's my lucky number."

I handed her the shovel, and she set down the lettuce and dug for several minutes.

"Do you want to try another square?" I asked her.

"I'm not *finished* yet," she said, and dug some more.

She stood up and surveyed the squares. "It's never in the corners," she said thoughtfully, "and it can't be Fourteen. It's never the date. Twelve," she said finally. "That's how old I am on my birthday."

She dug some more. "Are you certain you put the prizes in?" she said accusingly.

"Yes," I said. "Three shillings and a Grand Prize."

"You could *say* they were in there," she said, "and truly you'd kept them for yourself."

"They're in there," I said. "Which square do you want for your third try?"

"I don't," she said, handing me the shovel. "I want to think for a little."

"As you wish, miss," I said.

She held out her hand. "I want my tuppence back. For my third try."

I wondered if she were somehow related to Lady Schrapnell. Perhaps Elliott Chattisbourne, despite appearances, *was* Mr. C after all.

"I haven't any change," I said.

She flounced off, I raked the squares flat again, and leaned against a tree, waiting for more customers.

None came. They were apparently all hitting the jumble sale first. Business was so slow for the first hour I could easily have sneaked off to the drop, except for Eglantine, who hovered nearby, plotting which square to use her last tuppence on.

And, as it developed when she had finally decided on Number Seventeen and dug to no avail, keeping her eye on me. "I think you move the prizes when no one's looking," she said, brandishing the toy shovel. "That's why I've been watching you."

"But if you've been watching me," I said reasonably, "how could I have moved the prize?"

"I don't know," she said darkly, "but you must have. It's the only explanation. It's always in Seventeen."

Now that she was out of money, I'd hoped she would move on, but she hung about, watching a little boy choose Six (his age) and his mother pick Fourteen (the date).

"Perhaps you never put the prizes in at all," Eglantine said after they'd left, the little boy sobbing because he hadn't found a prize. "Perhaps you only said you did."

"Wouldn't you like to have a nice pony ride?" I said. "Mr. St. Trewes is giving pony rides over there."

"Pony rides are for infants," she said disdainfully.

"Have you had your fortune told?" I persisted.

"Yes," she said. "The fortuneteller said she saw a long journey in my future."

The sooner the better, I thought.

"They have some lovely penwipers in the fancy goods stall," I said shamelessly.

"I don't want a penwiper," she said. "I want a Grand Prize."

She kept an eagle eye on me for another half hour, at which point Professor Peddick came over.

"Looks exactly like the plain at Runnymede," he said, gesturing to include the lawn with its stalls and tea tent. "The lords, with their marquees and their banners spread out across the plain, waiting for King John and his party to arrive."

"Speaking of Runnymede," I said, "shouldn't we be going on downriver and then back to Oxford to see your sister and your niece? No doubt they will be missing you."

"Pah!" he said. "There's plenty of time. They'll be staying all summer, and the Colonel's ordered a red-spotted silver tancho that is to arrive tomorrow."

"Terence and I could run you home tomorrow on the train, just to check on things at home, and then you could come back to see the red-spotted silver tancho."

"Not necessary," he said. "Maudie's a capable girl. I'm certain she has things well in hand. And I doubt Terence would be willing to go, now that he's engaged to Miss Mering." He shook his head. "I can't say I entirely approve of these hasty engagements," he said. "What's your opinion of them, Henry?"

"That little pitchers have big ears," I said, looking at Eglantine, who was standing next to the Treasure Hunt, her hands behind her back, looking earnestly at the squares.

"Pretty little thing, but knows scarcely any history," Professor Peddick went on, not taking the hint. "Thought Nelson lost his arm fighting the Spanish Armada."

"Are you going to dig?" Eglantine said, coming over to him.

"Dig?" Professor Peddick said.

"For treasure," she said.

"As Professor Schliemann dug at ancient Troy," he said, picking up the little shovel. " '*Fuimus Troes; fuit Ilium.*' "

"You must pay tuppence first," Eglantine said. "And choose a number."

"Choose a number?" Professor Peddick said, bringing out two pennies. "Very well. Fifteen for the day *and* the year of the signing of the Magna Carta." He plunked down the pennies. "The fifteenth of June, 1215."

"That's tomorrow," I said. "What an excellent occasion for us to go down to Runnymede, on the very anniversary of the signing. We could telegram your sister and your niece to meet us there, and we could go down by boat tomorrow morning."

"Too many sightseers," Professor Peddick said. "They'd spoil the fishing."

"Fifteen's a very poor number," Eglantine said. "*I* would have chosen Nine."

"Here," Professor Peddick said, handing her the shovel. "You dig for me."

"May I keep anything I find?" she asked.

"We shall share the spoils," he said. " '*Fortuna belli semper anticipiti in loco est.*' "

"What do I get for digging if it isn't in Fifteen?"

"Lemonade and cakes in the tea tent," he said.

"It isn't in Fifteen," Eglantine said, but she began digging.

"A fateful day, the fifteenth of June," Professor Peddick said, watching her. "Napoleon marched his army into Belgium on the fifteenth of June in 1814. Had he pressed on to Ligny instead of stopping in Fleurus, he would have split Wellington's and Blücher's armies apart and won the battle of Waterloo. A day that changed history forever, the fifteenth of June."

"I *told* you it wasn't in Fifteen," Eglantine said. "*I* don't think it's in any of them. When do I get my lemonade and cakes?"

"Now, if you like," Professor Peddick said, taking her arm and leading her off toward the tea tent, and now I could go through and report in to Mr. Dunworthy.

I started for the gazebo, and hadn't made it three steps before I was stopped by Mrs. Chattisbourne. "Mr. Henry," she said, "have you seen Eglantine?"

I told her she was in the tea tent.

"I suppose you have heard the delightful news of Miss Mering's and Mr. St. Trewes's engagement," she said.

I said I had.

"I always think June is the perfect month for engagements, don't you, Mr. Henry? And so many *lovely* young girls about. I shouldn't be surprised if you were to become engaged, too."

I told her Eglantine was in the tea tent.

"Thank you," she said. "Oh, and if you see Mr. Finch, will you please tell him we are nearly out of parsnip wine at the baked goods stall?"

"Yes, Mrs. Chattisbourne," I said.

"Finch is such a wonderful butler," she said. "So thoughtful. Did you know he went all the way to Stowcester for seed cake for the stall? He spends every spare moment travelling the countryside, looking for delicacies for our table. Yesterday he walked to Farmer Bilton's for strawberries. He's quite simply amazing. The best butler we have ever had. I worry night and day that he will be stolen away from me."

A legitimate worry under the circumstances, I thought, and wondered what Finch was really up to at Stowcester and Farmer Bilton's. And whether Mrs. Chattisbourne would ever leave.

She did, but not before Pansy and Iris showed up, giggling, and spent tuppence apiece on Three and Thirteen (their lucky numbers). By the time I got rid of them, it had been nearly half an hour, and Eglantine was liable to be back at any moment.

I sprinted over to the driveway and the Pony Ride and asked Terence if he could watch the Treasure Hunt for me for a few minutes.

"What does it involve?" he asked suspiciously.

"Handing people a shovel and taking their tuppences," I said, skipping the part about Eglantine.

"I'll do it," Terence said, tying the pony to a tree. "It sounds like a soft job compared to this. I've spent all morning being kicked."

"By the pony?" I said, eyeing it warily.

"By the children."

I showed him the layout of the Treasure Hunt and gave him the shovel. "I'll be back in a quarter of an hour," I promised.

"Take as long as you like," he said.

I thanked him and took off for the gazebo. And nearly made it. At the edge of the lilacs, the curate caught me and said, "Are you enjoying the fête, Mr. Henry?"

"Tremendously," I said. "I—"

"Have you had your fortune told?"

"Not yet," I said. "I—"

"Then you must this very instant," he said, grabbing me by the arm and propelling me back toward the fortunetelling tent. "It and the jumble sale are the high point of the fête."

He shoved me through a red-and-purple flap into a tiny enclosed tent in which sat Mrs. Mering and the crystal ball, which she had apparently bullied Felpham and Muncaster's into delivering on time.

"Sit down," she said. "You must cross my palm with silver."

I handed her the lone gold coin she'd left me. She handed me back several silver coins in change and then passed her hands over the crystal ball.

"I see . . ." she said in a sepulchral voice, ". . . you will live a very long life."

It only seems long, I thought.

"I see . . . a long journey, very long . . . you are seeking something. Is it an object of great worth?" She closed her eyes and ran a hand across her forehead. "The glass is murky . . . I cannot see whether you will be successful in your search."

"You can't see where it is, can you?" I said, leaning over to try to see into the ball. "The object?"

"No," she said, placing her hands over it, ". . . it . . . Things Are Not What They Seem. I see . . . trouble . . . the glass is becoming clouded . . . at the center I see . . . Princess Arjumand!"

I jumped a good foot.

"Princess Arjumand! Naughty puss!" she said, reaching under her robes. "You mustn't come in here, you naughty bad kitty. Mr. Henry, do be so good as to take her back to my daughter. She quite spoils the atmosphere."

She handed over Princess Arjumand, who had to be detached claw by claw from her robes. "Always causing trouble," she said.

I carried Princess Arjumand over to the jumble sale stall and asked Verity to keep an eye on her.

"What did you find out from Mr. Dunworthy?" she said.

"I haven't gone yet. I got waylaid by Mrs. Mering," I said. "However, she saw a long journey in my future, so perhaps it means I'll be able to go now."

"She saw a wedding in my future," Verity said. "Let's hope it's Tossie's to Mr. C."

I came round behind the counter, handed Princess Arjumand to her, and then ducked out the back way, sprinted down to the towpath and along it to the gazebo, and hid in the lilac bushes, waiting for the net to open.

It took forever to open, during which I worried about Eglantine or the curate catching me, and then, when the net finally began to shimmer, about Lady Schrapnell catching me.

I came through in a crouch, ready to bolt if Lady Schrapnell was in the lab. She wasn't, at least in the parts that I could see. The lab looked like it had been turned into a war room. All across the wall where I had sat—how many days ago?—there was a comp setup so big it dwarfed the net console. A tall bank of monitors and three-dimensional stack screens filled the entire part of the lab that wasn't taken up by the net.

Warder was at the console, interrogating the new recruit.

"All I know is," the new recruit said, "he said, 'I'm not risking you being left behind again. Get in the net,' and I did."

"And Carruthers didn't say anything about doing anything before he followed you?" Warder asked. "Checking on something?"

He shook his head. "He said, 'I'm right behind you.' "

"Was there anyone about?"

He shook his head again. "The sirens had gone. And there's nobody living in that part of the city. It's all burnt down."

"The sirens had gone?" Warder said. "Were you under attack? Could a bomb have hit—" She looked up suddenly and saw me. "What are you doing here?" she said. "What happened to Kindle?"

"Advanced time-lag, thanks to you people," I said, flailing my way out of the veils. "Where's Mr. Dunworthy?"

"Over at Corpus Christi with the forensics expert," she said.

"Go tell him I'm here and need to talk to him now," I said to the new recruit.

"I'm *trying* to find out what happened to Carruthers," Warder said, flushing angrily. "You can't just come in here and—"

"This is important," I said.

"So is Carruthers!" she snapped. She turned to the new recruit. "Were there any delayed-action bombs in the area?"

The recruit looked uncertainly from her to me. "I don't know."

"What do you mean, you don't know?" Warder said angrily. "What about the buildings and ruins in the area, were they unstable? And don't tell me you don't know!"

"I'd best go fetch Mr. Dunworthy," the recruit said.

"All *right*," Warder snapped. "Come straight back. I've some more questions to ask you."

The recruit made his escape, brushing past T.J., who was on his way in with a stack of books, vids, and disks. "Oh, good," he said when he saw me. "I want to show you both—" He stopped, looking round. "Where's Verity?"

"In 1888," I said. "She got time-lagged doing all those drops for you."

"They didn't turn up anything," he said, trying to set the stack down without it falling over, "which doesn't make any sense. There's *got* to be increased slippage around the site. Here, let me show you."

He started to lead me over to the comp setup and then stopped and went over to the console and asked Warder, "Was there slippage on Ned's drop?"

"I haven't had time to calculate it," Warder said. "I've been *trying* to get Carruthers out!"

"Okay, okay," T.J. said, holding up his hands defensively. "Could you please calculate it?"

He turned to me. "Ned, I want to show you—"

"What's this about slippage on my drop?" I said. "There isn't any slippage on return drops."

"There was on Verity's last drop," he said.

"What's causing it?"

"We don't know yet," he said. "We're working on it. Come here. Let me show you what we're doing." He led me over to the comp setup. "Did Verity tell you about the Waterloo sims?"

"More or less," I said.

"Okay, it's very hard to make an accurate comp model of an historical event because so many factors are unknown, but Waterloo's an exception. The battle's been analyzed and every incident's been described down to a microscopic level. Also," he said, his black fingers typing rapidly, "it has several crisis points and a number of factors which could have made the battle go either way: the violent rainstorms on the sixteenth and seventeenth, General Grouchy's failure to come up—"

"Napoleon's bad penmanship," I said.

"Exactly. Napoleon's message to D'Erlon and the failure to take Hougoumont, among others."

He hit more keys, leaning round to see the bank of stack screens behind him.

"All right, here's what we've been looking at," he said, picking up a lightpen and walking over to the center screen. "This is a sim of Waterloo as it actually happened."

The screen showed a three-dimensional gray blur with lighter and darker areas. "This is the battle," he said, switching on the pen and pointing it into the center of the three-dimensional blur. "And here," he pointed at the edges, "are the surrounding temporal and locational areas the battle affected."

The light darted back to the center and rapidly pointed to several places. "Here you can see the battle at Quatre Bras, the fight for Wavre, the charge of the Old Guard, the retreat."

I couldn't see anything but assorted gray blurs. I felt the way I always do when a doctor shows me a scan. "Here you see the lungs, the heart—" I never see anything of the sort.

"What I've done is introduce simulated incongruities into the model and see how the sim changes," he said.

He moved to the screen on the left. As near as I could tell, it looked identical to the one in the center. "In this one, for example, Napoleon sent an illegible order to D'Erlon to turn toward Ligny, with the result that he brought his men up behind Napoleon's left flank instead of ahead of it and was mistaken for the enemy. I introduced a simulated historian here," he said, pointing at gray, "who substituted a legible order for Napoleon's note, and as you can see, it changed the picture radically."

I would have to take his word for it.

"When the incongruity's introduced, you get a pattern of radically increased slippage at the site," he pointed with the lightpen, "and then slightly lower levels here and here surrounding the site, and then smaller peripheral patches as the system corrects itself."

I squinted at the screen, trying to look intelligent.

"In this case, the system was able to self-correct almost immediately. D'Erlon issued the orders to his second-in-command, who gave them to a lieutenant, who couldn't hear him for the artillery fire, and sent the troops up on the left flank after all, and the situation reverted to its original pattern."

He pointed the lightpen at the top row of screens. "I tried a number of variables of varying severity. In this one, the historian breaks the lock on the gate at Hougoumont. In this one, he spoils an infantryman's shot so Letort isn't killed. In this one here, the historian intercepts a message between Blücher and Wellington," he said, pointing at one screen after another. "They vary greatly in their impact on the situation and in how long it takes the continuum to self-correct."

He pointed at more screens. "This one took a few minutes, this one took two days, and there doesn't seem to be a direct correlation between the seriousness of the incongruity and its consequences. In this one," he pointed at the far left bottom screen, "we shot Uxbridge to prevent his suicidal charge, and his second-in-command immediately took up the charge with the same result.

"On the other hand, in this one," he indicated a screen in the second row, "we had an historian dressed as a Prussian soldier stumble and fall during the fight for Ligny, and the self-correction was enormous, involving four regiments and Blücher himself."

He moved to a screen in the center. "In *this* one, we changed the circumstances at La Sainte Haye. The thatched roofs caught fire from the artillery shells, and a chain of men with soup kettles full of water managed to put the fires out."

He pointed at a spot near the center. "I introduced an historian here to steal one of the soup kettles. It created a major incongruity, and the interesting thing is that the self-correction didn't just involve increased slippage here and here," the light pointed at the top of the screen, "but here, before 1814."

"It went back in the past and corrected itself?"

"Yes," he said. "In the winter of 1812, there was a bad snowstorm, which caused a deep rut in the road in front of La Sainte Haye, which caused an oxcart passing over it to lose part of its load, including a small wooden keg full of beer, which a servant found and carried home to La Sainte Haye. The keg, with the top hacked off, was substituted for the missing soup kettle in the bucket brigade, the fires were put out, and the incongruity was repaired."

He went back to the comp, hit more keys, and brought up a new set of screens. "This one, where Gneisenau retreats to Liège, and this one, in which the historian helps push a cannon out of the mud, show self-corrections in the past, too."

"That's why you had Verity do drops in May?" I said. "Because you think the incongruity may have attempted to adjust itself before it happened?"

"But we haven't found any slippage anywhere except for your drop," he said, sounding frustrated. "Every one of these," he waved at the screen, "no matter how large or how small the self-correction, has the same basic pattern: radically increased slippage at the site, moderately increased slippage in the immediate area, and then isolated pockets of slippage farther from the site."

"Which doesn't match our incongruity at all," I said, staring at the screen.

"No," T.J. said, "it doesn't. The slippage on Verity's drop was nine minutes, and I haven't been able to find any radical increase in slippage anywhere near the site. The only slippage at all is the cluster in 2018, and it's much greater than it should be, that far from the site."

He went to the comp, typed something in, and came back to the left-hand screen, which had changed slightly. "The only one that's been close is this one," he said. "We had the historian fire an artillery shell that killed Wellington."

He felt in his pockets for the lightpen, couldn't find it, and settled for his finger. "See this? Here and here, you have radically increased slippage, but it can't contain the altering events and discrepancies which develop here and here and here," he said, pointing at three spots close to the focus, "and the amount of slippage drops off sharply *here,* and you can see *here,*" he pointed farther out, "the backups start to fail, and the net begins to malfunction as history starts to alter course."

"And Napoleon wins the battle of Waterloo."

"Yes," he said. "You can see the parallels to your incongruity *here*," he pointed at darker gray, "where there's a pocket of increased slippage nearly seventy years from the site, and here," he pointed at a spot of lighter gray, "in the lack of slippage at a short distance from the site."

"But there's still radically increased slippage *at* the site," I said.

"Yes," he said grimly. "In every single incongruity we've tried. Except yours."

"But at least you've been able to prove that incongruities are possible," I said. "That's something, isn't it?"

"What?" he said blankly. "These are all just mathematical sims."

"I know, but you've shown what would happen if—"

He was shaking his head violently. "What would happen if we really tried to send an historian to Waterloo to intercept a message or shoot a horse or give directions is that the net wouldn't open. Historians have been trying for over forty years. No one can get within two years and a hundred miles of Waterloo." He waved angrily at the banks of screens. "These sims are all based on a net without any safeguards."

So we were right back where we started.

"Could something have overridden the safeguards on Verity's drop?" I said. "Or made them malfunction?"

"That was the first thing we checked. There was no sign of anything but a perfectly normal drop."

Mr. Dunworthy came in, looking worried. "Sorry I took so long," he said. "I went to see if the forensics expert had made any progress on either the name or the date."

"Has she?" I said.

"Where's the recruit?" Warder cut in crabbily before Mr. Dunworthy could answer. "He was supposed to come back with you."

"I sent him over to the cathedral to keep Lady Schrapnell occupied so she wouldn't come over while Ned was here," he said.

And I trusted him to do that about as much as I trusted him to find his way home, so we'd better make this short.

"Has the forensics expert decoded Mr. C's name?"

"No. She's narrowed the number of letters down to eight, and she's located the Coventry entry, and is working on the date."

Well, that was something. "We need it as soon as possible," I said. "Terence and Tossie got engaged yesterday."

"Oh, dear," Mr. Dunworthy said, and looked around as if he would have liked to sit down. "Betrothal was a very serious matter in Victorian days," he said to T.J.

He turned back to me. "Ned, the two of you still don't have any leads as to Mr. C's identity?"

"No, and we still haven't been able to get hold of the diary," I said. "Verity's hoping Mr. C comes to the church fête today."

I tried to think if there was anything else I should tell or ask them. "T.J., you said something about slippage on the return drops?"

"Oh, yes. Warder!" he called across to the console, where she was violently pounding keys. "Have you figured the slippage yet?"

"I am *trying* to—"

"I know, I know, you're trying to get Carruthers out," T.J. said.

"*No,*" she said. "I am trying to bring Finch through."

"It can wait," T.J. said. "I need the slippage on Ned's return drop."

"All *right!*" she said, her seraphim's hundred eyes flashing. She beat on the keys for half a minute. "Three hours, eight minutes."

"Three hours!" I said.

"It's better than Verity's last drop," Mr. Dunworthy said. "That was two days."

T.J. held his hands out, palms up, and shrugged. "There hasn't been any on any of the sims."

I thought of something. "What day is it?"

"Friday," T.J. said.

"It's nine days till the consecration," Mr. Dunworthy said, thinking. "The fifth of November."

"Nine days!" I said. "Good Lord! And I don't suppose the bishop's bird stump has turned up?"

Mr. Dunworthy shook his head. "Things don't look good, do they, Ensign Klepperman?"

"There's one thing that does," T.J. said, darting back to the comp and hitting keys. "I did a bunch of scenarios on the Berlin bombing." The screens changed to a slightly different pattern of gray blurs. "Missing the target, plane getting hit, pilot getting hit, even eliminating the pilot and plane altogether, and none of them affects the outcome. London still gets bombed."

"That *is* good news," Mr. Dunworthy said wryly.

"Well, it's something anyway," I said, wishing I could believe it.

The net shimmered, and Finch appeared. He waited for Warder to raise the veils and then came straight over to Mr. Dunworthy and said, "I have excellent news regarding the—" He stopped and looked at me. "I will be in your office, sir," he said and went out hastily.

"I want to know what Finch is up to," I said. "Did you send him back to drown Princess Arjumand?"

"Drown—?" T.J. said, and started to laugh.

"Did you?" I demanded. "And don't tell me you're not at liberty to say."

"We are *not* at liberty to tell you what Finch's mission is," Mr. Dunworthy said, "but I can tell you, Princess Arjumand is perfectly safe, and that you will be pleased with the results of Finch's mission."

"If Henry's going back," Warder said irritably from the console, "I need to send him now so I can start the half-hour intermittent on Carruthers."

"We need the forensics expert's information as soon as you have it," I said to Mr. Dunworthy. "I'll try to come through tonight or tomorrow."

Mr. Dunworthy nodded.

"I don't have all day," Warder said. "I am *trying*—"

"All *right*," I said, and went over to the net.

"What time do you want to be sent back to?" Warder asked. "Five minutes after you left?"

Hope suddenly leaped up like one of Wordsworth's rainbows. "I can go back to whenever I want?"

"It's *time travel*," Warder said. "I haven't got all—"

"Half-past four," I said. With luck, there would be twenty minutes' slippage, and the fête would be completely over.

"Half-past four?" Warder said, looking belligerent. "Won't someone have missed you?"

"No," I said. "Terence will be delighted he doesn't have to go back to the Pony Ride."

Warder shrugged and began setting up the coordinates. "Step in the net," she said, and hit the "send" key.

The net shimmered, and I straightened my boater and tie and strode happily back to the fête. It was still overcast, so I couldn't see the sun to tell what time it was, and my watch was useless, but the crowd seemed a bit thinner. It must be at least half-past three. I went over to the jumble sale stall to report to Verity that I had nothing to report.

She wasn't there. The stall was being tended by Rose and Iris Chattisbourne, who tried to sell me a silver sugar hammer.

"She's in the tea tent," they said, but she wasn't there either.

Cyril was, hoping against hope someone would drop a sandwich, and giving the impression that he'd been there all day. I bought him a currant bun and myself a rock cake and a cup of tea and took them back over to the Treasure Hunt.

"You weren't gone very long," Terence said. "I told you to take as long as you liked."

"What time is it?" I said with a sinking feeling. "My watch—stopped."

" 'It was the very best butter,' " Terence quoted. "It's five past twelve. I don't suppose *you'd* like to take the Pony Ride for a bit?" he said hopefully.

"No," I said.

He wandered morosely off toward the drive, and I sipped my tea and ate my rock cake and thought about the unfairness of Fate.

It was a very long afternoon. Eglantine, who had cadged another fivepence from one of her sisters, spent most of the afternoon squatting next to the sand, plotting her strategy.

"I don't think any of the squares has the Grand Prize in it," she said, after she'd squandered tuppence on Number Two.

"It does," I said. "I put it in there myself, whether you believe me or not."

"I do believe you," she said. "The Reverend Mr. Arbitage saw you do it. But someone might have stolen up and taken it when nobody was here."

"Someone's been here the entire time."

"They might have sneaked in and out the back way," she said. "While we were talking."

She went back to squatting, and I went back to my rock cake, which was even harder than the rock cake I'd had at the Prayers for the RAF Service and Baked Goods Sale, and thought about the bishop's bird stump.

Had someone sneaked it out the back way when nobody was looking? I had said no one would want it, but look at the things people bought at jumble sales. Perhaps a looter had taken it out of the rubble, after all. Or perhaps Verity was right, and it had been taken out of the cathedral sometime before the raid. Either it had been in the cathedral during the raid, or it hadn't, I thought, looking at the squares of sand. Those were the only two possibilities. And either way it had to be somewhere. But where? In Number Eighteen? Number Twenty-five?

At half-past one the curate came to spell me so I could "have a proper luncheon" and "have a look at the fête." The "proper luncheon" consisted of a fish paste sandwich (which I gave half of to Cyril) and another cup of tea, after which I made the rounds of the stalls. I won a red glass ring at the fishing pond, bought a quilted tea cozy, a pomander made from an orange stuck full of cloves, a china crocodile, and a jar of calves' foot jelly, told Verity I hadn't got the date or Mr. C's name, and went back to the Treasure Hunt. When Eglantine wasn't looking, I buried the crocodile in Number Nine.

The afternoon wore on. People chose Four, Sixteen, Twenty-one, and Twenty-Nine, and actually found two of the shillings. Eglantine spent the rest of her fivepence to no avail and stomped off in a huff. At one point, Baine came up with Princess Arjumand and dumped her in my arms.

"Could you possibly watch her for a bit, Mr. Henry?" he said. "Mrs. Mering wishes me to run the coconut shy, and I fear Princess Arjumand *cannot be left alone even for a moment,*" he said, looking hard at her.

"The globe-eyed nacreous ryunkin again?" I said.

"Yes, sir."

A large box full of sand didn't seem like a terribly good place for her either. "Why can't you spend the entire day sleeping on the fancy goods display like that calico cat at the Nativity of the Virgin Mary jumble sale?" I said.

"More," she said, and rubbed her nose against my hand.

I petted her, thinking what a pity it was that she hadn't drowned and achieved nonsignificance, so that the net would have slammed shut when I tried to return her, and I could have kept her.

Of course, I couldn't really have kept her. Some billionaire would have snapped her up, and one cat couldn't replace an entire extinct species, even with cloning. But still, I thought, scratching her behind the ears, she was a very nice cat. Except, of course, for the nacreous ryunkin. And Professor Peddick's double-gilled blue chub.

Finch came hurrying up. He looked hastily round and then leaned forward and said, "I have a message for you from Mr. Dunworthy. He said to tell you he spoke to the forensics expert, and she's deciphered the date of the trip to Coventry. He said—"

"Mama says you're to let me have three more tries," Eglantine said, appearing out of nowhere, "and she will give you fivepence when the fête closes."

Finch looked nervously at Eglantine. "Is there somewhere we could speak privately, sir?" he said.

"Eglantine," I said. "How would you like to run the Treasure Hunt for a few minutes?"

She shook her head virtuously. "I wish to dig. The person in charge isn't allowed to win prizes. I wish Number Two."

"I'm sorry," I said. "This gentleman was ahead of you. Mr. Finch, what square would you like?"

"Square?" Finch said.

"A square to dig in," I said, indicating the sandbox. "As there are thirty squares, most people choose a *date*. If it's one of those listed here," I added, remembering the date might be the thirty-first. "Did you have a specific *date* in mind, Mr. Finch?"

"Oh," Finch said, the light dawning. "The date. I would like square Number—"

"He hasn't paid," Eglantine said. "You must pay tuppence first to dig."

Finch fished in his pockets. "I'm afraid I haven't any—"

"Butlers get a free try," I said. "What number—?"

"That isn't *fair*," Eglantine wailed. "Why should butlers get a free try?"

"It's a church fête rule," I said.

"You didn't give Mrs. Mering's butler a free try," she said.

"He took his on the coconut shy," I said, handing Finch the shovel. "The *date*, Mr. Finch?"

"Fifteen, please, Mr. Henry," he said quickly.

"Fifteen?" I said. "Are you certain?"

"You can't choose Fifteen," Eglantine said. "It's already been chosen. And so have Sixteen and Seventeen. You can't choose a number which has already been chosen. It's against the rules."

"Fifteen," Finch said firmly.

"But that's impossible." I said. "The fifteenth is tomorrow."

"And you can't buy Six or Twenty-two," Eglantine said, "because I'm going to buy them."

"Was she absolutely certain?" I said.

"Yes, sir," Finch said.

"What about the month? Could it have been July? Or August?" even though I knew it wasn't. Verity had told me that day at Iffley the trip to Coventry had been in June.

"I would pick one of the corners," Eglantine said. "Thirty or One."

"And you're certain it's the fifteenth? Tomorrow?"

"Yes, sir," Finch said. "Mr. Dunworthy sent me through immediately to tell you."

"I've got to tell Verity," I said. "Finch, shut up shop."

"You *can't*," Eglantine wailed. "I get three more chances."

"Let her dig in three more squares and then close down," I said and took off for the jumble sale stall before either of them could protest, skirting round the back way so I wouldn't be waylaid by Mrs. Mering or the Chattisbourne girls.

Verity was selling the stringless banjo to a young man in a derby and a handlebar mustache. I picked up an unidentifiable utensil with a large serrated wheel and two sets of curved blades and pretended to know what it was till the young man left.

"A Mr. Kilbreth," Verity said. "Spelled with a 'K.'"

"The forensics expert's deciphered the date of the trip to Coventry," I said before anyone could come up and interrupt us. "It's the fifteenth of June."

She looked shocked. "But that's impossible. The fifteenth is tomorrow."

"My sentiments exactly."

"How did you find out? Did you go through again?"

"No. Finch came and told me."

"And he's certain?"

"Yes. So what do we do?" I said. "I don't suppose I could simply suggest an outing to Coventry tomorrow morning? To see the sights?"

Verity shook her head. "The day after an activity like this is spent rehashing it with the Chattisbournes and the curate and the Widow Wallace. They'd never be willing to go off and miss that. It's the best part of the fête."

"What about fish?" I said.

"Fish?"

"We could tell the Colonel and Professor Peddick there are excellent shallows or deeps or gravel bottoms for bream or something. Isn't Coventry on a river? The Colonel and Professor Peddick can't resist anything with fish involved."

"I don't know," Verity said thoughtfully, "but you've given me an idea. I don't suppose you can crack your toes, can you?"

"What?"

"That's how the Fox sisters did it. Never mind, we can do it with—" She began rummaging through the jumble sale items, looking for something. "Oh, good, it's still here," she said, and picked up the metal sugared-violets box.

"Here, buy this," she said, thrusting it at me. "I haven't any money."

"What for?"

"I've got an idea," she said. "Buy it. It's fivepence."

I obligingly handed her a shilling.

"I was going to buy that," Eglantine said, appearing out of nowhere.

"I thought you were over at the Treasure Hunt digging," I said.

"I was," she said. "Squares Ten, Eleven, and Twenty-seven. The treasure wasn't in any of them. I don't believe it's in any of them. I don't believe you ever put the treasure in it." She turned to Verity. "I told you this morning I wanted to buy the sugared-violets box."

"You can't," Verity said. "Mr. Henry's already bought it. Be a good girl and go find Mrs. Mering for me. I need to speak with her."

"It is just the right size to keep buttons in," Eglantine said. "And I told you this morning I wanted to buy it."

"Wouldn't you rather have a nice book?" Verity said, offering her *An Old-Fashioned Girl.*

"Here's tuppence," I said. "If you'll go fetch Mrs. Mering, I'll tell you where the treasure is."

"That's against the rules," she said.

"Giving a clue isn't," I said. I leaned down and whispered in her ear, "The battle of Waterloo."

"The day or the year?"

"That's for you to figure out."

"Will you give me clues to the squares the shilling is in?"

"No," I said. "And fetch Mrs. Mering before you start digging."

She ran off.

"Quick, before she comes back," I said, "what's your idea?"

She took the sugared-violets box from me, removed the lid, and held the box and lid apart, like a pair of cymbals, and then brought them together with a tinny rap.

"A séance," she said.

"A séance?" I said. "That's your idea? I'm sorry I didn't let Eglantine buy the box."

"You said the Colonel and Professor Peddick couldn't resist anything having to do with fish," she said. "Well, Mrs. Mering can't resist anything to do with the spirits or séances—"

"Séance?" Mrs. Mering said, swooping up in her Coat of Many Colors. "Are you proposing a séance, Verity?"

"Yes, Aunt Malvinia," Verity said, hastily wrapping the box and lid in tissue paper, putting it in the wicker swan, and handing them both to me.

"I'm certain you'll enjoy your purchases, Mr. Henry," she said, and turned back to Mrs. Mering. "Mr. Henry was just telling me he has never sat in on a séance."

"Is that *true*, Mr. Henry?" Mrs. Mering said. "O, then we must certainly have one tonight just for you. I must ask the Reverend Mr. Arbitage if he can attend. Mr. Arbitage!" she called, and hurried off.

"Give me the violets box," Verity whispered.

I turned slightly so no one could see our hands and passed her the tissue-wrapped box. "What are you going to use it for?"

"Table-rapping," she whispered, sticking it in her reticule. "Tonight we are going to receive a spirit message telling us to go to Coventry."

"You're certain this will work?" I said.

"It worked for Madame Iritosky," she said. "And D. D. Home and the Fox sisters and Florence Cook. It fooled the scientist William Crookes *and* Arthur Conan Doyle. Mrs. Mering thought *you* were a spirit. It will work for us. What could possibly go wrong?"

Mrs. Mering bustled up, robes fluttering. "The Reverend Mr. Arbitage is conducting the cake raffle. I shall have to remember to ask him later. O, Mr. Henry," she said, taking my arm. "I know we shall have a good séance. I can feel the presence of the spirits hovering near already."

Actually it was Baine, who had come up behind her and was waiting for an opening to speak.

"Perhaps it is the same spirit you heard the night before last, Mr. Hen—what *is* it, Baine?" Mrs. Mering said impatiently.

"Madame Iritosky, madam," he said.

"Yes, yes, what about her?"

"She's here."

*"Into the Valley of Death...."*
*"The Charge of the Light Brigade"*
*Alfred, Lord Tennyson*

# CHAPTER SEVENTEEN

In the Foyer—A Summons—Baine Unpacks and Makes an Interesting
Discovery—In the Kitchen—Astounding Anecdotes of Jane's
Second Sight—Preparations for the Séance—I Sympathize with
Napoleon—Jewels—Dueling Mediums—A Ghostly Manifestation

Madame Iritosky was waiting in the foyer with nine pieces of luggage, a large black enameled cabinet, and Count de Vecchio.

"Madame Iritosky!" Mrs. Mering gushed. "What a delightful surprise! And Count! Baine, go and fetch the Colonel and tell him we have guests! He will be so pleased! You know Miss Brown," she said, indicating Verity, "and this is Mr. Henry."

We had followed her up to the house, Verity muttering, "What's *she* doing here? I thought she never left her house."

"Eet eez a pleasure, Signor Henree," Count de Vecchio said, bowing to me.

"Why did you not let us know you were coming?" Mrs. Mering said. "Baine could have met you at the station."

"I did not know myself until last night," Madame Iritosky said, "when I received a message from the Other Side. One cannot ignore a summons from the spirits."

She didn't look like I'd expected. She was a short dumpling of a woman with a button nose, untidy gray hair, and a rather threadbare brown dress.

Her hat was shabby, too, and the feathers on it looked like they had been appropriated from a rooster. The sort of person I would have expected Mrs. Mering to have turned up her nose at, but instead she was practically fawning over her.

"A message from the spirits!" Mrs. Mering said, clasping her hands. "How thrilling! What did they say?"

" '*Go!*' " Madame Iritosky said dramatically.

"*Avanti!*" Count de Vecchio said. "They rapped eet out on the table. 'Go.' "

" 'Go where?' I asked them," Madame Iritosky said, "and waited for them to rap an answer. But there was only silence."

"*Silencio,*" the Count said helpfully.

" 'Go where?' I asked again," Madame Iritosky said, "and suddenly, there on the table before me was a white light that grew and grew until it became . . ." She paused dramatically. ". . . your letter."

"My letter!" Mrs. Mering breathed, and I moved toward her, afraid we were going to have another swooning on our hands, but she recovered herself after swaying a moment. "I wrote to her, telling her of the spirits I had seen," she said to me. "And now they have sent for her!"

"They are trying to tell you something," Madame Iritosky said, gazing at the ceiling. "I feel their presence. They are here among us now."

So were Tossie and Terence and Baine. And Colonel Mering, looking extremely irritated. He was wearing waders and carrying a fishing net. "What's this all about?" he grumbled. "Better be important. Discussing the Battle of Monmouth with Peddick."

"Miss Mering, *amor mia,*" the Count said, going immediately over to Tossie. "I am delighted to meet with you again." He bowed over Tossie's hand like he was going to kiss it.

"How do you do?" Terence said, stepping in front of her and extending his hand stiffly. "Terence St. Trewes, Miss Mering's fiancé."

The Count and Madame Iritosky exchanged glances.

"Mesiel, you will never *guess* who's come!" Mrs. Mering said. "Madame Iritosky, allow me to introduce my husband, Colonel Mering!"

"Colonel Mering, thank you for welcoming us into your home," Madame Iritosky said, bobbing her head and her rooster feathers at him.

"Hrrumm," the Colonel muttered through his mustache.

"I told you I had seen a spirit, Mesiel," Mrs. Mering said. "Madame Iritosky has come to contact it for us. She says the spirits are among us even now."

"Don't see how," Colonel Mering grumbled. "No room for them in this damned foyer. Have a house. Don't see why we have to all stand out here with the bags."

"O, of course," Mrs. Mering said, seeming to notice for the first time how crowded the foyer had got. "Come, Madame Iritosky, Count, let us go into the library. Baine, have Jane bring tea, and take Madame Iritosky's and Count de Vecchio's things up to their rooms."

"Including the cabinet, madam?" Baine said.

"The—" Mrs. Mering said and looked, surprised, at the pile of luggage. "My, what a lot of luggage! Are you going on a journey, Madame Iritosky?"

She and the Count exchanged glances again. "Who can say?" Madame Iritosky said. "Whither the spirits command, I obey."

"O, of course," Mrs. Mering said. "No, Baine, Madame Iritosky will need her cabinet for our séance. Put it in the parlor."

I wondered where on earth it would fit, in among all the ottomans and firescreens and aspidistras.

"And take the rest of their things upstairs," Mrs. Mering went on, "and unpack them."

"No!" Madame Iritosky said sharply. "I prefer to unpack my own things. The psychic lines of force, you know."

"Of course," Mrs. Mering, who probably hadn't any more idea of what psychic lines of force were than the rest of us, said. "After tea, I want to take you out to the grounds and show you the place where I first saw the spirit."

"No!" Madame Iritosky said. "My powers are quite diminished by the long journey. Trains!" She shuddered. "After tea, I must rest. Tomorrow you may show me the entire house and grounds."

"Of course," Mrs. Mering said, sounding disappointed.

"We will examine Muchings End for spiritual habitation," Madame Iritosky said. "There is definitely a spirit presence here. We shall establish communications."

"Oh, what fun!" Tossie said. "Will there be manifestations?"

"Possibly," Madame Iritosky said, putting her hand to her forehead again.

"You are tired, Madame Iritosky," Mrs. Mering said. "You must sit down and have some tea." She led Madame Iritosky and the Count into the library.

"Why didn't you tell me about Count de Vermicelli?" Terence said earnestly to Tossie as they followed them.

"De Vecchio," Tossie said. "He's terribly handsome, isn't he? Iris Chattisbourne says all Italians are handsome. Do you think that's so?"

"Spirits!" the Colonel said, slapping his fishing net against his thigh. "Humbug! Lot of silly nonsense!" and stomped back out to the Battle of Monmouth.

Baine, who had been looking disapprovingly at the luggage, bowed and went down the corridor toward the kitchen.

"Well?" I said, when they had all gone. "What do we do now?"

"We get ready for tonight," Verity said. "Did that covered basket you had Princess Arjumand in survive the shipwreck?"

"Yes," I said. "It's in my wardrobe."

"Good," she said. "Go fetch it and put it in the parlor. I need to sew the sugared-violets box to my garters." She started up the stairs.

"You still plan to have the séance with Madame Iritosky here?"

"Tomorrow's the fifteenth. Do you have a better idea?"

"Couldn't we just suggest an excursion to Coventry to Tossie—like the one to see the church at Iffley?"

"She didn't go to see the church at Iffley, she went to see Terence, and you heard her. She's all agog to examine the grounds and see manifestations. She'd never be willing to miss that."

"What about Count de Vecchio?" I said. "Could he be Mr. C? He's certainly shown up at the right time, and if anyone ever looked like they'd have an alias, it's him."

"It can't be," she said. "Tossie was happily married to Mr. C for sixty years, remember? Count de Vecchio would spend all her money and leave her stranded in Milan in three months."

I had to agree. "What do you think they're doing here?"

Verity frowned. "I don't know. I assumed the reason Madame Iritosky never did séances away from home was that she had her house all set up with trapdoors and secret passages." She opened the door of the cabinet. "But some of her effects are portable." She shut the door. "Or perhaps she's here to do research. You know, snoop in drawers, read letters, look at family pictures."

She picked up a tintype of a couple standing next to a wooden sign that read "Loch Lomond." " 'I see a man in a top hat,' " she said, touching her fingertips to her forehead. " 'He's standing by . . . a body of water . . . a lake, I think. Yes, definitely a lake,' and then Mrs. Mering screams, 'It's Uncle George!' That's what they do, collect information to convince the gullible. Not that Mrs. Mering needs any convincing. She's worse than Arthur Conan Doyle. Madame Iritosky probably plans to spend her 'rest' sneaking into bedrooms and collecting ammunition for the séance."

"Perhaps we could get her to steal Tossie's diary for us," I said.

She smiled. "What exactly did Finch say about the diary? Did he say it was *definitely* the fifteenth?"

"He said Mr. Dunworthy said to tell us that the forensics expert had deciphered the date, and it was the fifteenth."

"Did Finch say how the forensics expert did it? A five looks a lot like a six, you know, or an eight. And if it were the sixteenth or the eighteenth, we'd have time to—I'm going to go talk to him," she said. "If Mrs. Mering asks where I've gone, tell her I went to ask the Reverend Mr. Arbitage to the séance. And see if you can find two pieces of wire about a foot and a half long."

"For what?"

"For the séance. Finch didn't happen to send a tambourine back with you in your luggage, did he?"

"No," I said. "Do you think you should do this? Remember what happened yesterday."

"I'm going to go talk to Finch, not the forensics expert." She pulled on her gloves. "At any rate, I'm completely recovered. I don't find you attractive at all," she said, and swept out the front door.

I went up to my room, got the covered basket, and put it in the parlor. Verity hadn't said what she wanted done with it, so I set it on the hearth behind the firescreen, where Baine wouldn't be likely to see it when he brought the cabinet in and put it efficiently away.

When I went back out in the corridor, Baine was waiting for me in the now luggage-less foyer.

"Might I have a word with you, sir?" he said. He looked anxiously in the direction of the library. "In private?"

"Of course," I said, and led him up to my room, hoping he wasn't going to ask me any more questions about conditions in the States.

I shut the bedroom door behind us. "You didn't throw Princess Arjumand in the river again, did you?"

"No, sir," he said. "It's about Madame Iritosky. In unpacking her things, sir, I found some extremely troubling items."

"I thought Madame Iritosky had said she'd unpack her own things."

"A *lady* never does her own unpacking," he said. "When I opened her trunks, I found a number of unfortunate items: reaching rods, trumpets, bells, slates, an accordion with a self-playing mechanism, wires, several yards each of black cloth and veiling, and a book of conjuring tricks. And *this!*" He handed me a small bottle.

I read the label aloud. "Balmain's Luminous Paint."

"I'm afraid Madame Iritosky is not a true medium, but a fraud," he said.

"It would seem so," I said, opening the bottle. It held a greenish-white liquid.

"I fear that her intentions and those of Count de Vecchio toward the Merings are dishonorable," he said. "I have taken the precaution of removing Mrs. Mering's jewels for safekeeping."

"Excellent idea," I said.

"But it is Madame Iritosky's influence over Miss Mering that I am most concerned about. I fear she may fall prey to some nefarious scheme of Madame Iritosky's and the Count's." He spoke passionately and with real concern. "While they were at tea, Madame Iritosky read Miss Mering's palm. She told her she saw marriage in her future. Marriage to a foreigner. Miss Mering is an impressionable young girl," he said earnestly. "She has not been trained to think scientifically or to examine her feelings logically. I fear she may do something foolish."

"You truly care about her, don't you?" I said, surprised.

His neck reddened. "She has many faults. She is vain and foolish and silly, but those qualities are due to her poor upbringing. She has been spoilt and pampered, but at heart she is sound." He looked embarrassed. "But she has little knowledge of the world. That is why I came to you."

"Miss Brown and I have been concerned as well," I said. "We are planning to attempt to persuade Miss Mering to accompany us on an excursion to Coventry tomorrow to get her away from the Count and Madame Iritosky."

"Oh," he said, looking relieved. "That is an excellent plan. If there is anything I can do to help—"

"You'd best put this back before Madame Iritosky finds it missing," I said, handing the bottle of Balmain's Luminous Paint back regretfully. It would have been perfect for writing "Coventry" on the séance table.

"Yes, sir," he said, taking the bottle.

"And it might be a good idea to lock up the silver."

"I have already done so, sir. Thank you, sir." He started for the door.

"Baine," I said. "There is something you can do. I'm convinced de Vecchio's not an authentic count. I believe there's a possibility he's travelling under an alias. When you unpack his things, if there are any papers or correspondence . . ."

"I understand, sir," he said. "And if there is anything else I can do, sir, please let me know." He paused. "I have only Miss Mering's best interests at heart."

"I know," I said, and went down to the kitchen to look for some strong, thin wire.

"Wire?" Jane said, wiping her hands on her apron. "What for, sorr?"

"To tie up my portmanteau," I said. "The clasp is broken."

"Baine'll fix it for you," she said. "Will they be having a séance tonight, now that this madam person's come?"

"Yes," I said.

"Will they have trumpets, do you think? My sister Sharon, she's in service in London, her mistress had a séance, and a trumpet floated right over the table and played 'Shades of Night Are Falling'!"

"I don't know if there will be trumpets," I said. "Baine's busy with Count de Vecchio's luggage, and I don't want to bother him. I need two lengths of wire about a foot and a half long."

"I can be giving you a piece of twine," she said. "Will that do?"

"No," I said, wishing I had simply told Baine to steal some out of Madame Iritosky's trunk. "It has to be wire."

She opened a drawer and began rummaging through it. "I've got the second sight, you know. Me mother had it, too."

"Umm," I said, looking into the drawer at a great assortment of unidentifiable utensils. But no wire.

"When Sean got his collar broke that time, I sorr it all in a dream. I get a funny feeling in the pit of me stomach whenever anything bad's goin' to happen."

Like this séance? I thought.

"Last night I dreamed I sorr a great ship. Mark my words, I told Cook this morning, somebody in this house will be going on a journey. And then this afternoon if this madam person didn't show up, and they'd come by *train!* Do you think they'll be having a manifestation tonight?"

I sincerely hope not, I thought, though there was no telling with Verity. "What exactly do you have planned?" I asked her when she got back just before dinner. "You're not going to dress up in veils or anything, are you?"

"No," she whispered, sounding regretful. We were standing outside the French doors to the parlor, waiting to go into dinner. On the sofa, Mrs. Mering was rehashing the sounds of Cyril's nocturnal breathings with Tossie—"The cry of a soul in hideous torment!"—and Professor Peddick and the Colonel were holding Terence captive with fishing stories in the corner by the hearth, so we had to talk softly. Neither Madame Iritosky nor the Count were down yet and were presumably still "resting." I hoped they hadn't caught Baine red-handed.

"I think the best thing to do is to keep it simple," Verity said. "Did you get the wires?"

"Yes," I said, taking them out of my jacket. "After an hour and a half of Jane's second-sight experiences. What are they for?"

"The table-tipping," she said, moving slightly so we couldn't be seen from inside. "Bend a hook in one end of each of them," she said, "and then, before the séance, put one wire up each sleeve. When the lights go out, you pull them down till they extend past your wrists and hook them under the edge of the table. That way you can lift the table and still be holding on to your partners' hands."

"Lift the table?" I said, putting them back inside my jacket. "What table? That massive rosewood thing in the parlor? No wire's going to lift that thing."

"Yes, it will," she said. "It works on a principle of leverage."

"How do you know?"

"I read it in a mystery novel."

Of course. "What if someone catches me in the act?"

"They won't. It'll be dark."

"What if someone says they want the lights on?"

"Light prevents the spirit forms from materializing."

"Convenient," I said.

"Extremely. They can't appear if there's an unbeliever present either. Or if anyone tries to interfere with the medium or with anyone in the circle. So no one will catch you when you lift the table."

"*If* I can tip it. That table weighs a ton."

"Miss Climpson did it. In *Strong Poison.* She had to. Lord Peter was running out of time. And so are we."

"You talked to Finch?" I said.

"Yes. Finally. I had to walk all the way over to Bakers' farm, where he'd gone to buy asparagus. What *is* he up to?"

"And the figure was definitely a five?"

"It wasn't a figure. It was written out. And there's no other number with two 'f's and two 'e's. It was definitely the fifteenth of June."

"The fifteenth of June," Professor Peddick said from the hearth. "The eve of the Battle of Quatre Bras and the fateful mistakes that led to the disaster of Waterloo. It was on that day that Napoleon made the error of trusting the taking of Quatre Bras to General Ney. A fateful day."

"It'll be a fateful day, all right, if we don't get Tossie up to Coventry," Verity murmured. "Here's what we'll do. You'll tip the table once or twice, then Madame Iritosky will ask if there's a spirit present, and I'll rap once for yes. And then she'll ask me if I have a message for someone, and I'll spell it out."

"Spell it out?"

"With raps. The medium recites the alphabet and the spirit raps on the letter."

"It sounds rather time-consuming," I said. "I thought on the Other Side they knew everything. You'd think they could come up with a more efficient means of communication."

"They did, the Ouija board, but it wasn't invented till 1891, so we'll just have to make do."

"How are you doing the raps?"

"I've got half of the sugared-violets box sewn to one garter and the other half to the other. When I hit my knees together, it makes a very nice, hollow sort of rap. I tried it upstairs in my room."

"How do you keep from rapping when you don't want to?" I said, looking down at her skirts. "In the middle of dinner, for instance."

"I've got one garter pulled higher than the other. I'll pull it down till they're at the same spot after we've sat down at the séance table. What I need you to do is keep Madame Iritosky from rapping."

"Has she got a sugared-violets box, too?"

"No. She does it with her feet. She cracks her toes like the Fox sisters. If you keep your leg pressed against hers so you can feel any movement, I don't think she'll try rapping herself, at least till after I've rapped out, 'Go to Coventry.' "

"Are you certain this will work?"

"It worked for Miss Climpson," she said. "Besides, it must have worked. You heard Finch. Tossie's diary says she went to Coventry on the fifteenth, so she must have gone. So we must have convinced her to go. So the séance must have been successful."

"That makes no sense," I said.

"This is the Victorian era," she said. "Women didn't have to make sense." She hooked her arm through mine. "Here are Madame Iritosky and the Count. Shall we go in to dinner?"

We went into dinner, which consisted of grilled sole, roast rack of lamb, and second-guessing Napoleon.

"Should never have stayed the night at Fleurus," Colonel Mering said. "If he had gone on to Quatre Bras, the battle would have taken place twenty-four hours earlier, and Wellington and Blücher would never have joined forces."

"Balderdash!" Professor Peddick said. "He should have waited for the ground to dry after the rainstorm. He should never have pressed forward in the mud."

It seemed grossly unfair. They had, after all, the advantage of knowing how things had turned out, while all Napoleon and Verity and I had to go on were a handful of battlefield communiqués and a date in a waterlogged diary.

"Rubbish!" Colonel Mering said. "Should have attacked earlier in the day and taken Ligny. Never would have been a battle of Waterloo if he'd done that."

"You must have seen a great many battles while you were out in India, Colonel," Madame Iritosky said. "And any number of fabulous treasures. Did you bring any of them home? A Rajah's emeralds, perhaps? Or a forbidden moonstone from the eye of an idol?"

"What?" Colonel Mering sputtered through his mustache. "Moonstone? Idol?"

"Yes, you know, Papa," Tossie said. "*The Moonstone.* It's a novel."

"Pah! Never heard of it," he muttered.

"By Wilkie Collins," Tossie persisted. "The moonstone was stolen, and there's a detective and quicksand and the hero did it, only he'd taken it without knowing it. You must read it."

"No point in it now that you've told me the ending," Colonel Mering said. "And no such thing as jeweled idols."

"But Mesiel brought me a lovely necklace of rubies," Mrs. Mering said, "from Benares."

"Rubies!" Madame Iritosky said, shooting a glance at Count de Vecchio. "Really!"

"What use can the *signora* have for rubies," Count de Vecchio said, "when she has such a jewel as her daughter? She ees like a diamond. No, like a *zaffiro perfetto,* how do you say, a flawless sapphire."

I looked at Baine, who was serving soup grimly.

"Madame Iritosky once contacted the spirit of a Rajah," Mrs. Mering said. "Do you think there will be manifestations at our séance tonight, Madame Iritosky?"

"Tonight?" Madame Iritosky said, alarmed. "No, no, there can be no séance tonight. Or tomorrow. These things must not be done in haste. I must have time to prepare myself spiritually."

And unpack your trumpets, I thought. I looked over at Verity, expecting an expression as grim as Baine's, but she was calmly eating her soup.

"And manifestations may not be possible here," Madame Iritosky went on. "Visible phenomena only occur near what we call portals, links between our world and the world beyond—"

"But there *is* a portal here," Mrs. Mering cut in. "I'm sure of it. I have seen spirits in the house and on the grounds. I'm *certain* if you will grant us a séance tonight, we shall have a manifestation."

"We mustn't overtire Madame Iritosky," Verity said. "She is quite right. Railway journeys *are* fatiguing, and we must not ask her to tax her wonderful psychic powers too far. We shall have to have tonight's séance without her."

"With*out* me?" Madame Iritosky said icily.

"We would not dream of taxing your spiritual powers for a poor, homely affair like ours. When you have recovered your strength, we will have a *true* séance."

Madame Iritosky opened her mouth, closed it, and opened it again, looking exactly like Colonel Mering's globe-eyed ryunkin.

"Fish?" Baine said, bending over her with the platter of sole.

Round One to our side. Now, if only the séance would go as well.

The Reverend Mr. Arbitage arrived at nine, I took the opportunity of the subsequent introductions to put the wires up my sleeves, and we all (except for Madame Iritosky, who had excused herself rather huffily and gone upstairs, and Colonel Mering, who had muttered, "Twaddle!" and gone off to the library to read his paper) trooped into the parlor and sat down around the rosewood table which there was no way on earth I was going to be able to lift, leverage or no leverage.

Verity motioned me to sit down next to her. I did and immediately felt a weight on my lap.

"What's that?" I whispered under cover of Terence, the Count, and the Reverend Mr. Arbitage all jockeying for position next to Tossie.

"Princess Arjumand's basket," Verity whispered back. "Open it when I give you the signal."

"What signal?" I said, and felt a sharp kick on my shin.

The Count and the Reverend Mr. Arbitage won the battle, and Terence was left with Mr. Arbitage and Mrs. Mering. Professor Peddick sat down next to me. "Napoleon was interested in spiritism," he said. "He held a séance in the Great Pyramid of Giza."

"We must join hands," the Count said to Tossie, taking her hand in his. "Like this. . . ."

"Yes, yes, we must all join hands," Mrs. Mering said. "Why, Madame Iritosky!"

Madame Iritosky was standing in the doorway, draped in a flowing purple robe with wide sleeves. "I have been summoned by the spirits to serve as your guide this evening in the parting of the veil." She touched the back of her hand to her forehead. "It is my duty, no matter what the cost to me."

"How wonderful!" Mrs. Mering said. "Do come sit down. Baine, pull up a chair for Madame Iritosky."

"No, no," Madame Iritosky said, indicating Professor Peddick's chair. "It is here that the teleplasmic vibrations converge." Professor Peddick obligingly changed chairs.

At least she hadn't sat down next to Verity, but she was next to Count de Vecchio, which meant she'd have one hand free. And next to me, which meant I was going to have an even harder time lifting tables.

"There is too much light," she said. "There must be dark—" She looked round the parlor. "Where is my cabinet?"

"Yes, Baine," Mrs. Mering said. "I told you to put it in here."

"Yes, madam," he said, bowing. "One of the doors was broken, so that it would not lock properly, and I removed it to the kitchen for repairs. I have repaired it. Would you like me to bring it in now?"

"No!" Madame Iritosky said. "That will not be necessary."

"As you wish," Baine said.

"I feel that there will not be manifestations tonight," she said. "The spirits wish to speak to us only. Join hands," she ordered, draping her voluminous purple sleeves over the table.

I grabbed her right hand and grasped it firmly.

"No!" she said, wrenching it away. "Lightly."

"So sorry," I said. "I'm new at this sort of thing."

She laid her hand back in mine. "Baine, turn down the lights," she said.

"The spirits can only come to us in candlelight. Bring a candle. Here." She indicated a flower-stand near her elbow.

Baine lit the candle and turned the lights down.

"Do not turn the lights up on any account," she ordered. "Or attempt to touch the spirits or the medium. It could be dangerous."

Tossie giggled, and Madame Iritosky began to cough. Her hand let go of mine. I took the opportunity to extend the wires from my wrists and hook them under the table.

"I beg your pardon. My throat," Madame Iritosky said, and slipped her hand in mine again. And if Baine had turned up the lights, it would have been dangerous, all right. I would have bet anything it would have revealed Count de Vecchio's hand in mine. Not to mention my own hanky-panky.

There was a faint rustling on my right. Verity, moving her garter into position.

"I've never been at a séance before," I said loudly to cover it. "We shan't hear bad news, shall we?"

"The spirits speak as they will," Madame Iritosky said.

"Isn't this exciting?" Mrs. Mering said.

"Silence," Madame Iritosky said in a sepulchral tone. "Spirits, we call you from the Other Side. Come to us and tell us of our fate."

The candle blew out.

Mrs. Mering screamed.

"Silence," Madame Iritosky said. "They are coming."

There was a long pause during which several people coughed, and then Verity kicked me on the shin. I let go of her hand and reached onto my lap, and lifted the lid off the basket.

"I felt something," Verity said, which wasn't true, because Princess Arjumand was brushing against *my* legs.

"I felt it, too," the Reverend Mr. Arbitage said after a moment. "It was like a cold wind."

"Oh!" Tossie said. "I felt it just now."

"Is there a spirit there?" Madame Iritosky said, and I leaned forward and lifted up with my wrists.

Amazingly, the table actually moved. Only a little, but enough to make Tossie and Mrs. Mering both give their little screamlets and Terence to exclaim, "I say!"

"If you are there, spirit," Madame Iritosky said, sounding irritated, "speak to us. Rap once for yes, twice for no. Are you a friendly spirit?"

I held my breath.

*Clack* went the sugared-violets box, and restored my faith in mystery novels.

"Are you Gitcheewatha?" Madame Iritosky asked.

"That's her spirit control," Mrs. Mering explained. "He's a Red Indian chief."

*Clack, clack.*

"Are you the spirit that I saw the other night?" Mrs. Mering said.

*Clack.*

"I *knew* it," Mrs. Mering said.

"Who are you?" Madame Iritosky said coldly.

There was a silence. "She wants us to use the alphabet," Verity said, and even in the dark I could sense Madame Iritosky glaring at her.

"Do you wish to communicate by means of the alphabet?" Mrs. Mering said excitedly.

*Clack.* And then a second clack, a different sound, like someone cracking a knuckle.

"You don't wish to communicate by alphabet?" Mrs. Mering said, confusedly.

*Clack,* and a sharp kick on the shins.

"She does," I said hastily. "A B C—"

*Clack.*

"C," Tossie said. "O, Madame Iritosky, you told me to beware of the sea."

"What else?" Mrs. Mering said. "Do go on, Mr. Henry."

Not while there was a foot loose in here. I slid forward in my chair, stretching my left leg till it touched Madame Iritosky's skirt, and pressed my foot hard against hers. "ABCDEFGHIJK," I said rapidly, my foot held tight against hers, "LMNO—"

*Clack.*

She pulled her leg back, and I wondered what would happen if I clamped my hand down hard on her knee.

It was too late. "ABCD—" Mrs. Mering said, and the rapping sounded again.

"C-O-D?" Mrs. Mering said.

"Cod," Professor Peddick said. "*Gadus callerias,* of which the most interesting variety is the Welsh whiting."

" 'Will you walk a little faster,' " Terence quoted, " 'said a whiting to a—' "

"Cod, coddle, cody," the Reverend Mr. Arbitage said. "Are you the ghost of Buffalo Bill Cody?"

"No!" I shouted before anyone could rap an answer. "I know what it is. It's not a C, it's a G. C and G look nearly alike," I said, hoping no one would notice the letters had been spoken, not written, and that they were nowhere near each other in the called-out alphabet. "G-O-D. She's trying to spell 'Godiva.' Are you the spirit of Lady Godiva?"

A very decisive *clack* and we were, thankfully, back on track.

"Lady Go*di*va?" Mrs. Mering said uncertainly.

Tossie said, "Is she the one who rode a horse without any—?"

"Tocelyn!" Mrs. Mering said.

"Lady Godiva was a very holy woman," Verity said. "She had only her people's best interests at heart. Her message must be very urgent."

"Yes," I said, pressing hard against Madame Iritosky's leg. "What are you trying to tell us, Lady Godiva? ABC—"

*Clack.*

I rattled through the alphabet again, determined not to leave any spaces this time for Madame Iritosky to insert a rap. "ABCDEFGHIJK—"

I made it as far as M. There was a sharp rap, like a very annoyed toe being cracked. I ignored it and pressed on to O, but to no avail.

"M," Mrs. Mering said. "CM."

"What sort of word begins with CM?" Terence said.

"Could she be saying 'come'?" Tossie said.

"Yes, of course," Mrs. Mering said. "But where does she wish us to come? ABC—" and Verity clacked on cue, but I didn't see what good it was going to do us. We'd never make it to "O," let alone "V."

"A—" Mrs. Mering said.

I stamped down hard on Madame Iritosky's foot, but it was too late. *Rap.* There was no mistaking the fury behind the rap this time. It sounded like she'd broken a toe.

"C-A—" Mrs. Mering said.

"Cat," Madame Iritosky pronounced. "The spirit is trying to communicate news of Miss Mering's cat." Her voice abruptly changed. "I bring you word of Princess Arjumand," she said in a low husky growl. "She is here with us on the Other Side—"

"Princess Arjumand? On the Other Side?" Tossie said. "But she can't be! She—"

"Do not grieve that she has passed over. She is happy here."

Princess Arjumand chose this moment to jump onto the table, scaring everyone and startling Tossie into a screamlet.

"O, Princess Arjumand!" Tossie said happily. "I knew you hadn't passed over. Why did the spirit say she had, Madame Iritosky?"

I didn't wait for her to come up with an answer. "The message was not 'cat.' C-A—What are you trying to say to us, spirit?" and rattled off the alphabet as fast as I could. "ABCDEFGHIJKLMNOPQRSTUV—"

Verity clacked, and Tossie said, "C-A-V? What does that spell? 'Cave'? She wishes us to come to a cave?"

"Cahv?" I said helpfully. "Cuhv?"

"Coventry," Mrs. Mering said, and I could have kissed her. "Spirit, do you wish us to come to Coventry?"

A fervent *clack.*

"Where in Coventry?" I said, put my full weight on Madame Iritosky's shoe, and started through the alphabet at a gallop.

Verity wisely decided not to try for "Saint." She clacked on M, I, and C, and, not sure how long I was going to be able to hold Madame Iritosky down, I said, "St. Michael's," got a *clack* of confirmation, asked, "Do you wish us to come to St. Michael's Church?" Another *clack,* and I withdrew my feet.

"St. Michael's Church," Mrs. Mering said. "Oh, Madame Iritosky, we must go first thing tomorrow morning—"

"Silence," Madame Iritosky said, "I sense a malicious spirit here," and I groped wildly for her foot with mine.

"Are you a wicked spirit?" she said.

*Rap.*

I waited for Verity to clack a second time, but there was nothing but a frantic rustling. She must have moved the sugared-violets box back up above her knee.

"Are you being controlled by an unbeliever?" Madame Iritosky asked.

*Rap.*

"Baine, bring up the lights," Madame Iritosky said commandingly. "There is someone rapping here who is not a spirit."

And I was going to be caught with wires sticking out of my wrists. I tried to pull my hand out of Madame Iritosky's (or the Count's), but whoever it was had an iron grip.

"Baine! The lights!" Madame Iritosky ordered. She struck a match and lit the candle.

There was a gust of air from the French doors, and the candle blew out.

Tossie screamed, and even Terence gasped. Everyone looked toward the billowing curtains. There was a sound, like a low moan, and something luminous appeared beyond the curtains.

"My God!" the Reverend Mr. Arbitage said.

"A manifestation," Mrs. Mering breathed.

The shape floated slowly toward the open French doors, canting slightly to port and glowing with a ghastly greenish light.

The hand holding mine relaxed, and I shoved the wires up my sleeves all the way to my elbows. Next to me, I could feel Verity pulling up her skirts and then reaching over and jamming the sugared-violets box down the side of my right boot.

"Count de Vecchio, go turn up the lights!" Madame Iritosky said.

"*Una fantasma!*" the Count exclaimed and crossed himself.

Verity straightened and took my hand. "O manifestation, are you the spirit of Lady Godiva?"

"Count de Vecchio," Madame Iritosky said, "I command you to turn up the gas!"

The shape reached the French doors and then seemed to rise and take shape as a face. A veiled face with large dark eyes. And a mashed nose. And jowls.

Verity's hand, holding mine, gave a little spasm. "O spirit," she said, her voice controlled, "do you wish us to come to Coventry?"

The shape drifted slowly back from the door, and then turned and vanished, as if a black cloth had been thrown over it. The French doors slammed shut.

"It bids us go to Coventry," I said. "We cannot ignore the spirit's summons."

"Did you *see* that?" Count de Vecchio said. "It was horrible, horrible!"

"I have seen a seraphim in the flesh," the Reverend Mr. Arbitage said rapturously.

The lights came up, revealing Baine standing calmly by the lamp on the marble-topped table, adjusting the flame.

"O, Madame Iritosky!" Mrs. Mering said, collapsing onto the carpet, "I have seen the face of my own dear mother!"

# CHAPTER EIGHTEEN

A Good Night's Sleep—An Alias—Sudden Departure—More
Aliases—Madame Iritosky's Future Predicted—The Mystery
of the Penwiper Solved—The Bishop's Bird Stump as Murder
Weapon—A Robbery—The Mystery of the Rubies Solved—The
Mystery of the Diary Solved—An Extended Departure—On the
Train to Coventry—A Setback

I t took the better part of an hour and a bottle of benzene to get the Balmain's Luminous Paint off Cyril, with Princess Arjumand assisting, and the fumes must have got to us, because the next thing I knew, Baine was shaking me and saying, "Sorry to wake you, sir, but it's past six, and Colonel Mering asked me to wake him and Professor Peddick at seven."

"Umm," I said, trying to come awake. Cyril burrowed deeper into the covers.

"Jimmy Slumkin, sir," Baine said, pouring hot water into the washbowl.

"What?"

"The true name of the Count. Jimmy Slumkin. It was on his passport."

Slumkin. Well, so much for the Count as the mysterious Mr. C, which was probably just as well, but I wished we had at least *one* suspect. Verity's Lord Peter's and Monsieur Poirot's problem was always that they had too many suspects. I had never heard of a mystery where the detective didn't have any.

I sat up and put my feet over the bed. "With an 'S' or a 'C'?"

Baine stopped setting the straight razors out and turned to look curiously at me. "I beg your pardon, sir?"

"Slumkin. Is it spelled with an 'S' or a 'C'?"

"An 'S,'" he said. "Why, sir?"

"Madame Iritosky told Miss Mering she would marry someone whose name began with a 'C,'" I said, stretching the truth a bit.

He turned back to his razors. "Really. Perhaps the 'C' stood for Count."

"No," I said, "she very definitely specified a *Mr.* C. You don't know of any eligible gentlemen in the area whose names begin with 'C,' do you?"

"Gentlemen?" he said. "No, sir."

I got shaved and dressed and then tried to get Cyril out of bed. "I am *not* going to carry you this time."

"It's rather cold and cloudy outside this morning," Baine said, not helping matters. "You'd best wear a coat."

"Cloudy?" I said, wrestling Cyril to the edge of the bed.

"Yes, sir," Baine said. "It looks as though it might rain."

Baine hadn't exaggerated. It looked like it might pour at any minute, and it felt like I had just made a drop into the middle of December. Cyril took one sniff out the door and bolted halfway up the stairs before I was able to catch him and carry him down again. "It's not that cold in the stable," I told him, which was a flat lie. It was freezing, and dark. The groom must have overslept, too.

I groped for matches and a lamp, and lit it. "Hullo," Verity said. She was sitting on a stack of hay bales, swinging her legs. "Where have you been?"

"What are you doing out here?"

"Madame Iritosky and the Count left at four. They bribed the groom to take them to the station."

Cyril, who claims he cannot make it up the height of a single stair tread without assistance, made a flying leap onto the hay bales and into Verity's lap.

"Hullo, Cyril," Verity said. "I thought perhaps you were right about Count de Vecchio being Mr. C, so I followed them out to make certain he didn't carry Tossie off with him."

"He's not Mr. C," I said. "He's Jimmy Slumkin."

"I know," she said, scratching Cyril behind the ears. "Also known as Tom Higgins, Comte de Fanaud, and Bob 'the Weasel' Wexford. I went through after they left and checked Scotland Yard's archives. I also know why they were here."

"To case the joint?"

"Probably," she said. Cyril turned on his side, sighing. Verity stroked his stomach. "It seems that night before last Madame Iritosky gave a special séance for the Psychic Research Society so they could test her authenticity. They bound her hands and feet and locked her in her cabinet, after which the spirit of Cleopatra appeared, played a tambourine, and danced around the table, touching the participants and telling them to beware the sea."

She grinned at me. "Unfortunately, one of the Psychic Research Society members was so overcome by Cleopatra's charms that, in spite of Madame Iritosky's warnings, he grabbed her wrist and attempted to pull her onto his lap."

"And then what?"

"The spirit yanked his hair and bit him. He yelped, and at that point another Psychic Research Society member turned up the lights, unlocked the cabinet—"

"Which was, oddly enough, empty."

"And tore the veils off Cleopatra, who turned out to be Madame Iritosky. Three days later she and her accomplice sailed for France, where she was exposed by Richet, who believed in *everybody*, and after that for Calcutta, where she learned a new set of tricks from an Indian fakir. In 1922, she went to America, just in time to be exposed as a fraud by Houdini, and thence back to Oxford, where Arthur Conan Doyle pronounced her 'the greatest medium I have ever seen. There can be no doubt of the truth of her mediumistic talents.' "

She looked fondly at Cyril. "When we've got Tossie safely connected to Mr. C," she said, scratching behind his ears, "I think I'll take you back with me."

She looked up at me impishly. "I'm kidding," she said. "I've sworn off incongruities. I would like to have a bulldog, though."

"Me, too," I said.

She ducked her head. "They haven't got Carruthers out yet," she said. "The net still won't open. Warder thinks perhaps it's a temporary blockage. She's switched to an accelerated four-hour intermittent to try and get past it."

"Has T.J. solved the mystery of why the incongruity was able to get past the net's defenses?" I asked.

"No. He's figured out why Napoleon lost the battle of Waterloo, though." She grinned, and then said more seriously, "And he was finally able to generate an incongruity."

"An incongruity?" I said. "Why didn't you tell me?"

"It was only a simulated incongruity. And it's not the right sort. It occurred as part of a self-correction. It was one of those sims where he had an historian kill Wellington. When he introduced a second historian into the sim, the historian was able to steal the rifle that the first historian was going to shoot Wellington with and bring it forward through the net, so that it prevented an incongruity rather than causing one. But he said to tell you that at least it proves bringing something forward through the net is theoretically possible, even if it didn't apply to our case."

Theoretically possible. It still didn't solve the problem of getting the net open to get the first historian through to kill Wellington in the first place.

"Anything else?" I asked.

"No. He and Mr. Dunworthy were happy that we'd managed to persuade Tossie to go to Coventry. They both think the fact that they haven't been able to find any increased slippage around the original drop means the incongruity was short-term and that all it needs to correct itself is for us to get her to St. Michael's on time."

She ducked her head again. "And, if it does, we'll be done here and have to go face Lady Schrapnell. And I promised I'd help you find the bishop's bird stump. So I decided to wait for you."

She shifted Cyril off her lap and pulled a pen, a bottle of ink, and some sheets of paper out of her pocket and set them on the hay.

"What's all that for?" I asked.

"For making a list of all the possibilities of what might have happened to the bishop's bird stump. Lord Peter Wimsey and Harriet Vane made a list in *Have His Carcase.*"

"There's no such thing as listing all the possibilities," I said. "The continuum's a chaotic system, remember?"

She ignored me. "In an Agatha Christie mystery, there's always one possibility you haven't considered, and that's the solution to the mystery. All right," she said, dipping her pen in the ink. "One, the bishop's bird stump was in the cathedral during the raid and was destroyed in the fire. Two, it was in the cathedral, survived the fire, and was found in the rubble. Three," she said, writing busily, "it was rescued during the raid."

I shook my head. "The only things saved were a flag, two sets of candlesticks, a wooden crucifix, and the altar books. There's a list."

"We are writing down *all* the possibilities," she said. "Later, we'll eliminate the ones that are impossible."

Which so far was all three.

"Four," she said, "it survived the raid, *even though* it didn't make the list for some reason, and it's stored somewhere."

"No," I said. "Mrs. Bittner went through all the things in the cathedral when they sold it, and it wasn't there."

"Lord Peter didn't keep contradicting Harriet when she was making a list," she said. "Five, it wasn't in the church during the raid. It was removed sometime between the tenth and the fourteenth of November."

"Why?" I said.

"For safekeeping. With the east windows."

I shook my head. "I went to Lucy Hampton rectory to see. The only things they had of Coventry's were the windows."

"Oh. Well, what if some member of the congregation took the bishop's bird stump home for safekeeping? Or to polish it or something, so that it just happened to be out of the cathedral that night?"

"If that happened, why didn't the person bring it back?"

"I don't know," she said, biting her lip. "Perhaps he was killed during the raid, by a high-explosive bomb, and whoever inherited it didn't know it belonged to the cathedral."

"*Or* he could have thought to himself, 'I can't do this to the people of Coventry. They're already going to have to suffer the loss of their cathedral. I can't inflict the bishop's bird stump on them as well.' "

"*Be* serious," she said. "What if he didn't bring it back because it was destroyed in the raid, by a bomb or something."

I shook my head. "Even a high-explosive bomb couldn't destroy the bishop's bird stump."

She flung the pen down. "I am *so* glad we're going to Coventry today so I can actually *see* the bishop's bird stump. It cannot possibly be as bad as you say."

She looked thoughtful. "What if the bishop's bird stump was involved in a crime? It was used as a murder weapon, and it got blood on it, so they stole it to keep anyone from finding out about the murder."

"You have been reading too many murder mysteries," I said.

She dipped her pen in the ink again. "What if it was stored in the cathedral, but *inside* something else, like Poe's 'The Purloined Letter'?" She started to write and then stopped and frowned at the pen. She pulled an orange dahlia penwiper out of her pocket.

"What are you doing?" I said.

"Wiping my pen," she said. She stuck the pen into the dahlia and wiped it off between the layers of cloth.

"It's a penwiper," I said. "A *pen wiper!* It's used to *wipe pens!*"

"Yes," she said, looking at me dubiously. "There was ink on the point. It would have blotted the paper."

"Of course! So you wipe it on a penwiper!"

"How many drops have you had, Ned?" she said.

"You're a wonderful girl, you know that?" I said, grabbing her by the shoulders. "You've solved a mystery that's been plaguing me since 1940. I could kiss—"

There was a bloodcurdling scream from the direction of the house, and Cyril buried his face in his paws.

"What now?" Verity said, looking disappointed.

I let go of her shoulders. "The daily swoon?"

She stood up and began brushing straw off her skirts. "This had better not be anything that keeps us from going to Coventry," she said. "You go first. I'll come in through the kitchen."

"Mesiel!" Mrs. Mering shrieked. "O, Mesiel!"

I took off for the house, expecting to find Mrs. Mering laid out among the bric-a-brac, but she wasn't. She was standing halfway down the stairs in her wrapper, clutching the railing. Her hair was in two operatic braids, and she was waving an empty velvet-lined box.

"My rubies!" she was wailing to the Colonel, who had apparently just come out of the breakfast room. He still had his napkin in his hand. "They've been stolen!"

"I *knew* it!" the Colonel, shocked into using a subject, said. "Should never have allowed that medium person in the house!" He threw down the napkin. "Thieves!"

"O, Mesiel," Mrs. Mering said, pressing the jewel case to her bosom, "surely you don't think Madame Iritosky had anything to do with this!"

Tossie appeared. "What's happened, Mama?"

"Tocelyn, go and see whether any of your jewelry is missing!"

"My diary!" Tossie cried and scampered off, nearly colliding with Verity, who must have come up the back stairs.

"What is it?" Verity said. "What's happened?"

"Robbed!" the Colonel said succinctly. "Tell Madame Whatever-Her-Name-Is and that Count person to come down immediately!"

"They've gone," Verity said.

"Gone?" Mrs. Mering gasped, and I thought she was going to pitch over the stairs.

I raced up and Verity hurried down, and we supported Mrs. Mering down the steps and into the parlor. We deposited her, sobbing, on the horsehair sofa.

Tossie appeared breathlessly at the top of the stairs. "O, Mama, my garnet necklace is missing!" she cried, pattering down the stairs, "and my pearls, and my amethyst ring!" But instead of running into the parlor, she disappeared down the corridor and reappeared a moment later, carrying her diary. "Thank goodness I hid my diary in the library, in amongst all the other books where no one would notice it!"

Verity and I looked at each other.

"Knew all this table-tipping nonsense would come to no good," Colonel Mering said. "Where's Baine? Ring for him!"

Verity started for the bellpull, but Baine was already there, carrying a chipped pottery jug.

"Put that down," Colonel Mering ordered, "and go fetch the constable. Mrs. Mering's necklace is missing."

"And my amethyst ring," Tossie said.

"I removed Mrs. Mering's rubies and the other pieces of jewelry last night for cleaning," Baine said. "I had noticed when the ladies wore them last, they seemed somewhat dimmed." He reached in the jug. "I left them to soak overnight in a solution of vinegar and baking soda." He pulled out the ruby necklace and handed it to Colonel Mering. "I was just returning the things to their cases. I would have mentioned it to Mrs. Mering, but she was busy with her guests."

"I knew it!" Mrs. Mering said from the sofa. "Mesiel, how could you have suspected dear Madame Iritosky?"

"Baine, check on the silver," Colonel Mering said. "And the Rubens."

"Yes, sir," Baine said. "What time would you like the carriages brought round?"

"Carriages? What for?" the Colonel said.

"To take us to Coventry," Tossie said. "We are going to St. Michael's Church."

"Pah!" Colonel Mering said. "No business going anywhere. Thieves in the neighborhood! No telling when they might come back!"

"But we have to go," Verity said.

"The spirits summoned us," Tossie said.

"Stuff and nonsense!" Colonel Mering sputtered. "Probably concocted the whole thing to get us all out of the house so they could come back and steal our valuables!"

"Concocted!" Mrs. Mering said, rising up majestically from the sofa. "Are you implying the spirit message we received last night was not genuine?"

Colonel Mering ignored her. "We won't need the carriages. And better make certain the horses are there. No telling what—" He looked suddenly stricken. "My Black Moor!"

I thought it unlikely that Madame Iritosky would steal the Colonel's goldfish, even if she had been foiled in the matter of the rubies, but it seemed like a bad idea to tell the Colonel that. I stepped back to let him pass as he shot out the door.

Mrs. Mering sank back down on the sofa. "O, that your father would doubt Madame Iritosky's genuineness! It is a mercy she's gone and is not here to suffer such vile accusations!" She thought of something. "What reason did she give for their departure, Baine?"

"I was unaware of their departure until this morning," Baine said. "It appears they left sometime during the night. I was extremely surprised. I had told Madame Iritosky that I felt certain you would write the Psychic Research Society this morning and ask them to come witness the manifestation, and I supposed of course that she would have stayed for that, but perhaps she had urgent business elsewhere."

"No doubt," Mrs. Mering said. "The spirits' summons may not be denied. But the Psychic Research Society *here!* How thrilling that would have been!"

The Colonel came back in, carrying Princess Arjumand under his arm and looking grim.

"Is your Black Moor safe, sir?" I asked anxiously.

"For the moment," he said, dumping the cat on the floor.

Tossie scooped her up.

"No coincidence that they arrived when they did, on the day before my red-spotted silver tancho was to arrive," the Colonel said. "Baine! Want you to stand guard over the fishpond all day. No telling when they might come back!"

"Baine is going with me," Mrs. Mering said, rising from the sofa, looking like a Valkyrie with her braids and the light of battle in her eyes. "And *we* are going to Coventry."

"Balderdash! Not going anywhere. Intend to stay here and defend the battlements!"

"Then we shall go without you," she said. "The spirits' summons cannot be denied. Baine, when is the next train to Coventry?"

"Nine-oh-four, madam," Baine said promptly.

"Excellent," she said, turning her back on the Colonel. "Bring the carriage round at a quarter past eight. We shall leave for the station at half-past."

He did, but we didn't. Or at half-past nine. Or ten. Luckily, there were trains at 9:49, 10:17, and 11:05, which Baine, the walking Bradshaw, rattled off each time we experienced a delay.

There were various delays. Mrs. Mering declared the drama of the morning had left her weak, and she could not go without a sustaining breakfast of blood sausage, kedgeree, and stuffed chicken livers. Tossie could not find her lavender gloves. Jane brought down the wrong shawl. "No, no, the cashmere is far too warm for June," Mrs. Mering said. "The tartan shawl, the one from Dunfermline."

"We're going to miss Mr. C," Verity said, standing waiting in the foyer while Mrs. Mering changed her hat again.

"No, we're not," I said. "We can leave in half an hour and still catch the 11:26, and the diary didn't say anything about what time of day it happened. Relax."

She nodded. "I've been thinking about the bishop's bird stump," she said. "What if someone hid something in it to keep someone else from stealing it? And they came back to take it out again, but there wasn't time, so they just took the whole thing?" She looked up the stairs. "What can be *taking* them so long? It's nearly eleven."

Tossie came tripping down the stairs in her lavender gloves and a medley of lavender frills. She looked out the open door.

"It looks like it's going to rain," she said, frowning. "We shan't be able to see any sights if it rains, Ma*ma*," she said to Mrs. Mering, who was descending the stairs. "Perhaps we should wait till tomorrow."

"No!" Verity said. "What if Lady Godiva has something urgent to tell us?"

"It *does* look like rain," Mrs. Mering said. "Has Baine packed the umbrellas?"

"Yes," I said. Also the guidebooks, the luncheon hamper, the smelling salts, a spirit lamp, Mrs. Mering's embroidery, Tossie's novel, Terence's Tennyson, several issues of the psychic weekly magazine, *The Light,* and an assortment of lap robes and rugs, all of which Baine had managed to pack so well there was still room for us in the two carriages, though it was probably a good thing Professor Peddick had decided to stay with the Colonel.

"I wished to discuss several points regarding the Battle of Thermopylae with the Colonel," he told Mrs. Mering.

"Well, don't let him stay out if it rains," she said, apparently softening a little toward her husband. "He'll catch his death."

Terence led Cyril over and hoisted him up onto the running board.

"Mr. St. Trewes," Mrs. Mering said in Wagnerian tones, "you cannot possibly be thinking of taking that *creature* with you."

Terence stopped in mid-hoist, Cyril's hind legs dangling in the air. "Cyril's a perfect gentleman on trains," Terence said. "He's been everywhere on them—London, Oxford, Sussex. He loves to look out the window, you know, at passing cats and things. And he always gets along famously with the railway guards."

But not with Mrs. Mering.

"A railway carriage is no place for an animal," she said.

"And I'm wearing my new travelling dress," Tossie said, patting at the frills with a lavender glove.

"But he'll be so disappointed," Terence said, reluctantly lowering him to the ground.

"Nonsense!" Mrs. Mering said. "Dogs haven't any feelings."

"Never mind, Cyril," Professor Peddick said. "You can come with me out to the fishpond. I've always been extremely fond of dogs. So has my niece, Maud. Feeds them from the table." They walked off together.

"Do get in, Mr. St. Trewes," Mrs. Mering said. "You will make us late for the train. Baine, did you pack my lorgnette?"

We finally left for the station at half-past ten. "Remember," Verity said to me as I helped her into the carriage, "Tossie's diary only says 'the trip to

Coventry.' It doesn't say which part of the trip. Mr. C could be someone at the station or on the train."

We arrived at the station at 11:09. The train had already gone, which was probably just as well since it took us nearly ten minutes to get everyone and everything out of the carriages. By the time we got out onto the platform, there was no one there.

"I don't see why the train couldn't have waited!" Mrs. Mering said. "A few minutes either way surely wouldn't make a difference. *So* inconsiderate!"

"I *know* it's going to rain and ruin my travelling dress," Tossie fretted, looking at the sky. "O, Terence, I do hope it doesn't rain on our wedding day."

" 'Ah festal day, so fair, so bright,' " Terence quoted, but absently, looking off toward Muchings End. "If it does rain, I hope Professor Peddick won't leave Cyril outside."

"I do hope they don't decide to go fishing in this weather," Mrs. Mering said, "what with Mesiel's weak chest. He caught a dreadful chill last spring. He was in bed for two weeks, and such a frightening cough! The doctor said it was a miracle it didn't go into pneumonia. Mr. Henry, do go and see if there's any sign of the train."

I walked down to the far end of the platform to check. When I came back, Verity was standing apart from the others. "I've been thinking about the bishop's bird stump," she said. "In *The Moonstone,* the jewel was taken by someone who didn't know he'd stolen it. He was sleepwalking, and he put it in something, and then a second person stole it from him. What if the person who took it—?"

"Was sleepwalking?" I said. "In Coventry Cathedral?"

"No. Didn't know they were committing a crime."

"Exactly how many drops have you done in the past week?" I asked.

Baine reappeared, with a porter who was at least seventy years old, and they and the groom began transferring our luggage from the carriages to the edge of the platform. Verity looked speculatively at the porter.

"No," I said. "She was married to him for over fifty years. That means he'd have to live to be a hundred and twenty."

"Did you see any sign of the train, Mr. Henry?" Mrs. Mering called.

"No, I'm afraid not," I said, walking over to her.

"Where *can* it be?" she said. "I hope its being late isn't an omen. Mr. Henry, have the carriages gone?"

"We *must* go to Coventry today," Verity said. "What would Madame Iritosky think of us if we ignored the spirits' message?"

"She herself thought nothing of departing in the middle of the night in response to a message she received," I said, wishing the bloody train would hurry up and come. "And I have no doubt the weather will be fine when we reach Coventry."

"And there are such lovely things in Coventry," Verity said and then obviously couldn't think of any.

"Blue dye," I said. "They are famous for their Coventry-blue dye. And ribbons."

"I might buy some for my trousseau," Tossie said.

"Professor Peddick tends to be absentminded," Terence said wistfully. "He won't go off and leave Cyril, do you think?"

"Azure ribbons, I think, for my going-away hat," Tossie said. "Or baby blue, perhaps. What do you think, Mama?"

"Why can't these trains arrive at the time listed on the schedule instead of making us wait for hours?" Mrs. Mering said.

And so on. The train arrived at exactly 11:32, pulling into the station with an impressive whoosh of steam, and Verity practically pushed everyone onto the train, keeping an anxious eye out for anyone who looked like he might be Mr. C.

Baine assisted Mrs. Mering up the steps and into our compartment and then ran back to supervise the porter in loading our belongings. Jane settled Mrs. Mering in her seat, gave her her lorgnette, her embroidery, found her handkerchief and her shawl, and then bobbed a curtsey and climbed down the steps.

"Where's she going?" I said to Verity, watching Jane hurry down the platform to the rear of the train.

"To second-class," she said. "Servants don't travel with their employers."

"How do they do without them?"

"They don't," she said, catching up her skirts and starting up the steps.

They certainly didn't. Baine came back as soon as everything was aboard to bring Mrs. Mering a lap robe and ask if there was anything else she needed.

"A cushion," she said. "These railway seats are so uncomfortable."

"Yes, madam," he said, and took off at a gallop. He returned in under a minute, disheveled and out of breath, with a brocade-covered cushion.

"The train from Reading is a corridor train, madam," he panted, "but this one has only compartments. I will, however, attend you at each stop."

"Were there no direct trains to Coventry?" she said.

"Yes, madam," Baine said. "At 10:17. The train is about to leave, madam. Is there anything else?"

"Yes, the Baedeker. And a rug to put my feet on. The condition of these railway compartment floors is disgraceful."

Mrs. Mering had obviously never been on the tube. It is a temporal universal that people never appreciate their own time, especially transportation. Twentieth-Century contemps complained about cancelled flights and gasoline prices, Eighteenth-Century contemps complained about muddy roads and highwaymen. No doubt Professor Peddick's Greeks complained about recalcitrant horses and chariot wheels falling off.

I had ridden on trains before, in the 1940s, most recently to Hampton Lucy to see if the bishop's bird stump was there with the east windows, but those trains had been packed with soldiers, the windows had been covered with blackout curtains, and all the fittings had been removed to make ammunition. And, even if it hadn't been wartime, they had been nothing to this.

The high-backed seats were upholstered in green velveteen, and the walls above were panelled in polished mahogany inlaid with a pattern of flowers. There were rich green plush curtains hung at the windows, and gas lamps in brackets on both sides, covered with etched-glass lampshades, and the luggage rack overhead, the hand rails, the arm rests, the curtain rings, were all of polished brass.

Definitely not the tube. And, as the train lurched slowly forward (with Baine making a last flying run to deliver the Baedeker and the rug and another back to second-class) and then picked up speed through the beautiful, misty countryside, definitely nothing to complain about.

That did not stop Mrs. Mering from complaining about the soot blowing in the window (Terence closed the window), about the stuffiness of the compartment (Terence opened the window again and drew the curtains), about the dimness of the day, the roughness of the ride, the hardness of the cushion Baine had brought her.

She gave a little screamlet each time the train stopped, started, or went round a curve, and a large one when the railway guard came in to take our tickets. He was even older than the porter, but Verity leaned forward to look at his name badge and subsided pensively in her seat after he'd gone.

"What was the guard's name?" I asked her when I helped her down at Reading Station, where we were to change trains.

"Edwards," she said, looking around the platform. "Do you see anyone who looks like he'd be willing to marry Tossie?"

"What about Crippen over there?" I said, nodding my head toward a pale, timid-looking young man who kept looking down the track and sticking his finger nervously in his collar.

"None of Crippen's wives managed to stay married to him for fifty years," she said, watching a large and irritable man with sidewhiskers who kept bellowing, "Porter! Porter!" to no avail. The efficient Baine had commandeered all of them before the train even stopped and was directing the disposition of the Mering effects.

"What about him?" I said, pointing at a five-year-old boy in a sailor suit.

A young man in a boater and a mustache came bolting onto the platform and looked wildly around. Verity gripped my arm. He saw Tossie, standing with Mrs. Mering and Jane, and started toward her, smiling.

"Horace!" A girl waved from another group of three ladies, and Horace raced over to her and began apologizing profusely for being late to meet them.

I looked guiltily over at Terence, thinking about the fateful meeting I'd made him miss.

The young man left with the three ladies, the sidewhiskered man grabbed up his own bags and stormed off, which left Crippen, now warily eyeing a station guard.

But even if he or the young man with the boater had been suddenly smitten, Tossie wouldn't have noticed them. She was too busy planning her wedding.

"I shall carry orange blossoms for my bouquet," she said, "or white roses. Which do you think, Terence?"

" 'Two roses on one stem on one slender spray,' " Terence quoted, looking longingly at a woman carrying a terrier, " 'in sweet communion grew.' "

"O, but orange blossoms have such a sweet smell."

"There are far too many trains," Mrs. Mering said. "They cannot possibly need all these trains."

Baine finally got everything and everyone on the train and arranged in an even more opulent compartment, and we started for Coventry. After a few minutes, a guard, this one much younger and actually quite good-looking, came along the corridor and punched our tickets. Tossie, deep in planning her trousseau, didn't so much as glance up, and what made us think that when we got to Coventry she would even *notice* Mr. C, engrossed as she was in her wedding plans with Terence? What made us think she would even notice the bishop's bird stump?

She would. She had to. The trip to Coventry had changed her life and inspired her great-great-great-great-granddaughter to make ours miserable.

After a few miles, Baine arrived, spread white linen napkins on our laps, and served us a sumptuous luncheon, which cheered everyone considerably (except possibly Baine, who had made approximately two hundred trips between first and second class, bringing us cold roast beef and cucumber sandwiches and Mrs. Mering a fresh handkerchief, her other gloves, her sewing scissors, and, for no discernible reason, Bradshaw's Railway Guide).

Terence looked out the window and announced it was clearing off, and then that he could see Coventry, and before Jane and Baine had time to gather up everything and fold up Mrs. Mering's lap robe, we were standing on the platform in Coventry, waiting for Baine to unload our luggage and find us a carriage. It had not cleared off, nor did it look like it was going to. There was a fine mist in the air, and the city's outline was blurred and gray.

Terence had thought of a poem suitable to the occasion and was declaiming it. " 'I waited for a train at Coventry,' " he quoted. " 'City of three spires . . .' " He stopped, looking puzzled. "I say, where are the three spires? I only see two."

I looked where he was pointing. One, two, and a tall box-like structure stood out against the gray sky.

"St. Michael's spire is being repaired," Baine said, struggling under a load of rugs and shawls. "The porter informed me that the church is undergoing extensive restorations at the moment."

"That explains why Lady Godiva spoke to us now," Mrs. Mering said. "The spirits' resting place must have been disturbed."

The mist deteriorated into a drizzle, and Tossie gave a screamlet. "My travelling dress!" she cried.

Baine appeared, unfurling umbrellas. "I have obtained a closed carriage, madam," he told Mrs. Mering, handing them to Terence and me to hold over the ladies.

Jane was put into a hack with the luncheon hamper and the rugs and shawls and told to meet us at the church, and we drove into town, the horses clattering along narrow brick-paved streets lined with old, half-timbered buildings that leaned out over the street. A Tudor inn with a painted sign hanging above the door, narrow brick shops selling ribbons and bicycles, narrower houses with mullioned windows and tall chimneys. The old Coventry. This would all be destroyed by fire along with the cathedral that November night in 1940, but it was hard to imagine it, clopping along the damp, placid streets.

The driver pulled the horses to a stop at the corner of St. Mary's Street, the street Provost Howard and his little band had paraded down, carrying the candlesticks and crosses and the regimental flag they'd rescued from the burning cathedral.

"Cahnt gawna fur thuhsahth dawblottuff," the driver said in an impenetrable dialect.

"He says he can't take the carriage any farther," Baine translated. "Apparently the route to the cathedral is blocked."

I leaned forward. "Tell him to go back along this street to Little Park Street. That will take us to the west doors of the church."

Baine told him. The driver shook his head and said something unrecognizable, but turned the horses around and started back up Earl Street.

"O, I can feel the spirits already," Mrs. Mering said, clutching her bosom. "Something is about to happen. I know it."

We turned up Little Park Street toward the cathedral. I could see the tower at the end of the street, and it was no wonder we hadn't been able to see the third spire from the railway station. It was encased in wooden scaffolding from a third of the way up all the way to the top, and, except that it had gray cloth tarps draped across it instead of blue plastic, it looked the way it had looked last week when I'd seen it from Merton's pedestrian gate. Lady Schrapnell was more authentic than she knew.

The piles of red sandstone blocks and heaps of sand in the churchyard looked the same, too, and I worried that the entire approach to the church might be blocked, but it wasn't. The driver was able to pull the carriage up directly in front of the west doors. On them was a large, hand-lettered sign.

"Iffley's churchwarden's been here," I said, and then saw what it said:

*"Closed for repairs.*
*1 June to 31 July."*

*"The heart is its own fate."*
*Philip James Bailey*

# CHAPTER NINETEEN

A Fateful Day—Another Conversation with a Workman—I
Sink to Promoting Jumble Sales—The Cathedral Ghost—A Tour—
I Attempt to Find Out Two Workmen's Names—The Bishop's
Bird Stump Is Found at Last—Tossie's Reaction—The
Execution of Mary Queen of Scots—Baine Expresses an Aesthetic
Opinion—Tossie's Reaction—The Albert Memorial, Beauties
of—Penwipers—Prevalence of Flower Names in Victorian Times—A
Premonition—I Attempt to Find Out the Curate's Name—A
Quarrel—An Abrupt Departure

Closed!" Tossie said.

"Closed?" I said and looked over at Verity. The color had drained from her face.

"Closed," Mrs. Mering said. "It's just as Madame Iritosky said. 'Beware,' and the letter 'C.' She was trying to warn us."

As if to prove her point, it began to drizzle.

"It can't be closed," Verity murmured, looking disbelievingly at the sign. "How can it be closed?"

"Baine," Mrs. Mering said. "What time is the next train?"

Don't let Baine know, I thought. If he didn't know the schedule, we had at least a quarter of an hour while he trotted back to the station to check and back, a quarter of an hour in which to think of something.

But this was Baine we were talking about, clearly the forerunner of Jeeves, and Jeeves had always known everything.

"2:08, madam," he said. "It goes to Reading. Or there's an express at 2:46 to Goring."

"We shall take the 2:08," Mrs. Mering said. "Goring is so common."

"But what about Lady Godiva?" Verity said desperately. "She must have had a reason for wanting you to come to Coventry."

"I am not at all convinced it was her spirit, particularly under the circumstances," Mrs. Mering said. "I believe Madame Iritosky was right about there being mischievous spirits at work. Baine, tell the driver to take us to the station."

"Wait!" I shouted, and jumped out of the carriage and squarely into a puddle. "I will be right back," I said. "Stay there," and took off along the tower wall.

"Where on earth is he going?" I heard Mrs. Mering say. "Baine, go and tell Mr. Henry to come back here immediately."

I sprinted round the corner of the church, holding my coat collar together against the wet.

I remembered from the rubble and the reconstruction that there was a door on the south side of the cathedral and another on the north, and if necessary I'd bang on the vestry door till someone answered.

But it wasn't necessary. The south door was open, and a workman was standing in it, under the porch just out of the rain, arguing with a young man in a clerical collar.

"You promised the clerestory would be completed by the twenty-second and here it is the fifteenth and you've not even begun the varnishing of the new pews," the curate, who was pale and rather pop-eyed, though that might have been from the workman, was saying.

The workman looked as though he had heard all this before and would hear it again. "We carn't start the varnishin', guv, till they're done in the clerestory 'cuz o' the dust."

"Well, then, complete the work in the clerestory."

He shook his head. "Carn't. Bill as wuz puttin' the steel girders in the beams is 'ome sick."

"Well, when will he be back? The work must be completed by next Saturday. That's the date of our church bazaar."

The workman gave him the identical shrug I had seen an electrician give Lady Schrapnell three weeks ago, and it occurred to me it was a pity she wasn't here. She'd have cuffed him smartly on the ear, and the work would have been done by Friday. Or Thursday.

"Cud be tomorra, cud be next month. Don't see wot you need new pews for anyways. I liked the aud box pews."

"*You* are not a member of the clergy," the curate said, getting more pop-eyed, "*or* an expert on modern church architecture. Next month is *not* good enough. The renovations must be completed by the twenty-second."

The workman spit on the damp porch and sauntered back into the church.

"Pardon me," I said, running up to the curate before he could disappear, too. "I wondered if we might tour the church."

"Oh, no!" the curate said, looking wildly round like a housewife surprised by unexpected guests. "We're in the midst of major renovations to the clerestory and the bell tower. The church is officially closed until the thirty-first of July, at which time the vicar would be delighted to conduct you on a tour."

"That's too late," I said. "And it's the renovations we've come to see. The church at Muchings End is badly in need of them. The altar's positively mediaeval."

"Oh, but," he said reluctantly, "the thing is, we're trying to prepare for the church bazaar, and—"

"Church bazaar!" I said. "What a wonderful coincidence! Mrs. Mering has just put on a bazaar at Muchings End."

"Mrs. Mering?" the curate said, looking back at the door as if he'd like to escape through it. "Oh, but the church is in no fit condition for ladies. You wouldn't be able to see the choir or the altar. There's sawdust everywhere, and workmen's tools."

"The ladies won't mind," I said, putting myself firmly between him and the door. "Sawdust is exactly what they've come to see."

Baine came running up with an umbrella, which he handed to me. I handed it back. "Go and bring the carriage round," I said to him. "Tell Mrs. Mering we can tour the church."

Which just goes to show you that hanging round Lady Schrapnell and her ancestors can teach you a thing or two about getting things done.

"Hurry!" I said to Baine, and he sprinted off through the drizzle, which was rapidly turning into rain.

"I really do not think a tour at this time is advisable," the curate said. "The workmen are installing a new choir railing, and I have an appointment to meet with Miss Sharpe regarding the fancywork table."

"You'll be having a jumble sale, of course," I said.

"A jumble sale?" the curate said uncertainly.

"It's the latest thing in bazaars. Ah, here they are." I bounded down the steps as the carriage pulled up, snatched Verity's hand, and pulled her out of the carriage. "What good luck! St. Michael's is open after all, and the curate's offered to give us a tour of the church. Quick," I muttered under my breath. "Before he changes his mind."

Verity tripped lightly up to the curate, smiled brightly at him, and peered in through the door. "Oh, do come look at this, Tossie," she said, and ducked inside.

Terence helped Tossie out and into the church, and I assisted Mrs. Mering, holding the umbrella Baine handed me over her head.

"Oh, dear," she said, looking anxiously at the clouds. "The weather looks very threatening. Perhaps we should start for home before the storm breaks."

"Some of the workmen say they've seen a spirit," I said rapidly. "One of them went home ill after the experience."

"How wonderful!" Mrs. Mering said.

We came up even with the curate, who was standing in the doorway, wringing his hands. "I'm afraid you will be sadly disappointed in St. Michael's, Mrs. Mering," he said. "We are—"

"—preparing for the annual bazaar. Mrs. Mering, you *must* tell him about your dahlia penwipers," I said shamelessly, maneuvering her around him and into the church. "So clever, and beautiful, besides."

There was a crack of thunder so loud I was convinced I'd been struck by lightning for lying.

"Oh, dear," Mrs. Mering said.

"I'm afraid this is an inauspicious time for a tour of the church," the curate said at the same time. "The vicar is away, and Miss Sharpe—"

I opened my mouth to say, "A brief tour, at least, since we're here," and didn't have to. There was a second crack of thunder, and the skies opened up.

Mrs. Mering and the curate stepped back into the church, away from the splashing raindrops, and Baine, the ever-ready, stepped forward and shut the door. "It looks like we'll be here awhile, madam," he said, and I could hear Verity sigh with relief.

"Well," the curate said, "as you're here, this is the nave. As you can see, we are undertaking renovations." He had not exaggerated about the sawdust or the mess. It looked nearly as bad as after the air raid. The chancel was blocked off with wooden hoardings. The pews were draped in dusty tarps. Stacks of lumber lay in front of the choir, from which there issued a loud banging.

"We are modernizing the church," the curate said. "The decorations were hopelessly out-of-date. I had hoped to have the bell tower replaced with a modern carillon, but the Renovations Committee refused to consider it. Hopelessly hidebound. But I was able to persuade them to remove the galleries and many of the old tombs and monuments, which were cluttering up the chapels. Some of them dated all the way back to the Fourteenth

Century." He rolled his eyes. "Simply ruined the look of the church."

He smiled a rather protruding smile at Tossie. "Would you care to see the nave, Miss Mering? We've put in all new electric lighting."

Verity came up next to me. "Get his name," she whispered.

"When our proposed plans are completed," the curate said, "the church will be a fully modern church which will last hundreds of years."

"Fifty-two," I muttered.

"I beg your pardon?" the curate said.

"Nothing," I said. "You're modernizing the tower, too?"

"Yes. It and the spire are being completely recased. It's rather rough here, ladies." He offered Tossie his arm.

Mrs. Mering took it. "Where is your crypt?" she asked.

"The crypt?" he said. "Over here," he pointed in the direction of the hoarding, "but it's not being modernized."

"Do you believe in the world beyond?" Mrs. Mering said.

"I . . . of course," he said, bewildered. "I'm a man of the cloth." He smiled protuberantly at Tossie. "I am of course merely a curate at present, but I hope to be offered a living next year in Sussex."

"Are you familiar with Arthur Conan Doyle?" Mrs. Mering demanded.

"I . . . yes," he said, looking even more bewildered. "That is, I've read *A Study in Scarlet*. Thrilling story."

"You have not read his writings on spiritism?" she said. "Baine!" she called to the butler, who was neatly standing the umbrellas next to the door. "Fetch the issue of *The Light* with Arthur Conan Doyle's letter in it."

Baine nodded, opened the heavy door, and disappeared into the deluge, pulling his collar up as he went.

Mrs. Mering turned back to the curate. "You have heard, of course, of Madame Iritosky?" she said, steering him firmly in the direction of the crypt.

The curate looked confused. "Is she something to do with jumble sales?"

"She was right. I can feel the presence of the spirits here," Mrs. Mering said. "Have you any history of ghosts here at St. Michael's?"

"Well, actually," the curate said, "there is a legend of a spirit having been seen in the tower. The legend dates back to the Fourteenth Century, I believe," and they passed beyond the hoardings to the Other Side.

Tossie looked after them uncertainly, trying to decide whether she should follow them.

"Come look at this, Tossie," Terence said, standing in front of a brass inscription. "It's a monument to Gervase Scrope. Listen to what it says, 'Here lies a poor tossed tennis ball/Was racketed from spring to fall.' "

Tossie obediently came over to read it, then to look at a small brass plate to the Botoners, who had built the cathedral.

"How quaint!" Tossie said. "Listen. 'William and Adam built the tower, Ann and Mary built the spire. William and Adam built the church, Ann and Mary built the choir.'"

She moved on to look at a large marble monument to Dame Mary Bridgeman and Mrs. Eliza Samwell, and then an oil painting of "The Parable of the Lost Lamb," and we proceeded round the nave, stepping over boards and bags of sand, and stopping at each of the chapels in turn.

"Oh, I do wish we had a guidebook," Tossie said, frowning at the Purbeck marble baptismal font. "How can one tell what to look at without a guidebook?"

She and Terence moved on to the Cappers' Chapel. Verity paused and gently tugged on my coat-tails, pulling me back. "Let them get ahead," she said under her breath.

I obediently stopped in front of a brass of a woman in Jacobean costume dated 1609. "In memory of Ann Sewell," it read. "A worthy stirrer-up of others to all holy virtues."

"Obviously an ancestor of Lady Schrapnell's," Verity said. "Have you found out the curate's name?"

When would I have had the chance to do that? I thought. "You think he's Mr. C?" I said. "He did seem taken with her."

"Every man seems taken with her," she said, looking at Tossie, who was hanging on Terence's arm and giggling. "The question is, is she taken with him? Do you see the bishop's bird stump?"

"Not yet," I said, looking round the nave. The flowers in front of the choir hoardings were in plain brass vases, and the sawdust-covered roses in the Cappers' Chapel were in a silver bowl.

"Where is it supposed to be?"

"In the fall of 1940, standing against the parclose screen of the Smiths' Chapel," I said. "In the summer of 1888, I have no idea. It could be anywhere." Including under one of those green tarps or somewhere behind the hoardings.

"Perhaps we should ask the curate where it is when he comes back," she said anxiously.

"We can't," I said.

"Why not?"

"First, it's not the sort of thing that would be in Baedeker. The average tourist, which is what we're supposed to be, would never have heard of it. Second, it's not the bishop's bird stump yet. It only became the bishop's bird stump in 1926."

"What was it till then?"

"A cast-iron footed pedestal firugeal urn. Or possibly a fruit compote."

The sound of hammering behind the hoardings stopped abruptly, and there was the ghostly sound of swearing.

Verity glanced at Tossie and Terence, who were pointing at a stained-glass window, and then asked, "What happened in 1926?"

"There was a particularly acrimonious Ladies' Altar Guild meeting," I said, "at which someone proposed the purchase of a bird stump, which was a sort of tall ceramic vase popular at the time, for the flowers in the nave. The bishop had recently instituted cost-cutting measures for the running of the cathedral, and the proposal was voted down on the grounds that it was an unnecessary expense and that there must be something around somewhere they could use; i.e., the cast-iron footed pedestal firugeal urn which had been in storage down in the crypt for twenty years. It was thereafter referred to somewhat bitterly as 'the bishop's notion of a bird stump,' and eventually shortened to—"

"The bishop's bird stump."

"But if it wasn't the bishop's bird stump when Tossie saw it, how does Lady Schrapnell know what she saw?"

"She described it in considerable detail in her diaries over the years, and when Lady Schrapnell first proposed her project, an historian was sent back to identify it in the spring of 1940 from the descriptions."

"Could the historian have stolen it?" she asked.

"No."

"How can you be certain?"

"It was me."

"Cousin," Tossie called. "Do come see what we've found."

"Perhaps she's found it without us," I said, but it was only another monument, this one with a row of four swaddled infants carved on it.

"Isn't it cunning?" Tossie said. "Look at the dearum-dearum babies."

The south door opened, and Baine came in, sopping wet and clutching the issue of *The Light* inside his coat.

"Baine!" Tossie called.

He came over, leaving a trail of water. "Yes, miss?"

"It's chilly in here. Fetch my Persian shawl. The pink one, with fringe. And Miss Brown's."

"Oh, that isn't necessary," Verity said, looking pityingly at Baine's bedraggled appearance. "I'm not cold at all."

"Nonsense," Tossie said. "Bring both of them. And see they don't get wet."

"Yes, miss," Baine said. "I shall fetch them as soon as I've brought your mother her book."

Tossie put her lips in a pout.

"Oh, look, Cousin," Verity said before she could demand Baine go get the

shawls *now.* "These misereres show the Seven Works of Mercy," and Tossie
obediently went into the Girdlers' Chapel to admire them, followed by the
black marble altar tomb, assorted fan vaulting, and a monument with a
particularly long and illegible inscription.

Verity took the opportunity to pull me ahead. "What if it isn't here?" she
whispered.

"It's here," I said. "It didn't disappear till 1940."

"I mean, what if it isn't here because of the incongruity? What if events
have changed, and they've already moved it down to the crypt or sold it at
a jumble sale?"

"The bazaar's not till next week."

"Which aisle did you say it was in in 1940?" she said, starting purposefully
toward the back of the nave.

"This aisle," I said, trying to catch up, "in front of the Smiths' Chapel,
but that doesn't mean that's where it is now—" I said, and stopped because
it was.

It was obvious why they had put the bishop's bird stump in this particular
aisle. In 1888 the light in this part of the nave had been very dim, and one
of the pillars blocked it from the view of the rest of the church.

And one of the ladies of the Altar Guild had done the best she could,
obscuring the upper levels with large, drooping peonies and twining ivy
over the centaurs and one of the sphinxes. It was also newer, and therefore
shinier, which tended to hide some of the details. It didn't look half bad.

"Good Lord," Verity said. "Is that it?" Her voice echoed back and forth
among the fan vaulting. "It's absolutely hideous."

"Yes, well, that's already been established. Keep it down." I pointed at a
pair of workmen at the back of the nave. One of them, in a blue shirt and
blackened neckerchief, was shifting boards from one pile to another. The
second, his mouth full of nails, was hammering loudly on a board laid across
a sawhorse.

"Sorry," Verity whispered contritely. "It was just rather a shock. I'd never
seen it before." She pointed gingerly at one of the decorations. "What *is* that,
a camel?"

"A unicorn," I said. "The camels are on this side, here, next to the
depiction of Joseph's being sold into Egypt."

"And what's that?" she said, pointing at a large group above a cast-iron
garland of roses and thistles.

"The execution of Mary, Queen of Scots," I said. "The Victorians liked
art that was representational."

"And crowded," she said. "No wonder Lady Schrapnell was having trouble getting a craftsman to make a reproduction."

"I had made sketches," I said. "I think the craftsmen refused on moral grounds."

Verity surveyed it intently, her head to one side. "That cannot possibly be a seahorse."

"Neptune's chariot," I said. "And this over here is the Parting of the Red Sea. Next to Leda and the Swan."

She reached out and touched the swan's outstretched wing. "You were right about it being indestructible."

I nodded, looking at its cast-iron solidity. Even the roof falling in on it would scarcely have dented it.

"And hideous-looking things are never destroyed," she went on. "It's a law. St. Pancras Station wasn't touched in the Blitz. And neither was the Albert Memorial. And it *is* hideous."

I agreed. Even the drooping peonies and the ivy couldn't hide that fact.

"Oh!" Tossie said behind us, in a transport of joy. "That's the loveliest thing I've ever seen!"

She fluttered up, Terence in tow, and stood gazing at it, her gloved hands clasped under her chin. "Oh, Terence, isn't it the most cunning thing you've ever seen?"

"Well . . ." Terence said dubiously.

"Look at the darling cupids! And the Sacrifice of Isaac! O! O!" She uttered a series of screamlets that made the workman doing the hammering look up in irritation. He saw Tossie, spit his nails out onto the floor, and nudged his companion. The companion looked up from his sawing. The hammerer said something to him that made him burst into a wide and toothless smile. He tipped his cloth cap to Tossie.

"I know," I murmured to Verity. "Get their names."

As the workmen were under the impression that I was going to report them to the curate for leering, it took some time, but when I got back, Tossie was still going on about the bishop's bird stump.

"O, look!" she mini-screamed. "There's Salome!"

"Widge and Baggett," I whispered to Verity. "They don't know the curate's name. They refer to him as Bug-Eyes."

"And look," Tossie exclaimed. "There's the platter, and there's John the Baptist's head!"

And this was all very well, but so far it didn't look like a life-changing experience. Tossie had ooh-ed and ahh-ed like this over the china wooden shoe at the jumble sale. And over Miss Stiggins's cross-stitched needlecases. And even if she was having an Epiphany (depicted above Neptune and his chariot on the side facing the pillar), where was Mr. C?

"O, I do wish I had one," Tossie enthused. "For our dear home, Terence, after we're married. One exactly like it!"

"Isn't it rather large?" Terence said.

The south door banged open, and Baine came in, looking like something from the wreck of the Hesperus, and carrying an oilcloth-wrapped parcel.

"Baine!" Tossie called, and he squelched his way over to us.

"I've brought your shawl, miss," he said, folding the tarp back from a corner of a pew and setting the bundle down and beginning to unwrap it.

"Baine, what do you think of this?" Tossie said, indicating the bishop's bird stump. "Don't you agree it's the most beautiful piece of art you've ever seen?"

Baine straightened and looked at it, blinking water out of his eyes.

There was a considerable pause while Baine wrung out his sleeve. "No."

"*No?*" Tossie said, making it into a screamlet.

"No." He bent over the pew, opening the oilcloth to reveal the shawls, neatly folded and perfectly dry. He straightened again, reached inside his coat for a damp handkerchief, wiped his hands on it, and picked the pink shawl up by the corners. "Your shawl, miss," he said, holding it out to her.

"I don't want it now," Tossie said. "What do you mean, 'no'?"

"I mean the sculpture is a hideous atrocity, vulgarly conceived, badly designed, and shoddily executed," he said, folding the shawl carefully and bending to lay it back in the bundle.

"How *dare* you say that?" Tossie said, her cheeks very pink.

Baine straightened. "I beg your pardon, miss. I thought you were asking my opinion."

"I *was,* but I expected you to tell me you thought it was beautiful."

He bowed slightly. "As you wish, miss." He looked at it, his face impassive. "It is very beautiful."

"I *don't* wish," she said, stamping her little foot. "How can you not think it's beautiful? Look at the cunning little Babes in the Wood! And the sweet little sparrow with a strawberry leaf in its mouth!"

"As you wish, miss."

"And *stop* saying that," she said, her ruffles quivering with rage. "*Why* do you say it's an atrocity?"

"This," he extended his hand toward the bishop's bird stump, "is cluttered, artificial, and," he looked pointedly at the Babes in the Wood, "mawkishly sentimental, intended to appeal to the aesthetically uneducated middle class."

Tossie turned to Terence. "Are you going to allow him to say such things?" she demanded.

"It is a bit cluttered," Terence said. "And what's that supposed to be?" he added, pointing to the Minotaur, "A horse or a hippopotamus?"

"A *lion*," Tossie said, outraged. "And there's Androcles taking a thorn out of its paw."

I looked at Verity. She was biting her lip.

"And it is *not* mawkishly sentimental," Tossie said to Baine.

"As you wish, miss."

His life was saved by the timely arrival of the curate and Mrs. Mering from behind the hoardings.

"The Roman cavalry," Verity murmured.

"Directly beneath Bacchus, holding a bunch of grapes," I murmured back.

"I do hope you will consider having a jumble sale at your bazaar," Mrs. Mering was saying, steering the curate toward us. "People have so many treasures in their attics that make excellent jumble sale items."

She stopped at the sight of the bishop's bird stump. "Something like this, for instance. Or an umbrella stand. Vases are so useful. We had a china one with a painted waterfall at our fête which sold for—"

Tossie interrupted her. "*You* think this is beautiful, don't you?" she said to the curate.

"Indeed I do," he said. "I consider it an example of all that is best in modern art," he said. "Excellent representations and a high moral tone. Particularly the depiction of the Seven Plagues of Egypt. It was donated a number of years ago by the Trubshaw family on the death of Emily Jane Trubshaw. She had purchased it at the Great Exhibition, and it was her most treasured possession. The vicar tried to dissuade them from donating. He felt it should remain in the family's possession, but they were adamant."

"I think it's the most beautiful thing I've ever seen," Tossie said.

"I quite agree," the curate said. "It has always reminded me of the Albert Memorial."

"I *adore* the Albert Memorial," Tossie said. "I glimpsed it when we went to Kensington to hear Mrs. Guppy speak on ectoplasm, and I couldn't rest until Papa had taken me to see it. I love the mosaics and the gilt spire!" She clasped her hands together. "And the statue of the Prince, reading the catalogue of the Great Exhibition!"

"It is an extraordinary monument," Terence said.

"And indestructible," Verity murmured.

"I find the sculptures representing the four continents particularly well-rendered," the curate said, "though in my opinion Asia and Africa are scarcely suitable for young ladies."

Tossie colored prettily. "I thought the elephant was absolutely cunning. And the frieze of great scientists and architects."

"Have you ever seen St. Pancras Railway Station?" the curate asked. "I consider that an extraordinary example of architecture as well. Perhaps you'd care to see the work we're doing on the church?" he asked her. "It is not, of course, on a par with the Albert Memorial, but J.O. Scott has done some excellent work." He took Tossie's arm and led her up to the choir. "The galleries have been cleared and all the box pews have been removed."

He pointed up at the clerestory arches above, still holding onto Tossie's arm. "Scott has had iron girders inserted in each of the timber beams to tie the clerestory walls together and make them much stronger. It is a classic example of how superior modern building materials are, compared to old-fashioned stone and wood."

"Oh, I think so, too," Tossie said eagerly.

Actually, it was a classic example of trying to turn the *Titanic*. When the cathedral caught fire on the night of November fourteenth, the iron girders had buckled and bent and then collapsed, taking the clerestory arches and the internal colonnades with them. Without the girders, the church might have remained standing. The outer walls and the tower, which hadn't been renovated to make them stronger, had.

"After we've completed the renovations," the curate was saying to Tossie, "we will have a church befitting this modern age, a church which will be treasured hundreds of years from now. Would you like to see the renovations we are doing on the tower?"

"Oh, yes," Tossie nodded, making her curls bob prettily.

There was a sound from over by the south door, and I looked up. It was a young woman in a gray dress. She had a large basket and a long nose, and she strode across the nave to the bishop's bird stump with sharp, staccato-sounding steps, like rifle shots.

"Miss Sharpe," the curate said, looking caught out. "Allow me to introduce—"

"I only came to deliver these for the bazaar," Miss Sharpe said. She thrust the basket at him and then withdrew it when she saw the curate was holding Tossie's arm. "It is penwipers. Two dozen." She turned. "I will leave them in the vestry."

"Oh, but can you not stay, Miss Sharpe?" the curate said, extricating his arm from Tossie's. "Miss Mering, allow me to introduce Miss Delphinium Sharpe."

I wondered if she was a relation of Mrs. Chattisbourne's.

"I was so hoping we could discuss the arrangement of the stalls for the bazaar, Miss Sharpe," the curate said.

"I shall not be able to attend the fête. I will leave these in the vestry," she said again. She turned and started her rifle-fire way back across the nave.

"We should love to see St. Pancras Railway Station, shouldn't we, Mama?" Tossie said. A door slammed loudly.

"It's a sterling example of neo-Gothic," the curate said, flinching a little. "I feel that architecture should reflect society, particularly churches and railway stations."

"Oh, so do I," Tossie said.

"I . . ." Mrs. Mering said, and Tossie and the curate both turned to look at her. She was looking at the bishop's bird stump, and she had an odd, tentative look on her face.

"What is it, Mama?" Tossie said.

Mrs. Mering put her hand uncertainly to her bosom and frowned slightly, the way people do when they are trying to decide whether they have chipped a tooth.

"Are you ill?" Terence said, taking hold of her arm.

"No," she said. "I've just had the oddest feeling . . . it . . ." She frowned. "I was looking at the . . ." she waved the hand that had been on her bosom at the bishop's bird stump, ". . . and all at once, I . . ."

"You received a spirit message?" Tossie said.

"No, not a message," Mrs. Mering said, probing at the tooth. "It . . . I had the oddest feeling. . . ."

"A premonition?" Tossie prompted.

"Yes," Mrs. Mering said thoughtfully. "You . . ." She frowned, as if trying to remember a dream, and then turned and stared at the bishop's bird stump. "It had . . . We must go home at once."

"Oh, but you can't go yet," Verity said.

"I so wanted to discuss the Treasure Hunt with you," the curate said, looking disappointedly at Tossie. "And the arrangement of the fancy goods tables. Can't you at least stay to tea?"

"Baine!" Mrs. Mering said, ignoring both of them.

"Yes, madam," Baine, who had gone back over by the south door, said.

"Baine, we must return home at once," Mrs. Mering said, and started across the nave toward him.

Baine hurried to meet her, bringing an umbrella. "Has something happened?" he said.

"I have had a Warning," Mrs. Mering said, looking much more like herself. "When is the next train?"

"In eleven minutes," he said immediately. "But it is a local train. The next express to Reading isn't till 4:18."

"Bring the carriage round," she said. "Then run ahead to the station and tell them to hold the train for us. And take down that umbrella. It's bad luck to have an open umbrella indoors. Bad luck!" She clutched her heart. "Oh, what if we are too late?"

Baine was struggling to get the umbrella furled. I took it from him, and he nodded gratefully and took off for the station, running.

"Wouldn't you like to sit down, Aunt Malvinia?" Verity asked.

"No, no," Mrs. Mering said, shaking off her hand. "Go and see if the carriage is here yet. Is it still raining?"

It was, and the carriage was. Terence and the driver helped her down the steps and bundled her and her travelling skirts into it.

I took advantage of the momentary delay to shake the curate's hand. "Thank you so much for showing us the church, Mr.—?" I said.

"Mr. Henry!" Mrs. Mering called from the carriage. "We shall miss our train."

The south door banged open, and Miss Sharpe emerged and walked rapidly down the steps past us and up Bayley Street. The curate looked after her.

"Goodbye," Tossie said, leaning out the window. "I should so love to see St. Pancras."

I tried again, my foot on the carriage step. "Good luck with your church bazaar, Mr.—?"

"Thank you," he said absently. "Goodbye, Mrs. Mering, Miss Mering. If you will excuse me—" He hurried after Miss Sharpe. "Miss Sharpe!" he called. "Wait! Delphinium! Dellie!"

"I don't believe I caught your name—" I said, leaning out the window.

"Mr. Henry!" Mrs. Mering snapped. "Driver!" And we rattled off.

# C H A P T E R   T W E N T Y

Retreat—I Attempt to Ascertain the Station Guard's Name—Mrs.
Mering's Premonition, Possible Meanings of—Shawls—Aliases
of Clergymen—Eglantine Has Her Future Predicted—John Paul
Jones—Tea, Unfortunate Revivifying Effects of—Apports—
Newspapers—Fans—Yet Another Swoon—Baine to the Rescue—
A Shocking Headline

The trip home closely resembled Napoleon's retreat from Waterloo: a great deal of panic, hurry, and confusion, followed by inaction and despair. Jane nearly got left behind in the scramble for the station, Mrs. Mering threatened to faint again, and there was another cloudburst just as we rolled up. Terence nearly poked Tossie in the eye trying to get the umbrellas up.

Baine was holding the train by brute force. "Hurry," I said to Mrs. Mering, helping her out of the hansom cab, "the train's pulling out."

"No, no, it mustn't leave without us," she said, sounding genuinely urgent. "My premonition—"

"Then we must hurry," Verity said, taking her other arm, and we propelled her across the platform to first-class.

The station guard, still arguing with Baine, gave up at the sight of Tossie struggling with her skirts and her ruffled parasol and helped her board, tipping his hat gallantly. "I know," I muttered. "Get his name."

There was no time to find a porter. Terence and I, ignoring the conventions of class, grabbed the hampers, satchel, parcels, rugs, and Jane out of the hansom cab and flung them willy-nilly into the second-class carriage.

I ran back to pay the driver, who tore off as soon as the money was in his hands as if Blücher's Prussians were after him, and ran back onto the platform. The train had started to move, its heavy wheels turning in a slow but mounting acceleration. The station guard stepped back from the edge of the platform, his hands clasped behind his back. "What's your name?" I gasped, running up.

Whatever he answered, the train's whistle drowned it out completely. The train began to pick up speed.

"What?" I shouted. The whistle blew again.

"What?" he shouted.

"Your name," I said.

"Ned!" Terence shouted from the first-class platform. "Come on then!"

"I'm coming. What's your *name?*" I shouted to the guard and jumped for it.

I missed. My right hand caught the brass railing and I hung there for an instant. Terence grabbed my left arm and hauled me up onto the step. I grasped the railing and turned around. The station guard was trotting toward the station, his head ducked into his pulled-up collar.

"Your *name!*" I shouted into the rain, but he had already disappeared into the station.

"What was that all about?" Terence said. "You very nearly ended up like Anna Karenina."

"Nothing," I said. "Which is our compartment?"

"Third back," he said and started down the corridor to where Verity stood, looking back at the platform, which was now rapidly receding from us. Rain poured down on its empty boards.

" 'Thy fate is the common fate of all,' " Terence quoted. " 'Into each life some rain must fall, Some days must be dark and dreary,' " and opened the compartment door. Mrs. Mering sat slumped against the cushions in a state of semicollapse, holding a lace-edged handkerchief to her nose.

"Are you certain Tossie's mother wasn't the one who had the life-changing experience?" I whispered to Verity.

"Mr. Henry, Verity, do come in and sit down," Mrs. Mering said, waving the handkerchief. I caught a blast of Parma violets. "And shut the door. You're causing a draft."

We came in. I shut the door. We sat down.

" 'And homeward bound we wend our merry way,' " Terence quoted, smiling at everyone.

No one smiled back. Mrs. Mering sniffed at her handkerchief, Verity looked worried, and Tossie, huddled in the corner, positively glared at him.

If she had had a life-altering experience, she certainly didn't look it. She looked tired and sulky and damp. Her ruffled organdy was limp and non-fluttering, and her golden curls had begun to frizz.

"We might at least have stayed for tea, Mama," she said fretfully. "The curate intended to ask us, I'm sure of it. It isn't as if this were the only train. If we'd taken the 5:36, we'd have had plenty of time for tea."

"When one has a dreadful premonition," Mrs. Mering said, obviously feeling better, "one does not stop for tea." She waved the handkerchief, and I got another staggering whiff of violets. "I tried to tell Mesiel he should come with us."

"Did your premonition specify it was Colonel Mering who was in danger?" Verity asked.

"No," Mrs. Mering said, and got that odd, probing-a-tooth look again. "It . . . there was . . . water—" She gave a tiny scream. "What if he's fallen in the fishpond and drowned? His new goldfish was to arrive today." She sank back against the cushions, breathing into the handkerchief.

"Papa knows how to swim," Tossie said.

"He might have hit his head on the stone edging," Mrs. Mering said stubbornly. "Something dreadful's happened. I can feel it!"

She wasn't the only one. I glanced sideways at Verity. She was looking calmly desperate. We needed to talk.

"Can I fetch you anything, Mrs. Mering?" I said. I wasn't sure how to get Verity out of the compartment. Perhaps I could get the railway guard to give her a message. I'd cross that railway bridge when I came to it. "It's rather chilly in here. Can I fetch you a travelling rug?"

"It is cold," she said. "Verity, go and tell Jane I want my Scottish shawl. Tossie, do you want yours?"

"What?" Tossie said uninterestedly, looking out the window.

"Your shawl," Mrs. Mering said. "Do you want it?"

"No!" Tossie said violently.

"Nonsense," Mrs. Mering said. "It's cold in here," and to Verity, "Bring Tossie's shawl."

"Yes, Aunt Malvinia," Verity said and went out.

"It is cold in here," I said. "Shall I ask the guard to bring in a stove? Or a heated brick for your feet?"

"No. Why on earth don't you want your shawl, Tossie?"

"I *want* my tea," Tossie said to the window. "Do you think I'm aesthetically uneducated?"

"Of course not," Mrs. Mering said. "You speak French. Where are you going, Mr. Henry?"

I took my hand off the compartment door. "I just thought I'd step out onto the observation platform for a moment," I said, taking out a pipe as proof.

"Nonsense. It's pouring rain out there."

I sat down, defeated. Verity would be back in a moment, and we'd have missed our chance. The way we had missed our chance in Coventry.

"Mr. St. Trewes," Mrs. Mering said, "go and tell Baine to bring us some tea."

"I'll do it," I said, and was out of the compartment before she could stop me. Verity would already be on her way back with the shawl. If I could stop her before she got to the end of the second-class carriage, we could—

A hand reached out of the second-to-last compartment, grabbed my sleeve, and yanked me inside. "Where *have* you been?" Verity said.

"It isn't easy to get away from Mrs. Mering," I said, taking a look down the corridor to make sure there was no one coming before I shut the compartment door.

Verity pulled down the shades. "The real question is, what do we do now?" She sat down. "I was sure getting her to Coventry would do the trick. She'd see the bishop's bird stump, she'd meet Mr. Whatever-His-Name-Is-Beginning-With-a-C, her life would be changed, and the incongruity would be fixed."

"We don't know that it wasn't. She may have had her life changed, and we just don't know it yet. There were those men on the platform in Reading, and the conductor, and the curate. And the one who looked like Crippen. And Cyril. We mustn't forget his name begins with a 'C.'"

She didn't even smile. "Tossie didn't let him come to Coventry, remember?"

I sat down opposite her. "Personally, my money's on the curate," I said. "A bit too pop-eyed and pompous for my taste, but then Tossie's already demonstrated how wretched *her* taste is, and you saw how he was ogling her. My bet is that he shows up at Muchings End tomorrow on some pretext or other—he's decided to become a spiritist, or he wants advice on the coconut shy, or something—they fall in love, she drops Terence like a hot potato, and the next thing you know, they're posting the banns for Miss Tossie Mering and the Reverend Mr.—"

"Dolt," Verity said.

"It's a perfectly legitimate theory," I said. "You heard the two of them cooing about the Albert Mem—"

"Doult. D-O-U-L-T," she said. "The Reverend Mr. Doult."

"Are you certain?"

She nodded grimly. "Mrs. Mering told me his name when we were getting into the carriage. 'A well-intended young man, the Reverend Mr. Doult,' she said, 'but lacking in intelligence. He refuses to see the logic of the afterlife.' "

"You're sure it was Doult, and not—"

"Colt?" she said. "I'm positive." She shook her head. "The curate wasn't Mr. C."

"Well, then, it must have been one of the men on the platform at Reading. Or Muchings End's curate."

"His name is Arbitage."

"So he says. What if he's operating under an alias?"

"An alias? He's a clergyman."

"I know, and the Church would be particularly unforgiving of youthful misbehavior and misdemeanors, which would be why he had to take an assumed name. And his constantly being at Muchings End shows he's interested in her. And, speaking of which, what is this peculiar fascination she has for curates?"

"They all need wives to help them with the Sunday school and the church fêtes."

"Jumble sales," I muttered. "I knew it. The Reverend Mr. Arbitage is interested in spiritism," I said to Verity. "He's interested in vandalizing old churches. He's—"

"He's not Mr. C," Verity said. "I looked him up. He married Eglantine Chattisbourne."

"Eglantine Chattisbourne?" I said.

She nodded. "In 1897. He became the vicar of St. Albans in Norwich."

"What about the station guard?" I said. "I didn't catch his name. He—"

"Tossie didn't even glance at him. She hasn't shown the slightest interest in anybody all day." She leaned tiredly back against the seat. "We have to face it, Ned. The life-changing experience didn't happen."

She looked so discouraged I felt I had to try and cheer her up. "The diary didn't say she had the life-changing experience in Coventry," I said. "All it said was, 'I shall never forget that *day* we went to Coventry.' It might have happened on the way home. Mrs. Mering had a premonition something terrible was going to happen," I said, and smiled at her. "Perhaps there'll be a train wreck, and Mr. C will pull Tossie out of the wreckage."

"A train wreck," she said longingly. She stood and picked up the shawl. "We'd better be getting back before Mrs. Mering sends someone to look for us," she said resignedly.

I opened the door. "Something will happen, you'll see. There's still the diary. And Finch's related project, whatever that is. And we've still got a half-dozen stations and a change of trains before Muchings End. Perhaps Tossie will collide with Mr. C on the platform in Reading. Or perhaps she already has. When you didn't come back, her mother sent her to look for you, and as the train swayed going round a curve, she fell into his arms. Dashing, titled, as insufferable as she is, *and* he happens to be the sculptor of the bishop's bird stump, and she's in his compartment right now, discussing Victorian art."

But she wasn't. She was still in her corner, looking moodily out at the rain, when we entered our compartment.

"*There* you are," Mrs. Mering said. "Where *have* you been? I'm nearly frozen."

Verity hastened to drape the shawl around Mrs. Mering's shoulders.

"Did you tell Baine we wanted our tea?" Mrs. Mering said.

"I am just on my way to do so now," I said, my hand on the door handle. "I met Miss Brown on my way there and accompanied her back," and ducked out.

I expected to find Baine deep in Toynbee's *The Industrial Revolution* or Darwin's *Descent of Man,* but his book lay open on the seat beside him, and he was staring out at the rain. And apparently thinking about his aesthetic outburst and what the consequences of it might be, because he said gloomily, "Mr. Henry, might I ask a question about the States? You have been there. Is it true America is the Land of Opportunity?"

I really should have studied Nineteenth Century. All I could remember was a civil war, and several gold rushes. "It is definitely a country where everyone is free to voice his opinion," I said, "and does so. Particularly in the western states. Mrs. Mering would like tea," I told him and then went out on the rear platform and stood there with my pipe, pretending to smoke and looking at the rain myself. It had subsided into a misty drizzle. Heavy clouds hung grayly over the muddy roads we rattled by. Retreating to Paris.

Verity was right. We had to face it. Mr. C wasn't going to show up at Reading or anywhere else. We had attempted to mend the tear in the continuum by tying the broken threads together again, getting Tossie to the appointed place on the appointed day.

But in a chaotic system, there was no such thing as a simple tear. Every event was connected to every other. When Verity waded into the Thames, when I walked down the tracks to the railway station, dozens, thousands of events had been affected. Including the whereabouts of Mr. C on 15 June, 1888. We had broken all the threads at once, and the fabric in the space-time loom had come apart.

" 'Out flew the web and floated wide,' " I said aloud. " ' "The curse is come upon me," cried the Lady of Shalott.' "

"Eh, what's that?" a man's voice said, opening the door and coming out on the platform. He was stout, with an enormous set of Dundreary whiskers and a meerschaum pipe which he tamped down violently. "Curse, did you say?" he said, lighting his pipe.

"Tennyson," I said.

"Poetry," he growled. "Lot of rot, if you ask me. Art, sculpture, music, what use are they in the real world?"

"Exactly," I said, extending my hand. "Ned Henry. How do you do?"

"Arthur T. Mitford," he said, crushing my hand in his grip.

Well, it was worth a try.

"Don't believe in curses," he said, sucking fiercely on his pipe. "Or Fate, or destiny. Lot of rot. A man makes his own destiny."

"I hope you're right," I said.

"Of course I'm right. Look at Wellington."

I knocked the tobacco out of my pipe onto the rails below, and started back to the compartment. Look at Wellington. And Joan of Arc at Orléans. And John Paul Jones. They had all succeeded when everything looked lost.

And the continuum was tougher than it looked. It had slippage and backups and redundancy. "Missing you one place, we meet another." And if so, what I'd told Verity might be true, and Mr. C might be on the platform at Reading. Or in our compartment at this very moment, punching our tickets or hawking sweetmeats.

He wasn't. Baine was, handing round china cups and dispensing tea, which was having an unfortunate reviving effect on Mrs. Mering. She sat up straight, arranged her plaid shawl around her, and set about making everyone miserable.

"Tossie," she said. "Sit up properly and drink your tea. You were the one who wanted tea. Baine, didn't you bring lemon?"

"I will see if there are any for sale in the station, madam," he said and departed.

"Why is this such a long stop?" Mrs. Mering said. "We should have taken an express. Verity, this shawl gives no warmth at all. You should have told Jane to bring the cashmere."

The train started up, and after several minutes, Baine reappeared, looking like he had had to run for it. "I'm afraid they hadn't any lemon, madam," he said, producing a bottle of milk from his pocket. "Would you care for milk?"

"From who knows what sort of cow? Hardly. This tea is lukewarm."

Baine produced a spirit lamp, and proceeded to heat more water while Mrs. Mering looked around at us for another victim. "Mr. St. Trewes," Mrs. Mering said to Terence, who had retreated behind his book of poems, "it's far too dark to read in here. You will ruin your eyes."

Terence closed the book and put it in his pocket, looking like a man who was just beginning to realize what he had let himself in for. Baine lit the lamps and poured more tea.

"What a dull group you all are," Mrs. Mering said. "Mr. Henry, tell us about the States. Mrs. Chattisbourne says you told her you were out West fighting Red Indians."

"Briefly," I said, wondering if she were going to ask about scalping next, but she was on a different course.

"Did you have the opportunity while you were in the West of attending one of Baroness Eusapia's séances in San Francisco?" she asked.

"I'm afraid not," I said.

"Pity," she said, and it was clear she thought I had missed all the best tourist attractions. "Eusapia is famous for her apports."

"Apports?" Terence asked.

"Objects transported through the air from distant locations," she said.

That's it, I thought. That's what happened to the bishop's bird stump. It was apported to a séance in San Francisco.

". . . flowers and photographs," Mrs. Mering was saying, "and once she apported a sparrow's nest all the way from China. With the sparrow in it!"

"How do you know it was a Chinese sparrow?" Terence said dubiously. "It didn't chirp in Chinese, did it? How do you know it wasn't a California sparrow?"

"Is it true that servants in America don't know their proper place," Tossie said, looking at Baine, "and that their mistresses actually allow them to express opinions on education and art as if they were equals?"

It looked like the universe was going to collapse right here in this compartment. "I . . . uh . . ." I said.

"Did you see a spirit, Mrs. Mering," Verity said, trying to change the subject, "when you had your premonition?"

"No, it . . ." she said, and got that odd, inward look again. "Baine, how many more stops does this horrid train make?"

"Eight, madam," he said.

"We shall be frozen before we reach home. Go and tell the conductor to bring us a stove. And fetch a rug for my knees."

And so on. Baine fetched the rug, and a warmed brick for Mrs. Mering's feet, and a powder for the headache which Mrs. Mering had given all of us, but which she took herself.

"I certainly hope you do not intend to keep *dogs* after you are married," she told Terence, and made him turn down the lamps because they hurt her eyes. At the next station, she sent Baine to purchase a newspaper. "My premonition said that something dreadful was going to happen. Perhaps there has been a robbery. Or a fire."

"I thought you said your premonition had something to do with water," Tossie said.

"Fires are put out with water," she said with dignity.

Baine came in, looking like he had nearly missed the train again. "Your newspaper, madam."

"*Not* the *Oxford Chronicle*," Mrs. Mering said, pushing it aside. "The *Times*."

"The newspaperboy did not have the *Times*," Baine said. "I will attempt to see if there is a copy in the smoking car."

Mrs. Mering sank back against the seat. Terence picked up the discarded *Oxford Chronicle* and began to read it. Tossie went back to looking uninterestedly out the window.

"It's stifling in here," Mrs. Mering said. "Verity, go fetch my fan."

"Yes, Aunt Malvinia," she said gratefully, and made her escape.

"Why do they insist on overheating these railway cars?" Mrs. Mering said, fanning herself with her handkerchief. "It really is a disgrace that we must travel in such uncivilized conditions." She glanced across at Terence's newspaper. "I simply do not see—"

She stopped, staring blindly at Terence.

Tossie looked up. "What is it, Ma*ma?*"

Mrs. Mering stood up and took a staggering step backward in the direction of the door. "That night at the séance," she said, and fainted dead away.

"Ma*ma!*" Tossie said, starting up. Terence peered round his paper and then dropped it in a rattling heap.

Mrs. Mering had fallen slantwise across the door, with her head fortunately on the plush seat and her arms flung out to either side.

Terence and I scooped her up and deposited her more or less on the seat, with Tossie fluttering around us.

"O, Ma*ma!*" she said, leaning over Mrs. Mering's inert form. "Wake up!"

She took off her mother's hat, which didn't seem particularly to the point, and began patting her cheek. "O, do wake up, Ma*ma!*"

There was no response.

"Speak to me, Ma*ma!*" Tossie said, gently patting her cheek. Terence picked up the newspaper he'd dropped and began fanning her with it.

Still no response.

"You'd better go and get Baine," I said to Terence.

"Yes. Baine," Tossie said. "He'll know what to do."

"Right," Terence said, handed Tossie the newspaper, and hurried off down the corridor.

"Ma*ma!*" Tossie said, picking up fanning where Terence had left off. "Speak to me!"

Mrs. Mering's eyes fluttered open. "Where am I?" she said faintly.

"Between Upper Elmscott and Oldham Junction," Tossie said.

"On the train from Coventry," I translated. "Are you all right?"

"O, Mama, you gave us *such* a fright!" Tossie said. "What happened?"

"Happened?" Mrs. Mering repeated, pushing herself to sitting. She felt at her hair. "Where's my hat?"

"It's here, Ma*ma*," Tossie said, handing me the newspaper and picking up the hat. "You fainted. Did you have another premonition?"

"Premonition?" Mrs. Mering said vaguely, trying to pin her hat back on. "I don't . . ."

"You were looking at Terence, and you stopped speaking, as though you'd seen a spirit, and then you fell to the floor in a faint. Was it Lady Godiva?"

"Lady Godiva?" Mrs. Mering said, sounding more like her old self. "Why on earth would Lady—" She stopped.

"Ma*ma?*" Tossie said anxiously.

"I remember," Mrs. Mering said. "We asked the spirits for news of Princess Arjumand, and the doors opened . . ." she said, her voice rising, ". . . it must have been just at that moment . . . I asked if she had been drowned. . . ."

And went out like a light again. Her head fell sideways onto the plush armrest, and her hat flopped forward over her nose.

"Ma*ma!*" Tossie shrieked.

"Do you have any smelling salts?" I asked, propping Mrs. Mering up.

"Jane has," she said. "I'll go and fetch them." She scampered off down the corridor.

"Mrs. Mering," I said, fanning her with one hand and holding her erect with the other. She had a tendency to flop over to one side. "Mrs. Mering!" I wondered if I should loosen her stays, or at the least her collar, but decided I'd better wait for Tossie. Or Verity. And where were they?

The door banged open and Terence galloped in, panting. "I couldn't find Baine anywhere. 'He has vanished from the sight of mortal men.' Perhaps he's been apported." He peered interestedly at Mrs. Mering. "She's still out?"

"Again," I said, fanning. "Any idea what brought this on?"

"Not a clue," he said, sitting down on the seat opposite. "I was reading the newspaper, and she suddenly looked at me as though I were Banquo's ghost. 'Is that a dagger that I see before me, its handle towards my hand?' only in this case it was the *Oxford Chronicle,* and went out like a light. Was it my choice of reading material, do you think?"

I shook my head. "She said something about Princess Arjumand, and about the spirits."

Verity came in, carrying the fan. "What—" she said blankly.

"She's fainted," I said. "Tossie's gone for the smelling salts."

Tossie hurried in, followed by Baine.

"Where's Jane?" I said, glancing briefly at her. "Did you bring the smelling salts?"

"I brought Baine," she said, her cheeks very pink from her haste.

Baine immediately took charge, kneeling in front of Mrs. Mering and taking off her hat. He unbuttoned her collar. "Mr. St. Trewes, open the window. Mr. Henry, if you could give me some room, please."

"Careful," I said, letting go of Mrs. Mering's arm. "She has a tendency to list to starboard," but he already had hold of both her shoulders. I stepped back next to Verity, still holding the folded newspaper.

"Now then," he said, and pushed her head down between her knees.

"Baine!" Tossie said.

"Oh," Mrs. Mering said, and tried to sit up.

"Take deep breaths," Baine said, keeping his hand firmly on the back of her neck. "That's it. Deep breaths. Good," he said, and let her sit up.

"What—" she said, bewilderedly.

Baine produced a flask of brandy from his coat pocket and a china teacup. "Drink this," he commanded, placing her gloved hands around it. "That's it. Good."

"Are you feeling better, Mama?" Tossie said. "What made you faint?"

Mrs. Mering took another sip of the brandy. "I don't remember—" she said. "Whatever it was, I feel much better now." She handed the teacup to Baine. "How much farther to Muchings End?"

Verity, standing next to me, whispered, "What happened?"

"I don't have the slightest idea. Terence was reading the newspaper," I said, holding it up for illustration, "and she suddenly—" I stopped, staring, just like Macbeth.

It was the second story down, just under an article about boating congestion on the Thames.

"BALLIOL PROFESSOR DROWNED," it read, and under it, in smaller caps, but still quite readable (this being the *Oxford Chronicle* and not the *Times*):

"HISTORY PROFESSOR MATTHEW PEDDICK KILLED IN RIVER ACCIDENT"

> " 'The curse has come upon me,' cried the Lady of Shalott."
>
> Alfred, Lord Tennyson

# CHAPTER TWENTY·ONE

Explanations and Recriminations—Another Premonition—Our
Corporeality Is Called in Question—A Thunderstorm—The
Mystery of the Telegrams Solved—A Quiet Evening at Home—An
Arrival—Childhood Nicknames—The Establishment of the Jumble
Sale as an Ongoing Tradition—Decline and Fall

The remainder of the trip consisted of explanations and recriminations.
"I thought you said he sent his sister a telegram," Terence said.

"I thought he had," I said. "I asked him, 'Did you send your telegrams?' and he said, 'Yes,' and waved the yellow receipt slips at me."

"Well, he must have forgotten to pay for them or something. The funeral's tomorrow at ten."

"Madame Iritosky *tried* to warn me," Mrs. Mering said, lying back against three cushions and a folded blanket Baine had been dispatched to fetch for her. " 'Beware the sea,' she said. 'Beware the sea!' She was trying to tell me Professor Peddick had drowned!"

"But he didn't drown," I said. "It's all a misunderstanding. He fell in the river, and Terence and I fished him out. Professor Overforce must have thought he drowned when he couldn't find him."

"Fell in the river?" Mrs. Mering said. "I thought your boat capsized."

"It did," Terence said, "but that was the next day. We heard this splash, and I thought it was Darwin, because there were a number of trees along the bank just there, but it wasn't. It was Professor Peddick, and it was a lucky thing we came along just at the right moment to save him or he would have been done for. Fate. 'Ah, happy fate, that grasped the skirts of happy chance!' Because he was going down for the third time, and we had the very devil of a time—"

"*Mr.* St. Trewes!" Mrs. Mering, obviously recovering, said. "There are ladies present!"

Terence looked chagrined. "Oh, I do beg your pardon. In the excitement of telling the story, I—"

Mrs. Mering nodded dismissively. "You say Professor Peddick fell in the river?"

"Well, actually, Professor Overforce—they were discussing history, you see, and Professor Peddick said . . ."

I had stopped listening and was staring blankly at the wall, the way Mrs. Mering had stared with her premonition. Something someone had said—for a moment I had almost had it, the solution to the mystery, the significant clue, and Verity was right, we had been looking at it the wrong way round—but I had only had it for an instant, and then it had slipped away. It was something that one of them had said. Mrs. Mering? Terence? I squinted at Terence, trying to remember.

". . . and then Professor Peddick said Julius Caesar wasn't irrelevant and that was when Professor Overforce went in the drink."

"Professor Overforce!" Mrs. Mering said, motioning to Verity for the smelling salts. "I thought you said Professor Peddick fell in."

"Actually, it was more that he was pushed," Terence said.

"Pushed!"

It was no use. Whatever my premonition had been, it was gone. And it was obviously time to intervene.

"Professor Peddick slipped and fell in," I said, "and we rescued him and intended to take him back home, but he insisted on coming with us downriver. We stopped in Abingdon so he could send a telegram to his sister, telling her of his plans, but it obviously went astray, and when he turned up missing, she assumed that he was dead. Whereas he was really alive and with us."

She took a deep whiff of the smelling salts. "With you," she said, looking speculatively at Terence. "There was a cold gust of wind, and I looked up, and there you were, standing in the doorway in the darkness. How do I know you're not all spirits?"

"Here. Feel," Terence said, offering his arm. " 'Too, too solid flesh.' " She squeezed his sleeve gingerly. "There, you see," he said. "Quite real."

Mrs. Mering looked unconvinced. "The spirit of Katie Cook felt solid. Mr. Crookes put his arm round her waist at a séance, and he said she felt quite human."

Yes, well, there was an explanation for that, and for the fact that spirits bore an unusual resemblance to people draped in cheesecloth, and with that sort of reasoning, we were never going to be able to prove we were alive.

"And they had Princess Arjumand with them," Mrs. Mering said, warming to her theory, "who Madame Iritosky said had crossed over to the Other Side."

"Princess Arjumand isn't a spirit," Verity said. "Baine caught her in the fishpond this morning, trying to catch Colonel Mering's Black Moor. Isn't that right, Baine?"

"Yes, miss," he said, "but I was able to remove her before there was any harm done."

I looked at him, wondering if he had removed her to the middle of the Thames, or if he'd been too frightened by the Verity incident to try it again.

"Arthur Conan Doyle says that spirits eat and drink in the afterlife just as we do here," Mrs. Mering said. "He says the afterlife is just like our world, but purer and happier, and the newspapers would never print anything that isn't true."

And so on, until we changed trains at Reading, at which terminus the topic switched to how disgracefully Professor Peddick had behaved.

"To put his loved ones through such dreadful anguish," Mrs. Mering said, standing on the platform watching Baine struggle with the luggage, "to leave them to sit by the window, anxiously watching for his return, and then, as the hours passed, to have all vestiges of hope fade, is the absolute height of cruelty! Had I but known how careless of his loved ones' affections he was, I should never have opened our home and our hospitality to him. Never!"

"Should we wire ahead and warn Professor Peddick of the impending storm?" I whispered to Verity as we walked up the steps to the other train.

"When I was gone to fetch the fan," she said, watching Tossie ahead of us with Terence, "did anyone come into the compartment, anyone at all?"

"Not a soul," I said.

"And Tossie stayed there the whole time?"

"She went to get Baine, after her mother fainted," I said.

"How long was she gone?"

"Only long enough to fetch Baine," I said, and then at her crestfallen look, "She might have bumped into someone in the corridor. And we're still not home. She might meet someone here. Or at the station at Muchings End."

But the guard who handed her into our compartment was at least seventy, and there wasn't a soul, departed or otherwise, on the rainy platform at Muchings End. Or at home. Except for Colonel Mering and Professor Peddick.

I should definitely have wired ahead.

"Had the most wonderful idea," Colonel Mering said, coming happily out to greet us in the rain.

"Mesiel, where is your umbrella?" Mrs. Mering cut in before he could get any farther. "Where is your *coat?*"

"Don't need 'em," the Colonel said. "Just been out to look at my new red-spotted silver tancho. Perfectly dry," even though he looked fairly damp and his mustache had gone limp. "Couldn't wait to tell you our idea. Absolutely splendid. Thought we'd come straight up to tell you, didn't we, Professor? Greece!"

Mrs. Mering, being helped out of the carriage by Baine, who was holding an umbrella over her, looked warily at Professor Peddick, as if still not quite sure of his corporeality. "Grease?"

"Thermopylae," the Colonel said happily. "Marathon, the Hellespont, the straits of Salamis. Laying out the battle today. Came to me. Only way to see the lay of the land. Envision the armies."

There was an ominous peal of thunder, which he ignored. "Holiday for the whole family. Order Tossie's trousseau in Paris. Visit Madame Iritosky. Got a telegram from her today saying she was going abroad. Pleasant tour." He stopped and waited, smiling, for his wife's response.

Mrs. Mering had apparently decided Professor Peddick was alive, at least for the moment. "Tell me, Professor Peddick," she said in a voice that could have used several shawls, "before departing on this 'tour,' did you intend to inform your family of your plans? Or allow them to continue to wear mourning, as you have done thus far?"

"Mourning?" Professor Peddick said, pulling out his pince-nez.

"Beg pardon, my dear?" the Colonel said.

There was another extremely apt peal of thunder.

"Mesiel," Mrs. Mering said, "you have been nursing a viper in your bosom." She extended an accusing finger toward Professor Peddick. "This man has deceived those who befriended him, who took him in, but far, far worse, he has deceived his own loved ones."

Professor Peddick took off his pince-nez and peered through them. "Viper?"

It occurred to me that we could stand here all night and Professor Peddick never get any closer to comprehending the calamity that had befallen him, and I wondered if I should attempt to intervene, particularly since the rain was starting up again.

I glanced at Verity, but she was looking hopefully up the empty drive.

"Professor Peddick," I began, but Mrs. Mering was already thrusting the *Oxford Chronicle* at him.

"Read that," she commanded.

"Feared drowned?" he said, putting on his pince-nez and then taking them off again.

"Didn't you send your sister a telegram?" Terence asked. "Telling her you were going downriver with us?"

"Telegram?" he said vaguely, turning over the *Chronicle* as though the answer might be on the back.

"Those telegrams you sent at Abingdon," I said. "I asked you if you'd sent your telegrams, and you said you had."

"Telegrams," he said. "Ah, yes, I remember now. I sent a telegram to Dr. Maroli, the author of a monograph on the signing of the Magna Carta. And one to Professor Edelswein in Vienna."

"You were supposed to send one to your sister and your niece," Terence said, "letting them know your whereabouts."

"Oh, dear," he said. "But Maudie's a sensible girl. When I didn't come home, she'd know I'd gone on an expedition. Not like most women, fretting and stewing and thinking you've been run over by a tram."

"They didn't think you'd been run over by a tram," Mrs. Mering said grimly. "They thought you'd drowned. The funeral is tomorrow at ten o'clock."

"Funeral?" he said, peering at the newspaper. "Services at ten o'clock. Christ Church Cathedral," he read. "Why on earth would they have a funeral? I'm not dead."

"So you say," Mrs. Mering said suspiciously.

"You must send them a telegram immediately," I said before she could ask to feel his arm.

"Yes, immediately," Mrs. Mering said. "Baine, fetch writing materials."

Baine bowed. "You would perhaps be more comfortable in the library," he said, and mercifully got us indoors.

Baine brought a pen, ink, paper, and a penwiper shaped like a hedgehog, and then tea, scones, and buttered muffins on a silver tray. Professor Peddick composed a telegram to his sister and another to the dean of Christ Church, Terence was dispatched to the village to send them, and Verity and I took advantage of his departure to sneak into the breakfast room and plot our next move.

"Which is what?" Verity said. "There wasn't anyone at the station. Or here. I asked the cook. Nobody's come to the door all day. As soon as it stops raining, I think we should go through and tell Mr. Dunworthy we've failed."

"The day's not over yet," I said. "There's still dinner and the evening. You'll see, Mr. C will burst in during the soup and announce they've been secretly engaged since Easter."

"Perhaps you're right," Verity said without conviction.

But nothing happened during dinner except Mrs. Mering's repeating of her premonition, which had now taken on elaborate embellishments. "And as I stood there in the church, I seemed to see the spirit of Lady Godiva before me—clothed, of course—in a robe of Coventry blue, with her long hair hanging down, and as I stood there, transfixed, she held up her glowing white hand in warning and said, 'Things Are Not What They Seem.' "

Nothing happened over cigars and port, either, except a full description of the merits of the Colonel's new red-spotted silver tancho. I found myself hoping that when we rejoined the ladies, they'd be sitting round a shipwrecked sailor or a disinherited duke, listening eagerly to his tale of having got lost in the rainstorm, but when Colonel Mering pulled the folding doors open, Mrs. Mering was draped on the settee, apparently overcome again and breathing deeply into a scented handkerchief, Tossie was sitting at the writing table and writing in her diary, and Verity, on the slipper chair, was looking up eagerly, as if she expected the sailor to come in with us.

There was a knock on the front door, and Verity half-stood up, letting her embroidery fall, but it was only Terence, back from sending the telegrams.

"I thought it best to wait for an answer to the one to your sister," he said, handing his wet coat and umbrella to Baine. He handed Professor Peddick two yellow envelopes.

The professor fumbled for his pince-nez, tore the telegrams open, and proceeded to read them aloud. " 'Uncle. Delighted to hear from you. Knew you were well. All love. Your niece.' "

"Dear Maudie," he said. "I knew she wouldn't lose her head. It shows what intelligent creatures women can be when properly educated."

"Educated," Tossie cut in. "Is she aesthetically educated?"

Professor Peddick nodded. "Art, rhetoric, the classics, mathematics." He tore open the other envelope. "None of your silly music and needlework." He read the second telegram out loud. " 'Horace. How could you? Mourning ordered. Flowers and pallbearers already arranged. Expect you on 9:32 train. Professor Overforce already engaged to give eulogy.' Professor Overforce!" He stood up. "I must leave for Oxford at once. When is the next train?"

"There are no more trains to Oxford tonight," Baine, the walking Bradshaw, said. "The first train tomorrow is the 7:14 from Henley."

"I must be on it," Professor Peddick said. "Pack my bags at once. Overforce! He does not want to give a eulogy. He wants to discredit my theory of history and advance his own. He's after the Haviland Chair. Natural forces! Populations! The murderer!"

"Murderer?" Mrs. Mering shrieked, and I thought we were going to have to go over the entire living-or-dead thing again, but Professor Peddick didn't give her so much as a chance to call for her smelling salts.

"Not that murder counts in his theory of history," he said, clutching the telegram. "The murder of Marat, of the two Little Princes in the Tower, the murder of Darnley, none of them had any effect on the course of history, according to Overforce. Individual action is irrelevant to the course of history. Honor doesn't matter in Overforce's theory, nor does jealousy, nor foolishness, nor luck. None of them have any effect on events. Not Sir Thomas More, nor Richard the Lionhearted, nor Martin Luther." And so on.

Mrs. Mering attempted to interrupt once or twice and then subsided against the settee. Colonel Mering took up his newpaper (not the *Oxford Chronicle*). Tossie, her chin propped on her hand, played idly with a large carnation penwiper. Terence stretched out his legs toward the fire. Princess Arjumand curled up in my lap and fell asleep.

Rain pattered against the window, the fire crackled, Cyril snored. Verity poked determinedly at her embroidery and kept glancing at the ormolu mantel clock, which appeared to have stopped.

"At the Battle of Hastings," Professor Peddick said, "King Harold was killed by an arrow in the eye. A lucky shot that determined the outcome of the battle. How does Overforce's theory of history account for luck?"

The front-door knocker banged, loudly, and Verity stabbed her finger with her embroidery needle. Terence sat up, blinking. Baine, adding logs to the fire, stood up and went to answer the door.

"Who can that be, at this hour?" Mrs. Mering said.

Please, I thought, let it be Mr. C.

"Natural forces! Populations!" Professor Peddick fumed. "How does the Siege of Khartoum fit into that theory?"

I could hear muffled voices in the vestibule, Baine's and another man's. I looked over at Verity, who was sucking her pricked finger, and then back at the parlor door.

Baine appeared in it. "The Reverend Mr. Arbitage," he said, and the curate bustled in, rain dripping from his flat-brimmed hat.

"Absolutely unforgivable to visit so late, I know," he said, handing his hat to Baine, "but I simply had to stop by and tell you how well the fête did. I was over at Lower Hedgebury at a meeting of the Slum Charities Committee and everyone was simply *agog* at our success. A success," he simpered, "which I consider to be entirely due to your idea of having a jumble sale, Mrs. Mering. Reverend Chichester wants to institute one for his Mission for Unfortunate Girls Midsummer Bazaar."

"Reverend Chichester?" I said, leaning forward.

"Yes," he said eagerly. "He wanted to know if you would be willing to lend your expertise to the enterprise, Mrs. Mering. And Miss Mering and Miss Brown, of course."

"Reverend Chichester," I said. "I believe I've heard of him. Young, unmarried, dark mustache?"

"Reverend Chichester?" the Reverend Arbitage said. "Good heavens, no. Ninety, if he's a day. Rather afflicted with palsy, I'm afraid, but still active in good works. And very interested in the Other Side."

"I shouldn't wonder," Colonel Mering muttered from the depths of his newspaper. "He's already got one foot over the line."

"The Final Judgment may be but a step away for all of us," the Reverend Arbitage said, pursing his lips. " 'Fear God, and give glory to him; for the hour of his judgment is come.' Revelation chapter fourteen, verse seven."

He truly was a toad. Prissy, self-righteous, humorless. The perfect mate for Tossie. And there didn't seem to be any other takers.

"Arbitage," I said. "Is that your full name?"

"I beg your pardon," he said.

"So many people have multiple names these days," I said. "Edward Burne-Jones, Elizabeth Barrett Browning, Edward Bulwer-Lytton. I thought perhaps Arbitage was short for Arbitage-Culpepper or Arbitage-Chutney."

"Arbitage is my full name," he said, drawing himself up. "Eustace Hieronymous Arbitage."

"And no pet names, I suppose, not for a man in your line of work," I said. "In childhood, though? My sisters' pet name for me was Curls, because of my baby locks. Did you have curly hair?"

"I believe," the Reverend Mr. Arbitage said, "I was quite bald until the age of three."

"Ah," I said. "Chuckles, perhaps? Or Chubby?"

"Mr. *Hen*ry," Mrs. Mering said, "Mr. Arbitage is trying to tell us the results of the fête."

"Yes, well," the Reverend Mr. Arbitage said, pulling a leather notebook from his pocket, "after expenses the receipts came to eighteen pounds, four shillings and eight pence, more than enough to paint over the wall murals and put in a new pulpit. We may even have enough to purchase an oil painting for the lady chapel. Perhaps a Holman-Hunt."

"What do you think the purpose of art is, Mr. Arbitage?" Tossie asked abruptly.

"To edify and instruct," he said promptly. "All art should point a moral."

"Like *The Light of the World*," she said.

"Indeed," he said. " 'For behold, I stand at the door and knock. . . .' Revelation chapter three, verse twenty." He turned to Mrs. Mering. "So may I tell the Reverend Mr. Chichester he can count on your assistance?"

"I'm afraid not," Mrs. Mering said. "We are leaving for Torquay the day after tomorrow."

Verity looked up, stricken, and the Colonel lowered his paper.

"My nerves," Mrs. Mering said, looking hard at Professor Peddick. "So many unsettling things have happened in the last few days. I feel the need to consult with Dr. Fawleigh. Perhaps you've heard of him. He's an expert in spiritism. Ectoplasm. And from there, we shall journey to Kent to meet Mr. St. Trewes's parents and make arrangements for the wedding."

"Ah," Mr. Arbitage said. "But you will be back by August, I do hope. Our summer fête was such a success I've decided we should have a St. Bartholomew's Day Fair, and we will of course want to have a fortuneteller. And a jumble sale. Mrs. Chattisbourne wanted to have a whist drive instead, but I told her the jumble sale was destined to become a *tradition*. And all thanks to you. I have already been collecting items for it. Miss Stiggins donated a boot rack, and my great-aunt is sending me an etching of *The Battle of Naseby!*"

"Ah, yes, Naseby!" Professor Peddick said. "Prince Rupert's cavalry charge. A classic example of how one can be within a hairsbreadth of success, only to see it turn into defeat, and all because of not using forethought."

There was some more discussion of the perils of acting without thinking, and then the Reverend Mr. Arbitage delivered a benediction and took his leave.

Tossie scarcely seemed to notice. "I am rather tired," she said as soon as Baine had shown him out. She kissed her father and then her mother.

"You're looking pale," Mrs. Mering said. "The sea air will do you good."

"Yes, Mama," she said as though she were thinking of something else. "Good night," and went upstairs.

"It is time we all retired," Mrs. Mering said, standing up. "It has been a long—" she fixed Professor Peddick with a gimlet eye, "—and *eventful* day for all of us, and, Mesiel, you will need to be up early to accompany Professor Peddick on his journey."

"Accompany Professor Peddick?" Colonel Mering said, stammering. "Can't leave my red-spotted silver tancho."

"I am certain you would wish to ensure that Professor Peddick does not drop from sight," Mrs. Mering said firmly. "I am certain you would not wish to be responsible for leaving a second family uninformed and bereft."

"No, of course not," Colonel Mering said, defeated. "Glad to see you home, Professor Peddick."

While they consulted with Baine about train times, I went over to Verity and whispered, "I'll report in in the morning when I take Cyril out to the stable."

She nodded numbly. "All right." She took one last look round, as if she hoped Mr. C might still appear. "Good night," she said and went upstairs.

"Come, Cyril," Terence said, looking meaningfully at me. "Time for you to go out to the stable," but I wasn't paying any attention.

I was looking at the writing table, where Tossie had left her diary.

"I'll be up in a moment," I said, sidling over in front of it. "I just want to find a book to read."

"Books!" Mrs. Mering said. "Entirely too many people read books these days," and swept from the room.

"Come along, Cyril," Terence said. Cyril staggered to his feet. "Still raining outside, Baine?"

"I'm afraid so, sir," Baine said and went to open the front door for them.

"Pickett's Charge!" Professor Peddick said to Colonel Mering. "At the American battle of Gettysburg. Another excellent example of acting without thinking! How would Overforce account for Pickett's Charge?" and they went out together.

I shut the parlor door behind them and hurried over to the writing desk. The diary was open, with the pen and the carnation penwiper covering the bottom two-thirds of the page. At the top was written, in a ruffly hand, "June the fifteenth," and below it, "Today we went to Cov—"

I lifted the penwiper. "—entry," it read, the "y" trailing off into blankness. Whatever she'd recorded for posterity about the great day, she hadn't done it yet, but there might be clues to Mr. C in earlier entries.

I shut the diary, grabbed Gibbon's *Decline and Fall of the Roman Empire,* Vols. One and Two, off the shelf behind, sandwiched the diary between them, and turned round with the books in my hands.

Baine was standing there. "I shall be glad to take Miss Mering's diary up to her so that you are not inconvenienced, sir," he said.

"Excellent," I said, and extricated it from between the Gibbon. "I was just taking it up to her."

"As you wish, sir."

"No, that's all right," I said. "You take it up. I think I shall take a walk before bed." A patently ridiculous remark with the rain beating against the French doors, and one he didn't believe any more than he believed I was taking Tossie's diary up to her. But he only said, "As you wish, sir," again.

"Did anyone come to the door tonight?" I said. "Besides the Reverend Mr. Arbitage?"

"No, sir."

"Or to the kitchen door? A peddler? Or someone seeking shelter from the storm?"

"No, sir. Will that be all, sir?"

Yes, that would be all. And in a few years, what? The Luftwaffe would finish off the RAF and commence landing at Dover, and Tossie and Terence's grandchildren would fight them on the beaches and in the ditches and in Christ Church Meadow and at Iffley, to no avail. They would hang Nazi banners from Buckingham Palace's balconies and goose-step through

Muchings End and Oxford and Coventry. Well, at least Coventry wouldn't burn down. Only the Houses of Parliament. And civilization.

And the space-time continuum would correct itself eventually. Unless Hitler's scientists discovered time travel.

"Will that be all, sir?" Baine said again.

"Yes," I said, "that will be all," and turned to open the door.

Rain blew in, and getting wet and cold seemed somehow fitting. I started out.

"I have taken the liberty of putting Mr. St. Trewes's friend in your room, sir," Baine said.

"Thank you," I said gratefully. I shut the door, turned, and started past him up the stairs.

"Mr. Henry," he said.

"Yes?" I said, but whatever he intended to say, he must have thought better of it.

"An excellent book," he said. "*The Decline and Fall.*"

"Edifying and instructive," I said, and went up to bed.

*"And kiss me, Kate! We will be married a Sunday."*

Petruchio

# CHAPTER TWENTY-TWO

Inherent Optimism of Time Travel—An Early Departure—A
Problem—Gladys and Gladys—Finch Is Missing—Anecdotes of
Cats' Maternal Resourcefulness—A Delayed Departure—
Eavesdropping—Cabbages—Verity Is Missing—Baine Quotes
Shakespeare—Illiteracy Laws Proposed—The Mystery of the
Waterlogged Diary Solved—A Premature Departure

I felt better in the morning. When I came down with Cyril at six, the rain had stopped, the sky was blue, and the wet grass glittered like diamonds.

And time travel is inherently hopeful. Failing to fix it once, you get innumerable other chances, or at least somebody does, and a week from now, or a year, when the forensics expert finally managed to decipher the diary, Carruthers or Warder or some addled new recruit could come back on the fifteenth and see to it that Mr. C made his entrance on cue.

We hadn't succeeded, but at this very moment they might have solved the Mystery of Waterloo and self-correction. At this very moment T.J. and Mr. Dunworthy might be sending someone through to intercept me on my way to Oxford's railway station and keep me from meeting Terence and mucking up his love life. Or to separate Professor Peddick and Professor Overforce. Or to stop Verity from wading into the Thames and rescuing Princess Arjumand in the first place. Or to send me to World War I to recover from my time-lag.

The cat would swim to shore, Terence would meet Maud, and the

Luftwaffe would bomb London. And I would never meet Verity. Small price to pay for saving the universe. Well worth the sacrifice.

And I wouldn't feel any loss because I wouldn't ever have met her. I wondered suddenly if Terence did, if he knew on some level that he hadn't met his true love. And if he did, what did he feel? Mawkish sorrow, like one of his Victorian poems? Or a gnawing of some need unsatisfied? Or just a grayness to everything?

I took Cyril out to the stable. Princess Arjumand had come down with us, and she stalked ahead across the wet grass, her tail in the air, coming back periodically to wind herself around Cyril's hind legs and my ankles. There was a sound over by the stable, and the big doors began to creak open.

"Hide," I said, scooping up Princess Arjumand and ducking back into the shelter of the kitchen door. The groom, looking like he'd just been awakened, pushed the doors open, and the driver led two horses, hitched to the carriage, out. The carriage to take Professor Peddick and Colonel Mering to the station.

I looked toward the house. Baine was bringing out the luggage and setting it on the front steps. Professor Peddick stood behind him in his academic gown and mortarboard, holding his kettle of fish against his stomach and talking to Terence.

"Come along," I whispered to Cyril and started toward the side of the stable. Princess Arjumand wriggled wildly in my arms, trying to get free, and I let her down. She took off like a shot across the lawn. I led Cyril in the groom's door.

"Make it look like you've been here all night," I said, and Cyril promptly went over to his burlap sacking, turned round three times, flopped down, and began to snore loudly.

"Good boy," I said, and let myself out of the stable. And collided with Terence.

"Have you got Cyril?" he said.

"I just brought him down," I said. "Why? Is something wrong? Did Mrs. Mering see me?"

He shook his head. "Baine came and knocked me up this morning and said Colonel Mering was ill and would I accompany Professor Peddick to Oxford. Seems he caught a chill yesterday fishing for trout, and Mrs. Mering wants to make certain Professor Peddick makes it home. Good idea, actually. He's likely to spot a hill that reminds him of the Battle of Hastings or something and get off the train. I thought I'd take Cyril. Thought it would be a bit of a holiday for him from—" he stopped and started again, "—especially as he didn't get to go to Coventry yesterday. Is he in the stable?"

"Next to the hay bales," I said, but when he opened the groom's door, Cyril was standing just inside, wagging his pudgy body.

"Would you like to take a journey by rail, old man?" Terence said, and the two of them set off happily for the house.

I waited till the carriage had set off and Baine had gone back into the house and then legged it out to the laburnum arbor before the groom came yawning back to the stables, and then went out through the herbaceous border and across the croquet lawn to the gazebo.

There was someone in it. I circled round the weeping willow and came up behind the lilacs. A dark figure was sitting hunched on one of the side benches. Who would be sitting out here at this hour? Mrs. Mering, hunting for ghosts? Baine, catching up on his reading?

I parted the lilac branches so I could see better, sending a shower of water over my blazer and flannels. Whoever it was, they had a cloak wrapped around them and a hood pulled up over their head. Tossie? Waiting for a rendezvous with her life-changing lover? Or the mysterious Mr. C himself?

I couldn't see the figure's face from there. I needed to be on the other side of the gazebo. I carefully let go of the branches, dousing myself again, and stepped back squarely on Princess Arjumand.

"Mrowrrrr!" she yowled, and the figure darted up, clutching the cloak. The hood fell back.

"Verity!" I said.

"Ned?"

"*Mreer!*" Princess Arjumand said. I scooped her up to see if I'd hurt her. "Mere," she said, and began to purr.

I carried her round the lilacs and over to where Verity was standing. "What are you doing out here?" I said.

Verity looked as pale as one of Mrs. Mering's spirits. The cloak, which must have been an evening cloak of some kind, was drenched, and under it she had on her white nightgown.

"How long have you been out here?" I said. Princess Arjumand was squirming. I put her down. "You didn't have to report in. I told you I'd do it when I brought Cyril down. What did Mr. Dunworthy say about—" and saw her face. "What is it?"

"The net won't open," she said.

"What do you mean, it won't open?"

"I mean, I've been out here for three hours. It won't open."

"Sit down and tell me exactly what happened," I said, indicating the bench.

"It *won't* open!" she said. "I couldn't sleep, and I thought the sooner we reported in, the better, and I could be back before anybody got up, so I came out to the drop, and the net wouldn't open."

"The drop's not there?"

"No, it's there. You can see the shimmer. But when I step into it, nothing happens."

"Could you be doing something wrong? Are you sure you were standing in the right place?"

"I've stood in a dozen different places," she said impatiently. "It *won't open!*"

"All right, all right," I said. "Could someone have been there? Someone who might have seen you? Mrs. Mering, or Baine, or—"

"I thought of that. After the second time, I walked down to the river and out to the fishpond and over to the flower garden, but no one was there."

"And you aren't wearing something from this era?"

"I thought of that, too, but this is the nightgown I brought through in my luggage, and, no, it hasn't been mended or had a new button sewn on."

"Maybe it's you," I said. "I'll try."

"I hadn't thought of that," she said more cheerfully. "The next drop should be any minute."

She led me out of the gazebo and around to the side to a patch of grass next to a cluster of pink peonies. There was already a faint glitter to the grass. I hastily checked my clothes. Blazer, flannels, socks, shoes, and shirt were all the ones I'd worn through.

The air shimmered, and I stepped into the very center of the grass. The light began to grow. "Is this what happened when you tried it?" I said.

The light abruptly died. Condensation glittered on the peonies.

"Yes," Verity said.

"Perhaps it's my collar," I said, unfastening it and handing it to her. "I can't tell mine from the ones Elliott Chattisbourne loaned me."

"It's not your collar," Verity said. "It's no use. We're trapped here. Just like Carruthers."

I had a sudden vision of staying here forever, playing croquet and eating kedgeree for breakfast and boating on the Thames, Verity trailing her hand in the brown water and looking up at me from under her beribboned hat.

"I'm sorry, Ned. This is all my fault."

"We're not trapped," I said. "All right. Let's be Harriet and Lord Peter and examine all the possibilities."

"I've already considered all the possibilities," she said tightly. "And the only one that makes any sense is that it's all breaking down, like T.J. said it would."

"Nonsense," I said. "It takes years for an incongruity to collapse the continuum. You saw the models. It may be breaking down in 1940, but not a week after the incongruity."

She was looking like she wanted to believe me.

"All right," I said, sounding more confident than I felt. "You go back to the house and get dressed before you compromise us both and I have to marry you."

That made her smile, at least. "And then have breakfast, so Mrs. Mering won't think you're missing and send out a search party for you. After breakfast, tell her you're going sketching and come back out here and wait for me. I'm going to go find Finch and get another opinion."

She nodded.

"This is probably nothing, a glitch, and Warder just hasn't noticed it yet. Or maybe she's shut down all return drops till she gets Carruthers back. Whatever it is, we'll get to the bottom of it."

She nodded again, a little more cheerfully, and I took off for the Chattisbournes', wishing I believed anything I'd just said, and that the Victorians hadn't lived so far apart.

A maid in a ruffled apron and cap answered the door.

"Gladys, I need to speak to Mr. Finch, the butler," I said, when I was able to catch my breath. I felt like Professor Peddick's runner from the battle of Marathon who'd run all the way to Sparta. He'd died, hadn't he, after delivering his message? "Is he here?"

"I'm very sorry, sir," the maid said, dropping an even worse curtsey than Jane's. "Mr. and Mrs. Chattisbourne are not at home. Would you wish to leave your card?"

"No," I said. "It's Mr. Finch I wish to speak to. Is he here?"

She had clearly not been briefed for this contingency.

"You may leave your calling card, if you wish," she said, and held out a small silver plate embossed with curlicues.

"Where did Mr. and Mrs. Chattisbourne go?" I persisted. "Did Mr. Finch drive them?"

She looked completely undone. "Mr. and Mrs. Chattisbourne are not at home," she said, and shut the door in my face.

I went round to the kitchen and knocked on the door. It was answered by another maid. This one had on a canvas apron and a kerchief and was armed with a potato peeler.

"I need to speak to the butler, Mr. Finch, Gladys," I said.

"Mr. and Mrs. Chattisbourne aren't here," she said, and I was afraid she was going to be equally unforthcoming, but she added, "They went over to Donnington. To the St. Mark's Fancy Works Sale."

"It's Mr. Finch I need to speak to. Did he accompany them?"

"No," she said. "He's up to Little Rushlade, buying cabbages. He left this morning carrying a big basket to fetch them home in."

"When?" I asked, wondering if I could catch up with him.

"Before breakfast. It was scarcely light out. What's wrong with Farmer Gamm's cabbages down the road I don't know, but he says only the best for

Mrs. Chattisbourne's table. *I* say one cabbage is as good as another." She made a face. "It's three hours' walk at the least."

Three hours' walk. There was no point in going after him, and he wouldn't be back soon enough to justify waiting. "When he gets back, would you be good enough to tell him that Mr. Henry from the Merings' was here and to please come see him at once?"

She nodded. "Though I should imagine he'll be all tuckered out by the time he gets back. Why he should have decided to go today, after the night we had, I don't know. Mrs. Marmalade had her kittens last night, and a time we had finding out where she'd hid them."

I wondered if the rules against discussing sex didn't apply to the servant classes, or if once the kittens were a fact, they became an acceptable topic.

"Last time it was the root cellar," she said, "and once their eyes are open, you can never find them all to drown them. And the time before we never did find where she'd hid them. That Mrs. Marmalade's a sly boots, she is."

"Yes, well, if you'd just please give him my message as soon as he gets back," I said, putting on my boater.

"The time before *that,* it was Miss Pansy's sewing box. And the time before that the linen drawer in the upstairs cupboard. The sly boots know you'll try to take their kittens, you know, and so they hide them in the most peculiar places. When the Merings' cat had her kittens last winter, she hid them in the wine cellar and they didn't find them for nearly three weeks! Christmas Day it was they finally found them, and what a time catching them all. When I was in service at the Widow Wallace's, the cat had her kittens in the oven!"

I managed to get away after several more anecdotes about resourceful cat mothers, and hotfooted it back to the gazebo.

At first I didn't see Verity, and I thought perhaps she'd tried it again while I was gone and been successful, but she was on the other side of the gazebo, sitting under a tree. She was wearing the white dress I'd first seen her in, and her neck was bent gracefully over her sketchbook.

"Any luck?" I said.

"Nothing." She got to her feet. "Where's Finch?"

"Off buying cabbages in a neighboring village," I said. "I left a message for him to come to Muchings End as soon as he gets back."

"A message," she said. "That's a good idea. We could try and send a message." She looked speculatively at her sketchbook. "You don't have any paper you brought through with you, do you?"

I shook my head. "Everything I brought through was washed away when the boat capsized. No, wait. I've got a bank note." I got it out of my pocket. "But what do we write with?"

"We take the chance that a milliliter or so of carbon is a nonsignificant article," she said, holding up her charcoal pencil.

"That's too thick," I said. "I'll go back to the house and fetch a pen and ink. When's the next rendezvous?"

"Now," Verity said, and pointed at the shimmering air.

There wasn't time to race to the house and back, let alone scrawl, "Can't get through," and our coordinates. "We'll need to wait till next time," I said.

Verity was only half-listening to me. She was watching the growing glow in the grass. She stepped into the center of it and handed me her sketchbook and pencil.

"You see?" she said. The glow immediately dimmed. "It still won't open," and disappeared in a shimmer of condensation.

Well, and that was that. The continuum hadn't broken down, at least not yet, and we weren't trapped here. Ah, well, it was probably for the best. I truly did hate kedgeree, and croquet matches were deadly. And if St. Michael's was any indication, the late summer would bring on hordes of jumble sales and fêtes.

I looked at my pocket watch. It was half past IX. I needed to get back to the house before somebody saw me and asked me what I was doing loitering out here, and with luck I might still be able to get some devilled kidneys or smoked kippers from the Stag at Bay.

I started for the rockery, and nearly ran into Baine. He was standing looking grimly out over the Thames, and I scanned the water, looking for Princess Arjumand out in the middle of it treading water with her white paws.

I didn't see her, but Baine was going to see me in a moment. I ducked back into the lilacs, trying not to rustle any leaves, and nearly stepped on Princess Arjumand.

"Muir," she said loudly. "Mrowr."

Baine turned and looked straight at the lilacs, frowning.

"Mere," Princess Arjumand said. Shhh, I said silently, putting my finger to my lips. She began rubbing up against my leg, meowing loudly. I stooped to pick her up and knocked against a dead branch. It snapped off, its brittle leaves rattling sharply.

Baine started toward the lilacs. I began thinking up excuses. A lost croquet ball? And what was I doing playing croquet by myself at nine o'clock in the morning? Sleepwalking? No, I was fully dressed. I looked longingly back at the gazebo, gauging the distance and time to the next rendezvous. Both too far. And, knowing Princess Arjumand, she'd saunter in at the last minute and cause *another* incongruity in the continuum. It would have to be a lost croquet ball.

"Mire," Princess Arjumand said loudly, and Baine raised his arms to part the lilac bushes.

"Baine, come here immediately," Tossie said from the towpath. "I wish to speak to you."

"Yes, miss," he said, and went over to where she was standing, dressed in ruffles, tucks, and lace, and holding her diary.

I took advantage of the distraction to scoop Princess Arjumand up and step farther into the depths of the lilacs. She snuggled against my chest and began purring loudly.

"Yes, miss?" Baine said.

"I insist that you apologize to me," Tossie said imperiously. "You had no right to say what you did yesterday."

"You are quite right," Baine said solemnly. "It was not my place to express my opinions, even though they were solicited, and I do apologize for speaking as I did."

"Meeee," Princess Arjumand said. In listening, I had forgotten to keep petting her, and she put her paw gently on my hand. "Mooorre."

Tossie looked round, distractedly, and I backed farther out of sight behind the bushes.

"Admit that it was a beautiful piece of art," Tossie said.

There was a long pause, and then Baine said quietly, "As you wish, Miss Mering."

Tossie's cheeks flushed pink. "Not 'as I wish.' The Reverend Mr. Doult said it was . . ." There was a pause, ". . . 'an example of all that was best in modern art.' I copied it down in my diary."

"Yes, miss."

Her cheeks went even pinker. "Are you daring to disagree with a man of the cloth?"

"No, miss."

"My fiancé Mr. St. Trewes said it was extraordinary."

"Yes, miss," Baine said quietly. "Will that be all, miss?"

"No, it will not be all. I demand that you admit you were wrong about its being an atrocity and mawkishly sentimental."

"As you wish, miss."

"*Not* as I wish," she said, stamping her foot. "*Stop* saying that."

"Yes, miss."

"Mr. St. Trewes and the Reverend Mr. Doult are gentlemen. How dare you contradict their opinions! You are only a common servant."

"Yes, miss," he said wearily.

"You should be dismissed for being insolent to your betters."

There was another long pause, and then Baine said, "All the diary entries and dismissals in the world cannot change the truth. Galileo recanted under threat of torture, but that did not make the sun revolve round the earth. If you dismiss me, the vase will still be vulgar, I will still be right, and your taste will still be plebeian, no matter what you write in your diary."

"Plebeian?" Tossie said, bright pink. "How dare you speak like that to your mistress? You are dismissed." She pointed imperiously at the house. "Pack your things immediately."

"Yes, miss," Baine said. *"E pur si muove."*

"What?" Tossie said, bright red with rage. "What did you say?"

"I said, now that you have dismissed me, I am no longer a member of the servant class and am therefore in a position to speak freely," he said calmly.

"You are not in a position to speak to me at all," Tossie said, raising her diary like a weapon. "Leave at once."

"I dared to speak the truth to you because I felt you were deserving of it," Baine said seriously. "I had only your best interests at heart, as I have always had. You have been blessed with great riches; not only with the riches of wealth, position, and beauty, but with a bright mind and a keen sensibility, as well as with a fine spirit. And yet you squander those riches on croquet and organdies and trumpery works of art. You have at your disposal a library of the great minds of the past, and yet you read the foolish novels of Charlotte Yonge and Edward Bulwer-Lytton. Given the opportunity to study science, you converse with conjurors wearing cheesecloth and phosphorescent paint. Confronted by the glories of Gothic architecture, you admire instead a cheap imitation of it, and confronted by the truth, you stamp your foot like a spoilt child and demand to be told fairy stories."

It was quite a speech, and after it, I fully expected Tossie to hit him over the head with the diary and sweep off in a flurry of ruffles, but instead she said, "You think I have a bright mind?"

"I do. With study and discipline, you would be capable of marvelous things."

From my mid-lilac vantage point, their faces were hidden from me, and I had a feeling seeing them was important. I moved over to the left to a thinner bush. And ran squarely into Finch. I nearly dropped Princess Arjumand. She yowled, and Finch yelped.

"Shh," I said to both of them. "Finch, did you get the message I left at the Chattisbournes'?" I whispered.

"No, I've been in Oxford," Finch said, beaming, "where, I'm delighted to say, my mission was a complete success."

"Shh," I whispered. "Keep your voice down. The butler and Tossie are having an argument."

"An argument?" he said, pursing his lips. "A butler never argues with his employer."

"Well, this one does," I said.

Finch was rustling under the lilacs. "I'm glad I ran into you," he said, coming up with a basket full of cabbages. "Where's Miss Kindle? I need to speak with both of you."

"What do you mean, 'Where's Miss Kindle?' I thought you said you just came through from the lab."

"I did," he said.

"Then you must have seen her. She just went through."

"To the laboratory?"

"Of course to the laboratory," I said. "How long were you there before you came through?"

"An hour and a half," Finch said. "We were discussing the next phase of my mission, but no one came through during that time."

"Could she have come through without you noticing?" I said. "While you were having this discussion?"

"No, sir. We were standing in the net area, and Miss Warder has been keeping a very close watch on the console because of Carruthers." He looked thoughtful. "Had you noticed any problem with the net?"

"*Problem?*" I said, forgetting we were supposed to keep our voices down. "We've been trying for the last five hours to get the bloody thing to open!"

"Shh," Finch said, "keep your voice down," but it scarcely mattered. Baine's and Tossie's voices had risen to shouting point.

"And don't quote Tennyson at me!" Tossie said furiously.

"That was not Tennyson," Baine shouted. "It was William Shakespeare, who is eminently quotable. 'Think you a little din can daunt mine ears? Have I not heard great ordnance in the field and heaven's artillery thunder in the skies?' "

"The net wouldn't open?" Finch said.

"That's what my message was about," I said. "It wouldn't open for either of us. Verity'd been trying since three o'clock this morning." A thought struck me. "When did you go through from here?"

"At half past two."

"That was just before Verity tried," I said. "How much slippage was there?"

"None," he said, looking worried. "Oh, dear, Mr. Lewis said something like this might happen."

"Something like what?"

"Some of his Waterloo models showed aberrations in the net, due to the incongruity."

"What sort of aberrations?" I said, raising my voice again.

"Failure to open, destination malfunction."

"What do you mean, 'destination malfunction'?"

"In two of the simulations, the historian was sent to some other des-tination on the return drop. Not just locational slippage, but an entirely different space-time location. Mexico in 1872, in one instance."

"I've got to go tell Mr. Dunworthy," I said, starting for the drop. "How long ago did you come through?"

"At twenty till ten," he said, scurrying after me, taking out his pocket watch. "Twelve minutes ago."

Good. That meant only four minutes till the next one. I reached the gazebo and went over to the spot where Verity had gone through.

"Do you think this is a good idea, sir?" Finch said worriedly. "If the net's not working properly—"

"Verity might be in Mexico or God knows where else," I said.

"But she'd have come back, sir, wouldn't she, as soon as she realized it was the wrong destination?"

"Not if the net wouldn't open," I said, trying to find the spot where Verity had stood.

"You're right," Finch said. "What can I do, sir? I'm expected back from Little Rushlade," he indicated the basket, "but I could—"

"You'd better take your cabbages to the Chattisbournes' and then meet me back here. If I'm not here, you go through and tell Mr. Dunworthy what's happened."

"Yes, sir," he said. "What if the net won't open, sir?"

"It'll open," I said grimly.

"Yes, sir," he said and hurried off with his basket.

I looked hard at the grass, willing the shimmer to start. I was still holding the cat, and I couldn't just put her down. She was liable to walk into the net at the last minute, and another incongruity was the last thing we needed.

There were still three minutes left. I pushed back through the lilacs to where Tossie and Baine had been, intending to put the cat down where they could see her.

Things had apparently not improved. "How *dare* you!" Tossie said.

" 'Nay, come, Kate, come!' " Baine said. " 'You must not look so sour.' "

"How dare you call me Kate, as if I were a common servant like you!"

I squatted down and tipped Princess Arjumand out of my hands. She sauntered off through the bushes toward Tossie, and I sprinted back to the drop.

"I intend to tell my fiancé how insolently you spoke to me," Tossie shouted. Apparently she hadn't noticed Princess Arjumand. "When Mr. St. Trewes and I are married, I intend to make him run for Parliament and pass a law making it a crime for servants to read books and have ideas."

There was a faint hum, and the air began to shimmer. I stepped into the center of it.

"And I intend to write down everything you said to me in my diary," she said, "so that my children and my children's children shall know what a rude, insolent, barbaric, common—what are you *doing?*"

The net began to shimmer in earnest, and I didn't dare step out of it. I craned my neck, trying to see over the lilacs.

"What are you doing?" Tossie cried. "Put me down!" A string of screamlets. "Put me down this instant!"

"I have only your best interests at heart," Baine said.

I looked at the growing light, trying to gauge how long I had. Not long enough, and I couldn't risk waiting for the next drop, not with Verity God-knew-where. Mexico had had a revolution in the 1870s, hadn't it?

"I shall have you arrested for this!" A series of thumps, as of someone beating on someone's chest. "You arrogant, horrid, uncivilized bully!"

" 'And thus I'll curb her mad and headstrong humour,' " Baine said. " 'He that knows better how to tame a shrew, now let him speak.' "

The air around me filled with light. "Not yet," I said, and, as if in response, it dimmed a little. "No!" I said, not knowing whether I wanted the net to open or not.

"*Put* me *down!*" Tossie demanded.

"As you wish, miss!" Baine said.

The light from the net flared and enfolded me. "Wait!" I said as it closed, and thought I heard a splash.

*"Can you row?" the Sheep asked, handing her a pair of*
*knitting-needles as she spoke.*
*"Yes, a little—but not on land—and not with needles—" Alice was*
*beginning to say, when suddenly the needles turned into oars in her hands,*
*and she found they were in a little boat, gliding along between banks:*
*so there was nothing for it but to do her best.*

*Lewis Carroll*

# CHAPTER TWENTY-THREE

Arrival—In the Lab—I Attempt to Ascertain My Space-Time
Location—I Hide—Zuleika Dobson—Eavesdropping—Treasures
of Various Cathedrals—In a Bookstore—Timelessness of Men's
Clothing—Timelessness of Books—More Eavesdropping—Spoiling
the Ends of Mysteries—In a Dungeon—Bats—I Attempt to Use
the Little Gray Cells—I Fall Asleep—Yet Another Conversation
with a Workman—Origin of Ghost Legend in Coventry
Cathedral—Arrival

W herever I was, it wasn't the lab. The room looked like one of Balliol's old
lecture rooms. There was a blackboard on one wall and, above it, the
mounting for an old-fashioned pull-down map, and on the door were
a number of taped-up notices.

But it was obviously being used as a lab. On a long metal table was a row
of primitive digital-processor computers and monitors, all linked together
with gray and yellow and orange cords and a clutch of adaptors.

I looked back at the net I had just come through. It was nothing but a chalked circle, with a large masking-tape "X" in the center. Behind it, and attached to it by an even more dangerous-looking tangle of cords and copper wires, was a frightening assortment of capacitors, metal boxes studded with dials and knobs, lengths of PVC pipe, thick cables, jacks, and resistors, all taped together with wads of wide silver tape, which had to be the mechanism of the net, though I could not have imagined trying to cross the street in such a contraption, let alone going back in time.

A horrible thought struck me. What if this was the lab after all? What if the incongruity had altered more than Terence and Maud's marriage and the bombing of Berlin?

I strode over to the door, hoping against hope the printed notices didn't say 2057. And weren't in German.

They weren't. The top one said, "Parking is forbidden on the Broad, Parks Road, and in the Naffield College car park. Violators will be towed," which sounded fascist, but then the Parking Authority always sounded fascist. And there were no swastikas on it, or on the railway schedule beside it. A large notice on pink paper read, "Fees for Hilary term are now past due. If you have not paid, please see the bursar immediately."

And, inevitably, below it, "Orphans of the Pandemic Jumble Sale and St. Michael's at the North Gate Charity Drive. April fifth, 10 A.M. to 4 P.M. Bargains. White elephants. Treasures."

Well, it definitely wasn't Nazi England. And the Pandemic had still happened.

I examined the notices. Not a sign of a year on any of them, no dates at all, except for the upcoming jumble sale at St. Michael's at the North Gate, and even that wasn't certain. I'd seen notices over a year old on the notice board at Balliol.

I went over to the windows, pried the tape off one corner, and pulled the paper aside. I was looking out at Balliol's front quad at a beautiful spring day. The lilacs outside the chapel were in bloom, and in the center of the quad a huge beech tree was just leafing out.

There was a chestnut tree in the center of the quad now, and it was at least thirty years old. Before 2020, then, but after the Pandemic, and the railway schedule meant it was before the Underground had reached Oxford. And after the invention of time travel. Between 2013 and 2020.

I went back over to the computers. The middle monitor was blinking, "Push 'reset.'"

I did, and the veils above the net descended with a thunk. They weren't transparent, they were dusty dark-red velvet that looked like they belonged in amateur theatricals.

"Destination?" the screen was blinking now. I had no idea what system of coordinates they'd used in the Twenties. Mr. Dunworthy had told me stories about the point-and-shoot time travel they'd done in the early days, without Pulhaski coordinates, without safeguards or parameter checks or any idea of where they were going or whether they'd get back. The good old days.

But at least the computer spoke English and not some primitive code. I typed in, "Current location?"

The screen went blank and then began blinking, "Error."

I thought a minute and then typed in, "Help screen."

The screen went blank again and stayed blank. Wonderful.

I began punching function keys. The screen began blinking, "Destination?"

There was a sound at the door. I looked round wildly for someplace to hide. There wasn't any. Except the net, which was no place at all. I dived into the red velvet curtains and yanked them together.

Whoever was at the door was having difficulty getting in. There was a good deal of rattling and jimmying before the door opened.

I retreated to the center of the net and stood very still. There was the sound of the door's closing, and then silence.

I stood there, listening. Nothing. Had whoever it was changed their mind and gone out again? I took a careful step toward the edge and pulled the curtains a millimeter apart. A beautiful young woman was standing by the door, biting her lip and looking straight at me.

I fought the impulse to jerk back. She hadn't seen me. I wasn't sure she was seeing the net either. She seemed lost in some inner vision of her own.

She was wearing a calf-length white dress that could have been from any decade from the 1930s on. Her red hair was long and looped up in the knotted ponytail of the Millennium era, but that didn't necessarily mean anything. Historians in the Fifties wore them, too, along with braids and snoods and coronets, anything to keep the long hair they had to have for their drops out of the way.

The young woman looked younger than Tossie, but probably wasn't. She was wearing a wedding ring. She vaguely reminded me of someone. It wasn't Verity, though her determined expression made me think of Verity. And not Lady Schrapnell or any of her ancestors. Somebody I'd met at one of my jumble sales?

I squinted at her, trying to get a fix. Her hair was wrong. Should it be lighter? Reddish-blonde, perhaps?

She stood there a long minute with the look Verity had had—frightened, angry, determined—and then walked rapidly in the direction of the computers and out of my line of sight.

Silence again. I listened for the quiet click of keys, hoping she wasn't setting up a drop. Or typing in directions for the veils to rise.

I couldn't see from this angle. I moved carefully to the next break in the curtain and peered through. She was standing in front of the comps, staring at them, or, rather, past them, through them, with that same look of determination.

And something else I'd never seen on Verity's face, not even when Terence had told us he and Tossie were engaged, an edge of reckless desperation.

There was a sound at the door. She turned and immediately started toward the door. And out of range again. And the person at the door obviously had a key. By the time I'd moved back to my original vantage point, he was standing in the open door, looking at her.

He was wearing jeans and a ragged sweater and spectacles. His hair was light brown and the longish indeterminate cut historians adopt because it can be maneuvered into almost any era's style, and he looked familiar, too, though it was probably just the expression on his face, which I would have known anywhere. I should. It was the expression I had every time I looked at Verity.

He was holding a fat stack of papers and folders, and he still had the key to the lab in his hand.

"Hullo, Jim," she said, her back to me, and I wished I could see her face, too.

"What are you doing here?" he said in a voice I knew as well as my own. Good Lord! I was looking at Mr. Dunworthy.

Mr. Dunworthy! He'd told me stories about the infancy of time travel, but I had always thought of him as, you know, Mr. Dunworthy. I hadn't imagined him as skinny or awkward. Or young. Or in love with somebody he couldn't have.

"I came to talk to you," she said. "And to Shoji. Where is he?"

"Meeting with the head," Mr. Dunwor—Jim said. "Again." He went over to the table and dumped his load of papers and folders on the end of it.

I switched peepholes, wishing they'd stay put.

"Is this a bad time?" she said.

"The worst of times," he said, looking through the stack for something. "We've got a new head of the history faculty since you left to marry Bitty. Mr. Arnold P. Lassiter. "P" for Prudence. He's so cautious we haven't done a drop in three months. 'Time travel is an endeavor that should not be undertaken without a complete knowledge of how it works.' Which means filling up forms and more forms. He wants complete analyses on every drop—the ones he's willing to authorize, that is, which are few and far between—parameter checks, slippage graphs, impact probability stats, security checks—" He stopped rummaging. "How did you get into the lab?"

"It was unlocked," she said, which was a lie. I twisted my head around, trying to find an angle from which I could see her face.

"Wonderful," Jim said. "If Prudence finds out, he'll have a fit." He found the folder he wanted and pulled it out of the stack. "Why isn't Bitty the Bishop with you?" he said, almost belligerently.

"He's in London, appealing the C of E's ruling."

Jim's face changed. "I heard about Coventry's being declared nonessential," he said. "I'm sorry, Lizzie."

Coventry. Lizzie. This was Elizabeth Bittner he was talking to, the wife of the last bishop of Coventry. The frail, white-haired lady I'd interviewed in Coventry. No wonder I'd thought her hair should be lighter.

"Nonessential," she said. "A cathedral nonessential. Religion will be ruled nonessential next, and then Art and Truth. Not to mention History." She walked toward the blacked-out windows and out of range.

*Will* you stand still? I thought.

"It's so unfair," she said. "They kept Bristol, you know. Bristol!"

"Why didn't Coventry make the cut?" Jim said, moving so I couldn't see him either.

"The C of E ruled that all churches and cathedrals have to be seventy-five percent self-supporting, which means tourists. And the tourists only come to see tombs and treasures. Canterbury's got Becket, Winchester's got Jane Austen and a black Tournai marble font, and St. Martin's-in-the-Fields is in London, which has the Tower and Madame Tussaud's. We used to have treasures. Unfortunately, they were all destroyed by the Luftwaffe in 1940," she said bitterly.

"There's the baptistry window of the new cathedral," Jim said.

"Yes. Unfortunately there's also a church that looks like a factory warehouse and stained-glass windows that face the wrong way and the ugliest tapestry in existence. Mid-Nineteenth Century was not a good period in art. Or architecture."

"They come to see the ruins of the old cathedral, don't they?"

"Some of them. Not enough. Bitty tried to convince the Appropriations Committee that Coventry's a special case, that it has historical importance, but it didn't work. World War II was a long time ago. Scarcely anybody remembers it." She sighed. "The appeal's not going to work either."

"What happens then? Will you have to close?"

She must have shaken her head. "We can't afford to close. The diocese is too far in debt. We'll have to sell." She abruptly moved back into my line of sight, her face set. "The Church of the Hereafter made an offer. It's a New

Age sect. Ouija boards, manifestations, conversations with the dead. It'll kill him, you know."

"Will he be completely out of a job?"

"No," she said wryly. "Religion's nonessential, which means clergy are hard to come by. Rats deserting a sinking ship and all that. They've offered him the position of senior canon at Salisbury."

"Good," Jim said, too heartily. "Salisbury's not on the nonessential list, is it?"

"No," she said. "It has plenty of treasures. And Turner. It's too bad he couldn't have come to Coventry to paint. But you don't understand. Bitty can't bear to sell it. He's descended from Thomas Botoner, who helped build the original cathedral. He loves the cathedral. He'd do anything to save it."

"And you'd do anything for him."

"Yes," she said, looking steadily at him. "I would." She took a deep breath. "That's why I came to see you. I have a favor to ask." She stepped eagerly toward him, and they both moved out of my line of sight.

"I was thinking if we could take people back through the net to see the cathedral," she said, "to see it burn down, they'd realize what it meant, how important it was."

"Take people *back?*" Jim said. "We have trouble getting Prudence to approve research drops, let alone tourist excursions."

"They wouldn't be tourist excursions," she said, sounding hurt. "Just a few select people."

"The Appropriations Committee?"

"And some vid reporters. If we had the public on our side—if they saw it with their own eyes, they'd realize—"

Jim must have been shaking his head, because she stopped and switched tactics. "We wouldn't necessarily have to go back to the air raid," she said rapidly. "We could go to the ruins afterward, or—or to the old cathedral. It could be in the middle of the night, when there wouldn't be anybody in the cathedral. If they could just see the organ and the Dance of Death miserere and the Fifteenth-Century children's cross for themselves, they'd realize what it meant to have lost Coventry Cathedral once, and they wouldn't let it happen again."

"Lizzie," Jim said, and there was no mistaking that tone. And she had to know it was impossible. Oxford had never allowed sightseeing trips, not even in the good old days, and neither had the net.

She did know it. "You don't understand," she said despairingly. "It'll kill him."

The door opened, and a short scrawny kid with Asian features came in. "Jim, did you run the parameter—"

He stopped, looking at Lizzie. She must have cut a real swath in Oxford. Like Zuleika Dobson.

"Hullo, Shoji," Lizzie said.

"Hullo, Liz," he said. "What are you doing here?"

"How'd the meeting with Prudence go?" Jim said.

"About like you'd expect," Shoji said. "Now it's the slippage he's worried about. What's its function? Why does it fluctuate so much?" His voice became prissy and affected, imitating Lassiter's voice, " 'We must consider all possible consequences before we initiate action.' " He reverted to his own voice. "He wants a complete analysis of slippage patterns on all past drops before he'll authorize any new ones." He crossed out of my line of sight and over to the computers.

"You're joking," Jim said, following him. "That'll take six months. We'll never go anywhere."

"I think that's the general idea," Shoji said, sitting down at the middle computer and beginning to type. "If we don't go anywhere, there's no risk. Why are the veils down?"

There was no record of a time traveller from the future *or* the past suddenly materializing in Balliol's lab. Which either meant I hadn't been caught or I'd come up with an extremely convincing story. I tried to think of one.

"If we don't *go* anywhere," Jim said, "how are we supposed to *learn* anything about time travel? Did you tell him science involves *experiments?*"

Shoji began hitting keys on the keyboard. " 'This is not a chemistry class we are talking about, Mr. Fujisaki,' " he said in the prissy voice as he typed. " 'This is the space-time continuum.' "

The curtains began, awkwardly, to rise.

"I *know* it's the continuum," Jim said, "but—"

"Jim," Lizzie said, still out of sight but not for long, and both of them turned to look at her. "Will you ask him at least?" she said. "It means—"

And I found myself in a corner of Blackwell's Book Store. Its dark woods and book-lined walls are not only instantly recognizable but timeless, and for a moment I thought I'd made it back to 2057, and getting to the lab was going to be a simple matter of sprinting up the Broad to Balliol, but as soon as I poked my head round the bookcase, I knew it wasn't going to be that simple. Outside Blackwell's bow windows it was snowing. And there was a Daimler parked in front of the Sheldonian.

Not Twenty-First Century, and now that I looked around, not the end of Twentieth either. No terminals, no paperbacks, no print-and-binds. Hardbacks, mostly without dust jackets, in blues and greens and browns.

And a shop assistant bearing down on me with a notebook in her hand and a yellow pencil behind her ear.

It was too late to duck back into a corner. She'd already seen me. Luckily, men's clothes, unlike women's, haven't changed that much over the years, and boating blazers and flannels can still be seen in Oxford, though usually not in the dead of winter. With luck, I could pass as a first-year student.

The shop assistant was wearing a slimmish navy-blue dress Verity would probably have been able to date to the exact month, but the mid-Twentieth-Century decades all look alike to me. 1950? No, her pencil-decked hair was put up in a severe knob, and her shoes laced. Early 1940s?

No, the windows were intact, there weren't any blackout curtains and no sandbags piled up by the door, and the clerk looked far too prosperous to be post-war. The Thirties.

Verity's regular assignment was the Thirties. Maybe the net had mistakenly sent me to the coordinates of one of her old drops. Or maybe she was here.

No, she couldn't be here. My clothes might pass, but not her long, high-necked dress and piled-up hair.

The range of times and places she could be without creating an incongruity just by her appearance was very limited, and most of them were civilized, thank goodness.

"May I help you, sir?" the shop assistant said, looking at my mustache disapprovingly. I'd forgotten about it. Had men been clean-shaven in the 1930s? Hercule Poirot had had a mustache, hadn't he?

"May I help you, sir?" she repeated, more severely. "Is there a particular book you are looking for?"

"Yes," I said. And what books would they have had in Blackwell's in Nineteen-Thirty- What? *The Lord of the Rings?* No, that was later. *Goodbye Mr. Chips?* That had been published in 1934, but what was this? I couldn't see a date on that salespad of the shop assistant's, and the last thing we needed, with the continuum falling down around our ears, was another incongruity.

"*The Decline and Fall of the Roman Empire,*" I said to be safe. "By Gibbon."

"That would be on the the first floor," she said. "In History."

I didn't want to go up to the first floor. I wanted to stay close to the drop. What was on this floor? Eighty years from now, it would be metafiction and self-writes, but I doubted they had either here. *Through the Looking Glass?* No, what if children's lit was already in a separate shop?

"The stairs up to the first floor are just there, sir," she said, removing her pencil from behind her ear and pointing with it.

"Have you Jerome's *Three Men in a Boat?*" I said.

"I will have to check," she said, and started toward the rear.

"*To Say Nothing of the Dog,*" I called after her, and, as soon as she had rounded a bookcase, darted back to my corner.

I had been half-hoping the net would be open, or faintly shimmering in preparation, but there was nothing in the ceiling-to-floor rows of books to indicate it had ever been there. Or to give me a clue to what year I was in.

I began taking down books and opening them to the title page. 1904. 1930. 1921. 1756. That's the trouble with books. They're timeless. 1892. 1914. No date. I flipped the page over. Still no date. I flipped the page back again and read the title. No wonder. Herodotus's *History,* which the Colonel and Professor Peddick had been reading only yesterday.

The bell over the door jangled. I peered carefully round the corner, hoping it was Verity. It was three middle-aged women in fur stoles and angle-brimmed hats.

They stopped just inside the door, brushing snow lovingly off their furs as if they were pets, and talking in high nasal tones.

". . . and eloped with him!" the one on the right said. Her fur looked like a flattened version of Princess Arjumand. "*So* romantic!"

"But a *farmer!*" the middle one said. Her fur looked more like Cyril and was nearly as wide.

"I don't care if he is a farmer," the third one said. "I'm glad she married him." She had the best fur of all, an entire string of foxes with their heads still on and bright little glass eyes. "If she hadn't, she'd still be trapped in Oxford, serving on church committees and running jumble sales. Now, what was it I wanted to buy? I said to Harold this morning, I must remember to buy that when I go to Blackwell's. Now, what could it have been?"

"I must get something for my godchild for her birthday," the one with Cyril on her shoulders said. "What should I get? *Alice,* I suppose, though I've never understood why children like it. Going from place to place with no rhyme or reason. Appearing and disappearing."

"Oh, look!" the string of foxes said. She had picked up a book with a green dust jacket from a display table. Her fox-colored gloved hand was over the title, but I could see the author's name: Agatha Christie.

"Have you read her latest?" she said to the others.

"No," the one with Cyril on her shoulders said.

"Yes," the Princess Arjumand said, "and it—"

"Stop," the string of foxes said, raising her gloved hand in warning. "Don't tell me the ending." She turned back to Cyril. "Cora always *ruins* the ending. Do you remember *The Murder of Roger Ackroyd*?"

"That was different. You wanted to know what all the fuss in the papers was about, Miriam," the Princess Arjumand said defensively. "I couldn't explain it without telling who the murderer was. At any rate, this one isn't anything like *Roger Ackroyd*. There's this girl who someone is attempting to murder, or at least that's what one's *supposed* to think. Actually—"

"*Don't* tell me the ending," the Little Foxes said.

"I didn't intend to," the Princess Arjumand said with dignity. "I was simply going to say that what you think is the crime, isn't, and things aren't at all what they seem."

"Like in *The Fountain Pen Mystery,*" the Cyril-draped one said. "What you think is the first crime turns out to be the second. The first one had happened years before. Nobody even knew the first crime had been committed, and the murderer—"

"*Don't* tell me," the Little Foxes said, clapping fox-gloved hands to her ears.

"The butler did it," the Cyril said.

"I thought you hadn't read it," the Little Foxes said, taking her hands down from her ears.

"I didn't," she said. "It's always the butler," and the lights went out.

But it was daytime, and even if something had happened to the electricity, there would still be enough light from Blackwell's bow windows to see by.

I put my hand out to the bookshelf in front of me and felt it cautiously. It felt clammy and hard, like stone. I took a cautious step toward it. And nearly pitched forward into emptiness.

My foot was half over a void. I reeled back, staggered, and sat down hard on more stone. A staircase. I felt around, patting the rough stone wall, reaching down. A winding staircase, with narrow wedge-shaped steps, which meant I was in a tower. Or a dungeon.

The air had a cold, mildewy smell, which probably meant it wasn't a dungeon. A dungeon would smell a good deal worse. But if it were a tower, light should be filtering in from a slit window somewhere above, and it wasn't. I couldn't see my hand in front of my face. A dungeon.

Or, I thought hopefully, the erratic bouncing had given me such a case of time-lag I'd gone completely blind.

I fumbled in my pockets for a match and struck it on the wall. No such luck. Rock walls, stone steps loomed up around me. Definitely a dungeon. Which meant I probably wasn't in Oxford in 2018. Or 1933.

The Seventeenth Century had been big on dungeons. Ditto the Sixteenth through the Twelfth. Before that England had run mostly to pigsties and stick huts. Wonderful. Trapped in a Norman dungeon in the Middle Ages.

Or a corner of the Tower of London, in which case tourists would come trooping up the stairs in a few minutes. But somehow I didn't think so. The steps, in the brief light of the match, had looked unworn, and when I felt along the wall, there weren't any safety railings.

"Verity!" I shouted down into the blackness. My voice echoed off stone and silence.

I stood, bracing myself against the wall with both hands, and started carefully up, feeling for the edge of the narrow step with my foot. One step. Two. "Verity! Are you here?"

Nothing. I felt for the next step. "Verity!"

I put my foot on the step. It gave under my weight. I started to fall, flailing wildly, trying to catch myself and scraping my hand. I slid two steps and came down hard on one knee.

And if Verity was here, she had to have heard that. But I called again. "Verity!"

There was an explosion of sound, a violent flapping and whirring of wings that sounded like it was diving straight for me. Bats. Wonderful. I flung an arm I couldn't see in front of my face.

The flapping intensified, but though my eyes strained through the darkness, I couldn't see.

The flapping was coming straight at me. A wing brushed my arm. Wonderful. The bats couldn't see either. I flailed at the darkness, and the flapping grew more frantic and then subsided, flying off above me, and I sat down very slowly and silently.

All right. Clearly the intelligent thing to do was sit here and wait for the net to open. And hope I wasn't permanently stuck like Carruthers.

"And meanwhile Verity's lost somewhere!" I shouted and was instantly sorry. The bats attacked again, and it was a good five minutes before they subsided.

I sat still and listened. Either this dungeon was completely soundproofed, or I wasn't anywhere in the last three centuries. The world hasn't been truly silent since the beginning of the Industrial Revolution. Even the Victorian era had had trains and steam launches to contend with, and in the cities, the rattle and clop of traffic which would shortly become a roar. And both Twentieth and Twenty-First Century have an electronic hum that's always present. Here, now that the bats had gone back to bed, there was no sound at all.

So what now? I'd probably kill myself if I tried any more exploration, and probably miss the net's opening in the process. Assuming it was going to open.

I felt in my pocket for another match and my watch. Half past X. Warder had had a half-hour intermittent on the drop at Muchings End and I had only been in the lab twenty minutes, in Blackwell's possibly fifteen. Which meant the net might open at any time. Or not at all, I thought, remembering Carruthers.

And in the meantime, what? Sit here and stare at the darkness? Worry about Verity? Try to figure out what had happened to the bishop's bird stump?

According to Verity, detectives weren't required to go anywhere or do anything. They could sit in an easy chair (or a dungeon) and solve the mystery just by using "the little gray cells." And I had more than enough mysteries to occupy me: Who on earth would have wanted to steal the bishop's bird stump? Who was Mr. C and why the bloody hell hadn't he shown up yet? What was Finch up to? What was I doing in the middle of the Middle Ages?

But the answer to that one was obvious. Verity and I had failed, and the continuum was starting to collapse. Carruthers trapped in Coventry and then the slippage on the return drops and then Verity—I should never have let her go through. I should have realized what was happening when the net wouldn't open. I should have realized what was going to happen when Tossie didn't meet Mr. C.

It was one of T.J.'s worst-case Waterloo scenarios, an incongruity too devastating for the continuum to be able to fix it. "See here," T.J. had said, pointing at the formless gray image, "and here, you have radically increased slippage, but it can't contain the incongruity, and you can see *here* where the backups start to fail, and the net begins to malfunction as the course of history starts to alter."

The course of history. Terence marries Tossie instead of Maud, and a different pilot flies the mission to Berlin, and he miscalculates the target or is hit by flak, or he thinks he hears something wrong with the engine and turns back, and the other planes, thinking he's received orders, follow him, or because of him they get lost, the way the German pilots had two nights before, or somehow the lack of their grandson's presence in the world affects the history of airplane development or the amount of gasoline in England or the weather. And the raid never happens.

The Luftwaffe doesn't retaliate by bombing London. It doesn't bomb Coventry. So there is no restoration project. And no Lady Schrapnell to send Verity back to 1888. And the paradoxes multiply and reach critical mass and the net begins to break down, trapping Carruthers in Coventry, sending me farther and farther afield. This is the cat that dropped the bomb that brought down the house that Jack built.

It was getting colder. I pulled the lapels of my blazer together, wishing it was the tweed.

But if it was a worst-case scenario, why hadn't there been any increased slippage on Verity's drop? "See here," T.J. had said, bringing up sim after sim after sim, "every single incongruity has this area of radically increased slippage around the focus." Except ours.

Nine minutes' slippage on that first drop, between two and thirty on all the others, an average of fourteen for all drops to the Victorian era. Only two areas of increased slippage, and one of those was due to Ultra.

I took my coat off and wrapped it around me like a blanket, shivering and thinking about Ultra.

Ultra had had a system of backups, too. The first line of defense was secrecy. But if there was a breach, they put their secondary system of defenses into action, like they had done in North Africa.

They'd been using Ultra to locate and sink convoys carrying fuel oil to Rommel, which could have roused suspicions that codes were being broken, so a spotter plane had been sent up each time to be seen by the convoy, so the Nazis could blame the sinking on having been spotted.

Except once, when heavy fog kept the plane from finding the convoy, and, in their panic to make certain the oil didn't make it to Rommel, the RAF and the Royal Navy had both shown up to sink it, and nearly blown the cover.

So the head of Ultra put a backup plan into operation, planting rumors in the port of Malta, sending an easily decodable message to a nonexistent agent, arranging for it to be intercepted. The message thanked the agent for his information on the convoy and gave him a raise. And the Nazis had spent the next six months tracking down rumors and looking for the agent. And not suspecting we had Ultra.

And if that plan had failed, they would have tried something else. And even if all the plans had failed, they would have failed *after*, not *during* the breach.

No matter how bad the incongruity was, the continuum should have tried to prevent it. Instead, it had added nine minutes' slippage, nine minutes that had sent Verity through at the exact moment to save the cat, when five minutes either way would have prevented it from happening at all. It was as if the continuum had taken one look at the incongruity and fainted dead away, like Mrs. Mering.

Verity had said to look for the one little fact that didn't fit, but none of it fit: Why, if the continuum was trying to repair itself, hadn't it sent me through at Muchings End so I could have returned the cat before Mrs. Mering went off to consult Madame Iritosky? Why had it sent me through three days late and just in time to prevent Terence from meeting Maud? And the biggest little fact of all, why had the net allowed the incongruity at all when it was supposed to shut down automatically?

"You understand these are all hypothetical scenarios," T.J. had said. "In all these cases, the net refused to open."

It was impossible to get anywhere near Waterloo. Or Ford's Theater. Or Franz-Joseph Street. If the cat was so pivotal to the course of history, why wasn't it impossible to get anywhere near Muchings End? Why wasn't there increased slippage on Verity's drop, where it was needed, and so much in

Oxford in April, 2018? And how, if the slippage was keeping everything away, had I gotten through?

It would have been nice if the answer had been there, in the lab in 2018, but it was obvious that, whatever had caused the slippage, it wasn't anything Jim Dunworthy or Shoji Fujisaki had done. They weren't doing any drops.

Doubtless, if Hercule Poirot were here, he'd have come up with a neat solution not only to the Mystery of the Baffling Incongruity, but also that of the Little Princes in the Tower, Jack the Ripper, and who blew up St. Paul's. But he wasn't, and neither was the dapper Lord Peter Wimsey, and if they were, I'd have taken their coats away from them and put them over my knees.

Somehow, during that reverie, I had realized I was staring at an un-evenness in the pitch-blackness opposite that might be the mortar between the stones, and that it meant light was coming from somewhere.

I flattened myself against the wall, but the light, or, rather, *very* slight absence of darkness, didn't flicker or grow, like a torch coming down from somewhere above.

And it wasn't the reddish-yellow of a lantern. It was only a grayer shade of black. And I must really be time-lagged, because it took another five minutes for the other possibility to occur to me: that the reason for the pitch-blackness was that it was night and I was in a tower, after all. And the way out was down.

And a near-fall and scraping of my right hand catching myself to realize that if I waited another half hour I'd be able to see where I was going and get out of here without killing myself.

I sat back down on the step, leaned my head against the wall, and watched the grayness grow.

I had made an assumption that darkness meant a dungeon, and as a consequence, I had been looking at things all wrong. Was that what we were doing in regard to the incongruity, too? Had we assumed something we shouldn't have?

History was full of mistaken assumptions—Napoleon's assuming Ney had taken Quatre Bras, Hitler's assuming the invasion would come at Calais, King Harold's Saxons' assuming William the Conqueror's men were retreating instead of leading them into a trap.

Had we made a mistaken assumption about the incongruity? Was there some way of looking at it which explained everything—from the lack of slippage on Verity's drop to the excess of it in 2018? Some way of looking at it in which everything fit—Princess Arjumand and Carruthers and the bishop's bird stump and all those bloody jumble sales and curates, to say nothing of the dog—and it all made sense?

I must have fallen asleep, because when I opened my eyes, it was fully daylight and there were voices coming up the stairs.

I looked wildly round the narrow tower, as if there might actually be somewhere to hide, and then sprinted up the stairs.

I had gone at least five steps before I realized I needed to count the steps so I would know where the drop was. Six, seven, eight, I counted silently, rounding the next curve of the steps. Nine, ten, eleven. I stopped, listening.

"*Hastyeh doon awthaslattes?*" the woman said.

It sounded like Middle English, which meant I'd been right about this being the Middle Ages.

"*Goadahdahm Boetenneher, thahslattes ayrnacoom,*" the man said.

"*Thahslattes maun bayendoon uvthisse wyke,*" the woman said.

"*Tha kahnabay,*" he said.

I couldn't understand what they were saying, but I had heard this conversation a number of times before, most recently in front of the south door of St. Michael's. The woman was demanding to know why something wasn't done. The man was making excuses. The woman, who must be an early ancestor of Lady Schrapnell's, was saying she didn't care, it had to be done in time for the jumble sale.

"*Thatte kahna bay, Goadahdahm Boetenneher,*" he said. "*Tha wolde hahvneedemorr holpen thanne isseheer.*"

"*So willetby, Gruwens,*" the woman said.

There was a clank of stone on stone, and the woman snapped, "*Lokepponthatt, Gruwens! The steppe bay loossed.*"

She was yelling at him for the loose step. Good. I hoped she read him out properly.

"*Ye charge yesette at nought,*" she said.

"*Ne gan speken rowe,*" the workman said placatingly.

They were still coming up. I looked up the tower's shaft, wondering if there might be a room or a platform above.

"*Tha willbay doone bylyve, Goadahdahm Boetenneher.*"

Botoner. Could the woman be Ann Botoner, or Mary, who had built the spire of Coventry Cathedral? And could this be the tower?

I started up again, trying not to make any noise and counting the steps. Nineteen, twenty.

There was a platform, overlooking an open space. I looked down at it. The bells. Or where the bells would be when they were installed. I had just ascertained my space-time location. It was the tower of Coventry Cathedral, the year it was built. 1395.

I couldn't hear them. I went back to the stairs and took two tentative steps down. And nearly ran into them.

They were right below me. I could see the top of a white-coiffed head. I leaped back up to the level of the platform, and on up the stairs, and nearly stepped on a pigeon.

It squawked and flew up, flapping like a bat at me and then past me and down onto the platform.

"Shoo!" Dame Botoner shouted. "Shoo! Thah divils minion!"

I waited, poised for flight and trying not to pant, but they didn't come any farther. Their voices echoed oddly, as if they had gone over to the far side of the platform, and after a minute I crept back down to where I could see them.

The man was wearing a brown shirt, leather leggings, and a pained expression. He was shaking his head. "Nay, Goadudahm Marree," he said. "It wool bay fortnicht ahthehlesst."

Mary Botoner. I looked wonderingly at this ancestor of Bishop Bittner's. She was wearing a reddish-brown shift, cut out in the wide sleeves to show a yellow underdress, and fastened with a metal belt that sank somewhat low. Her linen coif was pulled tight around her plump, middle-aged face, and she reminded me of someone. Lady Schrapnell? Mrs. Mering? No, someone older. With white hair?

She was pointing to things and shaking her head. "Thahtoormaun baydoon ah Freedeywyke," she said.

The workman shook his head violently. "Tha kahna bay, Goaduhdahm Boetenneher."

The woman stamped her foot. "So willetbay, Gruwens." She swept round the platform to the stairs.

I ducked back out of sight, ready to go up again, but the discussion was apparently over.

"Bootdahmuh Boetenneher—" the workman pleaded, following her.

I crept after them, keeping one turn above.

"Gottabovencudna do swich—" the workman said, trailing after her.

I was nearly back to the site of the drop.

"Whattebey thisse?" the woman said.

I cautiously came down one step, and then another, till I could see them. Mary Botoner was pointing at something on the wall.

"Thisse maun bey wroughtengain," she said, and, above her head, like a halo, I saw a faint shimmer.

Not now, I thought, not after waiting a whole night.

"Bootdahmuh Boetenneher—" the workman said.

"So willet bey," Mary Botoner said, jabbing her bony finger at the wall.

The shimmer was growing brighter. One of them would look up in a moment and see it.

"Takken under eft!" she said.

Come on, come on. Tell her you'll fix it, I thought.

"*Thisse maun bey takken bylyve,*" she said, and started, finally, down the stairs. The workman rolled his eyes, tightened his rope belt round his ample middle, and started after her.

Two steps. Three. Mary Botoner's coiffed head disappeared round the curve of the tower and then bobbed back into sight. "*Youre hyre isse neyquitte till allisse doone.*"

I couldn't wait any longer, even if it meant they saw me. People in the Middle Ages had believed in angels—with luck, they'd think I was one.

The shimmer began to glow. I shot down the steps, jumping over the pigeon, who took off into the air with a wild squawking.

"*Guttgottimhaben,*" the workman said, and they both turned to look up at me.

Mary Botoner crossed herself. "*Holymarr remothre—*"

And I dived for the already closing net and sprawled flat onto the blessed tiled floor of the lab.

# CHAPTER TWENTY-FOUR

In the Lab—A Long-Delayed Arrival—A Letter to the Editor—In
the Tower—I Ascertain My Space-Time Location—In the
Cathedral—I Act Without Thinking—Cigars—A Dragon—A
Parade—In the Police Station—In a Shelter—Fish—Verity Is
Found at Last—"Our beautiful, beautiful cathedral!"—An Answer

And let it be 2057, not 2018. I looked up, and yes, it was. Warder was bending over me, extending a hand to help me up.

When she saw it was me, she stood up and put her hands on her hips. "What are you doing here?" she demanded.

"What am I doing *here?*" I said, picking myself up. "What the bloody hell was I doing in 1395? What was I doing in Blackwell's in 1933? I want to know where Verity is."

"Get out of the net," she said, already moving back to the console and beginning to type. The veils on the net began to rise.

"Find out where Verity is," I said, following her. "She went through yesterday, and something went wrong. She—"

She moved her hand in a gesture of silencing. "Eleven December," she said into the console's ear. "Two P.M."

"You don't understand," I said. "Verity's missing. There's something wrong with the net."

"In a minute," she said, staring at the screen. "Six P.M. Ten P.M. Carruthers is stuck in Coventry," she said, her eyes never moving from the screen, "and I'm trying to—"

"*Verity* may be stuck in a dungeon. Or the middle of the Battle of Hastings. Or the lion's cage at the Zoo." I pounded on the console. "Find out where she is."

"In a *minute*," she said. "Twelve December. Two A.M. Six A.M.—"

"No!" I said, grabbing the ear of the console away from her. "Now!"

She stood up angrily. "If you do anything to jeopardize this rendezvous—"

Mr. Dunworthy and T.J. came in, their heads together worriedly over a handheld. "—another area of increased slippage," T.J. was saying. "See, here it—"

"*Give* me that ear," Warder said furiously, and they both looked up.

"Ned," Mr. Dunworthy said, hurrying over. "How did Coventry go?"

"It didn't," I said.

Warder snatched the ear back and began feeding times into it.

"No Mr. C, no 'life-changing experience,' " I said. "Verity tried to come through to tell you, but she didn't make it. Tell Warder she's got to find her."

"I'm running the accelerated," Warder said.

"I don't care what you're running," I said. "It can wait. I want you to find out where she is *now!*"

"In a minute, Ned," Mr. Dunworthy said quietly. He took my arm. "We're trying to pull Carruthers out."

"Carruthers can wait!" I said. "You know where he is, for God's sake! Verity could be anywhere!"

"Tell me what's happened," he said, still calmly.

"The net's starting to break down," I said. "That's what's happened. Verity went through to tell you we failed at Coventry, and right after she'd gone through, Finch came through and said she hadn't come through to the lab. So I tried to come through and tell you, but I ended up here in 2018, and then in Blackwell's in 1933, and then in a—"

"You were in the lab in 2018?" Mr. Dunworthy said, looking at T.J. "That's where the area of slippage was. What did you see, Ned?"

"—and then in the tower of Coventry Cathedral in 1395," I said.

"Destination malfunction," T.J. said worriedly.

"Two P.M. Six P.M.," Warder said, her eyes on the screen.

"The net's breaking down," I said, "and Verity's out there somewhere. You've got to get a fix on her and—"

"Warder," Mr. Dunworthy said. "Stop the accelerated. We need—"

"Wait, I'm getting something," she said.

"Now," Mr. Dunworthy said. "I want a fix on Verity Kindle."

"In a min—"

And Carruthers appeared in the net.

He was wearing the same thing he'd been wearing last time I'd seen him, his AFS coveralls and nonregulation helmet, except that they weren't covered with soot. "Well, it's about time!" he said, taking his tin helmet off.

Warder ran over to the net, pushed through the veils, and flung her arms around his neck. "I was *so* worried!" she said. "Are you all right?"

"I nearly got arrested for not having an identity card," Carruthers said, looking slightly taken aback, "and I was *this* close to being blown up when a delayed HE went off, but otherwise I'm fine." He disentangled himself from Warder's arms. "I thought something had gone wrong with the net, and I was going to be stuck there for the duration of the war. Where the bloody hell have you been?"

"Trying to get you out," Warder said, beaming at him. "We thought something had gone wrong with the net, too. Then I thought of running an accelerated to see if we could get past whatever the block was." She linked her arm through his. "Are you certain you're all right? Can I get you anything?"

"You can get *me* Verity. Now!" I said. "I want you to run a fix right *now*."

Mr. Dunworthy nodded.

"All right!" Warder snapped, and stomped over to the console.

"You didn't have any trouble coming back, did you?" T.J. said to Carruthers.

"Except that the bloody net wouldn't open for three weeks, no," Carruthers said.

"I mean, you didn't go to another destination before you came here?"

Carruthers shook his head.

"And you haven't any idea why the net wouldn't open?"

"No," Carruthers said. "A delayed HE went off a hundred yards from the drop. I thought perhaps it had done something to it."

I went over to the console. "Anything yet?"

"No," Warder said. "And don't stand over me like that. It keeps me from concentrating."

I went back over to Carruthers, who had sat down at T.J.'s sim setup and was pulling off his boots.

"One good thing came out of all this," he said, peeling off a very dirty sock. "I can definitely report to Lady Schrapnell that the bishop's bird stump wasn't in the rubble. We cleared every inch of the cathedral, and it wasn't there. But it *was* in the cathedral during the raid. The Head of the Flower Committee, this horrible old spinster sort named Miss Sharpe—you know the type, gray hair, long nose, hard as nails—saw it at five o'clock that afternoon. She was on her way home after a meeting of the Advent Bazaar and Soldiers' Parcel Effort Committee, and she noticed some of the chrys-anthemums in it were turning brown, and she stopped and pulled them out."

I was only half listening. I was watching Warder, who was hitting keys, glaring at the screen, leaning back thoughtfully, hitting more keys. She has no idea where Verity is, I thought.

"So you think it was destroyed in the fire?" Mr. Dunworthy said.

"*I* do," Carruthers said, "and everyone else does, except for this dreadful old harpy Miss Sharpe. *She* insists it was stolen."

"During the raid?" Mr. Dunworthy asked.

"No. She says as soon as the sirens went, she came back and stood guard, so it must have been stolen after five and before eight, and whoever took it must have known there was going to be a raid that night."

Numbers were coming up rapidly on the screen. Warder leaned forward, tapping keys rapidly. "Have you got the fix?"

"I'm *getting* it," she said irritably.

"She had an absolute bee in her bonnet about it," Carruthers said, peeling off his other sock and dumping it in his boot. "Interrogated everyone who'd been in or near the cathedral during the raid, accused the verger's brother-in-law, even wrote a letter to the editor of the local paper about it. Generally made everyone's lives miserable. I didn't have to do any detective work on it. She was doing it all. If somebody *had* stolen the bishop's bird stump, you can be certain she'd have found it."

"I've got it," Warder said. "Verity's in Coventry."

"Coventry?" I said. "When?"

"November fourteenth, 1940."

"Where?" I said.

She tapped the keys, and the coordinates came up.

"That's the cathedral," I said. "What time?"

She worked the keys some more. "Five past eight P.M."

"That's the raid," I said and started for the net. "Send me through."

"If the net's malfunctioning—" T.J. said.

"Verity's there," I said. "In the middle of an air raid."

"Send him through," Mr. Dunworthy said.

"We've tried this before, remember?" Carruthers said. "Nobody could get near the place, including you. What makes you think—"

"Give me your coveralls and helmet," I said.

He looked at Mr. Dunworthy and then started to strip them off.

"What was Verity wearing?" Mr. Dunworthy asked.

Carruthers handed me the coveralls, and I pulled them on over my tweeds. "A long white high-necked dress," I said, and realized I'd made an erroneous assumption. Her clothes wouldn't create an incongruity in the middle of an air raid. No one would even notice them. Or if they did, they'd think she was in her nightgown.

"Here, take this," T.J. said, handing me a raincoat.

"I want a five-minute intermittent," I said, taking the raincoat and stepping into the net. Warder lowered the veils.

"If you come through in the marrows field," Carruthers said, "the barn's to the west."

The net began to shimmer.

Carruthers said, "Watch out for the dogs. And the farmer's wife—"

And found myself right back where I'd started from. And in pitch-blackness. The darkness meant I was there the next night, or any of a thousand nights, a hundred thousand nights, while the cathedral sat its way through the Middle Ages. And meanwhile Verity was in the middle of an air raid. And all I could do was stay put and wait for the bloody net to open again.

"No!" I said, and smashed my fist against the rough rock. And the world exploded around me.

There was a whoosh and then a crump, and ack-ack guns started up off to the east. The darkness flared bluish-white and then the aftercolor of red, and I could smell smoke below me.

"Verity!" I shouted and ran up the stairs to the bells, remembering this time to count the steps. There was just enough orangish light to see by, and a faint smell of smoke.

I reached the bell platform and shouted up the stairs. "Verity! Are you up here?"

Pigeons, no doubt descendants of the one I'd disturbed six hundred years ago, flapped wildly down the upper tower and into my face.

She wasn't up there. I ran back down the stairs, shouting, till I reached the step where I'd come through, and began counting again.

Thirty-one, thirty-two. "Verity!" I shouted over the drone of planes and the wail of an air-raid siren that had, belatedly and unnecessarily, started up.

Fifty-three, fifty-four, I counted. "Verity! Where are you?"

I hit the bottom step. Fifty-eight. Remember that, I told myself and pushed the tower door open and came out into the west porch. The smell of smoke was stronger here, and had a rich, acrid scent to it, like cigar smoke.

"Verity!" I shouted, pushing open the heavy inner door of the tower. And came out into the nave.

The church was dark except for the rood light and a reddish light in the windows of the clerestory. I tried to estimate what time it was. Most of the explosions and sirens seemed to be off toward the north. There was a lot of smoke up near the organ, but no flames from the Girdlers' Chapel, which had been hit early. So it couldn't be later than half past eight, and Verity couldn't have been here more than a few minutes.

"Verity!" I called, and my voice echoed in the dark church.

The Mercers' Chapel had been hit in the first batch of incendiaries. I started up the main aisle toward the choir, wishing I'd brought a pocket torch.

The ack-ack stopped and then started up again with renewed effort, and the hum of the planes got louder. There was a thud, thud, thud of bombs just to the east, and flares lit the windows garishly. Half of them, the half that had had their stained glass removed for safekeeping, were boarded up or covered over with blackout paper, but three of the windows on the north were still intact, and the greenish flares made them light the church momentarily with a sickly red and blue. I couldn't see Verity anywhere. Where would she have gone? I would have expected her to stay close to the drop, but perhaps the raid had frightened her and she'd taken shelter somewhere. But where?

The drone of the planes became an angry roar. "Verity!" I shouted over the din, and there was a clatter above on the roof, like hail pattering, then a pounding and muffled shouts.

The fire watch, up on the roof putting out the incendiaries. Had Verity heard them and hidden somewhere so they wouldn't see her?

There was a crash overhead and then a whizzing, spitting sound. I looked up, and it was a good thing I did because I narrowly missed being hit by an incendiary.

It fell onto one of the pews, hissing and spitting molten sparks onto the wooden pew. I grabbed a hymnal out of the back of the next pew and knocked the incendiary off with it onto the floor. It rolled into the aisle and up against the end of the pew across the aisle.

I kicked it away, but the wood was already smoking. The incendiary spit and sparked, twisting like a live thing. It hit the kneeling rail and began to burn with a white-hot flame.

A stirrup pump, I thought, and looked around wildly, but they must have taken them all up on the roof. There was a bucket hanging by the south door. I ran back and grabbed it, hoping it had sand in it. It did.

I ran back up the nave and upended the bucket over the incendiary and the already-burning rail, and then stood back, waiting for it to spit.

It didn't. I used my foot to push the incendiary into the very middle of the aisle and check to make sure the fire on the kneeling rail was out. I had dropped the sand bucket and it had rolled under one of the pews. For the verger to find tomorrow and burst into tears.

I stood there looking at it, thinking about what I'd just done. I'd acted without thinking, like Verity, going after the cat in the water. But there was no chance here of changing the course of history. The Luftwaffe was already correcting any possible incongruities.

I looked up at the Mercers' Chapel. Flames were already licking through the carved wooden ceiling above it, and no amount of sand buckets would be able to put them out. In another two hours the entire cathedral would be in flames.

There was a dull boom as something landed outside the Girdlers' Chapel, lighting it for an instant. In the seconds before the light faded, I could see the fifteenth-century wooden cross with the carving of a child kneeling at the foot of it. In another half hour, Provost Howard would see it, behind a wall of flames, and the whole east end of the church would be on fire.

"Verity!" I shouted, and my voice echoed in the darkened church. "Verity!"

"Ned!"

I whirled around. "Verity!" I shouted and bolted back down the main aisle. I skidded to a stop at the back of the nave. "Verity!" I shouted and stood still, listening.

"Ned!"

Outside the church. The south door. I took off between the pews, stumbling over the rails, and across to the south door.

There was a knot of people gathered outside, looking anxiously up at the roof, and two tough-looking youths with their hands in their pockets, leaning casually against a lamp-post on the corner, discussing a fire off to the west. "What's that smell of cigars?" the taller one was asking, as calmly as if they were discussing the weather.

"Tobacconist's corner of Broadgate," the shorter one said. "We shoulda nipped in and pinched some cigs before it got going."

"Did you see a girl come out of the cathedral?" I asked the nearest person, a middle-aged woman in a kerchief.

"It's not going to catch, is it, do you think?" she said.

Yes, I thought. "The fire watch is up there," I said. "Did you see a girl run out of the church?"

"No," she said and went immediately back to looking up at the roof.

I ran down Bayley Lane and then back along the side of the church, but there was no sign of her. She must have come out one of the other doors. Not the vestry door. The fire watch came in and out that door. The west door.

I raced round to the west door. There was a cluster of people there, too, huddled inside the porch, a woman with three little girls, an old man wrapped in a blanket, a girl in a maid's uniform. A gray-haired woman with a sharp nose and a WAS armband stood in front of the doors, her arms crossed.

"Did you see anyone come out of the church in the last few minutes?" I asked her.

"No one's allowed inside the church except the fire watch," she said accusingly, and *her* voice reminded me of someone's, too, but I didn't have time to try to work out whose.

"She has red hair," I said. "She's wearing a long white . . . she's wearing a white nightgown."

"Nightgown?" she said disapprovingly.

A short, stout ARP warden came up. "I've got orders to clear this area," he said. "The fire brigade needs all avenues to the cathedral cleared. Come along."

The woman with the little girls picked up the littlest one and started out of the porch. The old man shuffled after her.

"Come along," the warden said to the maid, who seemed paralyzed with fright. "You too, Miss Sharpe." He waved to the gray-haired woman.

"I have no intention of going anywhere," she said, crossing her arms more militantly. "I am the vice-chairwoman of the Cathedral Ladies' Altar Guild and the head of the Flower Committee."

"I don't care who you are," the warden said. "I've got orders to clear these doors for the fire brigade. I've already cleared the south door, and now it's your turn."

"Warden, have you seen a young woman with red hair?" I interrupted.

"I have been assigned to guard this door against looters," the woman said, drawing herself up. "I have stood here since the raid began and I intend to stand here all night, if necessary, to protect the cathedral."

"And I intend to clear this door," the warden said, drawing *him-self* up.

I didn't have time for this. I stepped between them. "I'm looking for a missing girl," I said, drawing *myself* up. "Red hair. White nightgown."

"Ask at the police station," the warden said. He pointed back the way I'd come. "Down St. Mary's Street."

I took off at a trot, wondering who would win. My money was on the head of the Flower Committee. Who did she remind me of? Mary Botoner? Lady Schrapnell? One of the fur-bearing ladies in Blackwell's?

The warden hadn't done a very effective job of clearing the south door. The exact same knot of people was standing there, and the two youths were still holding up the lamp-post. I hurried along the south side of the cathedral toward Bayley Lane and straight into the processional.

I had read about what the police sergeant had called the "solemn little procession" when the fire watch had rescued what treasures they could grab and taken them across to the police station for safekeeping. And in my mind's eye, I had thought of it as that—a decorous parade, with Provost Howard leading, trooping the colors of the Warwickshire Regiment, and then the others, carrying the candlesticks and chalice and wafer box at a measured pace, and the wooden crucifix bringing up the rear—so that at first I didn't recognize it.

Because it wasn't a processional, it was a rabble, a rout, Napoleon's Old Guard frantically saving what they could from Waterloo. They stumbled down the road at a half-run, the canon with a candlestick under each arm and a load of vestments, a teenaged boy clutching a chalice and a stirrup pump for dear life, the provost charging with the colors thrust out before him like a lance and half-stumbling over the trailing flag.

I stopped, watching them just as if it were a parade, and that took care of one possibility Verity had proposed. None of them was carrying the bishop's bird stump.

They ran back into the police station. They must have dumped their treasures unceremoniously on the first surface they found, because they were back outside in under a minute and running back toward the vestry door.

A balding man in a blue coverall met them halfway up the stairs, shaking his head. "It's no good. There's too much smoke."

"I've got to get the Gospel and the Epistles," Provost Howard said and pushed past him and through the door.

"Where the bloody hell is the fire brigade?" said the teenaged boy.

"The fire brigade?" the canon said, looking up at the sky. "Where the bloody hell is the RAF?"

The teenaged boy ran back down St. Mary's to the police station to tell them to ring the fire brigade again, and I followed him.

The rescued treasures were sitting in a pathetic line on the sergeant's desk, the regimental colors propped up against the wall behind. While the teenaged boy was telling the sergeant, "Well, try them again. The whole chancel roof's on fire," I looked at them. The candlesticks, the wooden crucifix. There was a little pile of worn brown Books of Common Prayer, as well, that hadn't made the list, and a little bundle of offering envelopes and a choirboy's surplice, and I wondered how many other rescued items Provost Howard had left out of his list. But the bishop's bird stump wasn't there.

The boy darted out. The sergeant picked up the phone. "Have you seen a young woman with red hair?" I said before he could dial the fire brigade.

He shook his head, holding his hand over the receiver. "Most likely place she'd be is in one of the shelters."

A shelter. Of course. The logical place to be during an air raid. She'd have had more sense than to stay out in this. "Where's the nearest shelter?"

"Down Little Park Street," he said, cradling the phone. "Go back along Bayley and turn left."

I nodded my thanks and took off again. The fires were getting closer. The whole sky was a smoky orange, and there were yellow flames shooting up in front of Trinity Church. Searchlights crisscrossed the sky, which was getting brighter by the moment. It was getting colder, too, which seemed impossible. I blew on my icy hands as I ran.

I couldn't find the shelter. A house had taken a direct hit in the middle of the block, a mound of smoking rubble, and next to it, a greengrocer's shop was on fire. Everything else in the street was silent and dark.

"Verity!" I shouted, afraid I'd hear an answer from the rubble, and started back up the street, looking closely for a shelter sign on one of the buildings. I found it, lying in the middle of the road. I looked around helplessly, trying to determine which direction the blast might have blown it from. "Hello!" I shouted down stairway after stairway. "Is anyone there?"

I finally found it at the near end of the street, practically next to the cathedral, in a half-basement that offered no protection from anything, not even the cold.

It was a small, grubby room without any furniture. Possibly two dozen people, some of them in bathrobes, were sitting on the dirt floor against the sandbag-lined walls. A hurricane lamp hung at one end from a beam, swaying wildly every time a bomb landed, and under it a small boy in earmuffs and pajamas was playing a game of cards with his mother.

I scanned the dimness, looking for Verity, even though she obviously wasn't there. Where *was* she?

"Has anyone seen a girl in a white nightgown?" I said. "She has red hair."

They sat there as if they hadn't heard me, looking numbly ahead.

"Have you any sixes?" the little boy said.

"Yes," his mother said, handing him a playing card.

The bells of the cathedral began to chime, ringing out over the steady roar of the ack-ack guns and the whoosh and crump of the high explosives. Nine o'clock.

Everyone looked up at the sound. "That's the cathedral's bells," the little boy said, craning his neck at the ceiling. "Have you any queens?"

"No," his mother said, looking at her hand and then at the ceiling again. "Go fish. That's how you know our cathedral's all right, if you can hear the bells."

I had to get out of here. I plunged out the door and up the steps to the street. The bells rang out brightly, chiming the hours. They would do that all night, tolling the hours, reassuring the people of Coventry, while the planes droned overhead and the cathedral burned to the ground.

The knot of people had moved across the street from the south door for a better view of the flames shooting up from the cathedral roof. The two youths were still at their lamp-post. I ran up to them.

"It's no good," the tall one was saying. "They'll never get it out now."

"I'm looking for a young woman, a girl—" I said.

"Ain't we all?" the short one said, and they both laughed.

"She has red hair," I persisted. "She's wearing a white nightgown."

This, of course, got a huge laugh.

"I think she's in one of the shelters round here, but I don't know where they are."

"There's one down Little Park," the tall one said.

"I've already been to that one," I said. "She's not there."

They both looked thoughtful. "There's one up Gosford Street way, but you'll never get there," the short one said. "Land mine went off. Blocked the road."

"She might be in the crypt," the tall one said, and, at my expression, said, "The cathedral crypt. There's a shelter down there."

The crypt. Of course. Several dozen people had taken shelter down there the night of the raid. They'd stayed down there till eleven while the cathedral burned over their heads, and then been led out up the outside steps.

I tore past the gawkers to the south door and up the steps. "You can't go in there!" the woman in the kerchief shouted.

"Rescue squad," I shouted back and ran inside.

The west end of the church was still dark, but there was more than enough light in the sanctuary and the chancel. The vestries were ablaze, and the Girdlers' Chapel and, above, the clerestories were pouring out bronze-colored smoke. In the Cappers' Chapel, flames were licking at the oil painting of Christ with the lost lamb in his arms. Burning pages from the order of service were floating above the nave, drifting and dropping ash.

I tried to remember the layout from Lady Schrapnell's blueprints. The crypt lay under the St. Lawrence Chapel in the north aisle, just to the west of the Drapers' Chapel.

I started up the nave, ducking the fiery orders of service and trying to remember where the steps were. To the left of the lectern.

Far forward, in the choir, I caught a glimpse of something moving.

"Verity!" I shouted and ran up the nave.

The figure flitted through the choir toward the sanctuary. I caught its flash of white among the choir stalls.

Incendiaries clattered on the roof, and I glanced up and then back at the choir. The figure, if it had been a figure, had disappeared. Above the entrance to the Drapers' Chapel, an order of service, caught in the updraft, danced and dipped.

"Ned!"

I whirled around. Verity's faint voice seemed to come from behind me and far away, but was that a trick of the superheated air in the church? I ran along the choir. There was no one there or in the sanctuary. The order of service twirled in the draft from the Drapers' Chapel and then caught fire and sank, burning, onto the altar.

"Ned!" Verity shouted, and this time there was no mistaking it. She was outside the church. Outside the south door.

I tore out and down the steps, shouting her name, past the roof-watchers and the lamp-post-loungers. "Verity!"

I saw her almost immediately. She was halfway down Little Park Street, talking earnestly to the stout ARP warden, the skirt of her torn long white dress trailing behind her.

"Verity!" I called, but the din was too great.

"No, you don't understand," she was screaming at the warden. "I don't want a public shelter. I'm looking for a young man with a mustache—"

"Miss, my orders is to clear this area of all civilians," the warden said.

"Verity!" I shouted, practically in her ear. I grabbed her arm.

She turned. "Ned!" she said, and flung herself into my arms. "I've been looking all over for you."

"Ditto," I said.

"You've got no business being out here," the warden said sternly. There was a whistle, and a long drawn-out scream, during which I couldn't hear what he said. "This area is for official services only. Civilians aren't supposed to be—" There was a sudden deafening bang and the warden disappeared in a shower of dust and bricks.

"Hey!" I shouted. "Warden! Warden!"

"Oh, no!" Verity said, waving her hands as if trying to push the billowing dust aside. "Where is he?"

"Under here," I said, digging frantically through the bricks.

"I can't find him," Verity said, tossing bricks aside. "No, wait, here's his hand! And his arm!"

The warden shook her arm off violently and stood up, brushing dust off the front of his coveralls.

"Are you all right?" we both said in unison.

"Of course I'm all right," he said, coughing, "no thanks to you! Civilians! Don't know what you're doing. Could have killed someone, throwing bricks about like that. Interfering with the official duties of the ARP is an infraction punishable by—"

Planes began to drone overhead again. I looked up. The sky lit up with sharp flashes, and there was another, closer scream of a whistle.

"We'd better get out of this," I said. "Down here!" and pushed Verity ahead of me down a basement stairway and into the narrow shelter of a doorway.

"Are you all right?" I shouted, looking at her. Her hair had come down on one side, and her torn dress was streaked with soot. So was her face, and her left hand had a smear of blood on it. "Are you hurt?" I said, lifting it.

"No," she said. "I hit it on one of the arches in the church. It was dark, and I couldn't s-see where I was going." She was shivering. "How can it be so c-cold when the whole c-c-city's on fire?"

"Here," I said. "Put this on." I took off the raincoat and wrapped it round her shoulders. "Courtesy of T.J."

"Thanks," she said shakily.

There was another crash, and dirt rained down on us. I pulled her farther back into the doorway and put my arms around her. "We'll wait till this lets up a bit, and then go back to the cathedral and get out of this and back to a warmer climate," I said lightly, trying to make her smile. "We've got a diary to steal and a husband to find for Tossie. You don't suppose there's somebody around here who'd be willing to exchange all this," I waved my arm at the firelit sky, "for baby talk and Princess Arjumand? No, I suppose not."

The effect wasn't quite what I wanted. "Oh, Ned," Verity said, and burst into tears.

"What's wrong?" I said. "I know I shouldn't be making jokes in the middle of a raid. I—"

She shook her head. "It's not that. Oh, Ned, we can't go back to Muchings End. We're stuck here." She buried her face against my chest.

"Like Carruthers, you mean? They got him out. They'll get us out, too."

"No, you don't understand," she said, looking tearfully up at me. "We can't get to the drop. The fire—"

"What do you mean?" I said. "The tower didn't burn. It and the spire were the only things that didn't. And I know that dragon from the Flower Committee's guarding the west door, but we can get there from the south—"

"The tower?" she said blankly. "What do you mean?"

"You didn't come through in the tower?"

"No. In the sanctuary. I stayed there for nearly an hour, hoping it would open again, and then the fires started, and I was afraid the fire watch would catch me, so I went outside and looked for you—"

"How did you know I was here?"

"I knew you'd come as soon as you found out where I was," she said matter-of-factly.

"But—" I said, and decided not to tell her we'd tried to get here for two weeks and hadn't been able to even get close.

"—and when I got back to the church, the sanctuary was on fire. And the net won't open onto a fire."

"You're right," I said, "but we don't need it to. I came through in the tower, which only got a bit scorched. But we need to be able to get through the nave to the tower, so we'd better go."

"Just a minute," she said. She pulled the raincoat on over her arms and then took the tie belt off and used it to hitch her ripped, trailing skirt up to knee-length. "Will I pass for 1940 now?" she said, buttoning the coat.

"You look wonderful," I said.

We went up the stairs and back toward the cathedral. The east end of the roof was blazing. And the fire brigade had finally arrived. A fire engine was parked on the corner, and we had to step over a tangle of hoses and orange-lit puddles to get to the south door.

"Where are the firemen?" Verity asked as we reached the knot of people by the south door.

"There's no water," a ten-year-old boy in a thin sweater said. "Jerries got the water mains."

"They've gone round to Priory Row to find another hydrant."

"No water," Verity murmured.

We looked up at the cathedral. A good part of the roof was blazing now, shooting up in sparks at the near end near the apse, and there were flames in the blown-out windows.

"Our beautiful, beautiful cathedral," a man behind us said.

The boy tugged at my arm. "She's goin', ain't she?"

She was going. By ten-thirty, when they finally found a working hydrant, the roof would be completely ablaze. The firemen would attempt to play a hose on the sanctuary and the Lady Chapel, but the water would give out almost immediately, and after that it would just be a matter of time as the roof blazed and the steel rods J.O. Scott had put in to prevent strain on the arches, began to buckle and melt in the heat, bringing the fifteenth-century arches and the roof down on the altar and the carved misereres and Handel's organ and the wooden cross with the child kneeling at its foot.

Our beautiful, beautiful cathedral. I had always put it in the same class as the bishop's bird stump—an irritating antiquity—and there were certainly more beautiful cathedrals. But standing here now, watching it burn, I understood what it had meant to Provost Howard to build the new cathedral, modernist-ugly as it was. What it had meant to Lizzie Bittner not to see it sold for scrap. And I understood why Lady Schrapnell had been willing to fight the Church of England and the history faculty and the Coventry City Council and the rest of the world to build it back up again.

I looked down at Verity. Tears were running silently down her face. I put my arm around her. "Isn't there something we can do?" she said hopelessly.

"We'll build it back up again. Good as new."

But in the meantime we had to get back inside and into the tower. But how?

This crowd would never let us walk into a burning church, no matter what pretext I thought up, and the west door was being guarded by a dragon. And the longer we waited, the more dangerous it would be to get across the nave to the tower door.

There was a sound of clanging over the din of the ack-acks. "Another fire brigade!" someone shouted, and in spite of the fact that there was no water, everyone, even the two lamp-post-loungers, ran off toward the east end of the church.

"This is our chance," I said. "We can't wait any longer. Ready?"

She nodded.

"Wait," I said, and tore two long strips from the already-ripped hem of her dress.

I stooped and dipped them in the puddle left by one of the hoses. The water was ice-cold. I wrung them out. "Tie this over your mouth and nose," I said, handing her one. "When we get inside, I want you to head straight for the back of the nave and then go along the wall. If we get separated, the tower door's just inside the west door and to your left."

"Separated?" she said, tying on the mask.

"Wind this round your right hand," I ordered. "The door handles may be hot. The drop's fifty-eight steps up, not counting the floor of the tower."

I wrapped my hand in the remaining strip. "Whatever happens, keep going. Ready?"

She nodded, her greenish-brown eyes wide above the mask.

"Get behind me," I said. I cautiously opened the right side of the door a crack. No flame roared out, only a billow of bronze-colored smoke. I reared back from it and then looked inside.

Things weren't as bad as I'd been afraid they might be. The east end of the church was obscured by smoke and flames, but the smoke was still thin enough at this end to be able to see through, and it looked like this part of the roof was still holding. The windows, except for one in the Smiths' Chapel, had been blown out, and the floor was covered with shards of red and blue glass.

"Watch out for the glass." I pushed Verity ahead of me. "Take a deep breath and go! I'm right behind you," I said and opened the door all the way.

She took off running, with me right behind her, flinching away from the heat. She reached the door and yanked it open.

"The door to the tower's to your left!" I shouted, though she couldn't possibly have heard me above the furious roar of the fire.

She stopped, holding the door open.

"Go up!" I shouted. "Don't wait for me!" and started to sprint the last few yards. "Go up!"

There was a rumble, and I turned and looked toward the sanctuary, thinking one of the clerestory arches was collapsing. There was a deafening roar, and the window in the Smiths' Chapel shattered in a spray of sparkling fragments.

I ducked, shielding my face with my arm, thinking in the instant before it knocked me to my knees, "It's a high explosive. But that's impossible. The cathedral didn't sustain any direct hits."

It felt like a direct hit. The blast rocked the cathedral and lit it with a blinding white light.

I staggered up off my knees, and then stopped, staring out across the nave. The force had knocked the cathedral momentarily clear of smoke, and in the garish white afterlight I could see everything: the statue above the pulpit engulfed in flames, its hand raised like a drowning man's; the stalls in the children's chapel, their irreplaceable misereres burning with a queer yellow light; the altar in the Cappers' Chapel. And the parclose screen in front of the Smiths' Chapel.

"Ned!"

I started toward it. I only got a few steps. The cathedral shook, and a burning beam came crashing down in front of the Smiths' Chapel, falling across the pews.

"Ned!" Verity cried desperately. "Ned!"

Another beam, no doubt reinforced with a steel girder by J.O. Scott, crashed down across the first, sending up a blackish swell of smoke that cut off the whole north side of the church from view.

It didn't matter. I had already seen enough.

I flung myself through the door and through the tower door and up the firelit stairs, wondering what on earth I was going to say to Lady Schrapnell. In that one bright bomb-lit instant I had seen everything: the brasses on the walls, the polished eagle on the lectern, the blackening pillars. And in the north aisle, in front of the parclose screen, the empty wrought-iron flower stand.

It had been removed for safekeeping, after all. Or donated as scrap. Or sold at a jumble sale.

"Ned!" Verity shouted. "Hurry! The net's opening!"

Lady Schrapnell had been wrong. The bishop's bird stump wasn't there.

"No," said Harris, "if you want rest and change, you can't beat a sea trip."

Three Men in a Boat
Jerome K. Jerome

# CHAPTER TWENTY-FIVE

Back in the Tower—The Cask of Amontillado—In the Scullery,
the Kitchen, the Stables, and Trouble—Jane Is Completely
Incomprehensible—The Prisoner of Zenda—A Swoon, Not Mrs.
Mering This Time—Terence's New Understanding of Poetry—A
Letter—A Surprise—One Last Swoon, Involving Furniture—An
Even Bigger Surprise

Third time is not necessarily a charm. The net shimmered, and we were in pitch-blackness again. The din had disappeared, though there was still a strong smell of smoke. It was at least twenty degrees cooler. I took one arm away from around Verity and cautiously felt to the side. I touched stone.

"Don't move," I said. "I know where we are. I was here before. It's Coventry's belltower. In 1395."

"Nonsense," Verity said, starting up the steps. "It's the Merings' wine cellar."

She opened the door two steps above us a crack, and light filtered in, revealing wooden steps and racks of cobwebbed bottles below.

"It's daylight," she whispered. She opened the door a little wider and stuck her head out, looking both ways. "This passage opens off the kitchen. Let's hope it's still the sixteenth."

"Let's hope it's still 1888," I said.

She peeked out again. "What do you think we should do? Should we try to get out to the drop?"

I shook my head. "There's no telling where we'd end up. Or whether we could get back." I looked at her ragged, soot-streaked white dress. "You need to get out of those clothes. Especially the raincoat, which is circa 2057. Give it to me."

She shrugged out of it.

"Can you get up to your room without being seen?"

She nodded. "I'll take the back stairs."

"I'll go try to ascertain our space-time location. I'll meet you in the library in a quarter of an hour, and we'll go from there."

She handed me the raincoat. "What if we've been gone a week? Or a month? Or five years?"

"We'll claim we've been on the Other Side," I said, but she didn't laugh.

She said bleakly, "What if Tossie and Terence are already married?"

"We'll cross that bridge when we come to it," I said. "Or fall in."

She smiled back at me, one of those heart-turning smiles no amount of rest was ever going to render me immune to. "Thank you for coming to find me," she said.

"At your service, miss," I said. "Go put on a clean dress."

She nodded. "Wait a few minutes so we won't be seen together."

She opened the door and slid out, and I realized suddenly I hadn't told her what I'd gone all the way to the Fourteenth Century and back to tell her about.

"I found out how Tossie's diary—" I started, but she was already down the corridor and starting up the back stairs.

I peeled off the coveralls. My coat and trousers had been fairly well protected by them, but my hands, and presumably my face, were a mess. I wiped them on the lining of the coveralls, wishing wine cellars came equipped with mirrors. Then I rolled the coveralls into a bundle with the raincoat, and jammed them far back behind a rack of claret.

I took a cautious look and went out into the passage. There were four doors along it, one of which had to lead to the outside. The last one was covered in green baize, which meant it led to the main part of the house. I opened the first.

The scullery. It was full of Cinderella-like stacks of dirty dishes and piles of pots, and a row of unpolished shoes. The shoes had to mean it was after bedtime and before the family was up, which was good—it meant Verity wouldn't run into anyone on her way to her bedroom—but on second thought, it didn't make any sense. That first night, when I sneaked Cyril back to the stable, I had nearly run into Baine putting the polished shoes outside the doors, and it had still been dark out. And he hadn't collected them till after everyone had gone to bed. But it was clearly morning. Sun was streaming in on the pots and pans.

There was no newspaper and nothing else that might give a clue to our space-time location.

One of the pots had a copper bottom. I peered into it. There was a large smear of soot on my cheek and across my mustache. I pulled out my handkerchief, spit on it, dabbed at my face, smoothed my hair, and went back out into the passage, calculating. If this was the scullery, the next door must be the kitchen, and the one after that the door to the outside.

Wrong. It was the kitchen, and Jane and the cook were in it, whispering together in the corner. They moved apart guiltily. The cook went over to an enormous black stove and began stirring something briskly, and Jane put a piece of bread on a toasting fork and held it over the fire.

"Where's Baine?" I said.

Jane jumped about a foot. The bread fell off the toasting fork and into the ashes, flaring up brightly.

"What?" she said, holding the toasting fork in front of her like a rapier.

"Baine," I repeated. "I need to speak with him. Is he in the breakfast room?"

"No," she said frightenedly. "I swear by the Blessed Mother, I don't know where he is, sorr. He didn't tell us anything. You don't think the mistress will dismiss us, do you?"

"Dismiss you?" I said, bewildered. "Why? What have you done?"

"Nothing. But she'll say we must have known all about it, what with gossiping in the servants' hall and all that," she said, waving the toasting fork for emphasis. "That's what happened to my sister Margaret when young Mr. Val run off with Rose the scullery maid. Mrs. Abbott sacked the whole lot."

I took the toasting fork away from her. "Known all about what?"

"Never even guessed," the cook said from the stove. "All those fine airs and giving orders. It just goes to show you."

This wasn't getting anywhere, and I was running out of time. I decided to try the direct approach. "What time is it?" I asked.

Jane looked frightened all over again.

"Nine o'clock," the cook said, consulting a watch pinned to her bosom.

"Nine o'clock, and I've got to be taking it up to them," Jane said and burst into tears. "He said not to be taking it up till the morning post'd come, so as to give them enough time, and it's always here by nine o'clock." She wiped her eyes on the tail of her apron and straightened, steeling herself. "I'd best be going up and see if it's been."

I was going to ask, "Take what up?" but was afraid it would bring on a fresh round of tears and incoherencies. And there was no telling what the response might be if I asked them what *day* it was. "Tell Baine to bring me a copy of the *Times*. I'll be in the library," I said, and went outside.

At least it was still summer, and, on closer inspection, June. The roses were still in bloom, and the peonies, destined to serve as prototypes for countless penwipers, were still just coming out. As was Colonel Mering, carrying a burlap sack toward the fishpond. As oblivious and absorbed with his goldfish as he very likely was, I still didn't want to have an encounter with him until I knew how much time had elapsed.

Accordingly, I ducked around the side of the house. I'd go round to the groom's door, through the stable, and from there to the French doors and the parlor. I slipped in the groom's door. And nearly tripped over Cyril. He was lying on a burlap sack with his chin on his paws.

"You wouldn't happen to know the time, would you?" I said. "And the date?"

And here was another sign that something was wrong. Cyril didn't get up. He simply raised his head, looked at me with an expression like the Prisoner of Zenda, and lay it back down again.

"What is it, Cyril? What's wrong?" I said, and reached to tug on his collar. "Are you ill?" And saw the chain.

"Good Lord," I said to him. "Terence hasn't *married* her, has he?"

Cyril continued to gaze hopelessly at me. I unhooked the chain. "Come along, Cyril," I said. "We'll go straighten this out."

He staggered to his feet and trotted after me resignedly. I went out of the stables and around to the front of the house to find Terence. He was down at the Merings' dock, sitting in the boat and staring at the river, his head sunk nearly as low as Cyril's had been when he'd been left to guard the boat.

"What are you doing out here?" I said.

He looked up dully. " 'The mirror crack'd from side to side,' " he said. " 'Out flew the web and floated wide,' " which didn't exactly clarify things.

"Cyril was chained up in the stable," I said to him.

"I know," Terence said without moving his gaze. "Mrs. Mering caught me sneaking him upstairs last night."

So at least a full day and night had passed since our departure, and I'd better think of an explanation for my absence quickly before Terence asked me where I'd been.

But he simply went on gazing out at the river. "He was right, you know. About how it happens."

"How what happens?"

"Fate," he said bitterly.

"Cyril was *chained* up," I said.

"He's got to become accustomed to being in the stable," he said dully. "Tossie doesn't approve of animals in the house."

"*Animals?*" I said. "This is Cyril we're talking about. And what about Princess Arjumand? *She* sleeps on the pillows."

"I wonder if she woke up that morning, happy as a lark, no idea her doom was going to come upon her."

"Who?" I said. "Princess Arjumand?"

"I hadn't a clue, you know, even when we were pulling into the station. Professor Peddick was talking about Alexander the Great and the battle of Issus, something about the decisive moment and everything depending on it, and I'd no idea."

"You got Professor Peddick safely back to Oxford, didn't you?" I said, suddenly worried. "He didn't get off the train to go look for gravel bottoms?"

"No," he said. "I delivered him into the arms of his loved ones. Into the arms of his loved ones," he repeated anguishedly. "And just in time. Professor Overforce was about to deliver his funeral oration."

"What did he say?"

"He fainted dead away," Terence said, "and when he came to, he flung himself at Professor Peddick's knees, babbling about how he'd never have forgiven himself if he'd drowned and how he'd seen the error of his ways, how Professor Peddick was right, a single thoughtless action could change the course of history and he intended to go straight home and tell Darwin not to jump out of trees anymore. And yesterday he announced he was withdrawing his candidacy for the Haviland Chair in favor of Professor Peddick."

"Yesterday?" I said. "When did you take Professor Peddick to Oxford? The day before yesterday?"

"Yesterday?" Terence said vaguely. "Or was it an eon ago? Or a single moment? 'We shall all be changed in a moment, in the twinkling of an eye.' There one is on one's island, weaving away, and the next thing one knows . . . I didn't properly understand poetry, you know. I thought it was all just a way of speaking."

"What was?"

"Poetry. All that about dying for love. And mirrors cracking from side to side. It did, you know. Clean across." He shook his head sadly. "I never understood why she didn't just row down to Camelot and tell Lancelot she loved him." He stared gloomily out at the water. "Well, I know now. He was already engaged to Guinevere."

Well, not exactly engaged, since Guinevere was already married to King Arthur, and at any rate, there were more important things to be addressed.

"Cyril's too sensitive to be chained up," I said.

"We are all, all in chains. Bound, helpless and raging, in the adamantine chains of fate. Fate!" he said bitterly. "Oh, wretched Fate that let us meet too late. I thought she'd be one of those dreadful modern girls, all bloomers and bluestocking ideas. He told me I'd like her, you know. Like her!"

"Maud," I said, the light finally dawning. "You've met Professor Peddick's niece Maud."

"There she was, standing on the railway platform at Oxford. 'Did my heart love till now? Forswear it, sight! For I ne'er saw true beauty till this night.' "

"The railway platform," I said wonderingly. "You met her on the railway platform at Oxford. But that's wonderful!"

"Wonderful?" he said bitterly. " 'Too late I loved you, O Beauty ever ancient and ever new! Too late I loved you!' I am engaged to Miss Mering."

"But can't you break the engagement? Miss Mering surely wouldn't want you to marry her knowing you loved Miss Peddick."

"I am not free to love anyone. I bound that love to Miss Mering when I pledged my troth to her, and Miss Peddick would not want a love without honor, a love I had already promised to another. Oh, if I had only met Miss Peddick that day in Oxford, how different things—"

"Mr. Henry, sorr," Jane interrupted, running up to us, her cap askew and her red hair coming down. "Have you seen Colonel Mering?"

Oh, no, I thought. Mrs. Mering caught Verity on her way up the stairs. "What's wrong?" I said.

"I must find the Colonel first," she said, which was no answer. "He said I was to be giving it to him at breakfast but he isn't there, and the mail's come and all."

"I saw the Colonel going out to the fishpond," I said. "Give him what? What's happened?"

"Oh, sorr, you gentlemen had best both go inside," she said, in an agony. "They're in the parlor."

"Who? Is Verity there? What's happened?" I said, but she had already taken off at a run for the fishpond, her skirts flying.

"Terence," I said urgently. "What day is it?"

"What does it matter?" Terence said. " 'Tomorrow and tomorrow and tomorrow, Creeps in this petty pace from day to day, lighting fools the way to dusty death.' Fools!"

"This is important," I said, yanking him to his feet. "The date, man!"

"Monday," he said. "The eighteenth of June."

Oh, Lord, we'd been gone three days!

I took off for the house, Cyril at my heels.

" ' "The curse has come upon us," ' " Terence quoted, " 'cried the Lady of Shalott.' "

I could hear Mrs. Mering before we were in the front door. "Your behavior has truly been inexcusable, Verity. I should not have expected my cousin's daughter to have been so selfish and thoughtless."

She knew we'd been gone three days, and poor Verity didn't. I skidded down the corridor toward the parlor, Cyril hot on my heels. I had to tell her before she said anything.

"I had all the care of the patient," Mrs. Mering said. "I'm utterly exhausted. Three days and nights in that sickroom, and not so much as a moment to rest."

I had my hand on the doorknob. I stopped. Three days and three nights in a sickroom? Then she might not know after all, she was only chastising Verity for not helping. But who was ill? Tossie? She had looked wan and pale that night after Coventry.

I put my ear to the door and listened, hoping the eavesdroppees would be more informative than they usually were.

"You might at least have offered to sit with the patient for a few minutes," Mrs. Mering said.

"I am so sorry, Aunt," Verity said. "I thought you would be afraid of infection."

Why *can't* people say who and what they are talking about so the eavesdropper has a chance? I thought. The patient. Infection. Be more specific.

"And I thought she would insist on you and Tossie nursing him," Verity said.

Him? Had Mr. C shown up and promptly fallen ill? And fallen in love with his nurse Tossie?

"I would not *dream* of allowing Tocelyn in the sickroom," Mrs. Mering said. "She is such a delicate girl."

Down the corridor I saw Terence open the front door. I was going to have to go in, information or no. I looked down at Cyril. Mrs. Mering would no doubt demand to know what he was doing in the house. Then again, that might be a welcome diversion under the circumstances.

"Tocelyn has far too delicate a constitution for nursing," Mrs. Mering was saying, "and the sight of her poor father ill would be much too upsetting for her."

Her poor father. Then it was Colonel Mering who'd been ill. But then what was he doing heading down to the fishpond?

I opened the door.

"I thought you might show more concern for your poor uncle, Verity," Mrs. Mering said. "I am dreadfully disappointed in—"

"Good morning," I said.

Verity looked gratefully at me.

"And how is Colonel Mering this morning?" I said. "I trust he is feeling better. I saw him outside just now."

"Outside?" Mrs. Mering said, clutching at her bosom. "He was *told* not to come down this morning. He will catch his death. Mr. St. Trewes," she said to Terence, who had just come in and was standing, looking hangdog, by the parlor door. "Is it true? Has my husband gone outside? You must go and fetch him at once."

Terence turned obediently to go.

"Where is Tossie?" Mrs. Mering said petulantly. "Why isn't she down yet? Verity, tell Jane to fetch her."

Terence reappeared, with the Colonel and Jane behind him.

"Mesiel!" Mrs. Mering cried. "What did you mean by going outside? You have been deathly ill."

"Had to get out to the fishpond," the Colonel said, harrumphing. "Check on things. Can't just leave my Japanese demekins out there with that cat about. Stopped on my way out by that silly girl—can never remember her name—the maid—"

"Colleen," Verity said automatically.

"*Jane.*" Mrs. Mering glared at Verity.

"Told me I had to come in here immediately," Colonel Mering said. "Made a huge fuss. What's it all about?"

He turned to Jane, who swallowed, took a deep, sobbing breath, and stuck out a letter on a silver salver.

"Harrumph, what's this?" the Colonel said.

"The mail, sorr," Jane said.

"Why didn't Baine bring it?" Mrs. Mering demanded. She took the letter off the salver. "No doubt it is from Madame Iritosky," she said, opening it, "explaining why she had to leave so suddenly." She turned to Jane. "Tell Mr. Baine to come here. And tell Tossie to come down. She will want to hear this letter."

"Yes, ma'am," Jane said, and fled.

"I do hope she has enclosed her address," Mrs. Mering said, unfolding several closely written pages, "so that I can write and tell her of our experience with the spirits at Coventry." She frowned. "Why, it is not from Madame—" she stopped, reading the letter silently.

"Who is the letter from, my dear?" the Colonel said.

"O," Mrs. Mering said, and fainted dead away.

It was a real faint this time. Mrs. Mering crashed into the credenza, decapitated the potted palm, broke the glass dome over the feather arrangement, and ended up with her head on the velvet footstool. The pages of the letter fluttered down around her.

Terence and I dived for her. "Baine!" the Colonel thundered, yanking on the bellpull. "Baine!" Verity stuck a cushion under her head and began fanning her with the letter.

"Baine!" the Colonel bellowed.

Jane appeared in the door, looking terrified.

"Tell Baine to come here immediately," he shouted.

"I can't, sorr," she said, twisting her apron.

"Why not?" he bellowed.

She cringed away from him. "He's gone, sir."

"What do you mean, gone?" the Colonel demanded. "Gone where?"

She'd twisted her apron completely into a knot. "The letter," she said, wringing the ends of it.

"What do you mean, that he's gone to the postal office? Well, go and fetch him." He waved her out of the room. "Damn Madame Iritosky! Upsetting my wife even when she isn't here! Damned spiritist nonsense!"

"Our daughter," Mrs. Mering said, her eyelids fluttering. She focused on the letter Verity was fanning her with. "O, the letter! The fated letter . . ." and went out again.

Jane ran in with the smelling salts.

"Where's Baine?" Colonel Mering thundered. "Didn't you fetch him? And go tell Tossie to come down immediately. Her mother needs her."

Jane sat down on the gilt chair, flung her apron over her head, and began to bawl.

"Here, here, what's this?" Colonel Mering harrumphed. "Get up, girl."

"Verity," Mrs. Mering said, clutching weakly at Verity's arm. "The letter. Read it. I cannot bear—"

Verity obediently stopped fanning and held the letter up. " 'Dearest Papa and Darling Mumsy,' " she said, and looked like *she* was going to faint.

I started toward her, and she shook her head wordlessly at me and read on. " 'Dearest Papa and Darling Mumsy, By the time you read this I shall be a married woman.' "

"Married?" Colonel Mering said. "What does she mean, married?"

" '. . . and I shall be happier than I have ever been or ever thought of being,' " Verity read on. " 'I am very sorry to have deceived you in this way, especially Papa, who is ill, but I feared if you knew of our intentions, you would forbid my marrying, and I know that when you come to know dear Baine as I do,' " Verity's voice caught, and then she went on, pale as death, " 'as I do, you will see him not as a servant but as the dearest, kindest, best man in the world, and will forgive us both.' "

"Baine?" Colonel Mering said blankly.

"Baine," Verity breathed. She let the letter fall to her lap and looked up desperately at me, shaking her head. "No. She can't have."

"She's eloped with the butler?" Terence said.

"Oh, Mr. St. Trewes, my poor boy!" Mrs. Mering cried, clutching her bosom. "Are you quite destroyed?"

He didn't look destroyed. What he looked was blank, with that vague, undecided look soldiers get when they've just lost a leg or been told they're being shipped home and haven't yet taken it in.

"Baine?" Colonel Mering said, glowering at Jane. "How did a thing like this happen?"

"Read on, Verity," Mrs. Mering said. "We must know the worst."

"The worst," Verity murmured and picked up the letter. " 'No doubt you are curious as to how this all came about so quickly.' "

Which was putting it mildly.

" 'It all began with our trip to Coventry.' " She stopped, unable to go on.

Mrs. Mering snatched the letter from her impatiently. " '. . . our trip to Coventry,' " she read, " 'a trip I know now the spirits were guiding us to that I might find my true love.' Lady Godiva! I hold her entirely responsible for this!" She took the letter up again. " 'While we were there I admired a cast-iron footed pedestal firugeal urn which I know now to be in execrable taste, completely lacking in simplicity of form and design, but I had never been properly trained in matters of Artistic Sensibility or educated in Literature and Poetry, and was only an ignorant, thoughtless spoilt girl.

" 'I asked Baine, for that is how I still think of him, though now I must learn to call him William and beloved husband! Husband! How sweet the sound of that precious word! I asked him to concur in my praise of the footed firugeal urn. He would not. Not only would he not, but he called it hideous and told me that my taste in liking it was ignorant.

" 'No one had ever contradicted me before. Everyone around me had always indulged me in all my opinions and agreed with everything I said, except for Cousin Verity, who had corrected me once or twice, but I put that down to her not being married and having no prospects. I tried to help her to wear her hair in a more attractive way, but was unable to do much for her, poor thing.' "

"What is known as burning your bridges," I murmured.

" 'Perhaps now that I am wed, Mr. Henry will notice her,' " Mrs. Mering read. " 'I tried to promote her to him, but, alas, he had eyes only for me. They would make a good couple, not handsome or clever, but well-suited nonetheless.' "

"*All* her bridges."

" 'I was not at all used to being contradicted, and at first I was angry, but when you swooned on the train on the way home, Mama, and I went to fetch him, he was so strong and quick-witted and helpful in assisting you, Mama, that it was as if I saw him with new eyes, and I fell in love with him right there in the railway carriage.' "

"It's all my fault," Verity murmured. "If I hadn't insisted we go to Coventry—"

" 'But I was too stubborn to admit my feelings,' " Mrs. Mering read, " 'and the next day I confronted him and demanded he apologize. He refused, we quarreled, and he *threw me in the river,* and then he kissed me, and oh, Mama, it was so romantic! Just like Shakespeare, whose plays my beloved husband is having me read, beginning with *The Taming of the Shrew.*' "

Mrs. Mering flung the letter down. "Reading books! *That* is the cause of all this! Mesiel, you should never have hired a servant who read books! I blame you entirely for this. Always reading Ruskin and Darwin and Trollope. Trollope! What sort of name is that for an author? And *his* name. Servants should have solid English names. 'I used it when I worked for Lord Dunsany,' he said. 'Well, you're certainly not using it here,' I said. Of course what can one expect from a man who refused to dress for dinner? *He* read books, too. Dreadful socialist things. Bentham and Samuel Butler."

"Who?" the Colonel said, confused.

"Lord Dunsany. Dreadful man, but he has a nephew who will inherit half of Hertfordshire and Tossie could have been received at Court, and now . . . now . . ."

She swayed and Terence reached for the smelling salts, but she waved them irritatedly away. "Mesiel! Don't just sit there! Do something! There must be some way to stop them before it's too late!"

"It's too late," Verity murmured.

"Perhaps not. Perhaps they only left this morning," I said, gathering up the pages of the letter and scanning them. They were covered with Tossie's flowery hand and dozens of exclamation points and underlinings and badly blotted in places. She should have bought a penwiper at the jumble sale, I thought irrelevantly.

" 'It is no use to try and stop us,' " I read. " 'By the time you receive this we shall already have been married in Surrey at a registrar's office and will be on our way to our new home. My dearest husband—ah, that most precious of words!—feels that we will thrive better in a society less enslaved to the archaic class structure, a country where one can have whatever name he likes, and to that end, we sail for America, where my husband—ah, that sweet word again!—intends to earn his living as a philosopher. Princess Arjumand is accompanying us, for I could not bear to be separated from her as well as you, and Papa would probably kill her when he found out about the calico goldfish.' "

"My split-tailed nacreous ryunkin?" Colonel Mering said, starting up out of the chair. "What about it?"

" 'She ate the calico. Oh, dear, Papa, can you find it in your heart to forgive her as well as me?' "

"We must disown her," Mrs. Mering said.

"We certainly must," Colonel Mering said. "That ryunkin cost two hundred pounds!"

"Colleen!" Mrs. Mering said. "I mean, Jane! Stop snuffling and fetch my writing desk at once. I intend to write to her and tell her from this day forward we have no daughter."

"Yes, ma'am," Jane said, wiping her nose on her apron. I stared after her, thinking about Colleen/Jane and Mrs. Chattisbourne calling all her maids Gladys, and trying to remember exactly what Mrs. Mering had said about Baine. " 'I used it when I worked for Lord Dunsany.' " And what had Mrs. Chattisbourne said that day we went to fetch things for the jumble sale? "I have always felt it is not the name that makes the butler, but training."

Colleen/Jane came back into the room, carrying the writing desk and sniffling.

"Tocelyn's name shall never be spoken again in this house," Mrs. Mering said, sitting down at the writing table. "Henceforth her name shall never cross my lips. All of Tocelyn's letters shall be returned unopened." She took out a pen and ink.

"How will we know where to send the letter telling her she's disowned if we don't open her letters?" Colonel Mering said.

"It's too late, isn't it?" Verity said bleakly to me. "There's nothing we can do."

I wasn't listening. I gathered up the pages of the letter and turned them over, looking for the end.

"From this day forth I shall wear mourning," Mrs. Mering said. "Jane, go upstairs and press my black bombazine. Mesiel, when anyone asks you, you must say our daughter died."

I located the end of the letter. Tossie had signed the letter, "Your repentant daughter, Tocelyn," and then scratched "Tocelyn" out and signed her married name.

"Listen to this," I said to Verity, and began reading.

" 'Please tell Terence that I know he will never get over me, but that he must try, and not to begrudge us our happiness, for Baine and I were fated to be together.' "

"If she's truly gone and married this person," Terence said, the light dawning, "then I'm released from my engagement."

I ignored him. " 'My darling William does not believe in Fate,' " I persisted, " 'and says that we are creatures of Free Will, but he believes that wives should have opinions and ideas of their own, and what else can it have been but Fate? For had Princess Arjumand not disappeared, we should never have gone to Coventry—' "

"Don't," Verity said, "please."

"You have to hear the rest of it," I said, "'— to Coventry. And had I not seen the footed firugeal urn, we should never have come together. I will write when we are settled in America. *Your repentant daughter,*'" I read, emphasizing each word, "'*Mrs. William Patrick Callahan.*'"

*"Look here! I've an idea we've been working this thing from the wrong end."*

*Lord Peter Wimsey*

# CHAPTER TWENTY-SIX

An Anticlimax—How Mystery Novels End—Mrs. Mering Blames the Colonel—Realizing What It Means—A Happy Ending for Cyril—Mrs. Mering Blames Verity—A Séance Proposed—Packing—Premonitions—Mrs. Mering Blames Me—Finch Is Still Not at Liberty to Say—Waiting for the Train—Disappearance of the Bishop's Bird Stump—Realizing What It Means

Well, it wasn't exactly the ending of an Agatha Christie mystery, with Hercule Poirot gathering everyone together in the drawing room to reveal the murderer and impress everyone with his astonishing deductive powers.

And it definitely wasn't a Dorothy Sayers, with the detective hero saying to his heroine sidekick, "I say, we make a jolly good detectin' team. How about makin' the partnership permanent, eh, what?" and then proposing in Latin.

We weren't even a halfway decent detectin' team. We hadn't solved the case. The case had been solved in spite of us. Worse, we had been such an impediment, we'd had to be packed off out of the way before the course of history could correct itself. This is the way the world ends, not with a bang but an elopement.

Not that there wasn't whimpering. Mrs. Mering was doing a good deal of that, not to mention weeping, wailing, and clutching the letter to her bosom.

"O, my precious daughter!" she sobbed. "Mesiel, don't just stand there. *Do* something."

The Colonel looked around uneasily. "What can I do, my dear? According to Tossie's letter, they are already afloat."

"*I* don't know. Stop them. Have the marriage annulled. Wire the Royal Navy!" She stopped, grabbed her heart, and cried, "Madame Iritosky tried to warn me! She said, 'Beware of the sea!'"

"Pah! Seems to me if she'd truly had any contact with the Other Side, she could have given a better warning than that!" Colonel Mering said.

But Mrs. Mering wasn't listening. "That day at Coventry. I had a premonition—oh, if I had only realized what it meant, I might have saved her!" She let the letter flutter to the floor.

Verity stooped and picked it up. "'I will write when we are settled in America,'" she said softly. "'Your repentant daughter, Mrs. William Patrick Callahan.' William Patrick Callahan." She shook her head.

"What do you know?" she said softly. "The butler did it."

As she said it, I had the oddest sensation, like one of Mrs. Mering's premonitions, or a sudden shifting underfoot, and I thought suddenly of anti-cathedral protesters and Merton's pedestrian gate.

"The butler did it." And then something else. Something important. Who had said that? Verity, explaining the mystery novels? "It was always the least likely suspect," she had said in my bedroom that first night. "For the first hundred books or so, the butler did it, and after that *he* was the most likely, and they had to switch to unlikely criminals, you know, the harmless old lady or the vicar's devoted wife, that sort of thing, but it didn't take the reader long to catch on to that, and they had to resort to having the detective be the murderer, and the narrator, and . . ."

But that wasn't it. Someone else had said, "The butler did it." But who? Not anyone here. Mystery novels hadn't even been invented, except for *The Moonstone. The Moonstone.* Something Tossie had said about *The Moonstone,* about being unaware you were committing a crime. And something else. Something about disappearing into thin air.

"And the neighbors!" Mrs. Mering wailed. "What will Mrs. Chattis-bourne say when she finds out? And the Reverend Mr. Arbitage!"

There was a long moment during which only the sound of her sobbing could be heard, and then Terence turned to me and said, "Do you realize what this means?"

"Oh, Terence, you poor, poor boy!" Mrs. Mering sobbed. "And you would have had five thousand pounds a year!" and allowed herself to be led weeping from the room by Colonel Mering.

We watched them climb the stairs. Halfway up, Mrs. Mering swayed in her husband's arms. "We shall have to hire a new butler!" she said despairingly. "Where shall I ever find a new butler? I blame you entirely for this, Mesiel. If you had let me hire English servants instead of *Irish*—" She broke down, weeping.

Colonel Mering handed her his handkerchief. "There, there, my dear," he said, "don't take on so."

As soon as they were out of sight, Terence said, "Do you Realize What This Means? I'm not engaged. I'm free to marry Maud. 'Oh, frabjous day! Callooh! Callay!' "

Cyril clearly Realized What It Meant. He sat up alertly and began to wag his entire body.

"You do know, don't you, old fellow?" Terence said. "No more sleeping in the stable for you."

And no more baby talk, I thought. No more putting up with Princess Arjumand.

"It's the soft life for you from now on," Terence said. "Sleeping in the house and riding on trains and all the butcher's bones you like! Maud adores bulldogs!"

Cyril smiled a wide, drooling smile of pure happiness.

"I must go up to Oxford immediately. When's the next train? Pity Baine's not here. He'd know." He leaped up the stairs. At the top, he leaned down over the railing and said, "You do think she'll forgive me, don't you?"

"For being engaged to the wrong girl?" I said. "A minor infraction. Happens all the time. Look at Romeo. He'd been in love with some Rosalind person. It never seemed to bother Juliet."

" 'Did my heart love till now?' " he quoted, extending his hand dramatically down toward Verity. " 'Forswear it, sight! For I ne'er saw true beauty till this night.' " He disappeared down the upstairs corridor.

I looked at Verity. She stood with her hands on the newel post and was gazing sadly after Terence.

By tomorrow she'll be back in the 1930s, I thought, Realizing What It Meant. She would be back to documenting the Depression and reading mystery novels, her beautiful red hair in a pageboy, and her long legs, which I had never seen, encased in silk stockings with a seam down the back. And I would never see her again.

No, I would probably see her at the consecration. If I were still allowed to come. If Lady Schrapnell didn't permanently assign me to jumble sale duty when I told her that the bishop's bird stump hadn't been in the cathedral.

And if I did see Verity at the consecration, what exactly was I supposed to say to her? All Terence had to apologize for was thinking he'd been in love. I had to apologize for being such a liability in the scheme of things that I'd had to be shut up in a dungeon during the denouement. Not exactly something to be proud of. It was just as well I'd be stuck behind the fancy goods stall.

"I'm going to miss all this," Verity said, her eyes still on the stairs. "I should be glad it's all worked out so well, and that the continuum's not going to collapse . . ." She turned her beautiful naiad's eyes on me. "You do think the incongruity's repaired, don't you?"

"There's a train at 9:43," Terence said, racketing down the stairs with a valise in one hand and his hat in the other. "Baine thoughtfully left a Bradshaw in my room. Arrives at 11:02. Come along, Cyril, we're going to go get engaged. Where's he got to? Cyril!" He disappeared into the parlor.

"Yes," I said to Verity. "Completely repaired."

"Ned, you can arrange to have the boat sent back to Jabez, can't you?" Terence said, reappearing with Cyril. "And the rest of my things sent to Oxford?"

"Yes," I said. "Go."

He pumped my hand. "Goodbye. 'Friend, ahoy! Farewell, farewell!' I'll see you next term."

"I . . . I'm not certain about that," I said, and realized how much I was going to miss him. "Goodbye, Cyril." I leaned down to pat him on the head.

"Nonsense. You're looking much better since we've been at Muchings End. You'll be entirely cured by Michaelmas term. We'll have such jolly times on the river," Terence said, and was gone, Cyril trotting happily after him.

"I want them out of this house immediately," Mrs. Mering's voice said, overwrought, and we both looked up the stairs.

A door slammed overhead. "Absolutely out of the question!" Mrs. Mering said, and then the low sound of voices murmuring. ". . . and tell them . . ."

More murmuring. "I want you to go downstairs immediately and tell them. This is all due to them!"

More murmuring, and then, "If she'd been a proper chaperone this would never ha—"

A door shutting cut her off, and a minute later Colonel Mering came down the stairs, looking extremely embarrassed.

"All been too much for my poor dear wife," he said, looking at the carpet. "Her nerves. Very delicate. Rest and absolute quiet is what she needs. Think it best you go to your aunt in London, Verity, and you back to—" He looked at a loss.

"To Oxford," I said.

"Ah, yes, to your studies. Sorry about this," Colonel Mering said to the carpet. "Glad to arrange for the carriage."

"No, that's all right," I said.

"No trouble," he said. "Will have Baine tell—" he stopped, looking lost.

"I'll see that Miss Brown gets to the station," I said.

He nodded. "Must go see to my dear wife," he said, and started up the stairs.

Verity went after him. "Colonel Mering," she said, following him halfway up the stairs. "I don't think you should disown your daughter."

He looked embarrassed. "Afraid Malvinia's quite determined. Dreadful shock, you know. Butler and all that."

"Baine—I mean, Mr. Callahan—*did* prevent Tossie's cat from eating your Black Moor," she said.

Wrong thing to say. "He didn't prevent it from eating my globe-eyed nacreous ryunkin," he said angrily. "Cost two hundred pounds."

"But he did take Princess Arjumand with him so she can't eat any more of your goldfish," she said persuasively, "and he prevented Madame Iritosky from stealing Aunt Malvinia's ruby necklace. And he's read Gibbon." She put her hands on the newel post and looked up at him. "And she is your only daughter."

Colonel Mering looked down at me for support. "What do you think, Henry? Will this butler fellow make her a good husband?"

"He has her best interests at heart," I said firmly.

The Colonel shook his head. "Afraid my wife is quite determined never to speak to her again. Said from this moment forth, Tossie is dead to her." He went sadly up the stairs.

"But she's a spiritist," Verity said, pursuing him. "She is quite capable of speaking to the dead."

His face lit up. "Capital idea! Could have a séance." He went happily up the stairs. "Loves séances. Could rap out, 'Forgive.' Bound to work. Never thought all that medium poppycock would be of any use."

He rapped loudly three times on the banister. "Capital idea!"

He started down the corridor and then stopped and put his hand on Verity's arm. "Should pack and depart for the station as soon as possible. Your own best interests at heart. Nerves, you know."

"I quite understand," Verity said and opened the door to her room. "Mr. Henry and I shall be gone directly." She shut her door behind her.

Colonel Mering disappeared down the corridor. A door opened and shut, but not before Mrs. Mering's voice had boomed out like the Red Queen's, ". . . gone yet? I thought I told you—"

Time to depart.

I went upstairs and into my room. I opened the wardrobe and got out my carpetbag. I set it on the bed and then sat down beside it and thought about what had just happened. The continuum had somehow managed to correct the incongruity, pairing off lovers like the last act of a Shakespearean comedy, though just how it had managed it wasn't clear. What was clear was that it had wanted us out of the way while it was doing whatever it was doing. So it had done the time-travel equivalent of locking us in our rooms.

But why had it sent us to Coventry's air raid, a crisis point, where presumably we could do a lot more damage? Or *was* Coventry a crisis point?

Its being off-limits had seemed to indicate it was a crisis point, and logically Ultra's involvement should make it one, but perhaps the raid was only off-limits when we were looking for the bishop's bird stump, because Verity and I had already been there. Perhaps it had been off-limits to give us a clear field.

To do what? To watch Provost Howard take candlesticks and Regimental Colors to the police station and see that the bishop's bird stump wasn't among the things saved? To see that it wasn't in the church during the raid?

I would have given anything not to have seen that, not to have to tell Lady Schrapnell. But it was definitely not there. I wondered who had stolen it and when.

It had to have been that afternoon. Carruthers said the Flower Committee biddy Miss Sharpe had said she'd seen the bishop's bird stump when she left the cathedral after the Advent Bazaar and Soldiers' Christmas Parcel Effort meeting, that she'd stopped and pulled three dead flowers out of it.

Everything started to shift, the way it had when Finch said, "You're on Merton's playing fields," and I grabbed for the bedpost like it was the pedestrian gate.

A door slammed. "Jane!" Mrs. Mering's voice said from the corridor. "Where is my black bombazine?"

"Here, mum," Jane's voice said.

"O, this won't do at all!" Mrs. Mering's voice again. "It's entirely too heavy for June. We shall have to order mourning clothes from Swan and Edgar's. They had a lovely soft black crepe with jet trim on the bodice and a pleated underskirt."

A pause, either for weeping or wardrobe-planning.

"Jane! I want you to take this note over to Notting Hill. And not a word to Mrs. Chattisbourne. Do you hear?" Slam.

"Yes, mum," Jane said timidly.

I stood there, still clutching the bedpost, trying to recall the idea, the odd sensation I'd had a moment ago, but it was gone, as quickly as it had come, and that must have been what had happened to Mrs. Mering there in the cathedral. She hadn't had a message from the spirit world, or from Lady Godiva either. She had looked at Baine and Tossie, and for an instant things had shifted into their true orientation, and she had seen what was happening, what was going to happen.

And then she must have lost it, because otherwise she'd have dismissed Baine on the spot and sent Tossie off on a Grand Tour of Europe. It must have gone as instantly as it came, the way mine just had, and that odd, chipped-tooth-probing look of hers had been her trying to remember what had triggered it.

The butler did it. "If I can ever do anything to repay you for returning Princess Arjumand, I should be more than obliged," Baine had said, and he certainly had repaid me. In spades. "The butler did it," Verity had said, and he certainly had.

Only not Verity. The fur-bearing woman in Blackwell's. "The butler always does it," she said, and the other one, the one with the Cyril-like fur draped over her shoulders, had said, "What you think is the first crime turns out to be the second. The real crime had happened years before. Nobody even knew the first crime had been committed." The real crime. A crime the person was unaware of having committed. And something else. About someone marrying a farmer.

"But a butler!" Mrs. Mering's anguished voice cried from down the corridor, followed by placating murmurs.

"Never should have let them stay in the first place!" Colonel Mering said.

"If she hadn't met Mr. St. Trewes," Mrs. Mering wailed, "she'd never have been thinking about marriage." Her voice died away into sobbing murmurs, and it was nice to know other people second-guessed their actions, but it was definitely time to go.

I opened the bureau and looked at the clothes Baine had neatly stacked inside. The shirts all belonged to Elliott Chattisbourne and the Victorian era. And the collars and cuffs and nightshirt. I wasn't as certain of the socks, but I must have been wearing the pair I'd come through in or the net wouldn't have opened. Unless of course I was going to cause an incongruity, in which case there wouldn't even be any increased slippage.

And if the continuum had been trying to get rid of Verity and me, why hadn't the net just refused to open the first time we tried to come back from Oxford after we'd reported in? Why hadn't it refused to open when Verity tried to take Princess Arjumand through? Baine wasn't trying to drown the cat. He'd have been delighted to find Verity standing there by the gazebo with Princess Arjumand, delighted she'd waded in and rescued her. Why hadn't it refused to open when Verity tried to come through to Muchings End in the first place? It didn't make sense.

I opened the bottom drawer. Baine had thoughtfully folded my too-small shirts and waxed my too-small patent leather shoes. I put them in the carpetbag and looked round the room for any other stray items. Not the straight razors, thank goodness. Nor the silver-backed brushes.

My straw boater was lying on the nightstand. I started to put it on and then thought better of it. It was hardly the occasion for jauntiness.

None of it made sense. Why, if the continuum hadn't wanted us meddling, had it landed me forty miles away? And Carruthers in a marrows field? Why had it refused to open for Carruthers for three weeks after the raid? Why had it sent me to 2018 and 1395 and Verity to 1940? And, the most important question of all, why had it brought us back now?

"An American!" Mrs. Mering shrieked from the end of the corridor. "It's all Mr. Henry's fault. His disgraceful American ideas of class equality!"

Definitely time to go. I closed the carpetbag and went out into the corridor. I stopped at Verity's door and raised my hand to knock, and then thought better of that, too.

"*Where* is Jane?" Mrs. Mering's voice rang out. "Why isn't she back yet? Irish servants! This is all your fault, Mesiel. *I* wanted to hire—"

I made a speedy and quiet exit down the stairs. Colleen/Jane was standing at the foot of them, twisting her apron in her hands.

"Has she dismissed you?" I asked her.

"No, sorr, not yet," she said, looking up nervously in the direction of Mrs. Mering's room. "But she's that angry."

I nodded. "Has Miss Brown come down?"

"Yes, sorr. She said to tell you she would wait for you at the station."

"The station?" I said, and then realized she meant the drop. "Thank you, Jane. Colleen. And good luck."

"Thank you, sorr." She started up the stairs, crossing herself as she went.

I opened the front door, and there stood Finch, in his morning coat and butler's derby, his hand already reaching for the knocker.

"Mr. Henry," he said. "Just the person I came to see."

I shut the door behind me and led him over to where we couldn't be observed from the windows.

"I'm so glad I caught you before you left, sir," he said. "I have a dilemma."

"I'm hardly the person to ask," I said.

"You see, sir, my mission's nearly completed, and I might be able to depart as early as tomorrow morning, but Mrs. Chattisbourne is having a tea tomorrow afternoon to plan the St. Anne's Day Sale of Work. It's terribly important to her, and so I'd planned to stay on to see that everything went well. That kitchen maid of hers, Gladys, has the mind of a rabbit, and—"

"And you're afraid you'll miss the consecration if you stay a few more days?" I said.

"No. I asked Mr. Dunworthy and he said it was quite all right, they could bring me through at the same time. No, my dilemma is this." He held out a square envelope with the initials M.M. embossed in gold script on it. "It's an offer of employment from Mrs. Mering. She wants me to come and be her butler."

So that was why Colleen/Jane had her cloak on. With Mrs. Mering's only daughter gone, run off to elope with the butler, and her heart broken, the first thing she had done was to send Colleen/Jane over to the Chattisbournes' to filch Finch.

"It's a very good offer, sir," Finch said. "There are a number of advantages to taking it."

"And you're thinking of staying in the Victorian era permanently?"

"Of course not, sir! Although," he said wistfully, "there are moments when I feel I have found my true métier here. No, my dilemma is that Muchings End is much more convenient to my mission than the Chattisbournes'. If I am reading the signs correctly, I should be able to complete my mission tonight and it won't matter, but it might turn out to take several days. And if that were the case, my mission—"

"What *is* your mission anyway, Finch?" I said, exasperated.

He looked pained. "I'm afraid I'm not at liberty to say. I was sworn to secrecy by Mr. Lewis, and I have also witnessed events you are not yet aware of, and have access to information you have not, and I dare not jeopardize the success of either of our missions by speaking out of turn. As you know, sir, 'Loose lips sink ships.' "

I had that odd, disorienting sensation again, of things up-ending and reorienting themselves, and I tried to grab hold of it, like I had grabbed onto the pedestrian gate.

"Loose lips sink ships." I knew who had said that. I had, thinking about Ultra and Coventry and secrets as crisis points. It was something about Ultra, and what would have happened if the Nazis had found out we had broken their code—no, it was no use. Just as things were starting to shift, it was gone again.

"If the mission should go several days," Finch was saying, "Muchings End is much closer both to the vicarage and the drop. And it's not as if I would be leaving Mrs. Chattisbourne in the lurch. I have already found an excellent butler for her through an agency in London. I intend to telegraph him of the vacant position just before I leave. But it doesn't seem fair to accept the position with Mrs. Mering when I will not be staying. I suppose I could attempt to find a second but—"

"No," I said. "Take the position. And don't give any notice when you leave. Just disappear. Mrs. Mering needs to suffer the slings and arrows of unreliable domestic help so she can learn to appreciate her new son-in-law. Plus, it will teach her not to steal her friends' servants."

"Oh, good, sir," he said. "Thank you. I shall tell her I can take the position *after* Mrs. Chattisbourne's tea party." He started up to the door again. "And don't worry, sir. It's always darkest before the dawn."

He raised the knocker, and I hurried out to the gazebo. At the last minute, I remembered the coveralls and the Burberry and went back down to the wine cellar to collect them and put them in my carpetbag to take through. The coveralls had an ARP patch on them and Burberry hadn't begun manufacturing his raincoats till 1903, fifteen years from now, and the last thing we needed was another incongruity.

I shut up the carpetbag and started out to the drop again, wondering if Verity would be there or if she would have gone on ahead to Oxford to avoid awkward goodbyes.

But she was there, in the white hat, with her bags on either side of her, as if she were on a railway platform.

I came up beside her. "Well," I said, setting down my carpetbag.

She looked at me from behind her white veil, and I thought, it truly is too bad I didn't singlehandedly save the universe. Since I hadn't, I looked at the peonies behind the gazebo and said, "When's the next train?"

"Five minutes," she said. "If it opens."

"It will open," I said. "Tossie's married Mr. C, Terence is getting engaged to Maud, their grandson will fly a night raid to Berlin, the Luftwaffe will leave off bombing aerodromes and begin bombing London, and all's right with the continuum."

"In spite of us," she said.

"In spite of us."

We stared at the peonies.

"I suppose you're glad it's over," she said. "I mean, you'll finally be able to get what you wanted."

I looked at her.

She looked away. "Some sleep, I mean."

"I'm not nearly so enamored of it anymore," I said. "I've learned to do without."

We stared at the peonies some more.

"I suppose you'll go back to your mystery novels," I said after another silence.

She shook her head. "They're not very true-to-life. They always end by solving the mystery and righting the wrong. Miss Marple's never shuffled off to an air raid while they clean up the mess she's made." She tried to smile. "What will you do now?"

"Jumble sales, probably. I should imagine Lady Schrapnell will assign me to permanent coconut shy duty when she finds out the bishop's bird stump wasn't there after all."

"Wasn't where?"

"In the cathedral," I said. "I got a clear view of the north aisle as we were leaving. The stand was there, but no bishop's bird stump. I hate to tell her, she had her heart so set on its having been in the cathedral. You were right. Strange as it may seem, someone must have removed it for safekeeping."

She frowned. "Are you certain you were looking in the right place?"

I nodded. "In front of the parclose screen of the Smiths' Chapel, between the third and fourth pillars."

"But that's impossible," she said. "It was there. I saw it."

"When?" I said. "When did you see it?"

"Just after I came through," she said.

"Where?"

"In the north aisle. The same place it was when we were there yesterday."

There was a faint whisper of air, and the net began to shimmer. Verity stooped to pick up her bags and stepped down onto the grass.

"Wait." I grabbed her arm. "Tell me exactly when and where you saw it."

She looked anxiously at the shimmering net. "Shouldn't we—"

"We'll catch the next one," I said. "Tell me exactly what happened. You came through in the sanctuary—"

She nodded. "The sirens were going, but I couldn't hear any planes, and it was dark in the church. There was a little light on the altar and another one on the rood screen. I thought I'd better stay near the drop, in case it opened again right away. So I hid in one of the vestries and waited, and after a while I saw torches over by the vestry door, and the fire watch came in, going up to the roofs, and I heard one of them say, 'Had we better start carrying things out of the vestries?' so I sneaked into the Mercers' Chapel and hid. I could still see the drop from there."

"And then the Mercers' Chapel caught on fire?"

She nodded. "I started for the vestry door, but there was all this smoke, and I must have got turned around. I ended up in the choir. That's when I hit my hand on the arch and cut it. I remembered that the tower hadn't burned, so I got down on the floor and worked my way along the choir railing to the nave and then crawled down the nave till the smoke got less thick and I could stand up."

"And when was that?"

"I don't know," she said, looking anxiously at the net. "What if it doesn't open again? Perhaps we should discuss this in Oxford."

"No," I said. "When did you stand up in the nave?"

"I don't *know*. A little before they started carrying things out."

The shimmer flared into light. I ignored it. "All right. You crawled down the nave—" I prompted.

"I crawled down the nave and after I'd gone about halfway, the smoke started to thin out, and I could see the west door. I took hold of the pillar I was next to and stood up, and there it was, in front of the screen. On its stand. It had a big bouquet of yellow chrysanthemums in it."

"You're certain it was the bishop's bird stump?"

"It doesn't exactly look like anything else," she said. "Ned, what's this all about?"

"What did you do then?"

"I thought, well, at least I've accomplished something. I can tell Ned it was there during the raid. If I make it out of here. And I started toward the tower door. The aisle was blocked with a pew that had got knocked over, and I had to go round it, and before I could reach the tower, the fire watch came in and started carrying things out."

"And?" I prompted.

"I ducked across into the Cappers' Chapel and hid."

"How long were you in there?"

"I don't know. A quarter of an hour or so. One of the fire watch came back in and got the altar books. I waited till he was gone, and then I went out to look for you."

"Out the south door?" I said.

"Yes," she said, looking at the net. It was beginning to dwindle and fade.

"Were there people outside on the steps when you went out?"

"Yes. If we've missed our chance to go home—"

"Did any of the fire watch go near the bishop's bird stump?"

"No. They went into the sanctuary and the vestries and one of them ran down and got the altar cross and the candlesticks out of the Smiths' Chapel."

"And that's all he got?"

"Yes."

"You're certain?"

"I'm certain. He had to go round the back of the nave and up the south aisle with them, because of the smoke. He ran right past me."

"Did you see any of them in the Drapers' Chapel?"

"No."

"And you didn't go in the Drapers' Chapel?"

"I *told* you. I came through in the sanctuary, and I was in the Mercers' Chapel and then the choir. And that's all."

"Could you see the north door from where you were hiding?"

She nodded.

"And no one went out that way?"

"It was locked," she said. "I heard one of the fire watch tell another to unlock the north door, that the fire brigade would bring the hoses in that way, and he said they'd have to do it from the outside, because of the Smiths' Chapel being on fire."

"What about the west door? The tower door?"

"No. The fire watch all went out the vestry door."

"Did you see anyone else in the cathedral?" I said. "Besides the fire watch? And the firemen?"

"In the cathedral? Ned, it was on fire."

"What were the fire watch wearing?"

"Wearing?" she said bewilderedly. "I don't know. Uniforms. Coveralls. I . . . the verger was wearing a tin helmet."

"Were any of them wearing white?"

"White? No, of course not. Ned, what—?"

"Could you see the west door—the tower door—from where you were hiding?"

She nodded.

"And no one went out the west door while you were there? You didn't see anyone in the Drapers' Chapel?"

"No. Ned, what's this all about?"

The north door was locked, and Verity had a clear view of the south door, and there were people—that knot of roof-watchers and the two louts by the lamp-post—outside the whole time.

The fire watch was using the vestry door, and shortly after Provost Howard made it out with the altar books, it was blocked by fire. And there were people by the vestry door, too. And the stout ARP warden making the rounds. And the dragon lady head of the Flower Committee was standing militant guard outside the west door. There was no way out of the cathedral.

There was no way out of the cathedral. There was no way out of the lab. And no place to hide. Except the net.

I grabbed both of Verity's arms. I had hidden in the net, behind the theatrical curtains, and listened to Lizzie Bittner say, "I'd do anything for him." In Oxford in 2018. Where T.J. had discovered a region of increased slippage.

"It's because we don't have the treasures Canterbury and Winchester have," Lizzie Bittner had said. Lizzie Bittner, whose husband was a descendant of the Botoners who had built the church in 1395. Lizzie Bittner, who had lied about the lab's being open. Who had a key.

"What you think is the first crime turns out to be the second," the fur-bearing woman had said. "The first crime had happened years before." Or after. This was time travel, after all. And in one of the Waterloo sims, the continuum had gone back to 1812 to correct itself.

And the clue, the little fact that didn't fit, was the increased slippage. The increased slippage that hadn't happened on Verity's drop, that should have prevented her from rescuing the cat, from committing the incongruity in the first place. Five minutes either way would have done it, but instead there'd been nine minutes' worth. Nine minutes that had put her right at the scene of the crime.

"Every one of the simulated incongruities has increased slippage at the site," T.J. had said. Every single one of them. Even the ones in which the incongruity was too great for the continuum to correct it. Every single one. Except ours.

And all we had was a cluster of slippage in 2018, which T.J. had said was too great for being that far from the site. And Coventry. Which was a crisis point.

"Ned," Verity said urgently. "What's wrong?"

"Shh," I said, holding onto her arms like I had held onto the green metal uprights of Merton's pedestrian gate. I almost had it, and if I didn't jar it with any sudden movements or distractions, I would see the whole thing.

The slippage was too far from the site, and discrepancies were only found in the immediate vicinity of the incongruity. And the fur-bearing lady in Blackwell's had said, "I'm glad she married him." She had been talking about some woman who had married a farmer. "If she hadn't, she'd still be trapped in Oxford, serving on church committees and running jumble—"

"Ned?" Verity said.

"Shh."

"She was convinced the bishop's bird stump had been stolen," Carruthers had said, talking about the "bitter old spinster sort," Miss Sharpe, who had been in charge of the Flower Committee.

And the ARP warden had said, "Come along, Miss Sharpe," to the gray-haired woman guarding the west door. The gray-haired woman who had reminded me of someone, and she had said, "I have no intention of going anywhere. I am the vice-chairman of the Cathedral Ladies' Altar Guild and the head of the Flower Committee."

"Miss Sharpe," he had called her.

Miss Sharpe, who had been so upset she'd accused everyone of knowing about the raid in advance. Who'd even written a letter to the editor.

She'd sent a letter to the paper, saying someone had advance knowledge of the raid.

In Coventry, which had known about the raid in advance. Which, unlike Muchings End, wasn't an historical backwater. Which was a crisis point. Because of Ultra.

Because if the Nazis found out we had their Enigma machine, it could change the course of the war. The course of history.

And the only instance of something being brought forward through the net was as part of a self-correction.

I was gripping Verity's arms so hard it had to be hurting her, but I didn't dare let go. "That young woman in the cathedral," I said. "What was her name?"

"In the cathedral?" Verity said bewilderedly. "Ned, there wasn't anyone in the cathedral. It was on fire."

"Not during the raid," I said. "The day we went there with Tossie. The young woman who came to see the curate. What was her name?"

"I don't . . . It was a flower name," she said. "Geranium or—"

"Delphinium," I said. "Not her first name. Her last name."

"I . . . it began with an 'S.' Sherwood, no, Sharpe," she said, and the world shifted 180 degrees, and I wasn't at Balliol's gate, I was on Merton's playing fields, and there, in Christ Church Meadow, was Coventry Cathedral, the center of it all.

"Ned," Verity said urgently. "What is it?"

"We've been looking at this the wrong way round," I said. "You didn't cause an incongruity."

"But—the coincidences," she stammered, "and the increased slippage in 2018. There had to have been an incongruity."

"There was," I said. "And, thanks to my amazing little gray cells, I know when it happened. And what caused it."

"What?"

"Elementary, my dear Watson. I will give you a clue. Several clues, in fact. Ultra. *The Moonstone*. The Battle of Waterloo. Loose lips."

"Loose lips?" she said. "Ned—"

"Carruthers. The dog that didn't bark in the night. Penwipers. Pigeons. The least likely suspect. And Field General Rommel."

"Field General Rommel?"

"The battle of North Africa," I said. "We were using Ultra to locate Rommel's supply convoys and sink them, being careful to send out a reconnaissance plane to be seen by the convoy so the Nazis wouldn't get suspicious."

I told her about the fog and the plane being unable to find the convoy, the RAF and the Navy's simultaneous arrival, and about what Ultra had done afterward—the telegram, the planted rumors, the messages intended to be intercepted. "If the Nazis had found out we had Ultra, it would have changed the outcome of the war, so they had to set in motion an elaborate intelligence mission to correct the slip-up." I beamed at her. "Don't you see? It all fits."

It all fit. Carruthers being trapped in Coventry, my making Terence miss meeting Maud, Professor Overforce pushing Professor Peddick in the Thames, even all those bloody jumble sales.

The fur-bearing ladies in Blackwell's, Hercule Poirot, T.J., Professor

Peddick with his talk of the Grand Design, all of them had been trying to tell me, and I'd been too blind to see it.

Verity was looking worriedly at me. "Ned," she said, "exactly how many drops have you had?"

"Four," I said. "The second of which was to Blackwell's, where I overheard three fur-bearing matrons having an extremely enlightening discussion of a mystery novel, and the first of which was to the lab in 2018, where I heard Lizzie Bittner say she would do anything to keep Coventry Cathedral from being sold to a gaggle of spiritualists."

The net began to shimmer faintly.

"What if there was an incongruity?" I said. "A slip-up? And the continuum, trying to protect the course of history, set in motion a sophisticated system of secondary defenses to correct the problem? Like Ultra, sending out telegrams and false leads, implementing an elaborate plan involving the drowning of cats and séances and jumble sales and elopements. And dozens of agents, some of whom weren't even aware of the true purpose of the mission."

The peonies glittered brightly. "In the best detective tradition, I cannot prove any of this," I said. "Therefore, Watson, we must go collect evidence." I picked up Verity's bags and deposited them next to the peonies. " 'Quick, Watson! A hansom cab!' "

"Where are we going?" she said suspiciously.

"To the lab. 2057. To check the Coventry local papers and the cathedral's committee rosters for 1888 and 1940."

I took her arm, and we stepped into the shimmering circle. "And then," I said, "we will go to get the bishop's bird stump."

The light began to grow. "Hold on," I said and stepped out of the net to get the carpetbag.

"Ned!" Verity said.

"Coming," I said. I opened the carpetbag, took out the boater, shut the bag and carried it back into the circle. I set the bag down and put the boater on at a jaunty angle that would have made Lord Peter proud.

"Ned," Verity said, stepping back, her greenish-brown eyes wide.

"Harriet," I said, and pulled her back into the already shining net.

And kissed her for a hundred and sixty-nine years.

*"Quick, Hastings. I have been blind, imbécile. Quick, a taxi."*

*Hercule Poirot*

# CHAPTER TWENTY-SEVEN

I Fail to Ascertain My Space-Time Location—Carruthers Refuses
to Go to Coventry—The Mystery of Verity's Drop Solved—A
Complication—Carruthers Goes to Coventry—Finch is Still
Not at Liberty to Say—More Newspapers—On the Tube to
Coventry—Failure of Contemps to Appreciate Transportation of
Own Time—I Quote Poetry—The Criminal Confesses—The
Bishop's Bird Stump Is Found at Last

When, oh, when will I ever learn to ascertain my space-time location on arrival? Granted, I had a number of things on my mind, most particularly what I intended to say to Verity when I got the time, and what I needed to do right now, but that was no excuse.

"Where's Mr. Dunworthy?" I said to Warder the minute we came through. I didn't wait for the veils to rise. I grabbed Verity's hand and fought my way through them to the console.

"Mr. Dunworthy?" Warder said blankly. She was dressed up, in a print dress and a curly hairdo that made her look almost pleasant.

"He's in London," Carruthers said, coming in. He was dressed up as well and had washed all the soot off. "I see you found Verity." He smiled at her. "You didn't happen to see if the bishop's bird stump was there while you were in Coventry, did you?"

"Yes," I said. "What's Mr. Dunworthy doing in London?"

"Lady Schrapnell had a last-minute notion the bishop's bird stump might have been stored in the same place as the treasures from the British Museum were during the Blitz, in an unused tunnel of the Underground."

"It wasn't," I said. "Ring him up and tell him to come back here immediately. T.J. didn't go with him, did he?" I said, looking at the bank of stack screens he'd run his Waterloo models on.

"No," he said. "He's changing his clothes. He should be back in a minute. What's this all about?"

"Where's Lady Schrapnell?" I said.

"Lady Schrapnell?" Warder said, as if she'd never heard of her.

"Yes. Lady Schrapnell," I said. "Coventry Cathedral. The bane of our existence. Lady Schrapnell."

"I thought you were trying to avoid her," Carruthers said.

"I am trying to avoid her right now," I said. "But in a few hours, I may want her. Do you know where she is?"

He and Warder exchanged glances. "At the cathedral, I would imagine."

"One of you needs to find out for certain," I said. "Ask her what her schedule for the rest of the day is."

"Her *schedule?*" Carruthers said.

Warder, at the same time, said, "*You* go find her if you want her," and it would obviously take more than a few curls to make her pleasant. "I'm not running the chance of her giving me something else to do! She's already got me ironing all the altar cloths and—"

"Never mind," I said. I didn't need Lady Schrapnell right now, and there were other, more important things to check. "I need you to do something else for me. I need copies of the *Coventry Standard* and the *Midlands Daily Telegraph* for November fifteenth through—" I turned to Carruthers. "When did you come back from Coventry? What day?"

"Three days ago. Wednesday."

"What day in *Coventry?*"

"December the twelfth."

"From November the fifteenth through December the twelfth," I said to Warder.

"That's out of the question!" Warder said. "I've got the altar cloths to iron and three rendezvouses to bring in. And all the choir's surplices to press. Linen! There are any number of fabrics she could have had the choir wear that wouldn't wrinkle walking up the nave to the choir, but Lady Schrapnell *had* to have linen! 'God is in the details,' she said. And now you expect me to get copies of *newspapers*—"

"I'll do it," Verity said. "Do you want facsimiles or articles only, Ned?"

"Facsimiles," I said.

She nodded. "I'll do them at the Bod. I'll be back directly," she said, flashed me one of her naiad smiles, and was gone.

"Carruthers," I said. "I need you to go to Coventry."

"Coventry?" Carruthers said, backing up abruptly and crashing into Warder. "I'm not going back there. I had enough trouble getting out last time."

"You don't have to go to the air raid," I said. "What I need—"

"And I'm not going anywhere in the vicinity. Remember the marrows field? And those bloody dogs? Forget it."

"I don't need you to go back in time," I said. "All I need is some facts from the church archives. You can take the tube. I want you to find out—"

T.J. came in, and he was dressed up too, in a white shirt and his short academic robe. I wondered if Lady Schrapnell had imposed some sort of dress code.

"Just a minute, Carruthers," I said. "T.J., I need you to do something. The model you did of the incongruity. I want you to change the focus."

"Change the focus?" he said blankly.

"The site where the incongruity occurred," I said.

"Don't tell me there's been another incongruity," Warder said. "That's *all* we need right now. I've got fifty linen surplices to press, three rendezvouses—"

"You said a self-correction could extend into the past, right, T.J.?" I said, ignoring her.

T.J. nodded. "Some of the models showed preemptive self-corrections."

"And that the only instance you found of a significant object being removed from its space-time location was as part of a self-correction."

He nodded again.

"And you said that our incongruity didn't match any of the Waterloo models. I want you to see if it matches with the focus changed."

T.J. obligingly sat down at the bank of computers and pushed the sleeves of his robe up. "To what?"

"Coventry Cathedral," I said. "November the fourteenth—"

"November the fourteenth?" T.J. and Carruthers interrupted in unison. Warder gave me one of those "how-many-drops-have-you-had?" looks.

"November the fourteenth," I said firmly. "1940. I don't know the exact time. Sometime after 7:45 P.M. and before eleven. My guess is half-past nine."

"But that's during the air raid," Carruthers said, "the place none of us could get anywhere near."

T.J. said, "What's this all about, Ned?"

"*The Fountain Pen Mystery* and Hercule Poirot," I said. "We've been looking at this the wrong way round. What if the rescue of the cat wasn't the incongruity? What if it was part of the continuum's self-correction and the real incongruity had happened earlier? Or later?"

T.J. began feeding in figures.

"There wasn't any increased slippage on Verity's drop," I said, "even though five minutes either way would have kept her from rescuing Princess Arjumand. So would the net's failure to open, but neither line of defense worked. And why did the slippage on my drop send me to Oxford to meet Terence, keep him from meeting Maud, and loan him the money for the boat so he could go meet Tossie? What if it was because the continuum wanted those things to happen? And what if all the signs we saw as indications of breakdown—my being bounced to the Middle Ages, Carruthers being trapped in Coventry—were all part of the self-correction, as well?"

A table of coordinates came up. T.J. scanned the columns, fed in more figures, scanned the new patterns. "Only the focus?" he said.

"You said discrepancies only occurred in the immediate vicinity of the site," I said to T.J. "But what if the site wasn't Muchings End? What if it was the raid on the cathedral, and what Verity and I saw was a discrepancy, was the course of events that would have happened if the incongruity hadn't been repaired?"

"Interesting," T.J. said. He rapidly fed in more figures.

"Only the focus," I said. "Same events, same slippage."

"This will take a while," he said, feeding in more figures.

I turned to Carruthers. "Here's what I need you to find out in Coventry." I reached round Warder for a handheld and spoke into it. "I want the names of the cathedral staff, lay and clerical, in 1940," I said, "and the cathedral's marriage records for 1888 through—" I hesitated a moment, thinking, and then said, "—1888 through 1915. No, 1920, to be on the safe side."

"What if the records were destroyed in the raid?"

"Then get the C of E's list of church livings for 1940. That will have been on file in Canterbury and a number of other places. They can't all have been hit by the Blitz."

I hit the handheld's print key, watched it spit out the list, and tore it off. "I need these as soon as possible."

Carruthers stared at it. "You expect me to go *now?*"

"Yes," I said. "This is important. If I'm right, we'll have the bishop's bird stump in time for the consecration."

"Then you'd better hurry," Warder said dryly. "It's in two hours."

"The consecration?" I said blankly. "That's impossible," and finally asked what should have been my first question on stepping out of the net. "What day is it?"

Verity ran in, carrying an armful of facsimile sheets. She'd changed into a slat dress and plimsolls. Her legs were just as long as I'd imagined them. "Ned, the consecration's in a few hours!"

"I just found that out," I said, trying to think what to do. I'd counted on having a couple of days to collect evidence to support my theory, but now there would scarcely be time to get to Coventry and back—

"Can I help?" Verity said.

"We need proof the incongruity's been fixed," I said. "I intended to send Carruthers—"

"I can go," Verity said.

I shook my head. "There isn't time. When does the consecration start?" I asked Warder.

"Eleven o'clock," she said.

"And what time is it now?"

"A quarter past nine."

I looked over at T.J. "How long till you have the sim?"

"Another minute," T.J. said, his fingers flying. "Got it." He hit "return," the columns of coordinates disappeared, and the model came up.

I don't know what I'd expected. The model that came up on the screen looked just like all the others—a shapeless, shadowy blur.

"Well, will you look at that?" T.J. said softly. He hit some more keys. "This is the new focus," he said, "and this is a superimpose of the Waterloo soup kettle sim."

He spoke into the comp's ear. Both models came up, one over the other, and even I could see that they matched.

"Do they match?" Warder said.

"Yeah," T.J. nodded slowly. "There are a few minor differences. The slippage at the site isn't as great, and you can see it's not an exact match here and here," he said, pointing at nonexistent shapes. "And I don't know what this is," he pointed at nothing in particular, "but it definitely looks like a self-correction pattern. See how the slippage lessens as it approaches 1888, and then ceases altogether on—"

"June eighteenth," I said.

T.J. typed in some figures. "June eighteenth. I'll need to run slippage checks and probabilities, and find out what this is," he said, tapping the nothing-in-particular, "but it definitely looks like that was the incongruity."

"*What* was?" Carruthers said. "And who caused it?"

"That's what I needed you to find out in Coventry," I said, looking at my useless pocket watch. "But there's no time."

"Of course there's time," Verity said. "This is a time travel lab. We can send Carruthers back to get the information."

"He can't go back to 1940," I said. "He's already been there. And the last thing we need is to cause another incongruity."

"Not to 1940, Ned. To last week."

"He can't be in two places at once," I said and realized he wouldn't be.

Last week he'd been in 1940, not 2057. "Warder, how long will it take you to calculate a drop?" I said.

"A drop! I've already got three rendez—"

"I'll press the surplices," Verity said.

"I need him to go back for—how long do you think it'll take you? A day?"

"Two," Carruthers said.

"For two days. Weekdays. The church archives aren't open on weekends. And it has to be two days he was in 1940. And then bring him back here immediately."

Warder looked stubborn. "How do I know he won't get trapped in Coventry again?"

"Because of that," I said, pointing at the comp. "The incongruity's fixed."

"It's all right, Peggy," Carruthers said. "Go ahead and calculate it." He turned to me. "You've got the list of what I need to find out?"

I gave it to him. "And one other thing. I need a list of the heads of all the ladies' church committees in 1940."

"I don't have to look up the head of the Flower Committee. I know who it was," he said. "That harpy Miss Sharpe."

"All the ladies' church committees, *including* the Flower Committee," I said.

Verity handed him a pencil and a jotter. "So you won't be tempted to bring any paper from last week through the net with you."

"Ready?" Carruthers said to Warder.

"Ready," she said warily.

He positioned himself in the net. Warder came over and smoothed his collar. "You be careful," she said, straightening his tie.

"I'll only be gone a few minutes," he said, grinning fatuously. "Won't I?"

"If you're not," Warder said, smiling, "I'll come and get you myself."

"I wouldn't have believed it," I murmured to Verity.

"Time-lag," she said.

"I've got it set on a ten-minute intermittent," Warder cooed.

"I won't stay a minute longer than I have to," Carruthers said. "I've got to come back as soon as I can so I can take you to the consecration." He took her in his arms and gave her a lingering kiss.

"Look, I'm sorry to break up this tender scene," I said, "but the consecration's in two hours."

"All *right*," Warder snapped, gave one last smoothing to Carruthers's collar, and stomped back to the console. Love may conquer all, but old dispositions die hard, and I hoped Baine intended to live near a river in the States.

Warder lowered the veils and Carruthers disappeared. "If he's not back safely in ten minutes," she said, "I'm sending *you* to the Hundred Years' War." She turned on Verity. "You promised you'd press the surplices."

"In a minute," I said, handing Verity one of the facsimile sheets.

"What are we looking for?" Verity said.

"Letters to the editor. Or an open letter. I'm not certain."

I leafed through the *Midlands Daily Telegraph.* An article about the King's visit, a casualties list, an article beginning, "There is heartening evidence of Coventry's revival."

I picked up the *Coventry Standard.* An advertisement for ARP Sandbags, Genuine Government Size and Quality 36s 6d per hundred. A picture of the ruins of the cathedral.

"Here are some letters," Verity said, and handed me her sheet.

A letter praising the fire service for their courage. A letter asking if anyone had seen Molly, "a beautiful ginger cat, last seen the night of 14 November, in Greyfriars Lane," a letter complaining about the ARP wardens.

The outside door opened. Verity jumped, but it wasn't Lady Schrapnell. It was Finch.

His butler's frock coat and his hair were flecked with snow, and his right sleeve was drenched.

"Where have you been?" I asked. "Siberia?"

"I am not at liberty to say," he said. He turned to T.J. "Mr. Lewis, where is Mr. Dunworthy?"

"In London," T.J. said, staring at the comp screen.

"Oh," he said, disappointed. "Well, tell him—" he looked warily at us, "—the mission is completed," he wrung out his sleeve, "even though the pond was solid ice, and the water was freezing. Tell him the number of the—" another look at us, "—the number is six."

"And I don't have all day," Warder said. "Here's your bag." She handed him a large burlap sack. "You can't go through like that," she said disgustedly. "Come on. I'll get you dried off." She led him into the prep room. "I'm not even the tech. I'm only substituting. I've got altar cloths to iron, I've got a ten-minute intermittent to run—" The door shut behind them.

"What was that all about?" I said.

"Here," Verity said, handing me a facsimile sheet. "More letters to the editor."

Three letters commenting on the King's visit to Coventry, one complaining about the food at the mobile canteens, one announcing a jumble sale at St. Aldate's for the victims of the air raid.

Finch, dried and combed, came back in with Warder, who was still complaining. "I don't see why you have to bring them all through today," she said, marching over to the console to punch keys. "I've got *three* rendezvouses to bring in, fifty—"

"Finch," I said. "Do you know if Mrs. Bittner intends to attend the consecration?"

"Mr. Dunworthy had me send her an invitation," he said, "and I should have thought she, of all people, would have wanted to see Coventry Cathedral restored, but she wrote to say she was afraid it would be too fatiguing."

"Good," I said, and picked up the *Standard* for the twelfth and paged through it. No letters. "What about the *Telegraph?*" I asked Verity.

"Nothing," she said, putting them down.

"Nothing," I said happily, and Carruthers appeared in the net, looking bemused.

"Well?" I said, going over to him.

He reached in his pocket for the jotter and handed it to me through the veils. I flipped it open and started down the list of church officials, looking for a name. Nothing. I turned the page to the church livings.

"The head of the Flower Committee in 1940 was a Mrs. Lois Warfield," Carruthers said, frowning.

"Are you all right?" Warder said anxiously. "Did something happen?"

"No," I said, scanning the church livings. Hertfordshire, Surrey, Northumberland. There it was. St. Benedict's, Northumberland.

"There was no Miss Sharpe on any of the committees," Carruthers said, "or on the church membership roster."

"I know," I said, scribbling a message on one of the pages of the jotter. "Finch, ring up Mr. Dunworthy and tell him to come back to Oxford immediately. When he gets here, give him this." I tore it out, folded it over, and handed it to him. "Then find Lady Schrapnell and tell her not to worry, Verity and I have everything under control and not to begin the consecration till we get back."

"Where are you going?" Finch said.

"You promised you'd iron the choirboys' surplices," Warder said accusingly.

"We'll try to be back by eleven," I said, taking Verity's hand. "If we're not, stall."

"Stall!" Finch said, horrified. "The Archbishop of Canterbury's coming. And Princess Victoria. How am I supposed to stall?"

"You'll think of something. I have the highest faith in you, Jeeves."

He beamed. "*Thank* you, sir," he said. "Where shall I tell Lady Schrapnell you've gone?"

"To fetch the bishop's bird stump," I said, and Verity and I took off at a lope for the tube station.

The sky outside was gray and overcast. "Oh, I hope it doesn't rain for the consecration," Verity said as we ran.

"Are you joking?" I panted. "Lady Schrapnell would never allow it."

The tube station was jammed. Masses of people, wearing hats and ties and carrying umbrellas, poured up the steps.

"A cathedral!" a girl in braids carrying a Gaia Party sign grumbled as she swept past me. "Do you *know* how many trees we could have planted in Christ Church Meadow for the cost of that *building?*"

"At any rate, we're going out of town," I called to Verity, who'd gotten separated from me. "The trains *out* of Oxford should be less crowded."

We pushed our way over to the escalators. They were no better. I lost sight of Verity and finally found her a dozen steps below me. "Where's everyone going?" I called.

"To meet Princess Victoria," the large woman carrying a Union Jack on the step behind me said. "She's travelling up from Reading."

Verity had reached the bottom of the escalator. "Coventry!" I called to her, pointing over the heads of the crowd toward the Warwickshire Line.

"I know," Verity shouted back, already headed down the corridor.

The corridor was jammed, and so was the platform. Verity pushed her way over to me. "You're not the only one who's good at solving mysteries, Sherlock," she said. "I've even figured out what Finch is up to."

"What?" I said, but a train was pulling in. The crowd surged forward, pushing us apart.

I fought my way over to her again. "Where are all *these* people going? Princess Victoria's not in Coventry."

"They're going to the protest," a boy in braids said. "Coventry's holding a rally to protest the disgraceful theft of their cathedral by Oxford."

"Really?" Verity said sweetly. "Where's it being held? In the shopping center?" and I could have kissed her.

"You realize," she said, pushing a hand-painted sign that read, "Architects Against Coventry Cathedral" out of her face, "that there's probably a time-traveller from a hundred years in the future in this crowd who thinks this is all unbelievably quaint and charming."

"That's impossible," I said. "What *is* Finch up to?"

"He's been—" she started, but the doors were opening and people were jamming onto the train.

We got separated again in the process, and I found myself half a car away from her, shoved into a seat between an old man and his middle-aged son.

"But why rebuild Coventry Cathedral, of all things?" the son was complaining. "If they had to rebuild something that had been destroyed, why not the Bank of England? That would have been of some use at least. What good's a cathedral?"

" 'God works in a mysterious way,' " I quoted, " 'His wonders to perform.' "

Both of them glared at me.

"James Thomson," I said. "*The Seasons.*"

They glared some more.

"Victorian poet," I said, and subsided between them, thinking about the continuum and *its* mysterious ways. It had needed to correct an incongruity, and it had done so, putting into action its entire array of secondary defenses, and shutting down the net, shifting destinations, manipulating the slippage so that I would keep Terence from meeting Maud, and Verity would arrive at the exact moment Baine threw the cat in. To save the cat that killed the rat that ate the malt that lay in the house that Jack built.

"Coventry," the station sign read, and I fought my way out from between the bankers and off the train, motioning to Verity to get off, too. She did, and we fought our way up the escalators and out into Broadgate in front of the statue of Lady Godiva. It looked even more like rain. The protesters were putting their umbrellas up as they started for the shopping center.

"Should we ring her up first?" Verity said.

"No."

"You're sure she'll be at home?"

"I'm sure," I said, not at all certain.

But she was, though it took her a little time to open the door.

"Sorry, I'm having a bout of bronchitis," Mrs. Bittner said hoarsely, and then saw who we were. "Oh," she said.

She stood back so we could enter. "Come in. I've been expecting you." She held out her veined hand to Verity. "You must be Miss Kindle. I understand you are a fan of mystery novels, too."

"Only those of the Thirties," Verity said apologetically.

Mrs. Bittner nodded. "They are quite the best." She turned to me. "I read a great many mystery novels. I am particularly fond of those in which the criminal nearly gets away with the crime."

"Mrs. Bittner," I said, and didn't know how to go on. I looked helplessly at Verity.

"You've puzzled it out, haven't you?" Mrs. Bittner said. "I was afraid you would. James told me you were his two best pupils." She smiled. "Shall we go into the drawing room?"

"I . . . I'm afraid we haven't much time . . ." I stammered.

"Nonsense," she said, starting down the corridor. "The criminal is always given a chapter in which to confess his sins."

She led us into the room where I'd interviewed her. "Won't you sit down?" she said, indicating a chintz-covered sofa. "The famed detective always gathers the suspects together in the drawing room," she said, moving slowly toward a sideboard considerably smaller than the Merings', steadying herself on the furniture, "and the criminal always offers them a drink. Would you care for some sherry, Miss Kindle? Would you care for some sherry, Mr. Henry? Or *sirop de cassis?* That's what Hercule Poirot always drank. Dreadful stuff. I tried it once when I'd been reading Agatha Christie's *Murder in Three Acts*. Tastes like cough medicine."

"Sherry, thank you," I said.

Mrs. Bittner poured two glasses of sherry and turned to hand them to us. "It caused an incongruity, didn't it?"

I took the glasses from her, handed one to Verity, and sat down beside her. "Yes," I said.

"I was so afraid it had. And when James told me last week about the theory regarding nonsignificant objects being removed from their space-time location, I knew it must have been the bishop's bird stump." She shook her head, smiling. "Everything else that was in the cathedral that night would have burned to ashes, but I could see by looking at it that it was indestructible."

She poured herself a glass of sherry. "I tried to undo what I'd done, you know, but I couldn't get the net to open, and then Lassiter—that was the head of faculty—put on new locks, and I couldn't get into the lab. I should have told James, of course. Or my husband. But I couldn't bear to." She picked up the glass of sherry. "I told myself the net's refusing to open meant that there hadn't been an incongruity after all, that no harm had been done, but I knew it wasn't true."

She started for one of the chintz-covered chairs, moving slowly and carefully. I jumped up and took the glass of sherry for her till she had sat down.

"Thank you," she said, taking it from me. "James told me what a nice young man you were." She looked at Verity. "I don't suppose either of you have ever done something you were sorry for afterward? Something you'd done without thinking?"

She looked down at her sherry. "The Church of England was shutting down the cathedrals that couldn't support themselves. My husband loved Coventry Cathedral. He was descended from the Botoner family who built the original church."

And so are you, I thought, realizing now who it was Mary Botoner had reminded me of, standing there in the tower arguing with the workman. You're a descendant of the Botoners, too.

"The cathedral was his life," she went on. "He always said that it wasn't the church building that mattered, but what it symbolized, yet the new cathedral, ugly as it was, was everything to him. I thought if I could bring back some of the treasures from the old cathedral," she said, "it would be good publicity. The tourists would flock to see them, and the cathedral wouldn't have to be sold. I thought it would kill my husband if it had to be sold."

"But hadn't Darby and Gentilla proved it was impossible to bring things forward through the net?"

"Yes," she said, "but I thought since the things had ceased to exist in their own space-time, they might come through. Darby and Gentilla had never tried to bring through anything that didn't still exist in its own time." She twisted the stem of the glass in her hands. "And I was fairly desperate."

She looked up. "So I broke into the lab late one night, went back to 1940, and did it. And the next day, James telephoned to tell me that if I wanted a job, that Lassiter had authorized a series of drops to Waterloo, and then he told me—" She stopped, staring into the past. "—he told me that Shoji had had a breakthrough in temporal theory, that he'd discovered why it was impossible to bring things forward through the net, that such an action would cause an incongruity that could change the course of history, or worse."

"So you tried to take it back?" Verity said.

"Yes. And I went and saw Shoji and made him tell me as much as I could about incongruities without making him suspicious. It was all bad, but the worst was that he told me they'd been able to adapt the net to safeguard against them, and weren't we lucky one hadn't happened before we did, we could have caused the collapse of the entire space-time continuum."

I looked over at Verity. She was watching Mrs. Bittner, her beautiful face sad.

"So I hid the swag, as they say in the mystery novels, and waited for the world to end. Which it did. The cathedral was deconsecrated and sold to the Church of the Hereafter and then turned into a shopping center."

She stared into her sherry. "The irony is that it was all for nothing. My husband loved Salisbury. I had been so convinced that losing Coventry Cathedral would kill him, but it didn't. He truly meant that about churches being only a symbol. He didn't seem to mind even when they built a Marks and Spencer's on the ruins." She smiled warmly. "Do you know what he said when he heard Lady Schrapnell was rebuilding the old cathedral? He said, 'I hope this time they get the spire on straight.' "

She set her glass down. "After Harold died, I came back here. And two weeks ago James telephoned and asked me if I could remember anything about the drops we'd done together, that there was an area of increased slippage in 2018, and he was afraid it was due to an incongruity. I knew then it was just a matter of time before I was found out, even though he had the wrong incongruity." She looked up at us. "James told me about the cat and Tossie Mering. Did you manage to get Lady Schrapnell's great-great-grandmother married to the mysterious Mr. C?"

"Not exactly," I said. "She did marry him, but it was no thanks to us."

"It was the butler," Verity said, "under an assumed name."

"Of course," Mrs. Bittner said, clapping her veined hands together. "The old solutions are always the best. The butler, the case of mistaken identity, the least likely suspect—" She looked at us both meaningfully, "—the purloined letter." She stood up. "I hid it in the attic."

We started up the stairs. "I was afraid moving it might make things worse," she said, taking the steps slowly, "so I left the loot here when we went to Salisbury. I made certain it was well-hidden, and I took care to rent the house to people without children—children are so curious, you know—but I was always afraid someone would come up here and find it and do something that would change the course of history." She turned back, holding onto the banister, and looked at me. "But it already had, hadn't it?"

"Yes," I said.

She didn't say anything more. She seemed to be concentrating all her effort on climbing the stairs. When we reached the first floor, she led us down a corridor past a bedroom and opened a narrow door onto another, steeper flight of stairs. "This leads up to the attic," she said, panting a little. "I'm sorry. I need to rest a bit before going on. There's a chair in the bedroom."

I ran to fetch it, and she sat down on it. "Would you like a glass of water?" Verity asked.

"No, thank you, dear," she said. "Tell me about the incongruity I caused."

"You weren't the only person who considered the bishop's bird stump indestructible," I said. "So did the chairman of the Flower Committee named—"

"Delphinium Sharpe," Verity said.

I nodded. "She had been there the night of the raid, standing guard by the west door, and she knew the bishop's bird stump couldn't have been carried out. When it wasn't found in the rubble or among the things the fire watch had saved, she concluded it had been stolen some time before the raid and that the thief must have known about the raid in advance, knowing he could get away with it. She was quite vocal with her theory—"

"She even wrote a letter to the editor of one of the Coventry papers," Verity put in.

I nodded. "This next part is only a theory, like Miss Sharpe's," I said. "The only evidence we have is Carruthers's testimony, the list of ladies' church committees for 1940, and a letter to the editor that wasn't in either of the Coventry papers."

Mrs. Bittner nodded sagely. "The incident of the dog in the nighttime."

"Exactly," I said. "The Nazis made it a practice to obtain and read Allied newspapers, looking for any intelligence information that might be inadvertently revealed. I think Miss Sharpe's letter and the words 'advance warning of the raid' must have caught the eye of someone in Nazi intelligence who was worried about the Nazi code system being compromised, and that inquiries were subsequently made, inquiries that revealed the High Command had dispatched RAF fighters to Coventry that night and had attempted to jam the pathfinder beams."

"And the Nazis realized we had Ultra," Verity said, "and changed the Enigma machine."

"And we lost the campaign in North Africa," I said, "and possibly the D-Day invasion—"

"And the Nazis won the war," Mrs. Bittner said bleakly. "Only they didn't. You stopped them."

"The continuum stopped them with its system of secondary defenses, which is almost as good as Ultra's," I said. "The one thing that didn't fit in this whole mess was the slippage on Verity's drop. If there hadn't been any slippage, that might have meant the continuum's defenses had somehow broken down, but there had been. But not enough to fit Fujisaki's theory that incongruities occur when the slippage required is more than the net can supply. The net could easily have supplied fourteen minutes of slippage, or four, which would have been all that would have been necessary to keep the incongruity from ever happening. So the only logical conclusion was that it had intended for Verity to go through at that exact moment—"

"Are you saying the continuum arranged for me to save Princess Arjumand?" Verity said.

"Yes," I said. "Which made us think you'd caused an incongruity and we had to fix it, which is why we arranged a séance to get Tossie to Coventry to see the bishop's bird stump and write in her diary that the experience had changed her life—"

"And Lady Schrapnell would read it," Verity said, "and decide to rebuild Coventry Cathedral and send me back to Muchings End to find out what happened to the bishop's bird stump, so I could save the cat—"

"So I could be sent back to return it and overhear a conversation about mystery novels in Blackwell's and spend a night in a tower—"

"And solve the mystery of the bishop's bird stump," Mrs. Bittner said. She stood up and started up the stairs. "I'm glad you did, you know," she said, leading the way up the narrow stairs. "There is nothing heavier than the weight of a secret crime."

She opened the door to the attic. "I should have been found out soon at any rate. My nephew's been lobbying me to move into a single-floor flat."

Attics in books and vids are always picturesque places, with a bicycle, several large plumed hats, an antique rocking horse, and, of course, a steamer trunk for storing the missing will or the dead body in.

Mrs. Bittner's attic didn't have a trunk, or a rocking horse, at least that

I could see. Though they might easily have been there, along with the lost Ark of the Covenant and the Great Pyramid of Giza.

"Oh, dear," Mrs. Bittner said, looking round in dismay. "I'm afraid it's more *The Sittaford Mystery* than 'The Purloined Letter.' "

"Agatha Christie," Verity explained. "Nobody noticed the evidence because it'd been stuck in a cupboard with a bag of golf clubs and tennis rackets and a lot of other things."

"A lot of other things" was putting it mildly. The low-raftered room was crammed from end to end with cardboard cartons, stacked lawn chairs, old clothes hanging from an exposed pipe, jigsaw puzzles of the Grand Canyon and the Mars colony, a croquet set, squash rackets, dusty Christmas decorations, books, and an assortment of bedspread-draped furniture, all stacked on top of each other in sedimentary layers.

"Could you reach me down that chair?" Mrs. Bittner said, pointing at a Twentieth Century plastiform atrocity perched on top of a washing machine. "I have difficulty standing for very long."

I got it down, disentangling a trowel and several coat hangers from its aluminum legs, and dusted it off for her.

She sat down, easing herself into it gingerly. "Thank you," she said. "Hand that tin box to me."

I handed it to her reverently.

She set it down beside her on the floor. "And those large pasteboard boxes. Just push them aside. And those suitcases."

I did, and she stood up and walked down the little aisle my shifting the boxes had made and into darkness.

"Plug in a lamp," she said. "There's an outlet over there." She pointed at the wall behind an enormous plastic aspidistra.

I reached for the nearest lamp, a massive affair with a huge pleated shade and a squat, heavily decorated metal base.

"Not that one," she said sharply. "The pink one."

She pointed at a tall, early Twenty-First Century fringed affair.

I plugged it in and switched on the hard-to-find knob, but it didn't do much good. It lit the fringe and Verity's Waterhouse face, but not much else.

Apparently Mrs. Bittner thought so, too. She went over to the ornate metal lamp. "*The Masqued Murder*," she said.

Verity leaned forward. "Evidence disguised as something else," she murmured.

"Exactly," Mrs. Bittner said, and lifted the pleated shade off bishop's bird stump.

It was too bad Lady Schrapnell wasn't here. And Carruthers. All that time we had spent searching for it in the rubble, and it was here all along. Removed for safekeeping, as Carruthers had suggested, and not a mark on it. The Red Sea still parted; Springtime, Summer, Autumn, and Winter still held their respective garlands of apple blossoms, roses, wheat, and holly; John the Baptist, his head still on the platter, still stared reproachfully at King Arthur and his Knights of the Round Table. Gryphons, poppies, pineapples, puffins, the Battle of Prestonpans, all of it intact and not even dusty.

"Lady Schrapnell will be so pleased," Verity said. She squeezed down the aisle to look at it more closely. "Good heavens. That side must have been facing the wall. What are those? Fans?"

"Clams. Clams inscribed with the names of important naval battles," I said. "Lepanto, Trafalgar, the Battle of the Swans."

"It's difficult imagining it changing the course of history," Mrs. Bittner said, peering at Shadrach, Meshach, and Abednego in the fiery furnace. "It doesn't improve with age, does it? Like the Albert Memorial."

"With which it has a good deal in common," Verity said, touching an elephant.

"I don't know," I said, cocking my head to look at it sideways. "I'm beginning to feel a certain affection for it."

"He's time-lagged," Verity said. "Ned, the elephant's carrying a howdah full of pineapples and bananas to an eagle with a fish fork."

"It's not a fish fork," I said. "It's a flaming sword. And it's not an eagle, it's an archangel, guarding the entrance to the Garden of Eden. Or possibly the Zoo."

"It *is* truly hideous," Mrs. Bittner said. "I don't know what I was thinking of. After all those trips, I was probably a bit time-lagged myself. And there was a good deal of smoke."

Verity turned to stare at her, and then at me.

"How many trips did you make?" she said finally.

"Four," Mrs. Bittner said. "No, five. The first one didn't count. I came through too late. The whole nave was on fire, and I was nearly overcome by smoke inhalation. I still have trouble with my lungs."

Verity was still staring at her, trying to take it in. "You made five trips to the cathedral?"

Mrs. Bittner nodded. "I only had a few minutes between the time the fire watch left and the fire got out of hand, and the slippage kept putting me later than I wanted. Five was all I had time for."

Verity looked disbelievingly at me.

"Hand me down the bandbox," Mrs. Bittner told her. "The second time I nearly got caught."

"That was me," I said. "I saw you running toward the sanctuary."

"That was you?" she said, laughing, her hand on her chest. "I thought it was Provost Howard, and I was going to be arrested for a looter."

Verity handed her the bandbox, and she took off the lid and began rummaging through the tissue paper. "I took the bishop's bird stump on the last trip. I was trying to reach the Smiths' Chapel, but it was on fire. I ran across to the Dyers' Chapel and got the bronze candlesticks off the altar, but they were too hot. I dropped the first one, and it rolled away under one of the pews."

And I found it, I thought, and thought it had been blown there by concussion.

"I went after it," she said, digging matter-of-factly through tissue paper, "but the rafters were coming down, so I ran back up the nave, and I saw that the organ was on fire, it was all on fire—the woodwork and the choir and the sanctuary—that beautiful, beautiful cathedral—and I couldn't save any of it. I didn't think, I just grabbed the nearest thing I could find, and ran for the net, spilling chrysanthemums and water everywhere." She took out a wad of tissue paper and unwrapped a bronze candlestick. "That's why there's only one."

Mr. Dunworthy had said she was absolutely fearless, and she must have been, darting back and forth between crashing beams and falling incendiaries, the net opening on who-knows-what and no guarantee it would stay open, no guarantee the roof wouldn't fall in. I looked at her in admiration.

"Ned," she ordered, "bring me that painting. The one with the bedspread over it."

I did, and she pulled the bedspread off a painting of Christ with the lost lamb in his arms. Verity, standing beside me, clasped my hand.

"The rest of the things are over there," Mrs. Bittner said. "Under the plastic."

And they were. The embroidered altar cloth from the Smiths' Chapel. An engraved pewter chalice. A Sixteenth-Century wooden chest. A small statue of St. Michael. A mediaeval enameled pyx. A silver candelabrum with the candles still in it. A misericord carved with one of the Seven Works of Mercy. The capper's pall. A Georgian altar plate. And the wooden cross from the Girdlers' Chapel, with the image of a child kneeling at the foot of it.

All the treasures of Coventry Cathedral.

*"Harris said he thought it was a very fine maze, so far as he was a judge; and we agreed that we would try to get George to go into it, on our way back."*

Three Men in a Boat
Jerome K. Jerome

# CHAPTER TWENTY-EIGHT

Deliveries—Finch Stalls—Lady Schrapnell Is Missing—Realizing
What It Means—A Letter—The Mystery of Princess Arjumand
Solved—Proposing in English—Reasons to Get Married—The
Mystery of Finch's Mission Solved—A New Mystery—Lady
Schrapnell Sees the Bishop's Bird Stump—The San Francisco
Earthquake—Fate—A Happy Ending

Verity was the first one to recover. "It's forty-five minutes till the consecration," she said, looking at her watch. "We'll never make it."

"We'll make it," I said, grabbing up the handheld.

I rang up Mr. Dunworthy. "We've got it," I said. "We need you to get us back to Oxford. Can you send a heli?"

"Princess Victoria's attending the consecration," he said, which didn't seem to be an answer to my question.

"Security measures," Verity explained. "No helis, aircraft, or zoomers allowed in the vicinity."

"Can you arrange ground transport then?" I asked Mr. Dunworthy.

"The tube's faster than any ground transport that we can send," he said. "Why not just bring it on the tube?"

"We can't," I said. "We need at least," I looked over at the treasures, which Verity was already carting down the attic stairs, "270 to three hundred cubic feet of transport space."

"For the bishop's bird stump?" he said. "It hasn't grown, has it?"

"I'll explain when I get there," I said. I gave him Mrs. Bittner's address. "Have a crew waiting for us when we get there," I said. "*Don't* let the consecration begin till we arrive. Is Finch there?"

"No, he's over at the cathedral," Mr. Dunworthy said.

"Tell him to *stall*," I said. "And don't let Lady Schrapnell find out about this if you can help it. Ring me back as soon as you've arranged for transport."

I stuck the handheld in my blazer pocket, picked up the bishop's bird stump, and started down the stairs with it. The handheld rang.

"Ned," Lady Schrapnell said. "Where have you been? The consecration's in less than three-quarters of an hour!"

"I know," I said. "We're coming as fast as we can, but we need transport. Can you arrange for a lorry? Or tube transport?"

"Tube transport is only for cargo," she said. "I don't want you to let the bishop's bird stump out of your sight for one second. It's been lost once. I don't want it lost again."

"Neither do I," I said and rang off.

I picked up the bishop's bird stump again. The handheld rang.

It was Mr. Dunworthy. "You will not believe what that woman wants us to do! She wants you to take the bishop's bird stump to the nearest net and take it back in time to two days ago so it can be cleaned and polished before the consecration."

"Did you tell her that's impossible, that objects can't be in two places at the same time?"

"Of course I told her, and she said—"

" 'Laws are made to be broken,' " I said. "I know. Are you sending us a lorry?"

"There's not a single lorry in Coventry. Lady Schrapnell recruited every single one in four counties for the consecration. Carruthers is ringing up car and solar rental agencies."

"But we've got to have three hundred cubic feet," I said. "Can't you send a lorry from Oxford?"

"Princess Victoria," he said. "It would take hours to get there."

"Because of all the traffic," Verity interpreted.

"If there's too much traffic for a lorry to get to us, how are we supposed to get to the cathedral?"

"Everyone will be at the cathedral by the time you arrive. Oh, good," he said to someone else. "Carruthers has got hold of a rental agency."

"Good," I said, and thought of something. "Don't send a solar. It's overcast here, looks like it might rain at any minute."

"Oh, dear. Lady Schrapnell's determined to have the sun shining for the consecration," he said, and rang off.

This time I made it all the way down to the second floor with the bishop's bird stump before the handheld rang again. It was Mr. Dunworthy again. "We're sending a car."

"A car won't be big enough for—" I began.

"It should be there in ten minutes," he said. "T.J. needs to talk to you about the incongruity."

"Tell him I'll talk to him when I get back," I said, and rang off.

The handheld rang. I switched it off and finished carrying the bishop's bird stump down to the little foyer, which was already filled with things.

"They're sending a car," I said to Verity. "It should be here in ten minutes," and went in the parlor to see Mrs. Bittner.

"They're sending a car to take us to the consecration," I told her. She was sitting in one of the chintz-covered chairs. "Can I fetch you your coat? Or your bag?"

"No, thank you," she said quietly. "You're certain it's a good idea to take the bishop's bird stump out into the world, that it won't alter history?"

"It already has," I said. "And so have you. You realize what you've done means, don't you? Because of you, we've discovered a whole class of objects which can be brought forward through the net. Other treasures which were destroyed by fire. Artworks and books and—"

"Sir Richard Burton's writings," she said. She looked up at me. "His wife burnt them after he died. Because she loved him."

I sat down on the sofa. "Do you not want us to take the bishop's bird stump?" I said.

"No." She shook her white head. "No. It belongs in the cathedral."

I leaned forward and took her hands. "Because of you, the past won't be as irretrievable as we thought it was."

"Parts of the past," she said quietly. "You'd best go bring the rest of the things down."

I nodded and started back up to the attic. Halfway up the stairs I ran into Verity, carefully carrying down the capper's pall on her outstretched arms.

"It's simply *amazing*," she said in a very good imitation of Mrs. Mering's voice, "the treasures people have in their attics."

I grinned at her and went on up. I brought down the children's cross and the altar plate and was on my way down with the Sixteenth-Century wooden chest when Verity called up the stairs to me. "The car's here."

"It's not a solar, is it?" I called down to her.

"No," she said. "It's a hearse."

"Does it have the coffin in it?"

"No."

"Good. Then it should be large enough," I said, and carried out the chest.

It was an ancient fossil-fueled hearse which looked like it had been used in the Pandemic, but it was at least large and opened at the back. The driver was staring at the heap of treasures. "Having a jumble sale, are you?"

"Yes," I said, and put the chest in the back.

"It'll never all fit," he said.

I shoved the chest as far forward as it would go and took the silver candelabrum Verity handed me. "It'll fit," I said. "I am an old hand at packing. Give me that."

It all fit, though the only way we could make it work was by putting the statue of St. Michael in the front seat. "Mrs. Bittner can sit up front," I told Verity, "but you and I will have to sit in the back."

"What about the bishop's bird stump?" she said.

"It can sit on my lap."

I went back inside to the parlor. "We've got the car loaded," I said to Mrs. Bittner, "are you ready?" even though it was obvious she wasn't. She was still sitting quietly in the chintz-covered chair.

She shook her head. "I will not be going with you after all," she said. "My bronchitis—"

"Not going?" Verity said from the door. "But you're the one who saved the treasures. You should go and see them in the cathedral."

"I have already seen them in the cathedral," she said. "They cannot look any more beautiful than they did that night, among the flames."

"Your husband would want you there," Verity said. "He *loved* the cathedral."

"It is only an outward symbol of a larger reality," she said. "Like the continuum."

The driver stuck his head in the door. "I thought you said you were in a hurry."

"We're coming," I said over my shoulder.

"Please come," Verity said, kneeling beside the chair. "You should *be* there."

"Nonsense," Mrs. Bittner said. "You don't see the guilty party accompanying Harriet and Lord Peter on their honeymoon, do you? No. The guilty party is left alone to contemplate his sins and consider the consequences of his actions, which is what I intend to do. Although in my case, the consequences are not quite what one would have expected. They take a bit of getting used to. I have been wearing sackcloth and ashes so long."

She flashed us a sudden smile, and I saw all at once what Jim Dunworthy and Shoji Fujisaki and Bitty Bittner had all fallen in love with.

"You're certain you won't come?" Verity said, fighting back tears.

"Next week. When my bronchitis is better," she said. "I'll let you two give me a personal tour."

"You said you had to be in Oxford by eleven," the driver said. "You'll never make it."

"We'll make it," I said, and helped Mrs. Bittner to her feet so she could walk us out to the car.

"You're certain you'll be all right?" Verity said.

Mrs. Bittner patted Verity's hand. "Perfectly all right. Everything has turned out far better than could have been expected. The Allies have won World War II," she smiled that Zuleika Dobson smile again, "and I have got that hideous bishop's bird stump out of my attic. What could be better?"

"I couldn't see over the cross, so I put it up front," the driver said. "You two will have to sit in the back."

I kissed Mrs. Bittner on the cheek. "Thank you," I said and crawled in. The driver handed me the bishop's bird stump. I set it on my lap. Verity crawled in across from me, waving to Mrs. Bittner, and we were off and running.

I turned the handheld back on and rang up Mr. Dunworthy. "We're on our way," I said. "We should be there in about forty minutes. Tell Finch he needs to keep stalling. Have you arranged to have a crew there to meet us?"

"Yes," he said.

"Good. Is the archbishop there yet?"

"No, but Lady Schrapnell is, and she's having a fit. She wants to know where you found the bishop's bird stump and what sort of flowers are supposed to go in it. For the order of service."

"Tell her yellow chrysanthemums," I said.

I rang off. "All taken care of," I said to Verity.

"Not quite, Sherlock," she said, sitting against the side of the hearse with her knees hunched up. "There are still a few things that need explaining."

"I agree," I said. "You said you knew what Finch's related mission was. What is it?"

"Bringing back nonsignificant objects," she said.

"Nonsignificant objects? But we've only just found out that's possible," I said. "And nonsignificant objects didn't have anything to do with our incongruity."

"True," she said, "but for over a week, T.J. and Mr. Dunworthy thought they did and were trying all sorts of things."

"But nothing burned down in Muchings End or Iffley while we were there. What did Finch bring through? Cabbages?"

The handheld rang. "Ned," Lady Schrapnell said. "Where *are* you?"

"On our way," I said. "Between—" I leaned forward to our driver. "Where are we?"

"Between Banbury and Adderbury," he said.

"Between Banbury and Adderbury," I said. "We'll be there as soon as we can."

"I still don't see why we couldn't have shipped it back to the past," Lady Schrapnell said. "It would have been so much simpler. Is the bishop's bird stump in good shape?"

There was no answer to that. "We'll be there as soon as we can," I said again, and rang off.

"All right, it's my turn to ask the questions," Verity said. "There's still something I don't understand. How did getting Tossie to Coventry on the fifteenth of June to see the bishop's bird stump and fall in love with Baine fix the incongruity?"

"It didn't," I said. "That isn't why Tossie was there."

"But her seeing the bishop's bird stump inspired Lady Schrapnell to rebuild Coventry and send me back to read the diary, which led me to rescue Princess Arjumand—"

"Which was all part of the self-correction. But the *principal* reason Tossie had to be there on the fifteenth was so she could be caught flirting with the Reverend Mr. Doult."

"Oh!" she said. "By the girl with the penwipers."

"Very good, Harriet," I said. "The girl with the penwipers. Whose name was Miss Delphinium Sharpe."

"The woman in charge of the Flower Committee."

"Not anymore," I said. "When she saw Tossie flirting with the Reverend Mr. Doult, she was, you may remember, extremely upset. She flounced off with her penwipers, and as we were leaving the church, she was walking up Bayley Lane, her long nose in the air. I saw the Reverend Mr. Doult hurrying after her to placate her. And, now this is the part I'm not certain of, but my guess is, in the course of the argument that followed, she burst into tears, and he ended up proposing. Which meant that the Reverend Mr. Doult didn't stay in the cathedral position, but obtained a church living in some rural vicarage."

"That's why you wanted the list of church livings."

"*Very* good, Harriet. He was much quicker off the mark than I expected. He married her in 1891 and got a parish the following year in Northumberland."

"So she was nowhere near Coventry on the night of the fourteenth of November, 1940," she said. "And, being busy with parish jumble sales and scrap metal drives, paid no attention to a certain bishop's bird stump being missing."

"So she didn't write a letter to the editor," I said, "and everyone else just assumed it had burned up in the fire."

"And Ultra's secret was safe." She frowned. "And the whole thing, my rescuing Princess Arjumand and us going to Oxford to see Madame Iritosky and your preventing Terence from meeting Maud and loaning him the money for the boat and the séance and everything, it was all part of the self-correction? Everything?"

"Everything," I said, and then thought about what I'd said. Just how elaborate had the self-correction been and what all had been involved? Professor Peddick's and Professor Overforce's feud? The Psychic Research Society? The donation of the sugared-violets box to the jumble sale? The fur-bearing ladies in Blackwell's?

"I still don't understand," Verity said. "If all the continuum needed to do was to keep Delphinium Sharpe from writing a letter to the editor, there had to be simpler ways to do it."

"It's a chaotic system," I said. "Every event is connected to every other. To make even a small change would require far-reaching adjustments."

But how far-reaching? I wondered. Had the Luftwaffe been involved? And Agatha Christie? And the weather?

"I *know* it's a chaotic system, Ned," Verity was saying. "But there was an air raid going on. If the self-correction's an automatic mechanism, a direct hit would have corrected the incongruity much more simply and directly than some scheme involving cats and trips to Coventry."

A direct hit from a high-explosive bomb would have eliminated any threat Delphinium Sharpe posed to Ultra, and there wouldn't have been any consequences. Over five hundred people had been killed in Coventry that night.

"Perhaps Delphinium Sharpe, or one of the other people in the west door that night, had some other part to play in history," I said, thinking of the stout ARP warden and the woman with the two children.

"I'm not talking about Delphinium Sharpe," Verity said. "I'm talking about the bishop's bird stump. If the Smiths' Chapel had taken a direct hit, Miss Sharpe would have believed the bishop's bird stump was destroyed and wouldn't have written her letter. Or it could have taken a direct hit before Lizzie Bittner came through, so she couldn't cause the incongruity in the first place."

She was right. A direct hit was all it would have taken. Unless the high-explosive bomb would alter something else. Or unless the bishop's bird stump had some other part to play in the plan. Or the continuum had some other, subtler reason for using the correction it had.

Plans, intentions, reasons. I could hear Professor Overforce now. "I knew it! This is nothing but an argument for a Grand Design!"

A Grand Design we couldn't see because we were part of it. A Grand Design we only got occasional, fleeting glimpses of. A Grand Design involving the entire course of history and all of time and space that, for some unfathomable reason, chose to work out its designs with cats and croquet mallets and penwipers, to say nothing of the dog. And a hideous piece of Victorian artwork. And us.

"History is character," Professor Peddick had said. And character had certainly played a part in the self-correction—Lizzie Bittner's devotion to her husband and the Colonel's refusal to wear a coat in rainy weather, Verity's fondness for cats and Princess Arjumand's fondness for fish and Hitler's temper and Mrs. Mering's gullibility. And my time-laggedness. If they were part of the self-correction, what did that do to the notion of free will? Or was free will part of the plan as well?

"There's something else I don't understand," Verity said. "The incongruity was repaired when Tossie eloped with Baine, right?"

I nodded.

"Then why was Delphinium Sharpe there? Didn't T.J. say the probabilities collapsed into the true course of events as soon as the incongruity was repaired?"

"But the incongruity *hadn't* been repaired when we were there," I said. "Baine had thrown Tossie in the water, but they hadn't run off together yet. And until they did, the incongruity still wasn't completely repaired."

"Of course they had. They'd run off together on June eighteenth, 1888. And it was a foregone conclusion once he kissed her, so why were we sent to Coventry at all? It obviously wasn't to make Tossie elope with Baine."

I knew the answer to that one at least. "To find the bishop's bird stump," I said. "I needed to see the doors and the empty wrought-iron stand to realize what had happened."

"But why?" she said, still frowning. "It could have fixed it without even letting us know it had."

"Out of pity?" I said. "Because it knew Lady Schrapnell would kill me if I didn't find it in time for the consecration?"

But she was right. The bishop's bird stump could have continued to sit in Mrs. Bittner's attic, gathering dust, now that the incongruity was fixed and the Nazis hadn't found out about Ultra. So why had I been sent to the lab in 2018 and to Blackwell's and the air raid and been given such obvious clues if it hadn't mattered whether the bishop's bird stump was found or not? Would its eventual discovery after Mrs. Bittner's death have caused some other incongruity? Or was there some reason it needed to be in the cathedral for the consecration?

"We're coming up on Oxford," the driver said. "Where do you want me to go?"

"Just a minute," I said and rang up Mr. Dunworthy.

Finch answered. "Thank goodness," he said. "Take Parks Road to Holywell and Longwell and then turn south on the High and turn off onto Merton's playing fields. Take the access road. We'll be waiting for you at the vestry door. Do you know where that is?"

"Yes," I said. "Did you get that?" I asked the driver.

He nodded. "You're taking this lot to the cathedral?"

"Yes."

"Waste of money and everybody's time, if you ask me," he said. "I mean, what good is a cathedral?"

"You'd be surprised," Verity said.

"Turn in here," I said, looking for Merton's pedestrian gate. "Finch, we're here," I said into the handheld, and to the driver again, "Go round to the east end. The vestry door's on the south side."

He pulled up next to the vestry door, where Finch had a dozen people waiting for us. One of them opened the back door, and Verity scrambled out and started giving orders. "The altar cloth goes in the Smiths' Chapel," she said, "and so does this candlestick. Take care you don't get the reconstructions mixed up with the real things. Ned, hand me the capper's pall."

I laid it over her outstretched arms, and she started up the steps with it.

I picked up the handheld. "Finch, where are you?"

"Right here, sir," he said at the door of the hearse. He was still in his butler's frock coat, though his sleeve was now dry.

I handed him the enameled pyx. "The consecration hasn't begun yet, has it?"

"No, sir," he said. "There was an unfortunate jam-up in St. Aldate's. Fire engines and ambulances completely blocking the street. It turned out to have all been an unfortunate mix-up," he said, completely poker-faced, "but it took some time to clear up. No one was able to get near Christ Church Meadow for nearly an hour. And then the bishop was delayed. His driver took a wrong turn and ended up in Iffley. And now there seems to be some mix-up over the tickets."

I shook my head admiringly. "Jeeves would have been proud of you. To say nothing of Bunter. And the Admirable Crichton." I lifted out the bishop's bird stump.

"Can I take that for you, sir?"

"I want to deliver this myself." I nodded with my head at the children's cross. "That goes in the Girdlers' Chapel. And the statue of St. Michael goes in the choir."

"Yes, sir," he said. "Mr. Lewis is looking for you. He has something he needs to discuss with you concerning the continuum."

"Fine," I said, wrestling with the misericord. "As soon as this mess is over."

"Yes, sir," he said. "And at some point, sir, I need to speak with you about my mission."

"Just tell me one thing," I said, sliding the misericord out and handing it over to two first-year students. "Was your mission bringing back nonsignificant objects?"

He looked appalled. "It most certainly was not."

I picked up the bishop's bird stump. "Do you know where Lady Schrapnell is?"

"She was in the vestry a moment ago, sir." He looked up at the sky. "Oh dear, it's looking more and more like rain. And Lady Schrapnell wanted everything to be just as it was on the day of the raid."

I carried the bishop's bird stump up the steps and in the vestry door, and this was appropriate: carrying the bishop's bird stump in through the same door Provost Howard had carried the candlesticks and the crucifix and the Regimental Colors out of. The treasures of Coventry.

I opened the door and took it into the vestry. "Where's Lady Schrapnell?" I asked an historian I recognized from Jesus.

She shrugged and shook her head. "No," she called to someone in the sanctuary. "We still need hymnals for the last five rows of pews in the north aisle. And three Books of Common Prayer."

I went out into the choir. And chaos. People were running about, shouting orders, and there was a loud sound of hammering from the Mercers' Chapel.

"Who took the Book of the Epistles?" a curate shouted from the lectern. "It was here just a moment ago."

There was a chord from the organ, and the opening notes of "God Works in a Mysterious Way His Wonders to Perform." A thin woman in a green apron was sticking long pink gladiolas in a brass vase in front of the pulpit, and a stout woman in glasses with a sheet of paper was going up to person after person, asking them something. Probably she was looking for Lady Schrapnell, too.

The organ stopped, and the organist shouted up to someone in the clerestory, "The trumpet stop's not working." Choirboys in linen surplices and red cassocks were wandering about. Warder must have got the surplices ironed, I thought irrelevantly.

"I don't see what it matters whether the inside of the choir stalls is finished," a blonde with a long nose was saying to a boy lying half under one of the choir stalls. "Nobody will be able to see it from the congregation."

" 'Ours is not to reason why,' " the boy said. " 'Ours is but to do or die.' Hand me that laser, will you?"

"Pardon me," I said. "Can either of you tell me where Lady Schrapnell is?"

"The last time I saw her," the boy said from under the choir stall, "she was in the Drapers' Chapel."

But she wasn't in the Drapers' Chapel, or the sanctuary, or up in the clerestory. I went down into the nave.

Carruthers was there, sitting in a pew folding orders of service.

"Have you seen Lady Schrapnell?" I said.

"She was just here," he said disgustedly. "Which is how I got stuck doing this. She suddenly decided at the last minute that the orders of service had to be reprinted." He looked up. "Good Lord, you found it! Where was it?"

"It's a long story," I said. "Which way did she go?"

"Vestry. Wait. Before you go, I want to ask you something. What do you think of Peggy?"

"Peggy?"

"Warder," he said. "Don't you think she's the sweetest, most adorable creature you've ever seen?"

"Don't you have the orders of service folded yet?" Warder said, coming up. "Lady Schrapnell wants them for the ushers."

"Where is she?" I asked her.

"The Mercers' Chapel," Warder said, and I made my escape.

But Lady Schrapnell wasn't in the Mercers' Chapel or the baptistry, and there were signs of activity near the west door. I was going to have to return the bishop's bird stump myself.

I carried it across to the Smiths' Chapel, thinking, now the wrought-iron stand will have disappeared, but it was there, right where it was supposed to be, in front of the parclose screen. I set the bishop's bird stump carefully on it.

Flowers. It needed flowers. I went back up to the pulpit and the woman in the green apron. "The vase in front of the parclose screen of the Smiths' Chapel needs flowers in it," I said. "Yellow chrysanthemums."

"Yellow chrysanthemums!" she said, snatching up a handheld and looking at it in alarm. "Did Lady Schrapnell send you? The order didn't say anything about yellow chrysanthemums."

"It's a last-minute addition," I said. "You haven't seen Lady Schrapnell, have you?"

"Girdlers' Chapel," she said, jamming gladiolas in the pulpit vase. "Chrysanthemums! Where am I supposed to get yellow chrysanthemums?"

I started down the transept aisle. It was jammed with choirboys and people in academic dress. "All right!" a young man the spitting image of the Reverend Mr. Arbitage said. "Here's the order of procession. First, the censer, followed by the choir. Then the members of the history faculty, by college. Mr. Ransome, where is your robe? The instructions clearly said full academic regalia."

I sidled back along one of the pews to the north aisle and started up the nave. And saw Mr. Dunworthy.

He was at the entrance to the Girdlers' Chapel, standing against one of the arches and holding onto it for support. He was holding a sheet of paper, and as I watched, it fluttered from his hand onto the floor.

"What is it?" I said, hurrying up to him. "Are you all right?"

I put my arm round him. "Come here," I said, leading him to the nearest pew. "Sit down." I retrieved the piece of paper and sat down next to him. "What is it?"

He smiled a little wanly at me. "I was just looking at the children's cross," he said, pointing to where it hung in the Girdlers' Chapel. "And realizing what it means. We were so busy trying to solve the incongruity and pull Carruthers out and work with Finch, it never hit me till now what we've discovered."

He reached for the sheet of paper I had picked up. "I have been making a list," he said.

I looked at the sheet of paper in my hand. "The library at Lisbon," it read. "The Los Angeles Public Library. Carlyle's *The French Revolution*. The library at Alexandria."

I looked at him.

"All destroyed by fire," he said. "A maid burnt the only copy of Carlyle's *The French Revolution* by mistake." He took the paper from me. "This is what I was able to think of in just a few minutes."

He folded up the list. "St. Paul's Cathedral was vaporized by a pinpoint bomb," he said. "All of it. The painting of *The Light of the World*, Nelson's tomb, the statue of John Donne. To think that they might—"

The curate came up. "Mr. Dunworthy," he said. "You are supposed to be in line."

"Have you seen Lady Schrapnell?" I asked the curate.

"She was in the Drapers' Chapel a moment ago," he said. "Mr. Dunworthy, are you ready?"

"Yes," Mr. Dunworthy said. He took off his mortarboard, tucked the list inside, and put it back on again. "I am ready for anything."

I headed up the nave to the Drapers' Chapel. The transept aisle was full of milling dons, and Warder was in the choir, trying to line up the choirboys. "No, no, no!" she was shouting. "*Don't* sit down! You'll wrinkle your surplices. I've just ironed them. And line up. I don't have all day!"

I edged past her and over to the Drapers' Chapel. Verity was there, standing in front of the stained-glass window, her beautiful head bent over a sheet of paper.

"What's that?" I asked, going over to her. "The order of service?"

"No," she said. "It's a letter. Remember how, after we found Maud's letter,

I suggested to the forensics expert that she see if any letters Tossie might have sent to other people existed?" She held it up. "She found one."

"You're joking," I said. "And I suppose it's got Baine's name in it."

"No, Tossie's still calling him her 'beloved husband.' And she signs it 'Toots.' But there are some very interesting things in it," she said, sitting down in one of the carved pews. "Listen to this: 'My darling Terence—' "

"Terence?" I said. "What on earth's she doing writing to Terence?"

"He wrote to her," she said. "That letter's lost. This is Tossie's reply."

"Terence wrote her?"

"Yes," Verity said. "Listen: 'My darling Terence, Words cannot properly express how *happy* your letter of the third made me.' 'Happy' is underlined. 'I had given up all hope of ever hearing of my precious Princess Arjumand in this *world!!*' 'World'—"

"Is underlined," I said.

"And there are two exclamation points," Verity said. She read on: " 'We were already far out to sea when I discovered her missing. My beloved husband did *everything* in his power to convince the captain to return to port *at once*, but he *cruelly* refused, and I thought I would never see my dearum precious Juju *again* in this life or know of her *Fate*.' "

"Pretty much the whole thing's underlined," Verity said, "and Fate is capitalized." She read, " 'You cannot imagine my joy when I received your letter. It was my *great fear* that she had *perished in the briny deep*, and now to hear that she is not only *alive* but with *you!*' "

"What?" I said.

"The entire thing's underlined from here on out," Verity said. " 'To *think* of my *delicate darling* travelling *all the way* from Plymouth to *Kent* when Muchings End would have been much closer! But perhaps it is *for the best*. Mama has written that Papa recently acquired a new golden veiltail ryunkin. And I know that you will give her a good home.

" 'Thank you for your *kind offer* to send Princess Arjumand to me in the care of Dawson, but my beloved husband and I agree that, given her *dislike of water*, it is best that she remain in your care. I know that you and your bride Maud will *love* and *cherish* her as I have. Mama wrote me of your *marriage*. Though it seems to me to have been a bit *hasty*, and I sincerely *hope* that it was not done *on the rebound*, I am *gladder than I can say* that you have been able to *forget* me, and it is my *fervent hope* that you will be as *happy* as I and my beloved husband are! Kiss Princess Arjumand and stroke her dear sweet fur for me, and tell her that her muvver finks of her dearum dearums darling evewy day. Gratefully, Toots Callahan.' "

"Poor Cyril," I said.

"Nonsense," Verity said. "They were made for each other."

"So are we," I said.

She ducked her head.

"So, how's about it, Harriet?" I said. "We make a jolly good detectin' team, eh what? What say we make the partnership permanent?"

"No!" Warder shouted. "I told you not to sit down. Look at those wrinkles! Those surplices are linen!"

"Well, Watson?" I said to Verity. "What do you say?"

"I don't know," she said miserably. "What if it's just time-lag? Look at Carruthers. He thinks he's in love with Warder—"

"That is absolutely out of the question!" Warder snapped at a small boy. "You should have thought of that before you put your surplice on!"

"Look at her! What if, now that this is all over," Verity said, looking earnestly up at me, "you're able to get some rest, you recover from your time-lag, and decide the entire thing was a dreadful mistake?"

"Nonsense," I said, backing her against the wall. "Also balderdash, pish-tosh, stuff-and-nonsense, humbug, and pshaw! To say nothing of poppycock! In the first place, you know perfectly well that the first time I saw you, wringing out your sleeve on Mr. Dunworthy's carpet, it was 'The Lady of Shalott' to the life—webs flying, mirrors splintering, threads and glass all over the place."

I put my hand on the wall above her head and leaned toward her. "In the second place," I said, "it's your patriotic duty."

"My patriotic duty?"

"Yes. We're part of a self-correction, remember? If we don't get married, something dire's likely to happen: the Nazis will realize we have Ultra, or Lady Schrapnell will give her money to Cambridge, or the continuum will collapse."

"*There* you are," Finch said, hurrying in with a handheld and a large pasteboard box. "I've been looking for you everywhere. Mr. Dunworthy said you and Miss Kindle were to have one, but I didn't know if that meant one or two."

I had no idea what he was talking about, but after a week in the Victorian era I was no longer bothered by the fact. "One," I said.

"Yes, sir," he said. "One," he said into the handheld and set it down on a monument. "Mr. Dunworthy said that in light of your valuable contributions, you were to have first pick. Did you have a preference in color?" he said, opening the box.

"Yes," Verity said. "Black. With white paws."

"What?" I said.

"I told you he was bringing back nonsignificant objects," Verity said.

"I should hardly call them nonsignificant," Finch said, and lifted out a kitten.

It was the exact image of Princess Arjumand, down to the white pantaloons on her back feet, only in miniature.

"Where?" I said. "How? Cats are an extinct species."

"Yes, sir," he said, handing the kitten to Verity, "but there was an over-abundance of them in Victorian times, with the result that farmers frequently drowned litters of kittens in an attempt to keep the population down."

"And when I brought Princess Arjumand through," Verity said, holding the kitten in her hand and petting it, "T.J. and Mr. Dunworthy decided to see if the kittens, once they had been put in a bag and thrown in the pond, would be nonsignificant."

"So you were wandering all over the countryside looking for pregnant cats," I said, looking in the box. There were two dozen kittens inside, most with their eyes still closed. "Are any of these Mrs. Marmalade's?"

"Yes, sir," he said, pointing at several little balls of fur. "These three tabbies and this calico. They are of course all too young to be weaned, but Mr. Dunworthy said to tell you you could have yours in five weeks. Princess Arjumand's are slightly older since they were not found for nearly three weeks."

He took the kitten away from Verity. "The cat will not actually belong to you," Finch said, "and you will need to return it to the lab for cloning and regular breeding. There are not enough yet for a viable gene pool, but we have contacted the Sorbonne, Caltech, and the University of Thailand, and I will be returning to Victorian England for additional specimens." He put the kitten back in the box.

"Can we come and see it?" Verity said.

"Certainly," Finch said. "And you will need to be trained in its care and feeding. I recommend a diet of milk and—"

"Globe-eyed nacreous ryunkins," I said.

Finch's handheld bleeped. He looked at it and scooped up the pasteboard box. "The archbishop's here, and the usher guarding the west door says it's starting to rain. We're going to have to let the crowd in. I must find Lady Schrapnell. Have you seen her?"

We both shook our heads.

"I'd best go find her," he said, scooping up the pasteboard box. He bustled off.

"In the third place," I said to Verity, picking up where I had left off, "I happen to know from that day in the boat that you feel exactly the same way I do, and if you're waiting for me to propose in Latin—"

"*There* you are, Ned," T.J. said. He was carrying a small screen and a portable comp hookup. "I need to show you something."

"The consecration's about to start," I said. "Can't it wait?"

"I don't think so," he said.

"It's all right," Verity said, "I'll be right back," and slipped out of the chapel.

"What is it?" I said to T.J.

"It probably isn't anything," T.J. said. "It's very likely a mathematical error. Or a glitch in the system."

"What is it?" I repeated.

"All right, do you remember how you asked me to shift the focus of the incongruity to Coventry 1940, and I did, and I told you it matched the Waterloo soup-kettle sim nearly perfectly."

"Yes," I said warily.

"Yes, well, 'nearly' is the operative word." He brought one of his blurry gray models up on the screen. "It matched very well in the peripheral slippage, and along the main areas here, and here," he said, pointing at indistinguishable areas. "But not in the slippage surrounding the site. And although there was slippage at the site of Mrs. Bittner's bringing the bishop's bird stump through, it wasn't radically increased."

"There wouldn't have been room for radically increased slippage, would there?" I said. "Lizzie Bittner had to go in within a very narrow window of time—between the time the treasures were last seen and their destruction by the fire. She only had a few minutes. Increased slippage would have put her right in the middle of the fire."

"Yes, well, even taking that into consideration, there is still the problem of the surrounding slippage," he said, pointing at nothing. "So," he said, flicking some more keys, "I tried moving the focus forward." A nondescript gray picture came up.

"Forward?"

"Yes. Of course, I didn't have enough data to pick a space-time location like you did, so what I did was to consider the surrounding slippage to be peripheral and to extrapolate new surrounding slippage, and then extrapolate a new focus from that."

He called up another gray picture. "Okay, this is the model of Waterloo. I'm going to superimpose it over the model with the new focus." He did. "You can see it matches."

I could. "Where does that put the focus?" I said. "What year?"

"2678," he said.

2678. Over six hundred years in the future.

"The fifteenth of June, 2678," he said. "As I said, it's probably nothing. An error in the calculations."

"And if it isn't?"

"Then Mrs. Bittner's bringing the bishop's bird stump through isn't the incongruity."

"But if it isn't the incongruity . . . ?"

"It's part of the self-correction as well," T.J. said.

"The self-correction of what?"

"I don't know," he said. "Something that hasn't happened yet. Something that's going to happen in—"

"—in 2678," I said. "What's the focus's location?" I asked, wondering if it would be as far-flung as the date. Addis Ababa? Mars? The Lesser Magellanic Cloud?

"Oxford," he said. "Coventry Cathedral."

Coventry Cathedral. On the fifteenth of June. Verity had been right. We were intended to find the bishop's bird stump and return it to the cathedral. And all of it, the selling of the new cathedral and Lady Schrapnell's rebuilding of the old one and our discovery that nonsignificant treasures could be brought forward through the net were all part of the same huge self-correction, some Grand—

"I'm going to double-check all the calculations and run some logic tests on the model," T.J. said. "Don't worry. It'll probably turn out to be nothing more than a flaw in the Waterloo sim. It's only a rough model."

He touched some keys, and the gray disappeared. He began folding up the screen.

"T.J.," I said. "What do you think determined the outcome of the Battle of Waterloo? Napoleon's handwriting or his hemorrhoids?"

"Neither," he said. "And I don't think it was any of the things we did sims on—Gneisenau's retreat to Wavre or the lost messenger or the fire at La Sainte Haye."

"*What do* you think it was?" I asked curiously.

"A cat," he said.

"A cat?"

"Or a cart or a rat or—"

"—the head of a church committee," I murmured.

"Exactly," he said. "Something so insignificant no one even noticed it. That's the problem with models—they only include the details people think are relevant, and Waterloo was a chaotic system. *Everything* was relevant."

"And we're all Ensign Kleppermans," I said, "suddenly finding ourselves in positions of critical importance."

"Yeah," he said, grinning, "and we all know what happened to Ensign Klepperman. And what's going to happen to me if I don't get over to the vestry. Lady Schrapnell wants me to light the candles in the chapels." He hastily grabbed up the screen and the comp setup. "I'd better get busy lighting. It looks like they're about to begin."

It did. The choirboys and dons were more or less lined up, the woman in the green apron was gathering up scissors and buckets and flower-wrappings, the boy had come out from under the choir stall. "Is the trumpet stop working now?" a voice called down from the clerestory, and the organist shouted back, "Yes." Carruthers and Warder were standing by the south door, their arms full of orders of service and each other. I went out into the nave, looking for Verity.

"*Where* have you been?" Lady Schrapnell said, bearing down on me. "I have been looking all over for you." She put her hands on her hips. "Well," she demanded. "I thought you said you'd found the bishop's bird stump. Where is it? You haven't lost it again, have you?"

"No," I said. "It's in front of the parclose screen of the Smiths' Chapel where it's supposed to be."

"I want to see it," she said and started for the nave.

There was a fanfare, and the organist launched into "O God Who Doeth Great Things and Unsearchable." The choirboys opened their hymnals. Carruthers and Warder pulled apart and took up their positions by the south door.

"I don't think there's time," I said. "The consecration's about to start."

"Nonsense," she said, barging through the choirboys. "There's plenty of time. The sun isn't out yet."

She pushed through the dons, parting them like the Red Sea, and started down the north aisle to the Smiths' Chapel.

I followed her, hoping the bishop's bird stump hadn't mysteriously disappeared again. It hadn't. It was still there, on its wrought-iron flower stand. The woman in the green apron had filled it with a lovely arrangement of white Easter lilies.

"There it is," I said, presenting it proudly. "After untold trials and tribulations. The bishop's bird stump. What do you think?"

"Oh, my," she said, and pressed her hand to her bosom. "It really is hideous, isn't it?"

"*What?*" I said.

"I know my great-great-great-great-grandmother is supposed to have liked it, but my God! What is that supposed to be?" she said, pointing at the base. "Some kind of dinosaur?"

"The Signing of the Magna Carta," I said.

"I'm almost sorry I had you waste so much time looking for it," she said. She looked thoughtfully at it. "I don't suppose it's breakable?" she said hopefully.

"No," I said.

"Well, I suppose we have to have it for authenticity's sake. I certainly hope the other churches don't have anything this hideous in them."

"Other churches?" I said.

"Yes, haven't you heard?" she said. "Now that we're able to bring objects forward through the net, I have all sorts of projects planned. The San Francisco earthquake, the MGM back lot, Rome before the fire Julius Caesar set—"

"Nero," I said.

"Yes, of course. You will have to bring back the fiddle Nero played."

"But it didn't burn in the fire," I said. "Only objects that have been reduced to their component parts—"

She waved her hand dismissively. "Laws are made to be broken. We'll start with the fourteen Christopher Wren churches that were burned in the Blitz, and then—"

"We?" I said weakly.

"Yes, of course. I've already specifically requested you." She stopped and glared at the bishop's bird stump. "*Why* are those lilies? They are supposed to be yellow chrysanthemums."

"I think lilies are extremely appropriate," I said. "After all, the cathedral and all its treasures have been raised from the dead. The symbolism—"

She wasn't impressed with the symbolism. "The order of service says yellow chrysanthemums," she said. " 'God is in the details.' " She stormed off to find the poor defenseless woman in the green apron.

I stood there, looking at the bishop's bird stump. Fourteen Christopher Wren churches. And the MGM back lot. To say nothing of what she might come up with when she Realized What It Meant.

Verity came up. "What's wrong, Ned?" she said.

"I am fated to spend my entire life working for Lady Schrapnell and attending jumble sales," I said.

"Pish-tosh!" she said. "You are fated to spend your life with me." She handed me the kitten. "And Penwiper."

The kitten didn't weigh anything. "Penwiper," I said, and it looked up at me with gray-green eyes.

"Mere," it said, and began to purr, a very small purr. A purrlet.

"Where did you get this kitten?" I said to Verity.

"I stole it," she said. "Don't look like that. I intend to take it back. And Finch will never miss it."

"I love you," I said, shaking my head. "If I'm fated to spend my life with you, does that mean you've decided to marry me?"

"I have to," she said. "I just ran into Lady Schrapnell. She's decided what this cathedral needs is—"

"A wedding?" I said.

"No, a christening. So they can use the Purbeck marble baptismal font."

"I don't want you to do anything you don't want to," I said. "I could sic Lady Schrapnell on Carruthers and Warder, and you could make a run for it to someplace safe. Like the Battle of Waterloo."

There was a fanfare, the organ launched into "The Heavens Are Declaring the Glory of God," and the sun came out. The east windows burst into blue and red and purple flame. I looked up. The clerestory was one long unbroken band of gold, like the net at the moment of opening. It filled the cathedral with light, illuminating the silver candlesticks and the children's cross and the underside of the choir stalls, the choirboys and workmen and eccentric dons, the statue of St. Michael and the Dance of Death and the orders of service. Illuminating the cathedral itself—a Grand Design made of a thousand thousand details.

I looked at the bishop's bird stump, cradling the kitten in the crook of my arm. The stained-glass window behind outlined the bishop's bird stump in glorious colors, and the window of the Dyers' Chapel opposite tinted the camels and the cherubs and the Execution of Mary, Queen of Scots emerald and ruby and sapphire.

"It *is* hideous, isn't it?" I said.

Verity took my hand. *"Placet,"* she said.